THE GIANT BOOK

OF

GHOST STORIES

Edited by
Richard Dalby

This edition published and distributed by
Parragon Book Service Ltd, Bristol, in 1996

First published by Magpie Books,
an imprint of Robinson Publishing Ltd, in 1993

Previously published by Robinson Publishing Ltd as
The Mammoth Book of Ghost Stories 2

Robinson Publishing Ltd
7 Kensington Church Court
London W8 4SP

ISBN 0 75250 152 6

A copy of the British Library Cataloguing in Publication Data
is available from the British Library.

Printed and bound in Great Britain

THE GIANT BOOK OF
OF
GHOST STORIES

CONTENTS

Acknowledgements

For permission to print copyright material in this anthology, grateful acknowledgements are made to the following:

"Who or What Was It?" © 1972 by Kingsley Amis. First published in *Playboy*, 1972. Reprinted by permission of Jonathan Clewes Ltd., London, on behalf of Kingsley Amis.
"The Shadowy Escort" © 1928 by A.M. Burrage, reprinted by permission of J.S.F. Burrage.
"The Elemental" © 1974 by Ronald Chetwynd-Hayes.
"Something to Reflect Upon" © 1990 by Clare Colvin.
"The Second Passenger" © 1973 by Basil Copper.
"St. Bartholomew's Day" © 1975 by Edmund Crispin, reprinted by permission of Messrs. A.P. Watt Ltd.
"The Spirit of Christmas" © 1990 by Vivian Edwards.
"The Black Widow" © 1991 by John S. Glasby.
"Madelein" © 1991 by Roger Johnson.
"And Turns No More His Head" © 1985 by A.F. Kidd.
"Dance! Dance! The Shaking of the Sheets" © 1991 by Alan W. Lear.
"Haunted Air" © 1934 by L.A. Lewis, reprinted by permission of Richard Dalby.
"Things" © 1928 by John Moore, reprinted by permission of the Peters Fraser & Dunlop Group Ltd.
"The Face" © 1913 by Lennox Robinson, reprinted by permission of Curtis Brown Ltd.
"A Fisher of Men" © 1984 by David G. Rowlands.
"Ward 8" © 1991 by Pamela Sewell.
"A Dream of Porcelain" © 1991 by Derek Stanford.
"The Ash Track" © 1991 by Mark Valentine.
"In a Nursing Home" © 1972 by E.H. Visiak, printed by permission of Bolt & Watson Ltd.

Every effort has been made to trace copyright holders, but the publishers would be interested to hear from anyone not here acknowledged.

Preface

For me the great value of this splendid collection of ghost stories is that most of them are in the classic gothic vein, even those by contemporary authors.

To look at the list of writers concerned is to know that there is a veritable feast in store for the reader, as the stories are all the work of eminent authors and written over a period of time when, in my opinion, the genre was at its height. To be able to choose at random from Conan Doyle, Charles Dickens, Nathaniel Hawthorne, Washington Irving, Sheridan Le Fanu, de Maupassant and Edgar Allan Poe, E.F. Benson, Edmund Crispin, Rudyard Kipling, M.R. James and Edgar Wallace is surely a rarity.

I personally knew E.F. Benson and M.R. James. I have met Kingsley Amis and the grandaughter of Bram Stoker. I think I must have devoured every book by Edgar Wallace that I could lay my hands on over the years.

I am of course familiar with some of these stories, but a great many are new to me, so it is always an adventure to find oneself caught up in the spells cast by the Masters.

Since time immemorial, man has been fascinated by the unusual, the unseen, the inexplicable and the bizarre. When we see a film, we are inevitably looking at one interpretation of the story concerned, presented to us by the director and the cast. However, when we read a story, there is no limit whatever to our own imagination, which can roam at will over page after page. Our own conception can be far more vivid and disturbing than when we are looking at something on celluloid which may not resemble what we expected.

I have always said that what we do not see is far more suggestive than what we do see. The power of these stories lies in their ability to draw us inexorably into their grasp, even though some of us may hesitate in apprehension and dread. I cannot think of a better reason to delve into Richard Dalby's treasury and I wish the readers of this book many a quake and shudder as they turn each page.

Christopher Lee

London
March 1991

KINGSLEY AMIS
Who or What Was It?

The television adaption of Sir Kingsley Amis's *classic supernatural novel*, The Green Man (1969), *starring Albert Finney as Maurice Allington, thrilled millions last year on BBC 1. The sequel "Who or What Was It?" (a.k.a. "The Green Man Revisited") retains its original form of a radio script as originally written and read by the author in 1972. His intention was "to fool listeners into thinking it was a factual account until three-quarters of the way through and then, with luck, induce them to suspend their altogether necessary disbelief for the last few minutes". Nevertheless, the story proved to be so convincing that many listeners (including a television producer) assumed it to be entirely true!*

I want to tell you about a very odd experience I had a few months ago, not so as to entertain you, but because I think it raises some very basic questions about, you know, what life is all about and to what extent we run our own lives. Rather worrying questions. Anyway, what happened was this.

My wife and I had been staying the weekend with her uncle and aunt in Westmorland, near a place called Milnethorpe. Both of us, Jane and I that is, had things to do in London on the Monday morning, and it's a long drive from up there down to Barnet, where we live, even though a good half of it is on the M6. So I said, Look, don't let's break our necks trying to get home in the light (this was in August), let's take it easy and stop somewhere for dinner and reckon to get home about half-past ten or eleven. Jane said okay.

So we left Milnethorpe in the middle of the afternoon, took things fairly easily, and landed up about half-past seven or a quarter to eight at the . . . the place we'd picked out of one of the food guides before we started. I won't tell you the name of the place, because the people who run it wouldn't thank me if I did. Please don't go looking for it. I'd advise you not to.

Anyway, we parked the car in the yard and went inside. It was a nice-looking sort of place, pretty old, built a good time ago I mean, done up in a sensible sort of way, no muzak and no bloody silly blacked-out lighting, but no olde-worlde nonsense either.

Well, I got us both a drink in the bar and went off to see about a table for dinner. I soon found the right chap, and he said, Fine, table for two in half an hour, certainly sir, are you in the bar, I'll get someone to bring you the menu in a few minutes. Pleasant sort of chap, a bit young for the job.

I was just going off when a sort of paunchy business type came in and said something about, Mr. Allington not in tonight? and the young fellow said No sir, he's taken the evening off. All right, never mind.

Well, I'll tell you why in a minute, but I turned back to the young fellow, said, Excuse me, but is your name Palmer? and he said Yes sir, and I said, Not David Palmer by any chance? and he said No sir, actually the name's George. I said, or rather burbled, A friend of mine was telling me about this place, said he'd stayed here, liked it very much, mentioned you, anyway I got half the name right, and Mr. Allington is the proprietor, isn't he? That's correct, sir. See you later and all that.

I went straight back to the bar, went up to the barman and said, Fred? and he said Yes sir. I said, Fred Soames? and he said, Fred Browning, sir. I just said, Wrong Fred, not very polite, but it was all I could think of. I went over to where my wife was sitting and I'd hardly sat down before she asked, What's the matter?

What was the matter calls for a bit of explanation. In 1969 I published a novel called *The Green Man*, which was not only the title of the book but also the name of a sort of classy pub, or inn, where most of the action took place, very much the kind of establishment we were in that evening.

Now the landlord of the Green Man was called Allington, and his deputy was called David Palmer, and the barman was called Fred Soames. Allington is a very uncommon name—I wanted that for reasons nothing to do with this story. The other two aren't, but to have got Palmer and Fred right, so to speak, as well as Allington was a thumping great coincidence, staggering in fact. But I wasn't just staggered, I was very alarmed. Because

2

the Green Man wasn't only the name of the pub in my book; it was also the name of a frightening creature, a sort of solid ghost conjured up out of tree-branches and leaves and so on that very nearly kills Allington and his young daughter. I didn't want to find I was right about that, too.

Jane was very sensible, as always. She said stranger coincidences had happened and still been just coincidences, and mightn't I have come across an innkeeper called Allington somewhere, half forgotten about it and brought it up out of my unconscious mind when I was looking for a name for an innkeeper to put in the book, and now the real Allington's moved from wherever I'd seen him before to this place. And Palmer and Fred really are very common names. And I'd got the name of the pub wrong. I'm still not telling you what it's called, but one of the things it isn't called is the Green Man. And, my pub was in Hertfordshire and this place was . . . off the M6. All very reasonable and reassuring.

Only I wasn't reassured. I mean, I obviously couldn't just leave it there. The thing to do was get hold of this chap Palmer and see if there was, well, any more to come. Which was going to be tricky if I wasn't going to look nosy or mad or something else that would shut him up. Neither of us ate much dinner, though there was nothing wrong with the food. We didn't say much, either. I drank a fair amount.

Then halfway through, Palmer turned up to do his everything-all-right routine, as I'd hoped he would, and as he would have done in my book. I said yes, it was fine, thanks, and then I asked him, I said we'd be very pleased if he'd join us for a brandy afterwards if he'd got time, and he said he'd be delighted. Jolly good, but I was still stuck with this problem of how to dress the thing up.

Jane had said earlier on, why didn't I just tell the truth, and I'd said, since Palmer hadn't reacted at all when I gave him my name when I was booking the table—see what I mean?—he'd only have my word for the whole story and might still think I was off my rocker, and she said of course she'd back me up, and I'd said he'd just think he'd got two loonies on his hands instead of one. Anyway, *now* she said, *Some* people who've read *The Green Man* must have mentioned it,—fancy that, Mr. Palmer, you and Mr. Allington and Fred are all in a book by somebody called Kingsley Amis. Obvious enough

3

when you think of it, but like a lot of obvious things, you have got to think of it.

Well, that was the line I took when Palmer rolled up for his brandy, I'm me and I wrote this book and so on. Oh really? he said, more or less. I thought we were buggered, but then he said, Oh yes, now you mention it, I do remember some chap saying something like that, but it must have been two or three years ago—you know, as if that stopped it counting for much. I'm not much of a reader, you see, he said.

So. What about Mr. Allington, I said, doesn't he read? Not what you'd call a reader, he said. Well, that was one down to me, or one up, depending on how you look at it, because *my* Allington was a tremendous reader, French poetry and all that. Still, the approach had worked after a fashion, and Palmer very decently put up with being cross-questioned on how far this place corresponded with my place, in the book.

Was Mrs. Allington blonde? There wasn't a Mrs. Allington any more; she'd died of leukemia quite a long time ago. Had he got his widowed father living here? (Allington's father, that is.) No, Mr. Allington senior, and his wife, lived in Eastbourne. Was the house, the pub, haunted at all? Not as far as Palmer knew, and he'd been there three years. In fact, the place was only about two hundred years old, which completely clobbered a good half of my novel, where the ghosts had been hard at it more than a hundred years earlier still.

Nearly all of it was like that. Of course, there were some questions I couldn't ask, for one reason or another. For instance, was Allington a boozer, like my Allington, and even more so, had this Allington had a visit from God. In the book, God turns up in the form of a young man to give Allington some tips on how to deal with the ghosts, who he, God, thinks are a menace to him. No point in going any further into that part.

I said nearly all the answers Palmer gave me were straight negatives. One wasn't, or rather there were two points where I scored, so to speak. One was that Allington had a fifteen-year-old daughter called Marilyn living in the house. My Allington's daughter was thirteen and called Amy, but I'd come somewhere near the mark—too near for comfort.

The other thing was a bit harder to tie down. When I'm writing a novel, I very rarely have any sort of mental picture of any of the characters, what they actually look like. I think a lot of novelists would say the same. But, I don't know why, I'd had a very clear image of what my chap *David* Palmer looked like, and now I'd had a really good look at *George* Palmer, this one here, he was *nearly* the same as I'd imagined, not so tall, different nose, but still nearly the same. I didn't care for that.

Palmer, George Palmer, said he had things to see to and took off. I told Jane what I've just told you, about the resemblance. She said I could easily have imagined that, and I said I suppose I might. Anyway, she said, what do you think of it all?

I said it could still all be coincidence. What could it be if it isn't coincidence? she asked. I'd been wondering about that while we were talking to Palmer. Not an easy one. Feeling a complete bloody fool, I said I thought we could have strayed into some kind of parallel world that slightly resembles the world I made up, you know, like in a science-fiction story.

She didn't laugh or back away. She looked round and spotted a newspaper someone had left on one of the chairs. It was that day's *Sunday Telegraph*. She said, If where we are is a world that's parallel to the real world, it's bound to be different from the real world in all sorts of ways. Now you read most of the *Telegraph* this morning, the real *Telegraph*. Look at this one, she said, and see if it's any different. Well, I did, and it wasn't: same front page, same article on the trade unions by Perry, that's Peregrine Worsthorne, same readers' letters, same crossword down to the last clue. Well, that was a relief.

But I didn't stay relieved, because there was another coincidence shaping up. It was a hot night in August when all this happened—or did I mention that before? Anyway, it was. And Allington was out for the evening. It was on a hot night in August, after Allington had come back from an evening out, that the monster, the Green Man, finally takes shape and comes pounding up the road to tear young Amy Allington to pieces. That bit begins on page 225 in my book, if you're interested.

The other nasty little consideration was this. Unlike some novelists I could name, I invent all my characters, except for a few minor ones here and there. What I mean is, I don't go in for just renaming people I know and bunging them into a book. But of course, you can't help putting *something* of yourself into all your characters, even if it's only, well, a surly bus-conductor who only comes in for half a page.

Right, obviously, this comes up most of all with your heroes. Now none of my heroes, not even old Lucky Jim, are me, but they can't help having pretty fair chunks of me in them, some more than others. And Allington in that book was one of the some. I'm more like him than I'm like most of the others; in particular, I'm more like my Maurice Allington in my book than the real Allington, who by the way turned out to be called John, seemed (from what I'd heard) to be like my Maurice Allington. Sorry to be long-winded, but I want to get that quite clear.

So: if, by some fantastic chance, the Green Man, the monster, was going to turn up here, he, or it, seemed more likely to turn up tonight than most nights. And, furthermore, I seemed sort of better cast for the part of the young girl's father, who manages in the book to save her from the monster, than this young girl's father did. You see that.

I tried to explain all this to Jane. Evidently I got it across all right, because she said straight away, We'd better stay here tonight, then. If we can, I said, meaning if there was a room. Well, there was, and at the front of the house too, which was important, because in the book that's the side the monster appears on.

While one of the blokes was taking our stuff out of the car and upstairs, I said to Jane, I'm not going to be like a bloody fool in a ghost story who insists on seeing things through alone, not if I can help it—I'm going to give Bob Conquest a ring. Bob's an old chum of mine, and about the only one I felt I could ask to come belting up all this way (he lives in Battersea) for such a ridiculous reason. It was just after ten by this time, and the Green Man wasn't scheduled to put in an appearance till after one a.m., so Bob could make it all right if he started straight away. Fine, except his phone didn't answer; I tried twice.

Jane said, Get hold of Monkey; I'll speak to him. Monkey, otherwise known as Colin, is her brother; he lives with us in Barnet. Our number answered all right, but I got my son Philip, who was staying the weekend there. He said Monkey was out at a party, he didn't know where. So all I could do was the necessary but not at all helpful job of saying we wouldn't be home till the next morning. So that was that. I mean, I just couldn't start getting hold of George Palmer and asking him to sit up with us into the small hours in case a ghost came along. Could any of you? I should have said that Philip hasn't got a car.

Well, we stayed in the bar until it closed. I said to Jane at one point, You don't think I'm mad, do you? Or silly or anything? She said, On the contrary, I think you're being extremely practical and sensible. Well, thank God for that. Jane believes in ghosts, you see. My own position on that is exactly that of the man who said, I don't believe in ghosts, but I'm afraid of them.

Which brings me to one of the oddest things about this whole business. I'm a nervous type by nature, I never go in an aeroplane, I won't drive a car (Jane does the driving), I don't even much care for being alone in the house. But, ever since we'd decided to stay the night at this place, all the uneasiness and, let's face it, the considerable fear I'd started to feel as soon as these coincidences started coming up, it all just fell away. I felt quite confident, I felt I knew I'd be able to do whatever might be required of me.

There was one other thing to get settled. I said to Jane, we were in the bedroom by this time, I said, If he turns up, what am I going to use against him? You see, in the book, Maurice Allington has dug up a sort of magic object that sort of controls the Green Man. I hadn't. Jane saw what I was driving at. She said she'd thought of that, and took off and gave me the plain gold cross she wears round her neck, not for religious reasons, it was her grandmother's. That'll fix him, I thought, and as before I felt quite confident about it.

Well, after that we more or less sat and waited. At one point a car drove up and stopped in the car park. A man got out and went in the front door. It must have been Allington. I couldn't see much about him except he had the wrong colour hair, but when I looked at my watch it was eight minutes to midnight, the exact time when the Allington in the book got back after his evening out the night he coped with the creature. One more bit of . . . call it confirmation.

I opened our bedroom door and listened. Soon I heard footsteps coming upstairs and going off towards the back of the house and then a door shutting, and then straight away the house seemed totally still. It can't have been much later that I said to Jane, Look, there's no point in me hanging round up here. He might be early, you never know. It's a warm night, I might as well go down there now. She said, Are you sure you don't want me to come with you? Absolutely sure, I said, I'll be fine. But I do want you to watch from the window here. Okay, she said. She wished me luck and we clung to each other for a bit, and then off I went.

I was glad I'd left plenty of time, because getting out of the place turned out to be far from straightforward. Everything seemed to be locked and the key taken away. Eventually I found a scullery door with the key still in the lock.

Outside it was quite bright, with a full moon or not far off, and a couple of fairly powerful lights at the corners of the house. It was a pretty lonely spot, with only two or three other houses in sight. I remember a car went by soon after I got out there, but it was the only one. There wasn't a breath of wind. I saw Jane at our window and waved, and she waved back.

The question was, where to wait. If what was going to happen—assuming something was—if it went like the book, then the young girl, the daughter, was going to come out of the house because she'd thought she'd heard her father calling her (another bit of magic), and then this Green Man creature was going to, from one direction or the other he was going to come running at her. I couldn't decide which was the more likely direction.

A bit of luck, near the front door there was one of those heavy wooden benches. I sat down on that and started keeping watch first one way, then the other, half a minute at a time. Normally, ten minutes of this would have driven me off my head with boredom, but that night somehow it was all right. Then, after some quite long time, I turned my head from right to left on schedule and there was a girl, standing a few yards away; she must have come round that side of the house. She was wearing light green pyjamas—wrong colour again. I was going to speak to her, but there was something about the way she was standing. . . .

She wasn't looking at me, in fact I soon saw she wasn't looking at anything much. I waved my hand in front of her eyes, you know, the way they do in films when they think someone's been hypnotized or something. I felt a perfect idiot, but her eyes didn't move. Sleep-walking, presumably; not in the book. Do people walk in their sleep? Apparently not, they only pretend to, according to what a psychiatrist chum told me afterwards, but I hadn't heard that then. All I knew, or thought I knew, was this thing everybody's heard somewhere about it being dangerous to wake a sleepwalker.

So I just stayed close to the girl and went on keeping watch, and a bit more time went by, and then, sure enough, I heard, faintly but clearly, the sound I'd written about, the rustling, creaking sound of the movement of something made of tree-branches, twigs, and clusters of leaves. And there it was, about a hundred yards away, not really much like a man, coming up at a clumsy, jolting sort of jog-trot on the grass verge, and accelerating.

I knew what I had to do. I started walking to meet it, with the cross ready in my hand. (The girl hadn't moved at all.) When the thing was about twenty yards away I saw its face, which had fungus on it, and I heard another sound I'd written about coming from what I suppose you'd have to call its mouth, like the howling of wind through trees.

I stopped and steadied myself and threw the cross at it and it immediately vanished—immediately. That wasn't like the book, but I didn't stop to think about it. I didn't stop to look for the cross, either. When I turned back, the girl had gone. So much the better. I rushed back into the inn and up to the bedroom and knocked on the door—I'd told Jane to lock it after me.

There was a delay before she came and opened it. I could see she looked confused or something, but I didn't bother with that, because I could feel all the calm and confidence I'd had earlier, it was all just draining away from me. I sat her down on the bed and sat down myself on a chair and just rattled off what had happened as fast as I could. I must have forgotten she'd been meant to be watching.

By the time I'd finished I was shaking. So was Jane. She said, What made you change your mind? Change my mind?—what about? Going out there, she said; getting up again and going out. But, I said, I've been out there all the time. Oh no you haven't, she said, you came back up here after about twenty minutes, she said, and you told me the whole thing was silly and you were going to bed, which we both did. She seemed quite positive.

I was absolutely shattered. But it all really happened, I said, just the way I told you. It couldn't have, she said; you must have dreamed it. You certainly didn't throw the cross at anything, she said, because it's here, you gave it back to me when you came back the first time. And there it was, on the chain round her neck.

I broke down then. I'm not quite clear what I said or did. Jane got some sleeping pills down me and I went off in the end. I remember thinking rather wildly that somebody or other with a funny sense of humour had got me into exactly the same predicament, the same mess, as the hero of my book had been: seeing something that must have been supernatural and just not being believed. Because I knew I'd seen the whole thing; I knew it then and I still know it.

I woke up late, feeling terrible. Jane was sitting reading by the bed. She said, I've seen young Miss Allington. Your description of her fits and, she said, she used to walk in her sleep. I asked her how she'd found out and she said she just had; she's good at that kind of thing.

Anyway, I felt better straight away. I said it looked as if we'd neither of us been dreaming even if what I'd seen couldn't be reconciled with what she'd seen, and she agreed. After that we rather dropped the subject in a funny sort of way. We decided not to look for the cross I'd thrown at the Green Man. I said we wouldn't be able to find it. I didn't ask Jane whether she was thinking what I was thinking, that looking would be a waste of time because she was wearing it at that very moment. I'll come back to that point in a minute.

We packed up, made a couple of phone calls rearranging our appointments, paid the bill and drove off. We still didn't talk about the main issue. But then, as we were coming off the Mill Hill roundabout, that's only about ten minutes from home, Jane said, What do you think happened?—happened to sort of make it all happen?

I said, I think someone was needed there to destroy that monster. Which means I was guided there at that time, or perhaps the time could be adjusted, I said; I must have been, well, sent all that stuff about the Green Man and about Allington and the others.

To make sure you recognized the place when you got there and knew what to do, she said. Who did all the guiding and the sending and so on? she said. The same, the same chap who appeared in my book to tell Allington what he wanted done. Why couldn't he have fixed the monster himself? she said. There are limitations to his power. There can't be many, she said, if he can make the same object be in two places at the same time.

Yes, you see, she'd thought of that too. It's supposed to be a physical impossibility, isn't it? Anyway, I said probably the way he'd chosen had been more fun. More fun, Jane repeated. She looked very thoughtful.

As you'll have seen, there was one loose end, of a sort. Who or what was it that had taken on my shape to enter that bedroom, talk to Jane with my voice, and share her bed for at any rate a few minutes? She and I didn't discuss it for several days. Then one morning she asked me the question more or less as I've just put it.

Interesting point, I said; I don't know. It's more interesting than you think, she said; because when . . . whoever it was got into bed with me, he didn't just go to sleep.

I suppose I just looked at her. That's right, she said; I thought I'd better go and see John before I told you. (That's John Allison, our GP.)

It was negative, then, I said. Yes, Jane said.

Well, that's it. A relief, of course. But in one way, rather disappointing.

ROBERT ARTHUR
The Believers

From one spoof radio broadcast, we now move to another, again with an unforeseen twist in the tale. The author of this memorable tale contributed several chilling stories to the magazines Unknown *and* Weird Tales, *and wrote for the American radio series* The Mysterious Traveller *adapting several classics of the macabre by W. Hope Hodgson, Agatha Christie, Ray Bradbury, and others.*

"This is it," Nick Deene said with enthusiasm after he had stared down at the old Carriday house for a couple of minutes. "This is what I had in mind. Right down to the last rusty hinge and creaky floorboard."

Danny Lomax heaved a sigh of relief.

"Praise be!" he said. "We've wasted almost a week finding a house that suited you just right, and that doesn't leave us much time to start the publicity. Although I'll admit"—Danny squinted down at the brooding old pile of stone and lumber that still retained some traces of a one-time dignity—"I'll admit you've really turned up a honey. If that isn't a haunted house, it'll do until one comes along."

Nick Deene stood for a moment longer, appraising the Carriday mansion, on whose arched entrance the carved figure 1784 still defied the corroding elements. The building was a long, L-shaped Colonial-type house, with stone foundations and hand-sawed clapboard upper structure. It had been painted some dark colour once, but the colour had gone with the years, leaving the structure a scabrous, mottled hue.

The building was two-storied, with attics, and seemed to contain a number of rooms. Woods, once cut back, had crept up almost to the walls and gave the place a cramped, crowded feeling. A weed-grown dirt carriage drive connecting with a half-impassable county road, and the tumbled ruins of a couple of outbuildings, finished off the scene.

"It has everything, Danny!" Nick Deene went on, with animation. "Absolutely everything but a ghost."

"Which is just fine with me," asserted the technical assistant allotted him by his radio hour sponsors—*So-Pure Soaps present Dare Danger with Deene!* "Of course, I don't believe in ghosts, as the hillbilly said about the hippopotamus, but that's all the more reason I don't want to go meeting one. I'm too old to go around revising my beliefs just to please a spook."

"That's just it," Nick Deene told him. "A resident haunt that somebody or other had seen, or thought he'd seen, and described, would cramp my style. Of course, nobody comes out here, and it's spooky enough to make any casual passer-by take another road, but there's no definite legend attached to it. That's what I've been looking for—that, plus a proper background. And this has the proper background. Three generations of Carridays died here—of malaria, probably; look at the swamp back there. The last Carriday ran away to sea and died in Java. The place has been empty fifteen years now, except for a tramp found in it one winter, dead of pneumonia. Nobody's going to buy it, not away out here in a swampy section of woods. For a couple thousand dollars the estate agent will be glad enough to let us have the key and do anything we want to it, including furnishing it with a nice, brand-new ghost. Which is just what I'm going to do."

"Nicholas Deene, Hand-Tailored Spooks, Ghost Maker to the Nobility," Danny Lomax grunted. "You know, I used to read your books and believe 'em. That chapter where you told about the doomed dancing girl in the old temple at Angkor Vat, and how you saved her just before the priests came for her, gave me a big kick once. I was young enough to think it had really happened!"

"Well, there *is* a temple at Angkor Vat." Nick Deene grinned. "And dancing girls too. So if you enjoyed the story, why complain? You believed it when you read it, didn't you?"

"Yeah," Danny Lomax agreed, stamping out a cigarette. "I believed it."

"Then you got your money's worth," the tall, bronzed man asserted. (Sun lamp treatments every evening, carefully timed by his valet, Walters, kept that bronze in good repair.) "And a million people still believe that story. Just as ten million people are going to believe in the Carriday Curse."

"All right," the small, wiry man assented. "I'm not here to argue. Even if the Carriday Curse is strictly a Nick Deene fake, I don't like this place. If I had a lot of baby spooks I wanted to raise, I'd bring 'em here and plant 'em. The atmosphere is so unhealthy!"

Nick Deene smiled the flashing toothed smile that had won him indulgence all around the globe, had been photographed against the columns of the Athenaeum, halfway up Mount Everest, atop an elephant going over the Alps, and too many other places to list. He brushed back the jet-black hair that lay so smoothly against his skull, and started back toward the road. Danny Lomax followed, making plans out loud.

"We can have 'em run a mobile unit up to the road, here," he decided. "You'll have a portable sender on your back, and the unit will pick it up and retransmit to Hartford. Hartford will pipe it into New York and out through the network. We'll give the equipment a thorough check so there's not much chance of anything going wrong. Your rating has been falling off lately, but this'll hypo the box office up to the top again. Most of your listeners have already read the stuff you've been dramatizing on the ether, you know. This one, a direct broadcast from a haunted house on the night of Friday the 13th will pull 'em in. You're a fake, Deene, but you got some good ideas, and this is one of the better ones. *If*."

"If what?" Nick demanded challengingly, as they reached the road and prepared to clamber into a waiting car.

"If you put it over." Danny Lomax took the right-hand seat and slammed the door. "A lot of newspaper men don't like you any too well, and if there's any stink to this thing they'll horse-laugh it to death. There has to be a ghost, and your audience has to believe in it. Don't make any mistake about that."

"There'll be a ghost," Nick Deene shrugged, putting the car into motion. "And they'll believe in it. I'll be right in the room with 'em. I'm working on the script now. I'm going to ask them to turn out the light when they listen, and imagine they're with me, waiting in the dark for the Thing that for a hundred years has been the Curse of the Carridays to appear. I'll be armed only with a flashlight, a Bible, and——"

"And a contract," Danny interrupted. "Sorry. But I've lost all my illusions since meeting you."

"And a crucifix," Deene continued, a little nettled by now. "They'll hear boards creaking, and a death-watch beetle ticking in the wall. And plenty of other details. I'll make them up as I go along. Spontaneity always gives the most convincing effect, I've found. And they'll be convinced. Aren't they always?"

"Yes," the advertising man agreed reluctantly. "When you go into your act, old ladies swoon with excitement and little kids scream all night in their cribs. There was one heart-failure—an old maid in Dubuque—after last month's show, the one in which you were fighting an octopus forty feet beneath the surface, down in the Malay pearling waters."

"There'll be half a dozen this time," Nick Deene prophesied complacently. "When I start into the Carriday house to meet the Thing with a face like an oyster——"

"A face like an oyster, huh?" Danny Lomax repeated, and swallowed hard. "That's what it's going to look like?"

Nick Deene chuckled and nodded.

"If there's anything deader looking than a watery blue oyster that's been open too long," he said, "I don't know what it is. Where was I? Oh, yes. Well, when I start into that house to wait for the approach of the Thing with an oyster face, I'm going to scare the living daylights out of ten million people, if you guys do your jobs right."

"We will, we will," Danny promised. "We'll ship out photos of the house, I'll plant the story the locals should repeat to a couple of fellows in the village, we'll ballyhoo you all the way down the line. The only thing we won't do is try to fix the weatherman to make it a stormy night. You'll have to take your chances on that."

"It's generally foggy down here in the swamps at night," Deene replied, quite seriously. "Fog is as good as a storm any time."

"Yeah," Danny Lomax agreed, twisting around to look down at the house in the hollow below—the road having taken them up a slope behind it. Fog was already forming in tenuous grey wisps, as the disappearance of the sun brought cool air currents rolling down into the swampy dell. "Fog's good enough for me, any time. You know, Deene, maybe it's a good thing you don't believe in spooks yourself."

"Maybe it is, at that." Nick Deene grinned as they topped a rise and the Carriday house disappeared from view.

It was not a foggy night. Yet there were mists about the Carriday house as Danny Lomax, Nicholas Deene, and two newspaper men—Ken Blake and Larry Miller—prepared to enter it.

Sitting as it did in the very bottom of a little glen, it was wrapped in pale vapour that danced and shifted in slow, stately movements. A quarter moon thrust a weak finger of radiance down into the woods. It was eleven o'clock, and time for *Dare Danger With Deene* to hit the air with its special broadcast.

Danny Lomax had earphones clamped to his ears, tentacles of wire trailing back from them to the broadcast unit pulled up beside the road. The house was four hundred yards away, and Danny was conscious of a vague regret it wasn't four million as he snatched off the earphones and dropped his hand.

Nick Deene caught the signal, which meant that the theme music was finished, as well as the lengthy announcement outlining the circumstances of the broadcast. His deep, expressive voice took up the tale without a hitch.

"This is Nicholas Deene speaking," he said easily into the mike attached to his chest and connected to the pack broadcaster slung over his shoulder. "The old Carriday mansion lies in a depression below me, some four hundred yards away. Wan moonlight illuminates it. Veils of fog wrap around it as if to hide it from man's gaze. For fifteen years no human being has spent a night beneath its roof—alive."

His voice paused significantly, to let his unseen audience experience its first prickle of pleasurable terror.

"But tonight I am going to brave the curse of the Carridays. I am going to enter the house. And in the great master bedroom where three generations of Carridays died, I am going to wait for the unknown Thing that legends tell of to appear.

"I am going toward the house now, with two reputable newspaper men at my side. One of them has a pair of handcuffs, the other the key. They are going to handcuff me to the sturdy bedposts of the dust-covered ancient four-poster that can be seen through the window in the master bedroom. That is to insure that I shall not leave before midnight strikes—before this ill-omened Friday the thirteenth passes away into the limbo of the vanished days."

Nick Deene's voice went on, rising and falling in carefully cadenced rolls, doing little tricks to the emotions of listeners a mile, a thousand miles, three thousand miles away. He and Danny Lomax and the two reporters trudged on downhill toward the house.

This was a last-minute inspiration of Nick Deene's, this handcuff business. The press had taken a somewhat scoffing note toward the stunt broadcast. But Nick Deene's showman's instinct had risen to the occasion. There was a compellingness to the idea of a man being chained in a deserted house, haunted or not—being unable to leave—which had impressed the critics.

Deene kept on talking as they approached the old mansion, flashlight beams dancing ahead of them. He described the woods, the night sounds, the dancing mist, the appearance of the empty, silent mansion ahead of them, and did a good job. Not that it was necessary for the three men with him. Even before they reached the house, the carefully cultivated skepticism which Blake and Miller had sported was gone from their faces. Cynical though they were, Danny Lomax thought he could catch traces of uneasiness on their countenances.

"We are standing on the rotten, creaking porch now," Deene was telling his audience. "One reporter is unlocking the door with the key given us reluctantly by the white-haired agent for the property, a man whose expression tells us that he knows many things about this house his closed lips will not reveal.

"The door creaks open. Our lights probe the black throat of the hall. Dust is everywhere, inches thick. It rises and swirls about us as we enter——"

They went in, and Nick Deene's tread was the firmest of the four as they strode the length of a narrow hall and reached the stairs. Their lights showed side rooms, filled with old furniture whose dust covers had not been removed in almost two decades. The stairs were winding, and creaked. The air was as musty as it always is in houses long closed.

They reached the second floor where a finger of moonlight intruded through an end window. Their flashlights reflected off a dusty mirror, and Larry Miller jumped uneasily. Nick Deene chuckled into the microphone, and a million listeners nodded in quick approval of his courage.

"My friends are nervous," Nick Deene was telling them. "They feel the atmosphere that hangs so heavy in these silent rooms trod only by creatures of the unseen.

"But we are now in the bedroom where I shall wait——"

The bedroom was big. The door leading into it, though, was low and narrow, and the windows were small. A broken shutter hanging outside creaked in an unseen air current.

There were two old chairs, a bureau, a cedar chest, a rag rug — and the four-poster bedstead. A coverlet, grey with dust, lay over the mattress. Nick Deene grimaced as he saw it, but his voice did not falter.

Danny Lomax snatched the coverlet off the bed and shook it. Dust filled the air, and he coughed as he put the coverlet back into place. He slid a chair up beside the bed, and Nick Deene, without disturbing the broadcast, slid off his pack transmitter and placed it on the chair.

He lay down on the bed, and Larry Miller, with a pair of handcuffs from his pocket, linked one ankle to the left bed-post. Danny Lomax adjusted the mike so that Nick Deene could speak into it without having to hold it, and Deene waved his hand in a signal of preparedness.

"My friends are preparing to depart," he told his audience. His words leaped from the room to the waiting mobile unit, from there to Hartford, twenty miles away, thence to New York, and then to the world, or whatever part of it might be listening. "In a moment I shall be alone. I have a flashlight, but to conserve the batteries I am going to turn it out.

"May I make a suggestion? Why don't you, who are listening, turn out your lights too, and we will wait together in darkness for the approach of the creature known as the Curse of the Carridays — a creature which I hope, before the next hour is over, to describe to you.

"What it is or what it looks like, I do not know. The one man who could tell — the agent for the property — faithful to his trust though the last Carriday died long since in far-off Java, will not speak. Yet, if the portents are favourable, we — you and I — may see it tonight."

Clever, Danny Lomax thought, his trick of identifying the audience with himself, making them feel as if they were on the spot, too. One of the big secrets of his success.

"Now," Nick Deene was saying, "I take my leave of my companions——"

Then Danny and the two reporters were leaving. Nick Deene kicked his leg, the chain of the handcuff rattled, and Larry Miller jumped. Nick waved a sardonic hand after them.

They went downstairs, not dawdling, and no one spoke until they were outside. Then Blake drew a deep breath.

"He's a phony," he said, with reluctant admiration. "And you know as well as I do that if he sees anything tonight, it'll be strictly the product of his imagination. But just the same, I wouldn't spend an hour in that place, handcuffed to the furniture, for a month's pay."

Without hesitating, they set off for the waiting unit, and the small knot of men — technicians, reporters, and advertising agency men — clustered around it. And as they hurried, lights went out in a house here, another there — in Boston, in Sioux Falls, Kalamazoo, Santa Barbara and a thousand other towns — as some of Nick Deene's farflung audience obeyed his melodramatic suggestion to listen to him in the darkness. And two million families settled themselves to wait with him, hanging on his every word, their acceptance of everything he said complete, their belief utter.

When the three men reached the mobile unit again, the little group of half a dozen men there were clustered about the rear, where a half-circle of light burned through the darkness and a loud-speaker repeated Nick Deene's every word.

Deene was still building atmosphere. His resonant voice was picturing the house, the shadows, the dust, the darkness that seemed to crouch within the hallways.

"Listen," Nick Deene was saying, and Danny Lomax could visualize the big bronze man grinning sardonically as he spoke, "and hear with me the small night sounds that infest this ancient, spirit-ridden dwelling. Somewhere a board is creaking — perhaps for no tangible cause. I cannot tell. But it comes to me clearly——"

Listening, they could hear it, too. The eerie, chill-provoking creak of a floorboard or stairway, in midnight silence. Nick Deene had two bits of wood in his pocket that he rubbed together to get that effect, but only Danny Lomax knew that. And even knowing, he did not like the sound.

"I hear the creaking——" Nick Deene's voice was low, suspense-filled now—"I hear the creaking, and something else. A monotonous tick-tick-tick that seems to become louder and louder as I listen to it, the frightening beat of the death-watch beetle within the walls of this room——"

19

They could hear that too, as Nick Deene's voice died out. Hear it, and their own breathing become faster as if they too were in that room, listening with a man bound to the great four-poster there.

And in Atlanta, in Rochester, in Cincinnati, in Memphis, Mobile, Reno, Cheyenne, and a thousand other cities and towns, Nick Deene's listeners heard it too in the hushed silence in which they listened. They swallowed a little harder, looked about them a little uneasily, and smiled — smiles that were palpably artificial. And they believed—

Danny Lomax would have believed, too, if he hadn't known of the small metal contrivance by which Nick Deene managed the "death-watch beetle" noises. Even knowing, he admitted to himself that it was an impressive performance. When Nick Deene had boasted that he would make ten million people believe in the "curse of the Carridays" he had exaggerated — but not about their believing. His audience probably didn't number more than five million. But he had most of that five million by now in a complete state of belief for anything he might want to say next.

Danny glanced at his watch, turning his wrist so that the timepiece caught the light. Thirty-five minutes gone. Twenty-five to go. Time now for Deene to start turning on the heat. Time for the sock punch to start developing. He'd built up his background and sold his audience. Now he ought to begin to deliver.

He did. A moment later, Nick Deene's voice paused abruptly. The sudden silence held more suspense than any words he could have spoken. It held for ten seconds, twenty, thirty. Then he broke it only with a half-whispered announcement.

"I think I can hear something moving outside the house——"

Around the unit there was utter silence, save for the hum of the generator that was pumping the broadcast over the hills and woods to Hartford.

"Whatever it is—" Nick Deene's voice was still low, still that of a man who whispers an aside even while intent upon something else—"whatever it is, it's coming closer. It seems to be moving slowly up from the small patch of swamp just south of the house."

Absently, Danny Lomax reached for a cigarette. Nick was sticking to the general script they'd outlined. Almost at the last minute, they'd decided against a spiritual manifestation, a ghost pure and simple.

Instead, with his usual instinct for getting the right note, Nick Deene had switched to a *Thing*. Something nameless, something formless, something unclassifiable. Something out of the night and the swamp and the unknown. Something that might be alive and might not be alive. But something that, when Nick Deene got through describing it, would be very, very real——

"Whatever it is, it's coming closer," Nick Deene reported then. "I hear a dragging, dull sound, as of something heavy moving through dead brush and over rough ground. It may be just an animal, perhaps even a stray cow, or a horse, or a wild pig escaped from a pen somewhere on an adjacent farm——"

Five million listeners held their breath a moment. Of course, just a stray horse, or a cow. Something warm, something familiar, something harmless. Then——

"It's pulling at the boards which cover the cellar windows!" Nick Deene exclaimed. "It's trying to get into the house!"

Danny Lomax held his cigarette unlighted, until the flaring match burned his fingers. In spite of their determined skepticism, there was an intentness to the faces of the reporters and technicians gathered around the end of the mobile unit. They knew or guessed this was a phony. Yet the sudden jolt, after Deene had given their nerves a moment in which to relax, got them all. Just as it was getting the whole great, unseen audience.

Danny Lomax, from years of listening to radio programmes behind the scenes, had developed a sixth sense of his own. He could tell almost to a degree just how a programme was going over — whether it was smashing home or laying an egg. He could feel the audience that listened reacting, and he could sense what their reactions were.

Now something was pulling at him — something strained and tense and uneasy. Several million people or more were listening, were believing, were living through the scene with Nicholas Deene. Crouched there in the chilly night beside the broadcast unit, Danny Lomax could feel the waves of their belief sweeping past him, impalpable but very real.

Nick Deene's voice had quickened. He was reporting now the sound of nails shrieking as they pulled free, as boards gave way. He described a heavy, squashy body forcing its way through the tiny window. He made his listeners hear the soft, squashy sounds of something large and flabby moving through the darkness of the cellar of the house, finding the stairs, going up them slowly, slowly, slowly——

"Now it's in the hall." The big man's words were short, sharp, electric. "It's coming toward the door. I hear boards creaking beneath its weight. It senses that I'm here. It's searching for me. I confess I'm frightened. No sane man could fail to be. However, I am convinced it can't hurt me. If it's a psychic manifestation, it's harmless, however horrifying its appearance may be. So I am keeping a firm grip on my nerves. Only if they betray me can I be endangered.

"Whatever it is, it's just outside the doorway now. The room is in darkness. The moon has set. I have my flashlight, though, and I am going to turn it full on the thing in the doorway.

"I can smell a musty, damp odour, as of swamps and wet places. It is very strong. Almost overpowering. But now I'm going to turn on the light——"

Nick Deene's voice ceased. Danny Lomax's wrist-watch ticked as loudly as an alarm clock. The seconds passed. Ten. Twenty. Thirty. Forty. Someone shifted position. Someone's breath was rasping like that of a choking sleeper.

Then—"It's going!" Nick Deene's voice was a whisper. "It looked at me, and would have entered. I could sense what it wished. It wished — *me*. But I have the Bible and crucifix I brought tightly in my hand, the light has been shining full into its — its face, if I can call it that. I did not lower my gaze, and now it's going. I can no longer see it. The light of my flash falls on the black, empty frame of the doorway. *It* is slithering back down the hall, toward the steps. It is returning to the swamp from which it came when it sensed my presence here.

"I can hardly describe it. I don't know what it was. It stood as high as a man, yet its legs were only stumps of greyness without feet of any kind. Its body was long and bulbous, like a misshapen turnip, its flesh greyish and uneven. It shone a little, as if with slime, and I saw droplets of water on it catch the light of my torch.

"It had a head, a great round head that was as hairless as the rest of it. And a face — I cannot make you see it as I saw it. Staring into it, I could only think of an oyster. A monstrous, wet, blue-grey oyster, with two darker spots that must have been eyes.

"It had arms. At least, two masses of matter attached to either side of its body reached out a little toward me. There were no hands on the ends of them. Just strings of — corruption.

"That was all I could see. Then it turned. Now it has gone. It has reached the bottom steps, going down with a shuffling, bumping noise. It is moving toward the cellar stairs, the floor creaking beneath it, back to the cellar window through which it forced itself, back to the depths of the swamp from which it emerged. Yet the sense of it still hangs in this room, and I know that if my will should slacken, it could feel it, and return. But it must not. I will not let it. It *must* return to the bottomless muck from which it came——"

Danny Lomax touched his dry lips with his tongue. This was it. This was the high spot. This was where Nick Deene got over, or fell flat on his face. Danny knew that whichever it was, he'd be able to sense it.

And he did. Not failure. Success! The unseen currents that eddied around him were belief. The belief of millions of people, wrapped in a skein spun of words. The belief of millions of listeners seeing in their minds something that had never existed, but which Nick Deene had created and put there.

Tomorrow they might laugh. They might belittle and ridicule the very fact that they had listened. But they'd never be able to forget how they had felt. And now, for the moment at least, they believed. Completely.

Danny let out a breath, and looked at his watch. Almost midnight. Nick Deene was speaking again.

"It's gone now. It's outside again, seeking the swamp from which it came. This is Nicholas Deene speaking. I'm going to sign off now. I've been through quite a nerve strain. Thanks for listening, everybody. I'm glad that you weren't disappointed, that something happened tonight to make this broadcast worth your listening. Good night, all. This is Nicholas Deene saying goodnight."

Danny Lomax saw the chief engineer throw a switch, and nod to him. He leaned forward toward a secondary mike in the unit, and slipped on a pair of headphones.

"All right, Nick," he said. "You're off the air. We're coming down to unlock you now."

"Okay," Nick Deene's voice came back, a little ragged. "Hurry, will you? The last couple of minutes, I could swear I *have* heard noises outside. Maybe I'm too good. I'm believing myself. How'd it go?"

"Went fine," Danny told him. "They ate it up. Five million people are sitting in their parlours this minute, getting the stiffness out of their muscles, and trying to pretend they didn't believe you."

"I told you they would." Deene's voice was momentarily complacent. Then it became edged again. "Listen, hurry, will you? There *is* something moving around outside this house—You say they ate it up?"

"Straight," Danny Lomax told him. "I could feel it. They're all still seeing that Thing you described, with the oyster face, crawling in through the cellar window, slithering up the stairs, standing in your doorway——"

"Cut it!" Deene ordered abruptly. "And come down here. *There's something coming in the cellar window where we loosened the boards for the reporters to find!*"

Lomax turned.

"Oh, Joe," he called to the driver. "Take the unit down in front of the house, will you? Save walking. . . . What did you say then, Nick? I missed it."

"I said there's something coming in the cellar window!" Nick Deene's voice was almost shrill. "It's knocking around in the cellar. It's coming toward the stairs!"

"Steady, Nick, steady," Danny Lomax cautioned. "Don't let your nerves go now. You and I know it's just a gag. Don't go and——"

"Good grief!" Deene's breath was coming in gasps. *"There's something coming up the stairs!* Come and get me out of here!"

Danny looked up, a frown between his eyes.

"Joe, get going, will you?" he snapped, and the driver looked around in annoyed surprise.

"Right away," he grunted, and the unit jerked forward. "This fast enough to suit you?"

Danny Lomax didn't answer.

"Nick, you all right?" he demanded of the mike, and Deene's voice, almost unrecognizable, came back.

"Danny, Danny," it gobbled, "there's something coming up the stairs with a sort of thump-thump. I can smell marsh gas and ammonia. There's something making a slithery sound. *I tell you something has got into this house from the swamp and is after me!*"

The unit was jolting down the long unused road. The reporters had swung on. They were staring at Danny, sensing something, they didn't know what, going wrong. Danny, the earphones tight, hung over the mike.

"Take it easy, take it easy," he soothed. "We wrote all that down. It's just on paper. You just said it. Five million people believed it, but you and I don't have to, Nick. We——"

"Listen to me!" Nick cried. "There's something in the hall. Something that scrapes and thumps. The floorboards are creaking. Danny, you know I'm chained here. It's coming after me. It is! It is!" Nick Deene's voice was hysterical. "It's at the doorway. It's——"

The voice was drowned out by a scraping of gravel as the brakes went on abruptly. Wheels fought for traction, lost it. A muddy spot had slewed the broadcast unit to one side. The long-untended road gave no hold. The rear wheels slid toward the ditch beside the road. The unit jolted, toppled, was caught as the hubs dug into a clay bank. The newspaper men were jolted off. Danny Lomax was bounced away from the mike, his earphones torn off his head.

He scrambled back toward the mike. The earphones were cracked. He threw a switch cutting in the speaker.

"Nick!" he cried. "Nick!"

"*—in the doorway now!*" came the terror-shrill wail from the speaker. "Coming in! Oyster-face—great, blank, watery oyster-face—Danny, Danny, put me back on the air, tell 'em all it's just a joke, tell 'em it isn't so, tell 'em not to believe, not to believe. Danny, do you hear, tell 'em *not to believe*!

"It's coming in! It wants me! It smells, and it's all wet and watery and its face—its *face!* Danny, tell 'em not to believe! It's 'cause they believe. It didn't exist. I thought it up. But they all believed me. You said they did! Five million people, all believing at the same time! Believing strong enough for you to feel! They've made it, Danny, they've brought it to life! It's doing just what I said it did, and it looks just like I—like I—*Danny! Help me!* HELP ME!"

The loud-speaker screamed, vibrated shrilly at the overload and was silent. And in the sudden hush, an echo came from the night. No, not an echo, but the scream itself they had been hearing. Faint, and dreadful, it reached them, and Danny Lomax was quite unable to move for an instant.

Then he galvanized into action, and as he ran into the darkness, the others followed. With horrifying finality, Nick Deene's screams had ceased. Danny could see the Carriday house ahead, dark, silent, tomb-like. It was three hundred yards away, and the curve of the road hid it momentarily.

The three hundred yards took almost a minute to make. Then Danny, gasping, turned into the old carriage drive, Nick Deene's words still screaming in his mind.

"They've made it, Danny! They've brought it to life! Five million people, all believing at the same time——"

Could—- Could— Danny's mind wouldn't ask itself the question, or answer it. But he had felt the currents of belief. In a million homes or more, five million people had sat, and listened, and believed. In the concentrated power of their believing, had they stirred some spark of force into life, had they jelled into the form of their belief a creature that——

Feet pounded behind him. Someone had a flashlight. The beam of it played over the house, and for a moment darted into the darkness beyond and to one side.

And Danny Lomax caught a glimpse of movement.

A vague, grey-white glimmer of motion, a half-seen shape that moved with speed through the dense vegetation toward the four-acre swamp south of the house and for an instant shone faintly, as if with slime and wetness.

If there was any sound of movement, Danny Lomax did not hear it, because the scuffle of running feet and the hoarse breathing of running men behind drowned it out. But as he listened intently, he thought he heard a single scream, muffled and cut abruptly short. It was as though a man had tried to cry out with his mouth almost covered by something wet and soft and pulpy——

Danny Lomax pulled up and stood quite still, as the newspaper men and technicians came up with him and ran past. He scarcely heard them, was scarcely aware of them, for his whole body was cold. Something was squeezing his insides with a giant hand, and he knew that in just an instant he was going to be deathly sick.

And he knew already that the bedroom upstairs was empty. That the searchers would find only half a handcuff hanging from the footboard of the bed, its chain twisted in two, some marks in the dust, and a few drops of slimy water to tell where Nick Deene had gone.

Only those, and an odour hanging pungent and acrid in the halls——

SABINE BARING-GOULD
A Happy Release

Sabine Baring-Gould (1834–1924), *squire-parson of Lew Trenchard in Devon for many years, will always be remembered for the great hymns he wrote, especially "Onward, Christian Soldiers"; but he was also amazingly prolific in other branches of literature, including biographies, travel books, folklore, novels, and ghost stories. The latter were collected in* A Book of Ghosts *(1904).*

Mr. Benjamin Woolfield was a widower. For twelve months he put on mourning. The mourning was external, and by no means represented the condition of his feelings; for his married life had not been happy. He and Kesiah had been unequally yoked together. The Mosaic law forbade the union of the ox and the ass to draw one plough; and two more uncongenial creatures than Benjamin and Kesiah could hardly have been coupled to draw the matrimonial furrow.

She was a Plymouth Sister, and he, as she repeatedly informed him whenever he indulged in light reading, laughed, smoked, went out shooting, or drank a glass of wine, was of the earth, earthy, and a miserable worldling.

For some years Mr. Woolfield had been made to feel as though he were a moral and religious pariah. Kesiah had invited to the house and to meals, those of her own way of thinking, and on such occasions had spared no pains to have the table well served, for the elect are particular about their feeding, if indifferent as to their drinks. On such occasions, moreover, when Benjamin had sat at the bottom of his own table, he had been made to feel that he was a worm to be trodden on. The topics of conversation were such as were far beyond his horizon, and concerned matters of which he was ignorant. He attempted at intervals to enter into the circle of talk. He knew that such themes as football matches, horse races, and cricket were taboo,

28

but he did suppose that home or foreign politics might interest the guests of Kesiah. But he soon learned that this was not the case, unless such matters tended to the fulfilment of prophecy.

When, however, in his turn, Benjamin invited home to dinner some of his old friends, he found that all provided for them was hashed mutton, cottage pie, and tapioca pudding. But even these could have been stomached, had not Mrs. Woolfield sat stern and silent at the head of the table, not uttering a word, but giving vent to occasional, very audible sighs.

When the year of mourning was well over, Mr. Woolfield put on a light suit, and contented himself, as an indication of bereavement, with a slight black band round the left arm. He also began to look about him for someone who might make up for the years during which he had felt like a crushed strawberry.

And in casting his inquiring eye about, it lighted upon Philippa Weston, a bright, vigorous young lady, well educated and intelligent. She was aged twenty-four and he was but eighteen years older, a difference on the right side.

It took Mr. Woolfield but a short courtship to reach an understanding, and he became engaged.

On the same evening upon which he had received a satisfactory answer to the question put to her, and had pressed for an early marriage, to which also consent had been accorded, he sat by his study fire, with his hands on his knees, looking into the embers and building love-castles there. Then he smiled and patted his knees.

He was startled from his honey reveries by a sniff. He looked round. There was a familiar ring in that sniff which was unpleasant to him.

What he then saw dissipated his rosy dreams, and sent his blood to his heart.

At the table sat his Kesiah, looking at him with her beady black eyes, and with stern lines in her face. He was so startled and shocked that he could not speak.

"Benjamin," said the apparition, "I know your purpose. It shall never be carried to accomplishment. I will prevent it."

"Prevent what, my love, my treasure?" he gathered up his faculties to reply.

"It is in vain that you assume that infantile look of innocence," said his deceased wife. "You shall never — never — lead her to the hymeneal altar."

29

"Lead whom, my idol? You astound me."

"I know all. I can read your heart. A lost being though you be, you have still me to watch over you. When you quit this earthly tabernacle, if you have given up taking in the *Field*, and have come to realise your fallen condition, there is a chance — a distant chance — but yet one of our union becoming eternal."

"You don't mean to say so," said Mr. Woolfield, his jaw falling.

"There is — there is that to look to. That to lead you to turn over a new leaf. But it can never be if you become united to that Flibbertigibbet."

Mentally, Benjamin said: "I must hurry up with my marriage!" Vocally he said: "Dear me! Dear me!"

"My care for you is still so great," continued the apparition, "that I intend to haunt you by night and by day, till that engagement be broken off."

"I would not put you to so much trouble," said he.

"It is my duty," replied the late Mrs. Woolfield sternly.

"You are oppressively kind," sighed the widower.

At dinner that evening Mr. Woolfield had a friend to keep him company, a friend to whom he had poured out his heart. To his dismay, he saw seated opposite him the form of his deceased wife.

He tried to be lively; he cracked jokes, but the sight of the grim face and the stony eyes riveted on him damped his spirits, and all his mirth died away.

"You seem to be out of sorts to-night," said his friend.

"I am sorry that I act so bad a host," apologised Mr. Woolfield. "Two is company, three is none."

"But we are only two here to-night."

"My wife is with me in spirit."

"Which, she that was, or she that is to be?"

Mr. Woolfield looked with timid eyes towards her who sat at the end of the table. She was raising her hands in holy horror, and her face was black with frowns.

His friend said to himself when he left: "Oh, these lovers! They are never themselves so long as the fit lasts."

Mr. Woolfield retired early to bed. When a man has screwed himself up to proposing to a lady, it has taken a great deal out of him, and nature demands rest. It was so with Benjamin; he was sleepy. A nice little fire burned in his grate. He undressed and slipped between the sheets.

Before he put out the light he became aware that the late Mrs. Woolfield was standing by his bedside with a nightcap on her head.

"I am cold," said she, "bitterly cold."

"I am sorry to hear it, my dear," said Benjamin.

"The grave is cold as ice," she said. "I am going to step into bed."

"No — never!" exclaimed the widower, sitting up. "It won't do. It really won't. You will draw all the vital heat out of me, and I shall be laid up with rheumatic fever. It will be ten times worse than damp sheets."

"I am coming to bed," repeated the deceased lady, inflexible as ever in carrying out her will.

As she stepped in Mr. Woolfield crept out on the side of the fire and seated himself by the grate.

He sat there some considerable time, and then, feeling cold, he fetched his dressing-gown and enveloped himself in that.

He looked at the bed. In it lay the deceased lady with her long slit of a mouth shut like a rat-trap, and her hard eyes fixed on him.

"It is of no use your thinking of marrying, Benjamin," she said. "I shall haunt you till you give it up."

Mr. Woolfield sat by his fire all night, and only dozed off towards morning.

During the day he called at the house of Miss Weston, and was shown into the drawing-room. But there, standing behind her chair, was his deceased wife with her arms folded on the back of the seat, glowering at him.

It was impossible for the usual tender passages to ensue between the lovers with a witness present, expressing by gesture her disapproval of such matters and her inflexible determination to force on a rupture.

The dear departed did not attend Mr. Woolfield continuously during the day, but appeared at intervals. He could never say when he would be free, when she would not turn up.

In the evening he rang for the housemaid. "Jemima," he said, "put two hot bottles into my bed to-night. It is somewhat chilly."

"Yes, sir."

"And let the water be boiling—not with the chill off."

31

"Yes, sir."

When somewhat late Mr. Woolfield retired to his room he found, as he had feared, that his late wife was there before him. She lay in the bed with her mouth snapped, her eyes like black balls, staring at him.

"My dear," said Benjamin, "I hope you are more comfortable."

"I'm cold, deadly cold."

"But I trust you are enjoying the hot bottles."

"I lack animal heat," replied the late Mrs. Woolfield.

Benjamin fled the room and returned to his study, where he unlocked his spirit case and filled his pipe. The fire was burning. He made it up. He would sit there all night. During the passing hours, however, he was not left quite alone. At intervals the door was gently opened, and the night-capped head of the late Mrs. Woolfield was thrust in.

"Don't think, Benjamin, that your engagement will lead to anything," she would say, "because it will not. I shall stop it."

So time passed. Mr. Woolfield found it impossible to escape this persecution. He lost spirits; he lost flesh.

At last, after sad thought, he saw but one way of relief, and that was to submit. And in order to break off the engagement he must have a prolonged interview with Philippa. He went to the theatre and bought two stall tickets, and sent one to her with the earnest request that she would accept it and meet him that evening at the theatre. He had something to communicate of the utmost importance.

At the theatre he knew that he would be safe; the principles of Kesiah would not suffer her to enter there.

At the proper time Mr. Woolfield drove round to Miss Weston's, picked her up, and together they went to the theatre and took their places in the stalls. Their seats were side by side.

"I am so glad you have been able to come," said Benjamin. "I have a most shocking disclosure to make to you. I am afraid that—but I hardly know how to say it—that—I really must break it off."

"Break what off?"

"Our engagement."

"Nonsense. I have been fitted for my trousseau."

"Your what?"

"My wedding-dress."

"Oh, I beg pardon. I did not understand your French pronunciation. I thought—but it does not matter what I thought."

"Pray what is the sense of this?"

"Philippa, my affection for you is unabated. Do not suppose that I love you one whit the less. But I am oppressed by a horrible nightmare— daymare as well. I am haunted."

"Haunted, indeed!"

"Yes; by my late wife. She allows me no peace. She has made up her mind that I shall not marry you."

"Oh! Is that all? I am haunted also."

"Surely not?"

"It is a fact."

"Hush, hush!" from persons in front and at the side. Neither Ben nor Philippa had noticed that the curtain had risen and that the play had begun.

"We are disturbing the audience," whispered Mr. Woolfield. "Let us go out into the passage and promenade there, and then we can talk freely."

So both rose, left their stalls, and went into the *couloir*.

"Look here, Philippa," said he, offering the girl his arm, which she took, "the case is serious. I am badgered out of my reason, out of my health, by the late Mrs. Woolfield. She always had an iron will, and she has intimated to me that she will force me to give you up."

"Defy her."

"I cannot."

"Tut! these ghosts are exacting. Give them an inch and they take an ell. They are like old servants; if you yield to them they tyrannise over you."

"But how do you know, Philippa, dearest?"

"Because, as I said, I also am haunted."

"That only makes the matter more hopeless."

"On the contrary, it only shows how well suited we are to each other. We are in one box."

"Philippa, it is a dreadful thing. When my wife was dying she told me she was going to a better world, and that we should never meet again. *And she has not kept her word.*"

The girl laughed. "Rag her with it."

"How can I?"

"You can do it perfectly. Ask her why she is left out in the cold. Give her a piece of your mind. Make it unpleasant for her. I give Jehu no good time."

"Who is Jehu?"

"Jehu Post is the ghost who haunts me. When in the flesh he was a great admirer of mine, and in his cumbrous way tried to court me; but I never liked him, and gave him no encouragement. I snubbed him unmercifully, but he was one of those self-satisfied, self-assured creatures incapable of taking a snubbing. He was a Plymouth Brother."

"My wife was a Plymouth Sister."

"I know she was, and I always felt for you. It was so sad. Well, to go on with my story. In a frivolous mood Jehu took to a bicycle, and the very first time he scorched he was thrown, and so injured his back that he died in a week. Before he departed he entreated that I would see him; so I could not be nasty, and I went. And he told me then that he was about to be wrapped in glory. I asked him if this were so certain. 'Cocksure' was his reply; and they were his last words. And *he has not kept his word.*"

"And he haunts you now?"

"Yes. He dangles about with his great ox-eyes fixed on me. But as to his envelope of glory I have not seen a fag end of it, and I have told him so."

"Do you really mean this, Philippa?"

"I do. He wrings his hands and sighs. He gets no change out of me, I promise you."

"This is a very strange condition of affairs."

"It only shows how well matched we are. I do not suppose you will find two other people in England so situated as we are, and therefore so admirably suited to one another."

"There is much in what you say. But how are we to rid ourselves of the nuisance—for it is a nuisance being thus haunted. We cannot spend all our time in a theatre."

"We must defy them. Marry in spite of them."

"I never did defy my wife when she was alive. I do not know how to pluck up courage now that she is dead. Feel my hand, Philippa, how it trembles. She has broken my nerve. When I was young I could play spellikins—my hand was so steady. Now I am quite incapable of doing anything with the little sticks."

"Well, hearken to what I propose," said Miss Weston. "I will beard the old cat——"

"Hush, not so disrespectful; she was my wife."

"Well, then, the ghostly old lady, in her den. You think she will appear if I go to pay you a visit?"

"Sure of it. She is consumed with jealousy. She had no personal attractions herself, and you have a thousand. I never knew whether she loved me, but she was always confoundedly jealous of me."

"Very well, then. You have often spoken to me about changes in the decoration of your villa. Suppose I call on you to-morrow afternoon, and you shall show me what your schemes are."

"And your ghost, will he attend you?"

"Most probably. He also is as jealous as a ghost can well be."

"Well, so be it. I shall await your coming with impatience. Now, then, we may as well go to our respective homes."

A cab was accordingly summoned, and after Mr. Woolfield had handed Philippa in, and she had taken her seat in the back, he entered and planted himself with his back to the driver.

"Why do you not sit by me?" asked the girl.

"I can't," replied Benjamin. "Perhaps you may not see, but I do, my deceased wife is in the cab, and occupies the place on your left."

"Sit on her," urged Philippa.

"I haven't the effrontery to do it," gasped Ben.

"Will you believe me," whispered the young lady, leaning over to speak to Mr. Woolfield, "I have seen Jehu Post hovering about the theatre door, wringing his white hands and turning up his eyes. I suspect he is running after the cab."

As soon as Mr. Woolfield had deposited his bride-elect at her residence he ordered the cabman to drive him home. Then he was alone in the conveyance with the ghost. As each gaslight was passed the flash came over the cadaverous face opposite him, and sparks of fire kindled momentarily in the stony eyes.

"Benjamin!" she said, "Benjamin! Oh, Benjamin! Do not suppose that I shall permit it. You may writhe and twist, you may plot and contrive how you will, I will stand between you and her as a wall of ice."

Next day, in the afternoon, Philippa Weston arrived at the house. The late Mrs. Woolfield had, however, apparently obtained an inkling of what was intended, for she was already there, in the drawing-room, seated in an armchair with her hands raised and clasped, looking stonily before her. She had a white face, no lips that showed, and her dark hair was dressed in two black slabs, one on each side of the temples. It was done in a knot behind. She wore no ornaments of any kind.

In came Miss Weston, a pretty girl, coquettishly dressed in colours, with sparkling eyes and laughing lips. As she had predicted, she was followed by her attendant spectre, a tall, gaunt young man in a black frock-coat, with a melancholy face and large ox-eyes. He shambled in shyly, looking from side to side. He had white hands and long, lean fingers. Every now and then he put his hands behind him, up his back, under the tails of his coat, and rubbed his spine where he had received his mortal injury in cycling. Almost as soon as he entered he noticed the ghost of Mrs. Woolfield that was, and made an awkward bow. Her eyebrows rose, and a faint wintry smile of recognition lighted up her cheeks.

"I believe I have the honour of saluting Sister Kesiah," said the ghost of Jehu Post, and he assumed a posture of ecstasy.

"It is even so, Brother Jehu."

"And how do you find yourself, sister—out of the flesh?"

The late Mrs. Woolfield looked disconcerted, hesitated a moment, as if she found some difficulty in answering, and then, after a while, said: "I suppose, much as do you, brother."

"It is a melancholy duty that detains me here below," said Jehu Post's ghost.

"The same may be said of me," observed the spirit of the deceased Mrs. Woolfield. "Pray take a chair."

"I am greatly obliged, sister. My back——"

Philippa nudged Benjamin, and unobserved by the ghosts, both slipped into the adjoining room by a doorway over which hung velvet curtains.

In this room, on the table, Mr. Woolfield had collected patterns of chintzes and books of wall-papers.

There the engaged pair remained, discussing what curtains would go with the chintz coverings of the sofa and chairs, and what papers would harmonise with both.

"I see," said Philippa, "that you have plates hung on the walls. I don't like them: it is no longer in good form. If they be worth anything you must have a cabinet with glass doors for the china. How about the carpets?"

"There is the drawing-room," said Benjamin.

"No, we won't go in there and disturb the ghosts," said Philippa. "We'll take the drawing-room for granted."

"Well— come with me to the dining-room. We can reach it by another door."

In the room they now entered the carpet was in fairly good condition, except at the head and bottom of the table, where it was worn. This was especially the case at the bottom, where Mr. Woolfield had usually sat. There, when his wife had lectured, moralised, and harangued, he had rubbed his feet up and down and had fretted the nap off the Brussels carpet.

"I think," remarked Philippa, "that we can turn it about, and by taking out one width and putting that under the bookcase and inserting the strip that was there in its room, we can save the expense of a new carpet. But—the engravings—those Landseers. What do you think of them, Ben, dear?"

She pointed to the two familiar engravings of the "Deer in Winter," and "Dignity and Impudence."

"Don't you think, Ben, that one has got a little tired of those pictures?"

"My late wife did not object to them, they were so perfectly harmless."

"But your coming wife does. We will have something more up-to-date in their room. By the way, I wonder how the ghosts are getting on. They have let us alone so far. I will run back and have a peep at them through the curtains."

The lively girl left the dining apartment, and her husband-elect, studying the pictures to which Philippa had objected. Presently she returned.

"Oh, Ben! such fun!" she said, laughing. "My ghost has drawn up his chair close to that of that late Mrs. Woolfield, and is fondling her hand. But I believe that they are only talking goody-goody."

"And now about the china," said Mr. Woolfield. "It is in a closet near the pantry—that is to say, the best china. I will get a benzoline lamp, and we will examine it. We had it out only when Mrs. Woolfield had a party of her elect brothers and sisters. I fear a good deal is broken. I know that the soup tureen has lost a lid, and I believe we are short of vegetable dishes. How many plates remain I do not know. We had a parlour-maid, Dorcas, who was a sad smasher, but as she was

37

one who had made her election sure, my late wife would not part with her."

"And how are you off for glass?"

"The wine-glasses are fairly complete. I fancy the cut-glass decanters are in a bad way. My late wife chipped them, I really believe out of spite."

It took the couple some time to go through the china and the glass.

"And the plate?" asked Philippa.

"Oh, that is right. All the real old silver is at the bank, as Kesiah preferred plated goods."

"How about the kitchen utensils?"

"Upon my word I cannot say. We had a rather nice-looking cook, and so my late wife never allowed me to step inside the kitchen."

"Is she here still?" inquired Philippa sharply.

"No; my wife, when she was dying, gave her the sack."

"Bless me, Ben!" exclaimed Philippa. "It is growing dark. I have been here an age. I really must go home. I wonder the ghosts have not worried us. I'll have another look at them."

She tripped off.

In five minutes she was back. She stood for a minute looking at Mr. Woolfield, laughing so heartily that she had to hold her sides.

"What is it, Philippa?" he inquired.

"Oh, Ben! A happy release. They will never dare to show their faces again. They have eloped together."

NUGENT BARKER
One, Two, Buckle My Shoe

Nugent Barker (1888–1955) *wrote many strange and memorable short stories which enjoyed a vogue between the wars, and were later collected in a (now very scarce) volume entitled* Written with My Left Hand, *published in 1951. Among the best examples of his work are "Whessoe" (in* The Mammoth Book of Ghost Stories), *"The Curious Adventure of Mr. Bond", and the unusual tale reprinted here.*

"**A**nd now," said Harlock solemnly, pushing back his chair, "and now to business."

We rose to our feet at the far end of the studio, and watched him delicately pinching out the half-burnt candles on the shining dinner table. It was a scene that we had all been waiting for, from past experience—a transformation from the choice and orderly to the grotesque, for it left us standing in the large and leaping firelight.

Sitting at the chimney-side, ready to have our breaths caught by Harlock while we filled our chairs with comfort, we were in another room altogether. Witticisms lay behind us, arguments had been thrashed out and buried, the bowl, for the time being, had flowed; and towering shadows, the perfect background for ghost-stories, had taken their place.

We waited for our host's thin, fire-crimsoned face to reveal to us that his mounting list of horrors was about to be capped by an effort supremely terrifying for a Christmas occasion . . . but the slow, grim smile never came. He kicked the pine logs into a fiercer blaze; then fell to groping in the remotest corner of his studio.

When he returned, bringing from the shadows an unframed canvas, we supposed that the supreme effort had surely arrived: the story was to be too disturbing for even the remotest of smiles. He stood the canvas on a chair at one end of the fireplace, so that we all had a fairly good view of it. The quality

39

of the painting and the subject of the picture appeared to give to each other a dark and sinister life under the shifting light of the flames; but it was not until the clock had struck, bringing him up with a start, that Harlock began to tell us the following story:

"I found it in a corner of a shop in Fulham Road. It's a good piece of painting, as you can see—even by firelight; but that was not the reason why I bought it. The reason was not so — so aesthetic as that. I bought it because I knew the subject, and because I knew why the painter had painted it. *His* reason was not aesthetic, either— the man is quite unknown to me, by the way—and I don't expect he cared how little he got for his picture. He wanted to thrust it out of his sight . . . and he got rid of it because it had served its turn—the painting of it had prevented him from going mad."

Harlock put his finger tips together.

"I myself had done the same thing, you see. But I never sold my picture. I never tried. Perhaps my professional instinct is not so developed as his. As soon as I had painted it, from memory, putting in that finishing touch, that pinpoint of light in the landscape, I took a knife, and slashed the thing to pieces.

"No doubt," he continued, hesitatingly, looking round briefly at our row of faces, "you are wondering why, having got rid of it in such a deliberate manner, I bought its counterpart the moment I saw one in a shop. The reason is very simple. I was overjoyed at finding that another person besides myself had been to the place. . . . I always think of it as the loneliest *inhabited* house in England. The atrocious puffball weed told me that the house was indeed the very same. Without doubt, *he* had tasted the cheese and cider there . . . had stayed there half the night . . . had handled the same set of instruments. . . ."

Harlock stared into the heart of the fire.

"Very vividly," he continued, in a thoughtful voice, "I remember that slow and oddly clear September evening when, having walked for the better part of a day, I found myself, with the sea waves at my back, staring inland at a house, a cottage, a habitation— call it what you like— that sprawled beneath a thin protection of stunted and ragged trees at the back of a field of washed-out poppies, under a rising moon. A solitary light was shining below the thatched eaves, and I walked towards it over the poppy field.

"A nice sort of place to come upon when you're tired and hungry and have lost your way! Look for yourselves. Did you ever see a more god-forsaken spot, such ragged trees, such a sprawling and shapeless dwelling? And yet, you know, because of its very shapelessness it *had* a shape—the picture has caught it perfectly, and so did mine. Can you imagine such a ridiculous combination of things as a bloated pancake with a blanket of heavy thatch on the top of it? That's how it looked, in detail, when I was right up to it. All the straw colour had been soaked out by the sea-wind. And look at that feathery, puff-ball weed! It shows like a ground-mist in the picture, doesn't it? Up to the thatched eaves in many places; even higher. Heaven knows how I found the door at last, and the courage to thump it. I shall never forget that dead and dismal thumping on the door. Then I tried the latch, and found myself at once in a room that seemed to spread over the whole house. For all I knew, it *was* the house. The endless sagging beams helped to make it look like that, I think. And at first I could see nothing else in particular—nothing but the lamp on the huge round table, and a multitude of tiny windows with that weed shining beyond them. Then I saw some plates and dishes on the wall, the swinging of a pendulum—and after that . . . I always wish I had never seen the large and pale and flabby woman who was moving towards me from the far end of the room. She was unspeakably large. I stood my ground, staring, and I believe I counted the thumping clicks of the pendulum clock; they must have been, at any rate, the only links between myself and the busy world outside. They pulled me together at last, I suppose, for suddenly I blurted out that I had lost my way and had seen her light; and as she approached the table, smiling at me enormously, she sucked in her tiny lips until they almost disappeared. But the horridest thing about her was that she seemed to have earth in her hair."

Here Harlock paused; but only a stranger would have broken the silence. "I have never seen a fatter woman," our host continued. "She panted at the slightest exertion—gently enough —it was the only sound that ever came from her—but sufficiently to show me that she was certainly flesh and blood. Otherwise I might have had my doubts about her. For even at a distance the house had looked haunted. Something in the very set of the trees—the flock of feathers on the evening light—and the soughing of the sea. . . . And because of her shortness of breath

41

I began to suspect that her fatness was constitutional. Oh, you mustn't think that I was working it out as clearly as this! It was merely a matter of instinct, I suppose, roused by my hopes of a good square meal. And in the end, of course, I found I was right: my spirits had risen too high. Risen at the prospect of a well-stocked larder, I mean. For she motioned me up to the table, and I sat on a stool, an antique thing, hollowed and polished with years of sitting; and then she took a loaf of bread and half a cheese from a cupboard, and poured me out a bowl of cider, and I wanted to cry. Or very nearly.

"She sat there facing me across the table, large and still and silent in her wan, robe-like dress, while in my hunger I tried to swallow my tough bread and crumbly cheese and to wash them down with hurried gulps of cider from the bowl; and whenever I glanced at her over the rim I saw her horrid smile. My hostess sat with her clasped plump hands on the table, smiling at unknown things. Hostess? What a funny word to use! I watched her get up noiselessly, and then—I wish I could make you hear the sound that followed. She went round the room, swishing the little window-curtains on their metal rings and rods: swish, swish, swish, swish, a ripple passing round the room, blotting out the moonlight, blotting out those pictures of feathery, puff-ball weed.

"She left me abruptly after that—abruptly for her, I mean—and I wondered, with rather mixed feelings, whether she had gone to prepare a room for me—a bed. Perhaps it was because of her unbroken silence, and the even flow of her movements, that I took her hospitality, such as it was, as a matter of course. I don't remember asking myself whether she would expect to be paid for my night's lodging; she and money seemed so utterly unrelated to each other, I suppose. But I do remember that this sudden and welcome change in the evening's entertainment left me somewhat breathless—a bit frightened. Should I run away? While there was time? The same old situation that you come across in books. Such nonsense! But that's exactly how I felt, just then. The cider didn't help me. The cheese was appalling. Dry, crumbly stuff. Sour, too. Tasting rather of earth.

"I was to get many things into my head that night, but never the cider. This woman's flowing bowl was not of that kind. I could have shattered the silence without an effort, if it had been. In the end I made my effort, and succeeded—but what a fool I felt! 'I must do my best,' I thought, 'to keep my spirits up. *I shall see it out!*'—and the sudden sound of my voice startled me and made me laugh. I began at once to examine the room with deep interest. Here and there the ceiling bulged to such an extent that I *knew* I would bump my head against it sooner or later—running from the house in a moment of panic, for instance—it's funny what nerves will do! I liked the clock high up on the wall—and that was scarcely higher than head-level. It was one of those ancient timepieces built when time was really slow, with a round, brass face, a leisurely pendulum, and two brass weights on chains—by which I gathered that the clock would strike at any moment now—it was nearly nine—and I was curious to hear its voice. The plates and dishes on the cloudy dresser gave out a sort of phosphorescent light. They had no other use, I thought, but to be seen and wondered at; for a large oak chest was standing in front of the range. The mouth of the chimney above the chest was hollow, dark, and dead. There was no fireside. No chimney corner. Nowhere to sit and tell stories. . . .

"I never heard it strike," he said, with a kind of regret. "She came back before that happened. I heard the last of its loud ticks as she closed the door upon them; and I felt quite lonely then, lonely and rather bewildered, for while I was following her along the countless passages and ups and downs of her strange residence she looked like a thick mist rolling in front of me . . . if you can imagine such a silly thing as a solid mist panting for breath."

Harlock turned, and gazed for several moments—with a certain look of distress, I thought—at the picture in the chair. "I want you," he said, "I want you to get the hang of that room she took me to. I mean especially the feeling of it. But to begin with, it was a very big room, and she had lighted it with six or seven candles. Quite a showy display! Three of them were standing on a large, square table in the middle of the floor. The floor itself was covered with some kind of cork matting. She had stood two candles on a chest of drawers. She had even placed a candle on a chair in one of the corners, near the huge, painted, wooden bed. All the furniture was very massive, and painted. After the candles, it was the colour of the room that I noticed chiefly. The walls were panelled—shallow panels from wainscot to cornice—and painted a bluish green—I may as well call it viridian; a very light and faded but still rather shiny viridian. The furniture was of the same colour; so was the bed-linen, and the billowy eider-down; so were the heavy, shallow window-curtains; and because of this prevalent colouring, and in spite of the size of the furniture, the room looked empty and asleep. I sat on the edge of the high bed, on the top of the thick eiderdown, with the toes of my shoes just touching the floor. My mind was all on the room in which I was sitting. I was trying to get the feeling of it. And do you know what it was? You can't. It was *children*.

"It had been a nursery. But whose children, whose nursery, how can we ever know? Hers? That would be the most natural thing in the world . . . and the most horrible. And in any case," said Harlock thoughtfully, after a pause, "the question didn't seem to matter very much to me then, and I don't know that it does now. The feeling was there—the feeling of the nursery itself, I mean, of—merely of children long departed. And that also—I remember thinking to myself after a time—didn't matter any longer. The history of the room was over. Over and done with. Or was it, perhaps, only 'over', and not yet 'done with'?

"At this point in my speculations I took off my heavy walking-shoes, and lay flat on the bed, under the thick eider-down, which I pulled up to my chin. I had left all the candles burning, for I was afraid to sleep. I spent some time tracing with my eyes the very faded pattern on the ceiling, pretending that the pattern was a maze and that I was walking about in it, a game that I never get tired of; but even if I had gone to sleep I suppose the little bell would have woken me. You know how it is, in a strange room—things are watching you all the night, and you awaken early, suddenly, all alert: you wake up to listen for something that you have just heard. For some time I had been listening to the far off flump of the slow waves on the shore; and suddenly I heard the tinkle of a bell on the beach. They had washed up a bell? In a few moments, of course, I knew that it had tinkled in the room. I let the thought sink in. Then I threw off the eiderdown!

"It was only a momentary panic. One of those unreasoning fears that children do have, you know. In fact, as I roved about in my socks, searching for a toy, the room appeared quite friendly. I felt that I had known it all my life—The Viridian Room. I heard the bell tinkling again, jerkily, intermittently.

At last I stood in front of a tall cupboard. It wasn't locked. And there were no shelves in it—nothing to throw shadows. On the floor, at the back, I saw the bell shining in the candlelight. It was one of those tiny, round bells that toy reins have on them. I couldn't see why it had rung. By that, I mean, of course, *how* the bell had rung . . . the material reason. . . . I took it out," said Harlock, "I took it out and tinkled it; and presently I went and looked at the box of chalks on the table.

"It was open. I had seen it all the time—seen it without realising exactly what it was, I mean—seen just its existence, and not its purpose; for who would expect a box like that to contain chalks all of the same colour? After tinkling my bell for some time I dropped it on to the table and sat there facing the open cupboard and toying with my chalks, and presently I wanted a sheet of paper to write on. I found it in the drawer beside me, an exercise-book. I pulled up my chair, spread my elbows, and wrote at once, in viridian green, on a new page:

> One, two, buckle my shoe;
> Three, four, knock at the door;
> Five, six, pick up sticks;
> Seven, eight, lay them straight;
> Nine, ten, a fine fat hen;
> Eleven, twelve, dig and delve.

You remember that nursery rhyme? Until then I had forgotten it. I used to think it was full of sense, even when taken in a lump; and while I was still sitting at the table, looking across it into the open, lighted cupboard, and thinking over the words that I had just written down, I saw the mouse. At the back of the cupboard, against the wall, I saw a mousehole. Clearly the source of the tinkling! While I watched, two black shiny eyes appeared, and the furry shadow glided along the floor of the cupboard and into the room, where it took to moving in fits and starts.

" 'Hi there! What are you up to, you little beggar?' I called out, starting off in pursuit, and brandishing one of my heavy walking-shoes—but not with any serious purpose; you know I would never hit a creature, don't you? I simply followed the mouse across the room as far as the chest of drawers; and there I found a pair of shoes on the floor . . . kicked off into the corner between the chest and the wall.

'One, two, buckle my shoe.'"

Harlock had dropped into his gentlest voice.

"They *did* have buckles on them. Buckles as bright as silver. So I put on the shoes, and buckled them up, and found that in them I could walk as stealthily as a cat. I prowled with such gentleness over the room that I hardly made a candle quiver; and presently I stopped in front of the narrow door, the door that I haven't yet told you about.

"You see it the moment you enter the room—a rather low and narrow door on the far side of the table; but you don't *really* see it until later, when you are standing right in front of it, looking at the little knocker—the kind that you sometimes see on the study door in a vicarage.

'Three, four, knock at the door.'

"I knocked at the door.

"'Come in!' called an incredibly high-pitched, thin, and windy voice. I went in, shutting the door behind me."

At this point, Harlock jumped to his feet, and proposed loudly a round of drinks. He switched on a blaze of light, and we heard him boiling his electric kettle behind our backs.

"All that I could see at first," he continued, in a steady voice, a minute or so after he had returned to his chair, and while we were still sipping our whisky toddies in the restored fire-light, "was a regiment of moonbeams slanting into the room through uncurtained lattice windows, and a man facing me across the floor, motionless, waiting—myself, in a mirror. What a fool one feels, when one's two selves are brought thus face to face—each of them scared of the other! The first movement—the sudden tentative trial—and the spell is broken, and you turn eagerly to look for the thing that you *expect* to find. I saw her, at hand, lying on her large bed, slowly kneading the eiderdown beneath her with her fat fingers, pulling in her lips, watching me with her small eyes; and the floor and the bed and the woman were patterned with lattice windows. The bars of shadow and light showed me her rounded, massive bulk to perfection. Five, six, pick up sticks.

"And where do you think I found them? Why, on the bed itself, of course! A couple of bedstaffs. Do you know what a bedstaff is? It's a loose cross-piece of antique bedsteads, often

46

used as a handy weapon. I took them from the head and foot of the bed, and while I was doing so the face of my hostess was twisting about with a kind of cringing, mock terror. Five, six, pick up sticks—seven, eight—lay them straight! I remember that while I was wielding my cudgels I glanced in the mirror and saw the shadows of the window bars slipping along them. Lay them straight, lay them straight! Seven, eight, lay them straight! I laid them good and straight. Once I felt a shiver in my arm—I had hit the ceiling.

"As soon as I had satisfied myself that the flutters of her heart had ceased—I can still feel her wrist between my finger and thumb, you know—I dropped my bedstaffs for good, and hurried off to open one of the two other doors in the room—The Garden Door, I fancied the children had called it. How breathless was the scene through The Garden Door! I held my breath and gazed all over the great neglected garden; then I returned to the woman and picked her up, and I swear she was no heavier than a puff-ball. But what an armful she made! What an armful! What a fine fat hen! I carried her into the garden and over the rank grass and plunged with her into the cluster of weed beyond. I had seen it through The Garden Door, shimmering in the moonlight. The stuff stood higher than my head, and was here in great profusion—a forest of weed. I don't know how long I took to reach my destination. Probably not very long; but when you're pretending to be a pirate—or something of that kind—carrying your booty into the depths of the woods, to bury it, well, you don't care at all how long you take to reach the burial place. I came upon it in a moment, without warning—a sudden breaking from the weed into broad moonlight. "This is the place," I remember saying—"this is the spot they have chosen."

"A spade lay ready to my hand, and fluff from the surrounding weed was drifting and settling all the while on to the tumbled earth.

'Eleven, twelve,
Dig and delve.'

I put down my burden, and took up the spade; and in that spot I dug and delved.

"When I came out of the weed," said Harlock, in his softest voice, "I saw that the feathers were sticking to my clothes like splashes of plaster." The fire had burnt low, we could scarcely see each other's faces, and only his voice was holding our little group together. "And I think it was the sight of those feathers," he said, "that sent me tearing back in a panic over the lawn, slapping my clothes all the time. Escape! I had no other thought but that. The children's rhyme had worked its way with me. Escape from the house and the clump of weed and the infamous thing that I had buried there. I ran through the bedroom and into the viridian nursery and kicked off the buckled shoes—kicked them into the corner, as all the others had done!—and while I was sitting on the bed, putting on my walking shoes, and looking towards the open cupboard, I saw the mouse returning to his hole beside the little bell. . . .

"What was the use of my shutting the cupboard door with a bang? The Viridian Room hardly echoed to it. And even the loudest noise would not have convinced me that in that silent house such a sudden crash must certainly have brought things to an end. I even took steps to prove to my satisfaction that I was right. I ran back into the bedroom, back into all those spears of moonlight; and then—I wish I had never opened the Garden Door again. It was not what I actually saw, but what I knew I would see if I stayed for more than a very few moments. . . . Looking across the wild, moonlit grass, I saw at least a *shaking* in the tops of the weed—and it wasn't the wind, you know—the movement was working its way towards me, slowly, jerkily, inch by inch. . . .

"Fear, of course, won in the end. It sent me racing back into the depths of the house, where I caught my head a whack against the ceiling of the living-room, for the lamp was out. She had put it out. The clock was thumping loudly; and I was scared to death that she might find me there before I got away.

"I hardly know how I got away in time. Hunting for the door, plunging through the puff-balls, sprinting over the poppy field —have you ever seen poppies by moonlight? Sanity! That's what I was after! Sanity, and the breath of the sea! Well, there was no breath, the wind was dead, there were no waves; but I scooped up the water in my two hands, and cooled the bump on my head. . . . And after that I went back to the foreshore and watched the house until I saw her light gleaming again. . . ."

Harlock stared at the dying fire.

"I suppose I ought to have known it at once," he said, as if to himself. "Especially from a distance. Known that the spot was haunted, I mean. It was there, staring me in the face—the queer shape, the mist of puff-balls, the heavy thatch, the very set of the trees."

Then one of us, softly, as if to take the edge off the silence that followed, ventured a remark.

"I suppose the real ghost was the children."

"*She* was not!" Harlock burst out. "She was something far worse than that!"

Nothing further was said while we watched our host returning his picture to the remote corner.

E.F. BENSON
The Man Who Went Too Far

Edward Frederic Benson (1867–1940), now best known for his Mapp and Lucia novels (recently dramatised on TV), was a prolific writer of ghost stories for the leading popular monthly magazines. The majority of these were published in four classic collections: The Room in the Tower (1912), Visible and Invisible (1923), *Spook Stories* (1928) and More Spook Stories (1934).

"The Man Who Went Too Far" first appeared in the Pall Mall Magazine *June* (1904).

The little village of St. Faith's nestles in a hollow of wooded hill up on the north bank of the river Fawn in the county of Hampshire, huddling close round its grey Norman church as if for spiritual protection against the fays and fairies, the trolls and "little people," who might be supposed still to linger in the vast empty spaces of the New Forest, and to come after dusk and do their doubtful businesses. Once outside the hamlet you may walk in any direction (so long as you avoid the high road which leads to Brockenhurst) for the length of a summer afternoon without seeing sign of human habitation, or possibly even catching sight of another human being. Shaggy wild ponies may stop their feeding for a moment as you pass, the white scuts of rabbits will vanish into their burrows, a brown viper perhaps will glide from your path into a clump of heather, and unseen birds will chuckle in the bushes, but it may easily happen that for a long day you will see nothing human. But you will not feel in the least lonely; in summer, at any rate, the sunlight will be gay with butterflies, and the air thick with all those woodland sounds which like instruments in an orchestra combine to play the great symphony of the yearly festival of June. Winds whisper in the birches, and sigh among the firs; bees are busy with their redolent labour among the heather, a myriad birds chirp in the green temples of the forest trees, and the voice of the river prattling over stony places, bubbling into pools, chuckling and gulping round corners, gives you the sense that many presences and companions are near at hand.

Yet, oddly enough, though one would have thought that these benign and cheerful influences of wholesome air and spaciousness of forest were very healthful comrades for a man, in so far as Nature can really influence this wonderful human genus which has in these centuries learned to defy her most violent storms in its well-established houses, to bridle her torrents and make them light its streets, to tunnel her mountains and plough her seas, the inhabitants of St. Faith's will not willingly venture into the forest after dark. For in spite of the silence and loneliness of the hooded night it seems that a man is not sure in what company he may suddenly find himself, and though it is difficult to get from these villagers any very clear story of occult appearances, the feeling is widespread. One story indeed I have heard with some definiteness, the tale of a monstrous goat that has been seen to skip with hellish glee about the woods and shady places, and this perhaps is connected with the story which I have here attempted to piece together. It too is well known to them; for all remember the young artist who died here not long ago, a young man, or so he struck the beholder, of great personal beauty, with something about him that made men's faces to smile and brighten when they looked on him. His ghost they will tell you "walks" constantly by the stream and through the woods which he loved so, and in especial it haunts a certain house, the last of the village, where he lived, and its garden in which he was done to death. For my part I am inclined to think that the terror of the Forest dates chiefly from that day. So, such as the story is, I have set it forth in connected form. It is based partly on the accounts of the villagers, but mainly on that of Darcy, a friend of mine and a friend of the man with whom these events were chiefly concerned.

The day had been one of untarnished midsummer splendour, and as the sun drew near to its setting, the glory of the evening grew every moment more crystalline, more miraculous. Westward from St. Faith's the beechwood which stretched for some miles toward the heathery upland beyond already cast its veil of clear shadow over the red roofs of the village, but the spire of the grey church, over-topping all, still pointed a flaming orange finger into the sky. The river Fawn, which runs below, lay in sheets of sky-reflected blue, and wound its dreamy devious course round the edge of this wood, where a rough two-planked bridge crossed from the bottom of the garden of the last house in the village, and communicated by means of a little wicker gate with the wood itself. Then once out of the shadow of the wood the stream lay in flaming pools of the molten crimson of the sunset, and lost itself in the haze of woodland distances.

This house at the end of the village stood outside the shadow, and the lawn which sloped down to the river was still flecked with sunlight. Garden-beds of dazzling colour lined its gravel walks, and down the middle of it ran a brick pergola, half-hidden in clusters of rambler-rose and purple with starry clematis. At the bottom end of it, between two of its pillars, was slung a hammock containing a shirt-sleeved figure.

The house itself lay somewhat remote from the rest of the village, and a footpath leading across two fields, now tall and fragrant with hay, was its only communication with the high road. It was low-built, only two stories in height, and like the garden, its walls were a mass of flowering roses. A narrow stone terrace ran along the garden front, over which was stretched an awning, and on the terrace a young silent-footed man-servant was busied with the laying of the table for dinner. He was neat-handed and quick with his job, and having finished it he went back into the house, and reappeared again with a large rough bath-towel on his arm. With this he went to the hammock in the pergola.

"Nearly eight, sir," he said.

"Has Mr. Darcy come yet?" asked a voice from the hammock.

"No, sir."

"If I'm not back when he comes, tell him that I'm just having a bathe before dinner."

The servant went back to the house, and after a moment or two Frank Halton struggled to a sitting posture, and slipped out on to the grass. He was of medium height and rather slender in build, but the supple ease and grace of his movements gave the impression of great physical strength: even his descent from the hammock was not an awkward performance. His face and hands were of very dark complexion, either from constant exposure to wind and sun, or, as his black hair and dark eyes tended to show, from some strain of southern blood. His head was small, his face of an exquisite beauty of modelling, while the smoothness of its contour would have led you to believe that he was a beardless lad still in his teens. But something, some look which living and experience alone can give, seemed to contradict that, and finding yourself completely puzzled as to his age, you would next moment probably cease to think about that, and only look at this glorious specimen of young manhood with wondering satisfaction.

He was dressed as became the season and the heat, and wore only a shirt open at the neck, and a pair of flannel trousers. His head, covered very thickly with a somewhat rebellious crop of short curly hair, was bare as he strolled across the lawn to the bathing-place that lay below. Then for a moment there was silence, then the sound of splashed and divided waters, and presently after, a great shout of ecstatic joy, as he swam upstream with the foamed water standing in a frill round his neck. Then after some five minutes of limb-stretching struggle with the flood, he turned over on his back, and with arms thrown wide, floated down-stream, ripple-cradled and inert. His eyes were shut, and between half-parted lips he talked gently to himself.

"I am one with it," he said to himself, "the river and I, I and the river. The coolness and splash of it is I, and the water-herbs that wave in it are I also. And my strength and my limbs are not mine but the river's. It is all one, all one, dear Fawn."

A quarter of an hour later he appeared again at the bottom of the lawn, dressed as before, his wet hair already drying into its crisp short curls again. There he paused a moment, looking back at the stream with the smile with which men look on the face of a friend, then turned towards the house. Simultaneously his servant came to the door leading on to the terrace, followed by a man who appeared to be some half-way through the fourth decade of his years. Frank and he saw each other across the bushes and garden-beds, and each quickening his step, they met suddenly face to face round an angle of the garden walk, in the fragrance of syringa.

"My dear Darcy," cried Frank, "I am charmed to see you."

But the other stared at him in amazement.

"Frank!" he exclaimed.

"Yes, that is my name," he said, laughing; "what is the matter?"

Darcy took his hand.

"What have you done to yourself?" he asked. "You are a boy again."

"Ah, I have a lot to tell you," said Frank. "Lots that you will hardly believe, but I shall convince you——"

He broke off suddenly, and held up his hand.

"Hush, there is my nightingale," he said.

The smile of recognition and welcome with which he had greeted his friend faded from his face, and a look of rapt wonder took its place, as of a lover listening to the voice of his beloved. His mouth parted slightly, showing the white line of teeth, and his eyes looked out and out till they seemed to Darcy to be focussed on things beyond the vision of man. Then something perhaps startled the bird, for the song ceased.

"Yes, lots to tell you," he said. "Really I am delighted to see you. But you look rather white and pulled down; no wonder after that fever. And there is to be no nonsense about this visit. It is June now, you stop here till you are fit to begin work again. Two months at least."

"Ah, I can't trespass quite to that extent."

Frank took his arm and walked him down the grass.

"Trespass? Who talks of trespass? I shall tell you quite openly when I am tired of you, but you know when we had the studio together, we used not to bore each other. However, it is ill talking of going away on the moment of your arrival. Just a stroll to the river, and then it will be dinner-time."

Darcy took out his cigarette case, and offered it to the other. Frank laughed.

"No, not for me. Dear me, I suppose I used to smoke once. How very odd!"

"Given it up?"

"I don't know. I suppose I must have. Anyhow I don't do it now. I would as soon think of eating meat."

"Another victim on the smoking altar of vegetarianism?"

"Victim?" asked Frank. "Do I strike you as such?"

He paused on the margin of the stream and whistled softly. Next moment a moor-hen made its splashing flight across the river, and ran up the bank. Frank took it very gently in his hands and stroked its head, as the creature lay against his shirt.

"And is the house among the reeds still secure?" he half-crooned to it. "And is the missus quite well, and are the neighbours flourishing? There, dear, home with you," and he flung it into the air.

"That bird's very tame," said Darcy, slightly bewildered.

"It is rather," said Frank, following its flight.

During dinner Frank chiefly occupied himself in bringing himself up-to-date in the movements and achievements of this old friend whom he had not seen for six years. Those six years, it now appeared, had been full of incident and success for Darcy; he had made a name for himself as a portrait painter which bade fair to outlast the vogue of a couple of seasons, and his leisure time had been brief. Then some four months previously he had been through a severe attack of typhoid, the result of which as concerns this story was that he had come down to this sequestered place to recruit.

"Yes, you've got on," said Frank at the end. "I always knew you would. A.R.A. with more in prospect. Money? You roll in it, I suppose, and, O Darcy, how much happiness have you had all these years? That is the only imperishable possession. And how much have you learned? Oh, I don't mean in Art. Even I could have done well in that."

Darcy laughed.

"Done well? My dear fellow, all I have learned in these six years you knew, so to speak, in your cradle. Your old pictures fetch huge prices. Do you never paint now?"

Frank shook his head.

"No, I'm too busy," he said.

"Doing what? Please tell me. That is what everyone is for ever asking me."

"Doing? I suppose you would say I do nothing."

Darcy glanced up at the brilliant young face opposite him.

"It seems to suit you, that way of being busy," he said. "Now, it's your turn. Do you read? Do you study? I remember you saying that it would do us all—all us artists, I mean—a great deal of good if we would study any one human face carefully for a year, without recording a line. Have you been doing that?"

Frank shook his head again.

"I mean exactly what I say," he said. "I have been *doing* nothing. And I have never been so occupied. Look at me; have I not done something to myself to begin with?"

"You are two years younger than I," said Darcy, "at least you used to be. You therefore are thirty-five. But had I never seen you before I should say you were just twenty. But was it worth while to spend six years of greatly-occupied life in order to look twenty? Seems rather like a woman of fashion."

Frank laughed boisterously.

"First time I've ever been compared to that particular bird of prey," he said. "No, that has not been my occupation—in fact I am only very rarely conscious that one effect of my occupation has been that. Of course, it must have been if one comes to think of it. It is not very important. Quite true my body has become young. But that is very little; I have become young."

Darcy pushed back his chair and sat sideways to the table looking at the other.

"Has that been your occupation then?" he asked.

"Yes, that anyhow is one aspect of it. Think what youth means! It is the capacity for growth, mind, body, spirit, all grow, all get stronger, all have a fuller, firmer life every day. That is something, considering that every day that passes after the ordinary man reaches the full-blown flower of his strength, weakens his hold on life. A man reaches his prime, and remains, we say, in his prime for ten years, or perhaps twenty. But after his primest prime is reached, he slowly, insensibly weakens. These are the signs of age in you, in your body, in your art probably, in your mind. You are less electric than you were. But I, when I reach my prime—I am nearing it—ah, you shall see."

The stars had begun to appear in the blue velvet of the sky, and to the east the horizon seen above the black silhouette of the village was growing dove-coloured with the approach of moon-rise. White moths hovered dimly over the garden-beds, and the footsteps of night tip-toed through the bushes. Suddenly Frank rose.

"Ah, it is the supreme moment," he said softly. "Now more than at any other time the current of life, the eternal imperishable current runs so close to me that I am almost enveloped in it. Be silent a minute."

He advanced to the edge of the terrace and looked out, standing stretched with arms outspread. Darcy heard him draw a long breath into his lungs, and after many seconds expel it again. Six or eight times he did this, then turned back into the lamplight.

"It will sound to you quite mad, I expect," he said, "but if you want to hear the soberest truth I have ever spoken and shall ever speak, I will tell you about myself. But come into the garden if it is not too damp for you. I have never told anyone yet, but I shall like to tell you. It is long, in fact, since I have even tried to classify what I have learned."

They wandered into the fragrant dimness of the pergola, and sat down. Then Frank began:

"Years ago, do you remember," he said, "we used often to talk about the decay of joy in the world. Many impulses, we settled, had contributed to this decay, some of which were good in themselves, others that were quite completely bad. Among the good things, I put what we may call certain Christian virtues, renunciation, resignation, sympathy with suffering, and the desire to relieve sufferers. But out of those things spring very bad ones, useless renunciations, asceticism for its own sake, mortification of the flesh with nothing to follow, no corresponding gain that is, and that awful and terrible disease which devastated England some centuries ago, and from which by heredity of spirit we suffer now, Puritanism. That was a dreadful plague, the brutes held and taught that joy and laughter and merriment were evil: it was a doctrine the most profane and wicked. Why, what is the commonest crime one sees? A sullen face. That is the truth of the matter.

"Now all my life I have believed that we are intended to be happy, that joy is of all gifts the most divine. And when I left London, abandoned my career, such as it was, I did so because I intended to devote my life to the cultivation of joy, and, by continuous and unsparing effort, to be happy. Among people, and in constant intercourse with others, I did not find it possible; there were too many distractions in towns and work-rooms, and also too much suffering. So I took one step backwards or forwards, as you may choose to put it, and went straight to Nature, to trees, birds, animals, to all those things which quite clearly pursue one aim only, which blindly follow the great native instinct to be happy without any care at all for morality, or human law or divine law. I wanted, you understand, to get all joy first-hand and unadulterated, and I think it scarcely exists among men; it is obsolete."

Darcy turned in his chair.

"Ah, but what makes birds and animals happy?" he asked. "Food, food and mating."

Frank laughed gently in the stillness.

"Do not think I became a sensualist," he said. "I did not make that mistake. For the sensualist carries his miseries pick-a-back, and round his feet is wound the shroud that shall soon enwrap him. I may be mad, it is true, but I am not so stupid anyhow as to have tried that. No, what is it that makes puppies play with their own tails, that sends cats on their prowling ecstatic errands at night?"

He paused a moment.

"So I went to Nature," he said. "I sat down here in this New Forest, sat down fair and square, and looked. That was my first difficulty, to sit here quiet without being bored, to wait without being impatient, to be receptive and very alert, though for a long time nothing particular happened. The change in fact was slow in those early stages."

"Nothing happened?" asked Darcy, rather impatiently, with the sturdy revolt against any new idea which to the English mind is synonymous with nonsense. "Why, what in the world *should* happen?"

Now Frank as he had known him was the most generous but most quick-tempered of mortal men; in other words his anger would flare to a prodigious beacon, under almost no provocation, only to be quenched again under a gust of no less impulsive kindliness. Thus the moment Darcy had spoken, an apology for his hasty question was half-way up his tongue. But there was no need for it to have travelled even so far, for Frank laughed again with kindly, genuine mirth.

"Oh, how I should have resented that a few years ago," he said. "Thank goodness that resentment is one of the things I have got rid of. I certainly wish that you should believe my story—in fact, you are going to—but that you at this moment should imply that you do not does not concern me."

"Ah, your solitary sojournings have made you inhuman," said Darcy, still very English.

"No, human," said Frank. "Rather more human, at least rather less of an ape."

"Well, that was my first quest," he continued, after a moment, "the deliberate and unswerving pursuit of joy, and my method, the eager contemplation of Nature. As far as motive went, I daresay it was purely selfish, but as far as effect goes, it seems to me about the best thing one can do for one's fellow-creatures, for happiness is more infectious than small-pox. So, as I said, I sat down and waited; I looked at happy things, zealously avoided the sight of anything unhappy, and by degrees a little trickle of the happiness of this blissful world began to filter into me. The trickle grew more abundant, and now, my dear fellow, if I could for a moment divert from me into you one half of the torrent of joy that pours through me day and night, you would throw the world, art, everything aside, and just live, exist. When a man's body dies, it passes into trees and flowers. Well, that is what I have been trying to do with my soul before death."

The servant had brought into the pergola a table with syphons and spirits, and had set a lamp upon it. As Frank spoke he leaned forward towards the other, and Darcy for all his matter-of-fact common sense could have sworn that his companion's face shone, was luminous in itself. His dark brown eyes glowed from within, the unconscious smile of a child irradiated and transformed his face. Darcy felt suddenly excited, exhilarated.

"Go on," he said. "Go on. I can feel you are somehow telling me sober truth. I daresay you are mad; but I don't see that matters."

Frank laughed again.

"Mad?" he said. "Yes, certainly, if you wish. But I prefer to call it sane. However, nothing matters less than what anybody chooses to call things. God never labels his gifts; He just puts them into our hands; just as he put animals in the garden of Eden, for Adam to name if he felt disposed."

"So by the continual observance and study of things that were happy," continued he, "I got happiness, I got joy. But seeking it, as I did, from Nature, I got much more which I did not seek, but stumbled upon originally by accident. It is difficult to explain, but I will try.

"About three years ago I was sitting one morning in a place I will show you to-morrow. It is down by the river brink, very green, dappled with shade and sun, and the river passes there through some little clumps of reeds. Well, as I sat there, doing nothing, but just looking and listening, I heard the sound quite distinctly of some flute-like instrument playing a strange unending melody. I thought at first it was some musical yokel on the highway and did not pay much attention. But before long the strangeness and indescribable beauty of the tune struck me. It never repeated itself, but it never came to an end, phrase after

59

phrase ran its sweet course, it worked gradually and inevitably up to a climax, and having attained it, it went on; another climax was reached and another and another. Then with a sudden gasp of wonder I localised where it came from. It came from the reeds and from the sky and from the trees. It was everywhere, it was the sound of life. It was, my dear Darcy, as the Greeks would have said, it was Pan playing on his pipes, the voice of Nature. It was the life-melody, the world-melody."

Darcy was far too interested to interrupt, though there was a question he would have liked to ask, and Frank went on:

"Well, for the moment I was terrified, terrified with the impotent horror of nightmare, and I stopped my ears and just ran from the place and got back to the house panting, trembling, literally in a panic. Unknowingly, for at that time I only pursued joy, I had begun, since I drew my joy from Nature, to get in touch with Nature. Nature, force, God, call it what you will, had drawn across my face a little gossamer web of essential life. I saw that when I emerged from my terror, and I went very humbly back to where I had heard the Pan-pipes. But it was nearly six months before I heard them again."

"Why was that?" asked Darcy.

"Surely because I had revolted, rebelled, and worst of all been frightened. For I believe that just as there is nothing in the world which so injures one's body as fear, so there is nothing that so much shuts up the soul. I was afraid, you see, of the one thing in the world which has real existence. No wonder its manifestation was withdrawn."

"And after six months?"

"After six months one blessed morning I heard the piping again. I wasn't afraid that time. And since then it has grown louder, it has become more constant. I now hear it often, and I can put myself into such an attitude towards Nature that the pipes will almost certainly sound. And never yet have they played the same tune, it is always something new, something fuller, richer, more complete than before."

"What do you mean by 'such an attitude towards Nature'?" asked Darcy.

"I can't explain that; but by translating it into a bodily attitude it is this."

Frank sat up for a moment quite straight in his chair, then slowly sunk back with arms outspread and head drooped.

"That;" he said, "an effortless attitude, but open, resting, receptive. It is just that which you must do with your soul."

Then he sat up again.

"One word more," he said, "and I will bore you no further. Nor unless you ask me questions shall I talk about it again. You will find me, in fact, quite sane in my mode of life. Birds and beasts you will see behaving somewhat intimately to me, like that moor-hen, but that is all. I will walk with you, ride with you, play golf with you, and talk with you on any subject you like. But I wanted you on the threshold to know what has happened to me. And one thing more will happen."

He paused again, and a slight look of fear crossed his eyes.

"There will be a final revelation," he said, "a complete and blinding stroke which will throw open to me, once and for all, the full knowledge, the full realisation and comprehension that I am one, just as you are, with life. In reality there is no 'me', no 'you,' no 'it'. Everything is part of the one and only thing which is life. I know that that is so, but the realisation of it is not yet mine. But it will be, and on that day, so I take it, I shall see Pan. It may mean death, the death of my body, that is, but I don't care. It may mean immortal, eternal life lived here and now and for ever. Then having gained that, ah, my dear Darcy, I shall preach such a gospel of joy, showing myself as the living proof of the truth, that Puritanism, the dismal religion of sour faces, shall vanish like a breath of smoke, and be dispersed and disappear in the sunlit air. But first the full knowledge must be mine."

Darcy watched his face narrowly.

"You are afraid of that moment," he said.

Frank smiled at him.

"Quite true; you are quick to have seen that. But when it comes I hope I shall not be afraid."

For some little time there was silence; then Darcy rose.

"You have bewitched me, you extraordinary boy," he said. "You have been telling me a fairy-story, and I find myself saying, 'Promise me it is true.' "

"I promise you that," said the other.

"And I know I shan't sleep," added Darcy.

Frank looked at him with a sort of mild wonder as if he scarcely understood.

"Well, what does that matter?" he said.

61

"I assure you it does. I am wretched unless I sleep."

"Of course I can make you sleep if I want," said Frank in a rather bored voice.

"Well, do."

"Very good: go to bed. I'll come upstairs in ten minutes."

Frank busied himself for a little after the other had gone, moving the table back under the awning of the verandah and quenching the lamp. Then he went with his quick silent tread upstairs and into Darcy's room. The latter was already in bed, but very wide-eyed and wakeful, and Frank with an amused smile of indulgence, as for a fretful child, sat down on the edge of the bed.

"Look at me," he said, and Darcy looked.

"The birds are sleeping in the brake," said Frank softly, "and the winds are asleep. The sea sleeps, and the tides are but the heaving of its breast. The stars swing slow, rocked in the great cradle of the Heavens, and——"

He stopped suddenly, gently blew out Darcy's candle, and left him sleeping.

Morning brought to Darcy a flood of hard common sense, as clear and crisp as the sunshine that filled his room. Slowly as he woke he gathered together the broken threads of the memories of the evening which had ended, so he told himself, in a trick of common hypnotism. That accounted for it all; the whole strange talk he had had was under a spell of suggestion from the extraordinary vivid boy who had once been a man; all his own excitement, his acceptance of the incredible had been merely the effect of a stronger, more potent will imposed on his own. How strong that will was, he guessed from his own instantaneous obedience to Frank's suggestion of sleep. And armed with impenetrable common sense he came down to breakfast. Frank had already begun, and was consuming a large plateful of porridge and milk with the most prosaic and healthy appetite.

"Slept well?" he asked.

"Yes, of course. Where did you learn hypnotism?"

"By the side of the river."

"You talked an amazing quantity of nonsense last night," remarked Darcy, in a voice prickly with reason.

"Rather. I felt quite giddy. Look, I remembered to order a dreadful daily paper for you. You can read about money markets or politics or cricket matches."

Darcy looked at him closely. In the morning light Frank looked even fresher, younger, more vital than he had done the night before, and the sight of him somehow dinted Darcy's armour of common sense.

"You are the most extraordinary fellow I ever saw," he said. "I want to ask you some more questions."

"Ask away," said Frank.

For the next day or two Darcy plied his friend with many questions, objections and criticisms on the theory of life, and gradually got out of him a coherent and complete account of his experience. In brief, then, Frank believed that "by lying naked," as he put it, to the force which controls the passage of the stars, the breaking of a wave, the budding of a tree, the love of a youth and maiden, he had succeeded in a way hitherto undreamed of in possessing himself of the essential principle of life. Day by day, so he thought, he was getting nearer to, and in closer union with, the great power itself which caused all life to be, the spirit of nature, of force, or the spirit of God. For himself, he confessed to what others would call paganism; it was sufficient for him that there existed a principle of life. He did not worship it, he did not pray to it, he did not praise it. Some of it existed in all human beings, just as it existed in trees and animals; to realise and make living to himself the fact that it was all one, was his sole aim and object.

Here perhaps Darcy would put in a word of warning.

"Take care," he said. "To see Pan meant death, did it not."

Frank's eyebrows would rise at this.

"What does that matter?" he said. "True, the Greeks were always right, and they said so, but there is another possibility. For the nearer I get to it, the more living, the more vital and young I become."

"What then do you expect the final revelation will do for you?"

"I have told you," said he. "It will make me immortal."

But it was not so much from speech and argument that Darcy grew to grasp his friend's conception, as from the ordinary conduct of his life. They were passing, for instance, one morning down the village street, when an old woman, very bent and decrepit, but with an extraordinary cheerfulness of face, hobbled out from her cottage. Frank instantly stopped when he saw her.

"You old darling! How goes it all?" he said.

But she did not answer, her dim old eyes were riveted on his face; she seemed to drink in like a thirsty creature the beautiful radiance which shone there. Suddenly she put her two withered old hands on his shoulders.

"You're just the sunshine itself," she said, and he kissed her and passed on.

But scarcely a hundred yards further a strange contradiction of such tenderness occurred. A child running along the path towards them fell on its face and set up a dismal cry of fright and pain. A look of horror came into Frank's eyes, and, putting his fingers in his ears, he fled at full speed down the street, and did not pause till he was out of hearing. Darcy, having ascertained that the child was not really hurt, followed him in bewilderment.

"Are you without pity then?" he asked.

Frank shook his head impatiently.

"Can't you see?" he asked. "Can't you understand that that sort of thing, pain, anger, anything unlovely, throws me back, retards the coming of the great hour! Perhaps when it comes I shall be able to piece that side of life on to the other, on to the true religion of joy. At present I can't."

"But the old woman. Was she not ugly?"

Frank's radiance gradually returned.

"Ah, no. She was like me. She longed for joy, and knew it when she saw it, the old darling."

Another question suggested itself.

"Then what about Christianity?" asked Darcy.

"I can't accept it. I can't believe in any creed of which the central doctrine is that God who is Joy should have had to suffer. Perhaps it was so; in some inscrutable way I believe it may have been so, but I don't understand how it was possible. So I leave it alone; my affair is joy."

They had come to the weir above the village, and the thunder of riotous cool water was heavy in the air. Trees dipped into the translucent stream with slender trailing branches, and the meadow where they stood was starred with midsummer blossomings. Larks shot up carolling into the crystal dome of blue, and a thousand voices of June sang round them. Frank, bare-headed as was his wont, with his coat slung over his arm and his shirt sleeves rolled up above the elbow, stood there like some beautiful wild animal with eyes half-shut and mouth half-open, drinking in the scented warmth of the air. Then suddenly he flung himself face downwards on the grass at the edge of the stream, burying his face in the daisies and cowslips, and lay stretched there in wide-armed ecstasy, with his long fingers pressing and stroking the dewy herbs of the field. Never before had Darcy seen him thus fully possessed by his idea; his caressing fingers, his half-buried face pressed close to the grass, even the clothed lines of his figure were instinct with a vitality that somehow was different from that of other men. And some faint glow from it reached Darcy, some thrill, some vibration from that charged recumbent body passed to him, and for a moment he understood as he had not understood before, despite his persistent questions and the candid answers they received, how real, and how realised by Frank, his idea was.

Then suddenly the muscles in Frank's neck became stiff and alert, and he half-raised his head.

"The Pan-pipes, the Pan-pipes," he whispered. "Close, oh, so close."

Very slowly, as if a sudden movement might interrupt the melody, he raised himself and leaned on the elbow of his bent arm. His eyes opened wider, the lower lids drooped as if he focussed his eyes on something very far away, and the smile on his face broadened and quivered like sunlight on still water, till the exultance of its happiness was scarcely human. So he remained motionless and rapt for some minutes, then the look of listening died from his face, and he bowed his head satisfied.

"Ah, that was good," he said. "How is it possible you did not hear? Oh, you poor fellow! Did you really hear nothing?"

A week of this outdoor and stimulating life did wonders in restoring to Darcy the vigour and health which his weeks of fever had filched from him, and as his normal activity and higher pressure of vitality returned, he seemed to himself to fall even more under the spell which the miracle of Frank's youth cast over him. Twenty times a day he found himself saying to himself suddenly at the end of some ten minutes' silent resistance to the absurdity of Frank's idea: "But it isn't possible; it can't be possible," and from the fact of his having to assure himself so frequently of this, he knew that he was struggling and arguing with a conclusion which already had taken root in his mind. For in any case a visible living miracle confronted him, since it was equally impossible that this youth, this boy, trembling on the verge of manhood, was thirty-five. Yet such was the fact.

July was ushered in by a couple of days of blustering and fretful rain, and Darcy, unwilling to risk a chill, kept to the house. But to Frank this weeping change of weather seemed to have no bearing on the behaviour of man, and he spent his days exactly as he did under the suns of June, lying in his hammock, stretched on the dripping grass, or making huge rambling excursions into the forest, the birds hopping from tree to tree after him, to return in the evening, drenched and soaked, but with the same unquenchable flame of joy burning within him.

"Catch cold?" he would ask; "I've forgotten how to do it, I think. I suppose it makes one's body more sensible always to sleep out-of-doors. People who live indoors always remind me of something peeled and skinless."

"Do you mean to say you slept out-of-doors last night in that deluge?" asked Darcy. "And where, may I ask?"

Frank thought a moment.

"I slept in the hammock till nearly dawn," he said. "For I remember the light blinked in the east when I awoke. Then I went—where did I go—oh, yes, to the meadow where the Pan-pipes sounded so close a week ago. You were with me, do you remember? But I always have a rug if it is wet."

And he went whistling upstairs.

Somehow that little touch, his obvious effort to recall where he had slept, brought strangely home to Darcy the wonderful romance of which he was the still half-incredulous beholder. Sleep till close on dawn in a hammock, then the tramp—or probably scamper—underneath the windy and weeping heavens to the remote and lonely meadow by the weir! The picture of other such nights rose before him; Frank sleeping perhaps by the bathing-place under the filtered twilight of the stars, or the white blaze of moon-shine, a stir and awakening at some dead hour, perhaps a space of silent wide-eyed thought, and then awandering through the hushed woods to some other dormitory, alone with his happiness, alone with the joy and the life that suffused and enveloped him, without other thought or desire or aim except the hourly and never-ceasing communion with the joy of nature.

They were in the middle of dinner that night, talking on indifferent subjects, when Darcy suddenly broke off in the middle of a sentence.

"I've got it," he said. "At last I've got it."

"Congratulate you," said Frank. "But what?"

"The radical unsoundness of your idea. It is this: 'All Nature from highest to lowest is full, crammed full of suffering; every living organism in Nature preys on another, yet in your aim to get close to, to be one with Nature, you leave suffering altogether out; you run away from it, you refuse to recognise it.' And you are waiting, you say, for the final revelation."

Frank's brow clouded slightly.

"Well," he asked, rather wearily.

"Cannot you guess then when the final revelation will be? In joy you are supreme, I grant you that; I did not know a man could be so master of it. You have learned perhaps practically all that Nature can teach. And if, as you think, the final revelation is coming to you, it will be the revelation of horror, suffering, death, pain in all its hideous forms. Suffering does exist: you hate it and fear it."

Frank held up his hand.

"Stop; let me think," he said.

There was silence for a long minute.

"That never struck me," he said at length. "It is possible that what you suggest is true. Does the sight of Pan mean that, do you think? Is it that Nature, take it altogether, suffers horribly, suffers to a hideous inconceivable extent? Shall I be shown all the suffering?"

He got up and came round to where Darcy sat.

"If it is so, so be it," he said. "Because, my dear fellow, I am near, so splendidly near to the final revelation. To-day the pipes have sounded almost without pause. I have even heard the rustle in the bushes, I believe, of Pan's coming. I have seen, yes, I saw to-day, the bushes pushed aside as if by a hand, and piece of a face, not human, peered through. But I was not frightened, at least I did not run away this time."

He took a turn up to the window and back again.

"Yes, there is suffering all through," he said, "and I have left it all out of my search. Perhaps, as you say, the revelation will be that. And in that case, it will be good-bye. I have gone on one line. I shall have gone too far along one road, without having explored the other. But I can't go back now. I wouldn't if I could; not a step would I retrace! In any case, whatever the revelation is, it will be God. I'm sure of that."

The rainy weather soon passed, and with the return of the sun Darcy again joined Frank in long rambling days. It grew extraordinarily hotter, and with the fresh bursting of life, after the rain, Frank's vitality seemed to blaze higher and higher. Then, as is the habit of the English weather, one evening clouds began to bank themselves up in the west, the sun went down in a glare of coppery thunder-rack, and the whole earth broiling under an unspeakable oppression and sultriness paused and panted for the storm. After sunset the remote fires of lightning began to wink and flicker on the horizon, but when bed-time came the storm seemed to have moved no nearer, though a very low unceasing noise of thunder was audible. Weary and oppressed by the stress of the day, Darcy fell at once into a heavy uncomforting sleep.

He woke suddenly into full consciousness, with the din of some appalling explosion of thunder in his ears, and sat up in bed with racing heart. Then for a moment, as he recovered himself from the panic-land which lies between sleeping and waking, there was silence, except for the steady hissing of rain on the shrubs outside his window. But suddenly that silence was shattered and shredded into fragments by a scream from somewhere close at hand outside in the black garden, a scream of supreme and despairing terror. Again and once again it shrilled up, and then a babble of awful words was interjected. A quivering sobbing voice that he knew said:

"My God, oh, my God; oh, Christ!"

And then followed a little mocking, bleating laugh. Then was silence again; only the rain hissed on the shrubs.

All this was but the affair of a moment, and without pause either to put on clothes or light a candle, Darcy was already fumbling at his door-handle. Even as he opened it he met a terror-stricken face outside, that of the man-servant who carried a light.

"Did you hear?" he asked.

The man's face was bleached to a dull shining whiteness.

"Yes, sir," he said. "It was the master's voice."

Together they hurried down the stairs, and through the dining-room where an orderly table for breakfast had already been laid, and out on to the terrace. The rain for the moment had been utterly stayed, as if the tap of the heavens had been turned off, and under the lowering black sky, not quite dark, since the moon rode somewhere serene behind the conglomerated thunder-clouds, Darcy stumbled into the garden, followed by the servant with the candle. The monstrous leaping shadow of himself was cast before him on the lawn; lost and wandering odours of rose and lily and damp earth were thick about him, but more pungent was some sharp and acrid smell that suddenly reminded him of a certain châlet in which he had once taken refuge in the Alps. In the blackness of the hazy light from the sky, and the vague tossing of the candle behind him, he saw that the hammock in which Frank so often lay was tenanted. A gleam of white shirt was there, as if a man were sitting up in it, but across that there was an obscure dark shadow, and as he approached the acrid odour grew more intense.

He was now only some few yards away, when suddenly the black shadow seemed to jump into the air, then came down with tappings of hard hoofs on the brick path that ran down the pergola, and with frolicsome skippings galloped off into the bushes. When that was gone Darcy could see quite clearly that a shirted figure sat up in the hammock. For one moment, from sheer terror of the unseen, he hung on his step, and the servant joining him they walked together to the hammock.

It was Frank. He was in shirt and trousers only, and he sat up with braced arms. For one half-second he stared at them, his face a mask of horrible contorted terror. His upper lip was drawn back so that the gums of the teeth appeared, and his eyes were focussed not on the two who approached him, but on something quite close to him, his nostrils were widely expanded, as if he panted for breath, and terror incarnate and repulsion and deathly anguish ruled dreadful lines on his smooth cheeks and forehead. Then even as they looked the body sank backwards, and the ropes of the hammock wheezed and strained.

Darcy lifted him out and carried him indoors. Once he thought there was a faint convulsive stir of the limbs that lay with so dead a weight in his arms, but when they got inside, there was no trace of life. But the look of supreme terror and agony of fear had gone from his face, a boy tired with play but still smiling in his sleep was the burden he laid on the floor. His eyes had closed, and the beautiful mouth lay in smiling curves, even as when a few mornings ago, in the meadow by the weir, it had quivered to the music of the unheard melody of Pan's pipes. Then they looked further.

Frank had come back from his bathe before dinner that night in his usual costume of shirt and trousers only. He had not dressed, and during dinner, so Darcy remembered, he had rolled up the sleeves of his shirt to above the elbow. Later, as they sat and talked after dinner on the close sultriness of the evening, he had unbuttoned the front of his shirt to let what little breath of wind there was play on his skin. The sleeves were rolled up now, the front of the shirt was unbuttoned, and on his arms and on the brown skin of his chest were strange discolorations which grew momently more clear and defined, till they saw that the marks were pointed prints, as if caused by the hoofs of some monstrous goat that had leaped and stamped upon him.

AMBROSE BIERCE
The Secret of Macarger's Gulch

Ambrose Bierce (1842–1914?), *noted for his satirical black humour, wrote some of the finest short stories of the American Civil War—enshrined for posterity in* Tales of Soldiers and Civilians *(1891). His obsession with the ghostly and inexplicable, seen to best effect in* Can Such Things Be *(1893), dated back to his grim childhood dreams which he always remembered with great clarity. To critics of his horror stories, he would respond: "If it scares you to read that one imaginary person killed another, why not take up knitting?" The American writer H.L. Mencken later commented that "the reputation of Bierce has always radiated an occult, artificial drug-store scent." Bierce was recently portrayed on screen by Gregory Peck in* Old Gringo.

Northwestwardly from Indian Hill, about nine miles as the crow flies, is Macarger's Gulch. It is not much of a gulch—a mere depression between two wooded ridges of inconsiderable height. From its mouth up to its head—for gulches, like rivers, have an anatomy of their own—the distance does not exceed two miles, and the width at bottom is at only one place more than a dozen yards; for most of the distance on either side of the little brook which drains it in winter, and goes dry in the early spring, there is no level ground at all; the steep slopes of the hills covered with an almost impenetrable growth of manzanita and chemisal, are parted by nothing but the width of the watercourse. No one but an occasional enterprising hunter of the vicinity ever goes into Macarger's Gulch, and five miles away it is unknown, even by name. Within that distance in any direction are far more conspicuous topographical features without names, and one might try in vain to ascertain by local inquiry the origin of the name of this one.

71

About midway between the head and the mouth of Macarger's Gulch, the hill on the right as you ascend is cloven by another gulch, a short dry one, and at the junction of the two is a level space of two or three acres, and there a few years ago stood an old board house containing one small room. How the component parts of the house, few and simple as they were, had been assembled at that almost inaccessible point is a problem in the solution of which there would be greater satisfaction than advantage. Possibly the creek bed is a reformed road. It is certain that the gulch was at one time pretty thoroughly prospected by miners, who must have had some means of getting in with at least pack animals carrying tools and supplies; their profits, apparently, were not such as would have justified any considerable outlay to connect Macarger's Gulch with any centre of civilization enjoying the distinction of a saw-mill. The house, however, was there, most of it. It lacked a door and a window frame, and the chimney of mud and stones had fallen into an unlovely heap, over-grown with rank weeds. Such humble furniture as there may once have been and much of the lower weather-boarding, had served as fuel in the camp fires of hunters; as had also, probably, the kerbing of an old well, which at the time I write of existed in the form of a rather wide but not very deep depression near by.

One afternoon in the summer of 1874, I passed up Macarger's Gulch from the narrow valley into which it opens, by following the dry bed of the brook. I was quail-shooting and had made a bag of about a dozen birds by the time I had reached the house described, of whose existence I was until then unaware. After rather carelessly inspecting the ruin I resumed my sport, and having fairly good success prolonged it until near sunset, when it occurred to me that I was a long way from any human habitation—too far to reach one by nightfall. But in my game bag was food, and the old house would afford shelter, if shelter were needed on a warm and dewless night in the foothills of the Sierra Nevada, where one may sleep in comfort on the pine needles, without covering. I am fond of solitude and love the night, so my resolution to "camp out" was soon taken, and by the time that it was dark I had made my bed of boughs and grasses in a corner of the room and was roasting a quail at a fire that I had kindled on the hearth. The smoke escaped out of the ruined chimney, the light illuminated the room with a kindly glow, and as I ate my simple meal of plain bird and drank the remains of a bottle of red wine which had served me all the afternoon in place of the water, which the region did not supply, I experienced a sense of comfort which better fare and accommodations do not always give.

Nevertheless, there was something lacking. I had a sense of comfort, but not of security. I detected myself staring more frequently at the open doorway and blank window than I could find warrant for doing. Outside these apertures all was black, and I was unable to repress a certain feeling of apprehension as my fancy pictured the outer world and filled it with unfriendly entities, natural and supernatural—chief among which, in their respective classes, were the grizzly bear, which I knew was occasionally still seen in that region, and the ghost, which I had reason to think was not. Unfortunately, our feelings do not always respect the law of probabilities, and to me that evening, the possible and the impossible were equally disquieting.

Every one who has had experience in the matter must have observed that one confronts the actual and imaginary perils of the night with far less apprehension in the open air than in a house with an open doorway. I felt this now as I lay on my leafy couch in a corner of the room next to the chimney and permitted my fire to die out. So strong became my sense of the presence of something malign and menacing in the place, that I found myself almost unable to withdraw my eyes from the opening, as in the deepening darkness it became more and more indistinct. And when the last little flame flickered and went out I grasped the shotgun which I had laid at my side and actually turned the muzzle in the direction of the now invisible entrance, my thumb on one of the hammers, ready to cock the piece, my breath suspended, my muscles rigid and tense. But later I laid down the weapon with a sense of shame and mortification. What did I fear, and why?—I, to whom the night had been

> a more familiar face
> Than that of man—

I, in whom that element of hereditary superstition from which none of us is altogether free had given to solitude and darkness and silence only a more alluring interest and charm! I was unable to comprehend my folly, and losing in the conjecture the thing conjectured of, I fell asleep. And then I dreamed.

I was in a great city in a foreign land—a city whose people were of my own race, with minor differences of speech and costume; yet precisely what these were I could not say; my sense of them was indistinct. The city was dominated by a great castle upon an overlooking height whose name I knew, but could not speak. I walked through many streets, some broad and straight with high, modern buildings, some narrow, gloomy, and tortuous, between the gables of quaint old houses whose overhanging stories, elaborately ornamented with carvings in wood and stone, almost met above my head.

I sought some one whom I had never seen, yet knew that I should recognize when found. My quest was not aimless and fortuitous; it had a definite method. I turned from one street into another without hesitation and threaded a maze of intricate passages, devoid of the fear of losing my way.

Presently I stopped before a low door in a plain stone house which might have been the dwelling of an artisan of the better sort, and without announcing myself, entered. The room, rather sparely furnished, and lighted by a single window with small diamond-shaped panes, had but two occupants: a man and a woman. They took no notice of my intrusion, a circumstance which, in the manner of dreams, appeared entirely natural. They were not conversing; they sat apart, unoccupied and sullen.

The woman was young and rather stout, with fine large eyes and a certain grave beauty; my memory of her expression is exceedingly vivid, but in dreams one does not observe the details of faces. About her shoulders was a plaid shawl. The man was older, dark, with an evil face made more forbidding by a long scar extending from near the left temple diagonally downward into the black moustache; though in my dreams it seemed rather to haunt the face as a thing apart—I can express it no otherwise—than to belong to it. The moment that I found the man and woman I knew them to be husband and wife.

What followed, I remember indistinctly; all was confused and inconsistent—made so, I think, by gleams of consciousness. It was as if two pictures, the scene of my dream, and my actual surroundings, had been blended, one overlying the other, until the former, gradually fading, disappeared, and I was broad awake in the deserted cabin, entirely and tranquilly conscious of my situation.

My foolish fear was gone, and opening my eyes I saw that my fire, not altogether burned out, had revived by the falling of a stick and was again lighting the room. I had probably slept only a few minutes, but my commonplace dream had somehow so strongly impressed me that I was no longer drowsy; and after a little while I rose, pushed the embers of my fire together, and lighting my pipe proceeded in a rather ludicrously methodical way to meditate upon my vision.

It would have puzzled me then to say in what respect it was worth attention. In the first moment of serious thought that I gave to the matter I recognized the city of my dream as Edinburgh, where I had never been; so if the dream was a memory it was a memory of pictures and description. The recognition somehow deeply impressed me; it was as if something in my mind insisted rebelliously against will and reason on the importance of all this. And that faculty, whatever it was, asserted also a control of my speech. "Surely," I said aloud, quite involuntarily, "the MacGregors must have come here from Edinburgh."

At the moment, neither the substance of this remark nor the fact of my making it, surprised me in the least; it seemed entirely natural that I should know the name of my dreamfolk and something of their history. But the absurdity of it all soon dawned upon me: I laughed aloud, knocked the ashes from my pipe and again stretched myself upon my bed of boughs and grass, where I lay staring absently into my failing fire, with no further thought of either my dream or my surroundings. Suddenly the single remaining flame crouched for a moment, then, springing upward, lifted itself clear of its embers and expired in air. The darkness was absolute.

At that instant—almost, it seemed, before the gleam of the blaze had faded from my eyes—there was a dull, dead sound, as of some heavy body falling upon the floor, which shook beneath me as I lay. I sprang to a sitting posture and groped at my side for my gun; my notion was that some wild beast had leaped in through the open window. While the flimsy structure was still shaking from the impact I heard the sound of blows, the scuffling of feet upon the floor, and then—it seemed to come from almost within reach of my hand — the sharp shrieking of a woman in mortal agony. So horrible a cry I had never heard nor conceived; it utterly unnerved me; I was conscious for a moment of nothing but my own terror! Fortunately my hand now found the weapon of which it was in search, and the familiar touch somewhat restored me. I leaped to my feet, straining my eyes to pierce the darkness. The violent sounds had ceased, but more terrible than these, I heard, at what seemed long intervals, the faint intermittent gasping of some living, dying thing!

As my eyes grew accustomed to the dim light of the coals in the fireplace, I saw first the shapes of the door and window looking blacker than the black of the walls. Next, the distinction between wall and floor became discernible, and at last I was sensible to the form and full expanse of the floor from end to end and side to side. Nothing was visible and the silence was unbroken.

With a hand that shook a little, the other still grasping my gun, I restored my fire and made a critical examination of the place. There was nowhere any sign that the cabin had been entered. My own tracks were visible in the dust covering the floor, but there were no others. I relit my pipe, provided fresh fuel by ripping a thin board or two from the inside of the house—I did not care to go into the darkness out of doors—and passed the rest of the night smoking and thinking, and feeding my fire; not for added years of life would I have permitted that little flame to expire again.

Some years afterward I met in Sacramento a man named Morgan, to whom I had a note of introduction from a friend in San Francisco. Dining with him one evening at his home I observed various "trophies" upon the wall, indicating that he was fond of shooting. It turned out that he was, and in relating some of his feats he mentioned having been in the region of my adventure.

"Mr. Morgan," I asked abruptly, "do you know a place up there called Macarger's Gulch?"

"I have good reason to," he replied; "it was I who gave to the newspapers, last year, the accounts of the finding of the skeleton there."

I had not heard of it; the accounts had been published, it appeared, while I was absent in the East.

"By the way," said Morgan, "the name of the gulch is a corruption; it should have been called 'MacGregor's.' My dear," he added, speaking to his wife, "Mr. Elderson has upset his wine."

That was hardly accurate—I had simply dropped it, glass and all.

"There was an old shanty once in the gulch," Morgan resumed when the ruin wrought by my awkwardness had been repaired, "but just previously to my visit it had been blown down, or rather blown away, for its *débris* was scattered all about, the very floor being parted, plank from plank. Between two of the sleepers still in position I and my companion observed the remnant of a plaid shawl, and examining it found that it was wrapped about the shoulders of the body of a woman; of course but little remained besides the bones, partly covered with fragments of clothing, and brown dry skin. But we will spare Mrs. Morgan," he added with a smile. The lady had indeed exhibited signs of disgust rather than sympathy.

"It is necessary to say, however," he went on, "that the skull was fractured in several places, as by blows of some blunt instrument; and that instrument itself—a pick-handle, still stained with blood—lay under the boards near by."

Mr. Morgan turned to his wife. "Pardon me, my dear," he said with affected solemnity, "for mentioning these disagreeable particulars, the natural though regrettable incidents of a conjugal quarrel—resulting, doubtless, from the luckless wife's insubordination."

"I ought to be able to overlook it," the lady replied with composure; "you have so many times asked me to in those very words."

I thought he seemed rather glad to go on with his story.

"From these and other circumstances," he said, "the coroner's jury found that the deceased, Janet MacGregor, came to her death from blows inflicted by some person to the jury unknown; but it was added that the evidence pointed strongly to her husband, Thomas MacGregor, as the guilty person. But Thomas MacGregor has never been found nor heard of. It was learned that the couple came from Edinburgh, but not—my dear, do you not observe that Mr. Elderson's boneplate has water in it?"

I had deposited a chicken bone in my finger bowl.

"In a little cupboard I found a photograph of MacGregor, but it did not lead to his capture."

"Will you let me see it?" I said.

The picture showed a dark man with an evil face made more forbidding by a long scar extending from near the temple diagonally downward into the black moustache.

"By the way, Mr. Elderson," said my affable host, "may I know why you asked about 'Macarger's Gulch'?"

"I lost a mule near there once," I replied, "and the mischance has—has quite—upset me."

"My dear," said Mr. Morgan, with the mechanical intonation of an interpreter translating, "the loss of Mr. Elderson's mule has peppered his coffee."

H.T.W. BOUSFIELD
The God with Four Arms

Henry Thomas Wishart Bousfield *was another of the very talented writers of bizarre and occult tales published in* Queen, Nash's Magazine *and other notable periodicals of the 1930s. This tale was the title story of his collection*, The God with Four Arms and other stories (1939).

I have drawn on my own imagination just enough to turn my father's voluminous notes into a connected narrative. And no more. Indeed there was little to add to them. My father was a careful man—in everything but money, as I discovered when he died a couple of years ago.

He was a doctor with rather a fashionable practice in West London which was slightly handicapped by his insatiable curiosity. He spent an incredible amount of time in the slums, in the foreign quarters, down by the docks, getting into conversation with every type of every race. He was a brilliant linguist, so he missed few opportunities, and whenever he came upon something unusual he carefully noted it down.

In his later years, when, fortunately, a couple of capable partners did most of his work for him, he spent very little time indeed at his proper business. He even, I understand, established a sort of free surgery where a man could get expert medical attention in return for a good story.

That description will identify him to anybody familiar with Rotherhithe. He was not known there by his real name. He called himself Doctor James.

John Maxton was one of my less respectable acquaintances on London's seaboard. He was an interesting ruffian, however, and I tolerated him for the sake of his reminiscences. He had been to a thousand places and seen ten thousand sights that I could never hope to see. Probably a good many police forces would have been glad to know his address, but in London he was extremely careful. The London police considered him not only harmless but respectable.

His ostensible business was a licensed grocery. He also owned a certain amount of house property dotted here and there—slum properties, of course, and one or two shops. One of his tenants was an elderly Eurasian, most inappropriately named Smith, who ran a sort of general junk-shop close to East India Docks.

I knew Smith as well as I knew Maxton. Both of them had a habit of calling at my surgery to swop a good story for some simple medical treatment. I knew they hated each other, and I knew there was something more between them than the normal relations of tenant and landlord. But what it was I never discovered.

Apparently Smith did a good trade. He was known to the whole shifting population of deep-sea sailors as a man who would pay a fair price for a bit of K'ang Hs'i or Ch'ien Lung, a Netsuké or an old bronze. I know for a fact that he made some wonderful bargains, and his best finds ultimately gravitated to Bond Street and the collections of the respectably rich.

It's impossible to find out all about those weird types—unless one can give one's whole time to them, and I have a practice that I cannot entirely neglect—since I live by it—although I have now got two most excellent fellows to help me. I must have missed a thousand tales by the necessity of earning my living.

In 1926 I was particularly busy throughout the summer—my most valuable patient really got ill and nearly died—and I neglected the wilderness for months at a time. At last, however, I got her safely out of the country, full of gratitude and a mild tonic, and I managed to spend a whole week undisturbed in my aromatic slum.

I arrived unobtrusively enough, but I had not been back an hour before Maxton called.

He accepted a cigarette and a drink.

"No, doctor," he said, "I'm not here to do any cadging this time. Just a friendly visit. We've missed you down here. Yes, you must have been making a lot of money out of the rich fools."

"If I didn't," I said, "I should starve. You people consider it's a privilege for anyone to doctor you."

"Well, sir, not a privilege, but sometimes amusing. Not?

"You're going to be here some days. Good. Perhaps you haven't heard about poor Smith?"

"Why 'poor.' Do you mean he's dead?"

"No, not dead. Only, Smith is a very foolish man. He has gone a little bit mad, I think. You know he is a tenant of mine. Well, lately he has been gambling or betting or something—I do not know what"—a curious chi-chi accent always crept into Maxton's speech when he got excited—"but it is serious. He comes to me first to borrow money. I lend it. Then he comes to put off paying his rent. I put it off one week, then two. After that it is no good.

"I tell Smith it is no good. That man has a very fine business, I tell him. Everyone knows the pretty things he gets from the sailors and sells to Murasaki in Bond Street who sells them to the rich people—your friends, doctor."

"Then why does he have to borrow?"

Maxton shrugged his shoulders.

"I don't know. He gambles, or his brother gambles, perhaps. Anyway, the money goes, and I have great trouble."

He looked quite guilty and uneasy.

"In the end," he said, "I sell him up. At least, I take his shop and his stock as against what he owes me. Quite fair. I get it in law against his written promises. How can I wait for ever? I am a poor man."

"How sick you'd be, Maxton," I remarked, "if anybody else said that, and seriously."

Maxton essayed an uneasy smile.

"I am taking over his stock this afternoon," he said, and paused.

"And where's Smith?" I demanded.

"He threw himself in front of a train at Aldgate Station," said Maxton, with his eyes on the floor.

"But you said he wasn't dead."

"Ah, maybe not then. That was a little time ago. But he is now. Yes. He was with me when it happened. I met him—that was bad luck. He asked me for more and yet more money. Me. And why? I acknowledge no reason why I should keep him, whether it is he or his brother who throws money away.

"So I say I will not, and Smith goes down on the line as a west-bound train comes in. They drag him out, very bloody, and carry him away. He is conscious, and he calls most unpleasant things out at me."

Maxton shuddered a little.

"What did he say?" I asked.

"Oh, I don't know. Some nonsense.

"Now, doctor, will you come with me to Smith's shop? I have the order and the keys in my pocket. Maybe you will make me an offer for some of his pretty things."

"You're frightened, Maxton," I said. "Now I shall expect some bargains if I pander to your superstitious fears and come with you. You're frightened because Smith cursed you. And probably you deserved it. I know you always hated him."

Maxton was silent.

"Did he leave any dependants? If so, and you're so scared, you'd better buy his ghost off by providing for them."

"He left nobody. I do not know his brother—if he really had a brother, I don't know."

"Very well," I said, "I'll come and protect you. But, mind, I shall expect very special treatment if I see something I want to buy."

Maxton beamed all over his ambiguous face.

"You shall have it, doctor," he said fervently.

It was growing dusk when we arrived at Smith's little shop. Maxton unlocked the door with some difficulty and turned up the light. The place was empty.

"The damn swine!" cried Maxton. "But what did he *do* with his money?"

"He must have had other creditors besides you, my friend," I remarked. "They've got ahead of you, that's all."

Maxton proceeded into the inner room. "Doctor!" he called.

I followed him. At first sight the room appeared to be full of stuff, and indeed it was full, but of rubbish. All the cheap imitation curios of modern Japan that sell in Blackpool and Margate and Southend were heaped on the little table. Twenty pounds for the lot would have been a generous estimate.

"I hope you didn't finance him to any great extent," I remarked, "because if you did, this is the best fulfilment of his curse that you need expect."

"The damn swine!" said Maxton again.

"We have adopted a Latin proverb," I said, "which, translated, states that one should not speak ill of the dead. Look the stuff over; it can't all be utter rubbish."

I poked into the confusion as I spoke.

"Look at this," I said.

Under a heap of fake ivories I unearthed a most perfect little gilded bronze. It was plainly of southern India, a four-armed figure, holding spears and thunderbolts—a typical Indra.

"Look at this," I said. "The best Indra I've ever seen. Any collector would give you twenty-five for this. He must have forgotten it."

"Twenty-five!" cried Maxton, now thoroughly infuriated. "Twenty-five! And he owed me two hundred. Yes, and much more beside." He laughed bitterly.

"I know nothing of these Indian things, doctor," he said. "Porcelain, yes, carpets, yes, and perhaps *afyun*— though no doubt I ought not to mention that."

He steadily regarded the bronze.

"Would you care for this, doctor? I might let you have it cheap."

But I, too, had been regarding it. I am not an unnecessarily superstitious man, but I did not care for the appearance of that image.

According to some authorities, Indra is the greatest of the gods, and there are other aspects of his personality. In the curious confusion that prevails in that Holy College, Indra has certain aspects that are demoniacal. I did not want the bronze.

"No, thank you, Maxton," I said. "Indian bronzes are not in my line. Now if you could produce, let us say, a Hsüan Te altar cup, that would be a different thing.

"I didn't know Smith ever bothered about Indian or Persian art."

"That man," said Maxton, still furiously rummaging in the rubbish, "bothered with anything that could be made to lose money for other people."

I'm afraid I laughed.

"Well," I said. "It's getting late. Why not go over this stuff to-morrow? Nothing here for anybody to steal except that Indra."

"I take that," said Maxton. "Shaitan!" he muttered ferociously, and picked it up and actually slapped it!

"I shouldn't do that," I said. "After all, Indra has done you no harm, and he is the greatest of the gods—when he is not also (incognito) a demon."

It was no longer getting late, it had got late. I went home.

And that was the last I saw of Maxton. What follows I laboriously pieced together from the report of the police and the missionary and the prison doctor, amplified by notes taken down in shorthand from Maxton in the prison infirmary.

After I left, Maxton stayed in the shop for perhaps another hour, exhaustively going through what remained of the stock in hopes of finding enough to reimburse him for what he claimed he had lent to Smith. Apparently nothing so good as the bronze Indra could be found, so he picked it up and, carrying it under his arm, walked to his own place.

It is a little difficult to establish just what happened then, except that Maxton seems to have drunk a good deal of brandy to drown his disappointment.

Brandy, however, does not agree with certain temperaments after a number of glasses. It appears that Maxton's constitution was, from a brandy-drinker's point of view, ill-chosen. By ten-thirty he was quarrelsome, slightly tipsy, and by no means well. He decided to go for a walk. As he left he made a final ill-tempered assault upon the bronze Indra, so that it fell to the floor and smashed one of its four arms. Incensed further by this, Maxton then kicked it, and a second arm fell off.

He stamped down the road feeling partly avenged.

At that hour not many people were about. He paused at a coffee-stall and ordered a sandwich and a cup of what is surprisingly called coffee in those parts. Two down-and-outs and a prosperous-looking Chinese were the only other customers. The Chinese was on Maxton's right.

Maxton, with a sandwich in one hand and a cup of coffee in the other, felt a slight stirring at his right side. He glanced down. A hand—his hand—dipped ever so gently into the Chinaman's pocket and withdrew a note-case. This he saw placed in his own pocket.

Yet in his right hand was all the time a cup of coffee, and in his left a sandwich.

The world for a moment swam before his eyes. Then one of the down-and-outs on his left purchased a packet of cigarettes and put it in the right pocket of his tattered jacket. Maxton saw and felt a hand go out from his left side and take that packet of cigarettes and thrust it into his own coat.

Yet in his left hand was still the remnant of a sandwich.

Hastily he finished the sandwich and the coffee, paid for them and hurried away. Neither the Chinese nor the out-of-works took the slightest notice of him. Round the corner, he felt in his right pocket. A note-case. He brought it out and examined it under a street-lamp. Not his. A handsome notecase, with twenty pounds inside it!

In his left-hand pocket was a packet of cheap cigarettes.

Maxton nearly fainted. Indeed he staggered. He clutched at the lamp-post to steady himself, and clutching that lamp-post he saw not two hands, but four.

As if the iron standard were red-hot, he snatched his hands away and thrust them in his trousers pockets. Before him were still two idle hands, his own hands. He could see the flamboyant ruby ring that he always wore whilst he *felt* the left hand that it must be upon in his pocket.

Where he went next from that place he did not know, but an hour later he found himself at Donovan's in Limehouse.

Since opium smoking has been so much discouraged by the police, Donovan's is not what it was. It is even difficult to get opium there, and opium was what Maxton decided he needed. Old Donovan, who might have obliged him, was out—an ominous indication that a raid was possible. However, a game was going on and there was a fairly full house.

Maxton stood looking on for a while, fatalistically waiting till someone should notice his infirmity or confirm that he was drunk. Two hands were in his pockets, he knew, and two others lit him a cigarette.

Whilst he was actually lighting a cigarette he saw a hand—his hand—ever so gently enter the pocket of one of the players and emerge with a pound note. He dare not stir, an incautious movement would have betrayed him. His victim saw nothing, felt nothing. The pound note entered his pocket.

Maxton felt his knees giving way under him. He sat down by himself against the wall. No one was within reach of his hands there.

He may have been drunk when he left his house, but I am quite prepared to believe that he was, by this time, stone-cold sober. He collected his thoughts. No one apparently had noticed that he had four arms instead of two. He wished—how he wished!—he were home so that he could count his members and decide whether he were mad or not. He must not attract attention. He called the potman.

"Joe, where's Donovan?"

"Not come in yet, Mr. Maxton."

"I want to see him. Business. Important. Guess you'd better let me sit in his room till he comes. I'll wait there."

"Yes, Mr. Maxton."

Maxton was well known. Joe unlocked the little cubby-hole at the back of the bar.

"And will I bring you a drink, Mr. Maxton?"

"Double brandy, Joe."

Keeping his hands firmly in his pockets—two of them, at any rate—Maxton went in. He stood with an air of preoccupation gazing at a fly-blown calendar till the drink arrived and the door was shut.

Then, ignoring the drink, he stretched his hands out before him.

Although everything else in the room was as clear-cut and certain as if he had never had a drink in his life, he could not ever be quite sure about his hands. He picked up at random his hat. There was a glimpse of the same hands, reaching of themselves for the inkstand. He dropped the hat. He was holding the inkstand. He had not four hands, but two. He took his coat off. It had, of course, two sleeves. Yet those extra hands—had he seen them?—were attached to arms in sleeves. He put his coat on again. He felt normal. He stood by the absent Donovan's desk and breathed a sigh of relief.

A small sound caught his attention.

A drawer of the desk was opening, of itself. At least he was not consciously touching it. In a new access of horror he glanced down. Still opening. He saw a hand—his hand—swiftly take out a knife and slip it into his pocket—an open knife with a long, thin blade—and close the drawer again.

Yet all the time his own hands—his real hands—were clutching his head!

He fled away from that desk. But he had to come back to it, for this time he needed the drink. He drank it.

He was still drinking it when Donovan came in.

"Good evening, Mr. Maxton," said Donovan. "You want to see me? No trouble, I hope? You have had a good game? Ah, Mr. Maxton, you are a great business man."

With an effort Maxton pulled himself together.

"Donovan, look at me. Do you think I am a fool?"

"A fool?" said Donovan (who, by the way, whatever his nationality, was certainly no Irishman). "Why, Mr. Maxton, you have not come here—at this time—about our little loan, our little business together?

"A fool! No, Mr. Maxton. But business is not good. First I cannot keep opium any longer, then I must not sell even a drink or hold a game for my friends. To-night, perhaps, there would again be a raid, but now I think not. I hear it will not be.

"So here I am."

He smiled sadly, and spread out his hands.

Maxton finished his drink and carefully put the glass on the table. He came closer.

"Donovan," he said. "Do you see anything strange about me?"

He came closer still. Donovan backed away.

"So!" he said. "You come here because you know I see you this morning. You know I see you push Smith on the line. And you come here to talk business, eh? There will be none of *that* business between us any more, Mr. Maxton. Oh, no. If I tell the police I saw you trip up Smith—push him—so that he fall on the line—what then?" He laughed.

"Strange about you? You are uneasy.

"But rest assured, I shall not give you away. Just give me that receipt you hold, and . . . For God's sake, Mr. Maxton—sir——"

Maxton had got him by the shoulders and was shaking him backwards and forwards.

"It's a lie," he said, "a lie, a lie, a lie!"

Violently he shook Donovan to and fro. "I never touched him. Blackmail, eh, Donovan? I'll see you in hell first."

Then he almost shrieked. As his hands still clutched Donovan's shoulders, another hand, his hand, appeared. It took the long, thin knife out of his pocket, and as he still gripped Donovan, drove that knife into Donovan's heart.

Donovan died, but before he died he screamed. There was no escape for Maxton.

Later, at the police station, they found the pocket-book that the prosperous Chinese had reported as stolen from him at the coffee-stall. The proprietor of the stall—and the two down-and-outs who had also been arrested on suspicion—duly identified him.

Several things came to light then. No; there was no hope for Maxton. He was hanged. His lawyer pleaded insanity, and even adduced Maxton's own story about a curse and a quadrumanous idol in evidence thereof. But Maxton, said the doctors, was perfectly normal. He had drunk enough, they said, to make him careless; that was all. His association with the worst of Donovan's activities was proved.

Maxton was hanged.

But sometimes I wonder. And I wonder what junk-shop now has a painted, bronze image of Indra with two missing hands.

A.M. BURRAGE
The Shadowy Escort

Alfred McLelland Burrage (1889–1956) was one of the finest ghost story writers this country has produced, alongside James, Benson and Wakefield. He also wrote the classic War is War, *a passionate and unforgettable novel based on his personal horrific experiences of trench warfare in the Great War, published in 1930 under the pseudonym "Ex-Private X". The following story, similarly based on the horrors of war, was first published in the* London Magazine, *May 1928.*

Almost everybody has at one time or another wanted to write a detective story, but, for the greater well-being of publishers and publishers' readers, not everybody has tried. Among those who have, with varying degrees of success, must be numbered a lot of men and women who would not have attempted to enter the realm of letters by any other frontier. Detective fiction has a fascination for nearly every type of mind. Thus it may happen that the butcher's boy cannot bring himself to deliver the meat until he has read the explanation of what really did happen in Chapter Six, and the Cabinet Minister, also immersed in another copy of the same work, forgets to protest because his dinner is late.

This is due to the age-old, natural, human love of a puzzle; and the ambition to create a puzzle of one's own, instead of merely trying to solve other peoples', is a natural after-growth.

Serrald had read detective fiction for years as a mental relaxation. When he dined out he talked about the Russian School and the influence of the Arthurian Legend upon our early poets; when he got home he went on reading "The Mystery of Bloodshot Grange." This he regarded as a secret vice, and did not own to it until he discovered that many of his intellectual friends, who also should have known better, made similar concessions to their lower natures.

Serrald was a man in the middle thirties who liked to pose as an intellectual. He was employed in one of the higher branches of the Civil Service, and had been immune from any other service during the early years of the War. But when the newspapers had invented "Cuthbert," and printed rude remarks about Government Rabbit Warrens, he had joined the Army as a private, and later received a commission after several months' service in France. Apparently he had done very well in the Army, but he rarely spoke about those days. The War had been too vulgar a brawl for a young man with a taste for intellectualism.

It was some years after the War that Serrald confided to his friend Masters his intention of writing a detective novel. He said that it might be better fun than continuing to read them, and that there must be a lot of fun to be had in laying false clues and finding for them sound and logical reasons for being included in the tale.

"I mean," he added, "to write a perfectly insoluble mystery story—insoluble, that is, until the reader has reached the last page."

Masters smiled at this modest ambition.

"Any ideas?" he asked.

"Oh, yes. My murder is going to be an act of omission, not of commission. The murderer turns out to be only a murderer in the sense that he has found his victim in a predicament in which death must supervene if he refuses help—and he just refuses help and leaves him to die. There is another strong criminal interest in the story, but before I can get on with it I've got to invent something new in the way of ciphers. I want a cipher that doesn't look like a cipher. It must, of course, be very difficult to solve and be very innocent in appearance, so that anybody finding it would scarcely guess that it conveyed a message at all."

Masters considered.

"Short or long messages?" he asked.

"Oh, short would do. Just something by which criminals could warn each other of danger, and make appointments, and all that."

"I'll have a good think," said Masters, "and tell you if anything occurs to me."

Two evenings later he came round to Serrald's rooms.

"I've got your cipher," he said, with the smile of one who anticipates praise.

"Oh? Got the key written down?"

"No. It hasn't to be written down. That's the beauty of it. It can be memorized in exactly one second. And nobody—except, of course, the super-human detective you intend to create—could possibly guess that it was a cipher. I think I'll take ten per cent commission on what you get out of your book."

"We'll see," said Serrald smiling.

"All right. Well, when one of your villains wants to communicate with another villain he just sends him a pack of cards. Or perhaps cards out of two or three packs. It depends on the length of the message required. And, of course, other cards might be added after the message was complete in order to ally suspicion in the event of the package going astray."

"I don't quite follow you."

"Well, my dear chap, there are twenty-six letters in the alphabet, and fifty-two cards to a pack. You take them in the order of their value at auction bridge. Thus the Ace of Spades is A, and the Two of Hearts is Z. Then we start again and the Ace of Diamonds becomes A and the Two of Clubs Z. That gives you two of every letter in one pack of cards.

"When one of your villains wants to tell another to 'Beware' he sends him a pack of cards with the cipher ones at the top, in the order in which he will slide them off the pack. If the word were 'Beware' the top card would be the King of Spades, then would come the Ten, W would be the Five of Hearts, A the Ace of Spades—or Diamonds if you like——"

"By Jove!" Serrald exclaimed in genuine admiration.

"And the best of it is that the man who receives the message can instantly destroy all traces of it by merely shuffling the cards. Similarly anybody who guessed that the cards meant something, and started monkeying with them, would spoil his own chance of deciphering the message as soon as he altered their sequence."

Serrald nodded.

"That's quite a brilliant idea. You go from the top to the bottom of the Spades, and then from the top to the bottom of the Hearts, and that gives you the alphabet. Ace of Hearts would be the fourteenth letter, which is—er—N——"

"Ace of Hearts and Ace of Clubs are both N's. You go straight down the Spades and then straight down the Hearts. That's one alphabet of letters. Then straight down the Diamonds and straight down the Clubs, and that's another. Of course, one pack of cards wouldn't go far if you wanted a longish message, because so many letters get duplicated so quickly. Your crooks would have to keep about ten packs of cards each, all of the same pattern, to send longish messages to each other without anybody who might casually see the cards suspecting there was a code."

"I've got it. Well, I've got stacks of cards here, red-backs, and blue-backs, all of the same pattern. I get them from the stores for bridge, you know, and about twice a year I send the old ones to a hospital. I'll get some out and spell you a message to see if I've got it right."

He went to a drawer and pulled out fourteen or fifteen discarded packs which had been thrust back into their cardboard cases, and poured them all out upon the table, pack after pack, after which he began stirring the heap with his hands.

"Let's see," he said. "I'll pull out a few cards at random first of all, and see if I can remember which letters they represent. Here's the Two of Diamonds. What's that?"

"M," said Masters. "Two of Spades and Two of Diamonds are both M's. What's that you've got there now? King of Hearts? That's O. Ace of Hearts is an N. Four of Diamonds—that's K. Hullo, we've fluked a word already—Monk. Carry on. That's an L. Ace of Spades—that's an A. Not too quick. 'Nother Ace of Hearts is another N. Knave of Diamonds D. That's funny. Two words come out running—Monk and Land."

Serrald pushed the cards away from him with an impatient gesture. He had turned suddenly pale and a cold sweat shone on his face.

"Yes," he said, quickly and unsteadily. "I understand it now. It's—yes, it's devilish clever. Have a drink, will you? No, I don't want to know any more about it. A child could understand it once he'd been told. Yes, it's devilish clever—devilish clever."

Masters stared at his friend with sudden anxiety and a kind of dismay.

"You're feeling all right, aren't you?" he asked.

"Oh, quite. Quite all right. Why? Whisky for you?"

"Thanks. But you do look a bit green, you know. I thought perhaps——"

"What?"

"Oh, nothing. Because the cards you pulled out at random happen to spell two words, it looked as if you thought there might be something uncanny about it. They're not very significant words, and I don't see how they could be tacked together to start a sentence. I invented the code last night and amused myself in the same way, to help me memorize it, by drawing cards at random and seeing if they'd form words. But I never got anything of more than four letters. Some promising starts at ambitious words, and then gibberish."

Serrald had risen. He poured out two drinks and swallowed his own quickly.

"I'm a bit tired," he said, "that's all." He kept his face averted. "Of course, one might go on picking out cards at random for ever without finding sequences which would spell words. That's what makes it so—so excellent as a cipher, when one knows the key. It's a really excellent idea of yours. I shall certainly use it in my story."

The two men met frequently, and it was natural after that for Masters, who felt almost a proprietary interest in the detective romance, to inquire after its progress. But, like that of so many would-be authors, Serrald's enthusiasm seemed to have set sharp upon its rising. He explained that he wasn't well, and that it was no use making a start on the job until he felt fit to tackle it properly. Indeed, he had taken to looking ill, and to drinking a great deal more than was good for a man with a nervous temperament. Masters regarded him with the dispassionate pity of one who sees disaster looming ahead for another—a disaster for which the spectator is neither responsible nor able to avert.

"That chap's in for some sort of a break-down," he thought.

About a month later Masters had occasion one evening to go and pay Serrald a call. Serrald lived on the second floor of a large "apartments" house in Bloomsbury, of which the street door was always kept open until late at night. He mounted the dark stairs and had reached the second-floor landing, when he became aware of a figure moving away from the door of Serrald's sitting-room. Masters made way for it with a muttered word of apology and watched it descend half a dozen of the stairs before he turned and tapped at Serrald's door. Something quite inexplicable in the sight of the figure that had passed him filled him with a kind of cold dismay.

The sound of his knuckles on the door provoked loud and startled exclamation from within.

"*Who's there? Who's there?*"

"It's only I," said Masters, and pushed open the door.

Inside the room Serrald, wild-haired and wild-eyed, had swung round in his chair to face the door. He was sitting before a large central table on which was piled a great muddled heap of playing cards.

"Hullo," said Masters in a level and pleasant voice. "Hope you don't mind my butting in. I know I didn't drive your other visitor away, because he'd started to go before I got here."

Lines grew on Serrald's white face. For a moment he showed the whites of his eyes.

"My other visitor?" he repeated.

"Army chap."

Serrald drew breath noisily.

"Army chap—how do you know?"

"Wore the uniform of an officer. Sorry, I expect I made a mistake. Thought he was moving away from your door."

"Officers don't wear uniform in peace time, except when they're on duty," Serrald said thickly.

"I know. But this one was wearing his. I dare say he's a London Terrier just come from his drill-hall."

Serrald gulped.

"What was he like?" he faltered. "Tall?"

"Tall, yes, and broad. Couldn't see much what he was like apart from that. But he looked—well, the general impression I got was—that his uniform wasn't exactly smart enough for the parade ground."

Serrald leaned over the table, his face between his hands.

"So it's true," he said drearily, as if to himself. "It isn't that I'm going mad. All this hasn't been subjective. Sit down, Masters. I know whom you've seen. You're right, too. He *was* a Territorial officer, and he's just come from his drill-hall. But his drill-hall's in hell."

Masters stared at him and privately reflected that he was going mad.

"You're full of happy thoughts to-night," he remarked pleasantly. "Made a start on that book? No, of course you haven't! But I see you're still experimenting with that cipher I invented."

"*You* didn't invent it!" Serrald snarled.

"My dear fellow! Don't rob me of my only claim to literary fame."

"*You* didn't invent it. It was put into your head so that you could come and torture me with it. I've always avoided spiritualists and clairvoyants, and people who think they get messages from the dead by automatic writing and ouijah boards, and —and so forth. And that night, when I pulled out cards at random and applied your beastly code——"

Masters interrupted him with a half-angry laugh.

"Oh, don't be a fool! You happened when I was there that night to make two inconsequent words——"

"I didn't!" Serrald interrupted fiercely. "I made one, and that wasn't inconsequent to me. Monkland is a man's name, you know."

Masters stood and stared at him.

"I don't see why I shouldn't tell you," Serrald continued drearily. "I don't feel any shame now. I'm in a state of terror, and terror, if you get it badly enough, carries you miles beyond shame. Some fellows got like that in the War. I didn't, though I was bad enough, Heaven knows!

"I think you know most of my War history. I didn't join until pretty late—my department kept me—and when I did, I went to one of those Territorial regiments which had a reputation for being 'particular,' and for filling up with professional men and old public schoolboys. And in due time I got drafted out to France, and found myself under Monkland.

"Monkland had been out almost from the beginning. He'd been wounded twice, and after he'd risen to the rank of sergeant he'd been gazetted. Nobody denied that he was a good soldier, but everybody hated him. He was a swine to the men, and that worst kind of military brute—a martinet with a sneer. But he differed from most sneerers and loud-mouthed parade-ground flunkies. They were nearly always cowards, but he wasn't. He didn't know what fear was, and he hadn't the slightest sympathy with those who did.

"He took a special delight in bullying me and holding me up to ridicule. I'd joined late and come out of a Government office, and I suppose I couldn't help showing how I loathed the filth and the hardship and the danger. He was the bane of my life in the rest-camps, and in the trenches. If ever there were a dirty or a dangerous job going, he put me on to it if he could. One's life, Heaven knows, was foul enough out there, without having a personal tormentor. I was in for a commission—which meant coming home for further training—but I knew he'd put a stop to that if he had the chance. And I wasn't the only one who prayed that he'd be killed.

"For all that he seemed to have a charmed life. He wasn't one of those officers who were always away on courses whenever there was any dirty work expected—because they weren't fit to lead their men. He was always on the spot, thoroughly fearless and efficient, and he seemed to love night raids. When he took one out he nearly always detailed me, because he knew how I hated them. I dare say he's listening to all this, but I don't care—I'm only telling you the truth. There's only the stark truth left between him and me now."

He paused for breath. Masters drew his own breath slowly.

"Mad," he thought, "quite mad."

"One night when we were in the Arras sector," Serrald resumed, "Brigade ordered a reconnaissance raid. Wanted to know if the German front line was occupied at night, and if it were they wanted a couple of prisoners—alive, if possible—as samples. Of course, Monkland got the job, and, of course, he chose me for first bayonet man. That was the kind of work I loathed—sneaking over in the dark into Heaven only knew what death-trap to try to kidnap a couple of armed men. Monkland knew how I loathed it, and it gave him a special pleasure to take me with him.

"Well, not only was the German front line occupied, but we found a machine-gun post as well. It opened out on us suddenly, and we all dodged and scattered all over the place in search of cover. The Germans must have thought that there was more considerable mischief afoot than there really was, for up went an S O S and down came a barrage.

"I lay in a shell-hole until long after everything was quiet again, not daring to come out, and at last, when I ventured, I couldn't see any of our people. Then I guessed correctly that those who were left had managed to get back to our line, and I started to try to find my way.

"It was very easy to make mistakes in the dark in No Man's Land. I must have wandered a good deal out of my way when I stumbled on a shell-hole, and there was Monkland lying in it smoking a cigarette. He was pretty badly hurt and couldn't move. He told me that he'd tried single-handed to approach the machine-gun post from the flank and bomb it, but that he'd been seen and sniped. He told me to take careful bearings of where he was and send out a stretcher party when I got back. So I left him.

"I don't know what you think of me, Masters, and I've gone a good way beyond caring. I told myself that it wasn't fair that two stretcher-bearers should risk their lives for a brute like that. All that the man had done to me clamoured in my blood for vengeance. You can guess what I did, I suppose—or what I didn't do? When I got back into our trench I didn't say anything.

"I knew it was very unlikely that Monkland would be found where he was lying. None of the raiding party seemed to know what had become of him, and the general impression was that he'd been killed or captured. A search party went out, but it only covered the ground we were supposed to have covered. So nobody ever saw Monkland alive again.

"But afterwards, long afterwards when the War was over, I knew that the cruel soul of that man still existed, that it hated me with the hatred of a devil, that it was trying desperately to make me aware of its close presence to me and its bitter enmity. For that reason I always avoided clairvoyants and people who claim to receive messages from the dead. I knew that I should get a message from Monkland. I'd been trying for years *not* to receive it.

"Then you brought me your cipher with the playing-cards and I pulled out some at random, and, according to your code, they spelt 'Monkland.' I knew that it was hopeless then. He'd got through to me. And I got bitten by an accursed morbid craving to find out what he wanted to say to me. I've hardly been able to leave the cards alone since. I've sat here by the hour, shuffling them up and picking them out at random and decoding his malignant messages to me——"

"Oh, nonsense!" Masters cried, no longer able to restrain himself. "This is sheer madness. It's unthinkable! Your mind's unhinged, Serrald."

Serrald uttered one short, bitter laugh.

"You think so, do you? You see that heap of cards? None of them are marked, are they? Shuffle them as you like. I won't look. I'll close my eyes and turn my back. I've never been able to do a card-trick in my life. Then I'll pick out cards one by one at random and you shall see what I get."

Masters had heard that the best way to cure a madman of his delusions was simply to disprove them to his face.

"Very well," he said; and when Serrald had turned his back he stirred up the great heap of cards. "What sort of messages do you generally get?" he asked unsteadily.

"The sort you might expect. Threatening, and bitter with irony and hatred. He isn't happy where he is. He wants me with him so that he can bully and pester me as he used. Are you ready? I'll close my eyes as I pick out the cards, and you shall name the code letters as I turn them."

Masters took out a notebook and a pencil, and wrote down the letter for each card as it was turned up. He was quickly aware that actual words were being spelled, and a cold wave of horror engulfed him as soon as he began to space them. The complete message read as follows:

"Since you did not send for me, I will come for you."

Masters uttered a sharp cry and recoiled from the table as if the cards were living and evil things.

On his way downstairs Masters met the proprietor of the house, who knew him by sight and greeted him civilly.

"Good evening, sir. Mr. Serrald is pretty well, I hope?"

"No—yes," said Masters hurriedly.

"I didn't think he had been very well lately. He has been keeping indoors a great deal and playing Patience. Is the officer gentleman with him?"

"What officer gentleman?" Masters asked through his teeth.

"The one I am always meeting on the stairs. I made sure it was Mr. Serrald he's been coming to see."

Masters said nothing, but staggered past him and out into the night.

Serrald was found dead of heart failure a few mornings later, sitting at the table before a great heap of playing-cards. It seemed that he had suspected that he might die suddenly, for he had left instructions that in such an event none of his belongings was to be touched until Masters had been sent for.

The proprietor of the house met Masters in the hall, and addressed him in a hushed voice appropriate to a house of death.

"Very sudden and very sad, sir. Yes, very, very sad. He must have died some time last night, for he was quite cold when I found him this morning. You may go up to his sitting-room, if you please, sir. He's been taken away now, but nothing else has been touched except—well, I did have the floor swept a bit. You see, sir, somebody must have come to see him last night in very muddy boots. My son, who's been a soldier and done his bit during the War, he said it was just like trench mud all over the room. You know the way up, sir?"

Masters went upstairs carrying a heart which beat harder than he had ever before known it to beat.

The chair in which Serrald had died lay on its back close to the table, on which was spread a great heap of cards lying face downwards. But along the edge of the table a few were turned face upwards in a row. Masters bent over them and shudderingly spelled out the last message which Serrald had received:

"To-night at midnight—Monkland."

BERNARD CAPES
The Widow's Clock

*Bernard Capes (1854–1918) was one of the
most gifted and imaginative writers of mystery and
supernatural literature at the turn of the century.
Over thirty of his poetic and macabre tales were
collected in* At a Winter's Fire (1899), From
Door to Door (1900), Plots (1902), Loaves and
Fishes (1906), Bag and Baggage (1913) *and*
The Fabulists (1915); *and there were many* more
*uncollected gems. "The Widow's Clock" first ap-
peared in the* Pall Mall Magazine *in May 1900.*

I was moved to pause outside the premises of Bull & Hacker,
auctioneers. Unaccountable excitement exhaled from their
very windows, grew intricate on their steps, congested at their
doorway. Something out of the common, it was evident, was
passing within.

I accosted a young man who was battling his way forth at the
moment. The young man's face was a red mask of hilarity.

"What's up?" said he. "Oh, Lord! go and look. Old Bull's took
mad, and he's knocking down the lots like skittles. There's some
stuff goin' cheap there, there is."

He was borne past me, and I fought my way into the auction-
room. I had a hard struggle to get within view of the rostrum; and
then I saw a figure, with eyes like a Cheshire cat's, standing—or
rather dancing—therein. It (the figure) was that, assuredly, of
the urbane Mr. Bull; but he had put a copper saucepan on his
head, and tied up his side-whiskers with ribbons.

Two grinning, embarrassed-looking men in shirt-sleeves had
just placed upon the long table under the pulpit a very present-
able plaster cast of the Capitoline Venus. The auctioneer
addressed the company with quite exaggerated suavity.

"Look at that, gentlemen," said he: "pray don't look at
me! My better half, gentlemen, and much better worth your
consideration. A little stiff and cold, but a rare bargain if you

100

keep her from putting rat poison in the soup.—How much for Mrs. Bull, now?—how much for the hard, unsympathetic lady? She's given me many a dressing, gentlemen, or she'd be better accommodated in that respect herself. A charitable soul indeed."

Here he cocked his saucepan over one eye, folded his arms, and ogling the company insinuatingly, suddenly bent down and bonneted with his hammer an old white-hatted broker who sat chuckling just underneath.

"The property of a gentleman going abroad!" he bellowed, recovering himself. "Must sell—must sell! Start your bids, and earn a reputation for gallantry in the Babylonian marriage market."

"A shillun," sniggered a sheepish-faced individual at the table.

Mr. Bull snatched off his saucepan and beat it flat on the desk.

"Gone for a shilling!" he roared, "and dear at the price."

There had been a flank movement up the room. Blue-coated figures now rose from the crowd and seized the madman. A scene of wild uproar and confusion ensued. Presently I found myself in the street.

"How did it come about?" I said to a neighbour, as I endeavoured to coax the creases out of a crumpled tile.

"Drink," said he laconically. "Old Bull was always a soaker, he was."

"The sales won't hold, I suppose?" said I.

"They'll hold tight enough for them as cut their lucky with the stuff afore he was found out," answered my friend gruffly. "Why, he was a-selling things for songs at fust—rail good things, mind you," he said.

I departed, wondering; and certain inquiries I prosecuted set me wondering yet more.

The following day I made occasion to call upon my acquaintance Aubrey Standish. He is a curioso, and a young man of a most fastidious and delicate dilettanteism—of Catholic taste also, within the liberal limits of Art. At the same time he holds (or held) it his particular principle that, given such tact and knowledge as his own, an extreme virtuosity could be indulged on nothing larger than an ordinary household income, so to speak; in illustration of which his rooms (he had but three) were shrines containing treasures of heavenly *marqueterie* and *bijouterie*. Enamels, by Jean Petitot; cinquecento intaglios in amethyst, and earlier cameos by Dioscorides; unique bits of gomroon porcelain ware from Chelsea; pot-pourri in old Nanking vases; fragments of tapestry; exquisite painted fans from the studios of M. Duvelleroy; swords in niello; a bronze fish, presumptively by Benvenuto Cellini, —such and varied bric-a-brac, sleeking from the chestnut glooms of Chippendale corner cupboards, disposed with a crafty affectation of *insouciance* on Louis XV commodes, blinking soft slumberous eyes from green plush-lined showcase tables, was the practical expression of Aubrey's boasted principle. And he would assure you, with all the enthusiasm of a nervous, lisping speech, that it needed but the knowledge of how to sit effectively in the sunshine for the rarest butterflies of Art to settle on one's hand. That was his rendering of the *Tout vient à qui sait attendre*, which was a proverb too much in the common way for one of his ultra-refinement; yet he was not exalted above the exercise of some particularly mean qualities—or, at least, so my Philistinism interpreted him.

Now he came skipping, in a Japanese silk dressing-gown, from his bedroom, and put a thin, scented hand on each of my shoulders.

"What a sweet tie!" said he. "Permit me. It tones, with your face, into the very aurelian tints of Giovanni Bellini."

"Oh, go to the devil!" said I crossly. "If I'm jaundiced, I'm jaundiced, that's all."

"My dear friend," said he, releasing me, "you're fretful. You take life at too high a pressure. You exhale a humanity before which I seem to shrink like a sensitive plant. I can never escape the feeling when you visit me, that my little museum will fly into prismatic splinters, like an opal too rudely unearthed."

I wanted, of course, to kick him; but bethought myself that this was scarcely the way to enforce a certain mission on which I had entered.

"Standish——" said I.

"Now, now," said he, lifting his hands, palms to me, and closing his eyes; "not the Charity Organisation again, my very sweet fellow! Not some malodorous citizen with a compound fracture of his tail, or a widow respectable in everything but the possession of twins. You wouldn't besmirch my preserves with such smut?"

"I'm to be bought out."

"Oh dear!" he said, with a little deprecating smile. "This is terrible. Do let me entreat your attention to that exquisite

Bartolozzi. I picked it up last week for a mere song—literally, the merest swan-song of a dying consumptive."

"Standish, I want to put it to you——"

He sank upon an Adams settee, sniffed at a tiny filagree vinaigrette, and fluttered a whisp of a handkerchief.

"I have learned to gather flowers of the wilderness. I have made a rose-crown of patience, till it blossoms about my head. Go on!" he murmured faintly.

"Standish, I will take no denial that you were at Bull & Hacker's sale yesterday."

"The subtlest penetration!" he whispered. "Were you there too?"

"Yes."

"Then," said he, "you were witness of a strange seizure."

"Not of yours," said I—"for it amounts to nothing else."

He only shrugged his eyebrows—a momentary spasm of astonishment.

"Was it not?" said I. "There is the very article, I see."

I had already 'spotted,' standing in the corner, what I sought—a lank "grandfather" clock in a Chippendale case. I nodded towards it significantly.

"It's by Smith of Crowland," said Standish, rallying, in the excitement of the collector. "His work was unique—the best of its kind. I assure you, I cannot recall a more vital illustration of my principles than is presented in that bargain."

"It is unique, you say?"

"I believe entirely. My one regret is, it doesn't go—or, at least, as yet I haven't been able to make it. And it was the durable quality of the Crownland clocks that gained them their reputation."

"Shall I examine it? I have a clever mechanical turn."

"By all means. I can trust you to handle it, I am sure."

He did not look as if he meant it; but I went and unbuttoned the door in the belly of the thing, and felt with my hand up along the pendulum.

"What would you say," said I, as I was thus engaged, "that this might have fetched under favourable conditions?"

"Eighty pounds," said Standish, with all the decision of a dealer.

"And you gave for it yesterday?"

"Eighteen pence."

His whole face creased with goblin merriment. His laugh was always a little hoarse, as if it were only the broken-out expression of what had been choking him for some time internally. Suddenly he came to his feet.

"You have set it going?" he cried.

"The pendulum was merely wired high up to the case. What time is it?"

He affected a fob, with dangling seals. He drew out what the Regency bucks called a warming-pan. "Twenty minutes to twelve," he said.

Fortuitously, I had but to move the hands of the bargain a minute or two.

"There's your clock going," said I, and shut the case.

"You are a genius!" he cried. "My happiness is complete. What an engaging possession is a practical head!"

"I'm glad you think so. It can always command its price, you mean; and so I may as well state it."

"Ha, ha! to be sure. The service of a friend is beyond price."

"Not in the least. I want eighty pounds for mine."

"Oh! of course. You're rating yourself higher than you do to the Income Tax assessors."

"I'm perfectly serious. I want eighty pounds—less eighteen-pence."

He was beginning to laugh—checked himself, and stared at me in amazement, already with a touch of anger in it.

"Are you daft?" he said.

"Not in the least. I'll explain myself. In taking advantage of that man's madness yesterday, Standish, I'm not at all sure you didn't give your economic principles an ugly look of felony."

His lip lifted, and he did not answer for a moment. Then said he, in a straitened voice: "I see, I see. This is a blackmailing affair."

I kept my temper royally.

"No," I said. "And I shan't be at the trouble to refute such a charge. I appeal only to your sense of fair-play. You must have it, Standish, for all your virtuosity. Will you listen while I tell you the facts of the case?"

"Oh! I'll listen," he said.

"Very well. Now, I'll explain. That clock was the property of a wretched widow—a woman once in decent circumstances, but at last reduced to the hardest necessity. I've come across her in the way of my work on behalf of the Society; and a certain association of guess and inquiry had led me to the truth. Her husband was a Liverpool-Irish 'patriot' of '81. I believe he was mixed up in the dynamite business. He died, however, years ago in prison. Piece by piece she has parted with every stick of their common property, till at last only the clock remained. That she could not find it in her heart to sell. *He* had always shown such an affection for it. No doubt even the worst of us have our little emotional associations. Perhaps it had once stood in his father's cottage. And so—though from the date of his arrest it had proved useless as a timepiece"—("Ha!" murmured Standish, with a happy nod to me)—"she stuck to it. Then, at last, hunger and the devil broke her loyalty. Mr. Bull happened on the relic in a professional way, presumed its value, and being for all his sins something better than a collector, didn't offer to buy it for eighteenpence, but proposed, like an honest man, to include it, with a reserve, in one of his sales."

I came to an end, and looked at Standish.

"*Without* reserve, I think," said he.

"*With*," said I. "The man was as mad as a hatter. He had to be removed in the end."

"You greatly interest me," said Standish. "I assure you that—though, of course, I thought there was something a little exceptional about our friend's conduct—I had no inkling, at that early stage, that things would reach so disastrous a climax."

"I am quite ready to believe it. And, now you know, you will draw the widow a cheque for eighty pounds."

Standish shook his head, with quite a rippling little laugh.

"You are a sweet, droll fellow," he said: "the dearest utilitarian, by way of your friends' pockets. If I could materialise such a rare piece of Quixotism and put it in a case, I would give you the money on the spot—if I had it."

"At least send back the clock and let it be re-sold."

He looked at me, as if politeness alone restrained him from a positive guffaw.

"Unconscious humourist!" he murmured thickly. Then he explained very kindly. "The whole text of my capital is sunk in these things—these glorious trifles, every one of which represents an opportunity most patiently coveted. The margin only stands for my living expenses. Now, do you really imagine I will forego the little rewards, when they reach me, of such devotion?—and for the benefit of a dead savage's widow?" he added, with an irrepressible laugh.

"It was an accident, Standish."

"Such is our chance."

"Is it hopeless my trying to move you?"

"You have moved me already, my dear soul. Positively, a new value attaches in my eyes to this bargain in the knowledge that it is pronounced, in a certain sense, historical. Pray look at the matter impartially. Why should all the unselfishness be demanded of me who make no profession of dealing in these common virtues? Probably your bombazine widow is much better equipped with the article than I am. Comfort her with the Christian assurance that my expectations are realised, if hers are not. Now, pray don't say any more. It is painful and unprofitable to both of us. Let me show you an almost perfect example of a *gemma potaria*—a sardonyx drinking-cup that I picked——"

I burst out, without more ado.

"Hang your drinking-cup!" I shouted; "you're just an inhuman swindler. Hang your drinking-cup, I say!"—and I made for the door.

Standish followed me, with imperturbable unconcern, down the stairs. At the moment, the liberated clock above began to strike midday.

"Hear it!" he cried triumphantly, pausing on a step. "It proclaims its emancipation! It speaks to its deliverer with a voice of silver! 'A bargain is a bargain,' it shrills. 'A——'"

Where was I! My brain was stuffed with wool, it seemed, and my eyes were mere balls of smoked glass. In a moment I staggered to my feet. Another shape was poised tottering just above me. The stairway rolled with choking vapour, through which—as it slowly dissipated by way of an open skylight—a wreck of burst paper and broken banister rails was revealed.

As sight returned to me, I stared up at Standish. He looked like nothing so much as a torn Japanese doll. Then with one impulse we laboured up through the inferno, and stood at the doorway of the shattered museum.

I think there cannot have remained two consecutive inches of sound material anywhere in the room. The entire show was exploded into shivers. Porcelain, tapestry, enamels, with the cabinets that had enshrined them—all were committed in undistinguishable fragments to a common ruin. *Tout vient à qui sait attendre:* Everything comes to him that knows how to wait—even a very lively retribution for his sins.

"Standish," I said (I could only speak in croaks)—"the patriot's clock, Standish—it must have been set to midday! Standish—you have been a good angel to the bombazine widow!"

ROBERT W. CHAMBERS
A Pleasant Evening

Robert William Chambers (1865–1933) *was one of the most popular American writers who carried on the superb tradition of horror and fantasy literature pioneered by Poe, O'Brien, Hawthorne and Bierce. His outstanding classic* The King in Yellow (1895) *was one of the most influential books in the genre. "A Pleasant Evening" is taken from his second collection* The Maker of Moons *(1896).*

> Et pis, doucett'ment on s'endort,
> On fait sa carne, on fait sa sorgue,
> On ronfle, et, comme un tuyau d'orgue,
> L'tuyau s'met à ronfler plus fort. . . .
> ARISTIDE BRUANT.

As I stepped upon the platform of a Broadway cable-car at Forty-second Street, somebody said; "Hello, Hilton, Jamison's looking for you."

"Hello, Curtis," I replied, "what does Jamison want?"

"He wants to know what you've been doing all the week," said Curtis, hanging desperately to the railing as the car lurched forward; "he says you seem to think that the *Manhattan Illustrated Weekly* was created for the sole purpose of providing salary and vacations for you."

"The shifty old tom-cat!" I said, indignantly, "he knows well enough where I've been. Vacation! Does he think the State Camp in June is a snap?"

"Oh," said Curtis, "you've been to Peekskill?"

"I should say so," I replied, my wrath rising as I thought of my assignment.

"Hot?" inquired Curtis, dreamily.

"One hundred and three in the shade," I answered. "Jamison wanted three full pages and three half pages, all for process work, and a lot of line drawings into the bargain. I could have faked them—I wish I had. I was fool enough to hustle and break my neck to get some honest drawings, and that's the thanks I get!"

"Did you have a camera?"

"No. I will next time—I'll waste no more conscientious work on Jamison," I said sulkily.

"It doesn't pay," said Curtis. "When I have military work assigned me, I don't do the dashing sketch-artist act, you bet; I go to my studio, light my pipe, pull out a lot of old *Illustrated London News*, select several suitable battle scenes by Caton Woodville—and use 'em too."

The car shot around the neck-breaking curve at Fourteenth Street.

"Yes," continued Curtis, as the car stopped in front of the Morton House for a moment, then plunged forward again amid a furious clanging of gongs, "it doesn't pay to do decent work for the fat-headed men who run the *Manhattan Illustrated*. They don't appreciate it."

"I think the public does," I said, "but I'm sure Jamison doesn't. It would serve him right if I did what most of you fellows do—take a lot of Caton Woodville's and Thulstrup's drawings, change the uniforms, 'chic' a figure or two, and turn in a drawing labelled 'from life.' I'm sick of this sort of thing anyway. Almost every day this week I've been chasing myself over that tropical camp, or galloping in the wake of those batteries. I've got a full page of the 'camp by moonlight,' full pages of 'artillery drill' and 'light battery in action,' and a dozen smaller drawings that cost me more groans and perspiration than Jamison ever knew in all his lymphatic life!"

"Jamison's got wheels," said Curtis,—"more wheels than there are bicycles in Harlem. He wants you to do a full page by Saturday."

"A what?" I exclaimed, aghast.

"Yes he does—he was going to send Jim Crawford, but Jim expects to go to California for the winter fair, and you've got to do it."

"What is it?" I demanded savagely.

"The animals in Central Park," chuckled Curtis.

I was furious. The animals! Indeed! I'd show Jamison that I was entitled to some consideration! This was Thursday; that gave me a day and a half to finish a full-page drawing for the paper, and, after my work at the State Camp I felt that I was entitled to a little rest. Anyway I objected to the subject. I intended to tell Jamison so—I intended to tell him firmly. However, many of the things that we often intended to tell Jamison were never told. He was a peculiar man, fat-faced, thin-lipped, gentle-voiced, mild-mannered, and soft in his movements as a pussy cat. Just why our firmness should give way when we were actually in his presence, I have never quite been able to determine. He said very little—so did we, although we often entered his presence with other intentions.

The truth was that the *Manhattan Illustrated Weekly* was the best paying, best illustrated paper in America, and we young fellows were not anxious to be cast adrift. Jamison's knowledge of art was probably as extensive as the knowledge of any "Art editor" in the city. Of course that was saying nothing, but the fact merited careful consideration on our part, and we gave it much consideration.

This time, however, I decided to let Jamison know that drawings are not produced by the yard, and that I was neither a floor-walker nor a hand-me-down. I would stand up for my rights; I'd tell old Jamison a few things to set the wheels under his silk hat spinning, and if he attempted any of his pussy-cat ways on me, I'd give him a few plain facts that would curl what hair he had left.

Glowing with a splendid indignation I jumped off the car at the City Hall, followed by Curtis, and a few minutes later entered the office of the *Manhattan Illustrated News*.

"Mr. Jamison would like to see you, sir," said one of the compositors as I passed into the long hallway. I threw my drawings on the table and passed a handkerchief over my forehead.

"Mr. Jamison would like to see you, sir," said a small freckle-faced boy with a smudge of ink on his nose.

"I know it," I said, and started to remove my gloves.

"Mr. Jamison would like to see you, sir," said a lank messenger who was carrying a bundle of proofs to the floor below.

"The deuce take Jamison," I said to myself. I started toward the dark passage that leads to the abode of Jamison, running over in my mind the neat and sarcastic speech which I had been composing during the last ten minutes.

Jamison looked up and nodded softly as I entered the room. I forgot my speech.

"Mr. Hilton," he said, "we want a full page of the Zoo before it is removed to Bronx Park. Saturday afternoon at three o'clock the drawing must be in the engraver's hands. Did you have a pleasant week in camp?"

"It was hot," I muttered, furious to find that I could not remember my little speech.

"The weather," said Jamison, with soft courtesy, "is oppressive everywhere. Are your drawings in, Mr. Hilton?"

"Yes. It was infernally hot and I worked like the devil—"

"I suppose you were quite overcome. Is that why you took a two days' trip to the Catskills? I trust the mountain air restored you—but—was it prudent to go to Cranston's for the cotillion Tuesday? Dancing in such uncomfortable weather is really unwise. Good-morning, Mr. Hilton, remember the engraver should have your drawings on Saturday by three."

I walked out, half hypnotized, half enraged. Curtis grinned at me as I passed—I could have boxed his ears.

"Why the mischief should I lose my tongue whenever that old tom-cat purrs!" I asked myself as I entered the elevator and was shot down to the first floor. "I'll not put up with this sort of thing much longer—how in the name of all that's foxy did he know that I went to the mountains? I suppose he thinks I'm lazy because I don't wish to be boiled to death. How did he know about the dance at Cranston's? Old cat!"

The roar and turmoil of machinery and busy men filled my ears as I crossed the avenue and turned into the City Hall Park.

From the staff on the tower the flag drooped in the warm sunshine with scarcely a breeze to lift its crimson bars. Overhead stretched a splendid cloudless sky, deep, deep blue, thrilling, scintillating in the gemmed rays of the sun.

Pigeons wheeled and circled about the roof of the grey Post Office or dropped out of the blue above to flutter around the fountain in the square.

On the steps of the City Hall the unlovely politician lounged, exploring his heavy underjaw with wooden toothpick, twisting his drooping black moustache, or distributing tobacco juice over marble steps and close-clipped grass.

My eyes wandered from these human vermin to the calm

scornful face of Nathan Hale, on his pedestal, and then to the grey-coated Park policeman whose occupation was to keep little children from the cool grass.

A young man with thin hands and blue circles under his eyes was slumbering on a bench by the fountain, and the policeman walked over to him and struck him on the soles of his shoes with a short club.

The young man rose mechanically, stared about, dazed by the sun, shivered, and limped away. I saw him sit down on the steps of the white marble building, and I went over and spoke to him. He neither looked at me, nor did he notice the coin I offered.

"You're sick," I said, "you had better go to the hospital."

"Where?" he asked vacantly—"I've been, but they wouldn't receive me."

He stooped and tied the bit of string that held what remained of his shoe to his foot.

"You are French," I said.

"Yes."

"Have you no friends? Have you been to the French Consul?"

"The Consul!" he replied; "no, I haven't been to the French Consul."

After a moment I said, "You speak like a gentleman."

He rose to his feet and stood very straight, looking me, for the first time, directly in the eyes.

"Who are you?" I asked abruptly.

"An outcast," he said, without emotion, and limped off thrusting his hands into his ragged pockets.

"Huh!" said the Park policeman who had come up behind me in time to hear my question and the vagabond's answer; "don't you know who that hobo is?—An' you a newspaper man!"

"Who is he, Cusick?" I demanded, watching the thin shabby figure moving across Broadway toward the river.

"On the level you don't know, Mr. Hilton?" repeated Cusick, suspiciously.

"No, I don't; I never before laid eyes on him."

"Why," said the sparrow policeman, "that's 'Soger Charlie';— you remember—that French officer what sold secrets to the Dutch Emperor."

"And was to have been shot? I remember now, four years ago—and he escaped—you mean to say that is the man?"

"Everybody knows it," sniffed Cusick, "I'd a-thought you newspaper gents would have knowed it first."

"What was his name?" I asked after a moment's thought.

"Soger Charlie—"

"I mean his name at home."

"Oh, some French dago name. No Frenchman will speak to him here; sometimes they curse him and kick him. I guess he's dyin' by inches."

I remembered the case now. Two young French cavalry officers were arrested, charged with selling plans of fortifications and other military secrets to the Germans. On the eve of their conviction, one of them, Heaven only knows how, escaped and turned up in New York. The other was duly shot. The affair had made some noise, because both young men were of good families. It was a painful episode, and I had hastened to forget it. Now that it was recalled to my mind, I remembered the newspaper accounts of the case, but I had forgotten the names of the miserable young men.

"Sold his country," observed Cusick, watching a group of children out of the corner of his eyes—"you can't trust no Frenchman not dagoes nor Dutchmen either. I guess Yankees are about the only white men."

I looked at the noble face of Nathan Hale and nodded.

"Nothin' sneaky about us, eh, Mr. Hilton?"

I thought of Benedict Arnold and looked at my boots.

Then the policeman said, "Well, solong, Mr. Hilton," and went away to frighten a pasty-faced little girl who had climbed upon the railing and was leaning down to sniff the fragrant grass.

"Cheese it, de cop!" cried her shrill-voiced friends, and the whole bevy of small ragamuffins scuttled away across the square.

With a feeling of depression I turned and walked toward Broadway, where the long yellow cable-cars swept up and down, and the din of gongs and the deafening rumble of heavy trucks echoed from the marble walls of the Court House to the granite mass of the Post Office.

Throngs of hurrying busy people passed up town and down town; slim sober-faced clerks, trim cold-eyed brokers, here and there a red-necked politician linking arms with some favourite heeler, here and there a City Hall lawyer, sallow-faced and saturnine. Sometimes a fireman, in his severe blue uniform, passed through the crowd, sometimes a blue-coated policeman, mopping his clipped hair, holding his helmet in his white-gloved hand. There were women too, pale-faced shop girls with pretty eyes, tall blonde girls who might be typewriters and might not, and many, many older women whose business in that part of the city no human being could venture to guess, but who hurried up town and down town, all occupied with *something* that gave to the whole restless throng a common likeness—the expression of one who hastens toward a hopeless goal.

I knew some of those who passed me. There was little Jocelyn of the *Mail and Express*; there was Hood, who had more money than he wanted and was going to have less than he wanted when he left Wall Street; there was Colonel Tidmouse of the 45th Infantry, N.G.S.N.Y., probably coming from the office of the *Army and Navy Journal*, and there was Dick Harding who wrote the best stories of New York life that have been printed. People said his hat no longer fitted,—especially people who also wrote stories of New York life and whose hats threatened to fit as long as they lived.

I looked at the statue of Nathan Hale, then at the human stream that flowed around his pedestal.

"*Quand même*," I muttered and walked out into Broadway, signalling to the gripman of an uptown cable-car.

I PASSED into the Park by the Fifth Avenue and 59th Street gate; I could never bring myself to enter it through the gate that is guarded by the hideous pigmy statue of Thorwaldsen.

The afternoon sun poured into the windows of the New Netherlands Hotel, setting every orange-curtained pane a-glitter, and tipping the wings of the bronze dragons with flame.

Gorgeous masses of flowers blazed in the sunshine from the grey terraces of the Savoy, from the high grilled court of the Vanderbilt palace, and from the balconies of the Plaza opposite.

The white marble façade of the Metropolitan Club was a grateful relief in the universal glare, and I kept my eyes on it until I had crossed the dusty street and entered the shade of the trees.

Before I came to the Zoo I smelled it. Next week it was to be removed to the fresh cool woods and meadows in Bronx Park, far from the stifling air of the city, far from the infernal noise of the Fifth Avenue omnibuses.

A noble stag stared at me from his enclosure among the trees as I passed down the winding asphalt walk. "Never mind, old fellow," said I, "you will be splashing about in the Bronx River next week and cropping maple shoots to your heart's content."

On I went, past herds of staring deer, past great lumbering elk and moose, and long-faced African antelopes, until I came to the dens of the great carnivora.

The tigers sprawled in the sunshine, blinking and licking their paws; the lions slept in the shade or squatted on their haunches, yawning gravely. A slim panther travelled to and fro behind her barred cage, pausing at times to peer wistfully out into the free sunny world. My heart ached for caged wild things, and I walked on, glancing up now and then to encounter the blank stare of a tiger or the mean shifty eyes of some ill-smelling hyena.

Across the meadow I could see the elephants swaying and swinging their great heads, the sober bison solemnly slobbering over their cuds, the sarcastic countenances of camels, the wicked little zebras, and a lot more animals of the camel and llama tribe, all resembling each other, all equally ridiculous, stupid, deadly uninteresting.

Somewhere behind the old arsenal an eagle was screaming, probably a Yankee eagle; I heard the "tchug! tchug!" of a blowing hippopotamus, the squeal of a falcon, and the snarling yap! of quarrelling wolves.

"A pleasant place for a hot day!" I pondered bitterly, and I thought some things about Jamison that I shall not insert in the volume. But I lighted a cigarette to deaden the aroma from the hyenas, unclasped my sketching block, sharpened my pencil, and fell to work on a family group of hippopotami.

They may have taken me for a photographer, for they all wore smiles as if "welcoming a friend," and my sketch block presented a series of wide open jaws, behind which shapeless bulky bodies vanished in alarming perspective.

The alligators were easy; they looked to me as though they had not moved since the founding of the Zoo, but I had a bad time with the big bison, who persistently turned his tail to me, looking stolidly around his flank to see how I stood it. So I pretended to be absorbed in the antics of two bear cubs, and the dreary old bison fell into the trap, for I made some good sketches of him and laughed in his face as I closed the book.

There was a bench by the abode of the eagles, and I sat down on it to draw the vultures and condors, motionless as mummies among the piled rocks. Gradually I enlarged the sketch, bringing in the gravel plaza, the steps leading up to Fifth Avenue, the sleepy park policeman in front of the arsenal—and a slim, white-browed girl, dressed in shabby black, who stood silently in the shade of the willow trees.

After a while I found that the sketch, instead of being a study of the eagles, was in reality a composition in which the girl in black occupied the principal point of interest. Unwittingly I had subordinated everything else to her, the brooding vultures, the trees and walks, and the half indicated groups of sun-warmed loungers.

She stood very still, her pallid face bent, her thin white hands loosely clasped before her. "Rather dejected reverie," I thought, "probably she's out of work." Then I caught a glimpse of a sparkling diamond ring on the slender third finger of her left hand.

"She'll not starve with such a stone as that about her," I said to myself, looking curiously at her dark eyes and sensitive mouth. They were both beautiful, eyes and mouth—beautiful, but touched with pain.

After a while I rose and walked back to make a sketch or two of the lions and tigers. I avoided the monkeys—I can't stand them, and they never seem funny to me, poor dwarfish, degraded caricatures of all that is ignoble in ourselves.

"I've enough now," I thought; "I'll go home and manufacture a full page that will probably please Jamison." So I strapped the elastic band around my sketching block, replaced pencil and rubber in my waistcoat pocket, and strolled off toward the Mall to smoke a cigarette in the evening glow before going back to my studio to work until midnight, up to the chin in charcoal grey and Chinese white.

Across the long meadow I could see the roofs of the city faintly looming above the trees. A mist of amethyst, ever deepening, hung low on the horizon, and through it, steeple and dome, roof and tower, and the tall chimneys where thin fillets of smoke curled idly, were transformed into pinnacles of beryl and flaming minarets, swimming in filmy haze. Slowly the enchantment deepened; all that was ugly and shabby and mean had fallen away from the distant city, and now it towered into the evening sky, splendid, gilded, magnificent, purified in the fierce furnace of the setting sun.

The red disk was half hidden now; the tracery of trees, feathery willow and budding birch, darkened against the glow; the fiery rays shot far across the meadow, gilding the dead leaves, staining with soft crimson the dark moist tree trunks around me.

Far across the meadow a shepherd passed in the wake of a huddling flock, his dog at his heels, faint moving blots of grey.

A squirrel sat up on the gravel walk in front of me, ran a few feet, and sat up again, so close that I could see the palpitation of his sleek flanks.

Somewhere in the grass a hidden field insect was rehearsing last summer's solos; I heard the tap! tap! tat-tat-t-t-tat! of a woodpecker among the branches overhead and the querulous note of a sleepy robin.

The twilight deepened; out of the city the music of bells floated over wood and meadow; faint mellow whistles sounded from the river craft along the north shore, and the distant thunder of a gun announced the close of a June day.

The end of my cigarette began to glimmer with a redder light; shepherd and flock were blotted out in the dusk, and I only knew they were still moving when the sheep bells tinkled faintly.

Then suddenly that strange uneasiness that all have known— that half-awakened sense of having seen it all before, of having been through it all, came over me, and I raised my head and slowly turned.

A figure was seated at my side. My mind was struggling with the instinct to remember. Something so vague and yet so familiar—something that eluded thought yet challenged it, something—God knows what! troubled me. And now, as I looked, without interest, at the dark figure beside me, an apprehension, totally involuntary, an impatience to *understand*, came upon me, and I sighed and turned restlessly again to the fading west.

I thought I heard my sigh re-echoed—I scarcely heeded; and in a moment I sighed again, dropping my burned-out cigarette on the gravel beneath my feet.

"Did you speak to me?" said some one in a low voice, so close that I swung around rather sharply.

"No," I said after a moment's silence.

117

It was a woman. I could not see her face clearly, but I saw on her clasped hands, which lay listlessly in her lap, the sparkle of a great diamond. I knew her at once. It did not need a glance at the shabby dress of black, the white face, a pallid spot in the twilight, to tell me that I had her picture in my sketch-book.

"Do—do you mind if I speak to you?" she asked timidly. The hopeless sadness in her voice touched me, and I said: "Why, no, of course not. Can I do anything for you?"

"Yes," she said, brightening a little, "if you—you only would."

"I will if I can," said I, cheerfully; "what is it? Out of ready cash?"

"No, not that," she said, shrinking back.

I begged her pardon, a little surprised, and withdrew my hand from my change pocket.

"It is only—only that I wish you to take these,"—she drew a thin packet from her breast—"these two letters."

"I?" I asked astonished.

"Yes, if you will."

"But what am I to do with them?" I demanded.

"I can't tell you; I only know that I must give them to you. Will you take them?"

"Oh, yes, I'll take them," I laughed, "am I to read them?" I added to myself, "It's some clever begging trick."

"No," she answered slowly, "you are not to read them; you are to give them to somebody."

"To whom? Anybody?"

"No, not to anybody. You will know whom to give them to when the time comes."

"Then I am to keep them until further instructions?"

"Your own heart will instruct you," she said, in a scarcely audible voice. She held the thin packet toward me, and to humour her I took it. It was wet.

"The letters fell into the sea," she said. "There was a photograph which should have gone with them but the salt water washed it blank. Will you care if I ask you something else?"

"I? Oh, no."

"Then give me the picture that you made of me to-day."

I laughed, again, and demanded how she knew I had drawn her.

"Is it like me?" she said.

"I think it is very like you," I answered truthfully.

"Will you not give it to me?"

Now it was on the tip of my tongue to refuse, but I reflected that I had enough sketches for a full page without that one, so I handed it to her, nodded that she was welcome, and stood up. She rose also, the diamond flashing on her finger.

"You are sure that you are not in want?" I asked, with a tinge of good-natured sarcasm.

"Hark!" she whispered; "listen!—do you hear the bells of the convent!"

I looked out into the misty night.

"There are no bells sounding," I said, "and anyway there are no convent bells here. We are in New York, mademoiselle"—I had noticed her French accent—"we are in Protestant Yankee-land, and the bells that ring are much less mellow than the bells of France."

I turned pleasantly to say good-night. She was gone.

"HAVE you ever drawn a picture of a corpse?" inquired Jamison next morning as I walked into his private room with a sketch of the proposed full page of the Zoo.

"No, and I don't want to," I replied, sullenly.

"Let me see your Central Park page," said Jamison in his gentle voice, and I displayed it. It was about worthless as an artistic production, but it pleased Jamison, as I knew it would.

"Can you finish it by this afternoon?" he asked, looking up at me with persuasive eyes.

"Oh, I suppose so," I said, wearily; "anything else, Mr. Jamison?"

"The corpse," he replied, "I want a sketch by to-morrow—finished."

"What corpse?" I demanded, controlling my indignation as I met Jamison's soft eyes.

There was a mute duel of glances. Jamison passed his hand across his forehead with a slight lifting of the eyebrows.

"I shall want it as soon as possible," he said in his caressing voice.

What I thought was, "Damned purring pussy-cat!" What I said was, "Where is this corpse?"

"In the Morgue—have you read the morning papers? No? Ah,—as you very rightly observe you are too busy to read the

119

morning papers. Young men must learn industry first, of course, of course. What you are to do is this: the San Francisco police have sent out an alarm regarding the disappearance of a Miss Tufft—the millionaire's daughter, you know. To-day a body was brought to the Morgue here in New York, and it has been identified as the missing young lady—by a diamond ring. Now I am convinced that it isn't, and I'll show you why, Mr. Hilton."

He picked up a pen and made a sketch of a ring on a margin of that morning's *Tribune*.

"That is the description of her ring as sent on from San Francisco. You notice the diamond is set in the centre of the ring where the two gold serpents' *tails* cross!

"Now the ring on the finger of the woman in the Morgue is like this," and he rapidly sketched another ring where the diamond rested in the *fangs* of the two gold serpents.

"That is the difference," he said in his pleasant, even voice.

"Rings like that are not uncommon," said I, remembering that I had seen such a ring on the finger of the white-faced girl in the Park the evening before. Then a sudden thought took shape—perhaps that was the girl whose body lay in the Morgue!

"Well," said Jamison, looking up at me, "what are you thinking about?"

"Nothing," I answered, but the whole scene was before my eyes, the vultures brooding among the rocks, the shabby black dress, and the pallid face,—and the ring, glittering on that slim white hand!

"Nothing," I repeated, "when shall I go, Mr. Jamison? Do you want a portrait—or what?"

"Portrait—careful drawing of the ring, and—er—a centre piece of the Morgue at night. Might as well give people the horrors while we're about it."

"But," said I, "the policy of this paper—"

"Never mind, Mr. Hilton," purred Jamison, "I am able to direct the policy of this paper."

"I don't doubt you are," I said angrily.

"I am," he repeated, undisturbed and smiling; "you see this Tufft case interests society. I am—er—also interested."

He held out to me a morning paper and pointed to a heading.

I read: "Miss Tufft Dead! Her Fiancé was Mr. Jamison, the well known Editor."

"What!" I cried in horrified amazement. But Jamison had left the room, and I heard him chatting and laughing softly with some visitors in the press-room outside.

I flung down the paper and walked out.

"The cold-blooded toad!" I exclaimed again and again; "making capital out of his fiancée's disappearance! Well, I—I'm darnd! I knew he was a bloodless, heartless, grip-penny, but I never thought—I never imagined—" Words failed me.

Scarcely conscious of what I did I drew a *Herald* from my pocket and saw the column entitled: "Miss Tufft Found! Identified by a Ring. Wild Grief of Mr. Jamison, her Fiancé."

That was enough. I went out into the street and sat down in City Hall Park. And, as I sat there, a terrible resolution came to me; I would draw that dead girl's face in such a way that it would chill Jamison's sluggish blood, I would crowd the black shadows of the Morgue with forms and ghastly faces, and every face should bear something in it of Jamison. Oh, I'd rouse him from his cold snaky apathy! I'd confront him with Death in such an awful form, that, passionless, base, inhuman as he was, he'd shrink from it as he would from a dagger thrust. Of course I'd lose my place, but that did not bother me, for I had decided to resign anyway, not having a taste for the society of human reptiles. And, as I sat there in the sunny park, furious, trying to plan a picture whose sombre horror should leave in his mind an ineffaceable scar, I suddenly thought of the pale black-robed girl in Central Park. Could it be her poor slender body that lay among the shadows of the grim Morgue! If ever brooding despair was stamped on any face, I had seen its print on hers when she spoke to me in the Park and gave me the letters. The letters! I had not thought of them since, but now I drew them from my pocket and looked at the addresses.

"Curious," I thought, "the letters are still damp; they smell of salt water too."

I looked at the address again, written in the long fine hand of an educated woman who had been bred in a French convent. Both letters bore the same address, in French:

CAPTAIN D'YNIOL.
(Kindness of a Stranger.)

"Captain d'Yniol," I repeated aloud—"confound it, I've heard that name! Now, where the deuce—where in the name

121

of all that's queer—" Somebody who had sat down on the bench beside me placed a heavy hand on my shoulder.

It was the Frenchman, "Soger Charlie."

"You spoke my name," he said in apathetic tones.

"Your name!"

"Captain d'Yniol," he repeated; "it is my name."

I recognized him in spite of the black goggles he was wearing, and, at the same moment, it flashed into my mind that d'Yniol was the name of the traitor who had escaped. Ah, I remembered now!

"I am Captain d'Yniol," he said again, and I saw his fingers closing on my coat sleeve.

It may have been my involuntary movement of recoil—I don't know—but the fellow dropped my coat and sat straight up on the bench.

"I am Captain d'Yniol," he said for the third time, "charged with treason and under sentence of death."

"And innocent!" I muttered, before I was even conscious of having spoken. What was it that wrung those involuntary words from my lips, I shall never know, perhaps—but it was I, not he, who trembled, seized with a strange agitation, and it was I, not he, whose hand was stretched forth impulsively, touching his.

Without a tremor he took my hand, pressed it almost imperceptibly, and dropped it. Then I held both letters toward him, and, as he neither looked at them nor at me, I placed them in his hand. Then he started.

"Read them," I said, "they are for you."

"Letters!" he gasped in a voice that sounded like nothing human.

"Yes, they are for you—I know it now——"

"Letters!—letters directed to *me*?"

"Can you not see?" I cried.

Then he raised one frail hand and drew the goggles from his eyes, and, as I looked, I saw two tiny white specks exactly in the centre of both pupils.

"Blind!" I faltered.

"I have been unable to read for two years," he said.

After a moment he placed the tip of one finger on the letters.

"They are wet," I said; "shall—would you like to have me read them?" For a long time he sat silently in the sunshine, fumbling with his cane, and I watched him without speaking. At last he said, "Read, Monsieur," and I took the letters and broke the seals.

The first letter contained a sheet of paper, damp and discoloured, on which a few lines were written:

My darling, I knew you were innocent——

Here the writing ended, but, in the blur beneath. I read:

Paris shall know—France shall know, for at last I have the proofs and I am coming to find you, my soldier, and to place them in your own dear brave hands. They know, now, at the War Ministry—they have a copy of the traitor's confession—but they dare not make it public—they dare not withstand the popular astonishment and rage. Therefore I sail on Monday from Cherbourg by the Green Cross Line, to bring you back to your own again, where you will stand before all the world, without fear, without reproach.

ALINE.

"This—this is terrible!" I stammered; "can God live and see such things done!"

But with his thin hand he gripped my arm again, bidding me read the other letter; and I shuddered at the menace in his voice.

Then, with his sightless eyes on me, I drew the other letter from the wet, stained envelope. And before I was aware—before I understood the purport of what I saw, I had read aloud these half effaced lines:

"The *Lorient* is sinking—an iceberg—mid-ocean—good-bye —you are innocent—I love——"

"The *Lorient*!" I cried; "it was the French steamer that was never heard from—the *Lorient* of the Green Cross Line! I had forgotten—I——"

The loud crash of a revolver stunned me; my ears rang and ached with it as I shrank back from a ragged dusty figure that collapsed on the bench beside me, shuddered a moment, and tumbled to the asphalt at my feet.

The trampling of the eager hard-eyed crowd, the dust and taint of powder in the hot air, the harsh alarm of the ambulance clattering up Mail Street—these I remember, as I knelt there, helplessly holding the dead man's hands in mine.

123

"Soger Charlie," mused the sparrow policeman, "shot hisself, didn't he, Mr. Hilton? You seen him, sir—blowed the top of his head off, didn't he, Mr. Hilton?"

"Soger Charlie," they repeated, "a French dago what shot hisself;" and the words echoed in my ears long after the ambulance rattled away, and the increasing throng dispersed, sullenly, as a couple of policemen cleared a space around the pool of thick blood on the asphalt.

They wanted me as a witness, and I gave my card to one of the policemen who knew me. The rabble transferred its fascinated stare to me, and I turned away and pushed a path between frightened shop girls and ill-smelling loafers, until I lost myself in the human torrent of Broadway.

The torrent took me with it where it flowed—East? West?—I did not notice nor care, but I passed on through the throng, listless, deadly weary of attempting to solve God's justice—striving to understand His purpose—His laws—His judgments which are "true and righteous altogether."

"MORE to be desired are they than gold, yea, than much fine gold. Sweeter also than honey and the honey-comb!"

I turned sharply toward the speaker who shambled at my elbow. His sunken eyes were dull and lustreless, his bloodless face gleamed pallid as a death mask above the blood-red jersey—the emblem of the soldiers of Christ.

I don't know why I stopped, lingering, but, as he passed, I said. "Brother, I also was meditating upon God's wisdom and His testimonies."

The pale fanatic shot a glance at me, hesitated, and fell into my own pace, walking by my side. Under the peak of his Salvation Army cap his eyes shone in the shadow with a strange light.

"Tell me more," I said, sinking my voice below the roar of traffic, the clang! clang! of the cable-cars, and the noise of feet on the worn pavements—"tell me of His testimonies."

"Moreover by them is Thy servant warned and in keeping of them there is great reward. Who can understand His errors? Cleanse Thou me from secret faults. Keep back Thy servant also from presumptuous sins. Let them not have dominion over me. Then shall I be upright and I shall be innocent from the great transgression. Let the words of my mouth and the meditation of my heart be acceptable in Thy sight—O Lord! My strength and my Redeemer!"

"It is Holy Scripture that you quote," I said; "I also can read that when I choose. But it cannot clear for me the reasons—it cannot make me understand——"

"What?" he asked, and muttered to himself.

"That, for instance," I replied, pointing to a cripple, who had been *born* deaf and dumb and horridly misshapen—a wretched diseased lump on the sidewalk below St. Paul's Churchyard—a sore-eyed thing that mouthed and mowed and rattled pennies in a tin cup as though the sound of copper could stem the human pack that passed hot on the scent of gold.

Then the man who shambled beside me turned and looked long and earnestly into my eyes. And after a moment a dull recollection stirred within me—a vague something that seemed like the awakening memory of a past, long, long forgotten, dim, dark, too subtle, too frail, too indefinite—ah! the old feeling that all men have known—the old strange uneasiness, that useless struggle to remember when and where it all occurred before.

And the man's head sank on his crimson jersey, and he muttered, muttered to himself of God and love and compassion, until I saw that the fierce heat of the city had touched his brain, and I went away and left him prating of mysteries that none but such as he dare name.

So I passed on through dust and heat; and the hot breath of men touched my cheek and eager eyes looked into mine. Eyes, eyes, that met my own and looked through them, beyond—far beyond to where gold glittered amid the mirage of eternal hope. Gold! It was in the air where the soft sunlight gilded the floating moats, it was under foot in the dust that the sun made gilt, it glimmered from every window pane where the long red beams struck golden sparks above the gasping gold-hunting hordes of Wall Street.

High, high, in the deepening sky the tall buildings towered, and the breeze from the bay lifted the sun-dyed flags of commerce until they waved above the turmoil of the hives below—waved courage and hope and strength to those who lusted after gold.

The sun dipped low behind Castle William as I turned listlessly into the Battery, and the long straight shadows of the trees stretched away over greensward and asphalt walk.

Already the electric lights were glimmering among the foliage although the bay shimmered like polished brass and the topsails of the ships glowed with a deeper hue, where the red sun rays fall athwart the rigging.

Old men tottered along the sea-wall, tapping the asphalt with worn canes, old women crept to and from in the coming twilight— old women who carried baskets that gaped for charity or bulged with mouldy stuffs—food, clothing?—I could not tell; I did not care to know.

The heavy thunder from the parapets of Castle William died away over the placid bay, the last red arm of the sun shot up out of the sea, and wavered and faded into the sombre tones of the afterglow. Then came the night, timidly at first, touching sky and water with grey fingers, folding the foliage into soft massed shapes, creeping onward, onward, more swiftly now, until colour and form had gone from all the earth and the world was a world of shadows.

And, as I sat there on the dusky sea-wall, gradually the bitter thoughts faded and I looked out into the calm night with something of that peace that comes to all when day is ended.

The death at my very elbow of the poor blind wretch in the Park had left a shock, but now my nerves relaxed their tension and I began to think about it all—about the letters and the strange woman who had given them to me. I wondered where she had found them—whether they really were carried by some vagrant current in to the shore from the wreck of the fated *Lorient*.

Nothing but these letters had human eyes encountered from the *Lorient*, although we believed that fire or berg had been her fare; for there had been no storms when the *Lorient* steamed away from Cherbourg.

And what of the pale-faced girl in black who had given these letters to me, saying that my own heart would teach me where to place them?

I felt in my pockets for the letters where I had thrust them all crumpled and wet. They were there, and I decided to turn them over to the police. Then I thought of Cusick and the City Hall Park and these set my mind running on Jamison and my own work—ah! I had forgotten that—I had forgotten that I had sworn to stir Jamison's cold, sluggish blood! Trading on his fiancée's reported suicide—or murder! True, he had told me that he was satisfied that the body at the Morgue was not Miss Tufft's because the ring did not correspond with his fiancée's ring. But what sort of man was that!—to go crawling and nosing about morgues and graves for a full-page illustration which might sell a few extra thousand papers. I had never known he was such a man. It was strange too —for that was not the sort of illustration that the *Weekly* used; it was against all precedent—against the whole policy of the paper. He would lose a hundred subscribers where he would gain one by such work.

"The callous brute!" I muttered to myself, "I'll wake him up—I'll—"

I sat straight up on the bench and looked steadily at a figure which was moving toward me under the spluttering electric light.

It was the woman I had met in the Park.

She came straight up to me, her pale face gleaming like marble in the dark, her slim hands outstretched.

"I have been looking for you all day—all day," she said, in the same low thrilling tones—"I want the letters back; have you them here?"

"Yes," I said, "I have them here—take them in Heaven's name; they have done enough evil for one day!"

She took the letters from my hand; I saw the ring, made of the double serpents, flashing on her slim finger, and I stepped closer, and looked her in the eyes.

"Who are you?" I asked.

"I? My name is of no importance to you," she answered.

"You are right," I said, "I do not care to know your name. That ring of yours——"

"What of my ring?" she murmured.

"Nothing—a dead woman lying in the Morgue wears such a ring. Do you know what your letters have done? No? Well I read them to a miserable wretch and he blew his brains out!"

"You read them to a man!"

"I did. He killed himself."

"Who was that man?"

"Captain d'Yniol——"

With something between a sob and a laugh she seized my hand and covered it with kisses, and I, astonished and angry,

127

pulled my hand away from her cold lips and sat down on the bench.

"You needn't thank me," I said sharply; "if I had known that—but no matter. Perhaps after all the poor devil is better off somewhere in other regions with his sweetheart who was drowned—yes, I imagine he is. He was blind and ill—and broken-hearted."

"Blind?" she asked gently.

"Yes. Did you know him?"

"I knew him."

"And his sweetheart, Aline?"

"Aline," she repeated softly—"she is dead. I come to thank you in her name."

"For what?—for his death?"

"Ah, yes, for that."

"Where did you get those letters?" I asked her, suddenly.

She did not answer, but stood fingering the wet letters.

Before I could speak again she moved away into the shadows of the trees, lightly, silently, and far down the dark walk I saw her diamond flashing.

Grimly brooding, I rose and passed through the Battery to the steps of the Elevated Road. These I climbed, bought my ticket, and stepped out to the damp platform. When a train came I crowded in with the rest, still pondering on my vengeance, feeling and believing that I was to scourge the conscience of the man who speculated on death.

And at last the train stopped at 28th Street, and I hurried out and down the steps and away to the Morgue.

When I entered the Morgue, Skelton, the keeper, was standing before a slab that glistened faintly under the wretched gas jets. He heard my footsteps, and turned around to see who was coming. Then he nodded, saying: "Mr. Hilton, just take a look at this here stiff—I'll be back in a moment—this is the one that all the papers take to be Miss Tufft—but they're all off, because this stiff has been here now for two weeks."

I drew out my sketching-block and pencils.

"Which is it, Skelton?" I asked, fumbling for my rubber.

"This one, Mr. Hilton, the girl what's smilin'. Picked up off Sandy Hook, too. Looks as if she was asleep, eh?"

"What's she got in her hand—clenched tight? Oh—a letter. Turn up the gas, Skelton, I want to see her face."

The old man turned the gas jet, and the flame blazed and whistled in the damp, fetid air. Then suddenly my eyes fell on the dead.

Rigid, scarcely breathing, I stared at the ring, made of two twisted serpents set with a great diamond,—I saw the wet letters crushed in her slender hand—I looked, and —God help me!—I looked upon the dead face of the girl with whom I had been speaking on the Battery!

"Dead for a month at least," said Skelton, calmly.

Then, as I felt my senses leaving me, I screamed out, and at the same instant somebody from behind seized my shoulder and shook me savagely— shook me until I opened my eyes again and gasped and coughed.

"Now then, young feller!" said a Park policeman bending over me, "If you go to sleep on a bench, somebody'll lift your watch!"

I turned, rubbing my eyes desperately.

Then it was all a dream—and no shrinking girl had come to me with damp letters—I had not gone to the office—there was no such person as Miss Tufft—Jamison was not an unfeeling villain—no, indeed!—he treated us all much better than we deserved, and he was kind and generous too. And the ghastly suicide! Thank God that also was a myth—and the Morgue and the Battery at night where that pale-faced girl had—ugh!

I felt for my sketch-block, found it; turned the pages of all the animals that I had sketched, the hippopotami, the buffalo, the tigers—ah! where was that sketch in which I had made the woman in shabby black the principal figure, with the brooding vultures all around and the crowd in the sunshine—? It was gone.

I hunted everywhere, in every pocket. It was gone.

At last I rose and moved along the narrow asphalt path in the falling twilight.

And as I turned into the broader walk, I was aware of a group, a policeman holding a lantern, some gardeners, and a knot of loungers gathered about something—a dark mass on the ground.

"Found 'em just so," one of the gardeners was saying, "better not touch 'em until the coroner comes."

The policeman shifted his bull's-eye a little; the rays fell on two faces, on two bodies, half supported against a park bench.

On the finger of the girl glittered a splendid diamond, set between the fangs of two gold serpents. The man had shot himself; he clasped two wet letters in his hand. The girl's clothing and hair were wringing wet, and her face was the face of a drowned person.

"Well, sir," said the policeman, looking at me; "you seem to know these two people—by your looks——"

"I never saw them before," I gasped, and walked on, trembling in every nerve.

For among the folds of her shabby black dress I had noticed the end of a paper—my sketch that I had missed!

R. CHETWYND-HAYES
The Elemental

Ronald Chetwynd-Hayes (b.1919), "Britian's Prince of Chill", is one of this country's most prolific writers of ghost and horror stories, with paperback sales alone in excess of one million copies. "The Elemental" was one of four supernatural stories by Chetwynd-Hayes filmed together under the title From Beyond the Grave *in 1973, starring Margaret Leighton as Madame Orloff, Ian Carmichael as Reginald Warren, and Nyree Dawn Porter as Susan.*

"There's an elemental sitting next to you," said the fat woman in the horrible flower-patterned dress and amber beads.

Reginald Warren lowered his newspaper, glanced at the empty seats on either side, shot an alarmed look round the carriage in general, then took refuge behind his *Evening Standard* again.

"He's a killer," the fat woman insisted.

Reginald frowned and tried to think rationally. How did you tackle a nutty fat woman?

"Thank you," he said over the newspaper, "I'm obliged."

Then he tried to immerse himself in the exploits of a company secretary who had swindled his firm out of thirty thousand pounds. He had not progressed further than the first paragraph when the newspaper shook violently, and a little pyramid formed just above an advertisement for Tomkins Hair Restoring Tonic. He jerked the paper downwards and it was at once skewered on the sharp point of an extremely lethal ladies' umbrella.

"Look, madam," he spluttered, "this really is too much."

"And I really do think you should listen to me, ducks," the fat lady insisted, completely unmoved by his outburst. "This is a particularly nasty specimen—a real stinker, and he's growing stronger by the minute."

Reginald stared longingly at the communication cord, but he

had been conditioned from birth to regard this interesting facility as something never to be pulled. Apart from which the old dear looked harmless. She was just batty.

"Have you been feeling weak, run down, rather tired lately?" the fat lady enquired solicitously. "Don't bother to answer that—I can see you have. He's been feeding on you. They do, you know, nasty, vicious things. I must say I haven't seen a homicidal one before. Sex-starved ones, yes, alcoholic ones, quite often, but killers, they are rare. In a way you are privileged."

"What . . ." Reginald felt he should display some interest, if only to humour her, "What exactly is an el . . .?"

"An elemental?" The fat woman settled back and assumed the air of an expert revealing professional mysteries to a layman. "Generally speaking it is a spirit of air, fire and water, but the 'orrible thing that's attached itself to you, is something that's trapped between the planes. It sort of lusts after the pleasures of the flesh. It sucks—yes, that's the word—sucks the juices of the soul. You follow me?"

Reginald was incapable of coherent speech; he nodded.

"Good." She beamed, then fumbled in her handbag and produced a pair of spectacles. "Let's have a butcher's." She adjusted the spectacles firmly on her nose and stared intently at a spot immediately to Reginald's left. "Ah, yes, my word yes. Tut-tut. He's firmly embedded, I fear. His right arm is deep in your left shoulder—ah—he's not happy about my interest . . ." She shook a clenched fist. "Don't you glare at me, you dirty little basket, I've got your measure, me lad. Yes, I have."

A shocked expression made her lips pucker and she hurriedly removed the spectacles and replaced them in her bag.

"He spat at me," she stated.

"Oh dear, I am sorry," Reginald was completely powerless to subdue the urge to rub his left shoulder, and the fat lady smiled grimly.

"I'm afraid you won't rub 'im off, dear. Not in a lifetime will you rub 'im off."

The train roared into Hillside Station, and Reginald greeted its appearance much as a Red-Indian-besieged cowboy welcomed the arrival of the U.S. cavalry.

"My station." He pulled a suitcase from the luggage rack. "Thank you very much."

"Wait."

The fat lady was fumbling in her handbag. "I've got one somewhere."

She upturned the bag and its contents tumbled out on to the seat.

"Really, don't bother," Reginald had the door open, "Must go . . ."

"Ah!" She produced a scrap of pasteboard. "My professional card. 'Madame Orloff, Clairvoyant Extraordinary. Séances, private sitting, palmistry, full psychic service guaranteed.' I can take care of your little problem in no time at all . . ."

Reginald snatched the card from her outstretched hand, slammed the door, and sprinted for the ticket-barrier. Madame Orloff jerked down the carriage window and shouted after his retreating figure:

"Special reduced rates for five sittings, and a bumper free gift of a genuine crystal-ball if you sign up for ten!"

Susan was waiting for him at the station entrance; she was white and gold and wore a backless sun-suit. He instantly forgot the fat lady, banished the last lingering thought of elementals to that dark world which had always lurked at the back of his mind, and drank in her cool beauty. The blood sang through his veins when he kissed her, and he wanted to say beautiful words, but instead: "It was hot in town."

"Poor darling." She slid her hand over his arm and they walked slowly towards the car. "You look tired. But never mind, seven lazy days in the country is what you need."

"Seven days of mowing grass, clipping hedges, hoeing, and chopping wood." He laughed, and the sound was young, carefree. "What have you been doing today?"

She opened the car door.

"Get in, I'll drive. Doing? Cleaning windows, Hoovering carpets, airing the bed, everything that's needed in a cottage that hasn't been lived in for three months. Did you remember to turn off the gas and lock the flat door before you left?"

He climbed in beside her and settled back with a sigh of content.

"Yes, and I cancelled the milk and papers, turned on the burglar-alarm, and flushed the loo."

"Good."

She swung the car out of the station forecourt and they glided smoothly under an archway of trees that linked arms over the narrow road. He closed his eyes and the occasional beam of sunlight flashed across his round, pleasant face.

"I shall sleep tonight. God, I feel tired, drained dry, almost as if . . ."

He stopped, opened his eyes, then frowned.

"As if what?" Susan cast an anxious glance sideways. "Look, don't you think you ought to see a doctor? I mean it's not like you to be so whacked."

He forced a laugh.

"Nonsense. It's this hot weather and the stuffy atmosphere in town. No, give me three or four days of this country air, plus three square meals prepared by your fair hand, and I'll be raring to go."

"I don't cook *square* meals. They're very much *with-it* meals. But honestly, you do look peaky. I'm going to make you put your feet up."

He grinned. "I don't need any encouragement."

The car shot out from under the trees and the sunlight hit them like a blast from a furnace. Reginald opened the glove-compartment and took out two pairs of sunglasses. He handed one to Susan and donned the other himself.

"We must have anti-glare windscreens installed. Bloody dangerous when the light hits you like that."

Susan changed gear.

"Don't swear, darling. It's not like you."

"I'm not swearing. Bloody is a perfectly respectable word these days."

"But it doesn't sound right coming from you. You're not a bloody type."

"Oh!" He grimaced, then sank back in his seat. Presently Susan's voice came to him again.

"Darling, I don't want to nag, but don't hump your left shoulder. It makes me think of the Hunchback of Notre-Dame."

He jerked his head sideways and a little cold shiver rang down his spine.

"What?"

She laughed happily; she was gold and ivory in the afternoon sunlight.

"That made you sit up. 'Oh, man, your name is vanity.' "

They swept round a bend in the road, and there was the cottage nestling like a broody hen behind the neatly-trimmed privet hedge. Susan unlocked the front door and Mr. Hawkins barked happily and reared up on his hind legs, begging to have his ears tickled. "Down, you monster." She patted his silky head, then went quickly through the little hall and disappeared into the kitchen. Reginald said: "Hullo, boy, how are you?" and Mr. Hawkins began to wag his tail, but after one or two cautious sniffs turned about and ran into the living-room.

"I think Mr. Hawkins has gone off me," Reginald said on entering the kitchen where Susan was examining a roast that was half out of the oven.

"About fifteen minutes more," she announced. "What did you say?"

"I said, I think Mr. Hawkins has gone off me. Seems I don't smell right or something."

"Probably thinks you need a bath. Why not have one before dinner? I've laid out a pair of slacks, and a white shirt; you'll feel much fresher afterwards."

"Hey . . ." He crept up behind her. "Are you suggesting I stink?"

She looked back at him, her eyes laughing.

"If your best friend won't tell you, why should I?"

He was but two feet from her, his hand raised above her gleaming white shoulder, and he bellowed with mock rage.

"Is that the way you speak to your lord and master? I've a good mind to . . ."

She pulled a saucepan on to the gas ring, then reached up to a wall cupboard and took down two dinner-plates which she placed in the slotted plate-rack.

"Be a good boy and go have your bath."

"Right." He shrugged as he turned towards the door. "I'll wallow in soap suds and sprinkle *Eau-de-Cologne* under my armpits."

"Oh, don't! That hurt!"

He stared back at her in astonishment; she was rubbing her right shoulder, her face screwed up in a grimace of pain.

"What are you talking about?"

"Don't play the innocent. You know darn well—you hit me."

He laughed, imagining this to be some sort of joke, the point of which would become clear in due course.

"Don't be silly, I haven't touched you."

She was performing an almost comical convulsion in an effort to rub the afflicted shoulder. "Look, there's only two of us here, and I certainly didn't hit myself."

"I tell you, I was nowhere near you."

She turned back to the stove, adjusted the gas, then switched on an extractor-fan. "It's not important, so there's no need to lie."

Reginald took a deep breath, and made an effort to speak calmly.

"For the last time, I did not hit you, I was nowhere near you, and I don't like being called a liar."

She made a great business of opening and closing doors, her face set in angry lines. "Go and have your bath. Dinner will soon be ready."

Reginald stamped out of the kitchen. In the hall he almost trod on Mr. Hawkins, who yelped and streaked towards the living-room.

Dinner began in an atmosphere that would have gladdened the heart of an Eskimo; a thaw set in when the sweet was served, and warmth returned with the coffee.

"Darling," he murmured, "please believe me, I didn't . . ."

She interrupted with a radiant smile.

"Forget it. If a man can't beat his wife, who can he beat?"

"But . . ."

"Not another word. What are we going to do after dinner? Watch television, read, or go to bed?"

"Let's take Mr. Hawkins for a walk, then pop in the *Plough* for a quick one."

"OK." She began to collect the empty coffee cups. "I'll wash up, then we'll be off."

"Give you a hand?" Reginald half-rose from his chair.

"No, you don't, this lot won't take me more than ten minutes. In any case, you always break something. Sit in the armchair and read the local rag— there's an uplifting article on pig-raising."

"If you insist."

He got up from the table, then slumped down in an armchair, where, after a fruitless attempt at interest in local events, he tossed the newspaper to one side and closed his eyes. The muted sounds made by Susan in the kitchen were pleasant; they told him all was well in his safe little world. They reminded him he had an adoring, beautiful young wife, a good job that he tackled with ease, a flat in town, a cottage in the country, money in the bank. He smiled, and this wonderful sense of security drew him gently into the quiet realms of sleep.

He came awake with a start. The rattle of plates still came from the kitchen; far away on the main by-pass a heavy van sent its muted roar across fields that dozed in the hot evening sun; Mr. Hawkins sat under the table and glared at his owner. Reginald blinked, then yawned as he spoke.

"What's the matter with you?"

The dog's usually placid, brown velvet eyes were fierce; his body was rigid, and, even as Reginald spoke, he bared his teeth and growled.

"What the hell!"

Reginald sat upright, and instantly Mr. Hawkins retreated and took refuge under a chair, where he crouched, growling and watching his master with a terrible intensity.

"Susan!" Reginald called out, "what the hell's wrong with this dog?"

Susan came out of the kitchen wiping her hands on a towel, her face creased into an expression of amused enquiry.

"So far as I know, nothing. Why?"

"Well, look at him." Reginald pointed at the snarling dog, who backed farther away under the chair until all that could be seen was a pair of gleaming eyes and bared teeth. "Anyone would think I was Dracula's mother looking for her feeding bottle. I say, you don't suppose he's got rabies, do you?"

"Good heavens, no." Susan crouched down and called softly: "Mr. Hawkins, come on boy."

Mr. Hawkins ran to her, his tail wagging feebly, and he whimpered when she patted his head and stroked his soft coat.

"Poor old chap, has the heat got you down? Eh? Do you want nice walkies? Eh? Nice walkies?"

Mr. Hawkins displayed all the signs of intense pleasure at this prospect, and performed a little dance of pure joy.

"He's all right," Susan said, straightening up, "It must have been your face that put him off."

"Well, he put the fear of God into me," Reginald rose. "He hasn't been normal since I arrived. Perhaps we ought to take him to a vet."

"Nonsense, he's fine." Susan went out into the hall and the dog scampered after her. "It must have been the heat that got him down. Do you think I need a coat?"

"No, go as you are and shock the natives." Reginald grinned, then frowned when he saw a six-inch-long mark that marred her right shoulder. "No, come to think of it, perhaps you'd better put on a jacket or something. It may be chilly before we get back."

She took a thin satin shawl down from the hall stand.

"I'll wear this. There isn't a breath of wind, and I wouldn't be surprised if there's a storm before morning."

Mr. Hawkins was flattened against the front door, and when Reginald opened it, he growled low in his throat before scampering madly along the garden path and out through a hole in the hedge. Reginald smiled grimly as he closed the door and followed Susan towards the gate.

"There's something bothering that damned dog."

Out in the narrow road Susan took his arm and they walked slowly under a steel-blue sky.

"Don't be so silly. He's frisky. Just heat and sex."

"Ah!" Reginald nodded. "I know then how he feels. What a combination." They left the roadway, climbed a stile and walked ankle-deep through lush summer grass, as the dying sun painted the far-away hillsides golden-brown. Mr. Hawkins raced happily back and forth, sniffing at rabbit holes, saluting trees, reliving the days when his forebears acknowledged neither man nor beast as master, and Susan sighed.

"Heaven must be eternity spent in walking through an English field at sunset."

"And hell," Reginald retorted, "must be eternity spent in a tube train during the rush hour."

They walked for a few minutes in silence; Susan adjusted her shawl, and Reginald watched her, a tiny frown lining his forehead.

"Susan, did something really . . .?"

"Did something really what?"

He shook his head. "Nothing. Forget it."

"No, tell me. What were you going to say?"

"It wasn't important." He patted the hand that lay on his arm. "Just a passing thought."

The sun had set when they once again walked up the garden path, and a full moon lit up the cottage and surrounding countryside, painting the red-bricked walls, the neat little garden, with a cold silver hue. Susan was laughing softly, and Reginald was frowning; he looked tired and drawn.

"Honestly, you must admit it was funny." She inserted the latch-key, then opened the door and led the way into the hall. "That little girl . . ."

"Yes, yes, you've been through it three times before," Reginald snapped, but his irritability only provoked further laughter.

"But . . ." She opened the living-room door and switched on the light, "But in front of a crowd of beer-boozy layabouts this little mite pointed at you and said . . ." For a moment Susan could not continue, then she wiped her eyes . . . and said, "'Ugly man making faces at me.' "

"All right," Reginald glared at Mr. Hawkins, who was watching him from under the table. "All right, so it was funny. Let's forget it, shall we?"

"But you should have seen your face. I thought for a moment you were going to be sick."

Reginald slumped into a chair and absentmindedly rubbed his left shoulder.

"Say, ugly face, you don't want anything else to drink after all that beer, do you?"

"No, and cut it out."

"Come on, now." She sat on the arm of his chair. "Where's your sense of humour? She was only a little thing, and probably tired out. I mean to say, you weren't really making faces at her, were you?"

"Of course not."

"Well then, why so grumpy?"

"I don't know," He spoke softly, "I honestly don't know."

"Let's go to bed," she whispered, "and dream away the dark-footed hours."

"Yup." He rose, then smiled down at her; she slid an arm about his neck and laid a soft cheek against his own.

"You are the most beautiful man in the whole world," she said. He nodded.

"I guess you're right at that."

Their laughter mingled when he carried her up the stairs, and Mr. Hawkins stood in the hallway and watched their ascending figures with worried eyes.

The curtains were drawn back, the soft moonlight kept

shadows at bay, and they lay side by side and waited for the silence to summon sleep.

"Think of all the bunny-rabbits peacefully asleep in their burrows," she whispered.

"Or think of them eating Farmer Thing-a-bob's cabbages," he murmured.

She giggled.

"Are you sleepy?"

"Somewhat."

"Why do you insist on sleeping on the right hand side of the bed?"

"That's a darn fool question." He stirred uneasily and widened the space between them. "Because it's man's prerogative, I guess."

There was a full minute of blessed silence.

"Darling, if you must hold my hand, don't press so hard."

His voice came from the half world where sleep and consciousness hold an even balance.

"I'm not holding your hand."

"But, darling, you are, and you must cut your nails."

"Stop blathering and go to sleep."

Suddenly her body began to thresh wildly, and her cry of protest rose to a terrified scream.

"Reginald, what are you doing? No . . . oh, my God!"

For a second he imagined she must be playing some silly joke, that this was a not very subtle way of informing him she was not prepared to sleep, then the violent threshing of her legs, the choking gasps, made him sit up and fumble frantically for the light switch. As lamplight blasted darkness, hurled it back against the walls, she leapt from the bed and stood facing him, gasping, massaging her throat, staring with fear-crazed eyes. He was dimly aware of a faint smell, sweet, cloying, like dead flowers.

"What's wrong?" He climbed out of bed and she backed to the wall, shaking her head.

"Keep away from me."

"What the hell . . .?"

He moved round the foot of the bed then stopped when he saw her expression of terror deepen. At that moment, truth reared up in his brain, but he ignored it, crushed it under the weight of his disbelief, and he whispered:

"You know I would do nothing to hurt you."

Her whisper matched his and it was as though they were in some forbidden place, afraid lest a dreaded guardian heard their voices.

"You tried to choke me. Awful hands with nails like talons, and a foul breath that I can still smell."

He could scarcely utter the next words.

"Could that have been me?"

The awful fear on her face was dreadful to watch, and truth was uncoiling again, would not be denied.

"Then—who was it?"

"Get back into bed," he urged, "Please, I will sit on a chair. I won't come near you, I promise."

The beautiful eyes still watched him as she moved to obey, but the moment her hand touched the pillow, she recoiled.

"The smell—the stench, it's still here."

They went downstairs and seated themselves in the living-room, far apart, like strangers who may never meet again, and his voice bridged the great gulf that separated them.

"There was a woman on the train. She said she was a medium."

She waited for his next words as though they were venomous snakes being offered on a silver tray.

"She said I had an elemental attached to my left shoulder. Apparently it is feeding off me, growing stronger by the minute."

Susan did not move or betray the slightest sign she had understood or even heard what he said.

"A few hours ago, I guess, we would have laughed at the very idea." Reginald was staring at the empty fireplace, even giving the impression he was addressing it rather than the silent girl who sat clutching her dressing-gown with white fingers. "It would have been a great giggle, a funny story to tell our friends over a drink. Now . . ."

They sat opposite each other for the remainder of the dark hours. Once, Mr. Hawkins howled from his chosen place in the empty hall. They ignored him.

Reginald found the card in his jacket pocket and read the inscription aloud.

MADAME ORLOFF
Clairvoyant Extraordinary

15 Disraeli Road,
Clapham, London, S.W.4.

He dialled the telephone number at the foot of the card and waited; presently a voice answered.

"Madame Orloff, Clairvoyant Extraordinary, messages from beyond a speciality, speaking."

Reginald cleared his throat.

"My name is Reginald Warren. I don't suppose you remember me—we met on a train yesterday . . ."

"Yes, indeed I do." The voice took on a joyful tone. "You're the man with the nasty little E. I expect you want me to get cracking on the 'orrible little basket."

"Well," Reginald lowered his voice, "last night it tried to strangle my wife."

"What's that? Speak up, my dear man. It did what?"

"Tried to strangle my wife," Reginald repeated.

"Yes, I expect it did. I told you it was a homicidal. Now look, stay put, I'll have to belt down there. It's a bit of a bind because I had two table-tapping sessions and one poltergeist on the books for this afternoon. Still, it can't be helped. Let me have your address."

Reginald parted with his address with the same reluctance that he would have experienced had he given up his soul.

"The Oak Cottage, Hawthorne Lane, Hillside, Surrey."

"Right." The cheerful voice had repeated the address, word by word, "Be with you about three. I wouldn't eat too hearty if I were you. He seems to be putting on weight if he's been up to his little tricks so soon. You may have a materialization, although I doubt it at this stage. His main objective is to get inside you. Take over. Follow me?"

"Yes," Reginald swallowed, "I think so."

"Good man. See you at three. Can I get a cab at the station?"

"No, but I'll pick you up."

"Not on your nelly." The voice assumed a shocked tone. "He'll most likely try to run you off the road if he knows I'm coming. I'll hire a car—and add the cost to my bill, of course."

"Of course," Reginald agreed, "anything at all."

Madame Orloff arrived at five minutes past three; she crossed her fingers and waved at Mr. Hawkins, who promptly made a bolt for the stairs.

"Poor little dear," she sighed. "Animals always spot them first, you know. Animals and some small children: Now let's have a butcher's."

She put on her spectacles and studied Reginald with keen interest.

"My, my, we have grown. Yes indeed, he's sucking up the old spiritual fluids like a baby at its mother's breast. She bent forward and sniffed, looking rather like a well-fed bulldog who is eagerly anticipating its dinner. "Pongs too, don't he?"

"How did it become attached to me?" Reginald asked, aware that Susan was watching their visitor with an expression that was divided between horror and amazement, "I mean, I was all right up to yesterday."

"Been in a tube train lately?" Madame Orloff asked. He nodded.

"Thought so. That damned Underground is packed with them during the rush hour. I once saw a bank clerk with six of 'em clinging to him like limpets, and he picked up two more between Charing Cross and Leicester Square. Wouldn't listen to me, of course."

She turned her attention to Susan, who cringed as the heavy figure came towards her.

"You're a pretty dear, and sensitive too, I fear. You must watch yourself, poppet, keep off animal foods—and I should wear a sprig of garlic if I were you. They can't stand garlic or clean thoughts. Think clean and religious thoughts, dear. Try to picture the Archbishop of Canterbury taking a bath. Now . . ." She rolled up her sleeves. "Let's see if we can get 'im dislodged. Sit yourself down, lad. No, not in an easy-chair, this plain straight-backed one is the ticket, and angel-love, will you draw the curtains? Light is apt to put me off me stroke."

Reginald was seated on a dining-room chair, the sunlight was diffused through blue nylon curtains, and the room looked cool, peaceful, a place where one might doze away the years. Susan whimpered.

"I'm frightened. Don't let her do it."

"Hush, dear." Madame Orloff twisted her head round, "We must dislodge the basket, or he'll be at your throat again, as sure as a preggers cat has kittens."

She put a large beringed hand on either side of Reginald's head, and closed her eyes.

"I don't follow the usual formula, so don't be surprised at anything I might say. It's just ways and means of concentrating me powers."

She began to jerk Reginald's head backwards and forwards while intoning a little rhyming ditty in a high-pitched voice.

"Black, foul thing from down below,
"Get you hence, or I'll bestow
A two-footed kick right up your bum
That'll make your buttocks come through your tum."

She writhed, jerked, made the amber beads rattle like bones in a box, all the while jerking Reginald's head and pressing down on his temples, then gave vent to a roar of rage.

"No you don't, you black-hearted little basket! Try to bite, would you? Get out, out—out—out . . .

"Get right out or I'll bash your snout,
Go right under, or get your number,
No more kicks, or you'll pass bricks,
No more crying, it's no use trying,
Out-a-daisy, you're driving me crazy."

Madame Orloff snatched her hands from Reginald's head and flopped down in a chair, where she sat mopping her sweat-drenched face with a large red handkerchief.

"Must have a breather, dear. Strewth, he's made me sweat like a pig. I've tackled some 'ard ones in me time, but he takes the biscuit." She clenched her fist and shook it in Reginald's direction. "You can grin at me like a cat that's nicked the bacon, but I'll get your measure yet." She turned to Susan. "Get us a glass of water, there's a dear."

Susan ran from the room, and Madame Orloff shook her head.

"You'll have to watch that one. She's hot stuff, attracts 'em like flies to cow dung, if you get my meaning. She's soft and pliable, and they'll slide into her as easy as a knife going into butter. You back already, dear? Mustn't run like that, you'll strain something."

She drank greedily from the glass that Susan handed her then rubbed her hands.

"Thirsty work this. Well, as the bishop said to the actress 'let's have another go.' "

She got up and once again took Reginald's head between her hands. Her face wore an expression of grim determination.

"Now, dear, I want you to help me. Strain. That's the word, dear. Strain. Possession is rather like having constipation. You have to strain. Keep repeating 'Old Bill Bailey' to yourself. It'll help no end. Ready?"

Reginald tried to nod but was unable to do so due to Madame's firm hold, so he muttered, "Yes" instead.

"Right—strain.

> "Nasty horsie that's had no oats,
> This little bunny ain't afraid of stoats,

(Strain man—Old Bill Bailey)

> Coal black pussy, he's no tom,
> He's had his op, so get you gone."

Madame raised her voice to a shout, and a large blue vase on the mantelpiece suddenly crashed onto the tiled hearth.

"Strain—Old Bill Bailey—come on, we've got 'im! Out—out —get yer skates on . . .

> "Out of the window, out through the door,
> There's no marbles here, he'll keep you poor,
> Don't grind your teeth. . . ."

A chair went tumbling across the floor, books came hurling from their shelves, a rug left the floor and wrapped itself round the ceiling lamp, and a cold wind tugged at the window curtains. Madame Orloff lowered her voice, but it was still clear, unexpectedly sad.

> "Lonely wanderer of the starless night,
> You must not stay, it is not right,
> Blood is for flesh, and flesh is for blood,
> We live for an hour, then are lost in the flood
> That sweeps us away into fathomless gloom,
> We spend eternity in a darkened room."

"Please stop!" Susan's voice was lost amid the howling wind, but Madame Orloff's cry of triumph rang out.

"Strain—strain . . . he's coming out. Aye, he's coming out as smooth as an eye leaving its socket. He's fighting every inch of the way, but old Ma Perkins was one too many for him. Out you go, my beauty, out you go, down to the land where black mountains glow with never-quenched fire, and white worms crawl from the corrupt earth, even as maggots seethe from a carcass on a hot afternoon. Go . . . *go*. . . ."

The cold wind died, hot air seeped back into the room; all around lay wrecked pictures, scattered books, broken furniture. An ugly crack disfigured the polished surface of a table. Susan was crying softly, Reginald was white-faced, looking like a man who has survived a long illness. Madame Orloff rose, pulled open the window curtains, then looked about with an air of satisfaction.

"A bit of a ruddy mess, but then, as someone once said, you can't make an omelette without breaking eggs. 'Fraid me services come a bit high, dear. I'll want fifty nicker for this little do."

"Worth every penny," Reginald rose somewhat unsteadily to his feet. "I can't thank you enough, Madame, I feel like . . ."

"A feather, eh?" Madame Orloff beamed. "A great weight lifted off yer shoulders? I know what you mean. I remember an old geezer down in Epsom; he had a nasty attached to him that was as big as a house. Ruddy great thing, had a lust for rice puddings, made the poor old sod eat three at one sitting. When I got shot of it, he leapt about like a two-year-old. Said he felt like floating. Well . . ." She took up her handbag. "Mustn't keep that car waiting any longer—the fare will cost you a fortune." She put a hand under Susan's chin and tilted her head; the blue eyes were bright with tears.

"Cheer up, ducks. It's all over now. Nothing to worry your pretty little head about any more."

"You must stay for dinner," Susan said softly. "We can't let you go like this. . . ."

"Thanks all the same, but I've got a sitting laid on for six o'clock, so I'll leave you to clear up the mess. Don't trouble to see me out. I'm quite capable of opening and closing a door."

From the hallway she looked back.

"I should keep away from the Underground during the rush hour, Mr. Warren. The place is a cesspit—everything from a damn nuisance poltergeist to a vampire-elemental. See you."

The front-door slammed and Reginald gathered Susan up into his arms; he patted her shaking shoulders and murmured: "There, there, it's all over now. It's all over."

They sat in the twilight, younger than youth, older than time, and rejoiced in each other.

"You are wonderful," she said.

"True," he nodded.

"And awfully conceited."

"Self-confidence," he corrected. "The weak are vain, the strong self-confident."

"And what am I?"

"White, gold and tinged with pink."

"I like that." She snuggled up to him and Mr. Hawkins dozed peacefully on the hearthrug.

Presently——

"What's that?"

She sat up. Fear was in waiting, ready to leap into her eyes.

"Nothing." He pulled her back, "Just nerves. It's all over now."

"I thought I heard someone knocking."

"There's no one to come knocking at our door. No one at all."

Mr. Hawkins whimpered in his sleep, and somewhere above, a floorboard creaked.

"The wood contracting," he comforted her. "The temperature is falling, so the wood contracts. We must not let imagination run away with us."

"Reginald . . ." She was staring up at the ceiling. "Madame Orloff—she got it loose from you, and I am grateful, but suppose——"

Another floorboard creaked and a bedroom door slammed.

"Suppose—it's—still here?"

He was going to say "Nonsense", laugh at her fears, but Mr. Hawkins was up on his four legs, his coat erect, growling fiercely as he glared at the closed door. Heavy footsteps were on the landing, pacing back and forth, making the ceiling lamp shake, breaking now and again into a kind of skipping dance. Susan screamed before she collapsed into merciful oblivion, and at once the sounds ceased, to be replaced by a menacing silence.

Reginald laid Susan down upon the sofa and crept on tip-toe towards the door. When he opened it a wave of foul-smelling cold air made him gasp, then, with courage born of desperation, he went out to the hall and peered up into the gloom-haunted staircase.

It was coming down. A black blob that was roughly

human-shaped, but the face was real—luminous-green; the eyes, red; a bird's-nest thatch of black hair. It was grinning, and the unseen feet were making the stairs tremble. Reginald, aware only that he must fight, picked up a small hall table and flung it straight at the approaching figure. Instantly, something—some invisible force—hurled him against the front door, and he lay on the door-mat powerless to move. The Thing moved slowly down the stairs, and for a hell-bound second the red eyes glared down at the prostrate man before it clumped into the living-room. The door slammed, and Mr. Hawkins howled but once.

Minutes passed and Reginald tried to move, but the power had gone from his legs. Also, there was a dull pain in the region of his lower spine, and he wondered if his back were broken. At last, the living-room door slid open, went back on its hinges with a protesting creak as though wishing to disclaim all responsibility for that which was coming out. Susan walked stiff-legged into the hall, white-faced, clothes torn, but her face was lit by a triumphant smile, and Reginald gasped out aloud with pure relief.

"Darling, thank heavens you're safe. Don't be alarmed—it flung me against the door, but I think I've only sprained something. Give me a hand up and we'll get the hell out of here."

She moved closer, still walking with that grotesque stiff-legged gait. Her head went over to one side, and for the first time he saw her eyes. They were mad—mad—mad. . . . Her mouth opened, and the words came out in a strangled, harsh tone.

"Life . . . life . . . life . . . flesh . . . flesh . . . flesh . . . blood . . ."

"Susan!" Reginald screamed and tried to get up, but collapsed as a blast of pain seared his back; he could only watch with dumb horror as she swung her stiff left leg round and began to hobble towards the broken table that lay on the bottom stair. She had difficulty in bending over to pick up the carved walnut leg, and even more difficulty in straightening up, but she gripped the leg firmly in her right hand, and the grimace on her face could have denoted pleasure.

"You . . . denied . . . me . . . life," the harsh voice said. "You . . . denied . . . me . . . life . . ."

She, if the thing standing over Reginald could still be so called, looked down with red-tinted eyes, horror in ivory and gold, and he wanted even then to hold her, kiss away the grotesque lines from around the full-lipped mouth, murmur his great love, close those dreadful eyes with gentle fingers. Then the carved walnut leg came down and smashed deep into his skull, and the world exploded, sent him tumbling over and over into eternity.

Presently the Thing which had been Susan went out into the evening that was golden with the setting sun. It drank deep of the cool air, for storm clouds were pouring in from the west and soon there would be rain.

It went stiff-legged down the garden path, and out into the roadway. There was still much killing to be done.

CLARE COLVIN
Something to Reflect Upon

Clare Colvin has worked as a journalist for a number of national newspapers, from political and foreign reporting to dramatic and literary criticism. She is now working on a novel and a collection of short stories. "Something to Reflect Upon" was first published in Winter's Tales (New Series: 6, 1990).

T he Villa Mozart is one of the finest turn-of-the-century apartment buildings in the Seiziéme, possibly one of the finest in the whole of Paris. You go through mahogany and bevelled glass doors to the main entrance hall. At the end of the hall a curving stone staircase winds round a glass elevator and the stone walls meet the ceiling in a carved frieze of grapes and pomegranates. On the stained glass window a pre-Raphaelite nymph in semi profile, yearns towards the heavens. Her auburn hair snakes out behind her to merge with the surrounding leaves.

The apartment itself is on the third floor and protected by a double front door with an elaborate lock that sends metal bars into the door frame at an extra turn of the key. I unlock the metal bars and step into a world of polished parquet and double doors. Two sets of glass doors lead into the dining room and sitting room, which are linked by more doors. Both rooms have French windows leading on to narrow iron balconies. I stand in the centre and see in the sitting room, in front of me, a marble fireplace surmounted by a looking glass which is framed by white plaster garlands. Turning towards the dining room, there is a twin fireplace and glass. I am reflected in the reflections of the mirrors *ad infinitum*. The image is of a woman with a pale face and long fair hair tied back with a black ribbon. She is wearing a dark grey coat and a light grey patterned cashmere scarf. Her clothes look expensive, but unobtrusive.

My aunt, whose apartment it is, is called the French aunt, though she is English. She is married to a French diplomat

150

and they are abroad most of the time, letting the apartment to other diplomats. This is why it has such a formal, unlived-in air. The table, flanked by the elaborately simple curves of art nouveau dining chairs, is a dark, polished mirror, untouched by spilt wines or carelessly placed knives and forks, all the marks that an ordinary table acquires as its patina. The pale colours of the sofas divulge nothing of evenings past, of cigarette smoking, coffee drinking, not even an indentation to show that they have been used. The air of impersonality is such that you hesitate to make a mark, but just drift through the double doors, touching nothing.

I am here because a diplomat who should have taken the flat did not, after all, get posted to Paris, and I am staying until they find another diplomat. I am also here because I need to recover from, no, to recover *myself*. I look on my leaving Robert as an escape, a declaration that I will no longer live a sub-text. It should be a triumph, but everyone extends sympathy to me, as if I am ill. So perhaps it is a defeat, after all. The first old friend with whom I had lunch here, who took me to a panelled restaurant near the Place Vendôme where we had a wild mushroom salad and scallops poached in seaweed, suddenly became terribly solicitous and asked me how I felt. I couldn't speak, and he pressed my hand and said, "Of course, you feel numb."

"Yes," I said, and we talked about something else. It is not only numbness, but a vacuum. The person you were has melted away, leaving a non-person, about whom others make their own judgements, assigning you a character, feelings and motives you do not possess. On my own, all that seems left is a bank of memories. I cross the road to the Jeu de Paumes and meet myself many years ago, walking from the gallery with *nymphéas* in my eyes. Straight ahead of me is the Crillon, like a formal Government building. One of those windows overlooking the Place de la Concorde was where we spent the first night of our honeymoon ten years ago. It was there, after months of being drawn into marriage by all the pressures which eventually make people marry, that I sat up in bed in the early hours of the morning and thought, *What have I done?* The Place was a moving pattern of weaving and dipping car headlights, illuminating in their rays a drizzle of rain. I watched them from the window until the sky began to lighten. We returned to England a married couple, Robert and Alice. Robert's name was always in front, to do with the way they sounded together. I lost my surname, too, and with it my sense of identity.

I am growing cold as I stand in the Place de la Concorde, and I remember it was cold then, as well. It is New Year's Eve tomorrow and some friends of the aunt have asked me to a party. Memories of New Year's parties stretch back for years, the prospects for each year judged by that moment at midnight when you find whether you are where you want to be. This is the first time I have spent New Year in Paris.

I return to the quartier of the Seiziéme. It is a strangely quiet and self-contained part of Paris. You walk through canyons of late nineteenth century apartment buildings designed for the haute bourgeoisie. Each apartment block has a large carpeted front hall, polished brass fittings, and an office for the concierge. The area is inhabited only, it seems, by women of a certain age, wearing calf-length black mink coats and walking their dogs. I stop at the traiteur to buy pâté, olives and céleri rémoulade. As the assistant wraps each portion, he says inquiringly, "Et avec cèla?" I order an oeuf en gelée which I had not originally intended to do. My French seems to have deserted me totally, and I am pointing at things like a tourist. I am glad to get back to the apartment where I can think fluently, rather than fit into the role of the quartier's mental defective.

In the apartment, the silence is profound. The front looks on to a cul de sac ending in a garden, and onto a similar turn of the century stone building opposite. The bedrooms on the side look into a quiet street with little traffic. Opposite the bedrooms are more apartment buildings, less distinguished architecturally but still bearing the stamp of money and position. The silence is broken by shouting in the street—mad, furious shouting. I open the window and see, on the pavement, a bearded man in an anorak who is so beside himself with rage that he is practically falling into the gutter. "Espèce de con!" he shouts, and "Je vais vous tuer!" I cannot quite make out what he is on about, but he uses the verb *tuer* a great deal. The concierge in the apartment building opposite comes out in a patterned frock that spreads across her hips. She stands there impassively, watching him. Obviously she knows he is not going to *tuer* her. If anything, he is going to *tuer* the women in their black mink coats. Perhaps he is protesting at his anonymity. I shut the window again. Metal rods slide into both ends of the window frame.

Here in the apartment I am protected, living in a hermetically sealed vacuum. How quiet it is, and how different from the place I first stayed in in Paris, an attic room in one of those hotels where you were afraid, as you ascended the slanting stairs, that they might fall away from the walls and cascade you into the basement. It was on the Left Bank, and there was noise at all times, until four in the morning from the late night people, and beginning again soon after five with the dustbins and the streetcleaners. I suppose I must have had a certain courage to have come to Paris that first time, at about seventeen or so, but when I come to think of it, I did quite a few brave things when I was young. I grew cowardly as I grew older, afraid of the unknown, and then I married Robert. At seventeen, after taking a modelling course, which was an accepted finishing education for girls at the time, I had gone to work for the house of Duparc in Faubourg St Honoré. I spent three months sitting in a changing room with another English girl, occasionally being asked to parade in the salon in one of M. Duparc's dresses, hand stitched by shortsighted seamstresses in the basement. It was a small House and it was like being part of a tense, temperamental family. M. Duparc flew easily into a tantrum, and a few years later he had a heart attack and retired. No one carried on his name, he was not that important a couturier. And I, who had had barely acknowledged fantasies of taking Paris by storm, left at the end of three months. M. Duparc decided to return to having Parisiennes as models, and Mme Duparc told me with sympathy and tact that there was no more work for me. "You are charming, my dear, but you are too self-effacing with the clothes. They must be worn with panache. Ma petite, you must make a production of yourself, if you are to be successful. Otherwise no one will notice you, and the world will go on without you."

One way of not being noticed was to marry Robert, for he demanded all the attention and did all the talking. It was easier to say nothing than to compete, and so Robert began thinking for me as well. He would tell other people what was in my mind and although I did not necessarily agree, when he said it with such an air of decision, it seemed to become fact. So my thoughts became Robert's too, and when I left, I found it hard not to ring him up to find out what I should think. Whenever I bought clothes in neutral shades, I heard Robert's voice ringing in my mind, "For God's sake, why don't you wear some bright colours? No one will notice you dressed like that. You'll just fade into the wallpaper."

I felt bruised when I arrived at the flat, but now, as long as I stay indoors, I feel an expansiveness and calm. It's going out that is the problem. Simple things like buying a loaf of bread are difficult when the slightest contact with another person makes you wince. I left my skin behind when I left Robert. I expect he shows it to people as proof that I will return. Until I grow another, life is bound to be painful.

Oddly enough, going to a party is less difficult than everyday life. It is to do with the preparation. I prepare myself like an actress in a dressing room. I sit in front of the mirror for the ritual of making up. First you prime the canvas with foundation, then you add colour. Pale eyeshadow overlaid with grey, eyeliner, carefully blurred, lip gloss, masses of mascara, and a touch of what they used to call rouge and now call blusher. There, who's got a pretty mask, then? the model training was not for nothing. Now I decide on the clothes. The grey blouse, no, that's wallpaper dressing. Finally I wear the black dress with a low back, long earrings and beads. I hear Robert's voice saying, "I hate you wearing black."

I am now ready to go into the street. I close the door behind me and lock the iron bars into place with a turn of the key. No fumbling with mortice and Yale. One flick of the wrist and the door is secure as Fort Knox. I walk down the stairs and into the street. The world outside is not as frightening at night because the dim lighting shields you from the stranger's gaze, and in the quartier there is no one around anyway. The women in their mink coats have locked themselves into their fortresses.

A taxi pulls up and I get in and am suddenly transported into a world of window curtains with bobbles, and boogie music. The taxi driver has a collection of big band music from the forties and fifties. He holds the tapes up for inspection at the traffic lights. He doesn't trust modern music, he says, because it destroys the ears and the mind. He is going to celebrate the New Year in his cab. At midnight, the time when no passenger will be there, he will turn the boogie music up and clash a spanner against his spare hub cap. It sounds as good a way of spending New Year's Eve as any.

We boogie along to my aunt's friends' apartment near the Parc Monceau. I don't know them, but they heard I was in Paris on my own, so they told me to come to their party, because to be alone on New Year's Eve is a bad omen for the year ahead. A maid opens the door and takes my coat, and a shy young man, my hostess's son, shows me into the salon.

I am in a high-ceilinged room, even higher than the Villa Mozart, with a gilded mirror on one wall that reaches to the ceiling. The parquet floor is covered by a deep Aubusson carpet, and cream and gold leaf Louis Quinze chairs are placed at strategic intervals. Two women sit, straightbacked, conversing with each other, their chairs too far apart for the conversation to be private.

The young man has disappeared towards the front door, and the women are looking at me in an expectant way for an introduction. I shake hands with the fair-haired woman in a billowing pink dress, and she smiles graciously, then I shake hands with the dark-haired woman in black. She, too, smiles and looks friendly, but neither of them move from their chairs, and there are no other chairs nearby, so I move on. In the far corner, four men in dinner jackets are having a conversation, and from their lack of interest in a new arrival, it is evident that they wish to continue without interruption. On such occasions, a drinks table can save you, but there is no drinks table here. I stand in the middle of the Aubusson carpet, reflected in the mirror, in a slim black dress, and behind me the two women on their gold leaf chairs at a distance from each other, still conversing. I think, if I walk across the carpet, I shall hear the crunching of gravel.

The shy young man returns and asks what I would like to drink. Some wine, I say, and when he scurries off, I follow him. There is the drinks table in the hall, with its comforting array of bottles, so now I know my escape route. Madame, my hostess, is there too, smiling, gracious, slightly distrait, for she had set herself the task of preparing a four course dinner of the sort you would expect in a restaurant. Several times during the course of the evening she emerges from her hutch of a kitchen to supervise arrangements and then returns to the stove. The taxi driver in his cab and Madame in her kitchen have both, in their separate ways, decided to spend New Year's Eve alone.

I feel better for a glass of wine and more people are now arriving, noisier and jollier than the earlier guests. I am still the outsider, but that, after a couple of glasses, does not seem to matter as much. The room is warmer, less intimidating, and the pendants of the chandeliers sparkle like leaves in a heat wave. The mirror reflects people weaving in and out of groups, and the Louis Quinze chairs have been abandoned. The party is going to be fun, after all.

In the dining room with its magenta walls, the candles on the tables cast flickering pools of light. The central dining table, polished and dark like the one at the Villa Mozart, has a selection of dishes of smoked salmon, cray fish and pâté de foie gras. I am sitting next to an enthusiastic and friendly man, whose dinner jacket seems incongruous with his untidy thatch of hair and gold-rimmed spectacles. He is not at all worried by my lack of French, and launches, for no apparent reason, into a dissertation on the virtues of Akhnaton, the first reformist Pharaoh. A monotheist, too, he says, as if that were a further sign of virtue. The dissertation is fascinating and everyone listens as though it is a lecture on their chosen subject. What do French women do during their men's displays of virtuosity, I wonder? An Englishwoman would have been watching her husband's face with an expression either of maternal anxiety or of distaste. Mme Akhnaton, who has a Nefertiti profile, is doing none of these things. She is narrowing her Anouk Aimée eyes at a middleaged admirer who is still crazy about her after all these years. Everyone here has known each other since they were very young and they are still carrying on the same interchangeable relationships. Mme Akhnaton knew Edouard de Truc when he was a smooth young man with dark hair, but she married her enthusiastic Egyptologist. Edouard de Truc now has grey, thinning hair, though he is still smooth, and he fans the memories of their earlier affair.

It is midnight and the tables are abandoned, as everyone performs the first task of the New Year, circling the magenta room to shake hands with and kiss their fellow guests, murmuring "Bonne année." At the last stroke of midnight, a tall, wasted-looking young man with large eyes, whom I had not seen before, says to me, "Happy New Year," in a perfect accent, and kisses me on both cheeks. I feel like someone who has been struggling in the rapids of the French language, and who has now come to dry land.

Jean-Marc, our hostess's son, puts on a Stones record and someone rolls up the Aubusson, leaving a wide expanse of parquet. Jean-Marc has a veritable archive of English records— Rolling Stones, Beatles, Bill Haley. Edouard de Truc dances to the memories of his youth, and so do most of us, apart from Jean-Marc, who is too young, and possibly the man I am with, who may be too young, but I am not sure because of the damage he has done to his face. It reflects lack of food and sleep, and the possibility of drink or drugs. His name is Philippe and he has arrived late from another party with a similarly ravaged-looking woman and a pale young man who has taken up residence at the drinks table.

Philippe and I sit on the broad Directoire sofa, watching the dancers. They have mostly dispersed, except for the fair-haired woman in pink, whom I had first seen sitting straightbacked in a Louise Quinze chair, and who now dances by herself in front of the mirror, with an undulating body and balletic movements of the arms. She enjoys the way her body moves with an innocent shamelessness, and her face—she must be about thirty-five — has the pleased expression of a schoolgirl showing off. Whether people are watching is irrelevant to her, for she loves music, she loves dancing, and she loves herself. The floor is her stage, and this is her show, choreographed on the spur of the moment. After a while, she pirouettes away through the door with a final flourish, acknowledging the applause. Philippe offers me a truffle from a silver dish. I choke on the cocoa dust with which it is coated, and try to blow if off the chocolate. The fine dark dust goes all over my dress.

"That's why I wear black," I say, then notice that the cocoa dust has also settled on the cream brocade upholstery. I think, I won't be invited here again.

The pale young man, Michel, and the woman with the ravaged air, whose name is Brigitte, join us after circling the rest of the party. Brigitte has red hennaed hair, intense eyes and talks a great deal about herself. She says she is a photographer and had an exhibition a while ago in a small gallery in the Marais area. The photographs were of women in different walks of life—a well known writer, a film director, a dancer, an alcoholic prostitute in a café, a lavatory attendant.

"Who buys the photographs?" I ask.

She regards the question as insulting, as I would not have thought of buying a photograph as a work of art. It appears that, so far, the writer and the film director have bought their own photographs, but the alcoholic whore and the lavatory attendant have not. Michel disappears to the hall again to refill his glass and Philippe discusses Michel's drink problem with Brigitte, who seems if anything more drunk. I am not sure about Brigitte, but I like Philippe. He has sympathetic eyes and a way of drawing me into the conversation, and he seems to like me.

At three in the morning, the party is beginning to disperse, and Brigitte says she will give us a lift, as there are bound to be no taxis. Michel insists that we go back to his place for coffee, and we drive towards the Place de L'Etoile, a land of fir trees covered with false snow and white fairylights, like the glittering domain of the Snow Queen. Michel's flat is a former chambre de bonne's rooms at the top of a large apartment building off the Avenue Foch. He is clearly one of those drinkers who hates to be on their own. He pours a whisky for himself and makes some Nescafé for us. Brigitte, in whom drink has unleashed a streak of aggression, is angry that he does not have real coffee. How can he possibly live in a place without coffee? How dare he offer his guests Nescafé? She bullies Michel as if he is the owner of an indifferent restaurant. Philippe tries to intervene and she tells him to shut up. Michael says in a quiet, flat voice, "There is either whisky or Nescafé. The whisky is real." Brigitte has a whisky and begins a monologue on photography. Her face is square-jawed, her eyes fanatical. I think, I have drained the dregs of this particular New Year's Eve. It's time to go.

Philippe says he will walk me home, but I say, No, I'll take a taxi. Outside it is raining, and there are no taxis, only an occasional late partygoer swishes past, sending up a spray from the road.

"I'll walk you home," says Philippe. "I have an umbrella."

It is not really cold, just wet, and we walk along the avenue. Philippe's arm rests lightly on my waist, and after a few minutes I put my arm round his waist. He is so thin you can feel his ribs through the jacket and I think, It is so long since I walked with my arm around someone. Although we are both tired, we are still talking. I learn a little more about Philippe. He is only half French. The other half is Polish which is why he accepts with fatalistic grace the walk through the rain. It is nearly five by the time we reach the Villa Mozart, and we are the only people awake in the neighbourhood. I realise that Philippe cannot be left on the doorstep, with his sodden shoes and his hair in rats' tails dripping onto his collar.

"I'll stay until the Métro begins running," says Philippe. He takes off his shoes and puts them beside the sofa, and I drape his jacket over a chair by the radiator where it emanates a dank smell of wet wool. I make a pot of tea for us, and Philippe sits on the sofa, his eyelids half closed. His white shirt hangs loosely on his body, the cuffs rolled back. I tell him a little, though not much, about why I am here. He listens, his hand resting lightly on my shoulder, then he says he must sleep for a while. It seems entirely natural that he should sleep in my bed. He takes off his shirt and climbs into one side of the bed. He closes his eyes, and his face, in profile, looks exhausted. I get into my side of the bed and lie quite still. Then his hand reaches out for mine.

"Are you asleep, Alice?"

"Almost," I say.

"Goodnight, then, Alice," he says and is asleep a few minutes later.

After an hour or so, there is a grey light through the shutters and I lie there, too tired to move, aware of the body next to me. He is still sleeping and in the faint light he looks at peace. The wasted look about his face has gone and he looks younger than before. The eyelids stretch over the large eyes, like a marble angel in repose. I think about his sympathy and knowingness last night. He asked me very little about myself, yet he seemed to know more than I said. I think, None of this would have happened if I had not been in a strange city, dependent on other people's whims. I have been too long on my own and now I have made a connection.

I leave him to sleep and stand under the bathroom shower waiting for my mind to clear. Then I go into the kitchen to make some breakfast. There are croissants, which I warm in the oven, and orange juice in the fridge. I leave the coffee on the stove and return to the bedroom. The blankets have slipped halfway down his chest and he is lying on his back, one arm stretched behind his head. I sit on the edge of the bed as he begins to stir and then I notice, as he moves the arm, a mark like a bruise or perhaps more like a dark discoloration.

You would have to be out of contact with all newspapers for the last few years not to be wary of these marks, I think. Nowadays there is no looking for kindness from a stranger, no love from someone whose history is not known to you. A whole way of reassurance has gone. I exist because I am loved. Now that way is closed. We are all locked in our separate bodies, hardly daring to touch each other. Last night I had forgotten the new set of rules. I had been going back to the days of chance, when chance was safe. Now the plague is spreading through the land and the Masque is ended.

Philippe opens his eyes and sees me looking at him. He says, "Good morning, Alice. Tu as bien dormi?" Then he gives me a warm smile full of affection. "I smell coffee. How kind you are."

We have breakfast in the sitting room and Philippe sits on the sofa, wearing his dried clothes again. He seems content simply to watch me, looking at me with his large, grey eyes. For him, it is the beginning of something new, a special friendship. For me, this breakfast is a disengagement.

"I must get home, but I'll ring you later," says Philippe. He writes my phone number on the pad by the phone, tears off the page and then writes his own number on the next page, writing underneath "Philippe". At the door, he puts his hands on my shoulders and looks intently at my face, as if he is trying to read it. Then he says, "A demain," kisses me softly and fleetingly on the mouth, and turns and walks away. I shut the door and stand in the hall for several minutes, listening to the silence. There is an awareness in the apartment that someone has been here, that the emptiness has been momentarily filled. In the sitting room, I look at myself in the mirror. My face seems different, more the way it was a few years ago, a little softer, perhaps. I take the coffee cups into the kitchen. The flat is closing ranks around me again, as the hushed impersonality returns.

New Year comes quietly to Paris. For the past two or three weeks, the French have been sulking. They have been frightened out of shops and restaurants by terrorists' bombs, and they are furious about the train strike. I hear on the radio that the Métro may be next, and decide I must visit the Bibliothèque Nationale first. The state of the Métro reflects the fury with which the

French regard their inefficient Government. Once it was neat and clean, but now there is litter, which no one clears away, as if in a dirty protest, and the interconnecting subways are lined with beggars and buskers.

On my way home from the Bibliothèque I stop by at the traiteur and buy some rillettes and a salade de tomates. The weather has turned colder, and the central heating in the flat does not seem as stifling. I pour myself a St. Raphaël blanc with ice and soda water. I know from the times when Robert would go out without me that you have to be disciplined about drinking on your own. Only one before dinner, maybe more if you are cooking.

The phone rings and it is, as I thought, Philippe. No one else has my number here. I have a momentary feeling of dread, that fear of involvement brings, but it is not difficult to deal with the call for, after ten years of being married to a man who tried to control my thoughts, lying comes easily to me.

"I'm terribly sorry. I would have loved to have seen you, but I am going back to London tomorrow."

He sounds surprised and says he thought I was staying here for longer.

"I rang my husband, and we decided it would be a good idea if I went back now."

A pause at his end of the phone. Then he decides, obviously, that changes of plan are a natural part of life, and the fatalistic element re-asserts itself.

"I'm sorry you're going . . . Well, let me know when you come to Paris again. You have my telephone number, don't you?"

I do. It is still on the pad by the phone.

Two days later it begins to snow and the Métro goes on strike. Now I have all the time to myself in the world. I look out at the white-blanketed street from my window. No one is going anywhere, least of all me. The central heating insulates me, providing a world of warmth that denies the natural elements. The phone remains silent. I lose the desire to go out, even to the traiteur or the boulanger. I eat less and less, but I read a great deal, I listen to the radio, I make some notes, I rest. At night, occasionally, I take a sleeping pill, for though I am tired I find it hard to sleep. I spend much of the time thinking about how each step in my life has taken me to this still centre, this place of stasis. Each time I was given a choice, I took a path that led to a lessening of choice. Now I am at the centre of the maze, with no choices left, but a sense at least that I still desire to exist. On my way into Paris, along the Périphérique, I saw a cemetery of neat, crowded graves, with little stone houses to which the bodies were confined, and I had a sudden sense of claustrophobia. How terrible to be confined to that space, never to go anywhere again. My own confinement to this apartment is not a wish for non-existence, more a wish for non-feeling until I gain my strength. Things will take their course, I realise, if I have time on my own. In the middle of the night the phone rings, a loud, insistent ringing. It would not be Philippe at this hour. I let it ring until it ceases. How oppressive a large flat becomes when you are on your own. You begin to feel previous lives going on in other rooms. Space has to be filled and if you do not fill it yourself, the past returns and gains possession of its territory.

The next day it snows again. I stand at the window and watch it swirling down and sideways, so light that it sometimes spirals upwards again. It is dizzying, almost hypnotic, after a while. I open the window and look down at the street. An ambulance is drawing up at the Villa Mozart, and after a while the ambulance-men carry out from the building a covered figure on a stretcher. One of the black mink coats has lost its owner. I switch on the radio and hear that the Métro strike is still going on, and there is now fury at the police because they do not have any snow ploughs with which to clear the streets, only battering rams with which to knock down demonstrators. A government minister is making an emergency broadcast on the subject.

Some days I stay in bed most of the time, because I feel curiously tired, and if I am not going out, I may as well stay in bed as sit on the sofa. But as the days go by, I am aware of having turned a corner, of beginning to feel stronger. My legs no longer ache as if I had been walking for ever, and I need less sleep. I have just been tired, that's all it was, and now I'm getting better. The weather is improving too. It is lighter and brighter, and the snow is beginning to melt. When I open the window, there is a mildness in the air. It is almost time to go out again.

I begin to think of food, quite ravenously, and then, the next morning I awake with a feeling of purpose and determination. The time has come to put my house in order, to do some cleaning, to stock up with food, why, even to cook a meal. I have found a new purpose in simple household matters. But there is just the business of getting out of the house. This is going to be difficult, because I am simply not used to exercise any more.

It feels good to be in the fresh air again. The pavement is clear of snow, apart from the slush wedged against the wall. It is really quite an effort to walk the slightly upward rise to the traiteur. In his window the massed oeufs en gelée glisten invitingly, framed in chopped aspic. The shop assistant looks at me oddly. He has not seen me for a while, and I know I am pale and underweight. He inquires after my health and I say that I have had the grippe, but I am better now. I look at the dishes of the day, but he has only an insipid blanquette de veau. Time to do my own cooking again. I buy the first course from him, freshly cooked langoustes with a mayonnaise verte, and the final course, a crême brulée with a smooth crust of caramel in a heartshaped dish. Then I see that he has pink champagne on special offer. No, he says, they have no half bottles, and so I take a whole bottle. I don't care what they say about pink champagne—I love it. I buy a bottle of Bordeaux, some mineral water, and pâté and olives.

Next door the butcher has laid out pink and red flesh on the marble slab. I still think in terms of two rather than one when I am cooking, and I ask for two fillet-steaks without thinking, but I do not correct my mistake. I shall do a Tournedos Rossini, with some of the pâté. At the boulangerie I buy a baguette and croissants, then fruit and salad leaves at the greengrocer. Even if the rest of Paris has fallen apart, the shops in the Seiziéme hold fast to their standards. I am out of breath when I return to the Villa Mozart with my shopping bags. I am also short of cash. I unload the various packages into the fridge and then rest on the sofa.

Evenings are always reassuring. You draw the curtains and any obligation to be active has gone. At this time of the day, it is quite natural to be sitting at home. People working, people going to the shops, taking clothes to the laundry, all those obligations have gone and it is quite all right to do what I have been doing most days, which is nothing. But tonight I have something to set my mind to. I have a dinner to prepare. I go to the Dutch bureau in the dining room and find some linen place mats in the drawer. In the glass cabinet are some fine champagne glasses shaped like flutes, so I take one and then ease the cork off the champagne. It is more robust than white champagne. I have one glass and immediately feel lighthearted. Now to get the dinner together.

I really do not need more than the langoustes. I had not realised how your stomach adapts to lack of food. It does not want more, but on the other hand, I am hungry for different tastes, so I shall go on. I bought a raspberry feuilleté in the boulangerie, when I wasn't looking, which I shall have with the crême brulée. In the meantime there is the fillet steak, underdone, the bread cooked in the juices of the meat and coated with pâté. One last glass of champagne—I did need more than half a bottle—and I go on to the Bordeaux.

I pour it into a large wine glass. In my head a conversation is beginning with my companion for dinner. It is Philippe, and I try to explain why I have been here on my own for so long. It is, I tell his sympathetic eyes, to do with finding out if anything is there after all the responses to other people are gone. When you only see yourself reflected in other people's eyes, you are not sure if you exist without them. Once the self that responded to others in the way that others expected, once that self is gone, you wait to see what will emerge in place of the mirror image. And there is someone now who is different, someone who enjoys life and wants to talk and laugh and love. I am not Robert's person any more, closed into a mould that constrains me, aware of the closing walls of circumstance. Now that is sorted out, I am ready to build a new life. Everything is beginning to fall into place and I have a need for new places, new experiences. I am ready to leave the apartment.

Well, the raspberry feuilleté was a little too much, but never mind, what I shall have now is a digestif. That should settle matters. I pour myself an Armagnac and watch the news on television. Around midnight, the feuilleté strikes again. I have an awful stabbing pain in my chest, which continues after I have gone to bed. I take some Neutrose Vichy and a couple of sleeping pills, to sleep off my indigestion.

I am awake now, it is morning, and I feel better than ever before. The doubts have gone and the cloud has lifted. An intense love overwhelms me and focuses on Philippe. I forget my fears, and that I don't really know who he is. As in a fairy tale where the heroine is indissolubly tied to the first living creature she meets when she wakes from her sleep—so I feel tied to Philippe. It will be easy to telephone him, now that I feel lighthearted and warm again.

I have been lying on the bed, and I must have been very tired. It must be late in the day, too, because the light through the shutters is bright. A fine day, and there is a warmth that is not just from the central heating. I stretch my arms and look up at the ceiling and—that's curious—I can't think why I haven't noticed it before, a large discoloured stain, and some of the paper is peeling. It looks as if there has been a leak from upstairs but why did I not notice it before? I walk along the corridor to the sitting room. The shutters are closed, but bright shafts of light slant across the floor. It seems dusty. Then I see something alarming, or rather, I see an alarming absence. The Dutch bureau has gone and so has the glass cabinet. Someone has been in and taken the furniture. Not all of it, for the sofa is here and the dining table, but the valuable pieces have gone. And the vase with dried flowers on the mantelpiece has gone, too, so have the magazines on the coffee table. The flat, always so impersonal, is now denying that anybody lives here at all. Someone must have come here last night, but why have they done it? Have there been burglars, or has my aunt sent in someone for the furniture? Is she telling me to leave? I look at the telephone and the pad with Philippe's number on it has gone as well. I walk towards the front door, and that, too, seems different. Have I somehow got into the wrong flat? I hear voices outside and now there is a key turning in the lock. Either it is my aunt or one of her agents come to tell me they want the apartment back, or else I am in the wrong apartment and am about to be accused of trespass.

The door opens and a woman steps into the hall. She has long, blonde hair and an attractive, suntanned face. She is wearing a cream linen suit and everything about her is well-groomed and cared for. A man follows her, bulky with short hair, a dark blue suit and slightly piggy eyes. Behind them, just closing the door, is my aunt's agent, M. Maurice. Why couldn't he have telephoned, the rude young man? I say, Bonjour, m'sieur, but he walks past me, and so do the two people he is showing around. They are, as I first guessed, Americans. I follow them into the sitting room and when Maurice opens the shutters, letting in a flood of sunlight, I say, "Excuse me, M. Maurice, but I am still living here, you know." He is looking in my direction, but he does not seem to have registered what I have said.

"This is the sitting room," he tells his Americans. "You will observe the symmetry of the two marble fireplaces at either end, and the matching mirrors. An excellent room for entertaining, you will agree. With the double doors open, so, it is perfect for a large reception."

"It's really beautiful," says the woman. "One of the prettiest rooms I have seen, and so much space."

"Yeah, very nice," says the man. He obviously leaves domestic decisions to his wife. He looks around the room, his eyes sweeping past me, and says, "Let's see the rest of the apartment."

I wait to confront them when they return. It is quite extraordinary, just at the moment when I feel ready to meet the world again, the world refuses to acknowledge my existence. As I wait, I begin to feel angry about the furniture. It is all to do with M. Maurice. He must have removed it, and he doesn't want to speak to me about it. Perhaps he is stealing the whole flat from my aunt. I go and stand by the window, so that he must see me as soon as he comes in. I hear them returning, and M. Maurice ushers them back into the sitting room. The Americans sit on the sofa and M. Maurice draws up a dining chair. The tapestry armchair, I notice, is also missing.

"Really, M. Maurice," I say, tapping him on the shoulder, "may we please speak about the furniture."

M. Maurice is looking inquiringly at the couple. "Well, m'sieur, madame?"

"The trouble, as always, is the price," says the woman. "Paris prices seem to be way ahead of the States."

"Mme Lavalle has not been anxious to sell in the past, but it seems they would now rather live outside Paris when they retire and will sell at some point, but they are prepared to wait for the right price."

"Then there was that unfortunate business with her niece," says the woman. "That can't make her want to keep the apartment."

"An accident," says M. Maurice with a shrug of regret. "She had not been in good health for some time, and was taking too many medicaments. Fortunately, we found out quite soon because Mme Dumas upstairs was worried when there was no reply from this apartment after her bathroom had flooded. Otherwise it might have been a matter of weeks."

"How very sad," says the woman. "What a waste."

I do not believe them. Today, more than ever, I want to leave the apartment. I can see the trees outside, the new leaves ruffled by the breeze. I now know, more than anything, that I want to be part of life again. I can hear the pigeons in the nearby garden, and I am aware of the warmth of the sun on my skin. All this energy, all this love that I have been feeling, is evidence that I am still here. I am more alive than I have ever been.

"I think perhaps we ought to go on to 53 Rue de la Tour," says the woman. "Not that it's much cheaper. What do you think, Jack?"

"I'll see whatever you say," says Jack. M. Maurice smiles and nods and they get up to go.

"No," I cry out. "Don't go. Look at me. I'm still here."

How can they leave without even seeing me?

"Look at me! For God's sake, look at me!"

I have moved from the window to the centre of the room and am standing in front of the mirror. Reflected in it is the mirror opposite which reflects back the view of the room. That is all there is, an empty room.

"Please look at me." My voice has become faint and there is a chill going through me, a feeling of absolute coldness.

"I'm not sure I like this area, anyway," says the woman. "I want somewhere with more life going on."

By the door, she looks back and stares towards the fireplace. Her eyes are momentarily confused, then she turns away.

"What is it, Linda?" asks Jack. He is impatient to get on.

"That's odd, I thought I saw something move, for a moment. But it was only a shadow on the wallpaper."

They left the apartment and locked the door behind them. It was eleven on a fine morning in June.

BASIL COPPER
The Second Passenger

*Basil Copper (b.1924), described as "unquestion-
ably one of the greatest living macabre writers",
has had his best horror stories from the 1960s
and 70s collected in* Not After Nightfall (1967),
From Evil's Pillow (1973), When Footsteps Echo
(1975), And Afterward the Dark (1977), Here
Be Daemons (1978) *and* Voices of Doom (1980).
*One of his best ghost stories, "The Second Pas-
senger" was originally published in* The Dark
Brotherhood Journal (1973).

Mr. Reginald Braintree sat quite still in the corner of the
fusty third-class compartment, with his feet up on the
opposite seat and a copy of *The Times* spread-eagled on his lap.
The carriage was quite empty and had been since he left Charing
Cross so the liberty was pardonable. Outside, the blurred
scenery of wood and stream whirled effortlessly by, the white-
grey smoke from the engine fogging the windows and restricting
the vision. The noise of the wheels went monotonously on and
on, as though some tireless hand were rhythmically beating time
in some fantastic computation.

Dusk was closing in and the carriage lights shed their yellow
glare on to the wan face of Mr. Braintree, making his usually
pale features look macabre. They heightened the sombre effect
of his never genial eyes, distorting them into black pits, from
which his pupils gleamed, greenishly and balefully. His mouth
was a mere slit in the twilight, the shadow underneath making
it resemble a letter box which, metaphorically speaking, it was.

He was dressed in a faded suit of salt and pepper broadcloth.
His stout brown shoes were scratched and worn but they did not
look old; his hat was battered, yet it did not seem antique. In
short Mr. Braintree was a successful man who could afford to
dress well yet did not choose to, a thing not entirely unknown
among a certain class of business men.

His paper, stirred by some motion of the train, slipped unheeded to the floor, and he did not bother to pick it up. His figure slumped at the sudden motion when the carriage rounded a bend and then he automatically recovered himself as it regained the straight. In a way the railway was something like the course of Mr. Braintree's own career; it ploughed remorselessly on, unable to leave its designated route and when at length it came to a hill, instead of going round, it smashed an impetuous path through.

There were times when Mr. Braintree lapsed into compassion but they were few for he did not care to make a cult of weakness, as he called it. His first day as an office boy in a stockbroking firm in Cheapside many years before had taught him the efficacy of force, a lesson he had never forgotten; and which ever since he had used to determine the course of his life. The occasion was common enough, yet it left an everlasting impression.

It appeared that it was the duty of a certain Samuel Briggs, also a species of clerk, to fill the inkwells and run the errands, in addition to his other multifarious duties. However, being the type of person who will never do a thing if he can get someone else to do it for him, he somewhat naturally chose the moment of the newcomer's arrival to assert his authority. Unfortunately, from his point of view, the other clerks were big and determined men, not at all disposed to run his errands for him, but the entry of the diminutive Braintree altered the picture completely.

His first commissions were executed willingly enough and without suspicion, but later, one of the other employees having let something drop, young Braintree began to see the true situation, and not having a vacuum where his brain should be, sought to escape from this unwelcome and decidedly irksome yoke. The first hint of mutiny was met with black looks and a clenching of fists which, although subduing Braintree for a time, did not permanently dampen his resolution to be rid of his bondage.

The next time the dapper young gentleman told him to empty the waste paper baskets and be quick about it this spate of rhetoric being accompanied by a well-propelled kick in the rear, the youngster's temper flared. Impetuously turning, he flung the contents of the inkwell he was carrying full into the sneering, weakly handsome face of the clerk before him.

The next moments were somewhat hazy for he was picked up violently, shaken like a rat and, with a vicious back-handed slap in the face, hurled unceremoniously downstairs.

As he dazedly came to rest in the hallway he heard the malicious laughter of his contemporaries floating down towards him, and the sound was like gall to his already bitter soul. Spitting curses through the mask of blood that covered his features, he swore then and there to get even with his tormentor if it took him all his life. This resolve was interrupted by the appearance of the bedraggled form of Mr. Samuel Briggs at the head of the stairway, wiping some of the ink off his mottled countenance and transferring it to a convenient towel.

But although defeated physically, Braintree had gained an enormous moral victory over his opponent, for the confidence of the bully had been shaken, and from then on his manner was less assured. The younger boy received fewer commissions and they gradually stopped. But his dark brooding spirit still rankled over the day of his degradation and the promise he had compacted with himself remained as implacable as ever.

As he grew older his feelings became more subdued and subtle, and it would have needed a very shrewd and worldly person to see that the two clerks who worked so amicably together were in reality deadly enemies, each determined to usurp the other in the estimation of their employer, should the opportunity present itself. If it were Braintree who arrived early one morning, filled the inkwells, tidied the office and waded through arrears of work, then one could be sure that it was Briggs who sat up half the night sweating over a mountain of paper.

Was it not Briggs who cycled five miles through the pouring rain to old Mr. Steyning's house with some important documents that had been overlooked? And yet had not Braintree been just as meritorious in returning from a fortnight's holiday on his first day away, in order to tell Mr. Steyning of an important business speculation which he had learned en route? Who ran for the doctor when Mrs. Steyning was ill? Briggs, of course. And who summoned the courage to risk serious injury by rescuing the old man's daughter from the wheels of a bus? Braintree, naturally.

Finally, what cloak of generosity masked the actions of two unscrupulous men who eventually jointly subscribed the money needed to put the firm on its feet again? As sure as the earth revolves round the sun it was Briggs and Braintree, but that their actions were motivated by quixotic impulse is beyond imagination. Yet later it did not seem that they had been risking anything at all. For when their employer's anxiety with regard to the future of his organisation was allayed, he naturally turned to the men who had made this reversal possible.

The result was a junior partnership for both of them, an opportunity which neither of them neglected. From that time onwards their careers were set. With the passing of the years, while increasing in prosperity, they never forgot for a single moment that they were enemies, and though no one could have divined it, the germs of hatred were breeding and multiplying within their respective brains.

Things might have gone on like this for ever except for one fact. Mr. Steyning was growing old, his business prospering and with two capable junior partners to all appearances contentedly running things, he saw no reason why he should not sit back and put the reins unreservedly into their hands. So he retired and sealed their fates by so doing.

Without the old man's restraining influence the two men immediately fell apart again, and although no one would have seen any outward difference between them, their consuming passions were more openly manifest than usual. Their morning greeting was elaborately polite, almost to the verge of irony, while now and again, the masks slipping, cutting remarks would whip about the office, to the bewilderment of those who heard them.

Everyone began to suspect that something was wrong, and the clerks, on the same stools which had accommodated their employers years before, to whisper and gossip among themselves. The business too, began to suffer. Each of the partners, in his eagerness to outdo the other, eventually deprived himself of the benefits of their transactions. With the curb of Mr. Steyning's presence acting as a restraint to their impatient spirits they were safe; without him they were lost.

The affair swiftly progressed to an open rift, culminating in Braintree's discovery of Briggs' misdemeanours. The whole truth of the matter was never really discovered; some said women, some said horses were the reason, but the upshot of it was that Briggs had been spending above even his considerable income. Neither had families to tie them down in any way, for both men were bachelors, and thus there were no domestic questions.

For almost a year, considerable sums of money had been taken by Briggs and only covered by dexterous and skilful handling of the books. Perhaps it was a malicious and selfish ego that enjoyed and exulted in the fact of cheating a hated partner out of the money, or a pressing and desperate need, the step being taken only after long consideration; the truth will possibly never be known.

Discovery could not be postponed indefinitely; the misdemeanour uncovered some time. The denouement occurred on a cold March morning, when the rime sparkled on pavement and railing and fog hung like a thick yellow cloak over the city. Braintree was in an unusually foul temper, even for him, and strode through the outer office, looking neither right nor left, responding with a grunt to the chorus of salutations from the staff.

Briggs, a tall, sallow man with pock-marked cheeks was already seated at his desk sipping a measure of whisky from the cap of a silver hip flask, to take "the nip off the air", as he explained it.

"It would be more to the point if you attended more closely to the firm's affairs, instead of indulging in that debasing practice," Braintree sneered, for he was a strict teetotaller. The other, however, said nothing, which was unusual for him and the younger man commented on it.

Briggs' eyes were beginning to burn angrily and he half slewed on his seat, his right hand methodically screwing the cap of his flask; he twisted it savagely as though it were the thick head of his enemy. He opened his mouth to spit out a reply when the door was pushed back by the head clerk; he looked agitated and white.

"It's about the accounts, sir," he jerked hesitantly.

Braintree excused himself and went off irritably; if there was one thing he disliked it was any interruption to the smooth routine of the office. He was away a long time and Briggs sat staring moodily at the swirling fog outside the window; he made no attempt to deal with the jumble of documents on the desk before him. He was still sitting there when Braintree came back. He glanced coldly at his partner before crossing to his desk. He took something from a drawer and then re-locked it.

"I shall be some time," he told Briggs in a hostile voice.

The door clicked to behind him. Briggs took another swig from the flask and re-stoppered it. He toyed idly with a bunch of keys, his hands suddenly sweaty. Perhaps he did not move into the outer office because he was already acquainted with what would be found there. The clock ticked away while he listened with straining ears. There was the confused murmur of voices, mingled with the jingling of keys and rustling of papers.

The whispered consultations were still going on when Briggs left for lunch; they went on throughout the afternoon and eventually night fell again. Instead of leaving for his home as he usually did Briggs remained behind at his desk. The fog pressed sullenly against the window. He heard the outer office door close behind the last of the clerks, waited for the heavy footfall of his partner. It was nearly seven o'clock before the door of the inner office opened again.

The stocky form of the younger partner appeared. His manner was extremely mild when he spoke, yet the curious pose of his body suggested the coiling of a steel spring. Briggs had not moved; he gazed abstractedly across the office, as though trying to discern whether the Chinaman on the commercial calendar was grimacing or smiling. He felt like doing neither. He lifted his face, his forehead slightly shiny, and coughed; a nervous, startled cough, which sounded incongruous in the pregnant stillness.

"Well?"

It was Braintree who spoke. He stood by the back of the other's chair, his thick knuckles gleaming white where he clenched the woodwork.

"You know?" the other answered dully. "You've found out?"

Braintree nodded. He kept remarkable control. His voice was dry and smooth, as though a life's ambition had been achieved. "But twenty thousand, Briggs . . ."

He looked curiously at the still figure of his partner.

"How did you expect to get away with it?"

Briggs turned away from Braintree with a convulsive movement. He put his head in his hands.

"I wouldn't expect you to understand," he said. "What are you going to do?"

"Do?" said Braintree. He looked at his watch. "I've already done it. I've sent Simmonds round with a note to the station. The police should be here in twenty minutes."

"A bit premature aren't you?" Briggs sneered.

Red stood out in vivid patches on his cheeks and his breathing was becoming laboured.

"I don't think so," said Braintree smoothly. "It is a criminal matter, after all. Such a huge sum of money. And your personal accounts tally with the discrepancy."

He started back as Briggs got up with a sudden movement.

"You're enjoying this, aren't you?" said Briggs thickly.

Braintree declined to answer. He went to the window and watched the swirling fog. He toyed nervously with the heavy office ruler in his hand.

"I suppose it's no good asking you for an hour's grace?" said Briggs heavily.

Braintree shook his head. He had a sardonic smile on his lips. "None at all," he said. "You should have thought of this before. I must advise you against attempting to leave. I should be forced to prevent it."

He hefted the massive, metal-edged ruler in his hand uncertainly. Indeed, he was a somewhat incongruous figure and obviously ill-fitted for the self-appointed task. Briggs stared incredulously at him for a moment. Then he gave a short, barking laugh.

"I'm off," he said. "To blazes with you and your police."

He strode impetuously forward, thrusting Braintree aside. The partner fell against the window; he felt a sharp pain as his hand broke the glass. The sudden shock stung him into action. Briggs was at the door when Braintree reached him. The two men began a silent struggle; then Braintree was thrown aside. He fell against the desk this time and barked his shin; this second, unexpected pain sent a spurt of anger through him. Galvanised into action he struck at Briggs again and again with the heavy ruler.

Briggs gave a hoarse cry. The big man turned. Braintree saw blood on his face, the eyes filmy and horrified. He felt sick. The older man fell asprawl with a crash. His head caught the edge of the desk with a horrifying crack. He lay still. Braintree bent over him, searched for the steady pump of the heart, failed to find it. His own heart stood still.

Then another sound sent the adrenalin flooding through his own system. He started dragging the body of Briggs along the floor towards the cupboard as heavy footsteps sounded on the stair.

It was nearly eleven before Mr. Braintree reached the Essex marshes. It had been a long and tiring drive through East London and the little Morris was not behaving well. Braintree believed it might be the effect of the damp weather and one defective plug. He had not liked it at all when the vehicle had stalled completely at a traffic lights in Walthamstow.

But now he was clear of the more populous areas and he breathed more easily, the car positively humming along. The moon was up and its pallid light cast shadows across the humped form of Briggs on the back seat, covered by thick layers of motoring rugs. It had been a miracle that Briggs had driven his own car in from Surrey that day, Braintree reflected.

Once he had got rid of the police by telling them that Briggs had left, it had been fairly simple to bring the car to the seldom-used side alley and take the body down the back stair. Fairly simple, but how tiring, Braintree thought. Now, he had the perfect answer to the problem.

With Briggs' disappearance he had only to drive his car back to the nearest Tube and abandon it. When it was found it would merely add substance to the circumstance that Briggs had been unable to face the music and had fled. Braintree would have to stay in town tonight; that was the only flaw in his plan. By the time he got back to Central London his last train from Charing Cross would have gone and he had no desire to wait for the early morning paper train in this weather.

He must be careful, that was all; he had no luggage. He would simply register under another name, carefully choosing a small family hotel away from the city centre and tell them the truth; that he had missed his train. There must be many businessmen who were in a similar predicament, every evening. The more Braintree thought about it on his long, foggy drive, the more he liked it. He was free of the villages at last and making for a spot he remembered from years before. Unless it had been built up since then.

He took a rutted side road, the Morris protesting at the surface, and drove carefully along it. The fog had lifted with his clearing the city and he knew where he was. When he had driven as far as he could go, he left the car; the next hour, dragging Briggs' heavy form through the undergrowth was the most tiring he had ever known. When his feet began to squelch in mud he looked down; his prints were already beginning to fill with water. It was nearly time. He got his hands under Briggs' armpits and dragged him the last few yards to the top of the bank.

He was sweating as he gave the final push. The body rocked, sagged and then started to slide down the steep slope. The moon gilded the dead face as it slid to a halt; green scum parted, viscous mud sucked at the corpse. It began to sink slowly, bubbles of marsh gas bursting in foul, scummy pustules on the surface of the swamp. Mr. Braintree waited for twenty minutes until the entire corpse had been consumed. The last thing to go was one of Briggs' hands. It seemed to wave a valediction at Braintree as the fingers slowly disappeared beneath the surface.

Braintree shivered. It was growing cold again. Or the effect of his exercise was wearing off. He waited a few minutes more and finally the bubbles stopped coming to the top. The green scum of the surface resumed its interrupted sway. Mr. Braintree made his way heavily back to the road. No one would ever find Briggs now. That swamp was bottomless, he'd heard in years gone by; what it took it kept. He looked at his watch. It was already nearly one a.m. It seemed like a long drive back towards the city.

The train roared on through the night and still Mr. Braintree sat comfortably sprawled with his feet up and his antique hat poised beside him. Presently there came the hiss of brakes and the carriage shuddered and was still. Came the burst of escaping steam and a nervous little pulse beat somewhere under the floorboards. Figures went by in the corridor and, after glancing at the uninviting figure of the stockbroker, their owners passed on.

Carriage doors were slamming and the hoarse, inarticulate cry of a porter drifted up wind. "Sevenoaks, Sevenoaks."

A railway employee came down the carriages, slamming the doors. He caught sight of Mr. Braintree's recumbent form and slid back the door of the compartment, annoyance on his face.

"This train doesn't go any farther, sir."

Mr. Braintree's body sagged, asprawl at an awkward angle.

The porter bent over him, hesitated. His nostrils were assailed by a loathsome stench. He saw then, in the dim radiance of the carriage lighting, a patch of damp green slime on the floor. It glimmered wetly and the stench seemed to come from this. Fighting his nerves the porter seized Mr. Braintree by the shoulder.

The dead face fell forward and the man was conscious of the slime on the features; something like moss clustered round the nostrils and a thin driblet shuddered from the corner of the mouth. A shadow fell across the carriage and the figure of a tall, burly man passed in the corridor. The porter gave a hoarse shout and stumbled away from the corpse of Braintree.

"Just a minute, sir," he called after the tall figure. "There's been an accident."

On the platform the big man marched forward under the lamps without stopping. At every footprint green slime seemed to spring up on the surface of the platform. The porter cursed as he almost sprawled on the muck. There was that disgusting smell again. The big man went on. The porter increased his pace.

"Stop him!" he bawled at a group of railwaymen who were gossiping at one end of the platform.

They looked up curiously as the form of the big man went steadily up the steps of the bridge. He did not seem to be hurrying but the porter was unable to gain on him.

He shouted again and this time the group was stirred into action. Its members ran up the stairs, searching for the tall figure. One of them turned as the porter came up.

"What was it? What was it?" he said, his eyes wide with fear. There were patches of green slime on the steps of the bridge. A putrefying stench came to them down the wind. But the tall, hurrying figure of the big man was never seen again.

RALPH A. CRAM
No.252 Rue M. Le Prince

*Ralph Adams Cram (1863–1942) was one of
America's leading architects, reviving mediaeval
Gothic forms, particularly in the design of
churches. Among his many books were* The
Ruined Abbeys of Great Britain, The Gothic
Quest, My Life in Architecture, *and a collection
of weird and supernatural tales*, Black Spirits and
White (1895), *from which the following story is
taken.*

When in May, 1886, I found myself at last in Paris, I
naturally determined to throw myself on the charity of an
old chum of mine, Eugene Marie d'Ardeche, who had forsaken
Boston a year or more ago on receiving word of the death of
an aunt who had left him such property as she possessed. I
fancy this windfall surprised him not a little, for the relations
between the aunt and nephew had never been cordial, judging
from Eugene's remarks touching the lady, who was, it seems, a
more or less wicked and witch-like old person, with a penchant
for black magic, at least such was the common report.

Why she should leave all her property to d'Ardeche, no one
could tell, unless it was that she felt his rather hobbledehoy
tendencies towards Buddhism and occultism might some day
lead him to her own unhallowed height of questionable illumination. To be sure d'Ardeche reviled her as a bad old woman,
being himself in that state of enthusiastic exaltation which
sometimes accompanies a boyish fancy for occultism; but in
spite of his distant and repellent attitude, Mlle. Blaye de Tartas
made him her sole heir, to the violent wrath of a questionable
old party known to infamy as the Sar Torrevieja, the "King of
the Sorcerers". This malevolent old portent, whose grey and
crafty face was often seen in the Rue M. Le Prince during the
life of Mlle. de Tartas, had, it seems, fully expected to enjoy
her small wealth after her death; and when it appeared that

she had left him only the contents of the gloomy old house in the Quartier Latin, giving the house itself and all else of which she died possessed to her nephew in America, the Sar proceeded to remove everything from the place, and then to curse it elaborately and comprehensively, together with all those who should ever dwell therein.

Whereupon he disappeared.

This final episode was the last word I received from Eugene, but I knew the number of the house, 252 Rue M. Le Prince. So, after a day or two given to a first cursory survey of Paris, I started across the Seine to find Eugene and compel him to do the honours of the city.

Everyone who knows the Latin Quarter knows the Rue M. Le Prince, running up the hill towards the Garden of the Luxembourg. It is full of queer houses and odd corners—or was in '86—and certainly No. 252 was, when I found it, quite as queer as any. It was nothing but a doorway, a black arch of old stone between and under two new houses painted yellow. The effect of this bit of seventeenth century masonry, with its dirty old doors, and rusty broken lantern sticking gaunt and grim out over the narrow sidewalk, was, in its frame of fresh plaster, sinister in the extreme.

I wondered if I had made a mistake in the number; it was quite evident that no one lived behind those cobwebs. I went into the doorway of one of the new hotels and interviewed the concierge.

No, M. d'Ardeche did not live there, though to be sure he owned the mansion; he himself resided in Meudon, in the country house of the late Mlle. de Tartas. Would Monsieur like the number and the street?

Monsieur would like them extremely, so I took the card that the concierge wrote for me, and forthwith started for the river, in order that I might take a steamboat for Meudon. By one of those coincidences which happen so often, being quite inexplicable, I had not gone twenty paces down the street before I ran directly into the arms of Eugene d'Ardeche. In three minutes we were sitting in the queer little garden of the Chien Bleu, drinking vermouth and absinthe, and talking it all over.

"You do not live in your aunt's house?" I said at last, interrogatively.

"No, but if this sort of thing keeps on I shall have to. I like Meudon much better, and the house is perfect, all furnished, and nothing in it newer than the last century. You must come out with me tonight and see it. I have got a jolly room fixed up for my Buddha. But there is something wrong with this house opposite. I can't keep a tenant in it—not four days. I have had three, all within six months, but the stories have gone around and a man would as soon think of hiring the Cour des Comptes to live in as Number 252. It is notorious. The fact is, it is haunted the worst way."

I laughed and ordered more vermouth.

"That is all right. It is haunted all the same, or enough to keep it empty, and the funny part is that no one knows *how* it is haunted. Nothing is ever seen, nothing heard. As far as I can find out, people just have the horrors there, and have them so bad they have to go to the hospital afterwards. I have one ex-tenant in the Bicêtre now. So the house stands empty, and as it covers considerable ground and is taxed for a lot, I don't know what to do about it. I think I'll either give it to that child of sin, Torrevieja, or else go and live in it myself. I shouldn't mind the ghosts, I am sure."

"Did you ever stay there?"

"No, but I have always intended to, and in fact I came up here today to see a couple of rake-hell fellows I know, Fargeau and Duchesne, doctors in the Clinical Hospital beyond here, up by the Parc Mont Souris. They promised that they would spend the night with me some time in my aunt's house—which is called around here, you must know, 'la Bouche d'Enfer'—and I thought perhaps they would make it this week, if they can get off duty. Come up with me while I see them, and then we can go across the river to Véfour's and have some luncheon, you can get your things at the Chatham, and we will go out to Meudon, where of course you will spend the night with me."

The plan suited me perfectly, so we went up to the hospital, found Fargeau, who declared that he and Duchesne were ready for anything, the nearer the real "bouche d'enfer" the better; that the following Thursday they would both be off duty for the night, and that on that day they would join in an attempt to outwit the devil and clear up the mystery of No. 252.

"Does M. l'Américain go with us?" asked Fargeau.

"Why of course," I replied, "I intend to go, and you must not refuse me, d'Ardeche; I decline to be put off. Here is a chance for you to do the honours of your city in a manner which is faultless. Show me a real live ghost, and I will forgive Paris for having lost the Jardin Mabille."

So it was settled.

Later we went down to Meudon and ate dinner in the terrace room of the villa, which was all that d'Ardeche had said, and more, so utterly was its atmosphere that of the seventeenth century. At dinner Eugene told me more about his late aunt, and the queer goings on in the old house.

Mlle. Blaye lived, it seems, all alone, except for one female servant of her own age; a severe, taciturn creature, with massive Breton features and a Breton tongue, whenever she vouchsafed to use it. No one was ever seen to enter the door of No. 252 except Jeanne the servant and the Sar Torrevieja, the latter coming constantly from none knew whither, and always entering, *never leaving*. Indeed, the neighbours, who for eleven years had watched the old sorcerer sidle crab-wise up to the bell almost every day, declared vociferously that *never* had he been seen to leave the house. Once, when they decided to keep absolute guard, the watcher, none other than Maître Garceau of the Chien Bleu, after keeping his eyes fixed on the door from ten o'clock one morning when the Sar arrived until four in the afternoon, during which time the door was unopened (he knew this, for had he not gummed a ten-centime stamp over the joint and was not the stamp unbroken?) nearly fell down when the sinister figure of Torrevieja slid wickedly by him with a dry "Pardon, Monsieur!" and disappeared again through the black doorway.

This was curious, for No. 252 was entirely surrounded by houses, its only windows opening on a courtyard into which no eye could look from the hotels of the Rue M. Le Prince and the Rue de l'École, and the mystery was one of the choice possessions of the Latin Quarter.

Once a year the austerity of the place was broken, and the denizens of the whole quarter stood open-mouthed watching many carriages drive up to No. 252, many of them private, not a few with crests on the door panels, from all of them descending veiled female figures and men with coat collars turned up. Then followed curious sounds of music from within, and those whose houses joined the blank walls of No. 252 became for the moment popular, for by placing the ear against the wall strange music could distinctly be heard, and the sound of monotonous chanting voices now and then. By dawn the last guest would have departed, and for another year the hotel of Mlle. de Tartas was ominously silent.

Eugene declared that he believed it was a celebration of "Walpurgisnacht", and certainly appearances favoured such a fancy.

"A strange thing about the whole affair is," he said, "the fact that everyone in the street swears that about a month ago, while I was out in Concarneau for a visit, the music and voices were heard again, just as when my revered aunt was in the flesh. The house was perfectly empty, as I tell you, so it is quite possible that the good people were enjoying an hallucination."

I must acknowledge that these stories did not reassure me; in fact, as Thursday came near, I began to regret a little my determination to spend the night in the house. I was too vain to back down, however, and the perfect coolness of the two doctors, who ran down Tuesday to Meudon to make a few arrangements, caused me to swear that I would die of fright before I would flinch. I suppose I believed more or less in ghosts, I am sure now that I am older I believe in them, there are in fact few things I can *not* believe. Two or three inexplicable things had happened to me, although this was before my adventure with Rendel in Paestum I had a strong predisposition to believe some things that I could not explain, wherein I was out of sympathy with the age.

Well, to come to the memorable night of the twelfth of June, we had made our preparations, and after depositing a big bag inside the doors of No. 252, went across to the Chien Bleu, where Fargeau and Duchesne turned up promptly, and we sat down to the best dinner Père Garceau could create.

I remember I hardly felt that the conversation was in good taste. It began with various stories of Indian fakirs and Oriental jugglery, matters in which Eugene was curiously well read, swerved to the horrors of the great Sepoy mutiny, and thus to reminiscences of the dissecting-room. By this time we had drunk more or less, and Duchesne launched into a photographic and Zolaesque account of the only time (as he said) when he was possessed of the panic of fear; namely, one night many years ago, when he was locked by accident into the dissecting-room of the Loucine, together with several cadavers of a rather unpleasant nature. I ventured to protest mildly against the choice of subjects, the result being a perfect carnival of horrors, so that when we finally drank our last *crème de cacao* and started for "la Bouche d'Enfer", my nerves were in a somewhat rocky condition.

It was just ten o'clock when we came into the street. A hot dead wind drifted in great puffs through the city, and ragged masses of vapour swept the purple sky; an unsavoury night altogether, one of those nights of hopeless lassitude when one feels, if one is at home, like doing nothing but drink mint juleps and smoke cigarettes.

Eugene opened the creaking door, and tried to light one of the lanterns; but the gusty wind blew out every match, and we finally had to close the outer doors before we could get a light. At last we had all the lanterns going, and I began to look around curiously. We were in a long, vaulted passage, partly carriageway, partly foot-path, perfectly bare but for the street refuse which had drifted in with eddying winds. Beyond lay the courtyard, a curious place rendered more curious still by the fitful moonlight and the flashing of four dark lanterns. The place had evidently been once a most noble palace. Opposite rose the oldest portion, a three-storey wall of the time of Francis I., with a great wisteria vine covering half. The wings on either side were more modern, seventeenth century, and ugly, while towards the street was nothing but a flat unbroken wall.

The great bare court, littered with bits of paper blown in by the wind, fragments of packing cases, and straw, mysterious with flashing lights and flaunting shadows, while low masses of torn vapour drifted overhead, hiding, then revealing, the stars, and all in absolute silence, not even the sounds of the streets entering this prison-like place, was weird and uncanny in the extreme. I must confess that already I began to feel a slight disposition towards the horrors, but with that curious inconsequence which so often happens in the case of those who are deliberately growing scared, I could think of nothing more reassuring than those delicious verses of Lewis Carroll's——

> 'Just the place for a Snark! I have said it twice,
> That alone should encourage the crew.
> Just the place for a Snark! I have said it thrice,
> What I tell you three times is true——'

which kept repeating themselves over and over in my brain with feverish insistence.

Even the medical students had stopped their chaffing, and were studying the surroundings gravely.

"There is one thing certain," said Fargeau, "*anything* might have happened here without the slightest chance of discovery. Did ever you see such a perfect place for lawlessness?"

"And *anything* might happen here now, with the same certainty of impunity," continued Duchesne, lighting his pipe, the snap of the match making us all start. "D'Ardeche, your lamented relative was certainly well fixed; she had full scope here for her traditional experiments in demonology."

"Curse me if I don't believe that those same traditions were more or less founded on fact," said Eugene. "I never saw this court under these conditions before, but I could believe anything now. What's that?"

"Nothing but a door slamming," said Duchesne, loudly.

"Well, I wish doors wouldn't slam in houses that have been empty for eleven months."

"It is irritating"—and Duchesne slipped his arm through mine—"but we must take things as they come. Remember we have to deal not only with the spectral lumber left here by your scarlet aunt, but as well with the supererogatory curse of that hell-cat Torrevieja. Come on! Let's get inside before the hour arrives for the sheeted dead to squeak and gibber in these lonely halls. Light your pipes, your tobacco is a sure protection against 'your whoreson dead bodies'; light up and move on."

We opened the hall door and entered a vaulted stone vestibule, full of dust, and cobwebby.

"There is nothing on this floor," said Eugene, "except servants' rooms and offices, and I don't believe there is anything wrong with them. I never heard that there was, anyway. Let's go upstairs."

So far as we could see, the house was apparently perfectly uninteresting inside, all eighteenth century work, the façade of the main building being, with the vestibule, the only portion of the Francis I. work.

"The place was burned during the Terror," said Eugene, "for my great-uncle, from whom Mlle. de Tartas inherited it, was a good and true Royalist; he went to Spain after the Revolution, and did not come back until the accession of Charles the Tenth, when he restored the house, and then died, enormously old. This explains why it is all so new."

The old Spanish sorcerer to whom Mlle. de Tartas had left her personal property had done his work thoroughly. The house was absolutely empty, even the wardrobes and bookcases built in had been carried away; we went through room after room, finding all absolutely dismantled, only the windows and doors with their casings, the parquet floors, and the florid Renaissance mantels remaining.

"I feel better," remarked Fargeau. "The house may be haunted, but it don't look it, certainly; it is the most respectable place imaginable."

"Just you wait," replied Eugene. "These are only the state apartments, which my aunt seldom used, except, perhaps, on her annual 'Walpurgisnacht'. Come upstairs and I will show you a better *mise en scène*."

On this floor, the rooms fronting the court—the sleeping-rooms—were quite small ("They are the bad rooms all the same," said Eugene); four of them, all just as ordinary in appearance as those below. A corridor ran behind them connecting with the wing corridor, and from this opened a door, unlike any of the other doors in that it was covered with green baize, somewhat moth-eaten. Eugene selected a key from the bunch he carried, unlocked the door, and with some difficulty forced it to swing inward; it was as heavy as the door of a safe.

"We are now," he said, "on the very threshold of hell itself; these rooms in here were my scarlet aunt's unholy of unholies. I never let them with the rest of the house, but keep them as a curiosity. I only wish Torrevieja had kept out; as it was, he looted them, as he did the rest of the house, and nothing is left but the walls and ceiling and floor. They are something, however, and may suggest what the former condition must have been. Tremble and enter."

The first apartment was a kind of anteroom, a cube of perhaps twenty feet each way, without windows, and with no door except that by which we entered, and another to the right. Walls, floor, and ceiling were covered with a black lacquer, brilliantly polished, that flashed the light of our lanterns in a thousand intricate reflections. It was like the inside of an enormous Japanese box, and about as empty. From this we passed to another room, and here we nearly dropped our lanterns. The room was circular, thirty feet or so in diameter, covered by a hemispherical dome; walls and ceiling were dark blue, spotted with gold stars; and reaching from floor to floor across the dome stretched a colossal figure in red lacquer of a nude woman kneeling, her head touching the lintel of the door through which we had entered, her arms forming its sides, with the forearms extended and stretching along the walls until they met the long feet. The most astounding, misshapen, absolutely terrifying thing, I think, I ever saw. From the navel hung a great white object, like the traditional roc's egg of the Arabian Nights. The floor was of red lacquer, and in it was inlaid a pentagram the size of the room, made of wide strips of brass. In the centre of this pentagram was a circular disk of black stone, slightly saucer-shaped, with a small outlet in the middle.

The effect of the room was simply crushing, with this gigantic red figure crouched over it all; the staring eyes fixed on one, no matter what his position. None of us spoke, so oppressive was the whole thing.

The third room was like the first in dimensions, but instead of being black it was entirely sheathed with plates of brass, walls, ceiling, and floor—tarnished now, and turning green, but still brilliant under the lantern light. In the middle stood an oblong altar of porphyry, its longer dimensions on the axis of the suite of rooms, and at one end, opposite the range of doors, a pedestal of black basalt.

This was all. Three rooms stranger than these, even in their emptiness, it would be hard to imagine. In Egypt, in India, they would not be entirely out of place, but here in Paris, in a commonplace hotel, in the Rue M. Le Prince, they were incredible.

We retraced our steps, Eugene closed the iron door with its baize covering, and we went into one of the front chambers and sat down, looking at each other.

"Nice party, your aunt," said Fargeau. "Nice old party, with amiable tastes; I am glad we are not to spend the night in *those* rooms."

"What do you suppose she did in there?" inquired Duchesne. "I know more or less about black art, but that series of rooms is too much for me."

"My impression is," said d'Ardeche, "that the brazen room was a kind of sanutuary containing some image or other on the basalt base, while the stone in front was really an altar—what the nature of the sacrifice might be I don't even guess. The round room may have been used for invocations and incantations. The pentagram looks like it. Anyway it is all just as weird and *fin de siècle* as I can well imagine. Look here, it is nearly twelve, let's dispose of ourselves, if we are going to hunt this thing down."

The four chambers on this floor of the old house were those said to be haunted, the wings being quite innocent, and, so far as we knew, the floors below. It was arranged that we should each occupy a room, leaving the doors open with the lights burning, and at the slightest cry or knock we were all to rush at once to the room from which the warning sound might come. There was no communication between the rooms, to be sure, but, as the doors all opened into the corridor, every sound was plainly audible.

The last room fell to me, and I looked it over carefully.

It seemed innocent enough, a commonplace, square, rather lofty Parisian sleeping-room, finished in wood painted white, with a small marble mantel, a dusty floor of inlaid maple and cherry, walls hung with an ordinary French paper, apparently quite new, and two deeply embrasured windows looking out on the court.

I opened the swinging sash with some trouble, and sat down in the window seat with my lantern beside me trained on the only door, which gave on the corridor.

The wind had gone down, and it was very still without—still and hot. The masses of luminous vapour were gathering thickly overhead, no longer urged by the gusty wind. The great masses of rank wisteria leaves, with here and there a second blossoming of purple flowers, hung dead over the window in the sluggish air. Across the roofs I could hear the sound of a belated *fiacre* in the streets below. I filled my pipe again and waited.

For a time the voices of the men in the other rooms were a companionship, and at first I shouted to them now and then, but my voice echoed rather unpleasantly through the long corridors, and had a suggestive way of reverberating around the left wing beside me, and coming out at a broken window at its extremity like the voice of another man. I soon gave up my attempts at conversation, and devoted myself to the task of keeping awake.

It was not easy; why did I eat that lettuce salad at Père Garceau's? I should have known better. It was making me irresistibly sleepy, and wakefulness was absolutely necessary. It was certainly gratifying to know that I could sleep, that my courage was by me to that extent, but in the interests of science I must keep awake. But almost never, it seemed, had sleep looked so desirable. Half a hundred times, nearly, I would doze for an instant, only to awake with a start, and find my pipe gone out. Nor did the exertion of relighting it pull me together. I struck my match mechanically, and with the first puff dropped off again. It was most vexing. I got up and walked around the room. It was most annoying. My cramped position had almost put both legs to sleep. I could hardly stand. I felt numb, as though with cold. There was no longer any sound from the other rooms, nor from without. I sank down in my window seat. How dark it was growing! I turned up the lantern. That pipe again, how obstinately it kept going out! And my last match was gone. The lantern, too, was *that* going out? I lifted my hand to turn it up again. It felt like lead, and fell beside me.

Then I awoke—absolutely. I remembered the story of "The Haunters and the Haunted". *This* was the Horror. I tried to rise, to cry out. My body was like lead, my tongue was paralysed. I could hardly move my eyes. And the light was going out. There was no question about that. Darker and darker yet; little by little the pattern of the paper was swallowed up in the advancing night. A prickling numbness gathered in every nerve, my right arm slipped without feeling from my lap to my side, and I could not raise it—it swung helpless. A thin, keen humming began in my head, like the cicadas on a hillside in September. The darkness was coming fast.

Yes, this was it. Something was subjecting me, body and mind, to slow paralysis. Physically I was already dead. If I could only hold my mind, my consciousness, I might still be safe, but could I? Could I resist the mad horror of this silence, the deepening dark, the creeping numbness? I knew that, like the man in the ghost story, my only safety lay here.

It had come at last. My body was dead, I could no longer move my eyes. They were fixed in that last look on the place where the door had been, now only a deepening of the dark.

Utter night: the last flicker of the lantern was gone. I sat and waited; my mind was still keen, but how long would it last? There was a limit even to the endurance of the utter panic of fear.

Then the end began. In the velvet blackness came two white eyes, milky, opalescent, small, far away—awful eyes, like a dead dream. More beautiful than I can describe, the flakes of white flame moving from the perimeter inward, disappearing in the centre, like a never ending flow of opal water into a circular tunnel. I could not have moved my eyes had I possessed the power: they devoured the fearful, beautiful orbs that grew slowly, slowly larger, fixed on me, advancing, growing more beautiful, the white flakes of light sweeping more swiftly into the blazing vortices, the awful fascination deepening in its insane intensity as the white, vibrating eyes grew nearer, larger.

Like a hideous and implacable engine of death the eyes of the unknown Horror swelled and expanded until they were close before me, enormous, terrible, and I felt a slow, cold, wet breath propelled with mechanical regularity against my face, enveloping me in its fetid mist, in its charnel-house deadliness.

With ordinary fear goes always a physical terror, but with me in the presence of this unspeakable Thing was only the utter and awful terror of the mind, the mad fear of a prolonged and ghostly nightmare. Again and again I tried to shriek, to make some noise, but physically I was utterly dead. I could only feel myself go mad with the terror of hideous death. The eyes were close on me—their movement so swift that they seemed to be but palpitating flames, the dead breath was around me like the depths of the deepest sea.

Suddenly a wet, icy mouth, like that of a dead cuttle-fish, shapeless, jelly-like, fell over mine. The horror began slowly to draw my life from me, but, as enormous and shuddering folds of palpitating jelly swept sinuously around me, my will came back, my body awoke with the reaction of final fear, and I closed with the nameless death that enfolded me.

What was it that I was fighting? My arms sank through the unresisting mass that was turning me to ice. Moment by moment new folds of cold jelly swept round me, crushing me with the force of Titans. I fought to wrest my mouth from this awful Thing that sealed it, but, if ever I succeeded and caught a single breath, the wet, sucking mass closed over my face again before I could cry out. I think I fought for hours, desperately, insanely, in a silence that was more hideous than any sound—fought until I felt final death at hand, until the memory of all my life rushed over me like a flood, until I no longer had strength to wrench my face from that hellish succubus, until with a last mechanical struggle I fell and yielded to death.

Then I heard a voice say, "If he is dead, I can never forgive myself; I was to blame."

Another replied, "He is not dead, I know we can save him if only we reach the hospital in time. Drive like hell, *cocher!* Twenty francs for you, if you get there in three minutes."

Then there was night again, and nothingness, until I suddenly awoke and stared around. I lay in a hospital ward, very white and sunny, some yellow *fleurs-de-lis* stood beside the head of the pallet, and a tall sister of mercy sat by my side.

To tell the story in a few words, I was in the Hotel Dieu, where the men had taken me that fearful night of the twelfth of June. I asked for Fargeau or Duchesne, and by-and-by the latter came, and sitting beside the bed told me all that I did not know.

It seems that they had sat, each in his room, hour after hour, hearing nothing, very much bored, and disappointed. Soon after two o'clock Fargeau, who was in the next room, called to me to ask if I was awake. I gave no reply, and, after shouting once or twice, he took his lantern and came to investigate. The door was locked on the inside! He instantly called d'Ardeche and Duchesne, and together they hurled themselves against the door. It resisted. Within they could hear irregular footsteps dashing here and there, with heavy breathing. Although frozen with terror, they fought to destroy the door and finally succeeded by using a great slab of marble that formed the shelf of the mantel in Fargeau's room. As the door crashed in, they were suddenly hurled back against the walls of the corridor, as though by an explosion, the lanterns were extinguished, and they found themselves in utter silence and darkness.

As soon as they recovered from the shock, they leaped into the room and fell over my body in the middle of the floor. They lighted one of the lanterns, and saw the strangest sight that can be imagined. The floor and walls to the height of about six feet were running with something that seemed like stagnant water, thick, glutinous, sickening. As for me, I was drenched with the same cursed liquid. The odour of musk was nauseating. They dragged me away, stripped off my clothing, wrapped me in their coats, and hurried to the hospital, thinking me perhaps dead. Soon after sunrise d'Ardeche left the hospital, being assured

190

that I was in a fair way to recovery, with time, and with Fargeau went up to examine by day-light the traces of the adventure that was so nearly fatal. They were too late. Fire engines were coming down the street as they passed the Académie. A neighbour rushed up to d'Ardeche: "Oh Monsieur! What misfortune, yet what fortune! It is true *la Bouche d'Enfer*—I beg pardon, the residence of the lamented Mlle. de Tartas—was burned, but not wholly, only the ancient building. The wings were saved, and for that great credit is due to the brave firemen. Monsieur will remember them, no doubt."

It was quite true. Whether a forgotten lantern, overturned in the excitement, had done the work, or whether the origin of the fire was more supernatural, it was certain that "the Mouth of Hell" was no more. A last engine was pumping slowly as d'Ardeche came up; half a dozen limp, and one distended hose stretched through the *porte cochère*, and within, only the façade of Francis I. remained, draped still with the black stems of the wisteria. Beyond lay a great vacancy, where thin smoke was rising slowly. Every floor was gone, and the strange halls of Mlle. Blaye de Tartas were only a memory.

With d'Ardeche I visited the place last year, stead of the ancient walls was then only a new and ordinary in building, fresh and respectable; yet the wonderful stories of the old *Bouche d'Enfer* still lingered in the Quarter, and will hold there, I do not doubt, until the Day of Judgement.

191

EDMUND CRISPIN
St. Bartholomew's Day

From "No.252, Rue M.Le Prince", we move to another bizarre story set in the environs of Paris, coinciding with the 300th anniversary of the St. Bartholomew's Day Massacre. Edmund Crispin *(pseudonym of Robert Bruce Montgomery, 1921 –78) was one of Britain's most original post-war crime novelists, creator of detective Gervase Fen, and a devotee of the ghost stories of M.R. James. This story first appeared in* Ellery Queen's Mystery Magazine, *February 1975.*

T he town of Clauvères stands to the north of Paris, about seven miles in the direct line from the Arc de Triomphe. Today the metropolis, expanding, has engulfed it and passed beyond; but until recently it could lay some claim to a separate and independent existence. The traveller, if he pauses there at all, will see streets of cobbles, small ugly cafés, a Nineteenth Century church of no architectural interest, and beyond, the scattered peasant holdings on the low range of hills which rise from the banks of the Seine where it bends east toward St. Nicholas. Only if he turns left by the greystone *mairie*, and makes his way beyond the shops and the marketplace, will he find anything to reward him; for a twenty minutes' walk in this direction, along a white, straight, dusty road, lined with tall elms, will bring him to the Château de l'Echarpe.

The Château has long been deserted, long been a museum relic of the *grand siècle*. The tall rooms with their painted ceilings and gilded chairs may be inspected on payment of five francs by anyone curious to recreate the manners of an earlier age. But few are thus curious; there are better châteaux elsewhere, and Versailles itself can be reached in 25 minutes on the bus. For the rest, all that need be said of Clauvères for the purposes of this narrative is that it has one reasonably comfortable inn, the Coq d'Or.

To this inn, in the August of 1872, came an Englishman, a Mr. Rotherham. He seems to have been a man of about 50, of independent means, and a dabbler in the obscure corners of historical research. Despite the rather ostentatious parade of erudition in his letters, he apparently published nothing—if, that is, the catalogue of the Bodleian is to be trusted; and one conceives that his scholarship was less a serious preoccupation than an excuse to the world, and perhaps to himself, for the aimless life of travel which he led. He was unmarried, and his nearest relation was a young nephew to whom he wrote frequently and at length.

Clauvères, though he neither knew nor intended it, was to be the terminus of his last journey. He had caught a particularly slow train from Rouen and was in no very good temper when he drove in a carriage from the station to the inn. The shortage of food and the other discomforts consequent upon the recently concluded Franco-Prussian war further exacerbated him.

"The inn," he writes on the evening of his arrival, "is a mediocre enough place, but the best to be found here; and the poverty which afflicts Paris itself, together with the fatigue and inconvenience of the daily journey here, have decided me to remain until my work is finished. My hostess is a dark, sallow, elderly woman, a widow, with one son, who is of an anarchical disposition, and a fanatical devotee of the new decadent 'poetry' (so-called) represented by Baudelaire, Verlaine, and others of that tribe. This much I gather from the copy of an *advanced* periodical which I discovered him reading.

"My room, on the first story, has three tall windows looking out upon the street, and a large four-poster bed, which appears, however, to be comfortable enough; though I have had removed from it that insanitary abomination so dear to the Gallic mind, the *feather-mattress*. Fortunately the English currency is so valuable to these people in the present wretched plight of the country that I may count upon receiving every attention possible. The only disturbance which I am likely to encounter will be the noise of the market carts rattling over the cobbles in the early morning, and that I shall no doubt bear, since I do not anticipate being here more than a week at most.

"As you know, I am in hopes of completing here my investigations into the part played by the great family of Louvois in the religious wars of the Sixteenth Century, and I flatter myself that I shall have a number of fresh facts to offer to the Historical Research Society on my return. The immediate object of my interest is a relatively obscure collateral descendant of the great Charles de Louvois, one Raoul de Savigny, who would not be in any way notable were it not for the fact that he was the only member of that staunchly Catholic family to join forces with the Huguenots, and that he was a victim of the great massacre of St. Bartholomew's day (it is a whimsical thought, is it not, that the 300th anniversary of that event takes place in only a few days' time? I must be on the watch for *spectres!*)

"The standard text-books say nothing of him beyond the bare fact of his death and the information—hardly to be wondered at in the circumstances—that he lived in strict solitude and seclusion. But since his abode was the Château de l'Echarpe, hardly three miles from the inn-door, I anticipate it may be possible to obtain locally those details in which the libraries are so peculiarly barren. In any event, I plan to visit the Château for the first time after breakfast to-morrow."

This plan was duly put into effect. Mr. Rotherham records that the day was unusually hot, even for August, and that there were a great many flies. Apart from these trials his walk to the Château was untroubled, and in his letter that evening he dilates at some length on his impressions of the countryside and his first view of the Château standing high above the slow-moving river.

He roused the caretaker (whom he describes as a "surly, middle-aged peasant") from his cottage and was shown through the rooms. For the most part they bore witness to a period some 50 years later than that in which he was specially interested; but he was rewarded by discovering an authentic portrait of Viscount Raoul de Savigny hanging high above the fireplace in the great drawing room. This he describes in some detail.

"It is a thin, weak, effeminate face, with narrow eyes and an unusually red mouth, at first appearance the face of a man about 30 years of age; a closer inspection, however, convinced me that the sitter must have been nearer 40 when the portrait was painted. He wears a rich dress of red silk and velvet, and the chain and medal of some insignia (I could not at the distance discern what) hangs about his neck. An hour-glass, held horizontally so as to prevent the flow of sand from one end to the other, is in his right hand, and his left rests upon an open book, on one page of which some writing is discernible.

"Wishing to inspect the writing more closely, I asked our unamiable friend if a step-ladder could be procured; but he made so great a fuss over the difficulties attendant upon this—as I had supposed—simple operation, that I had to resign myself to waiting until my return on the morrow for my curiosity to be satisfied."

Evidently the caretaker proved unsatisfactory in other respects also. He knew nothing about the Château beyond information of the conventional guidebook variety, and that was concerned wholly with the family which succeeded the Savignys in occupancy. They had not remained there long, nor any subsequent tenants; and the place had been empty for the last 50 years.

"But if Monsieur wishes to know more, he should visit Monsieur le Curé, who understands about these things."

"Really." These priests were apt to fancy themselves as historians, Mr. Rotherham reflected. "Are there any documents connected with the Savignys to be seen locally?"

"Yes, Monsieur. They are in the possession of M. le Curé." The man hesitated. "Perhaps——"

"Well?"

"I was going to say that if Monsieur is interested in le Vicomte Raoul de Savigny, he should perhaps see these documents before he proceeds further in the matter."

"Certainly I must see them. If they are of historical importance, they should have been donated to one of the libraries. But I have noticed that the church is apt to have no conscience in these matters."

The tour of inspection over, they left the house and crossed the broad neglected lawn at the back. Rococo bowls and statuary were ranged beneath the windows. At its farthest extremity the lawn rose in a short precipitous slope to meet the first trees of the park. And among the trees something which winked in the morning sunlight caught Mr. Rotherham's eye as he was turning to leave.

"What is that?" he asked, pointing.

"It is nothing, Monsieur." The man's tone was guarded.

"Nonsense," said Mr. Rotherham. "I distinctly caught the sun's reflection in a window." He took a few steps. "A building."

"A mausoleum, Monsieur."

"Great heavens, man"—Mr. Rotherham was excited—"why

didn't you tell me? What sort of place is it? Who is buried there? You must take me to it at once."

"There is nothing of interest there, Monsieur."

"Surely I may be allowed to judge—" Mr. Rotherham hesitated, stopped, felt in his pocket, and produced a twenty-franc note. But the man shook his head.

"No, Monsieur, it is not that. If you insist, I will take you to it. But you cannot see the interior."

"There is no key?"

"Yes, Monsieur, there is a key. I could wish there was not. I should like to see it destroyed. But the family has forbidden visitors entrance to the tomb. And I was never curious to go in myself."

If these remarks struck Mr. Rotherham as strange, he does not mention the fact. He merely asked again, "And who is buried there?"

"Only one man, Monsieur. Raoul de Savigny."

"Raoul—! We must go there at once."

And so the two set off.

The mausoleum stood—and still stands—at the top of a slight eminence, surrounded and overshadowed by the trees of the park. It is circular in shape, and built in the neoclassical style which the renaissance made fashionable in France, with ornamental pillars surmounted by Ionic capitals all about it. The roof is of copper and there is a stout oak door, carved with the arms of the de Savignys. The only unusual feature is the circlet of low elongated windows set below the roof about twelve feet from the ground, occupying very much the same position as clerestory windows in a church. Upon these Mr. Rotherham gazed long and earnestly. Finally he asked if a ladder could be fetched.

"Monsieur wishes to look in at the windows? I should not advise it."

Mr. Rotherham was beginning to lose patience. "What is all this nonsense?" he snapped. "I trust you are not afraid of ghosts? In any case it is not you whom I am asking to ascend the ladder. For the last time, will you get it for me or will you not?"

The caretaker shrugged. "As Monsieur wishes."

The ladder was brought and set against the side of the mausoleum, and Mr. Rotherham began his climb. Halfway up he was assailed by a sudden misgiving: it would not be pleasant, on arriving at the window, to find someone looking out at you . . . But he braced himself and went on, and in fact no such eventuality occurred.

The windows were filthy, both inside and out, and it was difficult to make out much of what lay within. He could discern, however, the stone sarcophagus in the centre, and on the east side some kind of altar, with a brass crucifix on it. A little disappointed, he had turned away and was beginning to descend, when he was startled by a violent clanging noise from within the tomb. And when, conquering an unexpected reluctance, he looked in again, he saw that the brass crucifix had fallen onto the stone floor.

The caretaker was awaiting him at the bottom of the ladder, his face a little paler than before. "Monsieur heard?"

"Yes, of course," said Mr. Rotherham shortly. He was no doubt annoyed at having been so alarmed. "I shall be returning tomorrow," he went on quickly, "to look more closely at the portrait."

"If Monsieur could find it convenient to arrive before four o'clock—I shall be closing the grounds at that hour——"

Mr. Rotherham tut-tutted his annoyance. "Well, if it must be, it must be. It seems very early to have to leave."

"I am going away, Monsieur. The day after tomorrow is August the 24th. I shall return on the 25th, and shall be happy then to show Monsieur anything he pleases."

"A not unsatisfactory day," Mr. Rotherham concludes his letter, "and with promise of better to come to-morrow, when I visit the priest. The incident of the crucifix did, I confess, temporarily disturb me, but I think you know that I do not subscribe to the current superstitions on such subjects; and no doubt there is some perfectly natural explanation of the phenomenon."

His second night at the Coq d'Or was not as tranquil as he had anticipated. Whether it was due to the bed, or to the unfamiliar surroundings, or to some other reason, he got but little sleep, and that little was troubled with dreams.

"One in particular," he notes in his diary, "kept recurring. I seemed to be running along a dark cobbled street, with the high gables of houses on either side. And all the time a voice was speaking rapidly and continuously in my ear, in a sort of high, thin monotone. '*Je ne suis pas encore prêt,*' it said, '*l'experience n'est pas complete.*' ('I am not yet ready. The experiment is not complete.')

"At times it rose to a desolate wail which I do not, even now, like to think of. There were torches, I think, and a crowd of indistinct people who were trying to get hold of me. Then I was in a room, standing with my back to the wall, and there was a sudden sharp pain in my right side, and the people and the torches came up to me and were doing something to my mouth. The voice rose to a high, bubbling scream in the middle of a sentence, and then broke off, and I awoke."

I conjecture that Mr. Rotherham was a man not easily daunted, for he seems despite this to have been in high spirits when, after breakfast next morning, he set off to see the Curé, who proved to be a lean ascetic man, a very heavy smoker of yellow cigarettes which he rolled himself. He appeared oddly reluctant to further Mr. Rotherham's business, but was eventually persuaded to produce some faded sheets of yellow parchment, written in a crabbed Sixteenth Century hand.

"You will find here an account," he said, "of the death of le Vicomte Raoul de Savigny in the massacre of St. Bartholomew's day, 1572, together with other matters concerning him. It was written by one Jean de Tourcoing, at that time the priest of this parish, a few months after the events took place."

This really was a find. Mr. Rotherham took the parchment with hands which he could hardly prevent from trembling with excitement. "I may have your permission to copy this?"

The priest nodded. "But I would rather you copied it here, my son—it is not long. Please do not misunderstand me; I would of course trust you with the manuscript. But there are other reasons." He hesitated. "I must leave you now to say Compline. Please avail yourself of this room as much as you wish. And——"

Mr. Rotherham looked up from the parchment sheets. "Yes?"

"You will find something in those pages which may tempt you to a certain course of action. Resist that temptation, my son—resist it for your own good." The priest's manner was intent.

"Of course, of course," said Mr. Rotherham, who wished to be left alone with the manuscript. "Whatever you advise."

It is improbable that the priest can have been deceived by this hurried acquiescence, for he added, more kindly, "And remember, my son, at any time and in any emergency I am at your service." Then he turned and went out.

The account of Jean de Tourcoing, brief though it was, was undoubtedly authentic and contemporary. Mr. Rotherham found in it much to excite and a little to disturb him. It confirmed that Catherine de Medici was personally responsible for the massacre; it gave the number of victims in the Paris area as 13,000 (but this was probably guesswork and could not be relied on); and it repeated the legend—Mr. Rotherham smiled a little at this—that Charles IX was thereafter haunted by the spirits of dead Huguenots.

The number of the murdered in Clauvères itself was not large, but some considerable space was given up to the death of Raoul de Savigny, as by far the most notable among them. One passage is worth transcribing here in full.

"De Savigny, torturer, murderer, magician, and apostate, met his deserved end upon this same glorious night of August 24th. A man forever fearful of death, forever scheming by vile art to prolong his own wretched estate and keep earthbound his heretic soul in the middle career betwixt our Almighty Lord and His Adversary the Devil, and who, being cravenly terrified of both Heaven and Hell, sought to transgress and defy the inexorable decree of our going hence, he was hounded upon this same night like a dog through the streets, and struck to his own wall by a shaft in the right ribs.

"And the soldiers, being desirous of entertainment, were in mind—he being thus helpless—to torture him; in pursuance of which, his head, arms, and legs being clamped to the wall, his teeth were first drawn, singly, and his mouth slit back from the corners to the cheek-bone; he crying out the while that he was not yet ready for death, and imploring the soldiers to spare him. Then his finger-nails were torn out and the bones of his fingers separately broken. In all this he fainted often and was revived before the operation proceeded.

"At last, after five hours of continual mutilation, he was seen to be dead. And the parts of the body were assembled and embalmed in linen, and a tomb built in the park, and the remains placed there, and with them all the papers relating to his family and himself, and so at last he was left alone. All this I witnessed. Jean de Tourcoing *scripsit*, AD 1573, in the month of February, A.M.D.G."

199

When Mr. Rotherham left the priest's house with his transcript of this document he was thoughtful, and the subject of his reflections is revealed in a letter which he wrote to his nephew immediately on returning to his room at the inn.

"You will think less hardly of my intent," he says, "if you consider the immense additions to historical knowledge which will almost certainly be derived from the papers in the mausoleum. To ask permission to go in there would, I know, be a fruitless endeavour; there is too much superstition against it, and the caretaker made it clear that on this score the family which owns the Château is adamant. But I believe I am competent to carry through the business without leaving any traces. All depends upon whether the key has been left behind in the caretaker's cottage."

Mr. Rotherham's plan, in brief, was as follows: during the afternoon he would purchase in the town a length of rope and a good lantern, and when darkness fell he would leave the inn, giving as his excuse the desire for a moonlight walk, and make his way to the Château de l'Echarpe. There he would climb the wall, an operation which, from what he remembered, was likely to present few difficulties, search the cottage of the absent caretaker for the key to the mausoleum, make his way in there, take the documents referred to by Jean de Tourcoing, re-lock the tomb, restore the key carefully to the cottage, and return to the inn.

He anticipated no trouble in opening the sarcophagus, as he had noted that the lid was a light one of copper, and—a surprising feature—was not fastened down. Presumably the stout oak door was considered a sufficient safeguard against anyone's getting in or out.

Poor Mr. Rotherham! One may admire his courage, if not his wisdom. Curiously enough, he does not appear to have remembered the priest's warning, or if he did remember it, he was determined to ignore it. And when its full significance was at last borne in on him, it was far, far too late.

The story he was to tell subsequently was also prepared, for it would be impossible to conceal the fact that something criminal had been afoot, and after his visit to the Curé it was very likely that he would be connected with it. He would say that he had got into conversation with a stranger in a café (he would not, of course, know the stranger's name or be able to describe him minutely), and had chanced to mention to him the existence of the papers in the mausoleum, and his own regret at being unable to see them; that on the following day the stranger had reappeared, in possession of those same papers, and demanding payment for them; that, being incapable of dealing physically with the stranger, he had handed over the money; that the stranger had subsequently disappeared; and that, horrified by so flagrant a theft, he had hastened to return the papers to their owners—though not, he added to himself, before sufficient time had elapsed to allow him to make a copy of them. It is perhaps fortunate for Mr. Rotherham's reputation that so threadbare an account was never put to the test.

Darkness fell with the moon three-quarters toward the full, and a small wind crept in sudden gusts round the corners of the houses and over the cobbled streets, stirring the rich, dusty foliage in the trees which stood opposite the inn. Mr. Rotherham set out at about half-past ten, carrying his lantern and his rope in a suitcase. He was relieved that no one was about when he left the inn, for he would have been hard put to account for so unusual a piece of equipment for a moonlight stroll.

The journey to the Château was accomplished without incident; the only people he saw were a pair of lovers, too engrossed in their own concerns to pay any attention to him. The tall iron gates leading into the grounds were locked, but a convenient beech tree which stood by the wall made it unnecessary for him to use his rope—Mr. Rotherham, despite his 50 years, was an active, even an athletic man.

The grounds were silent and deserted. A windowpane smashed gave him access to the caretaker's cottage, and after a short search he found what he wanted—a huge, ancient key, rusted and corroding. Then he was out in the night air again, and making his way toward the mausoleum.

I can picture to myself his feelings as he stood before the tall oak door, the key in one hand, his lighted lantern in the other. It is not good, in the darkness, to be near places where dead people are. But whatever fears he may have had, he suppressed them, and went on with the job in hand. The lock was rusty from long disuse, and it was several minutes before the wards would turn. Then the door stood open, and he was inside.

The sarcophagus, a tall black mass, was in front of him, its copper lid illuminated by the straggling beams of moonlight which filtered through the windows, and the air was almost unbearably foul. In the light of the lantern he could see the brass crucifix on the floor where it had fallen the day before.

He took two steps forward, hesitantly, and all at once was overwhelmed by a dreadful and irresistible feeling that he was not alone. Another two steps, and with sudden violence the door of the mausoleum slammed to behind him, and he was conscious at the same moment of a voice gabbling softly and repeatedly in his left ear some such words as: "*Dorenavant tu seras assure de compagnie.*" ("From henceforth you may rest assured of having company.")

Blind with terror, he ran to the door, clawed it open, and somehow got outside. But the key was aged and rotten, and when he tried to turn it in the lock it broke off in his hand. Throwing everything aside, he made for the wall of the park, somehow scrambled over it, and dropped into the road beyond.

Of the journey back he afterward remembered nothing but an aching misery. But he no longer had the terrible sense that someone or something was with him, and he heard the clocks of Clauvères strike half-past eleven. It still wanted half an hour to St. Bartholomew's day.

Arrived at the inn, he drank some brandy, crept up to his room, and, in a futile endeavor to compose his mind, wrote down in his diary the events of the evening. "God have mercy on me," the entry concludes, "I did not know. I meant well. If only I could have locked the door after me . . ."

At this point the writing tails away. For now, at twenty-past midnight on the 24th of August, he knew again that he was not alone.

He turned, and saw what was in the big fourposter bed.

The rest shall be told in his own words. It is daylight again, and he is in another room of the inn, lying on the bed with a broken leg, and composing a letter—the last—to his nephew. The writing is that of an old man, and his fingers tremble so he can hardly hold the pen.

". . . the doctors say that it would be dangerous for me to be moved, and nothing will persuade them. Yet I would suffer the most dreadful physical pain conceivable to get away from this place. In the name of heaven, come to me as fast as train and boat will carry you.

"After that renewed and terrible conviction that I was again in the presence of something malevolent and evil, I looked towards the bed. Conceive of my extreme terror when I saw some creature sit up in it. It was swathed about with soiled linen like a mummy, with the arms close against the sides. There was no face, only ragged black holes where the eyes and mouth should have been, and that of the mouth dirtied and caked about with dry blood.

"Then the arms came away from the sides with a ripping and dust of rotten cloth, and it crawled off the bed and started towards me. I screamed out and ran for the door. There was a violent pain in my left leg, and blackness.

"I can write no more. Even in the sunlight, and with another person in the room, the memory of these things fills me with a worse horror than in my nightmares I had ever thought possible. For God's sake, come to me! The prospect of the brief hours of darkness before next midnight is unbearable to me."

On August 26th, Mr. Rotherham's nephew arrived at the inn. What he saw there sent him after a few moments running to the bathroom, where he threw up long and violently.

I was in Clauvères myself during the August of 1939, just before the war. The then landlord of the Coq d'Or was a grandson of the "anarchical young man" to whom Mr. Rotherham refers, and it was over a glass of beer with him in the inn parlour that I heard what became of Mr. Rotherham. He was reluctant to speak of it at first, but I scented some kind of mystery, and was eventually able to persuade him.

"I can only tell you, Monsieur," he said, "what my grandfather told me. The Englishman, you understand, would not be left for a moment alone, and it fell to my grandfather to stay with him in the room. As darkness approached, his agitation greatly increased, but towards midnight he fell silent for a short while. Then my grandfather, who was dozing off in his corner, was startled to hear him cry out in a terrible voice, 'Get the priest! For God's sake get the priest!'

"My grandfather hesitated, but so urgent was the request that he felt he must comply. As he left the room he was conscious of the smell of something that was decayed, and halfway down the passage he turned and saw that the door of the bedroom was opening slowly, and he heard the Englishman's voice cease abruptly. He hesitated, but"—the landlord shrugged—"he had no desire to go back then, and he ran to the priest's house. They returned a little after midnight, but there was nothing to do except cover the Englishman's face."

"How did he die?" I asked.

"That, Monsieur, my grandfather would never say."

Obviously the matter could not be allowed to rest there. I happened to remember that a friend of mine knew someone of the name of Rotherham, and since the name is not altogether common I wrote asking if he could give me any information on the subject. A week later I was rewarded by the arrival of a bulky package.

The Rotherham my friend knew was a son of the nephew to whom our Mr. Rotherham wrote, and enclosed were the letters, diary, and documents from which the preceding narrative has been pieced together.

"B—made no objection to lending them," my friend wrote. "All except the letters were returned to his father, as the nearest surviving relative, after his great-uncle's death. He says there was one thing among the personal effects which puzzled his father a good deal. It was found clutched in the unfortunate man's hand, and was a square gold medal, rather old and tarnished, with part of a heavy gold chain attached to it. On one side was an inverted crucifix, and on the other a clock face without hands, or from which the hands had been removed. B—tells me that he got it out to look at some time ago, but took such a dislike to it that he had it destroyed."

On the day following the arrival of this letter—it was August 23rd—I went out in the afternoon to the Château de l'Echarpe. The door of the mausoleum had been bricked up, but in other respects it was exactly as Mr. Rotherham had described it. I found the present caretaker, a pleasant young man who wore a black beret and smoked a cigarette.

"I am sorry, Monsieur," he said, "but——"

"But you're going away," I put in, "and won't be back until the 25th." And I explained my reasons for thinking that this would be so.

When I had finished, he nodded and looked at me shrewdly. "There is still an hour before my train leaves," he said. "If Monsieur would like to see the portrait—?" Naturally enough, Monsieur was delighted.

My guide, who was more obliging than Mr. Rotherham's, brought me a stepladder which enabled me to study the picture at close range. It was unsigned, probably the work of a clever amateur. The insignia round Viscount Raoul de Savigny's neck consisted of a square gold medal on a gold chain. The side which was not hidden showed (you will scarcely be surprised to hear it) a clock face from which the hands had been removed. And the writing in the book was a line from Ronsard: *"J'eviterai plaisir et damnation."* ("I shall avoid pleasure and damnation.")

The summer air was good after the musty uninhabited rooms of the Château.

"And now, Monsieur, I must leave," said the caretaker. "I was here once on St. Bartholomew's day, and no money would induce me to be in this neighbourhood again. It is the talking, you understand, and the mindless laughter, and the soft feeble pawing at the doors and windows . . ." He smiled suddenly. "If Monsieur will wait one moment, I will close my cottage and accompany him to the gates."

He went off, whistling, and I strolled idly toward the mausoleum. There is a thornbush which stands near the door, and although the day was windless, I saw that it was shaking violently. This induced me to change my plans and travel back to Paris on the evening train.

St. Bartholomew's day was still eight hours ahead and, looking back on it, I am fairly sure that the disturbance in the thornbush was caused by a cat. But in matters of this sort I consider it foolish to take unnecessary risks.

CHARLES DICKENS
The Ghost in Master B.'s Room

Charles Dickens (1812–70) *did more than any other writer to popularize the ghost story in the mid-nineteenth century, following the more antiquated Gothic horrors and "penny dreadfuls". The following story was one of Dickens's contributions (another was "The Mortals in the House") to his 1859 Christmas Number of* All the Year Round: The Haunted House.

It being now my own turn, I "took the word," as the French say, and went on:

When I established myself in the triangular garret which had gained so distinguished a reputation, my thoughts naturally turned to Master B. My speculations about him were uneasy and manifold. Whether his christian name was Benjamin, Bissextile (from his having been born in Leap Year), Bartholomew, or Bill. Whether the initial letter belonged to his family name, and that was Baxter, Black, Brown, Barker, Buggins, Baker, or Bird. Whether he was a foundling, and had been baptized B. Whether he was a lion-hearted boy, and B. was short for Briton, or for Bull. Whether he could possibly have been kith and kin to an illustrious lady who brightened my own childhood, and had come of the blood of the brilliant Mother Bunch?

With these profitless meditations I tormented myself much. I also carried the mysterious letter into the appearance and pursuits of the deceased; wondering whether he dressed in Blue, wore Boots (he couldn't have been Bald), was a boy of Brains, liked Books, was good at Bowling, had any skill as a Boxer, ever in his Buoyant Boyhood Bathed from a Bathing-machine at Bognor, Bangor, Bournemouth, Brighton, or Broadstairs, like a Bounding Billiard Ball?

So, from the first, I was haunted by the letter B.

It was not long before I remarked that I never by any hazard had a dream of Master B., or of anything belonging to him. But, the instant I awoke from sleep, at whatever hour of the night, my thoughts took him up, and roamed away, trying to attach his initial letter to something that would fit it and keep it quiet.

For six nights, I had been worried thus in Master B.'s room, when I began to perceive that things were going wrong.

The first appearance that presented itself was early in the morning, when it was but just daylight and no more. I was standing shaving at my glass, when I suddenly discovered, to my consternation and amazement, that I was shaving—not myself—I am fifty—but a boy. Apparently Master B.?

I trembled and looked over my shoulder; nothing there. I looked again in the glass, and distinctly saw the features and expression of a boy, who was shaving, not to get rid of a beard, but to get one. Extremely troubled in my mind, I took a few turns in the room, and went back to the looking-glass, resolved to steady my hand and complete the operation in which I had been disturbed. Opening my eyes, which I had shut while recovering my firmness, I now met in the glass, looking straight at me, the eyes of a young man of four or five and twenty. Terrified by this new ghost, I closed my eyes, and made a strong effort to recover myself. Opening them again, I saw, shaving his cheek in the glass, my father, who has long been dead. Nay, I even saw my grandfather too, whom I never did see in my life.

Although naturally much affected by these remarkable visitations, I determined to keep my secret, until the time agreed upon for the present general disclosure. Agitated by a multitude of curious thoughts, I retired to my room, that night, prepared to encounter some new experience of a spectral character. Nor was my preparation needless, for, waking from an uneasy sleep at exactly two o'clock in the morning, what were my feelings to find that I was sharing my bed with the skeleton of Master B.!

I sprang up, and the skeleton sprang up also. I then heard a plaintive voice saying, "Where am I? What is become of me?" and, looking hard in that direction, perceived the ghost of Master B.

The young spectre was dressed in an obsolete fashion: or rather, was not so much dressed as put into a case of inferior pepper-and-salt cloth, made horrible by means of shining buttons. I observed that these buttons went, in a double row, over each shoulder of the young ghost, and appeared to descend his back. He wore a frill round his neck. His right hand (which I distinctly noticed to be inky) was laid upon his stomach; connecting this action with some feeble pimples on his countenance, and his general air of nausea, I concluded this ghost to be the ghost of a boy who had habitually taken a great deal too much medicine.

"Where am I?" said the little spectre, in a pathetic voice. "And why was I born in the Calomel days, and why did I have all that Calomel given me?"

I replied, with sincere earnestness, that upon my soul I couldn't tell him.

"Where is my little sister," said the ghost, "and where my angelic little wife, and where is the boy I went to school with?"

I entreated the phantom to be comforted, and above all things to take heart respecting the loss of the boy he went to school with. I represented to him that probably that boy never did, within human experience, come out well, when discovered. I urged that I myself had, in later life, turned up several boys whom I went to school with, and none of them had at all answered. I expressed my humble belief that that boy never did answer. I represented that he was a mythic character, a delusion, and a snare. I recounted how, the last time I found him, I found him at a dinner party behind a wall of white cravat, with an inconclusive opinion on every possible subject, and a power of silent boredom absolutely Titanic. I related how, on the strength of our having been together at "Old Doylance's," he had asked himself to breakfast with me (a social offence of the largest magnitude); how, fanning my weak embers of belief in Doylance's boys, I had let him in; and how, he had proved to be a fearful wanderer about the earth, pursuing the race of Adam with inexplicable notions concerning the currency, and with a proposition that the Bank of England should, on pain of being abolished, instantly strike off and circulate, God knows how many thousand millions of ten-and-sixpenny notes.

The ghost heard me in silence, and with a fixed stare. "Barber!" it apostrophised me when I had finished.

"Barber?" I repeated—for I am not of that profession.

"Condemned," said the ghost, "to shave a constant change of customers—now, me—now, a young man—now, thyself as thou art—now, thy father—now, thy grandfather; condemned, too, to lie down with a skeleton every night, and to rise with it every morning——"

(I shuddered on hearing this dismal announcement.)
"Barber! Pursue me!"

I had felt, even before the words were uttered, that I was under a spell to pursue the phantom. I immediately did so, and was in Master B.'s room no longer.

Most people know what long and fatiguing night journeys had been forced upon the witches who used to confess, and who, no doubt, told the exact truth—particularly as they were always assisted with leading questions, and the Torture was always ready. I asseverate that, during my occupation of Master B.'s room, I was taken by the ghost that haunted it, on expeditions fully as long and wild as any of those. Assuredly, I was presented to no shabby old man with a goat's horns and tail (something between Pan and an old clothesman), holding conventional receptions, as stupid as those of real life and less decent; but, I came upon other things which appeared to me to have more meaning.

Confident that I speak the truth and shall be believed, I declare without hesitation that I followed the ghost, in the first instance on a broomstick, and afterwards on a rocking-horse. The very smell of the animal's paint—especially when I brought it out, by making him warm—I am ready to swear to. I followed the ghost, afterwards, in a hackney coach; an institution with the peculiar smell of which, the present generation is unacquainted, but to which I am again ready to swear as a combination of stable, dog with the mange, and very old bellows. (In this, I appeal to previous generations to confirm or refute me.) I pursued the phantom, on a headless donkey: at least, upon a donkey who was so interested in the state of his stomach that his head was always down there, investigating it; on ponies, expressly born to kick up behind; on roundabouts and swings, from fairs; in the first cab—another forgotten institution where the fare regularly got into bed, and was tucked up with the driver.

Not to trouble you with a detailed account of all my travels in pursuit of the ghost of Master B., which were longer and more wonderful than those of Sindbad the Sailor, I will confine myself to one experience from which you may judge of many.

I was marvellously changed. I was myself, yet not myself. I was conscious of something within me, which has been the same all through my life, and which I have always recognised under all its phases and varieties as never altering, and yet I was not the I who had gone to bed in Master B.'s room. I had the smoothest of faces and the shortest of legs, and I had taken another creature like myself, also with the smoothest of faces and the shortest of legs, behind a door, and was confiding to him a proposition of the most astounding nature.

This proposition was, that we should have a Seraglio.

The other creature assented warmly. He had no notion of respectability, neither had I. It was the custom of the East, it was the way of the good Caliph Haroun Alraschid (let me have the corrupted name again for once, it is so scented with sweet memories!), the usage was highly laudable, and most worthy of imitation. "Oh, yes! Let us," said the other creature with a jump, "have a Seraglio."

It was not because we entertained the faintest doubts of the meritorious character of the Oriental establishment we proposed to import, that we perceived it must be kept a secret from Miss Griffin. It was because we knew Miss Griffin to be bereft of human sympathies, and incapable of appreciating the greatness of the great Haroun. Mystery impenetrably shrouded from Miss Griffin then, let us entrust it to Miss Bule.

We were ten in Miss Griffin's establishment by Hampstead Ponds; eight ladies and two gentlemen. Miss Bule, whom I judge to have attained the ripe age of eight or nine, took the lead in society. I opened the subject to her in the course of the day, and proposed that she should become the Favourite.

Miss Bule, after struggling with the diffidence so natural to, and charming in, her adorable sex, expressed herself as flattered by the idea, but wished to know how it was proposed to provide for Miss Pipson? Miss Bule—who was understood to have vowed towards that young lady, a friendship, halves, and no secrets, until death, on the Church Service and Lessons complete in two volumes with case and lock—Miss Bule said she could not, as the friend of Pipson, disguise from herself, or me, that Pipson was not one of the common.

Now, Miss Pipson, having curly light hair and blue eyes (which was my idea of anything mortal and feminine that was called Fair), I promptly replied that I regarded Miss Pipson in the light of a Fair Circassian.

"And what then?" Miss Bule pensively asked.

I replied that she must be inveigled by a Merchant, brought to me veiled, and purchased as a slave.

[The other creature had already fallen into the second male place in the State, and was set apart for Grand Vizier. He afterwards resisted this disposal of events, but had his hair pulled until he yielded.]

"Shall I not be jealous?" Miss Bule inquired, casting down her eyes.

"Zobeide, no," I replied; "you will ever be the favourite Sultana; the first place in my heart, and on my throne, will be ever yours."

Miss Bule, upon that assurance, consented to propound the idea to her seven beautiful companions. It occurring to me, in the course of the same day, that we knew we could trust a grinning and good-natured soul called Tabby, who was the serving drudge of the house, and had no more figure than one of the beds, and upon whose face there was always more or less blacklead, I slipped into Miss Bule's hand after supper, a little note to that effect: dwelling on the blacklead as being in a manner deposited by the finger of Providence, pointing Tabby out for Mesrour, the celebrated chief of the Blacks of the Hareem.

There were difficulties in the formation of the desired institution, as there are in all combinations. The other creature showed himself of a low character, and, when defeated in aspiring to the throne, pretended to have conscientious scruples about prostrating himself before the Caliph; wouldn't call him Commander of the Faithful; spoke of him slightingly and inconsistently as a mere "chap," said he, the other creature, "wouldn't play"—Play!—and was otherwise coarse and offensive. This meanness of disposition was, however, put down by the general indignation of an united Seraglio, and I became blessed in the smiles of eight of the fairest of the daughters of men.

The smiles could only be bestowed when Miss Griffin was looking another way, and only then in a very wary manner, for there was a legend among the followers of the Prophet that she saw with a little round ornament in the middle of the pattern on the back of her shawl. But, every day after dinner, for an hour, we were all together, and then the Favourite and the rest of the Royal Hareem competed who should most beguile

211

the leisure of the Serene Haroun reposing from the cares of State—which were generally, as in most affairs of State, of an arithmetical character, the Commander of the Faithful being a fearful boggler at a sum.

On these occasions, the devoted Mesrour, chief of the Blacks of the Hareem, was always in attendance (Miss Griffin usually ringing for that officer, at the same time, with great vehemence), but never acquitted himself in a manner worthy of his historical reputation. In the first place, his bringing a broom into the Divan of the Caliph, even when Haroun wore on his shoulders the red robe of anger (Miss Pipson's pelisse), though it might be got over for the moment, was never to be quite satisfactorily accounted for. In the second place, his breaking out into grinning exclamations of "Lork you pretties!" was neither Eastern nor respectful. In the third place, when specially instructed to say "Bismillah!" he always said "Hallelujah!" This officer, unlike his class, was too good-humoured altogether, kept his mouth open far too wide, expressed approbation to an incongruous extent, and even once—it was on the occasion of the purchase of the Fair Circassian for five hundred thousand purses of gold, and cheap, too—embraced the Slave, the Favourite, and the Caliph, all round. (Parenthetically let me say God bless Mesrour, and may there have been sons and daughters on that tender bosom, softening many a hard day since!)

Miss Griffin was a model of propriety, and I am at a loss to imagine what the feelings of the virtuous woman would have been, if she had known, when she paraded us down the Hampstead-road two and two, that she was walking with a stately step at the head of Polygamy and Mahomedanism. I believe that a mysterious and terrible joy with which the contemplation of Miss Griffin, in this unconscious state, inspired us, and a grim sense prevalent among us that there was a dreadful power in our knowledge of what Miss Griffin (who knew all things that could be learnt out of book) didn't know, were the mainspring of the preservation of our secret. It was wonderfully kept, but was once upon the verge of self-betrayal. The danger and escape occurred upon a Sunday. We were all ten ranged in a conspicuous part of the gallery at church, with Miss Griffin at our head—as we were every Sunday—advertising the establishment in an unsecular sort of way—when the description of Solomon in his domestic glory, happened to be read. The moment that monarch was thus referred to, conscience whispered me, "Thou, too, Haroun!" The officiating minister had a cast in his eye, and it assisted conscience by giving him the appearance of reading personally at me. A crimson blush, attended by a fearful perspiration, suffused my features. The Grand Vizier became more dead than alive, and the whole Seraglio reddened as if the sunset of Bagdad shone direct upon their lovely faces. At this portentous time the awful Griffin rose, and balefully surveyed the children of Islam. My own impression was, that Church and State had entered into a conspiracy with Miss Griffin to expose us, and that we should all be put into white sheets, and exhibited in the centre aisle. But, so Westerly—if I may be allowed the expression as opposite to Eastern associations—was Miss Griffin's sense of rectitude, that she merely suspected Apples, and we were saved.

I have called the Seraglio united. Upon the question, solely, whether the Commander of the Faithful durst exercise a right of kissing in that sanctuary of the palace, were its peerless inmates divided. Zobeide asserted a counter-right in the Favourite to scratch, and the fair Circassian put her face, for refuge, into a green baize bag, originally designed for books. On the other hand, a young antelope of transcendent beauty from the fruitful plains of Camden-town (whence she had been brought, by traders, in the half-yearly caravan that crossed the intermediate desert after the holidays), held more liberal opinions, but stipulated for limiting the benefit of them to that dog, and son of a dog, the Grand Vizier—who had no rights, and was not in question. At length, the difficulty was compromised by the installation of a very youthful slave as Deputy. She, raised upon a stool, officially received upon her cheeks the salutes intended by the gracious Haroun for other Sultanas, and was privately rewarded from the coffers of the Ladies of the Hareem.

And now it was, at the full height of enjoyment of my bliss, that I became heavily troubled. I began to think of my mother, and what she would say to my taking home at Midsummer eight of the most beautiful of the daughters of men, but all unexpected. I thought of the number of beds we made up at our house, of my father's income, and of the baker, and my despondency redoubled. The Seraglio and malicious Vizier, divining the cause of their Lord's unhappiness, did their utmost to augment it. They professed unbounded fidelity, and declared that they would live and die with him. Reduced to the utmost wretchedness by these protestations of attachment, I lay awake, for hours at a time, ruminating on my frightful lot. In my despair, I think I might have taken an early opportunity of falling on my knees before Miss Griffin, avowing my resemblance to Solomon, and praying to be dealt with according to the outraged laws of my country, if an unthought-of means of escape had not opened before me.

One day, we were out walking, two and two—on which occasion the Vizier had his usual instructions to take note of the boy at the turnpike, and if he profanely gazed (which he always did) at the beauties of the Hareem, to have him bowstrung in the course of the night—and it happened that our hearts were veiled in gloom. An unaccountable action on the part of the antelope had plunged the State into disgrace. That charmer, on the representation that the previous day was her birthday, and that vast treasures had been sent in a hamper for its celebration (both baseless assertions), had secretly but most pressingly invited thirty-five neighbouring princes and princesses to a ball and supper: with a special stipulation that they were "not to be fetched till twelve." This wandering of the antelope's fancy, led to the surprising arrival at Miss Griffin's door, in divers equipages and under various escorts, of a great company in full dress, who were deposited on the top step in a flush of high expectancy, and who were dismissed in tears. At the beginning of the double knocks attendant on these ceremonies, the antelope had retired to a back attic, and bolted herself in; and at every new arrival, Miss Griffin had gone so much more and more distracted, that at last she had been seen to tear her front. Ultimate capitulation on the part of the offender, had been followed by solitude in the linen-closet, bread and water, and a lecture to all, of vindictive length, in which Miss Griffin had used the expressions: Firstly, "I believe you all of you knew of it;" Secondly, "Every one of you is as wicked as another;" Thirdly, "A pack of little wretches."

Under these circumstances, we were walking drearily along; and I especially, with my Moosulmaun responsibilities heavy on me, was in a very low state of mind; when a strange man accosted Miss Griffin, and, after walking on at her side for a little while and talking with her, looked at me. Supposing him to be a minion of the law, and that my hour was come, I instantly ran away, with a general purpose of making for Egypt.

The whole Seraglio cried out, when they saw me making off as fast as my legs would carry me (I had an impression that the first turning on the left, and round by the public-house, would be the shortest way to the Pyramids), Miss Griffin screamed after me, the faithless Vizier ran after me, and the boy at the turnpike dodged me into a corner, like a sheep, and cut me off. Nobody scolded me when I was taken and brought back; Miss Griffin only said, with a stunning gentleness, This was very curious! Why had I run away when the gentleman looked at me?

If I had had any breath to answer with, I dare say I should have made no answer; having no breath, I certainly made none. Miss Griffin and the strange man took me between them, and walked me back to the palace in a sort of state; but not at all (as I couldn't help feeling, with astonishment) in culprit state.

When we got there, we went into a room by ourselves, and Miss Griffin called in to her assistance, Mesrour, chief of the dusky guards of the Hareem. Mesrour, on being whispered to, began to shed tears.

"Bless you, my precious!" said that officer, turning to me; "your Pa's took bitter bad!"

I asked, with a fluttered heart, "Is he very ill?"

"Lord temper the wind to you, my lamb!" said the good Mesrour, kneeling down, that I might have a comforting shoulder for my head to rest on, "your Pa's dead!"

Haroun Alraschid took to flight at the words; the Seraglio vanished; from that moment, I never again saw one of the eight of the fairest of the daughters of men.

I was taken home, and there was Debt at home as well as Death, and we had a sale there. My own little bed was so superciliously looked upon by a Power unknown to me, hazily called "The Trade," that a brass coal-scuttle, a roasting-jack, and a birdcage, were obliged to be put into it to make a Lot of it, and then it went for a song. So I heard mentioned, and I wondered what song, and thought what a dismal song it must have been to sing!

Then, I was sent to a great, cold, bare school of big boys; where everything to eat and wear was thick and clumpy, without being enough; where everybody, large and small, was cruel; where the boys knew all about the sale, before I got there, and asked me what I had fetched, and who had bought me, and hooted at me, "Going, going, gone!" I never whispered in that wretched place that I had been Haroun, or had had a Seraglio: for, I knew that if I mentioned my reverses, I should be so worried, that I should have to drown myself in the muddy pond near the playground, which looked like the beer.

Ah me, ah me! No other ghost has haunted the boy's room, my friends, since I have occupied it, than the ghost of my own childhood, the ghost of my own innocence, the ghost of my own airy belief. Many a time have I pursued the phantom: never with this man's stride of mine to come up with it, never with these man's hands of mine to touch it, never more to this man's heart of mine to hold it in its purity. And here you see me working out, as cheerfully and thankfully as I may, my doom of shaving in the glass a constant change of customers, and of lying down and rising up with the skeleton allotted to me for my mortal companion.

ARTHUR CONAN DOYLE
The Brown Hand

The overwhelming popularity of Sherlock Holmes has always overshadowed Arthur Conan Doyle's other stories, especially those dealing with the occult and the supernatural, for which the author held a strong passion in real life. He eventually devoted himself full-time to the study of spiritualism and the paranormal.

One of his best ghost stories, "The Brown Hand", first appeared in the pages of the Strand *magazine in May 1899. Like Dr. Watson, the lead character served as a medical man in the mysterious East.*

Everyone knows that Sir Dominick Holden, the famous Indian surgeon, made me his heir, and that his death changed me in an hour from a hard-working and impecunious medical man to a well-to-do landed proprietor. Many know also that there were at least five people between the inheritance and me, and that Sir Dominick's selection appeared to be altogether arbitrary and whimsical. I can assure them, however, that they are quite mistaken, and that, although I only knew Sir Dominick in the closing years of his life, there were, none the less, very real reasons why he should show his goodwill towards me. As a matter of fact, though I say it myself, no man ever did more for another than I did for my Indian uncle. I cannot expect the story to be believed, but it is so singular that I should feel that it was a breach of duty if I did not put it upon record—so here it is, and your belief or incredulity is your own affair.

Sir Dominick Holden, C.B., K.C.S.I., and I don't know what besides, was the most distinguished Indian surgeon of his day. In the Army originally, he afterwards settled down into civil practice in Bombay, and visited, as a consultant, every part of India. His name is best remembered in connection with the Oriental Hospital which he founded and supported. The time came, however, when his iron constitution began to show signs of the long strain to which he had subjected it, and his brother practitioners (who were not, perhaps, entirely disinterested upon the point) were unanimous in recommending him to return to England. He held on so long as he could, but at last he developed nervous symptoms of a very pronounced character, and so came back, a broken man, to his native county of Wiltshire. He bought a considerable estate with an ancient manor-house upon the edge of Salisbury Plain, and devoted his old age to the study of Comparative Pathology, which had been his learned hobby all his life, and in which he was a foremost authority.

We of the family were, as may be imagined, much excited by the news of the return of this rich and childless uncle to England. On his part, although by no means exuberant in his hospitality, he showed some sense of his duty to his relations, and each of us in turn had an invitation to visit him. From the accounts of my cousins it appeared to be a melancholy business, and it was with mixed feelings that I at last received my own summons to appear at Rodenhurst. My wife was so carefully excluded in the invitation that my first impulse was to refuse it, but the interests of the children had to be considered, and so, with her consent, I set out one October afternoon upon my visit to Wiltshire, with little thought of what that visit was to entail.

My uncle's estate was situated where the arable land of the plains begins to swell upwards into the rounded chalk hills which are characteristic of the county. As I drove from Dinton Station in the waning light of that autumn day, I was impressed by the weird nature of the scenery. The few scattered cottages of the peasants were so dwarfed by the huge evidences of prehistoric life, that the present appeared to be a dream and the past to be the obtrusive and masterful reality. The road wound through the valleys, formed by a succession of grassy hills, and the summit of each was cut and carved into the most elaborate fortifications, some circular, and some square, but all on a scale which has defied the winds and the rains of many centuries. Some call them Roman and some British, but their true origin and the reasons for this particular tract of country being so interlaced with entrenchments have never been finally made clear. Here and there on the long, smooth, olive-coloured slopes there rose small, rounded barrows or tumuli. Beneath them lie the cremated ashes of the race which cut so deeply into the hills, but their graves tell us nothing save that a jar full of dust represents the man who once laboured under the sun.

It was through this weird country that I approached my uncle's residence of Rodenhurst, and the house was, as I found, in due keeping with its surroundings. Two broken and weather-stained pillars, each surmounted by a mutilated heraldic emblem, flanked the entrance to a neglected drive. A cold wind whistled through the elms which lined it, and the air was full of the drifting leaves. At the far end, under the gloomy arch of trees, a single yellow lamp burned steadily. In the dim half-light of the coming night I saw a long, low building stretching out two irregular wings, with deep eaves, a sloping gambrel roof, and walls which were criss-crossed with timber balks in the fashion of the Tudors. The cheery light of a fire flickered in the broad, latticed window to the left of the low-porched door, and this, as it proved, marked the study of my uncle, for it was thither that I was led by his butler in order to make my host's acquaintance.

He was cowering over his fire, for the moist chill of an English autumn had set him shivering. His lamp was unlit, and I only saw the red glow of the embers beating upon a huge, craggy face, with a Red Indian nose and cheek, and deep furrows and seams from eye to chin, the sinister marks of hidden volcanic fires. He sprang up at my entrance with something of an old-world courtesy and welcomed me warmly to Rodenhurst. At the same time I was conscious, as the lamp was carried in, that it was a very critical pair of light-blue eyes which looked out at me from under shaggy eyebrows, like scouts beneath a bush, and that this outlandish uncle of mine was carefully reading off my character with all the ease of a practised observer and an experienced man of the world.

For my part I looked at him, and looked again, for I had never seen a man whose appearance was more fitted to hold one's attention. His figure was the framework of a giant, but he had fallen away until his coat dangled straight down in a shocking fashion from a pair of broad and bony shoulders. All his limbs were huge and yet emaciated, and I could not take my gaze from his knobby wrists, and long, gnarled hands. But his eyes—those peering, light-blue eyes—they were the most arrestive of any of his peculiarities. It was not their colour alone, nor was it the ambush of hair in which they lurked; but it was the expression which I read in them. For the appearance and bearing of the man were masterful, and one expected a certain corresponding arrogance in his eyes, but instead of that I read the look which tells of a spirit cowed and crushed, the furtive, expectant look of the dog whose master has taken the whip from the rack. I formed my own medical diagnosis upon one glance at those critical and yet appealing eyes. I believed that he was stricken with some mortal ailment, that he knew himself to be exposed to sudden death, and that he lived in terror of it. Such was my judgment—a false one, as the event showed; but I mention it that it may help you to realize the look which I read in his eyes.

My uncle's welcome was, as I have said, a courteous one, and in an hour or so I found myself seated between him and his wife at a comfortable dinner, with curious, pungent delicacies upon the table, and a stealthy, quick-eyed Oriental waiter behind his chair. The old couple had come round to that tragic imitation of the dawn of life when husband and wife, having lost or scattered all those who were their intimates, find themselves face to face and alone once more, their work done, and the end nearing fast. Those who have reached that stage in sweetness and love, who can change their winter into a gentle, Indian summer, have come as victors through the ordeal of life. Lady Holden was a small, alert woman with a kindly eye, and her expression as she glanced at him was a certificate of character to her husband. And yet, though I read a mutual love in their glances, I read also mutual horror, and recognized in her face some reflection of that stealthy fear which I had detected in his. Their talk was sometimes merry and sometimes sad, but there was a forced note in their merriment and a naturalness in their sadness which told me that a heavy heart beat upon either side of me.

We were sitting over our first glass of wine, and the servants had left the room, when the conversation took a turn which produced a remarkable effect upon my host and hostess. I cannot recall what it was which started the topic of the supernatural, but it ended in my showing them that the abnormal in psychical experiences was a subject to which I had, like many neurologists, devoted a great deal of attention. I concluded by narrating my experiences when, as a member of the Psychical Research Society, I had formed one of a committee of three who spent the night in a haunted house. Our adventures were neither exciting nor convincing, but, such as it was, the story appeared to interest my auditors in a remarkable degree. They listened with an eager silence, and I caught a look of intelligence between them which I could not understand. Lady Holden immediately afterwards rose and left the room.

Sir Dominick pushed the cigar-box over to me, and we smoked for some little time in silence. That huge, bony hand of his was twitching as he raised it with his cheroot to his lips, and I felt that the man's nerves were vibrating like fiddle-strings. My instincts told me that he was on the verge of some intimate confidence, and I feared to speak lest I should interrupt it. At last he turned towards me with a spasmodic gesture like a man who throws his last scruple to the winds.

"From the little that I have seen of you it appears to me, Dr. Hardacre," said he, "that you are the very man I have wanted to meet."

"I am delighted to hear it, sir."

"Your head seems to be cool and steady. You will acquit me of any desire to flatter you, for the circumstances are too serious to permit of insincerities. You have some special knowledge upon these subjects, and you evidently view them from that philosophical stand-point which robs them of all vulgar terror. I presume that the sight of an apparition would not seriously discompose you?"

"I think not, sir."

"Would even interest you, perhaps?"

"Most intensely."

"As a psychical observer, you would probably investigate it in as impersonal a fashion as an astronomer investigates a wandering comet?"

"Precisely."

He gave a heavy sigh.

"Believe me, Dr. Hardacre, there was a time when I could have spoken as you do now. My nerve was a byword in India. Even the Mutiny never shook it for an instant. And yet you see what I am reduced to—the most timorous man, perhaps, in all this county of Wiltshire. Do not speak too bravely upon this subject, or you may find yourself subjected to as long-drawn a test as I am—a test which can only end in the madhouse or the grave."

I waited patiently until he should see fit to go farther in his confidence. His preamble had, I need not say, filled me with interest and expectation.

"For some years, Dr. Hardacre," he continued, "my life and that of my wife have been made miserable by a cause which is so grotesque that it borders upon the ludicrous. And yet familiarity has never made it more easy to bear—on the contrary, as time passes my nerves become more worn and shattered by the constant attrition. If you have no physical fears, Dr. Hardacre, I should very much value your opinion upon this phenomenon which troubles us so."

"For what it is worth my opinion is entirely at your service. May I ask the nature of the phenomenon?"

"I think that your experiences will have a higher evidential value if you are not told in advance what you may expect to encounter. You are yourself aware of the quibbles of unconscious cerebration and subjective impressions with which a scientific sceptic may throw a doubt upon your statement. It would be as well to guard against them in advance."

"What shall I do, then?"

"I will tell you. Would you mind following me this way?" He led me out of the dining-room and down a long passage until we came to a terminal door. Inside there was a large, bare room fitted as a laboratory, with numerous scientific instruments and bottles. A shelf ran along one side, upon which there stood a long line of glass jars containing pathological and anatomical specimens.

"You see that I still dabble in some of my old studies," said Sir Dominick. "These jars are the remains of what was once a most excellent collection, but unfortunately I lost the greater part of them when my house was burned down in Bombay in '92. It was a most unfortunate affair for me—in more ways than one. I had examples of many rare conditions, and my splenic collection was probably unique. These are the survivors."

I glanced over them, and saw that they really were of a very great value and rarity from a pathological point of view: bloated organs, gaping cysts, distorted bones, odious parasites—a singular exhibition of the products of India.

"There is, as you see, a small settee here," said my host. "It was far from our intention to offer a guest so meagre an accommodation, but since affairs have taken this turn, it would

222

be a great kindness upon your part if you would consent to spend the night in this apartment. I beg that you will not hesitate to let me know if the idea should be at all repugnant to you."

"On the contrary," I said, "it is most acceptable."

"My own room is the second on the left, so that if you should feel that you are in need of company a call would always bring me to your side."

"I trust that I shall not be compelled to disturb you."

"It is unlikely that I shall be asleep. I do not sleep much. Do not hesitate to summon me."

And so with this agreement we joined Lady Holden in the drawing-room and talked of lighter things.

It was no affectation upon my part to say that the prospect of my night's adventure was an agreeable one. I have no pretence to greater physical courage than my neighbours, but familiarity with a subject robs it of those vague and undefined terrors which are the most appalling to the imaginative mind. The human brain is capable of only one strong emotion at a time, and if it be filled with curiosity or scientific enthusiasm, there is no room for fear. It is true that I had my uncle's assurance that he had himself originally taken this point of view, but I reflected that the breakdown of his nervous system might be due to his forty years in India as much as to any psychical experiences which had befallen him. I at least was sound in nerve and brain, and it was with something of the pleasurable thrill of anticipation with which the sportsman takes his position beside the haunt of his game that I shut the laboratory door behind me, and partially undressing, lay down upon the rug-covered settee.

It was not an ideal atmosphere for a bedroom. The air was heavy with many chemical odours, that of methylated spirit predominating. Nor were the decorations of my chamber very sedative. The odious line of glass jars with their relics of disease and suffering stretched in front of my very eyes. There was no blind to the window, and a three-quarter moon streamed its white light into the room, tracing a silver square with filigree lattices upon the opposite wall. When I had extinguished my candle this one bright patch in the midst of the general gloom had certainly an eerie and discomposing aspect. A rigid and absolute silence reigned throughout the old house, so that the low swish of the branches in the garden came softly and smoothly to my ears. It may have been the hypnotic lullaby of this gentle susurrus, or it may have been the result of my tiring day, but after many dozings and many efforts to regain my clearness of perception, I fell at last into a deep and dreamless sleep.

I was awakened by some sound in the room, and I instantly raised myself upon my elbow on the couch. Some hours had passed, for the square patch upon the wall had slid downwards and sideways until it lay obliquely at the end of my bed. The rest of the room was in deep shadow. At first I could see nothing, presently, as my eyes became accustomed to the faint light, I was aware, with a thrill which all my scientific absorption could not entirely prevent, that something was moving slowly along the line of the wall. A gentle, shuffling sound, as of soft slippers, came to my ears, and I dimly discerned a human figure walking stealthily from the direction of the door. As it emerged into the patch of moonlight I saw very clearly what it was and how it was employed. It was a man, short and squat, dressed in some sort of dark-grey gown, which hung straight from his shoulders to his feet. The moon shone upon the side of his face, and I saw that it was chocolate-brown in colour, with a ball of black hair like a woman's at the back of his head. He walked slowly, and his eyes were cast upwards towards the line of bottles which contained those gruesome remnants of humanity. He seemed to examine each jar with attention, and then to pass on to the next. When he had come to the end of the line, immediately opposite my bed, he stopped, faced me, threw up his hands with a gesture of despair, and vanished from my sight.

I have said that he threw up his hands, but I should have said his arms, for as he assumed that attitude of despair I observed a singular peculiarity about his appearance. He had only one hand! As the sleeves drooped down from the upflung arms I saw the left plainly, but the right ended in a knobby and unsightly stump. In every other way his appearance was so natural, and I had both seen and heard him so clearly, that I could easily have believed that he was an Indian servant of Sir Dominick's who had come into my room in search of something. It was only his sudden disappearance which suggested anything more sinister to me. As it was I sprang from my couch, lit a candle, and examined the whole room carefully. There were no signs of my visitor, and I was forced to conclude that there had really been something outside the normal laws of Nature in his appearance. I lay awake for the remainder of the night, but nothing else occurred to disturb me.

I am an early riser, but my uncle was an even earlier one, for I found him pacing up and down the lawn at the side of the house. He ran towards me in his eagerness when he saw me come out from the door.

"Well, well!" he cried. "Did you see him?"

"An Indian with one hand?"

"Precisely."

"Yes, I saw him"—and I told him all that occurred. When I had finished, he led the way into his study.

"We have a little time before breakfast," said he. "It will suffice to give you an explanation of this extraordinary affair—so far as I can explain that which is essentially inexplicable. In the first place, when I tell you that for four years I have never passed one single night, either in Bombay, aboard ship, or here in England without my sleep being broken by this fellow, you will understand why it is that I am a wreck of my former self. His programme is always the same. He appears by my bedside, shakes me roughly by the shoulder, passes from my room into the laboratory, walks slowly along the line of my bottles, and then vanishes. For more than a thousand times he had gone through the same routine."

"What does he want?"

"He wants his hand."

"His hand?"

"Yes, it came about in this way. I was summoned to Peshawur for a consultation some ten years ago, and while there I was asked to look at the hand of a native who was passing through with an Afghan caravan. The fellow came from some mountain tribe living away at the back of beyond somewhere on the other side of Kaffiristan. He talked a bastard Pushtoo, and it was all I could do to understand him. He was suffering from a soft sarcomatous swelling of one of the metacarpal joints, and I made him realize that it was only by losing his hand that he could hope to save his life. After much persuasion he consented to the operation, and he asked me, when it was over, what fee I demanded. The poor fellow was almost a beggar, so that idea of a fee was absurd, but I answered in jest that my fee should be his hand, and that I proposed to add it to my pathological collection.

"To my surprise he demurred very much to the suggestion, and he explained that according to his religion it was an all-important matter that the body should be reunited after death, and so make a perfect dwelling for the spirit. The belief is, of course, an old one, and the mummies of the Egyptians arose from an analogous superstition. I answered him that his hand was already off, and asked him how he intended to preserve it. He replied that he would pickle it in salt and carry it about with him. I suggested that it might be safer in my keeping than his, and that I had better means than salt for preserving it. On realizing that I really intended to carefully keep it, his opposition vanished instantly. 'But remember, sahib,' said he, 'I shall want it back when I am dead.' I laughed at the remark, and so the matter ended. I returned to my practice, and he no doubt in the course of time was able to continue his journey to Afghanistan.

"Well, as I told you last night, I had a bad fire in my house at Bombay. Half of it was burned down, and, among other things, my pathological collection was largely destroyed. What you see are the poor remains of it. The hand of the hillman went with the rest, but I gave the matter no particular thought at the time. That was six years ago.

"Four years ago—two years after the fire—I was awakened one night by a furious tugging at my sleeve. I sat up under the impression that my favourite mastiff was trying to arouse me. Instead of this, I saw my Indian patient of long ago, dressed in the long, grey gown which was the badge of his people. He was holding up his stump and looking reproachfully at me. He then went over to my bottles, which at that time I kept in my room, and he examined them carefully, after which he gave a gesture of anger and vanished. I realized that he had just died, and that he had come to claim my promise that I should keep his limb in safety for him.

"Well, there you have it all, Dr. Hardacre. Every night at the same hour for four years this performance has been repeated. It is a simple thing in itself, but it has worn me out like water dropping on a stone. It has brought a vile insomnia with it, for I cannot sleep now for the expectation of his coming. It has poisoned my old age and that of my wife, who has been the sharer in this great trouble. But there is the breakfast gong, and she will be waiting impatiently to know how it fared with you last night. We are both much indebted to you for your gallantry, for it takes something from the weight of our misfortune when we share it, even for a single night, with a friend, and it reassures us to our sanity, which we are sometimes driven to question."

This was the curious narrative which Sir Dominick confided to me—a story which to many would have appeared to be a grotesque impossibility, but which, after my experience of the night before, and my previous knowledge of such things, I was prepared to accept as an absolute fact. I thought deeply over the matter, and brought the whole range of my reading and experience to bear upon it. After breakfast, I surprised my host and hostess by announcing that I was returning to London by the next train.

"My dear doctor," cried Sir Dominick in great distress, "you make me feel that I have been guilty of a gross breach of hospitality in intruding this unfortunate matter upon you. I should have borne my own burden."

"It is, indeed, that matter which is taking me to London," I answered; "but you are mistaken, I assure you, if you think that my experience of last night was an unpleasant one to me. On the contrary, I am about to ask your permission to return in the evening and spend one more night in your laboratory. I am very eager to see this visitor once again."

My uncle was exceedingly anxious to know what I was about to do, but my fears of raising false hopes prevented me from telling him. I was back in my own consulting-room a little after luncheon, and was confirming my memory of a passage in a recent book upon occultism which had arrested my attention when I read it.

"In the case of earth-bound spirits," said my authority, "some one dominant idea obsessing them at the hour of death is sufficient to hold them in this material world. They are the amphibia of this life and of the next, capable of passing from one to the other as the turtle passes from land to water. The causes which may bind a soul so strongly to a life which its body has abandoned are any violent emotion. Avarice, revenge, anxiety, love and pity have all been known to have this effect. As a rule it springs from some unfulfilled wish, and when the wish has been fulfilled the material bond relaxes. There are many cases upon record which show the singular persistence of these visitors, and also their disappearance when their wishes have been fulfilled, or in some cases when a reasonable compromise has been effected."

"*A reasonable compromise effected*"—those were the words which I had brooded over all the morning, and which I now verified in the original. No actual atonement could be made here—but a reasonable compromise! I made my way as fast as a train could take me to the Shadwell Seamen's Hospital, where my old friend Jack Hewett was house-surgeon. Without explaining the situation I made him understand what it was that I wanted.

"A brown man's hand!" said he, in amazement. "What in the world do you want that for?"

"Never mind. I'll tell you some day. I know that your wards are full of Indians."

"I should think so. But a hand——" He thought a little and then struck a bell.

"Travers," said he to a student-dresser, "what became of the hands of the Lascar which we took off yesterday? I mean the fellow from the East India Dock who got caught in the steam winch."

"They are in the *post-mortem* room, sir."

"Just pack one of them in antiseptics and give it to Dr. Hardacre."

And so I found myself back at Rodenhurst before dinner with this curious outcome of my day in town. I still said nothing to Sir Dominick, but I slept that night in the laboratory, and I placed the Lascar's hand in one of the glass jars at the end of my couch.

So interested was I in the result of my experiment that sleep was out of the question. I sat with a shaded lamp beside me and waited patiently for my visitor. This time I saw him clearly from the first. He appeared beside the door, nebulous for an instant, and then hardening into as distinct an outline as any living man. The slippers beneath his grey gown were red and heelless, which accounted for the low, shuffling sound which he made as he walked. As on the previous night he passed slowly along the line of bottles until he paused before that which contained the hand. He reached up to it, his whole figure quivering with expectation, took it down, examined it eagerly, and then, with a face which was convulsed with fury and disappointment, he hurled it down on the floor. There was a crash which resounded through the house, and when I looked up the mutilated Indian had disappeared. A moment later my door flew open and Sir Dominick rushed in.

"You are not hurt?" he cried.

"No—but deeply disappointed."

He looked in astonishment at the splinters of glass, and the brown hand lying upon the floor.

"Good God!" he cried. "What is this?"

I told him my idea and its wretched sequel. He listened intently, but shook his head.

"It was well thought of," said he, "but I fear that there is no such easy end to my sufferings. But one thing I now insist upon. It is that you shall never again upon any pretext occupy this room. My fears that something might have happened to you—when I heard that crash—have been the most acute of all the agonies which I have undergone. I will not expose myself to a repetition of it."

He allowed me, however, to spend the remainder of that night where I was, and I lay there worrying over the problem and lamenting my own failure. With the first light of morning there was the Lascar's hand still lying upon the floor to remind me of my fiasco. I lay looking at it—and as I lay suddenly an idea flew like a bullet through my head and brought me quivering with excitement out of my couch. I raised the grim relic from where it had fallen. Yes, it was indeed so. The hand was the *left* hand of the Lascar.

By the first train I was on my way to town, and hurried at once to the Seamen's Hospital. I remembered that both hands of the Lascar had been amputated, but I was terrified lest the precious organ which I was in search of might have been already consumed in the crematory. My suspense was soon ended. It had still been preserved in the *post-mortem* room. And so I returned to Rodenhurst in the evening with my mission accomplished and the material for a fresh experiment.

But Sir Dominick Holden would not hear of my occupying the laboratory again. To all my entreaties he turned a deaf ear. It offended his sense of hospitality, and he could no longer permit it. I left the hand, therefore, as I had done its fellow the night before, and I occupied a comfortable bedroom in another portion of the house, some distance from the scene of my adventures.

But in spite of that my sleep was not destined to be uninterrupted. In the dead of night my host burst into my room, a lamp in his hand. His huge, gaunt figure was enveloped in a loose dressing-gown, and his whole appearance might certainly have seemed more formidable to a weak-nerved man than that of the Indian of the night before. But it was not his entrance so much as his expression which amazed me. He had turned suddenly younger by twenty years at the least. His eyes were shining, his features radiant, and he waved one hand in triumph over his head. I sat up astounded, staring sleepily at this extraordinary visitor. But his words soon drove the sleep from my eyes.

"We have done it! We have succeeded!" he shouted. "My dear Hardacre, how can I ever in this world repay you?"

"You don't mean to say that it is all right?"

"Indeed I do. I was sure that you would not mind being awakened to hear such blessed news."

"Mind! I should think not indeed. But is it really certain?"

"I have no doubt whatever upon the point. I owe you such a debt, my dear nephew, as I have never owed a man before, and never expected to. What can I possibly do for you that is commensurate? Providence must have sent you to my rescue. You have saved both my reason and my life, for another six months of this must have seen me either in a cell or a coffin. And my wife—it was wearing her out before my eyes. Never could I have believed that any human being could have lifted this burden off me." He seized my hand and wrung it in his bony grip.

"It was only an experiment—a forlorn hope—but I am delighted from my heart that it has succeeded. But how do you know that it is all right? Have you seen something?"

He seated himself at the foot of my bed.

"I have seen enough," said he. "It satisfies me that I shall be troubled no more. What has passed is easily told. You know that at a certain hour this creature always comes to me. To-night he arrived at the usual time, and aroused me with even more violence than is his custom. I can only surmise that his disappointment of last night increased the bitterness of his anger against me. He looked angrily at me, and then went on his usual round. But in a few minutes I saw him, for the first time since his persecution began, return to my chamber. He was smiling. I saw the gleam of his white teeth through the dim light. He stood facing me at the end of my bed, and three times he made the low, Eastern salaam which is their solemn leave-taking. And the third time that he bowed he raised his arms over his head, and I saw his *Two* hands outstretched in the air. So he vanished, and, as I believe, for ever."

So that is the curious experience which won me the affection and the gratitude of my celebrated uncle, the famous Indian surgeon. His anticipations were realised, and never again was he disturbed by the visits of the restless hillman in search of his lost hand. Sir Dominick and Lady Holden spent a very happy old age, unclouded, so far as I know, by any trouble, and they finally died during the great influenza epidemic within a few weeks of each other. In his lifetime he always turned to me for advice in everything which concerned that English life of which he knew so little; and I aided him also in the purchase and development of his estates. It was no great surprise to me, therefore, that I found myself eventually promoted over the heads of five exasperated cousins, and changed in a single day from a hard-working country doctor into the head of an important Wiltshire family. I, at least, have reason to bless the memory of the man with the brown hand, and the day when I was fortunate enough to relieve Rodenhurst of his unwelcome presence.

H.B. DRAKE
Yak Mool San

Henry Burgess Drake wrote several interesting and curious novels including Cursed Be The Teasure (1926), The Shadowy Thing (1928), Hush-a-by Baby (1954), *and* The Book of Lyonne (1954), *illustrated by Mervyn Peake. He served as an intelligence officer during the Second World War in China and Korea, where the following weird tale is set.*

It was already late in March, towards the end, that is, of the hunting season in Korea. The winter had been disappointing, so, as the game laws still permitted another week or two, I was anxious to get in a last shoot. I could usually find a companion, but on this occasion it so happened there was no one free, so I was obliged either to forfeit my sport or to go alone. I decided to go alone.

I had heard at odd times of a somewhat forsaken mountain-range, known vaguely as the Tong San, at the Eastern Mountains, where good shooting was to be had. But as this meant a nine hours' rail journey to the nearest station, it was beyond the normal radius of my expeditions. Still, my winter's experience had convinced me that the country within three or four hours of the capital—where my business held me a prisoner—was shot out; so, though a longer journey meant less time with the gun, it seemed very possible that the sacrifice would pay. I found, too, on inquiry that there was a convenient night train, so by playing truant on Saturday I could leave on Friday evening and return by Monday morning and still have two clear days' shooting.

To avoid delay at the other end, I made what preliminary arrangements I could. The Japanese police, far from suggesting obstacles in their usual manner, were curiously at pains to be of service to me, showing indeed such an immediate interest at the mere mention of my destination that I did just wonder whether there was something peculiar about the place. There was a

Korean inn, they told me, where, though "veree inconvenyent," I could put up; also, though there were no professional beaters, yet they guaranteed to find me some half-dozen men who knew the country and the likeliest haunts of game. This was all I needed, as I could rapidly instruct them in the simple business of beating. Meanwhile, as the preparations went forward in this unexpected atmosphere of goodwill, I gathered considerable incidental information about the district. It was a wild place, mountainous, with patches of forest here and there—a rare thing in Korea—but, above all, it was deserted. This made game the more likely. So altogether I set out in good hope.

There would be no need to mention the train journey if I had not met with a certain Mr. Yi who gave me a piece of advice which transformed a mere shoot into a distinct adventure. My intention had been to turn in as soon as the boy-san had laid the bunks, and get all the sleep I could. The boy was already busy at the far end of the long coach, and I was half-way through a last pipe awaiting my turn to be bundled from my seat while he arranged the bed, when a Korean sat down opposite me, and with a dip of the head and an ingratiating smile said, "You go hunt, I think." I needn't reproduce all the conversation that followed. It was rather tedious. The fellow was dressed Western fashion, and refused to talk his own tongue, and I thought, to begin with, he was simply using me to practise his English on; but when I happened to mention my destination, he started with the same alert interest as had vaguely surprised me in the Japanese police. He at once began to press me with questions: "Why you go such a place? You hear something, yes? You veree brave?" I really woke up at that, and plied him with questions in my turn: What did he know of the place? Was there anything peculiar about it? Had he been there? "No, not been," he answered quickly, with something of a shudder. "Not want go. But you, you Engleesh. You like sport. You like danger. Yes, you Engleesh, you know——"

Yes, I knew that, I told him. But it was all hopelessly inconsequential. He threw out the most alarming suggestions. He even presented me with his visiting-card and made me promise to write to him if I returned alive. But the utmost I could draw from him was that the place had "how you say?—reputation." Still, as I've told you, he gave me one

233

piece of definite advice. If I wanted sport "more better than many," I ought to go "later."

Just at first this puzzled me. I couldn't go later, I explained, as the hunting season was nearly over. Just now the Japanese boy was busy converting my seat into a bed, and we were standing rather uneasily confined in the narrow passage-way between the double row of bunks. Mr. Yi became a little excited at my remark, and threw out a hand so vigorously that he nearly lost his balance in the rocking train, and repeated, "But later, later!"

I realized then that he was making a very common mistake in English. "Ah," I said, "you mean farther."

"Yes, farther," he agreed. "You go Yak Mool San. Medicine Water Mountain—you know," he translated the name. "You remember? Yak Mool San!"

We continued to talk some while after my bed was ready, but I could get nothing more out of him. To all my questions he opposed a tantalizing tilt of the head and a mask-like smile which might have concealed some profound secret or a complete vacuity. At last I dismissed him with a curt, "Well, I'm going to bed." He bowed himself away from me, leaving behind him as it were the ghost of an inane grin which slowly faded on the air.

Yak Mool San—I registered the name in my memory—Medicine Water Mountain; though I preferred to render it more poetically as the Mountain of the Healing Spring. Yet its delightful name was a disguise, I felt, for some elusive mystery.

The day was barely breaking when I left the train. The Japanese policeman on duty at the station was clearly expecting me. He welcomed me politely with the curious formula, "How do you do? I am sorry for you." I had heard it a hundred times before on the most commonplace occasions, yet now it harmonized so peculiarly with Mr. Yi's hints of the previous evening that I was prepared to suspect in it some hidden innuendo. But before I could answer the greeting—indeed, before I could show my shooting licence, which the man seemed to take for granted—he had swung round towards a white-pantalooned Korean porter, who was squatting dreamily on the platform, and chivvied him into getting busy with my kit. The fellow leapt into activity, and soon had my baggage corded to his *jigi*—a chair-like wooden structure on which the Koreans carry their loads—and hoisted on to his back. If it were my pleasure, he would now lead me to the inn.

I followed him into a shabby little town of thatched hovels, where diminutive black pigs nosed among the sewers. The inn was as mean as the town; yet the strange thing was to find an inn at all in such a forsaken spot. I was shown into a tiny room, some two yards square. And once again I found myself expected. Instead of the usual interminable wait, I found the room had been swept for me, and a fire laid beneath the floor, so I was comfortable enough squatting on a cushion and eating my breakfast, which was also in readiness.

My host squatted opposite me, white-robed, with a long grave face bearded like a goat, sedately drawing at a slender pipe. I tapped him immediately for information. There was game in plenty, he told me: pheasant and deer on the nearer slopes, goat and leopard higher up the mountains, and in the more forested places boar. "And where is Yak Mool San?" I asked him. I expected him to start at the name. But he didn't start. He removed his pipe from his lips and stared at me. Then he shook his head solemnly. "You cannot go to Yak Mool San," he said. My first impulse was to press him to explain. But in the yard outside I could hear the chattering of men whom I guessed to be my beaters. If the folk were in any way shy of the place, I knew that if I betrayed my intention of going there they would desert me. So I answered evasively, "No, no; I have been warned to keep away." At this he drew a deep breath. "It is a bad place," he said; "a bad place."

The beaters were ready for me—six, according to promise. One smiling old chap, radiant with the unaging infancy of the earth, seemed already to have been elected leader. There was, besides, a camp-following of urchins which increased as we passed through the town and out on to the hills. They were useful too; because the shoot was successful beyond my dreams, and one after another they were loaded with the kills and sent back to the inn.

It was a splendid country. At first a heavy mist lay over the earth, through which the hills loomed grey and ghostly like monstrous floating saurians. But as the sun strengthened, the mist gave way, and the land opened into the rolling Korean panorama of humpy hills and flat valleys climbing to a range of purple granite mountains which stood out steep and crenellated against the sky like some colossal rampart. When the landmarks were distinct, I drew out my map and located Yak Mool San.

Then, with no word as to my motive, I set the beaters to draw the valleys that would head the hunt that way. It was a wonderful day. The blue sky, the clear air, the free and spacious land would have set the blood singing of themselves; but with every beat starting its quarry there was the added zest of the perfect shoot which lifted joy to the pitch of intoxication.

It was well before evening when we reached the foot of Yak Mool San. The country over which we had passed had not been entirely deserted. We had come upon occasional squat little villages, and valleys terraced into rice-paddies; but habitation dwindled as we approached the mountains, and under Yak Mool San there was no human sign. Before us a ragged mass of granite, sparsely covered with scrubby pine, towered steeply to a naked cone of rock. But it was not inaccessible. A deep gorge, narrowing as it went, cut almost to the summit. The sides were matted with vegetation, but the bed was a tumble of boulders through which a trickle of clear water leaped and twisted to join a shallow river that flowed along the base. The beaters climbed a little way to a pool among the rocks, and, kneeling down, put their lips to the water and drank. "Yak Mool," they told me, inviting me to drink, "medicine water"; thus assuring me, if there had been any doubt, that I had not gone astray.

So far the men had shown no sign of uneasiness at the direction I had taken, but it became clear now that they were unwilling to push on. After wetting my lips in the pool, I was for setting off up the gorge, but they broke into an instant clamour calling on me to stop. It was a bad place; it was full of dragons; no one who went up Yak Mool San came down alive; he didn't come down at all—he vanished. I argued with them. I had shot plenty of deer, I told them, and a single goat; but I have shot no boar. They gabbled among themselves in an excited chorus, while the leader—his face for the first time that day no longer in a smile—told me we must return at once or we wouldn't reach the inn before nightfall. I pretended to understand their fear. Though tiger is rare enough now in Korea, yet the memory of tiger still keeps the Korean in terror of being overtaken by the dark. If there was tiger, I said, I had my gun. Moreover, I didn't intend to return to the inn. There must be caves in the mountains where we could sleep, and so be ready in the morning to continue the hunt. But at the talk of sleeping in a cave they went up in a single outcry of terror. A couple of them simply leapt down the gully, shouting as they ran. I took the leader by the arm. "See here," I told him deliberately, "if you will not come with me, then I go up the mountain alone. You can sleep in the nearest village and join me in the morning." He burst into a protest, and as I slipped on my pack, which one of the men had been carrying, and which contained some provisions and a blanket, and shouldering my gun began to climb the gorge, he tried to hold me back. But I shook myself free, and repeated, "You can join me in the morning." Poor old chap, there were tears in his eyes, and he fell suddenly dumb. Indeed, looking back from time to time as I ascended, I saw him still standing by the pool watching me in mute despair. I was none too happy when it became clear that I was to be left to my fate; but I couldn't lose face by returning now, and feeling more fool than hero, I pressed up alone.

It was steep going towards the top, but I came at last upon a saddle between two peaks and found myself on the crest. On the instant the country changed. Behind me I had left a rolling hill-land with patches of rice-fields and habitations, but before me was a deep hollow ringed in with fierce summits, and strewn at the bottom with a desolation of stones. I admit to a chill at the prospect; the place was so utterly lost and lonely. Moreover, the sun was setting. The air was grey, and it was cold. I felt like returning to where the water began—for I had climbed above the source of the healing spring—finding a cave, and turning in. But by an effort of will I determined to find my cave on the farther slope, and began to descend.

The darkness was gathering before I came upon what I wanted, a shelter among tumbled boulders with a thin stream gurgling by in a channel of stones. I set down my gun and threw off my pack, and was about to collect some fuel when I became aware of a shape on a rock above me silhouetted against the sky. It showed curiously pallid in the dim air, insubstantial like a shadow, and like a shadow without feature and without form. I felt myself arrested to a tense immobility, puzzled to resolve it to some known image. Then it moved, and at once I knew it for what it was. It was a boar, a monstrous boar such as I had never met with on the Korean mountains. And it was white. In a flush of excitement I reached back for my gun, levelled it, and pulled the trigger. But nothing happened. The gun was empty.

That was the first time I had been guilty of such carelessness. I thrust my hand into my pouch for a cartridge, loaded—but the creature had vanished. Yet I had heard no sound. I scrambled up to the rock where it had stood. But there was no sign of it. I listened; but couldn't locate it anywhere. It was too dark to look for spoor. In disgust I clambered back to my cave, lit my fire, cooked my supper, and laying up sufficient fuel to last me the night, huddled myself into my blanket and fell asleep.

2

I was up before the sun. I made a rapid breakfast, and again climbed to the rock where I had seen the white boar. The mountains were thick with mist, but if there were spoor I thought I could follow it. More than once I was tricked into believing that I had come across tracks, but the coarse, thin granite sand which lay over the rocks was too slight to hold any definite impression. I wandered, and was soon quite out of my bearings. I sat down and lit a pipe, deciding to wait for the sun. . . . Then again that shape was before me, like a patch of denser mist within the mist. It was rooting in the earth, presenting me its flank, and curiously enough, barely distinguishable as it was, I could yet make out a line of teats beneath its belly, and knew it for a sow. I brought my gun carefully to my shoulder, taking aim for its head. At that moment the mist seemed to thicken, and it faded from my sight. But it had had no time to move, and it was only some five paces from me. It was impossible to miss. I pulled the trigger, and all around me the hidden mountains echoed with the detonation. I jumped up and ran forward; but there was no trace of my quarry. I studied the ground in bewilderment, beat here and there; but it had completely vanished. Completely. There was only one explanation to the mystery. I had been cheated by an hallucination. Yet that didn't altogether satisfy me, possible as it was in such a mist with my mind working upon the image of the night before, because if I had imagined the thing I wouldn't have pictured it as a sow. Yet it had gone, dissolving before my eyes into nothingness. I sat down once more and relit my pipe, determined not to move again until the sun cleared the air.

I waited perhaps an hour; I don't really know. Then suddenly the sun struck through; and almost immediately the mist was sucked into the sky, and the mountains were all around me.

Then I became aware of something which surprised me in that forsaken place. It was full of graves; enormous graves, such as I had seen in the ancient capital of Kyung Ju. The graves of kings, rising in huge domed mounds like hills about the edge of the hollow, and showing here and there higher up among the slopes and gorges. I was in a vast mausoleum of departed royalty. That welter of stones below me, too, took on a new significance. They were the stones of fallen buildings, the ruins of a dead city. That also I had seen at Kyung Ju, but there at least some sort of town still stood amid the desolation. But here there was nothing to tell of human life. I couldn't so much as trace the outline of a fallen wall nor the passage of a buried street. I understood now the interest of the police, and the terror of the beaters. If ever a place were haunted, it would be such an abandoned wreckage as this, where life seemed paralysed out of hope beneath the spell of some monstrous visitation.

I stood for a long time looking at it all, distinguishing another hump and another as fresh graves asserted themselves on my view. Then, without thinking, I began to descend towards the hollow, coming almost at once upon yet a further grave which had lain so close beneath me that I had not noticed it. Like the rest, it was a great mound of earth, heaped on a platform which had been levelled across a widening in a gully. Guardian images of warriors and animals stood around it, enclosed within a low circular wall which opened only towards the valley; and before the opening was set a great flat block of granite for an altar stone. I paid it little attention, because it was an exact replica of other Korean tombs of consequence. I was more interested in the city below. So I found my cave and gathered my kit together, and set out to explore.

I needn't tell you of my wanderings. The place was more abandoned seen close to than seen from above. Though I came across some great base stones, hollowed out to sustain their cedar columns and so telling of palaces and temples, I realized of a sudden I was wasting my time, and struck back for the slopes. I didn't give a serious thought to returning for my beaters. I guessed well enough they would never follow me into that valley of tombs, and indeed had probably returned to the inn overnight to report my disappearance. There was nothing for it but to pick up what spoor I could and hunt alone. But you can imagine I had little success. The place was teeming with game, but with no one to beat it towards me while I lay in ambush on some convenient crest, I found myself all astray. The fact was, I hadn't the first idea of tracking and stalking, and the hours went by and my bag remained empty. So that can go unrecorded. But there are two things that I must record.

The first was the discovery of a grave which had been partially excavated. A great hole had been dug in the top, as though the thing had erupted like a miniature volcano. Clearly the Japanese had been at work; but the work had not been completed. I could only surmise that something in the atmosphere of the place had driven the coolies to desert. Indeed, it seemed surprising, knowing even the little that I did of the reputation of that haunted hollow, that any workmen had been induced at all to engage in such an undertaking. And it seemed likely there was a story behind that too, known to those interested Japanese police.

The second discovery was altogether astonishing. Mounting a ridge, I found myself looking down on a little terraced space of valley. The paddies looked shabby enough with their dykes half-fallen in and threatened on all sides by the invading shrub, but the stubble dotting their muddy surfaces witnessed to a last year's harvest of rice. So there was life here after all. And sure enough, higher up the slope was a miserable thatched hovel of mud and stones propped wryly against a boulder. I made straight towards it.

I found an old man there squatting just within the doorway, gazing out upon his forlorn estate. I suppose he was so inured to solitude that my figure looming suddenly up before him conveyed no intelligible impression to his mind. At any rate he eyed me with an unmoving vacancy, and even when I addressed him he didn't so much as move his lips to reply. Well, it was drawing towards noon, and as I had some provisions still remaining, I unslung my pack and began to prepare lunch. I gathered some fuel and, stepping past the old man and making free of the grate within the hut and of a brass bowl which stood beside it, I soon had a fire going and some broth on the boil. Still my recluse said nothing, observing my performance with an air of abstracted indifference. I poured out some soup and handed it to him. He put the bowl to his lips, sipped, swallowed a great mouthful, then, setting the bowl down, he turned a radiant face on me and said, "The spirits do not bring me food."

I might have guessed what was in his mind. He had lived among ghosts, that old fellow, and he had never seen a white face before. It needed the physical assurance of my food on his palate to waken him to the realization that I belonged to the world of men. After that he thawed. His face, drawn with hunger and loneliness, took on an amazing sweetness. And his voice, raucous at his first pronouncement, became soft and suave. I could detect in it, poor as was my accomplishment in the Korean tongue, the accents of a gentleman.

I should like to linger here in my narrative, as indeed I lingered with that remarkable old chap the better part of the afternoon. But without his gentle voice and patient face, and without that setting of inexorable desolation, you would find it a tedious delay. But this was his story.

He was a gentleman, as I had guessed, and a scholar. Misfortune had befallen his family. Unused though he was to working, he found himself compelled to work. He had hawked fish among the inland villages, scraped fuel from the hills and sold it in the cities, sat by the sides of streets behind a trayful of assorted trinkets, tried every shift, but nothing had prospered. He had become a beggar at last, scavenging for food at night among garbage-boxes, and sheltering during the winter in holes in the hillsides beneath a mat of straw. But at heart he was a scholar, and he had always kept with him a few of his favourite books. He showed me one, putting it reverently into my hands, and watching me anxiously as I turned the brittle yellow pages. I could make nothing of the script, which looked like the play of shadows through a fretted screen. But he interpreted the pictures. It was a history of the dynasty that had once ruled at Yak Mool San. Turning to a picture towards the end of the book, he slipped from his own story into a narrative of the disaster which had emptied the ancient city and left it to crumble into decay.

The picture was of a woman. Her name was Lady Ahn. She sat symmetrically posed, her hands on her lap, her feet, just showing beneath her wide dress, set exactly together. Her gown of pale clear blue, with ample sleeves striped vividly across with greens and reds and yellows, suggested in its decorous flatness no line of a living body beneath. Yet in spite of this formal rigidity there was something vital in the face. The cheeks indeed were dead enough, powdered to a blank whiteness in

241

the customary Eastern idealization of female beauty. And the vermilion lips were no more than the painted mouthpiece of an image. And the black hair, drawn severely back from the forehead and showing behind the neck the heads of elaborate amber pins, was utterly without lustre. It was the eyes that were alive. There was a penetrating devilry in their unswerving stare that made the rest of the picture of no consequence. That woman must have been consummately wicked.

Her story confirmed the impression. But the mere list of tortures and murders to her charge won't particularly interest you. You can read that in the history of any Eastern court. She was a concubine, plotting to be queen; that should explain her reputation. Yet that doesn't reach to the root of the matter. She bore a charmed life, evading assassination by such incredible devices that her enemies came to impute to her diabolical powers. She would be tracked to her chamber, surrounded, her assassins would burst in—but she would have vanished. She could change her shape, it was whispered, escaping over the roof like a leopard, gliding under the floor like a snake. The East can believe that readily enough; and the West has its legends, too, of snake-women and werwolves. Yet she was trapped at last, trapped in her summer pavilion "at the entrance to the mountain." She was found in the morning, deserted by her women, with a knife in her heart. And rumour had it that one arm had already changed to a bat's wing as she had attempted to transform herself and escape. But that time she had been too slow. She was dead without doubt when they found her. The pavilion was pulled down and a tomb erected in its place. "At the entrance to the mountain." I thought it must be the grave I had passed in the morning with such indifference. I would have studied it more carefully if I had guessed the drama it concealed.

But the story didn't end with the funeral rites. Lady Ahn's spirit still lived even if her body was dead, and it exacted a terrible revenge. You can imagine for yourself what calamities you please: floods and landslides and pestilence, wild beasts rooting up the paddies, devastating the crops, penetrating even into the palace by night and carrying away great men from their quilts, plagues of serpents coiling beneath cushions and striking in the dark, plagues of vampires unhindered by doors and shutters draining their victims to the last drop of blood. As much as you will in the same strain. And, of course, whatever the truth may have been, something portentous must have visited the city. And the explanation was simple: it was the vengeance of Lady Ahn. An exodus began. And when the king himself was found one morning dead without a wound in his body, the exodus became a stampede. Within five years the fear of a murdered concubine had turned a flourishing city into a wilderness.

The story was sufficiently impressive, told to me as it was in a voice of soft modulations, without hurry and without comment, like a statement of sorrowful fact. But it was a shock to hear that old chap say, "Her vengeance is not ended yet. Her spirit is still alive."

It was himself he was thinking of now, and of his misfortunes since he had settled in that place. Others had tried before him, but none had remained, driven away by the spirits that attended on Lady Ahn. He had known that, but it came to him that here was a spot where land was to be had without money. He sold one of his precious books and set himself up in the few necessary implements of the farmer, and had come there content, if fortune still proved unkind to him, to lie down and die. Fortune had been unkind, he told me, but he was not yet dead. It was the wild beasts that would not let him be. They ruined his seed-beds, trampled down his harvests. Yet he had managed to grow enough rice to keep himself alive. Also he had a bow, in the manner of his fathers, and could shoot a little. But he was getting old now, and watching by night over his crops he would fall asleep, and in the morning he would wake to find his paddies plashed with boar-hooves and his rice half-eaten. Yet when he was awake it was the same; for the wild beasts—they were spirits.

"Have you seen a white boar?" I asked. "A great white sow?"

At that he looked at me with a grave concern. "So soon," he said, "so soon you have seen her. Then you must go away."

Well, I had to go away if I wished to catch my train. I explained this to him, but he didn't appear to understand. It was clear that he imputed my hurried departure to my fear of the spirits.

My mind was full of that haunting story as I climbed the gorge to Lady Ahn's grave. And then for the third time I saw the white sow. I hadn't noticed it at first, because it was partly concealed behind the altar stone at the entrance to the tomb. But I detected a movement. It was still broad daylight, and there was no possibility of mistake. I levelled my gun, and almost at the same moment the creature lifted its head and looked straight upon me. I fired on the instant. It had no chance. The bullet took it full in the monstrous forehead; I was certain of it. The brute leaped up with a shrill squeal, fixing me with an unspeakable ferocity in its malicious devil's eyes; then collapsed behind the altar. I sprang towards it—and it had gone.

To be sure, there was blood on the ground; but the thing had gone. I ran round the great grave; but there was no sign of it, no trail of blood even. I had no time to continue my search. No stomach either. With something like panic in my heart I stumbled up to the ridge, down the farther slope, and stepped out for the station.

I had underestimated the distance and had to run at the end. I heard people in the town calling after me as I passed. Figures appeared at doorways ejaculating and gesticulating. I suppose I had the look of a man pursued by a ghost. I reached the station two minutes before the train. The policeman stared at me agape as I puffingly directed him to have my kills packed and sent on to me. I had to repeat my instructions several times before I could penetrate the barrier of his bewildered incredulity at seeing me alive. But he recovered; because as the train steamed in he was saying, "How do you do? I am sorry for you."

3

For one reason and another it was three years before I revisited Yak Mool San. This time my journey excited no interest. There was a different policeman at the station, who examined my licence with a meticulous scrutiny. At the inn, when I mentioned the haunted mountain, my host made no comment. The beaters raised no objection to following me up the gorge. And when I topped the ridge, I understood.

The hollow beneath me was populated now. The valleys were all terraced. There was a township below, with the stones mostly cleared into dividing-walls between fields. The fear had gone from the place. The ghost of Lady Ahn had been laid.

Indeed, the Japanese were excavating her tomb. I stopped a few minutes to watch the digging and shovelling. In two days, I was told, they would come to the coffin. Well, as it happened, I had two days to spare. I determined to be present when the coffin was opened. I wanted to see if the skeleton really bore a bat's wing in the place of an arm.

I looked up my friend the scholar. He was the same gentle fellow as I had known him at first. But he had a comely little house now, and his paddies were in good trim. He was well dressed too; and his face was fuller, and his body, though lean, was in excellent condition. He recognized me at once, and bowed me into his house, set a cushion for me on the floor, and offered me tobacco and wine. Fortune had been good to him, he told me, speaking not so much with exultation as with his old patience touched to a serene joy. Everything had changed since the day of my honourable visit. The wild beasts had left him in peace to cultivate his rice. He had had miraculous harvests, and had carried some over the mountain to sell. When people heard his story, they came to prospect; and some had remained. Others followed, and the place had grown into a colony. And all this was since the day of my honourable visit. He looked at me with a respectful questioning as though I might deign to explain the mystery. The implication was that I had somehow settled the business of Lady Ahn.

"And the white sow?" I asked. "Have you seen the white sow again?"

He didn't answer me at once, too intent on his own theme. He brought out his book instead, and turned to the picture of the evil woman. "She had a white face," he said; "and you have a white face. But yours is the face of a good man; yet you too must have a great power."

It was a pity I had nothing to tell him, because I knew he was chagrined at my silence. But I couldn't bring myself to impose on his simplicity.

I repeated my question.

"Ah," he sighed, as though he felt himself rebuked for having pried into my secret, "you need have no fear. If the white sow still lived—but you see . . ."

And he waved a benign white arm to indicate the prosperity that had sweetened the desolation.

I lodged with him while I remained on the mountain; but that I can pass over. I kept an eye on the excavation of Lady Ahn's grave, and took good care to witness the opening of the coffin. It was a great granite chest, and a crazy contraption of posts and pulleys had been erected to lift the lid. Some dozen Koreans hauled on ropes, singing in chorus. The stone shifted, rose, was swung aside. A perfect skeleton was disclosed, with amber pins beneath the neck, golden bracelets at the wrists, and a golden belt about the waist. The Japanese officials peering down let out a simultaneous "*Saa!*" of satisfaction. They were looking at the amber and the gold.

Well, there was no bat's wing, but two human arms as ordinary as you could wish. . . .

But the forehead was pierced with a single round hole, exactly the size of a bullet.

VIVIAN EDWARDS
The Spirit of Christmas

Vivian Edwards, *a doctor by profession, won the* Writers News *Ghost Story Competition with this excellent tale last Christmas.*

Debridges is undoubtedly an elite store, designed for the rich; those to whom money has relatively little meaning. That's why I enjoy working there over the Christmas period . . . the wages are good, and so are the tips. Rich parents, especially the foreign ones, are apt to slip several pounds into my capacious pocket. I do after all give their progeny enormous pleasure.

Let me explain myself.

I'm Father Christmas. I'm also a medical student. I think it was the extraordinary rubber-like mobility of my face, my capacity to smile, the deep throated laughter, that won the day when I was first interviewed, the last of one hundred applicants. The stethoscope dangling carelessly out of my pocket helped too. A doctor in the house, however junior, was a considerable asset.

The routine was always the same. A snowy bearded giant garbed in red, I'd have my own arena with its enormous Christmas tree, twinkling lights, gleaming decor, surrounded by sacks of gaily covered gifts . . . good ones too . . . for the entry tickets were fifteen pounds each; but then the area around that London branch of Debridges was exclusive.

Christmas was always a happy time for me. None of the pain, the sadness of hospital life; the disease; the awfulness of tragic accidents especially in the aftermaths of drunken driving. No glimpses of family tragedy; the horrors of child abuse. Quite the reverse. It was an artificial world. Quite unreal, but for me an escape. And although I say it myself, no-one could have been a jollier, or more popular Father Christmas. I exuded merriment.

Perhaps the most popular Father Christmas in London.

I'll never forget the Christmas of 1990. In spite of the snow sprinkling the streets, the bitter cold and swirling winds,

Debridges was packed. As usual, I was the focal point, sur-rounded by excited expectant faces. For each ticket had a number; one, preselected by the computer, would win a marvel-lous prize. For that day, it was a superb bicycle, worth all of three hundred pounds; that always produced anticipatory excitement . . . and of course each child had a present.

Suddenly, a small rather grubby girl emerged from the crowd, pushing her way to the head of the queue. Noisy chatter ceased, and no wonder, for her clothes were shabby. Defiantly she faced me, swinging her long yellow pigtails, her knees blue with cold. The bright red jumper pulled low over an orange skirt set a discordant note. Wide blue eyes dominating an oddly appealing face, looked directly into mine:

"A present . . . for my brother . . . he's five . . . *and* ill in bed." Tears trickled down her cheeks.

"Where's your ticket . . .?" I queried hesitantly.

The buzz of conversation ceased. All eyes were fixed on the girl.

"A *lady* . . . well . . . a *kind* of Mother Christmas . . . at the entrance . . . told me she'd give it to me . . . here . . ." she explained. Her voice was singularly sweet.

"There's *only me*, Father Christmas, here in Debridges."

"*She* told to come . . . to your magic cave. To get my present."

A difficult situation for me. One I'd never met before.

"It's my rule . . . no ticket . . . no present . . ."

A delighted smile suddenly spread across the girl's face. Gleefully she clapped her hands . . . pointing her fingers: "Look . . . there. *There*. I told you so. It's *Mother* Christmas . . ." Her high pitched voice slowed to a stop. Wonderingly she added . . . "Oh my. See . . . see her beautiful long hair . . . gold . . . gold like the sun."

For that moment in time, there was an ecstasy in the blueness of her eyes. She seemed transfigured; lost in joy.

There was a strange stillness around me. Everyone was looking in the same direction. I turned round disbelieving. There she was; a Mother Christmas. Large brown eyes gazed into mine. Held me. They were like deep pools. Long glittering golden hair had fallen loose from the enshrouding Christmas cowl. She held out her hands to me. Almost hypnotised, I took the proffered ticket.

248

"A present for Annie, and for her sick brother. They too need some Christmas magic."

Instantaneously there was a blinding flash. Almost as if from another world; only it wasn't. A press photographer had pushed his way to the front.

"A scoop," he shouted triumphantly.

"I told you . . . a ticket for me." Tears of joy streamed down Annie's face. "She promised me."

Immediately there was an excited buzz of conversation. Cries of wonder from the children crowding round me. "*Mother* Christmas . . . never seen *her* before . . . nobody ever told us about a Mother Christmas ."

There were more blinding flashes. Never had I received such publicity.

"It'll be a sensation," said the photographer. "Front page of the National News tomorrow . . ."

A most prestigious paper.

"Who told you she'd be here?" I asked, still puzzled.

"Mother Christmas herself of course . . . at the entrance of the store, just as Annie said."

I looked round again. Strange. That small figure, the golden hair, had seemingly melted into the background. Disappeared from sight, followed by the Oooos and Ahhhs from the children. For them it was a magic show, and I was their magician.

Still their Father Christmas.

"Come Annie," I said gently. Something told me she had that prize-winning number. I led her to the shining bike. "This is for your brother . . ."

"His name is Barrie," she whispered, awestruck.

"Annie has won the prize of the Day," I announced to the raised faces.

There were cheers; another blinding flash. Certainly Debridges would make its name.

Suddenly a voice pierced my ear-drums. The low soft voice of a woman.

"And Annie's present . . .?"

Strange. There was no-one around.

Almost mesmerized, I set a doll on the floor, surreptitiously setting the keys. Almost her size, it walked towards her.

"My name is Dolly . . . and I love you . . ." The voice sang, surprisingly lifelike.

249

Yet another blinding flash as Annie clasped the doll.

"Thank you, . . . "Thank you for ever Mother and Father Christmas." she said simply.

I shook myself. Feeling oddly impelled, I reached out for a large box of chocolates, tucking inside the wrapping four five pound notes; parents had been generous that day. I felt forced to part with it, though it had been designed for study books. No rich parents supplemented my meagre grant.

"For your mother Annie," I found myself saying. "Happy Christmas to you all."

What was the matter with me; I didn't easily part with money, yet here I was touched with tenderness, not only for Annie, but for all children poor like her.

When Annie left, clutching her bicycle, for she refused to let the store deliver it, the glow seemed to have gone out of the day. That crowd soon dispersed, yet more children came and went, each clutching their present, till the time came for the store to close.

I pondered over the conundrum. Who was Mother Christmas?

It was the Managing Director who supplied the answer. I was summoned to his office at the end of that wearing but strangely rewarding day.

"We do like to be kept informed," he said, somewhat sternly.

"Informed. . . I don't understand . . ."

"You, on your own initiative, organised a visit, by, I understand, a *Mother* Christmas; not perhaps in the best taste under the circumstances . . . and something with which I would not have agreed . . . it is I who must make decisions . . ." He frowned, adding "having said that, your day of course has been a brilliant success for Debridges . . . I'm told that photographs will appear in the national papers . . . tomorrow the store will be packed to capacity . . ."

I told him the whole story; recounted exactly what had taken place. After that he remained silent. Then he summoned George, who spent his time over Christmastide giving out balloons to every child visiting the store. The old man, near eighty, had once been the head porter at Debridges.

"Tell me again about Mother Christmas . . . you remember that nun don't you . . .?" The Director asked gently.

"Never forget *her* Sir. A proper Christian . . . real nun . . . worked twenty years for the store Sir, . . . independent like . . .

often as not she'd be giving a present to a poor child . . . one with no money . . . used to annoy the staff . . . specially, Sir the Managing Director, the one just before your time, Sir. *He* said her ragamuffins lowered the tone of the place . . . but *she* tooks no notice . . . proper angry he got, Sir . . . but the children loved her; like a magnet she was."

"Describe her to us."

"Small she was . . . but her hair Sir . . . like spun gold."

His description fitted mine exactly.

"What happened to her?" I asked.

"She died suddenly . . . after twenty years faithful service. That resolved Debridges' problem . . ." The Managing Director sighed thoughtfully. "But it seems she can no longer be ignored. In future, a *Mother* Christmas will be sent to our Children's Hospital; *and* somehow the store must put aside a day for the poorer children of the area with . . . Mother Christmas . . ."

"My wife is a student too, Sir . . . how about her?" I asked.

We all agreed that somehow seemed right; for the originator of Christmas, the baby Jesus, never had anything in the way of worldly goods.

And that is how the spirit of Christmas returned to Debridges.

ERCKMANN-CHATRIAN
Uncle Christian's Inheritance

"Erckmann-Chatrian" was the collaborative name of the most successful and popular writing team in France during the latter half of the nineteenth century: Emile Erckmann (1822–99) and Alexandre Chatrian (1826–90). Their most famous work, The Polish Jew, *was adapted for the London stage by Sir Henry Irving as* The Bells; *and many of their historical tales became accepted reading texts in British schools. "Uncle Christian's Inheritance" is one of a large number of Erckmann-Chatrian's mystery and supernatural stories originally gathered together as* Histoires et Contes Fantastiques.

When my excellent uncle Christian Hâas, burgomaster of Lauterbach, died, I had a good situation as maître de chapelle, or precentor, under the Grand Duke Yeri Peter, with a salary of fifteen hundred florins, notwithstanding which I was a poor man still.

Uncle Christian knew exactly how I was situated, and yet had never sent me a kreutzer. So when I learned that he had left me owner of two hundred acres of rich land in orchards and vineyards, a good bit of woodland, and his large house at Lauterbach, I could not help shedding tears of gratitude.

"My dear uncle," I cried, "now I can appreciate the depth of your wisdom, and I thank you most sincerely for your judicious illiberality. Where would now the money be, supposing you had sent me anything? In the hands of the Philistines, no doubt; whereas by your prudent delays you have saved the country, like another Fabius Cunctator—

'*Qui cunctando restituit rem*——'

I honour your memory, Uncle Christian! I do indeed!"

Having delivered myself of these deep feelings, and many

252

more which I cannot enter into now, I got on horseback and rode off to Lauterbach.

Strange, is it not, how the Spirit of Avarice, hitherto quite a stranger to me, came to make my acquaintance?

"Caspar!" he whispered, "now you are a rich man! Hitherto vain shadows have filled your mind. A man must be a fool to follow glory. There is nothing solid but acres, and buildings, and crown-pieces, put out in safe mortgages. Fling aside all your vain delusions! Enlarge your boundaries, round off your estate, heap up money, and then you will be honoured and respected! You will be a burgomaster as your uncle was before you, and the country folks, when they see you coming a mile off, will pull off their hats, and say—'Here is Monsieur Caspar Hâas, the richest man and the biggest *herr* in the country.'"

These notions kept passing and repassing in my mind like the figures in a magic-lantern, with grave and measured step. The whole thing seemed to me perfectly reasonable.

It was the middle of July. The lark was warbling in the sky. The crops were waving in the plain, the gentle breezes carried on them the soft cry of the quail and the partridge amongst the standing wheat; the foliage was glancing in the sunshine, and the Lauter ran its course beneath the willows; but what was all that to me, the great burgomaster? I puffed up my cheeks and rounded off my figure in anticipation of the portly appearance I was to present, and repeated to myself those delightful observations—

"This is Monsieur Caspar Hâas; he is a very rich man! he is the first *herr* in the country! Get on, Blitz!"

And the nag trotted forward.

I was anxious to try on my uncle's three-cornered hat and scarlet waistcoat. "If they fit me," I said, "what is the use of buying?"

About four in the afternoon the village of Lauterbach appeared at the end of the valley, and very proud I felt as I surveyed the tall and handsome house of the late Christian Hâas, my future abode, the centre of my property, real and speculative. I admired its situation by the long dusty road, its vast roof of grey shingle, the sheds and barns covering with their broad expanse the waggons, the carts, and the crops; behind, the poultry-yard, then the little garden, the orchard, the vineyards up the hill, the green meadows farther off.

I chuckled with delight over all these comforts and luxuries.

As I went down the principal street the old women with nose and chin nearly meeting at the extremity, the bare-pated children with ragged hair, the men in their otter-skin caps, and silver-chained pipes in their mouths, all gaze upon me, and respectfully salute me—

"Good day, Monsieur Caspar! How do you do, Monsieur Hâas?"

And all the small windows were filled with wondering faces. I am at home now; I seem as if I had always been a great landowner at Lauterbach, and a notable. My kapellmeister's life seems a dream, a thing of the past, my enthusiastic fondness for music a youthful folly! How money does modify men's views of things!

And now I draw bridle before the house of the village notary, Monsieur Becker. He has my title-deeds under his care, and is to hand them over to me. I fasten my horse to the ring at the door. I run up the steps, and the ancient scribe, with his bald head very respectfully uncovered, and his long spare figure clad in a green dressing-gown with full skirts, advances alone to receive me.

"Monsieur Caspar Hâas, I have the honour to salute you."

"Your servant, Monsieur Becker."

"Pray walk in, Monsieur Hâas."

"After you, sir, after you."

We cross the vestibule, and I find at the end of a small, neat, and well-aired room a table nicely and comfortably laid, and sitting by it a young maiden rosy and fresh-coloured, the very picture of modesty and propriety.

The venerable notary announced me—

"Monsieur Caspar Hâas!"

I bowed.

"My daughter Lothe!" added the good man.

And whilst I felt in myself a reviving taste for the beautiful, and was admiring Mademoiselle Lothe's pretty little chubby nose, the rosy lips, and the large blue eyes, her dainty little figure, and her dimpled hands, Maître Becker invited me to sit down at the table, informing me that he had been expecting me, and that before entering on matters of business it would be well to take a little refreshment, a glass of Bordeaux, &c., an invitation of which I fully recognised the propriety, and which I accepted very willingly.

And so we sit down. We talk first of the beautiful country. And I form opinions about the old gentleman, and wonder what a notary is likely to make at Lauterbach!

"Mademoiselle, will you take a wing?"

"Monsieur, you are very kind; thank you, I will."

Lothe looks down bashfully. I fill her glass, in which she dips her rosy lips. Papa is in good spirits; he tells me about hunting and fishing.

"Of course Monsieur Hâas will live as we do in the country. We have excellent rabbit-warrens. The rivers abound in trout. The shooting in the forests is let out. People mostly spend their evenings at the inn. Monsieur the inspector of woods and forests is a delightful young man. The *juge-de-paix* is a capital whist-player," and so on, and so on.

I listen, and think all this quiet life must be delightful. Mademoiselle Lothe pleases me a good deal. She does not talk much, but she smiles and looks so agreeable! How loving and amiable she must be!

At last the coffee came, then the kirschwasser. Mademoiselle Lothe retires, and the old lawyer gradually passes to business. He explains to me the nature of my uncle's property, and I listen attentively. There was no part of the will in dispute; there were no legacies, no mortgages. Everything is clear and straightforward. Happy Caspar! Happy man!

Then we went into the office to look over the deeds. The close air of this place of dry, hard business, those long rows of boxes, the files of bills—all these together put weak notions of love out of my head. I sat down in an armchair while Monsieur Becker, collecting his thoughts, puts his horn spectacles in their place upon his long, sharp nose.

"These deeds relate to your meadow-land at Eichmatt. There, Monsieur Hâas, you have a hundred acres of excellent land, the finest and best-watered in the commune; two and even three crops a year are got off that land. It brings in four thousand francs a year. Here are the deeds belonging to your vine-growing land at Sonnenthâl, thirty-five acres in all. One year with another you may get from this two hundred hectolitres (4,400 gals.) of light wine, sold on the ground at twelve or fifteen francs the hectolitre. Good years make up for the bad. This, Monsieur Hâas, is your title to the forest of Romelstein, containing fifty or sixty hectares (a hectare is 2½ acres) of excellent timber. This is your property at Hacmatt; this your pasture-land at Tiefenthal. This is your farm at Grüneswald, and here is the deed belonging to your house at Lauterbach; it is the largest house in the place, and was built in the sixteenth century."

"Indeed, Monsieur Becker! but is that saying much in its favour?"

"Certainly, certainly. It was built by Jean Burckhardt, Count of Barth, for a hunting-box. Many generations have lived in it since then, but it has never been neglected, and it is now in excellent repair."

I thanked Monsieur Becker for the information he had given me, and having secured all my title-deeds in a large portfolio which he was good enough to lend me, I took my leave, more full than ever of my vast importance!

Arriving before my house, I enjoyed introducing the key into the lock of the door, and bringing down my foot firmly and proudly on the first step.

"This is all mine!" I cried enthusiastically.

I enter the hall—"Mine!" I open the wardrobes—"Mine!" Mine—all that linen piled up to the top! I pace majestically up the broad staircase, repeating like a fool, "This is mine, and that is mine! Here I am, owner of all this! No more uneasiness about the future! Not an anxious thought for the morrow! Now I am going to make a figure in the world!—not on the weak ground of merit—not for anything that fashion can alter. I am a great man because I hold really and effectually that which the world covets.

"Ye poets and artists! what are you in comparison with the rich proprietor who has everything he wants, and who feeds your inspiration with the crumbs that fall from his table? What are you but ornamental portions of his feasts and banquets, just to fill up a weary interval? You are no more than the sparrow that warbles in his hedges, or the statue that figures in his garden-walk. It is by him and for him that you exist. What need has he to envy you the incense of pride and vanity—he who possesses the only solid good this world has to offer?"

At that moment of inflated conceit if the poor Kapellmeister Hâas had appeared before me I might very likely have turned and looked at him over my shoulder and asked, "What fool is that? What business has he with me?"

I threw a window open; evening was closing in. The setting sun gilded my orchards and my vines as far as I could see.

On the declivity of the hill a few white patches indicated the cemetery.

I turned round. A great Gothic hall, with rich mouldings decorating the ceiling, pleased my taste exceedingly. This was the Seigneur Burckhardt's hunting-saloon.

An old spinet stood between two windows; I ran my fingers absently over the keys, and the loose strings jingled with the disagreeable squeaking of a toothless old woman trying to sing like a young damsel.

At the end of this long apartment was an arched alcove closed in by deep red curtains, and containing a lofty four-post bedstead with a kind of grand baldacchino covering it in. The sight of this reminded me that I had been six hours on horseback, and undressing with a self-satisfied smirk on my face all the time—

"It is the first time," I said, "that I shall sleep in a bed of my own."

And laying myself comfortably down, with my eyes dreamily wandering over the distant plains on which the shadows of evening were settling down, I felt my eyelids gently yielding to the sweet influence of sleep. Not a leaf was stirring; the village noises ceased one by one, the last golden rays of the sun had disappeared, and I dropped into the unconsciousness of welcome sleep.

Dark night fell on the face of the earth, and then the moon was rising in all her splendour, when I awoke, I cannot tell why. The wandering scents of summer air reached me through the open window, fragrant with the sweet perfume of the new-mown hay. I gazed with surprise, then I made an effort to rise and open the window, but some obstacle prevented me. To my astonishment, though my head was perfectly free to move in any direction, my body was buried in a deep sleep like a lump of lead. Not a single muscle obeyed my repeated efforts to raise my body; I was conscious of my arms lying extended near me, and my legs being stretched out straight and immovable; but my head was swaying helplessly to and fro. My breathing, deep and regular—the breathing of my body went on all the same, and frightened me dreadfully. My head, exhausted with its vain efforts to obtain obedience from the limbs, fell back in despair, and I said, "What! is it paralysis?"

My eyes closed. I was reflecting with a feeling of horror upon this strange phenomenon, and my ears were listening intently to the agitated beating of my heart, over whose hurried flow of blood the mind had no power.

"What, what is this?" I thought presently. "Do my own body and limbs refuse to obey my will? Cannot Caspar Hâas, the undisputed lord of so many rich vineyards and fat pastures, move this wretched clod of earth which most certainly belongs to him? Oh, what does it all mean?"

As I was thus wondering and meditating I heard a slight noise. The door of my alcove opened, and a man clothed in some stiff material resembling felt, such as is worn by the monks in the chapel of St. Werburgh at Mayence, with a broad-brimmed hat and feather pushed off from the left ear, his hands buried up to the elbows in gauntlets of strong untanned leather, entered the room. This gentleman's huge jack-boots came over the knees, and were folded down again. A heavy chain of gold, with decorations suspended to it, hung from his shoulders. His tanned and angular countenance, his sallow complexion, his hollow eyes, bore an expression of bitterness and melancholy.

This dismal personage traversed the hall with a hard and sounding step as measured as the ticking of a clock, and placing his skinny hand upon the hilt of an immense long rapier, and stamping with his heel on the floor, he uttered in a horribly disagreeable creaking voice resembling the grating of an engine these words, which dropped in a dry mechanical fashion from his ashy lips:—

"This is mine—mine—Hans Burckhardt, Count of Barth!"

I felt a creeping sensation coming all over me.

At the same instant the door opposite flew open wide, and the Count of Barth disappeared in the next apartment; and I could hear his hard, dry automatic tread upon the stairs descending the steps, one by one, for a long time; there seemed no end to it, until at last the awful sounds died in the remote distance as if they had descended into the bowels of the earth.

But as I was still listening, and hearing nothing further, all in a moment the vast hall filled as if by magic with a numerous company; the spinet began to jingle; there was music and singing of love, and pleasure, and wine.

I gazed and saw by the bluish-grey moonlight ladies in the bloom of youth negligently floating over the floor, and chiefly about the old spinet; elegant cavaliers attired, as in the olden time, in innumerable dangling ribbons, and the very perfection of lace collars and ruffles, seated cross-legged upon gold-fringed stools, affectedly inclining sidelong, shaking their perfumed locks, making little bows, studying all kinds of graceful attitudes, and paying their court to the ladies, all so elegantly, and with such an air of gallantry, that it reminded me of the old mezzotint engravings of the graceful school of Lorraine in the sixteenth century.

And the stiff little fingers of an ancient dowager, with a parrot bill, were rattling the keys of the old spinet; bursts of thin laughter set discordant echoes flying, and ended in little squeaks with such a sharp discordant rattle of constrained laughter as made my hair stand on end.

All this silly little world—all this quintessence of fashion and elegance, long out of date, all exhaled the acrid odour of rose-water and essence of mignonette turned into vinegar.

I made new and superhuman exertions to get rid of this disagreeable nightmare, but it was all in vain. But at that instant a lady of the highest fashion cried aloud—

"Lords, you are at home here in all this domain—"

But she was cut short in her compliments; a silence like death fell on the whole assembly. They faded away. I looked, and the whole picture had vanished from my sight.

Then the sound of a trumpet fell on my listening ears. Horses were pawing the ground outside, dogs were barking, while the moon, calm, clear, inviting to meditation, still poured her soft light into my alcove.

The door opened as if by a blast of wind, and fifty huntsmen, followed by a company of young ladies attired as they were two centuries ago, in long trains, defiled with majestic pace out of one chamber into the other. Four serving-men passed amongst them, bearing on their brawny shoulders on a stout litter of oak boughs the bloody carcass of a monstrous wild boar, with dim and faded eye, and with the foam yet lying white on his formidable tusks and grisly jaws.

Then I heard the flourishes of the brazen trumpets redoubled in loudness and energy; but silence fell, and the pomp and dignity passed away with a sigh like the last moans of a storm in the woods; then—nothing at all—nothing to hear—nothing to see!

As I lay dreaming over this strange vision, and my eyes wandering vaguely over the empty space in the silent darkness, I observed with astonishment the blank space becoming silently occupied by one of the old Protestant families of former days, calm, solemn, and dignified in their bearing and conversation.

There sat the white-haired patriarch with the big Bible upon his knees; the aged mother, tall and pale, spinning the flax grown by themselves, sitting as straight and immovable as her own distaff, her ruff up to her ears, her long waist compressed in a stiff black bodice; then there sat the fat and rosy children, with serious countenances and thoughtful blue eyes, leaning in silence with their elbows on the table; the dog lay stretched by the great hearth apparently listening to the reading; the old clock stood in the corner ticking seconds; farther on in the shadow were girls' faces and young men, talking seriously to them about Jacob and Rachel by way of love-making.

And this good family seemed penetrated with the truth of the sacred story; the old man in broken accents was reading aloud the edifying history of the settlement of the children of Israel in the Land of Canaan—

"This is the Land of Promise—the land promised to Abraham and Isaac and Jacob your fathers—that you may be multiplied in it as the stars of heaven for multitude, and as the sand which is upon the seashore. And none shall disturb you, for ye are the chosen people."

The moon, which had veiled her light for a few minutes, reappeared, and hearing no more sounds of voices, I looked round, and her clear cold rays fell in the great empty hall. Not a figure, not a shade, was left. The moonlight poured its silver flood upon the floor, and in the distance the forms of a few trees stood out against the dark purple sky.

But now suddenly the high walls appeared lined with books, the old spinet gave way to the *secrétaire* of some man of learning, whose full-bottomed wig was peering above the back of a red-leather arm-chair. I could hear the quill coursing over the paper. The learned man, buried in thought, never moved; the silence was oppressive.

But fancy my astonishment when, slowly turning, the great scholar faced me, and I recognised the portrait of the famous lawyer Gregorius, marked No. 253 in the portrait-gallery at Darmstadt.

How on earth had this personage walked out of his grave?

I was asking myself this question when, in a hollow sepulchral voice, he pronounced these words:—

"*Dominorum, ex jurè Quintio, est jus utendi et abutendi quatenus naturalis ratio patitur.*"

As this sapient precept dropped oracularly from his lips, a word at a time, his figure faded and turned pale. With the last word he had passed out of existence.

What more shall I tell you, my dear friends? For hours, twenty generations came defiling past me in Hans Burckhardt's ancient mansion—Christians and Jews, nobles and commoners, fools and wise men of high art, and men of mere prose. Every one proclaimed his indefeasible right to the property; every one firmly believed himself sole lord and master of all he surveyed. Alas! Death breathed upon one after another, and they were all carried out, each as his turn came!

I was beginning to be familiar with this strange phantasmagoria. Each time that any of these honest folks turned round and declared to me, "This is mine!" I laughed and said, "Wait a bit, my fine fellow!—you will melt away just like the rest!"

At last I began to feel tired of it, when far away—very far—the cock crowed, announcing the dawn of day. His piercing call began to rouse the sleeper. The leaves rustled with the morning air; a slight shiver shook my frame; I felt my limbs gradually regaining their freedom, and, resting upon my elbow, I gazed with rapture upon the silent wide-spread land. But what I saw presently did not tend to exalt my spirits.

Along the little winding path to the cemetery were moving, in solemn procession, all the ghosts that had visited me in the night. Step by step they approached the decaying moss-grown door of the sacred inclosure; that silent, mournful march of spectres under the dim grey light of early morning was a gaunt and fearful sight.

And as I lay, more dead than alive, with gaping mouth and my face wet with cold perspiration, the head of the dismal line melted and disappeared among the weeping willows.

There were not many spectres left, and I was beginning to feel a little more composed, when the very last, my uncle Christian himself, turned round to me under the mossy gate and beckoned me to follow! A distant faint ironical voice said—

"Caspar! Caspar! come! Six feet of this ground belong to you!"

Then he too disappeared.

A streak of crimson and purple stretched across the eastern sky announced the coming day.

I need not tell you that I did not accept my uncle Christian's invitation, though I am quite aware that a similar call will one day arrive from One who must be obeyed. The remembrance of my brief abode at Burckhardt's fort has wonderfully brought down the great opinion I had once formed of my own importance, for the vision of that night taught me that though orchards and meadows may not pass away their owners do, and this fact compels to serious reflection upon the nature of our duties and responsibilities.

I therefore wisely resolved not to risk the loss of manly energy and of the best prizes of life by tarrying at that Capua, but to betake myself, without further loss of time, to the pursuit of music as a science, and I hope to produce next year, at the Royal Theatre of Berlin, an opera which, I hope, will disarm all criticism at once.

I have come to the final conclusion that glory and renown, which speculative people speak of as if they were mere smoke, is, after all, the most enduring good. Life and a noble reputation do not depart together; on the contrary, death confirms well-deserved glory and adds to it a brighter lustre.

Suppose, for instance, that Homer returned to life, no one would dispute with him his claim to be the author of the *Iliad*, and each would vie with the rest to do honour to the father of epic poetry. But if peradventure some rich landowner of that day came back to assert a claim to the fields, the woods, the pastures of which he used to be so proud, ten to one he would be received like a thief and perhaps die a miserable death.

JOHN S. GLASBY
The Black Widow

John Stephen Glasby (b. 1928), distinguished chemist and astronomer, joined the Imperial Chemical Industries (Nobel) Division in 1952, where he carried out research on detonation and rocket research. Among his books are The Dwarf Novae (1970) *and* The Variable Star Observer's Handbook (1971). *He has had over 500 stories published in various genres, mainly science fiction, crime and supernatural horror, most appearing under pseudonyms in the 1950s and 1960s.*

Philip Ransome put his foot down on the accelerator and the car rounded a corner with the shriek of rubber compressed to the utmost by the sudden turn. The long vista of forested slopes ahead suddenly reminded him strongly of a journey he had made once before when he had driven into a dark forest. But although the memory was so strong he couldn't remember where, or when, it had been. Certainly it was not here for this was the first time he had visited the south of France.

Beside him, Anne sat easily in the passenger seat, her gaze fixed on the dim road ahead with a curious lack of emotion.

"Philip," she said finally, "are you sure we did the right thing renting this villa without even seeing it?"

Philip squeezed her waist and then let go as the road abruptly narrowed, twisting and turning in a series of hairpin bends.

"Why? You think there may be something wrong with it?"

"I don't know."

"But, after all, we got it for next to nothing. One doesn't usually have that kind of luck."

"I suppose that's what's so . . . worrying." Anne gave him a resigned glance which made him smile uncertainly. "There must be something wrong. No one would rent it out for such an absurdly low price if it's everything they claim it to be."

Philip switched on the headlights as the trees shut out the overcast autumn sky. It wasn't like driving at night because he knew that the sky was still light somewhere above the thickly tangled branches.

"We've been through all this before, Anne," he said finally. "We'd be fools to turn down an offer like this."

Anne leaned back, eyes closed. "It isn't just the price. I've got a strange feeling about this place, that's all."

"But we haven't seen it yet," Philip insisted.

"I don't have to see it." Anne countered illogically.

"Another of your premonitions?"

"Call it that if you like." Her tone implied that she didn't want to discuss it any further.

Philip peered ahead, watching the road intently. They were now moving along the steep downgrade and it was so dark that he could only see clearly to the limit of the headlights. The twisted branches leaned over the road to form an impenetrable arch. Here and there were dips in the road and he had the odd feeling that the gloom was striving to drag them down whenever they passed over one.

In spite of his desire to be out in the open again, he was forced to drive slowly in third gear. Then, just as he rounded a bend he slammed his foot hard on the brake. Anne was hurled forward before the belt jerked her back into the padded seat.

"What the hell—" Philip stared incredulously through the windscreen. The twin beams picked out the figure standing in the middle of the road perhaps thirty yards away, thrusting forward a white face that stared at them from beneath the hood of a black cloak.

The engine had stalled and there was only the muted whirr of the interior air conditioning in the silence.

"What is it?" Anne asked in a hoarse whisper that seemed stuck in her throat.

Philip sucked in his breath in a long, heaving gasp. There was a chill dampness on his forehead and his fingers were trembling on the wheel.

"It's a woman." He got the words out with an effort. "But what's she doing out here, miles from anywhere. Damned fool. She could get herself killed."

He opened the door to get out and for an instant his glance left the black figure. Straightening, he looked back. The road was empty! He had a moment of panic as he continued to stare. Then he turned his head towards Anne. She, too, was peering into the gloom, a horrified expression on her face.

"Did you see where she went?" he asked.

Anne shook her head numbly. "She just vanished."

"Into the trees, you mean?" Philip could feel his heart jumping against his ribs.

"No. I'd have seen her if she had. One second she was there and the next she'd gone."

Philip strained his eyes to peer into the gloomy array of tree trunks on either side. All of his senses were intensified.

"You think we imagined it?" He willed himself to keep his voice down. The utter silence didn't help and he knew that Anne was closer to panic than he was. There had been something uncanny about that menacing shape.

"Maybe." Anne's muted whisper reached him from inside the car. "But it's gone now. Let's get the car started and get out of this place."

He slipped in beside her, slammed the door shut, welcoming the loud noise. Twisting the key in the ignition, he had to try the engine twice before it caught and he could feel the fear rising within him as he willed the engine to keep turning.

Engaging the gears, he drove forward, eyes flicking from side to side, expecting to see that ghostly figure in black emerge from the trees close at hand at any moment.

A hundred yards further on they passed between two large encroaching overhangs of rock which seemed intent on crushing them under their ponderous weight. Philip spun the wheel automatically as they came out into the open.

Down below lay the small village straddling the narrow road. By now it was early evening and most of the small windows gleamed with yellow lights. In places, the road narrowed as they crossed swift-rushing streams so that they barely scraped between the low parapets of ancient stone. Passing through the village, the road began rising as more trees showed on the rocky slopes. It was now almost completely dark but the moon, full and bright, allowed them to pick out the villa perched high above the road.

There was a screen of conifers fronting it, blocking their view a little, so they could not make out all of the details.

Two kilometres from the village, the headlights picked out the large metal gates on their right. Once through the gates the drive curved, then curved again. There was a wide lawn sloping down from the villa and Philip rolled down the window to get a better view as they approached.

Anne found herself wishing everything wasn't quite so still. There did not seem to be a breath of wind; she couldn't recall when she had last felt so deep a silence. It must have been the utter stillness which made her imagine she glimpsed movement among the trees on the far side of the grounds.

Her premonitory fears were working on her, she told herself; her yearning to fill the stillness and silence was making her think she saw someone walking among the shrubbery beyond the lawn.

The villa was supposed to be empty. The agent had written to say that if they required any help during the day they could engage someone from the village once they arrived. So there would be no one in the grounds, particularly at this time of night. It must be a bush bearing an oddly human shape, of course, and their own movement gave it the illusion of changing its position.

She didn't want to mention it to Philip, not after that frightening encounter on the forest road.

Philip was peering ahead, slowing the car as he drove around the neatly trimmed garden. He pulled up in front of the imposing entrance. Opening the door, he got out, breathing in the cool, crisp night air. Turning slowly, his brain seemed to fill up with the details of the villa. It looked more modern than he had expected. The photographs he had seen had not done it justice. So often, photographs painted a glowing picture which was not realized in reality.

He knew he ought to be pleased at getting a place like this for three months—and for much less than he would have had to pay for a much smaller place in England. But for some reason he couldn't fathom, there was a nagging little idea at the back of his mind that everything wasn't quite what it should be.

"Well, what do you think, Anne?"

"It *looks* all right," she said slowly, running her gaze over the building and grounds. "Somehow, it's different from what I imagined it would be like."

Philip took the cases from the car while Anne opened the door. They went inside, closing the door behind them. In spite of the pleasant, warm atmosphere inside the place, Philip felt a little flutter of panic in his mind as they walked down the hall into the front room. Instinctively, he tried to throw off the feeling that they were being watched. He had a sudden flash of conviction that they were being scrutinized by eyes peering from the stairway; unfriendly eyes.

Some part of his mind, curiously detached from the rest, seemed to reach out ahead of him, beyond Anne, and up the wide stairway, to detect a presence there.

"Is there anything wrong, Philip?"

With an effort, he pulled himself together and forced himself to meet Anne's worried gaze.

"Why . . . no." He put the cases down.

"You looked so strange. Almost—" Anne broke off momentarily, "Almost as if you were seeing something, or waiting for something. Yes, that's it. Waiting for something."

"Nothing like that." Giving a shrug, he forced conviction into his tone. "Just finding the place empty like this, I guess." He put an arm around her waist. "We'll soon settle in and enjoy our holiday."

Sometime during the night, Philip woke. He was instantly wide awake, his flesh tingling and his fingers gripping the coverlet in a convulsive grasp. White moonlight threw a maze of long shadows across the floor. Everything was absolutely still and silent except for the quiet sound of Anne's breathing next to him. Whatever had woken him so suddenly had not disturbed her.

He sat up slowly, tensed and rigid. His heart was palpitating wildly as if he had just woken from some frightful nightmare. But he was not a man prone to nightmares and he instinctively sought for some external reason for his awakening.

At that instant, he picked out the stealthy sound—unmistakably that of footsteps moving cautiously up the stairs. The idea that there was someone else in the villa started a little germ of panic screaming in his mind.

There had been several cases of foreign holidaymakers being murdered in France and if there was a burglar out there, he and Anne didn't stand a chance. There was no weapon in the room he could use to defend himself. But he couldn't simply sit there and wait for some killer to burst into the bedroom.

Somehow, he galvanized himself into action. Swinging his legs to the floor, he edged towards the door. The sound of someone moving outside was unmistakable now. They were deliberate, measured steps, those of someone who knew where he wanted to go and obviously was familiar with the interior of the villa.

Had the owner returned, not knowing they had already moved in? He tried to reassure himself with this possibility as he reached out and curled his fingers around the doorknob. The metal felt cold as ice to his touch.

Drawing in a deep breath, he pulled the door open sharply and stared out into the corridor. Through the wide windows at the end, brilliant moonlight flooded along the landing. He could see the whole of the corridor and the long sweep of the stairs quite clearly.

He could still hear the footsteps moving away and somehow he forced himself forward, leaning over the ornate banisters along the landing. There was a flicker of movement at the bottom. He had the unmistakable impression of a tall figure, dressed in black, that glided across the room below. Her back was towards him and he could see nothing of her features. But the sheer malevolence which shrouded the figure brought all of his fear back with a rush, together with instant recognition. He did not doubt it was the same figure they had encountered on the forest road. Philip realized he was holding his breath until the throbbing of blood in his throat threatened to choke him. He felt as if there was a cloud of darkness over him, pressing his head forward on his neck, forcing him forward over the banisters.

Gasping hoarsely, he succeeded in taking small, shallow breaths. He was trembling violently and it was only with a supreme effort of will that he managed to thrust himself backward and upright, otherwise he would surely have toppled into the room below.

The figure had vanished but the atmosphere of malignity, of something evil, remained. Somehow, he stumbled back into bed, taking care not to wake Anne. He lay there, staring rigidly at the ceiling, for more than an hour before he fell into an uneasy sleep.

When he woke the next morning, he had a splitting headache. Anne was already up and he could hear the clatter of dishes in the dining room downstairs. Dressing quickly, he swallowed a couple of aspirins and tried to force the events of the night into the background of his mind.

Splashing cold water onto his face, he rubbed himself dry, then went downstairs into the dining room at the rear. He told himself there had to be a logical explanation but the only reassuring one was that he had imagined, or dreamed, it all. He did not even want to consider the probability that the villa was haunted, nor did he want to frighten Anne. She was the one who had these strange premonitions. He had always been the earthy, practical type. Perhaps, if he got the opportunity, he would have a talk with one of the villagers. If there was anything strange about the villa, they would certainly know all of the details. Though whether they would be inclined to talk to a stranger was a different matter.

The kitchen door opened and Anne came in with two plates heaped with bacon and eggs. She set them down on the table and threw him a swift glance.

"Didn't you sleep well, Philip? You look ghastly."

"Not too well, I'm afraid." He would have to be careful what he said. "Being in a strange place, I guess."

"God, I slept like a log. Must have been the long drive." She sat down. "Funny how different everything looks in the sunlight."

Philip paused with his fork halfway to his mouth. "Then you've got over your doubts about the place?"

Anne laughed. "I'll admit it did look a little ghostly last night in the dark. But it looks beautiful now. And the agent has arranged everything for us. Plenty of food and drink and no trouble with the cooker. It's all so clean and tidy."

"He must have had someone from the village come in to get it all ready for us. I'll probably go down and have a word with him today."

"After breakfast I want to explore the whole place. Then I thought we might take a walk into the village."

Philip nodded in agreement. Already, he was feeling a little better, more easy in his mind. If Anne no longer felt there was anything odd about the place, it might have been nothing more than a nightmare when he had imagined he had heard those footsteps and seen that black, gliding shape.

Once the dishes had been washed and dried, they began their tour of the villa. It was soon obvious that it was much larger than either of them had imagined. Everything they saw indicated that the owner had to be extremely wealthy. Large crystal chandeliers hung from the ceilings, the furniture was of the best quality with a number of antiques, which would have fetched several thousand pounds at an auction.

Taking in all that he saw, Philip could not help wondering why such a place was let out to strangers. Not because the owner needed the money, nor merely for the purpose of keeping the place aired and clean. He was sure there had to be another, deeper reason.

As he went round with Anne, he found himself listening to every little sound the house made, every nerve and fibre in his body stretched almost to breaking point.

Relax, he told himself angrily as he followed his wife along a long, shadowy corridor. The idea that anything could be wrong here was ludicrous, utterly ridiculous.

Quite suddenly, he stopped. Out of the shadowed wall directly in front of him, a shape appeared—and in the shape, two eyes. Standing there, it seemed as though the night and the darkness were looking at him through those eyes.

Involuntarily, he staggered back a couple of paces, bumping into Anne.

"Philip—what's the matter?"

"Nothing, I . . ." He found himself stammering, barely able to get the words out. His tongue seemed jammed against the roof of his mouth. "It's just a picture. But it gave me quite a shock."

Somehow, he felt afraid to look at the large, full-length portrait. Even before he made it out clearly, he knew who it was.

"Oh, my God." Anne reached out and gripped his arm, her fingers biting deeply into the flesh. "That's—"

"The woman we saw on the road."

"Yes."

"Then there's only one explanation. She must be the present owner. The agent said something in his last letter about her being a widow."

He stood back a little, Anne still holding on to him. The woman in the portrait was seated at a table which he recognized as the one in the dining room along the corridor. She wore the same long black cloak he recalled from the previous day, the hood partly thrown back to reveal her face. There was, he realized, little remarkable about her features—apart from the eyes. Philip saw that they were fixed on him with a stare of calculated sardonic amusement as though daring him to look away and break the hypnotic spell they held for him.

For some reason he couldn't understand, his legs were shaking. There was an aura of evil malignancy surrounding the seated figure which almost overpowered him. It was like a dark nebulous shadow which seemed to emanate from the portrait, reaching out with cold, clammy tendrils, touching his skin and speeding up his heartbeat into an abnormally jerky rhythm.

Biting his lower lip, he pulled his gaze away, took Anne's arm and led her along the corridor. He hoped he had managed to convince her about the identity of the woman; that her own commonsense would tell her the owner now probably lived somewhere in the village and there was nothing supernatural about seeing her on that forest road.

Later that morning, they walked down the winding road into the village. The steep slopes glowed several different shades of grey and brown beneath the cloudless sky and the sun was hot on their shoulders. Overalled workers, the women with brightly coloured handkerchiefs around their heads, were working in the vineyards and several waved friendly greetings to them.

While Anne went on a tour of the quaint little village, Philip sought out Monsieur Reynault, the agent, checking the address on the last letter he had received before they had left England.

He found the small chalet on the very outskirts of the village, a neatly tended garden bordering the cobbled street. Going up to the door, he pushed the bell with his forefinger. There was a faint chime inside the house followed by the push of footsteps on the carpeted floor.

The door opened.

"Monsieur Reynault?"

"Oui." The man eyed him inquisitorially.

"I'm Philip Ransome. My wife and I rented the villa Couvier for the autumn."

271

"But, of course. Forgive me, I should have realized at once. Please come in."

Philip followed him into the small parlour where Reynault waved him to a chair. Taking a bottle from the table, Reynault poured out two glasses, handing one to Philip. "The local vintage." he said, raising his glass.

"Thanks." Philip sipped the wine appreciatively. He had noticed several bottles in the villa but so far, he and Anne had not tried any.

"Excellent," he said in answer to Reynault's inquiring glance.

"I'm glad you like it. But I presume you came to see me about something in particular. I trust you find everything to your satisfaction at the villa."

"Everything is perfect." Philip finished his wine and accepted a second glass. "There are, however, just one or two points I'd like to clear up."

"Certainly. If there's anything you wish to know, please ask."

Philip felt himself stiffen slightly. Was there a note of veiled uneasiness in the agent's tone, as if he had been taken by surprise by the remark?

"My wife is a little worried by the ridiculously low sum you're asking for renting the villa."

Reynault placed his glass on the small table with an exaggerated care before speaking. "I think I should point out that the sum you mention was fixed by the owner and has nothing to do with me. I merely carry out her instructions. Apparently she considers it to be reasonable." He paused significantly. "I should say that so far none of the other tenants have complained."

"So there have been others there?"

"Oh, yes. When Madame Couvier's husband died two years ago, she decided not to live there any longer but to rent the villa for three months each year during the autumn."

"Do you know where she lives now?"

"I'm afraid not. I've had no contact with her for over two years."

Philip stared at him in surprise. "Doesn't that strike you as odd?"

"Not really, Monsieur. Before she left she gave me specific instructions regarding the letting of the villa. All monies I receive are duly paid into her account. Any arrangements concerning food and maintainance I carry out myself."

"I see. And the painting hanging in the corridor. Is that of her?"

"Why, yes. But why do you ask?"

"Because as we were driving here, along the forest road, we saw a woman standing in the middle of the road. I realize it was dark among the trees and we only saw her for a few moments in the headlights, but she was wearing exactly the same kind of black cloak as that woman in the portrait."

"But that is impossible, Monsieur. You must have been mistaken. A shadow, perhaps, or the branch of a tree. It is so easy to be deceived, I assure you."

"Perhaps. But we both saw her."

Reynault spread his bony hands, then placed them on his knees. "Then I can offer no explanation."

Philip intended to tell him of his eerie experience during the night but decided against it, knowing it would only meet with the same response. Yet he felt certain the agent was hiding something, holding back some important information.

When he left five minutes later it was with a feeling of intense dissatisfaction. Anne was walking down the cobbled street towards him. She waved and quickened her step, hurrying up to him.

"Did you get anything out of him?"

"Not much." Briefly, he told her what he had learned from Reynault. When he had finished, she looked frustrated. "Do you agree with him that we both imagined what we saw on the road?"

"Either that, or this widow Couvier became eccentric after her husband's death and is living somewhere near the forest. These things sometimes happen, you know."

"I suppose so," Anne sighed. She fell into step with him as they walked back to the villa.

By early evening, the sun had been swallowed up by long bars of black cloud, building up into towering thunderheads over the mountains. The heat in the air became oppressive without a breath of wind and the suffocating silence was a dense blanket pressing the atmosphere against the ground. There came an occasional rumble of distant thunder but the storm didn't break until almost midnight.

By that time Anne had fallen asleep but Philip lay in the bed, wide awake, wincing each time the lightning flashed, lighting the room with a harsh, actinic glare. Each stroke was accompanied by a sharp crack, followed almost immediately by the crash of the thunder.

At times, he thought the entire building shook to its very foundations and he wondered how Anne could possibly sleep through it all, wishing he could close his eyes and not wake until morning. Maybe, he thought, if he closed the thick drapes across the windows they would blot out much of the lightning.

He hauled himself out of bed and padded to the windows. Oddly, there was no rain with the storm. The ground outside was as dry as a bone in the dazzling flash of a forked streak that speared from the clouds towards the peals. In the afterglow of that searing brilliance, he seemed to see everything in stark black and white like a photographic negative burned into his brain. Then pale blurs swarmed into his vision as his eyes watered but in that single instant he saw something which sent him reeling back from the windows.

The cloaked figure was standing in the middle of the lawn directly beneath the windows, head thrown back a little as if watching him. Savagely, he fought for self control and when a second flash came he forced himself to look again. The grounds were empty, yet he knew she had been there, that this time he had not been mistaken.

He spun frantically on his heel, jerkily, his heart racing, the blood pounding painfully in his temples. There had been something chill and dead about that figure and he felt the muscles of his stomach contract sharply as he realized it had not been a thing of flesh and blood.

But there was something he had to know, had to see for himself. He opened the bedroom door quietly although he doubted if it would make any difference. If Anne could sleep through the resounding din of the storm, the mere sound of the door opening wouldn't waken her. He almost fell as he ran down the stairs, taking them two at a time. For an instant, he expected to see that ghostly black figure waiting for him in the corridor. But there was nothing.

The place was in darkness but he felt his way along until his outstretched fingers touched the edge of the portrait on the wall. He jerked his hand back and edged away until his shoulders came up against the opposite wall. It was too dark to see anything but he didn't have to wait long for another vivid flash which lit up everything in stark detail.

The table and chair were there in the picture exactly as he remembered them from the previous morning. But where the woman had been there was simply a blank, grey space!

Philip was breathing faster than he liked by the time it dawned on him that he wasn't imagining things. The wall behind him bruised his shoulders but its solidity felt reassuring, as familiar as anything could be in this horrifying place. He knew he ought to wake Anne, get dressed as quickly as possible, and drive away from this haunted villa. Somehow, he forced his feet to move. There was only one thought in his mind now. They had to get away, in spite of the storm, if only to preserve their own lives and sanity.

He fell against the edge of the banister, hitting his side hard, but he scarcely noticed it. Madly, he scrambled up the stairs, thrusting open the bedroom door. Anne was still asleep, mercifully unaware of what was happening. Frenziedly, he shook her by the shoulder until she mumbled something drowsily and opened her eyes.

"Wake up, Anne." He realized he was shouting the words. "We've got to get out of here."

Anne sat up, shaking her head. "What's wrong, Philip?" she demanded.

"I've just seen that woman again, out there on the lawn." He knew the words were tumbling out in a rush but he couldn't help it any more than he could stop his hands from trembling. "She was staring up at the window, watching. Then—"

"Go on."

"Then I went downstairs to take a look at that portrait. She's not in it, Anne. There's just a blank space."

"Nonsense. You've been having a nightmare."

Philip stared down at her in shocked surprise. He had expected her to find it hard to believe him but not to be so vehemently dogmatic in her denial as this.

She threw back the covers and got out of bed. "Now try to calm yourself, Philip. I don't doubt you saw something out there. I thought I saw a figure the night we arrived. But it was only a bush which gave the appearance of moving."

"This was no bush." He swallowed hard, fought the muscles in his hands until they steadied. "I've seen and heard other things in this place."

"All right." Anne took his arm. "Let's go and take another look at this painting."

Wordlessly, he allowed her to lead him down the stairs and into the corridor.

"There," Anne said. "It's just as its always been."

Philip stared. Amused eyes looked down at him contemptuously from the picture.

"But I tell you I saw—" Something seemed to stick in his throat blocking off the rest of what he intended to say.

"Really, I don't know what's come over you, Philip. When we were on our way here it was me who thought there was something wrong with this place and you blamed it all on my premonitions. But now it's you imagining things. Come back to bed. You'll feel better in the morning."

There was a final crash of thunder as they made their way back to the bedroom. The storm was passing over, receding inland.

By mid-morning, the sun came out, hot and bright, and there was the smell of the vineyards in the air. Leaving Anne pottering around the villa, Philip climbed down the rocky slope to where the massive metal gates stood like grim sentinels on either side of the drive. There was the sound of a tractor somewhere in the distance and now and again he picked out a peal of laughter where some children were playing while their parents worked among the tall vines.

There was a normality about the scene and the sounds which contrasted starkly with the chaotic thoughts which continued to bubble away inside his mind. Over breakfast, he had tried his hardest to persuade Anne not to remain there any longer; had done his best to convince her the place really was haunted. But she had been adamant. As far as she was concerned, they were going to enjoy their holiday. They had paid for the tenancy and it was up to him to rid himself of this idiotic obsession about the villa.

He abruptly realized that even this strange change in her attitude was weird. There had been a number of occasions in the past when she had sensed some odd atmosphere about a place they were visiting and in every case, he remembered, it had subsequently come to light that some tragedy, or murder, had occurred there. Yet now, when the roles were reversed, she had sensed nothing out of the ordinary.

He started abruptly at a sudden movement. The man appeared without warning at the foot of the slope, beyond the gates; an old man leaning heavily on a stick. Philip eyed him curiously as he hobbled towards him, pausing just outside the gates as if reluctant to approach any closer.

"Monsieur Ransome?" The man spoke excellent English with scarcely a trace of accent.

"Why, yes." Surprised, Philip walked forward. "How do you know my name?"

"My old friend, Charles Reynault, told me some time ago you were renting the villa. Did he tell you anything about it?" He must have noticed Philip's blank stare for he went on quickly, "No, I see he didn't."

"If there's anything you can tell me, I'd certainly be grateful for any information." Philip motioned with his hand. "Won't you come inside while we talk?"

The old man shook his head vehemently. "I'll stay here if you don't mind." His rheumy eyes flicked from side to side as if he was regarding the looming gates as a boundary beyond which he dared not pass.

"As you wish."

"You've already heard something here—or seen something, haven't you?" The old man peered intently at him, a note of conviction in his voice.

Philip nodded slowly, taken aback by the old man's strange perception.

"I thought so. Maybe you've seen her—the Black Widow."

"Yes. But according to Monsieur Reynault she's the present owner."

"The present owner." The old Frenchman repeated the words like a curse and uttered a cackling laugh, his breath wheezing in his throat. "Oh, yes. There's no doubt about that. She's the owner, all right."

"I'm afraid I don't understand." Philip made his face expressionless, inwardly wondering if he was in the presence of a senile peasant.

"I was the gardener here when Monsieur Couvier was alive. Madame Couvier was much younger than him and there was a

277

lot of talk about her and some of the men in the village. I think he knew what was going on although he never said anything to my knowledge. But he was a very strange man and I was sure he was planning something.

"He had that portrait painted of her, you know. Nobody knows who the artist was except that he was a foreigner, came specially from somewhere in Eastern Europe, they say."

"But what had that got to do with—?"

The old man silenced him with a brusque motion of his stick. "Listen Monsieur and perhaps you may understand that there are some things in this world which we cannot explain rationally. Monsieur Couvier died very suddenly and mysteriously. There were rumours that he had been poisoned by his wife and I remember Madamoiselle Mignon saying that just as he died, he laughed and pointed a finger at his wife, telling her she would never be free."

Philip couldn't keep the little tremor out of his voice. "You believe he was murdered?"

"I believe it, Monsieur." The old man raised his stick to point down the hill. "He was buried yonder and she stood at the head of the grave, dressed in the same black cloak you see in the portrait. Then she returned to the villa, dismissed all of the servants and no one ever saw her again. Not alive, that is."

"Then she is dead?" Philip recalled what Reynault had told him, how he had had no contact with Madame Couvier since her husband's death.

"That depends on what you mean by dead." said the old man enigmatically. He placed both hands on his stick as if needing it to support him. "If you want to know what I believe—aye, and most of the villagers—her husband cursed her just before he died. I've heard rumours of some who've seen her in the churchyard and up on the forest road yonder. But it was no living creature they saw. Her black soul is imprisoned in that painting and she's doomed to wander until she can find someone else to take her place. Only then will she be free."

That froze Philip. He knew that, as a rational man, he ought not to believe a single word of this superstitious gossip. But in a strange and frightening way, all that the old man had just told him fitted everything together, slotted all that had happened since they had driven here into a coherent, but horrifying picture.

"My wife," he said hoarsely. "She's back there in the villa—alone."

Without waiting for any reply, he spun on his heel and ran back along the drive, accelerating his pace until his breath was ragged in his throat.

"Anne!"

He yelled her name as he reached the door and ran inside. His shout echoed around the walls. Wildly, he dashed into the kitchen and then the dining room. Both were empty and there was a silence all around him as if a vacuum had suddenly sucked up every sound.

Blindly, he stumbled along the corridor, staring at the painting, afraid of what he might see. For a moment it looked just as before. Then he peered closer and a low whimper bubbled from his shaking lips. It was Anne's face that stared at him from beneath the black hood, her eyes wide and filled with a mute pleading that drove all reasoning thought from his mind.

He felt as if he had passed beyond all horror. Staggering wildly, he scrambled backward. He didn't know where he was going, except away from that ghastly painting and out of the villa. Somehow, his stumbling footsteps carried him in the right direction. He found himself at the front door, his shaking fingers reaching out for the handle.

Before he could grasp it, the handle moved. Through the frosted glass he made out the shape which had suddenly materialized outside.

The door began to open slowly.

WILLIAM FRYER HARVEY
Across the Moors

*William Fryer Harvey (1885–1937), a gentle
Quaker doctor (awarded the Albert Medal for
Gallantry in the First World War), was a leading
master of the grim psychological horror story,
notably "The Beast With Five Fingers", "Miss
Cornelius" and "August Heat". His early tale
"Across the Moors", taken from* Midnight House
(1910), is one of his more traditional ghost stories.

I t really was most unfortunate.

Peggy had a temperature of nearly a hundred, and a pain
in her side, and Mrs. Workington Bancroft knew that it was
appendicitis. But there was no one whom she could send for
the doctor.

James had gone with the jaunting-car to meet her husband
who had at last managed to get away for a week's shooting.

Adolph, she had sent to the Evershams, only half an hour
before, with a note for Lady Eva.

The cook could not manage to walk, even if dinner could be
served without her.

Kate, as usual, was not to be trusted.

There remained Miss Craig.

"Of course, you must see that Peggy is really ill," said she, as
the governess came into the room, in answer to her summons.
"The difficulty is, that there is absolutely no one whom I can
send for the doctor." Mrs. Workington Bancroft paused; she
was always willing that those beneath her should have the
privilege of offering the services which it was her right to
command.

"So, perhaps, Miss Craig," she went on, "you would not mind
walking over to Tebbits' Farm. I hear there is a Liverpool doctor
staying there. Of course I know nothing about him, but we must
take the risk, and I expect he'll be only too glad to be earning
something during his holiday. It's nearly four miles, I know,

280

and I'd never dream of asking you if it was not that I dread appendicitis so."

"Very well," said Miss Craig, "I suppose I must go; but I don't know the way."

"Oh you can't miss it," said Mrs. Workington Bancroft, in her anxiety temporarily forgiving the obvious unwillingness of her governess' consent.

"You follow the road across the moor for two miles, until you come to Redman's Cross. You turn to the left there, and follow a rough path that leads through a larch plantation. And Tebbits' farm lies just below you in the valley."

"And take Pontiff with you," she added, as the girl left the room. "There's absolutely nothing to be afraid of, but I expect you'll feel happier with the dog."

"Well, miss," said the cook, when Miss Craig went into the kitchen to get her boots, which had been drying by the fire; "of course she knows best, but I don't think it's right after all that's happened for the mistress to send you across the moors on a night like this. It's not as if the doctor could do anything for Miss Margaret if you do bring him. Every child is like that once in a while. He'll only say put her to bed, and she's there already."

"I don't see what there is to be afraid of, cook," said Miss Craig as she laced her boots, "unless you believe in ghosts."

"I'm not so sure about that. Anyhow I don't like sleeping in a bed where the sheets are too short for you to pull them over your head. But don't you be frightened, miss, It's my belief that their bark is worse than their bite."

But though Miss Craig amused herself for some minutes by trying to imagine the bark of a ghost (a thing altogether different from the classical ghostly bark), she did not feel entirely at her ease.

She was naturally nervous, and living as she did in the hinterland of the servants' hall, she had heard vague details of true stories that were only myths in the drawing-room.

The very name of Redman's Cross sent a shiver through her; it must have been the place where that horrid murder was committed. She had forgotten the tale, though she remembered the name.

Her first disaster came soon enough.

Pontiff, who was naturally slow-witted, took more than five minutes to find out that it was only the governess he was escorting, but once the discovery had been made, he promptly turned tail, paying not the slightest heed to Miss Craig's feeble whistle. And then, to add to her discomfort, the rain came, not in heavy drops, but driving in sheets of thin spray that blotted out what few landmarks there were upon the moor.

They were very kind at Tebbits' farm. The doctor had gone back to Liverpool the day before, but Mrs. Tebbit gave her hot milk and turf cakes, and offered her reluctant son to show Miss Craig a shorter path on to the moor, that avoided the larch wood.

He was a monosyllabic youth, but his presence was cheering, and she felt the night doubly black when he left her at the last gate.

She trudged on wearily. Her thoughts had already gone back to the almost exhausted theme of the bark of ghosts, when she heard steps on the road behind her that were at least material. Next minute the figure of a man appeared: Miss Craig was relieved to see that the stranger was a clergyman. He raised his hat. "I believe we are both going in the same direction," he said. "Perhaps I may have the pleasure of escorting you." She thanked him. "It is rather weird at night," she went on, "and what with all the tales of ghosts and bogies that one hears from the country people, I've ended by being half afraid myself."

"I can understand your nervousness," he said, "especially on a night like this. I used at one time to feel the same, for my work often meant lonely walks across the moor to farms which were only reached by rough tracks difficult enough to find even in the daytime."

"And you never saw anything to frighten you—nothing immaterial I mean?"

"I can't really say that I did, but I had an experience eleven years ago which served as the turning point in my life, and since you seem to be now in much the same state of mind as I was then in, I will tell it you.

"The time of year was late September. I had been over to Westondale to see an old woman who was dying, and then, just as I was about to start on my way home, word came to me of another of my parishioners who had been suddenly taken ill only that morning. It was after seven when at last I started. A farmer saw me on my way, turning back when I reached the moor road.

"The sunset the previous evening had been one of the most lovely I ever remember seeing. The whole vault of heaven had been scattered with flakes of white cloud, tipped with rosy pink like the strewn petals of a full-blown rose.

"But that night all was changed. The sky was an absolutely dull slate colour, except in one corner of the west where a thin rift showed the last saffron tint of the sullen sunset. As I walked, stiff and footsore, my spirits sank. It must have been the marked contrast between the two evenings, the one so lovely, so full of promise (the corn was still out in the fields spoiling for fine weather), the other so gloomy, so sad with all the dead weight of autumn and winter days to come. And then added to this sense of heavy depression came another different feeling which I surprised myself by recognising as fear.

"I did not know why I was afraid.

"The moors lay on either side of me, unbroken except for a straggling line of turf shooting butts, that stood within a stone's-throw of the road.

"The only sound I had heard for the last half hour was the cry of the startled grouse—Go back, go back, go back. But yet the feeling of fear was there, affecting a low centre of my brain through some little used physical channel.

"I buttoned my coat closer, and tried to divert my thoughts by thinking of next Sunday's sermon.

"I had chosen to preach on Job. There is much in the old-fashioned notion of the book, apart from all the subtleties of the higher criticism, that appeals to country people; the loss of herds and crops, the break up of the family. I would not have dared to speak, had not I too been a farmer; my own glebe land had been flooded three weeks before, and I suppose I stood to lose as much as any man in the parish. As I walked along the road repeating to myself the first chapter of the book, I stopped at the twelfth verse.

"'And the Lord said unto Satan: Behold all that he hath is in thy power' . . .

"The thought of the bad harvest (and that is an awful thought in these valleys) vanished. I seemed to gaze into an ocean of infinite darkness.

"I had often used, with the Sunday glibness of the tired priest, whose duty it is to preach three sermons in one day, the old simile of the chess-board. God and the Devil were the players:

and we were helping one side or the other. But until that night I had not thought of the possibility of my being only a pawn in the game, that God might throw away that the game might be won.

"I had reached the place where we are now, I remember it by that rough stone water-trough, when a man suddenly jumped up from the roadside. He had been seated on a heap of broken road metal.

"'Which way are you going, guv'ner?' he said.

"I knew from the way he spoke that the man was a stranger. There are many at this time of the year who come up from the south, tramping northwards with the ripening corn. I told him my destination.

"'We'll go along together,' he replied.

"It was too dark to see much of the man's face, but what little I made out was coarse and brutal.

"Then he began the half-menacing whine I knew so well—he had tramped miles that day, he had had no food since breakfast, and that was only a crust.

"'Give us a copper,' he said, 'it's only for a night's lodging.'

"He was whittling away with a big clasp knife at an ash stake he had taken from some hedge."

The clergyman broke off.

"Are those the lights of your house?" he said. "We are nearer than I expected, but I shall have time to finish my story. I think I will, for you can run home in a couple of minutes, and I don't want you to be frightened when you are out on the moors again.

"As the man talked he seemed to have stepped out of the very background of my thoughts, his sordid tale, with the sad lies that hid a far sadder truth.

"He asked me the time.

"It was five minutes to nine. As I replaced my watch I glanced at his face. His teeth were clenched, and there was something in the gleam of his eyes that told me at once his purpose.

"Have you ever known how long a second is? For a third of a second I stood there facing him, filled with an overwhelming pity for myself and him; and then without a word of warning he was upon me. I felt nothing. A flash of lightning ran down my spine, I heard the dull crash of the ash stake, and then a very gentle patter like the sound of a far-distant stream. For a minute I lay in perfect happiness watching the lights of the house as they increased in number until the whole heaven shone with twinkling lamps.

"I could not have had a more painless death."

Miss Craig looked up. The man was gone; she was alone on the moor.

She ran to the house, her teeth chattering, ran to the solid shadow that crossed and recrossed the kitchen blind.

As she entered the hall, the clock on the stairs struck the hour. It was nine o'clock.

NATHANIEL HAWTHORNE
The Gray Champion

Nathaniel Hawthorne (1804–64) *is rightly celebrated for his classics about Puritan New England,* The Scarlet Letter *and* The House of the Seven Gables. *His early supernatural and weird short stories, highly praised by Longfellow and Poe, were collected as* Twice-Told Tales *in 1837.*

There was once a time when New England groaned under the actual pressure of heavier wrongs than those threatened ones which brought on the Revolution. James II, the bigoted successor of Charles the Voluptuous, had annulled the charters of all the colonies, and sent a harsh and unprincipled soldier to take away our liberties and endanger our religion. The administration of Sir Edmund Andros lacked scarcely a single characteristic of tyranny: a Governor and Council, holding office from the King, and wholly independent of the country; laws made and taxes levied without concurrence of the people, immediate or by their representatives; the rights of private citizens violated, and the titles of all landed property declared void; the voice of complaint stifled by restrictions on the press; and, finally, disaffection overawed by the first band of mercenary troops that ever marched on our free soil. For two years our ancestors were kept in sullen submission, by that filial love which had invariably secured their allegiance to the mother country, whether its head chanced to be a Parliament, Protector, or Popish Monarch. Till these evil times, however, such allegiance had been merely nominal, and the colonists had ruled themselves, enjoying far more freedom, than is even yet the privilege of the native subjects of Great Britain.

At length, a rumour reached our shores that the Prince of Orange had ventured on an enterprise, the success of which would be the triumph of civil and religious rights and the salvation of New England. It was but a doubtful whisper; it might be false, or the attempt might fail; and, in either case, the man that stirred against King James would lose his head. Still the intelligence produced a marked effect. The people smiled mysteriously in the streets, and threw bold glances at their oppressors; while, far and wide, there was a subdued and silent agitation, as if the slightest signal would rouse the whole land from its sluggish despondency. Aware of their danger, the rulers resolved to avert it by an imposing display of strength, and perhaps to confirm their despotism by yet harsher measures. One afternoon in April, 1689, Sir Edmund Andros and his favourite councillors, being warm with wine, assembled the red-coats of the Governor's Guard, and made their appearance in the streets of Boston. The sun was near setting when the march commenced.

The roll of the drum, at that unquiet crisis, seemed to go through the streets, less as the martial music of the soldiers, than as a muster call to the inhabitants themselves. A multitude, by various avenues, assembled in King Street, which was destined to be the scene, nearly a century afterwards, of another encounter between the troops of Britain, and a people struggling against her tyranny. Though more than sixty years had elapsed since the Pilgrims came, this crowd of their descendants still showed the strong and sombre features of their character, perhaps more strikingly in such a stern emergency than on happier occasions. There were the sober garb, the general severity of mien, the gloomy but undismayed expression, the scriptural forms of speech, and the confidence in Heaven's blessing on a righteous cause, which would have marked a band of the original Puritans, when threatened by some peril of the wilderness. Indeed, it was not yet time for the old spirit to be extinct; since there were men in the street, that day, who had worshipped there beneath the trees, before a house was reared to the God for whom they had become exiles. Old soldiers of the Parliament were here, too, smiling grimly at the thought, that their aged arms might strike another blow against the house of Stuart. Here, also, were the veterans of King Philip's war, who had burned villages and slaughtered young and old, with pious fierceness, while the godly souls throughout the land were helping them with prayer. Several ministers were scattered among the crowd, which, unlike all other mobs, regarded them with such reverence, as if there were sanctity in their very garments. These holy men exerted their influence to quiet the people, but not to disperse them. Meantime, the purpose of the Governor, in disturbing the peace of the town, at a period when the slightest commotion might throw the country into a ferment, was almost the universal subject of inquiry, and variously explained.

"Satan will strike his master stroke presently," cried some, "because he knoweth that his time is short. All our godly pastors are to be dragged to prison! We shall see them at a Smithfield fire in King Street!"

Hereupon the people of each parish gathered closer round their minister, who looked calmly upwards and assumed a more apostolic dignity, as well befitted a candidate for the highest honour of his profession, the crown of martyrdom. It was actually fancied, at that period, that New England might have a John Rogers of her own, to take the place of that worthy in the Primer.

"The Pope of Rome has given orders for a new St. Bartholomew!" cried others. "We are to be massacred, man and male child!"

Neither was this rumour wholly discredited, although the wiser class believed the Governor's object somewhat less atrocious. His predecessor under the old charter, Bradstreet, a venerable companion of the first settlers, was known to be in town. There were grounds for conjecturing, that Sir Edmund Andros intended, at once, to strike terror, by a parade of military force, and to confound the opposite faction, by possessing himself of their chief.

"Stand firm for the old charter Governor!" shouted the crowd, seizing upon the idea. "The good old Governor Bradstreet!"

While this cry was at the loudest, the people were surprised by the well-known figure of Governor Bradstreet himself, a patriarch of nearly ninety, who appeared on the elevated steps of a door, and, with characteristic mildness, besought them to submit to the constituted authorities.

"My children," concluded this venerable person, "do nothing rashly. Cry not aloud, but pray for the welfare of New England, and expect patiently what the Lord will do in this matter!"

The event was soon to be decided. All this time, the roll of the drum had been approaching through Cornhill, louder and deeper, till with reverberations from house to house, and the regular tramp of martial footsteps, it burst into the street. A double rank of soldiers made their appearance, occupying the whole breadth of the passage, with shouldered matchlocks, and matches burning, so as to present a row of fires in the dusk. Their steady march was like the progress of a machine, that would roll irresistibly over every thing in its way. Next, moving slowly, with a confused clatter of hoofs on the pavement, rode a party of mounted gentlemen, the central figure being Sir Edmund Andros, elderly, but erect and soldier-like. Those around him were his favourite councillors, and the bitterest foes of New England. At his right hand rode Edward Randolph, our arch-enemy, that "blasted wretch," as Cotton Mather calls him, who achieved the downfall of our ancient government, and was followed with a sensible curse, through life and to his grave. On the other side was Bullivant, scattering jests and mockery as he rode along. Dudley came behind, with a downcast look, dreading, as well he might, to meet the indignant gaze of the people, who beheld him, their only countryman by birth, among the oppressors of his native land. The captain of a frigate in the harbor, and two or three civil officers under the Crown, were also there. But the figure which most attracted the public eye, and stirred up the deepest feeling, was the Episcopal clergyman of King's Chapel, riding haughtily among the magistrates in his priestly vestments, the fitting representative of prelacy and persecution, the union of church and state, and all those abominations which had driven the Puritans to the wilderness. Another guard of soldiers, in double rank, brought up the rear.

The whole scene was a picture of the condition of New England, and its moral, the deformity of any government that does not grow out of the nature of things and the character of the people. On one side the religious multitude, with their sad visages and dark attire, and on the other, the group of despotic rulers, with the high churchman in the midst, and here and there a crucifix at their bosoms, all magnificently clad, flushed with wine, proud of unjust authority, and scoffing at the universal groan. And the mercenary soldiers, waiting but the word to deluge the street with blood, showed the only means by which obedience could be secured.

"O Lord of Hosts," cried a voice among the crowd. "provide a Champion for the people!"

This ejaculation was loudly uttered, and served as a herald's cry, to introduce a remarkable personage. The crowd had rolled back, and was now huddled together nearly at the extremity of the street, while the soldiers had advanced no more than a third of its length. The intervening space was empty—a paved solitude, between lofty edifices, which threw almost a twilight shadow over it. Suddenly, there was seen the figure of an ancient man, who seemed to have emerged from among the people, and was walking by himself along the centre of the street, to confront the armed band. He wore the old Puritan dress, a dark cloak and a steeple-crowned hat, in the fashion of at least fifty years before, with a heavy sword upon his thigh, but a staff in his hand to assist the tremulous gait of age.

When at some distance from the multitude, the old man turned slowly round, displaying a face of antique majesty, rendered doubly venerable by the hoary beard that descended on his breast. He made a gesture at once of encouragement and warning, then turned again, and resumed his way.

"Who is this gray patriarch?" asked the young men of their sires.

"Who is this venerable brother?" asked the old men among themselves.

But none could make reply. The fathers of the people, those of fourscore years and upwards, were disturbed, deeming it strange that they should forget one of such evident authority, whom they must have known in their early days, the associates of Winthrop, and all the old councillors, giving laws, and making prayers, and leading them against the savage. The elderly men ought to have remembered him, too, with locks as gray in their youth, as their own were now. And the young! How could he have passed so utterly from their memories—that hoary sire, the relic of long-departed times, whose awful benediction had surely been bestowed on their uncovered heads in childhood?

"Whence did he come? What is his purpose? Who can this old man be?" whispered the wondering crowd.

Meanwhile, the venerable stranger, staff in hand, was pursuing his solitary walk along the centre of the street. As he drew near the advancing soldiers, and as the roll of the drum came full upon his ear, the old man raised himself to a loftier mien, while the decrepitude of age seemed to fall from his shoulders, leaving him in gray but unbroken dignity. Now, he marched onward with a warrior's step, keeping time to the military music. Thus the aged form advanced on one side, and the whole parade of soldiers and magistrates on the other, till, when scarcely twenty yards remained between, the old man grasped his staff by the middle, and held it before him like a leader's truncheon.

"Stand!" cried he.

The eye, the face, and attitude of command; the solemn, yet warlike peal of that voice, fit either to rule a host in the battle field or be raised to God in prayer, were irresistible. At the old man's word and outstretched arm, the roll of the drum was hushed at once, and the advancing line stood still. A tremulous enthusiasm seized upon the multitude. That stately form, combining the leader and the saint, so gray, so dimly seen, in such an ancient garb, could only belong to some old champion of the righteous cause, whom the oppressor's drum had summoned from his grave. They raised a shout of awe and exultation, and looked for the deliverance of New England.

The Governor, and the gentlemen of his party, perceiving themselves brought to an unexpected stand, rode hastily forward, as if they would have pressed their snorting and affrighted horses right against the hoary apparition. He, however, blenched not a step, but glancing his severe eye round the group, which half encompassed him, at last bent it sternly on Sir Edmund Andros. One would have thought that the dark old man was chief ruler there, and that the Governor and Council, with soldiers at their back, representing the whole power and authority of the Crown, had no alternative but obedience.

"What does this old fellow here?" cried Edward Randolph, fiercely. "On Sir Edmund! Bid the soldiers forward, and give the dotard the same choice that you give all his countrymen—to stand aside or be trampled on!"

"Nay, nay, let us show respect to the good grandsire," said Bullivant, laughing. "See you not, he is some old round-headed dignitary, who hath lain asleep these thirty years, and knows nothing of the change of times? Doubtless, he thinks to put us down with a proclamation in Old Noll's name!"

"Are you mad, old man?" demanded Sir Edmund Andros, in loud and harsh tones. "How dare you stay the march of King James's Governor?"

"I have stayed the march of a King himself, ere now," replied the gray figure, with stern composure. "I am here, Sir Governor, because the cry of an oppressed people hath disturbed me in my secret place; and beseeching this favour earnestly of the Lord, it was vouchsafed me to appear once again on earth, in the good old cause of his saints. And what speak ye of James? There is no longer a Popish tyrant on the throne of England, and by to-morrow noon, his name shall be a byword in this very street, where ye would make it a word of terror. Back, thou that wast a Governor, back! With this night thy power is ended—tomorrow the prison!—back lest I foretell the scaffold!"

The people had been drawing nearer and nearer, and drinking in the words of their champion, who spoke in accents long disused, like one unaccustomed to converse, except with the dead of many years ago. But his voice stirred their souls. They confronted the soldiers, not wholly without arms, and ready to convert the very stones of the street into deadly weapons. Sir Edmund Andros looked at the old man; then he cast his hard and cruel eye over the multitude, and beheld them burning with that lurid wrath, so difficult to kindle or to quench; and again he fixed his gaze on the aged form, which stood obscurely in an open space, where neither friend nor foe had thrust himself. What were his thoughts, he uttered no word which might discover. But whether the oppressor were overawed by the Gray Champion's look, or perceived his peril in the threatening attitude of the people, it is certain that he gave back, and ordered his soldiers to commence a slow and guarded retreat. Before another sunset, the Governor, and all that rode so proudly with him, were prisoners, and long ere it was known that James had abdicated, King William was proclaimed throughout New England.

But where was the Gray Champion? Some reported, that when the troops had gone from King Street, and the people were thronging tumultuously in their rear, Bradstreet, the aged Governor, was seen to embrace a form more aged than his own. Others soberly affirmed, that while they marvelled at the venerable grandeur of his aspect, the old man had faded from their eyes, melting slowly into the hues of twilight, till, where he stood, there was an empty space. But all agreed, that the hoary shape was gone. The men of that generation watched for his reappearance, in sunshine and in twilight, but never saw him more, nor knew when his funeral passed, nor where his gravestone was.

And who was the Gray Champion? Perhaps his name might be found in the records of that stern Court of Justice, which passed a sentence, too mighty for the age, but glorious in all after times, for its humbling lesson to the monarch and its high example to the subject. I have heard, that whenever the descendants of the Puritans are to show the spirit of their sires, the old man appears again. When eighty years had passed, he walked once more in King Street. Five years later, in the twilight of an April morning, he stood on the green, beside the meeting house, at Lexington, where now the obelisk of granite, with a slab of slate inlaid, commemorates the first fallen of the Revolution. And when our fathers were toiling at the breastwork on Bunker's Hill, all through that night the old warrior walked his rounds. Long, long may it be, ere he comes again! His hour is one of darkness, and adversity, and peril. But should domestic tyranny oppress us, or the invader's step pollute our soil, still may the Gray Champion come; for he is the type of New England's hereditary spirit: and his shadowy march, on the eve of danger, must ever be the pledge, that New England's sons will vindicate their ancestry.

WASHINGTON IRVING
Governor Manco and the Soldier

Washington Irving (1783–1859), celebrated for the immortal "Rip van Winkle" and "The Legend of Sleepy Hollow", was a younger contemporary and close friend of Sir Walter Scott who helped and encouraged his talents for imaginative and supernatural literature. Among Irving's best short stories in this vein are "The Spectre Bridegroom" (1819), "The Devil and Tom Walker" (1824) and "Governor Manco and the Soldier" (from The Alhambra, *1832).*

W hen Governor Manco, or "the one-armed", kept up a show of military state in the Alhambra, he became nettled at the reproaches continually cast upon his fortress, of being a nestling place of rogues and contrabandistas. On a sudden, the old potentate determined on reform, and setting vigorously to work, ejected whole nests of vagabonds out of the fortress and the gipsy caves with which the surrounding hills are honeycombed. He sent out soldiers also, to patrol the avenues and footpaths, with orders to take up all suspicious persons.

One bright summer morning, a patrol, consisting of the testy old corporal who had distinguished himself in the affair of the notary, a trumpeter and two privates, was seated under the garden wall of the Generalife, beside the road which leads down from the mountain of the sun, when they heard the tramp of a horse, and a male voice singing in rough, though not unmusical tones, an old Castilian campaigning song.

Presently they beheld a sturdy sun-burnt fellow, clad in the ragged garb of a foot soldier leading a powerful Arabian horse, caparisoned in the ancient Moresco fashion.

Astonished at the sight of a strange soldier descending, steed in hand, from that solitary mountain, the corporal stepped forth and challenged him.

"Who goes there?"

"A friend."

"Who and what are you?"

"A poor soldier just from the wars, with a cracked crown and empty purse for a reward."

By this time they were enabled to view him more narrowly. He had a black patch across his forehead, which, with a grizzled beard, added to a certain dare-devil cast of countenance, while a slight squint threw into the whole an occasional gleam of roguish good-humour.

Having answered the questions of the patrol, the soldier seemed to consider himself entitled to make others in return. "May I ask," said he, "what city is that which I see at the foot of the hill?"

"What city!" cried the trumpeter; "come, that's too bad. Here's a fellow lurking about the mountain of the sun, and demands the name of the great city of Granada!"

"Granada! Madre di Dios! can it be possible?"

"Perhaps not!" rejoined the trumpeter; "and perhaps you have no idea that yonder are the towers of the Alhambra."

"Son of a trumpet," replied the stranger, "do not trifle with me; if this be indeed the Alhambra, I have some strange matters to reveal to the governor."

"You will have an opportunity," said the corporal, "for we mean to take you before him." By this time the trumpeter had seized the bridle of the steed, the two privates had each secured an arm of the soldier, the corporal put himself in front, gave the word, "Forward—march!" and away they marched for the Alhambra.

The sight of a ragged foot soldier and a fine Arabian horse, brought in captive by the patrol, attracted the attention of all the idlers of the fortress, and of those gossip groups that generally assemble about wells and fountains at early dawn. The wheel of the cistern paused in its rotations, and the slipshod servant-maid stood gaping, with pitcher in hand, as the corporal passed by with his prize. A motley train gradually gathered in the rear of the escort.

Knowing nods and winks and conjectures passed from one to another. "It is a deserter," said one; "A contrabandista," said another; "A bandalero," said a third;—until it was affirmed that a captain of a desperate band of robbers had been captured by the prowess of the corporal and his patrol. "Well, well," said the old crones, one to another, "captain or not, let him get out of the grasp of old Governor Manco if he can, though he is but one-handed."

Governor Manco was seated in one of the inner halls of the Alhambra, taking his morning's cup of chocolate in company with his confessor, a fat Franciscan friar, from the neighbouring convent. A demure, dark-eyed damsel of Malaga, the daughter of his housekeeper, was attending upon him. The world hinted that the damsel, who, with all her demureness, was a sly buxom baggage, had found out a soft spot in the iron heart of the old governor, and held complete control over him. But let that pass—the domestic affairs of these mighty potentates of the earth should not be too narrowly scrutinized.

When word was brought that a suspicious stranger had been taken lurking about the fortress, and was actually in the outer court, in durance of the corporal, waiting the pleasure of his excellency, the pride and stateliness of office swelled the bosom of the governor. Giving back his chocolate cup into the hands of the demure damsel, he called for his basket-hilted sword, girded it to his side, twirled up his mustachios, took his seat in a large high-backed chair, assumed a bitter and forbidding aspect, and ordered the prisoner into his presence. The soldier was brought in, still closely pinioned by his captors, and guarded by the corporal. He maintained, however, a resolute self-confident air, and returned the sharp, scrutinizing look of the governor with an easy squint, which by no means pleased the punctilious old potentate.

"Well, culprit," said the governor, after he had regarded him for a moment in silence, "what have you to say for yourself—who are you?"

"A soldier, just from the wars, who has brought away nothing but scars and bruises."

"A soldier—humph—a foot soldier by your garb. I understand you have a fine Arabian horse. I presume you brought him too from the wars, beside your scars and bruises."

"May it please your excellency, I have something strange to tell about the horse. Indeed I have one of the most wonderful things to relate. Something too that concerns the security of this fortress, indeed of all Granada. But it is a matter to be imparted only to your private ear, or in presence of such only as are in your confidence."

The governor considered for a moment, and then directed the corporal and his men to withdraw, but to post themselves outside the door, and be ready at a call. "This holy friar," said he, "is my confessor, you may say anything in his presence—and this damsel," nodding towards the handmaid, who had loitered with an air of great curiosity, "this damsel is of great secrecy and discretion, and to be trusted with anything."

The soldier gave a glance between a squint and a leer at the demure handmaid. "I am perfectly willing," said he, "that the damsel should remain."

When all the rest had withdrawn, the soldier commenced his story. He was a fluent, smooth-tongued varlet, and had a command of language above his apparent rank.

"May it please your excellency," said he, "I am, as I before observed, a soldier, and have seen some hard service, but my term of enlistment being expired, I was discharged, not long since, from the army of Valladolid, and set out on foot for my native village in Andalusia. Yesterday evening the sun went down as I was traversing a great dry plain of Old Castile."

"Hold," cried the governor, "what is this you say? Old Castile is some two or three hundred miles from this."

"Even so," replied the soldier coolly. "I told your excellency I had strange things to relate; but not more strange than true; as your excellency will find, if you will deign me a patient hearing."

"Proceed, culprit," said the governor, twirling up his mustachios.

"As the sun went down," continued the soldier, "I cast my eyes about in search of some quarters for the night; but, far as my sight could reach, there were no signs of habitation. I saw that I should have to make my bed on the naked plain, with my knapsack for a pillow; but your excellency is an old soldier, and knows that to one who has been in the wars such a night's lodging is no great hardship."

The governor nodded assent, as he drew his pocket handkerchief out of the basket hilt, to drive away a fly that buzzed about his nose.

"Well, to make a long story short," continued the soldier, "I trudged forward for several miles until I came to a bridge over a deep ravine, through which ran a little thread of water, almost dried up by the summer heat. At one end of the bridge was a Moorish tower, the upper end all in ruins, but a vault in the foundation quite entire. Here, thinks I, is a good place to make a halt; so I went down to the stream, took a hearty drink, for the water was pure and sweet, and I was parched with thirst; then opening my wallet, I took out an onion and a few crusts, which were all my provisions, and seating myself on a stone on the margin of the stream, began to make my supper; intending afterwards to quarter myself for the night in the vault of the tower; and capital quarters they would have been for a campaigner just from the wars, as your excellency, who is an old soldier, may suppose."

"I have put up gladly with worse in my time," said the governor, returning his pocket handkerchief into the hilt of his sword.

"While I was quietly crunching my crust," pursued the soldier, "I heard something stir within the vault; I listened—it was the tramp of a horse. By-and-by, a man came forth from a door in the foundation of the tower, close by the water's edge, leading a powerful horse by the bridle. I could not well make out what he was by the starlight. It had a suspicious look to be lurking among the ruins of a tower, in that wild solitary place. He might be a mere wayfarer, like myself; he might be a contrabandista; he might be a bandalero; what of that? thank heaven and my poverty, I had nothing to lose; so I sat still and crunched my crusts.

"He led his horse to the water, close by where I was sitting, so that I had a fair opportunity of reconnoitring him. To my surprise, he was dressed in a Moorish garb, with a cuirass of steel, and a polished skull-cap that I distinguished by the reflection of the stars upon it. His horse, too, was harnessed in the Moresco fashion, with great shovel stirrups. He led him, as I said, to the side of the stream, into which the animal plunged his head almost to the eyes, and drank until I thought he would have burst.

"'Comrade,' said I, 'your steed drinks well; it's a good sign when a horse plunges his muzzle bravely into the water.'

"'He may well drink,' said the stranger, speaking with a Moorish accent, 'it is a good year since he had his last draught.'

"'By Santiago,' said I, 'that beats even the camels that I have seen in Africa. But come, you seem to be something of a soldier, will you sit down and take part of a soldier's fare?' In fact I felt the want of a companion in this lonely place, and was willing to put up with an infidel. Besides, as your excellency well knows, a soldier is never very particular about the faith of his company, and soldiers of all countries are comrades on peaceable ground."

The governor again nodded assent.

"Well, as I was saying, I invited him to share my supper, such as it was, for I could not do less in common hospitality. 'I have no time to pause for meat or drink,' said he, 'I have a long journey to make before morning.'

"'In which direction?' said I.

"'Andalusia,' said he.

"'Exactly my route,' said I; 'so, as you won't stop and eat with me, perhaps you will let me mount and ride with you. I see your horse is of a powerful frame, I'll warrant he'll carry double.'

"'Agreed,' said the trooper; and it would not have been civil and soldier-like to refuse, especially as I had offered to share my supper with him. So up he mounted, and up I mounted behind him.

"'Hold fast,' said he, 'my steed goes like the wind.'

"'Never fear me,' said I, and so off we set.

"From a walk the horse soon passed to a trot, from a trot to a gallop, and from a gallop to a harum scarum scamper. It seemed as if rocks, trees, houses, everything, flew hurry scurry behind us.

"'What town is this?' said I.

"'Segovia,' said he; and before the word was out of his mouth, the towers of Segovia were out of sight. We swept up the Guadarama mountains, and down by the Escurial; and we skirted the walls of Madrid, and we scoured away across the plains of La Mancha. In this way we went up hill and down dale, by towers and cities, all buried in deep sleep, and across mountains, and plains, and rivers, just glimmering in the starlight.

"To make a long story short, and not to fatigue your excellency, the trooper suddenly pulled up on the side of a mountain. 'Here we are,' said he, 'at the end of our journey.' I looked about, but could see no signs of habitation; nothing but the mouth of a cavern. While I looked I saw multitudes of people in Moorish dresses, some on horseback, some on foot, arriving as if borne by the wind from all points of the compass, and hurrying into the mouth of the cavern, like bees into a hive. Before I could ask a question, the trooper struck his long Moorish spurs into the horse's flanks and dashed in with the throng. We passed along a steep winding way, that descended into the very bowels of the mountain. As we pushed on, a light began to glimmer up by little and little, like the first glimmerings of day, but what caused it I could not discern. It grew stronger and stronger, and enabled me to see everything around. I now noticed, as we passed along, great caverns, opening to the right and left, like halls in an arsenal. In some there were shields, and helmets, and cuirasses, and lances, and scimitars, hanging against the walls; in others there were great heaps of warlike munitions, and camp equipage lying upon the ground.

"It would have done your excellency's heart good, being an old soldier, to have seen such grand provision for war. Then, in other caverns, there were long rows of horsemen armed to the teeth, with lances raised and banners unfurled all ready for the field; but they all sat motionless in their saddles like so many statues. In other halls were warriors sleeping on the ground beside their horses, and foot-soldiers in groups ready to fall into the ranks. All were in old-fashioned Moorish dresses and armour.

"Well, your excellency, to cut a long story short, we at length entered an immense cavern, or I may say palace, of grotto work, the walls of which seemed to be veined with gold and silver, and to sparkle with diamonds and sapphires and all kinds of precious stones. At the upper end sat a Moorish king on a golden throne, with his nobles on each side, and a guard of African blacks with drawn scimitars. All the crowd that continued to flock in, and amounted to thousands and thousands, passed one by one before his throne, each paying homage as he passed. Some of the multitude were dressed in magnificent robes, without stain or blemish, and sparkling with jewels; others in burnished and enamelled armour; while others were in mouldered and mildewed garments, and in armour all battered and dented and covered with rust.

"I had hitherto held my tongue, for your excellency well knows, it is not for a soldier to ask many questions when on duty, but I could keep silent no longer.

"'Pr'ythee, comrade,' said I, 'what is the meaning of all this?'

"'This,' said the trooper, 'is a great and fearful mystery. Know, O Christian, that you see before you the court and army of Boabdil the last king of Granada.'

"'What is this you tell me?' I cried. 'Boabdil and his court were exiled from the land hundreds of years agone, and all died in Africa.'

"'So it is recorded in your lying chronicles,' replied the Moor: 'but know that Boabdil and the warriors who made the last struggle for Granada were all shut up in the mountain by powerful enchantment. As for the king and army that marched forth from Granada at the time of the surrender, they were a mere phantom train, of spirits and demons permitted to assume those shapes to deceive the Christian sovereigns. And furthermore let me tell you, friend, that all Spain is a country under the power of enchantment. There is not a mountain cave, not a lonely watch-tower in the plains, nor ruined castle on the hills, but has some spellbound warriors sleeping from age to age within its vaults, until the sins are expiated for which Allah permitted the dominion to pass for a time out of the hands of the faithful. Once every year, on the eve of St. John, they are released from enchantment, from sunset to sunrise, and permitted to repair here to pay homage to their sovereign: and the crowds which you beheld swarming into the cave are Moslem warriors from their haunts in all parts of Spain. For my own part, you saw the ruined tower of the bridge in Old Castile, where I have now wintered and summered for many hundred years, and where I must be back again by daybreak. As to the battalions of horse and foot which you beheld draw up in array in the neighbouring caverns, they are the spell-bound warriors of Granada. It is written in the book of fate, that when the enchantment is broken, Boabdil will descend from the mountain at the head of this army, resume his throne in the Alhambra and his sway of Granada, and gathering together the enchanted warriors, from all parts of Spain, will reconquer the peninsula and restore it to Moslem rule.'

"'And when shall this happen?' said I.

"'Allah alone knows: we had hoped the day of deliverance was at hand; but there reigns at present a vigilant governor in the Alhambra, a stanch old soldier, well known as Governor Manco. While such a warrior holds command of the very outpost, and stands ready to check the first irruption from the mountain, I fear Boabdil and his soldiery must be content to rest upon their arms.'"

Here the governor raised himself somewhat perpendicularly, adjusted his sword, and twirled up his mustachios.

"To make a long story short, and not to fatigue your excellency, the trooper, having given me this account, dismounted from his steed.

"'Tarry here,' said he, 'and guard my steed while I go and bow the knee to Boabdil.' So saying, he strode away among the throng that pressed forward to the throne.

"'What's to be done?' thought I, when thus left to myself; 'shall I wait here until this infidel returns to whisk me off on his goblin steed, the Lord knows where; or shall I make the most of my time and beat a retreat from this hobgoblin community?' A soldier's mind is soon made up, as your excellency well knows. As to the horse, he belonged to an avowed enemy of the faith and the realm, and was a fair prize according to the rules of war. So hoisting myself from the crupper into the saddle, I turned the reins, struck the Moorish stirrups into the sides of the steed, and put him to make the best of his way out of the passage by which he had entered. As we scoured by the halls where the Moslem horsemen sat in motionless battalions, I thought I heard the clang of armour and a hollow murmur of voices. I gave the steed another taste of the stirrups and doubled my speed. There was now a sound behind me like a rushing blast; I heard the clatter of a thousand hoofs: a countless throng overtook me. I was borne along in the press, and hurled forth from the mouth of the cavern, while thousands of shadowy forms were swept off in every direction by the four winds of heaven.

"In the whirl and confusion of the scene I was thrown senseless to the earth. When I came to myself I was lying on the brow of a hill with the Arabian steed standing beside me; for, in falling, my arm had slipt within the bridle, which, I presume, prevented his whisking off to Old Castile.

"Your excellency may easily judge of my surprise on looking round, to behold hedges of aloes and Indian figs and other proofs of a southern climate, and to see a great city below me with towers, and palaces, and a grand cathedral.

"I descended the hill cautiously, leading my steed, for I was afraid to mount him again, lest he should play me some slippery trick. As I descended I met with your patrol, who let me into the secret that it was Granada that lay before me; and that I was actually under the walls of the Alhambra, the fortress of the redoubted Governor Manco, the terror of all enchanted Moslems. When I heard this, I determined at once to seek your excellency, to inform you of all that I had seen, and to warn you of the perils that surround and undermine you, that you may take measures in time to guard your fortress, and the kingdom itself, from this intestine army that lurks in the very bowels of the land."

"And pr'ythee, friend, you who are a veteran campaigner, and have seen so much service," said the governor, "how would you advise me to proceed, in order to prevent this evil?"

"It is not for a humble private of the ranks," said the soldier modestly, "to pretend to instruct a commander of your excellency's sagacity, but it appears to me that your excellency might cause all the caves and entrances in the mountain to be walled up with solid mason work, so that Boabdil and his army might be completely corked up in their subterranean habitation. If the good father too," added the soldier reverently bowing to the friar, and devoutly crossing himself, "would consecrate the barricadoes with his blessing, and put up a few crosses and reliques and images of saints, I think they might withstand all the power of infidel enchantments."

"They doubtless would be of great avail," said the friar.

The governor now placed his arm akimbo with his hand resting on the hilt of his toledo, fixing his eye upon the soldier, and gently wagging his head from one side to the other.

"So, friend," said he, "then you really suppose I am to be gulled with this cock-and-bull story about enchanted mountains and enchanted Moors? Hark ye, culprit!—not another word. An old soldier you may be, but you'll find you have an older soldier to deal with, and one not easily outgeneralled. Ho! guards there! put this fellow in irons."

The demure handmaid would have put in a word in favour of the prisoner, but the governor silenced her with a look.

As they were pinioning the soldier, one of the guards felt something of bulk in his pocket, and drawing it forth, found a long leathern purse that appeared to be well filled. Holding it by one corner, he turned out the contents upon the table before the governor, and never did freebooter's bag make more gorgeous delivery. Out tumbled rings, and jewels, and rosaries of pearls, and sparkling diamond crosses, and a profusion of ancient golden coin, some of which fell jingling to the floor, and rolled away to the uttermost parts of the chamber.

For a time the functions of justice were suspended; there was a universal scramble after the glittering fugitives. The governor alone, who was imbued with true Spanish pride, maintained his stately decorum, though his eye betrayed a little anxiety until the last coin and jewel were restored to the sack.

The friar was not so calm; his whole face glowed like a furnace, and his eyes twinkled and flashed at sight of the rosaries and crosses.

"Sacrilegious wretch that thou art!" exclaimed he; "what church or sanctuary hast thou been plundering of these sacred relics?"

"Neither one nor the other, holy father. If they be sacrilegious spoils, they must have been taken in times long past, by the infidel trooper I have mentioned. I was just going to tell his excellency when he interrupted me, that, on taking possession of the trooper's horse, I unhooked a leathern sack which hung at the saddle-bow, and which I presume contained the plunder of his campaignings in days of old, when the Moors overran the country."

"Mighty well; at present you will make up your mind to take up your quarters in a chamber of the vermilion tower, which, though not under a magic spell, will hold you as safe as any cave of your enchanted Moors."

"Your excellency will do as you think proper," said the prisoner coolly. "I shall be thankful to your excellency for any accommodation in the fortress. A soldier who has been in the wars, as your excellency well knows, is not particular about his lodgings: provided I have a snug dungeon and regular rations, I shall manage to make myself comfortable. I would only entreat that while your excellency is so careful about me, you would have an eye to your fortress, and think on the hint I dropped about stopping up the entrances to the mountain."

Here ended the scene. The prisoner was conducted to a strong dungeon in the vermilion tower, the Arabian steed was led to his excellency's stable, and the trooper's sack was deposited in his excellency's strong box. To the latter, it is true, the friar made some demur, questioning whether the sacred relics, which were evidently sacrilegious spoils, should not be placed in custody of the church; but as the governor was peremptory on the subject, and was absolute lord in the Alhambra, the friar discreetly dropped the discussion, but determined to convey intelligence of the fact to the church dignitaries in Granada.

To explain these prompt and rigid measures on the part of old Governor Manco, it is proper to observe, that about this time the Alpuxarra mountains in the neighbourhood of Granada were terribly infested by a gang of robbers, under the command of a daring chief, named Manuel Borasco, who were accustomed to prowl about the country, and even to enter the city in various disguises, to gain intelligence of the departure of convoys of merchandise, or travellers with well-lined purses, whom they took care to waylay in distant and solitary passes of their road. These repeated and daring outrages had awakened the attention of government, and the commanders of the various posts had received instructions to be on the alert, and to take up all suspicious stragglers. Governor Manco was particularly zealous in consequence of the various stigmas that had been cast upon his fortress, and he now doubted not that he had entrapped some formidable desperado of this gang.

In the meantime the story took wind, and became the talk, not merely of the fortress, but of the whole city of Granada. It was said that the noted robber Manuel Borasco, the terror of the Alpuxarras, had fallen into the clutches of old Governor Manco, and been cooped up by him in a dungeon of the vermilion tower; and everyone who had been robbed by him flocked to recognise the marauder. The vermilion tower, as is well known, stands apart from the Alhambra on a sister hill, separated from the main fortress by the ravine down which passes the main avenue. There were no outer walls, but a sentinel patrolled before the tower. The window of the chamber in which the soldier was confined was strongly grated, and looked upon a small esplanade. Here the good folks of Granada repaired to gaze at him, as they would at a laughing hyena, grinning through the cage of a menagerie. Nobody, however, recognised him for Manuel Borasco; for that terrible robber was noted for a ferocious physiognomy, and had by no means the good-humoured squint of the prisoner. Visitors came not merely from the city, but from all parts of the country; but nobody knew him, and there began to be doubts in the minds of the common people whether there might not be some truth in his story. That Boabdil and his army were shut up in the mountain, was an old tradition which many of the ancient inhabitants had heard from their fathers. Numbers went up to the mountain of the sun, or rather to St. Elena, in search of the cave mentioned by the soldier; and saw and peeped into the deep dark pit, descending, no one knows how far, into the mountain, and which remains there to this day—the fabled entrance to the subterranean abode of Boabdil.

By degrees the soldier became popular with the common people. A freebooter of the mountains is by no means the opprobrious character in Spain that a robber is in any other country; on the contrary, he is a kind of chivalrous personage in the eyes of the lower classes. There is always a disposition, also, to cavil at the conduct of those in command; and many began to murmur at the high-handed measures of old Governor Manco, and to look upon the prisoner in the light of a martyr.

The soldier, moreover, was a merry, waggish fellow, that had a joke for everyone who came near his window, and a soft speech for every female. He had procured an old guitar also, and would sit by his window and sing ballads and love ditties, to the delight of the women of the neighbourhood, who would assemble on the esplanade in the evenings and dance boleros to his music. Having trimmed off his rough beard, his sunburnt face found favour in the eyes of the fair; and the demure handmaid of the governor declared that his squint was perfectly irresistible. This kind-hearted damsel had, from the first, evinced a deep sympathy in his fortunes, and having in vain tried to mollify the governor, had set to work privately to mitigate the rigour of his dispensations. Every day she brought the prisoner some crumbs of comfort which had fallen from the governor's table, or been abstracted from his larder, together with, now and then, a consoling bottle of choice Val de Peñas, or rich Malaga.

While this petty treason was going on, in the very centre of the old governor's citadel, a storm of open war was brewing up among his external foes. The circumstance of a bag of gold and jewels having been found upon the person of the supposed robber had been reported, with many exaggerations, in Granada. A question of territorial jurisdiction was immediately started by the governor's inveterate rival, the captain general. He insisted that the prisoner had been captured without the precincts of the Alhambra, and within the rules of his authority. He demanded his body therefore, and the *spolia opima* taken with him. Due information having been carried likewise by the friar to the grand Inquisitor of the crosses and rosaries, and other reliques contained in the bag, he claimed the culprit as having been guilty of sacrilege, and insisted that his plunder was due to the church, and his body to the next auto da fe. The feuds ran high, the governor was furious, and swore, rather than surrender his captive, he would hang him up within the Alhambra, as a spy caught within the purlieus of the fortress.

The captain general threatened to send a body of soldiers to transfer the prisoner from the vermilion tower to the city. The grand Inquisitor was equally bent upon despatching a number of the familiars of the Holy Office. Word was brought late at night to the governor of these machinations. "Let them come," said he, "they'll find me beforehand with them; he must rise bright and early who would take in an old soldier." He accordingly issued orders to have the prisoner removed at daybreak, to the donjon keep within the walls of the Alhambra. "And d'ye hear, child," said he to his demure handmaid, "tap at my door, and wake me before cock-crowing, that I may see to the matter myself."

The day dawned, the cock crowed, but nobody tapped at the door of the governor. The sun rose high above the mountain tops, and glittered in at his casement, ere the governor was wakened from his morning dreams by his veteran corporal, who stood before him with terror stamped upon his iron visage.

"He's off! he's gone!" cried the corporal, gasping for breath.

"Who's off—who's gone?"

"The soldier—the robber—the devil, for aught I know; his dungeon is empty, but the door locked,—no one knows how he has escaped out of it."

"Who saw him last?"

"Your handmaid, she brought him his supper."

"Let her be called instantly."

Here was new matter of confusion. The chamber of the demure damsel was likewise empty, her bed had not been slept in: she had doubtless gone off with the culprit, as she had appeared, for some days past, to have frequent conversations with him.

This was wounding the old governor in a tender part; but he had scarce time to wince at it, when new misfortunes broke upon his view. On going into his cabinet he found his strong box open,

307

the leather purse of the trooper abstracted, and with it, a couple of corpulent bags of doubloons.

But how, and which way, had the fugitives escaped? An old peasant who lived in a cottage by the road-side, leading up into the Sierra, declared that he had heard the tramp of a powerful steed just before daybreak, passing up into the mountains. He had looked out at his casement, and could just distinguish a horseman, with a female seated before him.

"Search the stables!" cried Governor Manco. The stables were searched; all the horses were in their stalls, excepting the Arabian steed. In his place was a stout cudgel tied to the manger, and on it a label bearing these words, "A gift to Governor Manco, from an Old Soldier."

M.R. JAMES
Rats

Montague Rhodes James (1862–1936), regarded by many contemporaries as the greatest scholar of his generation, succeeded—more than any other writer—in reviving and restyling the fine art of the ghost story at the turn of the century. His Ghost Stories of an Antiquary (1904) *is the single most important book in the twentieth-century literature of the supernatural.*

"And if you was to walk through the bedrooms now, you'd see the ragged, mouldy bedclothes a-heaving and a-heaving like seas." "And a-heaving and a-heaving with what?" he says. "Why, with the rats under 'em."

But was it with the rats? I ask, because in another case it was not. I cannot put a date to the story, but I was young when I heard it, and the teller was old. It is an ill-proportioned tale, but that is my fault, not his.

It happened in Suffolk, near the coast. In a place where the road makes a sudden dip and then a sudden rise; as you go northward, at the top of that rise, stands a house on the left of the road. It is a tall red-brick house, narrow for its height; perhaps it was built about 1770. The top of the front has a low triangular pediment with a round window in the centre. Behind it are stables and offices, and such garden as it has is behind them. Scraggy Scotch firs are near it: an expanse of gorse-covered land stretches away from it. It commands a view of the distant sea from the upper windows of the front. A sign on a post stands before the door; or did so stand, for though it was an inn of repute once, I believe it is so no longer.

To this inn came my acquaintance, Mr. Thomson, when he was a young man, on a fine spring day, coming from the University of Cambridge, and desirous of solitude in tolerable quarters and time for reading. These he found, for the landlord and his wife had been in service and could make a visitor

309

comfortable, and there was no one else staying in the inn. He had a large room on the first floor commanding the road and the view, and if it faced east, why, that could not be helped; the house was well built and warm.

He spent very tranquil and uneventful days: work all the morning, an afternoon perambulation of the country round, a little conversation with country company or the people of the inn in the evening over the then fashionable drink of brandy and water, a little more reading and writing, and bed; and he would have been content that this should continue for the full month he had at disposal, so well was his work progressing, and so fine was the April of that year—which I have reason to believe was that which Orlando Whistlecraft chronicles in his weather record as the "Charming Year."

One of his walks took him along the northern road, which stands high and traverses a wide common, called a heath. On the bright afternoon when he first chose this direction his eye caught a white object some hundreds of yards to the left of the road, and he felt it necessary to make sure what this might be. It was not long before he was standing by it, and found himself looking at a square block of white stone fashioned somewhat like the base of a pillar, with a square hole in the upper surface. Just such another you may see at this day on Thetford Heath. After taking stock of it he contemplated for a few minutes the view, which offered a church tower or two, some red roofs of cottages and windows winking in the sun, and the expanse of sea—also with an occasional wink and gleam upon it—and so pursued his way.

In the desultory evening talk in the bar, he asked why the white stone was there on the common.

"A old-fashioned thing, that is," said the landlord (Mr. Betts), "we was none of us alive when that was put there." "That's right," said another. "It stands pretty high," said Mr. Thomson, "I dare say a sea-mark was on it some time back." "Ah! yes," Mr. Betts agreed, "I 'ave 'eard they could see it from the boats; but whatever there was, it's fell to bits this long time." "Good job too," said a third, "'twarn't a lucky mark, by what the old men used to say; not lucky for the fishin', I mean to say." "Why ever not?" said Thomson. "Well, I never see it myself," was the answer, "but they 'ad some funny ideas, what I mean, peculiar, them old chaps, and I shouldn't wonder but what they made away with it theirselves."

It was impossible to get anything clearer than this: the company, never very voluble, fell silent, and when next someone spoke it was of village affairs and crops. Mr. Betts was the speaker.

Not every day did Thomson consult his health by taking a country walk. One very fine afternoon found him busily writing at three o'clock. Then he stretched himself and rose, and walked out of his room into the passage. Facing him was another room, then the stair-head, then two more rooms, one looking out to the back, the other to the south. At the south end of the passage was a window, to which he went, considering with himself that it was rather a shame to waste such a fine afternoon. However, work was paramount just at the moment; he thought he would just take five minutes off and go back to it; and those five minutes he would employ—the Bettses could not possibly object—to looking at the other rooms in the passage, which he had never seen. Nobody at all, it seemed, was indoors; probably, as it was market day, they were all gone to the town, except perhaps a maid in the bar. Very still the house was, and the sun shone really hot; early flies buzzed in the window-panes. So he explored. The room facing his own was undistinguished except for an old print of Bury St. Edmunds; the two next him on his side of the passage were gay and clean, with one window apiece, whereas his had two. Remained the south-west room, opposite to the last which he had entered. This was locked; but Thomson was in a mood of quite indefensible curiosity, and feeling confident that there could be no damaging secrets in a place so easily got at, he proceeded to fetch the key of his own room, and when that did not answer, to collect the keys of the other three. One of them fitted, and he opened the door. The room had two windows looking south and west, so it was as bright and the sun as hot upon it as could be. Here there was no carpet, but bare boards; no pictures, no washing-stand, only a bed, in the farther corner: an iron bed, with mattress and bolster, covered with a bluish check counterpane. As featureless a room as you can well imagine, and yet there was something that made Thomson close the door very quickly and yet quietly behind him and lean against the window-sill in the passage, actually quivering all over. It was this, that under the counterpane someone lay, and not only lay, but stirred. That it was some *one* and not some *thing* was certain, because the shape of a head was unmistakable on the bolster; and yet it was all covered, and no one lies with covered head but a dead person; and this was not dead, not truly dead, for it heaved and shivered. If he had seen these things in dusk or by the light of a flickering candle, Thomson could have comforted himself and talked of fancy. On this bright day that was impossible. What was to be done? First, lock the door at all costs. Very gingerly he approached it and bending down listened, holding his breath; perhaps there might be a sound of heavy breathing, and a prosaic explanation. There was absolute silence. But as, with a rather tremulous hand, he put the key into its hole and turned it, it rattled, and on the instant a stumbling padding tread was heard coming towards the door. Thomson fled like a rabbit to his room and locked himself in: futile enough, he knew it was; would doors and locks be any obstacle to what he suspected? but it was all he could think of at the moment, and in fact nothing happened; only there was a time of acute suspense—followed by a misery of doubt as to what to do. The impulse, of course, was to slip away as soon as possible from a house which contained such an inmate. But only the day before he had said he should be staying for at least a week more, and how if he changed plans could be avoid the suspicion of having pried into places where he certainly had no business? Moreover, either the Bettses knew all about the inmate, and yet did not leave the house, or knew nothing, which equally meant that there was nothing to be afraid of, or knew just enough to make them shut up the room, but not enough to weigh on their spirits: in any of these cases it seemed that not much was to be feared, and certainly so far he had had no sort of ugly experience. On the whole the line of least resistance was to stay.

Well, he stayed out his week. Nothing took him past that door, and, often as he would pause in a quiet hour of day or night in the passage and listen, and listen, no sound whatever issued from that direction. You might have thought that Thomson would have made some attempt at ferreting out stories connected with the inn—hardly perhaps from Betts, but from the parson of the parish, or old people in the village; but no, the reticence which commonly falls on people who have had strange experiences, and believe in them, was upon him. Nevertheless, as the end of his stay drew near, his yearning after some kind of explanation grew more and more acute. On his solitary walks he persisted in planning out some way, the least obtrusive, of getting another daylight glimpse into that room, and eventually arrived at this scheme. He would leave by an afternoon train—about four o'clock. When his fly was waiting, and his luggage on it, he would make one last expedition upstairs to look round his own room and see if anything was left unpacked, and then, with that key, which he had contrived to oil (as if that made any difference!), the door should once more be opened, for a moment, and shut.

So it worked out. The bill was paid, the consequent small talk gone through while the fly was loaded: "pleasant part of the country—been very comfortable, thanks to you and Mrs. Betts—hope to come back some time," on one side: on the other, "very glad you've found satisfaction, sir, done our best—always glad to 'ave your good word—very much favoured we've been with the weather, to be sure." Then, "I'll just take a look upstairs in case I've left a book or something out—no, don't trouble, I'll be back in a minute." And as noiselessly as possible he stole to the door and opened it. The shattering of the illusion! He almost laughed aloud. Propped, or you might say sitting, on the edge of the bed was—nothing in the round world but a scarecrow! A scarecrow out of the garden, of course, dumped into the deserted room. . . . Yes; but here amusement ceased. Have scarecrows bare bony feet? Do their heads loll on to their shoulders? Have they iron collars and links of chain about their necks? Can they get up and move, if never so stiffly, across a floor, with wagging head and arms close at their sides? and shiver?

The slam of the door, the dash to the stair-head, the leap downstairs, were followed by a faint. Awaking, Thomson saw Betts standing over him with the brandy bottle and a very reproachful face. "You shouldn't a done so, sir, really you shouldn't. It ain't a kind way to act by persons as done the best they could for you." Thomson heard words of this kind, but what he said in reply he did not know. Mr. Betts, and perhaps even more Mrs. Betts, found it hard to accept his apologies and his assurances that he would say no word that could damage the good name of the house. However, they *were* accepted. Since the train could not now be caught, it was arranged that Thomson should be driven to the town to sleep there. Before he went the Bettses told him what little they knew. "They says he was landlord 'ere a long time back, and was in with the 'ighwaymen that 'ad their beat about the 'eath. That's how he come by his end: 'ung in chains, they say, up where you see that stone what the gallus stood in. Yes, the fishermen made away with that, I believe, because they see it out at sea and it kep' the fish off, according to their idea. Yes, we 'ad the account from the people that 'ad the 'ouse before we come. 'You keep that room shut up,' they says, 'but don't move the bed out, and you'll find there won't be no trouble.' And no more there 'as been; not once he haven't come out into the 'ouse, though what he may do now there ain't no sayin'. Anyway, you're the first I know on that's seen him since we've been 'ere: I never set eyes on him myself, nor don't want. And ever since we've made the servants' rooms in the stablin', we ain't 'ad no difficulty that way. Only I do 'ope, sir, as you'll keep a close tongue, considerin' 'ow an 'ouse do get talked about": with more to this effect.

The promise of silence was kept for many years. The occasion of my hearing the story at last was this: that when Mr. Thomson came to stay with my father it fell to me to show him to his room, and instead of letting me open the door for him, he stepped forward and threw it open himself, and then for some moments stood in the doorway holding up his candle and looking narrowly into the interior. Then he seemed to recollect himself and said: "I beg your pardon. Very absurd, but I can't help doing that, for a particular reason." What that reason was I heard some days afterwards, and you have heard now.

ROGER JOHNSON
Mädelein

Roger Johnson (b.1947) has written several ghost stories in the Jamesian tradition, some of which ("The Wall-Painting" and "The Scarecrow") have appeared in the annual Year's Best Horror *anthologies. A librarian by profession, he also edits an invaluable newsletter,* The District Messenger, *for the Sherlock Holmes Society.*

I'm getting old. It was something of a shock to realise recently that it's over fifty years since Valerie Beddoes died.

Fifty years. Just another unsolved murder case. And of course events took place shortly afterwards that rather pushed a single death to the back of the public mind. So why raise the matter now? Well, facts that I ought to have known about long ago have at last come to my notice and made some sort of sense of the affair. Some sort. If I'm right, then the whole business is even stranger than we'd thought back in 1939.

The relationship that Valerie and I shared is difficult to define. It's such a tedious cliché to say that we were "just good friends", but really that's about the truth of it. It was only after we'd said goodbye for the last time that some inkling came to me of why I'd been able to maintain a strong friendship with such a very good-looking girl without a sexual element in the relationship. We were—well, not like sister and brother, perhaps, but like close cousins.

And Valerie was an exceptionally attractive creature. Tall, shapely, blue-eyed and blonde—the Aryan fallacy taken to a perfect extreme, but one could hardly blame her for the looks she'd inherited from her Saxon forebears. And since she was intelligent and well-educated, I think that occasionally she found her beauty something of a disadvantage. Strangely, as it seemed to me then (at twenty-two I was naive in many ways, but then my generation was like that), she found it hardest to

315

get other women to take her seriously. Margaret Pennethorne, for instance.

Playgoers under fifty are unlikely to know of Margaret Pennethorne. Even those familiar with her work may not recognise the name, since she didn't use it professionally, but she had a considerable reputation in the thirties and forties for strong historical dramas written under the pseudonym of Richard Border. *The Stone Queen* was the one that made her reputation—about Eleanor of Aquitaine—and although it hasn't been performed for years that particular play is still remembered because it also made the reputation of the young Celia Hesketh, who played Eleanor.

I was not a regular theatregoer in 1938, but I had recently seen the revival of *The Stone Queen* at the Arcadian Theatre, and when my cousin Jack Fellowes told me that he'd been invited to a party at which Richard Border was to be present I begged him to take me along. I wondered at the time why his agreement seemed to hide a sort of secret amusement. When he pointed "Richard Border" out to me the reason became clear—at least, once I'd stopped looking for a man who might perhaps have been concealed in the corner behind the two striking-looking women who were chatting so earnestly together.

Somehow I got myself introduced to the author of *The Stone Queen*. Striking? Yes, she was, if not in any obvious way. Aged about forty, I suppose, dark-haired and with an expression of rather disconcerting amusement in her eyes. She was some inches shorter than her companion, but gave the impression of being the bigger personality. I found her then rather overwhelming. The companion, on the other hand . . .

The companion was introduced to me as "my secretary, Valerie Beddoes".

Well, you already have some idea of what Valerie looked like. After we three had chatted for a while about Queen Eleanor and her brood of kings, and my halting contributions had persuaded Miss Pennethorne that I wasn't just a celebrity-seeker, I was very pleased when Valerie took my arm and said, "Meg wants to have a word with Dolly Tappan about the design for her next play. Come along—we'll go and get another drink."

I remember trying to conceal my appraisal of her face and figure, blushing when I realised that she had caught me out. I remember joining in her delighted laughter as she said, "Like

Cecily, I am very fond of being looked at. Well, by nice people, anyway. What about that drink?"

I had recently experienced a messy love affair, ending in a broken engagement. Will it surprise you to learn that I saw the lovely Valerie Beddoes not as a possible lover but as a sympathetic friend who would listen to my troubles? It seemed strange to me only in retrospect, after Jack and I had left the party, when there was only Valerie's picture in my mind. There was something about her presence that didn't allow thoughts of a sexual relationship. Odd. The very idea just didn't occur to me while we were together.

We became, as I've said, good friends. There were several interests that we shared: the music of Mozart, Thackeray's novels—other things too, including, of course, the plays of Richard Border. I visited Border's—Margaret Pennethorne's—house at Bray several times, though it was an experience that never quite pleased me because of the seemingly permanent sardonic amusement in Miss Pennethorne's eyes. She was always friendly, in a way that suggested some underlying motive, and I couldn't quite get used to the rather patronising way she would say, "I have work to do, I'm afraid. Val, why don't you two children settle down in the sitting-room and chat?"

Once she was out of the way, though, and we could hear the faint click of her typewriter through the study door, I felt more at ease. Valerie would produce cigarettes and perhaps a bottle of sherry, then she would sprawl elegantly on the couch while I took one of the big armchairs or walked restlessly about. I was young and full of serious ideas. Valerie, actually a year or two younger than I, somehow seemed more mature. She was certainly a wise conversationalist, able to listen and comment seriously on my profound political thoughts. I like to think that she was fond of me. I know that I've had no such good friends since.

We shared an interest in certain subjects, as I've indicated, but her near-obsession with the supernatural was something that quite escaped me. She had little time for ghost stories of the sort that appeared in the lurid magazines, but was fascinated (the word has lost most of its true magical force these days) by supposedly true accounts of the occult and bizarre. Perhaps it was this streak that made it inevitable that, at Margaret Pennethorne's request, Valerie should go to central Europe in search of the Bloody Countess of the Carpathians.

At that time I knew nothing of the Countess Elisabeth Bathory, though I have learned much in recent months. I was more concerned about my friend's safety in the uneasy atmosphere of a Europe that had so recently seen—how easily the word came to mind!—*Anschluss*. It was February 1939, and there was much to worry about for a sober-minded young idealist.

None of this seemed to matter to Valerie, though, nor to Margaret Pennethorne. I remember clearly how the news was broken to me when I called at the house in Bray, full of gloomy thoughts about the instability of the Munich agreement and the weakness of Neville Chamberlain. These ideas were quickly driven from me by Valerie's delighted smile and her words, "Darling! isn't it marvellous? Meg's got a new play on the boil, about a Hungarian vampire, and it's going to be even bigger than *The Stone Queen*—and I'm to do all the first-hand research for it!"

"A vampire?" I said cautiously. "Isn't that a bit outside her usual field?"

Margaret herself broke in here. The twinkle in her eyes seemed more metallic as she spoke: "Not really. I've always concentrated on the historical stuff—Eleanor, Barbarossa, Theodora—and this is really in the same vein. For heavens' sake, boy, I really believe you've never heard of Elisabeth Bathory!"

"Bathory? It—er—well, no . . ."

If there was something not quite sincere about the chuckle that greeted my reply, Valerie seemed not to notice. She took my arm and said, "I'll tell you about it. Come on. I've got coffee on the boil—and I'm sure Meg wants to be shot of us."

Still smiling, Margaret nodded and left. That smile seemed to be fixed onto her face.

(Elisabeth Bathory was a monster. Not physically, for she was held to be very beautiful, but mentally and spiritually. Her family, one of the most noble in eastern Europe, had intermarried for generations, and become marked by epilepsy, hereditary syphilis and madness. The madness erupted in this slim, dark, lovely woman.)

"I leave in two days' time," said Valerie at last. "Meg's fixed it all up. Boat-train to Dover, then Calais, Paris and across to

318

Buda-Pesth. It'll be wonderful to get away—to be working on my own."

"Two *days*? That's a bit—"

"Oh, I'll miss you, of course, and a few other friends, but it's such an opportunity! And, you know—" (she lowered her voice a little) "— I shall be so glad just to get away from Meg for a while." She tossed a cigarette over to me, smiling at my expression. "I know it's sudden, but I think Meg's actually had the idea in mind for some time. You know how she likes to keep her work to herself until she's quite sure of it."

"Two days," I said again.

"This really will be big, you know. I told her I thought that the life of the Bloody Countess would make a stunning exercise in *Grand Guignol*. She said, 'Never mind *Grand Guignol*. This will be positively *Gross Guignol*.'"

(Elisabeth Bathory was a sadist. She is believed to have been directly responsible for the murders of over 650 young women, having them cut, slashed or burned so that their blood flowed. She would bathe in the blood of virgins in the belief that it would prolong her youth and beauty.)

"You're going alone? I suppose Margaret will provide the money, but how will you manage otherwise?"

"I'll be safe enough. Hungary may be rather unsettled, but I'm hoping also to get into Austria and Czechoslovakia. The Germans seem to have clamped down pretty firmly on crime there. Besides, my German is pretty fluent. I'll manage all right."

It was true that the private atrocities that had seemed to flourish in the uneasy Germany of the twenties had no place in Adolf Hitler's Third Reich. Peter Kürten, Karl Denke, Fritz Haarmann, Georg Grossman—they were not part of the new German Empire. It was only rumour to us that private atrocity had given way to official atrocity, on a scale that made the activities of Elisabeth Bathory seem almost petty.

(Elisabeth Bathory was a devoted wife to her noble husband, the Count Francis Nadasdy, and a devoted mother to their children. She seemed to have no difficulty in keeping her domestic life quite separate from the bloodlust and magic of her darker nature.)

"What time do you leave Victoria?"

"The train's due out at 9.25 in the morning."

"Hell! I've got to go to Birmingham tomorrow and I shan't be back till Friday evening. I can't even come to see you off. How long do you expect to be away?"

"No telling. I'm to start at the state archives in Buda-Pesth, and then if I can I go on to Elisabeth's castle in eastern Czechoslovakia and to Vienna, where she had a town house. There's a special research that Meg wants me to carry out, besides just gathering details of the Countess' life. She's heard from a correspondent in Austria that a torture device made for the Countess may still exist. I'm to track it down if I can and try to buy it."

(Elisabeth Bathory had special torture rooms installed in most of her several houses and castles. She would also indulge herself in private rooms when she visited friends or relatives. In the cellar of her mansion in Vienna was a spiked cage, in which her naked victim would be hauled up on a rope and pulley and prodded with hot irons until she impaled herself in her torment. The beautiful Countess, herself naked, stood beneath the cage, bathing in the shower of fresh blood.)

"Good God! That's horrible."

Valerie shrugged. "Morbid, I agree, but after all, it's all in the distant past."

"You know as well as anyone that Margaret Pennethorne can make the past come alive. I suppose there's no changing your mind?"

"Not likely! I'm looking forward to this. It's a pity we shan't be able to meet again—but it isn't the end of the world, you know. I'll keep in touch, and we'll get together again as soon as I come back."

(After her eventual trial, at which in deference to her noble family she was referred to only as 'a blood-thirsty, bloodsucking Godless woman, caught in the act at Csejthe Castle, Elisabeth Bathory was sentenced to lifelong imprisonment at that same castle. She was immured in a small room without doors or windows, and only a small hatch for food to be passed to her. In August 1614 she died, "suddenly and without a crucifix and without light". For three and a half years she had seen nobody and nothing.)

Two weeks later, I happened to meet Margaret Pennethorne in Hatchard's bookshop. Naturally, I asked whether she'd had word yet from Valerie. Her quizzical smile was unchanged as she shook her head.

"Aren't you worried about her at all? I mean, with Europe so volatile—?"

"Oh, no. She's a capable enough girl. She'll cope. Besides, just now I'm rather relieved to have got her off my hands. Protracted love-affairs become tedious, don't you think?"

Much later that day I understood her remark. A love affair. They had been lovers. Of course! The notion just hadn't occurred to me before (didn't I say that I was a very naïve young man?), but it explained one thing at least. In spite of her obvious and very feminine good looks, I had never been able to think of Valerie in terms of a heterosexual love. Now I knew what it was about her that had precluded such thoughts.

(Elisabeth Bathory was bisexual, and all her perversities tended toward the lesbian side of her nature. She began by mistreating the peasant girls on her estates, who were in a very real sense her own property. The Hungarian peasants' revolt of a generation before had been savagely crushed, and the peasants of Elisabeth's time had no rights—even life itself was merely a privilege. Later she became convinced that only aristocratic virgins could provide the blood she needed. Her preferred victims were under eighteen years of age, blonde and buxom, in contrast to her own dark and slender beauty.)

A day or so later, the first letter arrived from Valerie, having taken four days in the post. My own feelings towards her were changed only in that they were now quite straightforward: she was and would remain the best friend I had. I read the letter with great interest.

She had succeeded in gaining admittance to the state archives in Buda-Pesth, and had obtained (helped no doubt by her own charm and Margaret Pennethorne's money) an abridged transcript of the trial records. This was in Latin, and she intended to spend some of the time while travelling in translating as much of it as she could. Meanwhile, she was now headed for what had recently become the independent state of Slovakia, to visit that same castle of Csejthe which had been the Countess Bathory's principal residence. All was going well, and she had encountered no difficulties of any sort. Everyone she had met had been kind and helpful. I must *stop worrying*.

321

There was a post-script: "I quite forgot to tell you just what the object is that Meg wants me to try and find. It's an Iron Maiden."

(The Iron Maiden was not a particularly common device, even in the great age of torture. The most famous example to be seen today is at Nuremberg, a bulky machine, very crudely shaped like a woman, and with a woman's face roughly depicted on the head. A section of the front is hinged like a door, and can be opened by means of a rope and pulley to reveal a hollow just large enough for a man to be placed. On the inside of the door are several long spikes, so arranged that when the door closed the upper ones would pierce the victim's eyes and the lower ones his heart and vitals.)

Unfortunately, Valerie didn't tell me where in Slovakia she would be staying, and I was unable to find Csejthe on any map available to me. Later events drove the question from my mind, and it was only within the last few years that I learned that the place is now called Cachtice.

The next letter came about ten days later. Since the postmark was unreadable, I still had no clear notion of just where Valerie was; somehow I felt reluctant to approach Margaret Pennethorne again.

The castle, itself ruined, stands on a high green hill surrounded by level and fertile country. The late Sir Iain Moncreiffe of That Ilk described it as "like a land-girt St Michael's Mount"—which is more pithy and probably as accurate as Valerie's longer description. If there was any local superstition attaching to the place, Valerie doesn't mention it; she seems to have had no trouble in finding someone to act as a guide. This woman, Anna, was presumably a native Czech speaker, but she had more than a smattering of German—of a sort . . . At least she was able, with little prompting, to show Valerie the very room in which the Bloody Countess had passed so many months in a living death.

(Elisabeth's family and that of her husband were Protestants —Calvinists in fact—but enjoyed the support of the Holy Roman Emperor. The estates at Csejthe were not subject to any interference from the Emperor or from the neighbouring Prince of Transylvania. Elisabeth herself was a Calvinist, a complete believer in predestination. As a noble with absolute authority, and a Christian already chosen for salvation, she had no cause to justify her acts to herself or to anyone else. Even when she turned to the devil for help—it was a sorceress who advised her that the blood of noble maidens was necessary—she remained a convinced Christian. One can only wonder whether John Calvin himself would have approved.)

Anna even told her that the Countess' house in Vienna had been situated in the Augustienerstrasse, near the Imperial Palace. As to the Iron Maiden—why, the *gnädiges Fraülein* could hardly expect a poor peasant woman to know much about that. Certainly it had existed at this castle, and she hadn't heard that it had been destroyed. Maybe it wasn't there when the authorities came at last to arrest the beautiful Countess. Maybe it had been sent away to one of her other houses. The house in Vienna, perhaps?

Fortunately, this fitted in nicely with Valerie's plans, since Margaret Pennethorne's reticent correspondent had also suggested that the torture machine might have been taken into Austria. As they said goodbye, Anna looked for a moment at Valerie and said (so Valerie thought), "You will find it, I think. You are the right sort."

(Elisabeth Bathory was given to torturing her young companions while making the long, slow journey from one house or castle to another. Later, unable to wait until she had reached her destination, she would kill the girls who travelled with her. The bodies were simply interred by the roadside, though in earlier years she had insisted upon a Christian burial for her victims.)

Even at the Austrian frontier, Valerie encountered no real difficulty. She had to be rather circumspect in writing from Vienna, but I understood that the passport officer, a true Nazi, had been most impressed by her evident Nordic beauty and fluent German. The only thing that slightly disturbed her was that more than once—at the frontier, and again a couple of times before reaching Vienna—she thought she caught a glimpse of the old peasant woman, Anna.

I never knew Vienna before the war. The only time I've spent there was in 1946 as an officer in the British occupation force. Even so, I doubt that my Vienna was any more unlike the city that Elisabeth Bathory knew. I try to put the great neo-classical and baroque structures of the Inner Stadt out of my mind but I find that there's nothing left. If I'd hoped for some sort of imaginative guidance from Valerie's letters, I was to be disappointed. A curious and disconcerting vagueness seemed to affect her—she who had always impressed me with the clarity and balance of her thoughts.

The accounts became at last almost dreamlike. I gathered that for at least a week after her arrival in the city she had more or less wandered around the Inner Stadt, admiring the Hofburg, the Opera House, the churches—and wondering, with a feeling that she couldn't quite define, whether she would meet Anna again. During these days, she must have passed many times the corner of the Augustienerstrasse and the Dorotheergasse. It didn't seem to occur to her, though, that there was anything special about the place.

(Elisabeth Bathory's mansion stood hard by the Austin Friary. As her blood-lust grew rapidly out of control, she abandoned nearly all rational precautions. The appalling screams of the tortured and dying were so loud that the good friars sometimes protested by hurling pots and pans at her windows.)

Almost every week brought a letter from Valerie—to which I couldn't reply, as, infuriatingly, she gave no address. Several times I tried to telephone Margaret Pennethorne, but there was no reply. Valerie knew that there was something particular she ought to be doing, something connected with a person she'd known in England. Or in Hungary. The letters would contain disturbing, almost surrealist, descriptive imagery of a city that was unlike any I had ever encountered. Yet, among these accounts, there were the names and descriptions of recognisable places. And then there were the people.

Soldiers, German and Austrian, goose-stepping, heel-clicking, saluting. The ominous *Heil Hitler* that seemed to have replaced the homely *Grüss Gott*. There was something in the eyes of the men that rather frightened her. All the men. The women, on the other hand . . .

It was never made clear whether she actually met Anna again, but there were many references to her, brief and inconsequential, often questioning. Was her face in every crowd, or could it just be nervous imagination? Was she only one person? But there was no need to pursue that sinister line. Whatever hold Anna might have over her, she could always go to Dorothy for comfort. Dear old Dorothy, so solid and motherlike. Besides, if it hadn't been for Dorothy—

Dorothy. Dorothea. Something about the name. Something meaningful?

If it hadn't been for Dorothy, she would never have met—
She was here to find something. Someone.
— would never have met Mädelein.

There was that odd, stunted little man who often seemed to be near when she was with Dorothy. She didn't like the glances he gave her, but at least Mädelein treated him with scornful tolerance. She must do the same. Darling lovely Mädelein.

The very last letter—like the rest, it was undated, but it reached me on the 21st of June—contains one very clear statement. Valerie was in love. Irrevocably, over head and ears in love. With Mädelein. They had hardly even met—just seen each other in the street; and it was all so *proper*. Perhaps that was a part of the spell. Nothing that had happened in England (what *had* happened in England?) had been like this. How wise Dorothy had been to keep them apart at first. Not a word exchanged, but when Mädelein had smiled, showing those beautiful white, even teeth, and her eyes shining the clearest blue, then Valerie *knew*. She'd found what she was looking for.

Now, what was I to make of all this? I had been against the journey from the start. Not only was the journey itself unsafe, I thought, but the reason for it was plainly morbid and mentally unhealthy. Was I right? Something had clouded my friend's mind; I couldn't doubt that she'd become (the word repels me, but I must use it) insanely obsessed by her mad search and by the mad world in which she'd arrived. Her descriptions of Mädelein in no way eased my mind, for they were clearly descriptions of Valerie herself.

Again I tried to telephone Margaret Pennethorne. This time, at least, she answered, but it was with a brusque, "Oh, it's you. Well, you're Valerie's friend; perhaps you can tell me where the wretched kid's got to?"

"But for heaven's sake! Isn't she in Vienna?"

"You tell me. She's out somewhere spending my money, and I haven't had a word from her in weeks."

I was horrified. And somehow, I just couldn't bring myself to mention Valerie's letters to me, which were the reason why I'd called in the first place. I said something vague about passing on any news that reached me and I put the telephone down.

Fear for my friend inspired me to boldness. I wrote to the British Embassy in Vienna, explaining that I was very concerned for a young Englishwoman whom I believed to be alone in the city and possibly in some kind of trouble. If someone from the Embassy staff could find her and assure me that she was all right, I should be most grateful.

The reply came nearly two weeks later.

The body of Valerie Beddoes, identified by her passport and her belongings, had been found in her room at a small *pension* near the Rotenturmstrasse. The manageress, having been alarmed by a single dreadful scream from the room, had awoken her husband and one of the male residents and with much reluctance entered the room. When she had realised what the viscous liquid was that her bare feet were treading in, she had become hysterical and had to be sedated. The police were called at once.

Valerie Beddoes lay upon the floor of the little room, her spine broken and four ribs crushed. She was naked, so that the appalling wounds inflicted upon her could be clearly seen. Her breasts and genitals had been savagely stabbed with some sharp, thick instrument like a chisel.

The police surgeon declared that he had come across nothing like it in Viennese criminal history. He could only compare it to the Whitechapel murders of 1888. Plainly it was *Lustmörden*, the work of a sexual psychopath. The coroner could only agree. Despite the landlady's stories of visitors to the young woman's room that night, whom she was unable to describe in any detail—even to being unsure of their number—it was plain that these visitors were women, and neither coroner nor police could credit that this horrible act was the work of a woman. The verdict was: murder by person or persons unknown.

It was all so sad, said the landlady; the English girl had been a little vague, perhaps, but so sweet and so very pretty.

The person or persons remained unknown. As soon as I felt able to, I sent a copy of the letter from the Embassy to Margaret Pennethorne. I expected no reply, and received none. Nor did I hear again from Vienna.

On the 3rd of September, Great Britain declared war against Germany. My time and thoughts were occupied for a long while with other matters, and when I returned at last to civilian life I deliberately put Valerie's death from my mind, preferring to remember our friendship and the good times. The wound healed, though it ached horribly at times.

And now it has opened again, all because of a suspicious voice that will not be silenced.

Over fifty years ago, I considered Valerie's pursuit of a sadistic murderess to be morbid and unhealthy. I think so still. For that reason I made no attempt to research further into the blood-soaked career of the Countess Elisabeth Bathory. Only Valerie mattered, and Valerie was dead. My only link with her had been Margaret Pennethorne, the enigmatic "Richard Border", and she was dead too, killed in the Blitz. So it was chance and not design that led me to realise that I'd made a false assumption all those years ago.

The Iron Maiden. The thing that Valerie had been looking for. Quite recently I discovered that the machine made for Elisabeth Bathory, to her own specifications (and which almost certainly was destroyed after her arrest at Csejthe), had been something rather different from the crude device preserved at Nuremberg. It was made in the form of an attractive and shapely young woman, life-sized and naked, complete with full breasts and pubic hair. The blue eyes could open and close, and the pink lips part to reveal even white teeth. The flowing blonde hair was real, and so were the teeth—they had been torn from the head of one of Elisabeth's victims. When the chosen subject, who must have looked like its living image, approached this hellish doll, its arms would enfold her in an embrace, at first amusing, swiftly bone-crushing. Meanwhile, from the genitals and the nipples, sharp spikes would spring to pierce the young woman's body.

I thought then that Valerie's mind had become clouded, and that "Mädelein" was merely a narcissistic projection of her own self. I think otherwise now, since I have discovered that "Mädelein", literally translated, is a diminutive of "Mädel"—a maid.

Valerie Beddoes did find what she was looking for after all . . .

A.F. KIDD
And Turns No More His Head

A.F.Kidd (b.1953) is an advertising copywriter and freelance artist whose interests include astronomy and campanology. She has written many excellent supernatural stories, published in three separate collections: Bell Music, In and Out of the Belfry, *and* Change and Decay *(from which the following story is taken).*

I used to work in an advertising agency—not one of the big ones, but one with a good solid reputation, all the same. Now most people in advertising work very hard, but there are some—mainly those who've been in the business for a number of years—who just sit back on their achievements and think they don't ever need to create anything original again. (You can usually recognise them by their habit of prefacing most of their remarks with "I've been in this business twenty years . . .")

Unfortunately for the rest of us, they often get taken on by agencies on the strength of a reputation gained twenty years before—then they spend their time going to conferences and giving talks which were amusing twenty years ago, leaving everyone else to do the work.

We had one of these at my agency. His name was Gerald Honeywell, and he was fairly typical of the breed, although he did at least seem to have wider interests than most. He would have been quite interesting to talk to except for his attitude. He treated everyone, with the exception of the managing director and of his sycophants, as congenital idiots—women more so than men.

One day, not long after he joined the agency, he saw me writing out Cambridge Major, which I was trying to learn, but instead of saying, as everyone else did, "What the hell's that?" he said, "Oh, bellringing."

"Are you a ringer?" I asked with great incredulity.

"No," he said, with an I-wouldn't-demean-myself air. "But

I've written an article about it being done by computer. I'll bring it in for you."

That was the first time I'd heard of it being done, so I was quite interested—not to mention surprised at Gerald Honeywell speaking to me almost like a human being.

The article—a photostat from some magazine—was presented to me with the air of a monarch bestowing a favour upon a lowly subject, a few days later.

It was headed *"SPECTRUM meets Cambridge Major"*, and I read it with fascination—and growing alarm. Not only had a computer been programmed to play changes through its loudspeaker, but Gerald Honeywell was proposing a system by which computers could be used to do away with ringers altogether! I found it a curious article for a non-ringer to have written, in view of the technicalities involved; but as I said, he had wide interests—and after all, it hadn't been his programme.

Now it so happened that, soon after I had read this subversive piece of literature, the local church where I rang held an open day.

I knew what that probably meant—spending half the day escorting parties up to the belfry, and the other half making sure that the local kids didn't nick the handbells or hang themselves with the ropes.

In the end, of course, it wasn't nearly as bad as I expected, and we all got a fair bit of a ring, so the day wasn't wasted.

But nobody was more surprised than I when Gerald Honeywell turned up and expressed a wish to see the bells.

I eyed his rotund form dubiously until it occurred to me that with a bit of luck he might get stuck halfway up the spiral staircase. So I prudently got him to precede me; but unfortunately he negotiated the narrow bits as if greased for cross-channel swimming, and reached the belfry unscathed.

Once inside, having perched him precariously on the narrow platform and restrained an urge to tell him not to hit his beer-gut on the four, which was nearest, I pointed out the tenor and the treble, and then started to explain about wheels, headstocks, stays and sliders; but it transpired that his purpose in wanting to see the bells was to work out how best to implement his computer ideas.

On the way down, he added the final heresy: "Probably be able to do away with bells altogether before long."

Dusk was gathering as he left the church, and as he passed through the graveyard on his way to the gate, I thought I saw something like a patch of deeper shade detach itself from the shadow of a tombstone and merge itself oddly with Honeywell's own shadow. But it may have been a trick of the light.

That Sunday we got the quarter-peal I'd been practising and studying for—my first of Cambridge—so I forgot about Gerald Honeywell.

But first thing on the following Monday morning he marched straight into my office without even removing his coat, and demanded accusingly, "I expect it was you ringing those bloody bells all Sunday."

I looked up, surprised at his tone. For all his faults, he was not a belligerent person.

"They're still ringing in my head," he complained. "The sooner we can control the sound, the better."

He looked ill and tired: and his appearance, never very prepossessing at the best of times, became more and more unlovely as the days went by.

The following week he was absent altogether. I didn't worry about him, merely concluded (not unreasonably) that too much beer, too many expense-account meals, and far too many "borrowed" cigarettes (he never bought his own, though he must have earned twice as much as anyone he took them from) had brought on a well-deserved attack of gout or dyspepsia.

The next practice night, I found the outside tower door locked, so had to go in through the main door. I was walking carefully through the darkness inside the church when I heard a movement.

"Who's that?" I called, but there was no reply, just an odd noise—like a ponderous scurrying, if you can imagine that. Like an enormous rat trying to be silent, but failing because of its bulk. At that thought I leapt for the light switch, only to draw my hand back with a gasp from something soft and rotten—my fingers sank into it.

When I turned on the light I found a decaying apple on the shelf, no doubt left over from the Harvest Festival. I would have laughed with relief—if I hadn't still been aware of that great, furtive tread in the shadows.

Then began a ghoulish game of hide-and-seek. Whether I was pursuing a human marauder or something monstrous, I had no idea, nor could I catch a glimpse of whatever it was.

Until someone began to raise the bells. The treble and the two started to go up, and a despairing sob came from behind one of the pews. At that, though I'd been apprehensive, there was such pain in it that I ran straight towards the noise. It sounded like the cry of some creature which had crawled into the nearest shelter to die from terrible wounds.

I didn't recognise the pathetic figure crouched on the floor at first. Apart from a constant shudder that ran through it, all that now moved were the eyes. Gerald Honeywell's eyes—staring wildly, ceaselessly moving.

I couldn't think of anything to do. I just stood there. Then he staggered to his feet, pushed past me, and ran towards the door. The sound of his running feet echoed oddly—it sounded like two sets of footsteps; though when I followed, mine didn't echo at all.

Outside, it was quite dark, but I could see him by the streetlight beside the gate. Following him, with a curious lurching, bobbing movement, was an odd, humped figure. It was completely covered by a kind of robe or cloak, made from some material which gleamed wetly where the light shone on it. It didn't run normally—it limped. But it was gaining on him.

I wanted to shout a warning, but the thought that it might notice me kept me silent. I didn't want to see it clearly.

When it reached the gate, it stopped, and moved its cloaked head to and fro, like an animal casting round for a scent which eluded it.

Then I heard the band begin to raise the rest of the bells in peal, and the creature apparently did too, for it stopped its searching movements and slid into the shadows with what seemed, somehow, to be a satisfied air.

Worrying about Gerald Honeywell wouldn't have helped, and not only was he out of sight, nothing would have induced me to pass the place where the thing had been—not on my own, anyway—so I went back into the church and climbed up to the ringing chamber.

When I got there, the bells were up and the ringers were all looking at something on the table. I moved over to see what, and found that it was an old book.

"Hi Maggie," I was greeted.

"Hi. What's that?" I asked.

"It's a sort of guide-book to the church. Printed in 1850."

"Where did you find that?"

"Junkshop down the road."

The book, naturally, was open at the section headed The Church Bells and Bell Tower. A paragraph caught my eye:

"A new Tenor Bell was given in 1792 by Mr. Giles Wood, to replace that one which was cracked and unringable. Upon it he caused to be engraved the following Rhyme:-

'When my Tones the World doth heare,
Let no man Dare to interfeare.'

"According to popular legend, a dreadful retribution would visit anyone who attempted to prevent the ringing of the bells; although whether the ghostly shade of Mr. Wood or some other supernatural visitant is supposed to enact this, is not known to this writer."

I turned over the pages, looking for more information, but that was all there was. The only other thing I could think of was to look for Giles Wood's grave, or see if there were any inscriptions in the church. (I didn't know its interior very well, because, like quite a few other ringers I could mention, I tend to think of churches as just buildings attached to bell-towers. Not, perhaps, laudable; but that's me.)

Quite what this would accomplish, if anything, I didn't know: if Gerald Honeywell had incurred some kind of supernatural vengeance by his silly ideas about doing away with bells, what could I do about it? Come to that, what could he do about it—apologise somehow? Would that be enough? I had no idea.

And then another avenue of investigation occurred to me, while I was reading *The Ringing World*. You know they have a "40 years ago" paragraph in it—well, that particular one was about the lifting of the wartime ban on ringing. It took a moment to hit me: what happened when the ban was in force? Did that creature slither round the churchyard—and did it go away when the bells began to be rung once more?

I was quite excited by this. But the problem was finding someone to ask. The obvious person should have been the vicar, but I didn't really relish the idea of going to him and asking in all seriousness about something that sounded as if it had been invented by M R James. Besides, the vicar viewed us as a godless lot who were only there on sufferance to ring the bells; at the very best he would have thought I was pulling his leg.

But I didn't know of any ringers who had been around forty years before. Our band were all quite young, and more than half (including me) were comparitive newcomers to the area.

Then I vaguely remembered something on one of the peal-boards in the tower, so the next time I was there I made a point of looking for it: and there it was. A peal of Stedman Triples, rung two years previously as "An 80th birthday compliment to Harold P Warwick, for 65 years a ringer in this tower".

Harold P Warwick was not difficult to find, for which I was greatly thankful: I had expected to be directed to his tombstone. But he proved to be an extremely robust old gent, confined to a wheelchair but in full possession of all his marbles. I couldn't recall ever having seen him, but he knew I was a ringer, and, moreover, congratulated me on the quarter.

"Well, my dear," he said, having insisted on making me a cup of tea which I didn't particularly want, "what can I do for you?"

"I wanted to ask you about during the war, when they banned ringing."

"Oh, you've been hearing about the Guardian, have you?"

"The guardian?"

"Don't act so surprised. Why else would you ask me that? I may be old, but I'm not daft."

So I told him about Gerald Honeywell.

". . . and I saw something following him.—"

"Now, you don't need to describe it. I know what it's like. A hopping, limping thing, all wet and nasty like it'd been in the river—with eyes like a beast's, but intelligent."

"I didn't see its face. I didn't want to, either."

"Well, I can tell you a bit about it—but I don't think I've any notion of how to stop it pestering this Honeywell fellow. You guessed right, though—it was lurking around all the time the bells weren't rung; and there's many a woman, and man too, that it gave a nasty fright. But it went away when we began to ring again: I never heard tell of it being seen since then, till now."

"Is it anything to do with Giles Wood who had a new tenor cast in seventeen-something?"

"Old Master Giles, they called him. 1792's the date on his bell. Yes, indeed, it all goes back to Old Master Giles."

He leaned back in his wheelchair and stared at the fire for a moment; then he went on.

"I suppose you looked for his grave, did you? I thought so. It's what I'd have done. And d'you know why you couldn't find it? I'll tell you. It's because he's not buried in the churchyard, nor in any holy ground, for that matter."

"Why not?"

"Don't interrupt me, young lady," he said with a flash of asperity (he must have been a real martinet in the ringing chamber) "You'll have the whole tale soon enough, just as I had it from my father, and he from his, right back to when it all happened.

"He was a strange old soul, by all accounts, was Master Giles. Never married nor seen with a woman, yet there was enough lasses, all the same, claimed they'd borne his bastards; nor never went to church, that anyone knew. But he did love to hear the bells. The money that man gave to the tower!

"He hardly ever stirred out of his house, that used to stand hard by the churchyard. People said he sat in there and spoke with the dead: those were the only neighbours he had, true enough, but they were a superstitious lot in those days. Still believed in witches and suchlike. And there was many folk that even said he dabbled in witchcraft, sat there alone in that house of his: he always had the money to give, for all he never seemed to do any work. It must have come by sorcery, they reasoned. And he'd pay for it—Old Scratch'd come for him in the end.

"Well, enough of that. When he had the old tenor replaced he had a verse put on it—you've read it? It wasn't the words he first wanted. There might be a clue in them, I can't exactly remember what they were. I'll find 'em in a while, they're wrote down somewhere.

"As the years went by, Master Giles kept to his house more and more. Folks said that strange lights were to be seen inside, and voices heard when there was none to speak to. There was talk of burning—as I said, they still believed in witches. This place was still way out in the country in those days, you know!

"It was my great-great-grandfather told this tale, and passed it on, for he was the only one who saw the end. He was churchwarden then.

"Nobody had seen Master Giles for a long while—some said weeks, others a matter of months. And one evening a group came to the churchwarden's home, near panic, and demanded he do something about the lights and the voices, since parson wouldn't.

"So, most reluctantly, he went across to Master Giles' house, the townsfolk following a way behind. And, indeed, there was a light inside; but it seemed to be no more than normal lamplight. But he was urged forward, and he tapped gently on the door. He heard nothing in reply, but a strange sound disturbed him slightly: like something damp being dragged across stone flags.

"And so he opened the door. And what he saw remained with him to the end of his life. Crawling towards the door, as if in pain or as if being restrained by something unseen, was a figure that may once have been human, but was now barely recognisable as such. Hunched, halting, its soft rotten flesh sloughing from yellow bones, it hugged to itself a cloth sodden with the fluids of dissolution. Whether it was all that remained of Old Master Giles, he never knew; but it stared at him with eyes so despairing that he was moved not by horror, but only by pity.

"But he jumped back in alarm, and in doing so, knocked over the lamp; barely escaping before the house went up like tinder.

"So now you see why Master Giles has no grave. And if I can find that paper —" he broke off, and propelled his chair dextrously towards an old roll-top bureau. After a short search, he handed me a yellowing piece of paper, upon which were written the barely legible lines:

"When this Tenor Bell soundes cleare
No Man need feel any feare.
But if any man my Voice prevent,
As Messenger I shal be sent. (This line was scratched out and the following substituted:)
Suffer then till thou Repent.
If thou Repent not with thy Soule
Nevermore shalt thou be whole.
In Pennance thou must pull my Rope
Until thy Soule be filld with Hope."

"Well—that seems clear enough," the old man commented. "Whether it's Old Master Giles himself, or some summoning of his, that has to be appeased, it looks as though this Honeywell has to ring the tenor to do it."

"But is it just the tenor?" I asked.

"That's all he mentions."

I had visions of disaster should Gerald Honeywell try to learn to ring: broken stays, discord in the tower, and who knows what else. But it was not to happen. The following morning he was found dead in his bed, apparently from a heart attack. I was dismayed to hear this. Could I, perhaps, have helped him, if I'd acted sooner?

The curious fact that his bedclothes were sopping wet was explained by the conclusion that the window had been open during the night, but had blown shut. Those who had thought about it might have been puzzled, for it had not rained that night; but, perhaps, not so puzzled as those who heard me tolling Old Master Giles' bell for Gerald Honeywell.

RUDYARD KIPLING
By Word of Mouth

Rudyard Kipling (1865–1936), *like many other great names in English literature, constantly returned to the allegorical world of fantasy and the supernatural. "By Word of Mouth", described by Kipling's biographer Charles Carrington as "a thoroughly convincing ghost story", was also totally believed by readers when it first appeared in the* Civil and Military Gazette *(Lahore) on 10 June 1887. The story was one of Kipling's very popular* Plain Tales from the Hills, *which delighted generations of his admirers.*

Not though you die to-night, O Sweet, and wail,
    A spectre at my door,
Shall mortal Fear make Love immortal fail—
    I shall but love you more,
Who, from Death's house returning, give me still
One moment's comfort in my matchless ill.

Shadow Houses

T his tale may be explained by those who know how souls are made, and where the bounds of the Possible are put down. I have lived long enough in this India to know that it is best to know nothing, and can only write the story as it happened.

Dumoise was our Civil Surgeon at Meridki, and we called him "Dormouse," because he was a round little, sleepy little man. He was a good Doctor and never quarrelled with any one, not even with our Deputy Commissioner who had the manners of a bargee and the tact of a horse. He married a girl as round and as sleepy-looking as himself. She was a Miss Hillardyce, daughter of "Squash" Hillardyce of the Berars, who married his Chief's daughter by mistake. But that is another story.

A honeymoon in India is seldom more than a week long; but there is nothing to hinder a couple from extending it over two or three years. India is a delightful country for married folk who are wrapped up in one another. They can live absolutely alone and without interruption—just as the Dormice did. Those two little people retired from the world after their marriage, and were very happy. They were forced, of course, to give occasional dinners, but they made no friends thereby, and the Station went its own way and forgot them; only saying, occasionally, that Dormouse was the best of good fellows though dull. A Civil Surgeon who never quarrels is a rarity, appreciated as such.

Few people can afford to play Robinson Crusoe anywhere— least of all in India, where we are few in the land and very much dependent on each other's kind offices. Dumoise was wrong in shutting himself from the world for a year, and he discovered his mistake when an epidemic of typhoid broke out in the Station in the heart of the cold weather, and his wife went down. He was a shy little man, and five days were wasted before he realised that Mrs. Dumoise was burning with something worse than simple fever, and three days more passed before he ventured to call on Mrs. Shute, the Engineer's wife, and timidly speak about his trouble. Nearly every household in India knows that Doctors are very helpless in typhoid. The battle must be fought out between Death and the Nurses minute by minute and degree by degree. Mrs. Shute almost boxed Dumoise's ears for what she called his "criminal delay," and went off at once to look after the poor girl. We had seven cases of typhoid in the Station that winter and, as the average of death is about one in every five cases, we felt certain that we should have to lose somebody. But all did their best. The women sat up nursing the women, and the men turned to and tended the bachelors who were down, and we wrestled with those typhoid cases for fifty-six days, and brought them through the Valley of the Shadow in triumph. But, just when we thought all was over, and were going to give a dance to celebrate the victory, little Mrs. Dumoise got a relapse and died in a week, and the Station went to the funeral. Dumoise broke down utterly at the brink of the grave, and had to be taken away.

After the death Dumoise crept into his own house and refused to be comforted. He did his duties perfectly, but we all felt that he should go on leave, and the other men of his own Service told him so. Dumoise was very thankful for the suggestion—he was thankful for anything in those days—and went to Chini on a walking-tour. Chini is some twenty marches from Simla, in the heart of the Hills, and the scenery is good if you are in trouble. You pass through big, still deodar forests, and under big, still cliffs, and over big, still grass-downs swelling like a woman's breasts; and the wind across the grass, and the rain among the deodars say—"Hush—hush—hush." So little Dumoise was packed off to Chini, to wear down his grief with a full-plate camera and a rifle. He took also a useless bearer, because the man had been his wife's favourite servant. He was idle and a thief, but Dumoise trusted everything to him.

On his way back from Chini, Dumoise turned aside to Bagi, through the Forest Reserve which is on the spur of Mount Huttoo. Some men who have travelled more than a little say that the march from Kotegarh to Bagi is one of the finest in creation. It runs through dark wet forest, and ends suddenly in bleak, nipped hillside and black rocks. Bagi dâk-bungalow is open to all the winds and is bitterly cold. Few people go to Bagi. Perhaps that was the reason why Dumoise went there. He halted at seven in the evening, and his bearer went down the hillside to the village to engage coolies for the next day's march. The sun had set, and the night-winds were beginning to croon among the rocks. Dumoise leaned on the railing of the verandah, waiting for his bearer to return. The man came back almost immediately after he had disappeared, and at such a rate that Dumoise fancied he must have crossed a bear. He was running as hard as he could up the face of the hill.

But there was no bear to account for his terror. He raced to the verandah and fell down, the blood spurting from his nose and his face iron-grey. Then he gurgled—"I have seen the *Memsahib!* I have seen the *Memsahib!*"

"Where?" said Dumoise.

"Down there, walking on the road to the village. She was in a blue dress, and she lifted the veil of her bonnet and said—'Ram Dass, give my *salaams* to the *Sahib*, and tell him that I shall meet him next month at Nuddea.' Then I ran away, because I was afraid."

What Dumoise said or did I do not know. Ram Dass declares that he said nothing, but walked up and down the verandah all the cold night, waiting for the *Memsahib* to come up the hill, and stretching out his arms into the dark like a madman. But no *Memsahib* came, and, next day, he went on to Simla cross-questioning the bearer every hour.

Ram Dass could only say that he had met Mrs. Dumoise, and that she had lifted up her veil and given him the message which he had faithfully repeated to Dumoise. To this statement Ram Dass adhered. He did not know where Nuddea was, had no friends at Nuddea, and would most certainly never go to Nuddea, even though his pay were doubled.

Nuddea is in Bengal, and has nothing whatever to do with a Doctor serving in the Punjab. It must be more than twelve hundred miles south of Meridki.

Dumoise went through Simla without halting, and returned to Meridki, there to take over charge from the man who had been officiating for him during his tour. There were some Dispensary accounts to be explained, and some recent orders of the Surgeon-General to be noted, and, altogether, the taking-over was a full day's work. In the evening Dumoise told his *locum tenens*, who was an old friend of his bachelor days, what had happened at Bagi; and the man said that Ram Dass might as well have chosen Tuticorin while he was about it.

At that moment a telegraph-peon came in with a telegram from Simla, ordering Dumoise not to take over charge at Meridki, but to go at once to Nuddea on special duty. There was a nasty outbreak of cholera at Nuddea, and the Bengal Government being short-handed, as usual, had borrowed a Surgeon from the Punjab.

Dumoise threw the telegram across the table and said—"Well?"

The other Doctor said nothing. It was all that he could say.

Then he remembered that Dumoise had passed through Simla on his way from Bagi; and thus might, possibly have heard first news of the impending transfer.

He tried to put the question and the implied suspicion into words, but Dumoise stopped him with—"If I had desired *that*, I should never have come back from Chini. I was shooting there. I wish to live, for I have things to do . . . but I shall not be sorry."

The other man bowed his head, and helped, in the twilight to pack up Dumoise's just opened trunks. Ram Dass entered with the lamps.

"Where is the *Sahib* going?" he asked.

"To Nuddea," said Dumoise softly.

Ram Dass clawed Dumoise's knees and boots and begged him not to go. Ram Dass wept and howled till he was turned out of the room. Then he wrapped up all his belongings and came back to ask for a character. He was not going to Nuddea to see his *Sahib* die and, perhaps, to die himself.

So Dumoise gave the man his wages and went down to Nuddea alone, the other Doctor bidding him good-bye as one under sentence of death.

Eleven days later he had joined his *Mensahib*: and the Bengal Government had to borrow a fresh Doctor to cope with that epidemic at Nuddea. The first importation lay dead in Chooadanga Dâk-Bungalow.

MARGERY LAWRENCE
The Curse of the Stillborn

Margery Lawrence (1889–1969) specialised in Gothic and romantic melodramas (The Madonna of Seven Moons was successfully filmed in 1944). She was also a strong believer in the occult and spiritualism, and many of her ghost stories were based on accounts she heard at seances. "The Curse of the Stillborn", written soon after Howard Carter's discovery of Tutankhamen's tomb in Egypt, appeared in her Nights of the Round Table (1926), a collection of masterly horror tales related by various members of a club.

"**D**ammit—why can't you let 'em bury their dead in their own way?"

The words were blurted out. Mrs. Peter Bond raised her sandy eyebrows and stared at the speaker with outraged virtue written large upon her square determined face, burnt brick-red with the Egyptian sun. Little Michael Frith wilted, but stuck to his point.

"I'm sorry—didn't mean to swear, Mrs. Bond—but *don't* you see what I mean, really?" His brown wrinkled brow was lined with distress.

Mrs. Bond pursed her lips disapprovingly. Upright and heavily built, in uncompromisingly stiff white piqué, her thick waist well-belted, her weatherbeaten face surmounted by a pith helmet, she looked impregnably solid and British, reflected Frith exasperatedly—three years among these people and no nearer comprehending them. He tried again.

"You see—Mefren's a child of the desert . . . and her old mother's a pure-bred nomad . . . wild as a hawk. Why can't you let 'em bury their dead in peace?"

"I am surprised at your attitude, Mr. Frith! I'm sorry, but I can't undertake to advise my husband any differently. These people are ignorant, childish, superstitious. . . . I and my husband stand here to try and teach them better. And you

342

actually suggest that I allow Mefren to bury her baby as she likes—presumably in the Desert, with I don't know what awful sort of heathen rites—when my husband is here, a minister of the Lord, ready and anxious to give the poor little thing decent Christian burial! I must say I don't think this side of it can have struck you, Mr. Frith!"

Mrs. Bond's voice was genuinely shocked. Restlessly little Michael Frith stirred and kicked a booted foot against the whitewashed wall. He frowned—how *could* he explain? The native point of view . . . and this good-hearted, narrow, stubborn woman!

Vaguely his mind fled to Mefren, small, slender brown creature, and her mother, Takkari, silent and haggard, with black burning eyes beneath her voluminous haik. Wanderers both, they had appeared at the door of his tent one dawn with a request for food . . . he was encamped on the lip of the Valley of Blue Stones, a deep cleft between two ridges a few miles away from the tiny town of Ikh Nessan, where Peter Bond's little white-washed church brooded over the tangle of mud huts like a white hen mothering a scattered handful of brown and alien chicks. Always soft-hearted, Frith had fed them both; and seeing the girl's condition and obvious exhaustion, had sent them into Ikh Nessan with a note to Mrs. Bond—of whose kind heart, despite her irritating ways, none of the tiny colony had the least doubt. Food and shelter were at once forthcoming, and none too soon, for it came to pass, only a few days after the wanderers' arrival at Ikh Nessan, that the girl's time came upon her, but too soon . . . and a child was born, but dead—stillborn.

Full of well-meaning sympathy and a genuine desire to help, Mrs. Bond had hurried to inform Takkari, grimly silent, crouched in the shadows of the mud hut that sheltered the weeping girl, that despite the fact that the child, poor little soul, had died too early for baptism, her husband was ready at once to conduct the burial service. She was met by blank silence and a vigorous shake of the head. Dashed, and considerably annoyed, the Englishwoman demanded her reasons. Glowering silence again, but repeated attacks elicited the brusque information, in halting English, that "Kistian bury no good. Come night, her bury self—come night, her go aways." Naturally Mrs. Bond was outraged, and withdrew to consult her husband. I fear, had it not been for Nature, whose heavy hand on the young mother forbade anything in the way of flight, Takkari and her daughter would have been away, lost in the heart of the Desert they came from, before that night. But the evening brought little Peter Bond, full of anxious sympathy for this frail member of the flock he genuinely loved, though shocked beyond measure at his wife's report of Takkari's refusal, and the sullen, stubborn silence with which she faced him. It was while awaiting the result of this, Mrs. Bond felt, most momentous interview, standing at the rickety gate of the little walled garden, the evening sun warm on the tamarisks that sprawled, green and lusty, across the whitewashed wall, that Michael Frith, dusty and hot, trudged by and paused with a cheery word. Full of her story, she had poured it forth, and her surprise and indignation were great to meet his gaze at the end—a look in which politeness warred with frank disapproval. His sympathies were entirely with Mefren and her dour, free-striding old nomad mother; why should they who were, at best, mere birds of passage, be obliged to conform to the hidebound ideas of this stupid Englishwoman? Left to himself "Peterkin," as the little chaplain was affectionately known, would have been a sympathetic, understanding father to these wayward children of his—it was the insistent domination of this well-meaning, sincerely religious, but supremely narrow-minded wife of his that drove him into insisting on the "Church's rights." The phrase was on Mrs. Bond's lips as Frith aroused himself from his reverie; she was still talking, her square, hard-featured face stern with strong disapproval as she eyed him.

"Towards a member of his flock—I told my husband he must not admit argument on the subject. As a Father, he must be Firm. . . ."

"But surely, it's not as if Mefren was a Christian," objected Frith drily; "if it was a member of your husband's congregation . . ."

"Oh, but she *is!*" Mrs. Bond was eagerly assertive. "They are both Christians . . . I took care to inquire about that when they came first, and Takkari assured me that both she and Mefren had been baptised!"

Michael Frith smiled drily. He could see Takkari's sombre eyes at that first interview, summing up the unconscious Mrs. Bond, and assenting gruffly to any suggestion put forward—anything for a shelter and good food for her ewe-lamb in her trouble. But what was there to say? He shrugged, none too politely.

"Well . . . I don't agree, I'm afraid, Mrs. Bond. You see, I know these people pretty well. And frankly, I warn you again—I should let them have their own way."

As he spoke there was a quick step from the house, and the Rev. Peter appeared on the threshold. Wiping his moist forehead with a large red handkerchief, he smiled uncertainly on Michael Frith, and turned with a mild air of triumph to his wife. She asked eagerly:

"Well—have you succeeded?"

"With the blessing of the Lord," said Peterkin solemnly. "Poor child—poor child! I feel for her ignorance, and for her mother, though I fear Takkari is still stubborn. But I wrought mightily with Mefren for the soul of her child, and at last I prevailed. . . ."

A shadow seemed to fall upon the group. Old Takkari stood behind them, her lean, muscular feet muffled in the dusty earth. From the dark hooding of her brown haik, pulled close about her head, her uncanny eyes shone out, moving from one face to the other in silence. Mrs. Bond started and drew a sharp breath—the woman was standing at her elbow before she had seen her, and the grim wrinkled face was pregnant with meaning. There was a moment's tense silence, then, turning to Frith, Takkari said something in a low tone, ending with a sardonic laugh . . . and was gone, flitting through the open gate and down the dusty road towards the little town. The group moved, and Mrs. Bond found her tongue.

"Well, really!" she began, then curiosity fought indignation and conquered. "Whatever did she say to you, Mr. Frith?"

Frith, feeling his patience, like his politeness, nearing its end, moved away in the track of the tireless brown feet that had left delicate tracks, like a greyhound's, in the white dust.

"Nothing in particular," he said over his shoulder, "only a warning. An old Arabic proverb to the effect that your blood must be upon your own head."

As he strode away he saw Mrs. Bond beckon to Said Ullah, idling with a few cronies under the nodding palms, to come and dig the grave.

Like a lean dark wolf returning to its lair at evening. Takkari crept back to her daughter's side that night. Burials are not things, in the tropical heat of Egypt, to be postponed, and already a newly-turned mound beneath a clump of aloes marked the cradle—first and last—of the poor little scrap of humanity that never saw the sun. Alone the chaplain and his wife had committed the tiny body to the warm earth, watched Said Ullah, lean and nonchalant, fill in the grave as they prayed. . . . Mefren was still in a semi-delirious state, and the sound of her distant moaning was disturbing. Mrs. Bond walked down after supper with offers of help, but was confronted by a silent, scowling Takkari in the doorway, whose determined headshake and glowering expression frankly daunted her. She retired, huffed, but somehow not feeling sufficiently sure of herself to adopt the attitude of dignity she felt the situation needed . . . defeated by the grim silence, the dark hut with its sinister single light spreading a dull red carpet behind the still dark figure of Takkari in her hooded draperies. The stealthy rustle of the bushes that brushed her skirts, the crooning of the faint wind that crept about the garden, combined with the velvet darkness of the night to defeat Mrs. Bond completely, and she beat a retreat to the shelter of the little "parson-house" as graceless Said Ullah called it, in a state of nerves very unusual with her. In fact, she took herself severely to task for her weakmindedness in not reproving Takkari for her lack of manners, but a curious feeling of reluctance to face that silent hut again kept her from a second attempt, and with a frown at herself and a mental note to rectify this leniency by increased severity on the morrow, Mrs. Bond settled herself down to write.

She was a most efficient clerk, in truth, and all the financial affairs, indeed the entire organisation of the secular side of her husband's life, was in her large and capable hands; every evening she set aside an hour at least for checking every item of the day, entering up accounts, engagements made for herself or her husband, requests for help, the thousand and one minor arrangements that make up a parson's life, who, like a doctor, can scarcely dare to call an hour his own. Laboriously on the opposite side of the table little Peter Bond, his high forehead grotesquely wrinkled under the pushed-up glasses, sat writing out his next Sunday's sermon; he was a painstaking preacher, and spent days upon one sermon—conscientious, entirely ineffective orations. It was a pleasant little room, despite the cheap and horrid "Eastern" bazaar stuff with which it was crammed. An oil lamp with a preposterous red shade, not unlike a rakishly poised hat, stood at the chaplain's elbow between him and his wife—the contrast between his slowly scratching pen and frequent pauses and her swiftly decisive scribbling was curiously symbolical of both characters. The room was silent, and outside the lazy, fat-bodied, night moths lunged and bumped against the pane. As a rule the intrusion of the insect tribe after lamp-time was the one thing that maddened Mrs. Bond, but to-night, oddly enough, the room was entirely empty, the churring of the myriad flies that usually found their way in to circle wildly round the lampshade was absent. It may have been the unwonted silence—one misses even a nuisance quite amazingly at first—but once or twice Mrs. Bond stopped her rapid writing, and raising her head, listened intently. The third time she frowned, and spoke.

"Peter—doesn't it strike you how quiet it is? Is there a storm gathering? I feel there must be."

The Rev. Peter raised his large mild blue eyes and regarded her solemnly. In the dead stillness of the room her voice had sounded curiously loud and harsh.

"A storm—I really couldn't say, my dear. There may be one of those desert storms brewing . . ." He stared over at the window, screwing up his eyes. "You may be correct, my dear. Indeed, I think there is something electrical in the air to-night. For instance, the lamp is burning very badly—very low indeed. Yes."

"Electricity—rubbish!" Mrs. Bond's voice was snappy; now she remembered that the unusually poor light had struck her, subconsciously, and for some obscure reason this worried her faintly. After the manner of many women, the inexplicable always had the effect of sharpening her temper; she hated any deviation from the ordinary as a cat hates getting wet. "Electric conditions can't affect an oil lamp, Peter. Don't be silly—oh!"

The exclamation was, as it were, wrung out of her, for suddenly the lamp, already perceptibly lower, sank to a mere pool of faint light on the table; even as they both exclaimed, though, it flared up again, and irritably Mrs. Bond pulled off the shade to examine it.

"Light the other lamp, Peter. There must be something in the oil, or the wick's a bad one, or something . . ." Mrs. Bond was an expert at managing a lamp, as she was at most household tasks, and the room sank into silence again as the Rev. Peter resumed his labours beneath a fresh lamp, and his better half wrestled with the internal secrets of the red-shaded one at a little table.

After ten minutes or so spent in patient analysis of the erring lamp, however, she pushed it on one side with an annoyed "Tcha! . . . There's nothing wrong with it, as far as I can see—it must have been the oil. Well, I can't waste any more time over it."

The Rev. Peter, deep in his sermon, grunted absently, and silence fell again upon the room. Outside the night brooded over the little group of buildings, huts, chapel, the few low-roofed bungalows that, greatly daring, clustered together at the very threshold of the dour, stark Desert. The wind rose among the whispering tamarisks, and the brushing of their green-tufted branches made a dry siffling sound against the low window-sill of the lighted room; the wide sky, a sheet of black-purple velvet, patterned sequin-like with stars, yawned above the Desert, vast, illimitable, a dome of immensity which was at once comforting and menacing. Comforting, at least, it had till now always been to Mrs. Bond, a sincerely pious woman in her stern way. Many a night in her first six months in Egypt she had gazed up at that wide dark peace, and telling herself that that same sky had shone above the Birth at Bethlehem—a star like those immense, unwinking stars had led the Wise Men over hill and dale to their goal at last—the same age-old silence shrouded Joseph and Mary on their flight from Herod's blood-drenched swords. She had gazed up at the stars and felt contentment, peace, a solace in the thought that she, too, lay beneath the Shelter that had made the stars . . . but for the first time, something faint, tiny, unexplained, seemed to have jarred the usual peaceful spell of the night.

Mrs. Bond felt, bit by bit, her attention wander from her work; irritated, she shrugged the feeling off at first, but it returned, slyly persistent, jogging her shoulder, whispering in her ear—the utter absence of the usual buzz and murmur of the circling insects worried her, at first subconsciously, then consciously. She found herself concentrating on this problem, to the exclusion of anything else; her writing became spasmodic, erratic, and at last ceased altogether. Pushing back her chair with an irritated sigh, she rose from the table.

"Peter—I really think I must have a touch of the sun! Can't concentrate in the least to-night somehow—it must be the heat."

The Rev. Peter looked up solicitously.

"Try an aspirin, my dear," he suggested mildly. His wife shook her head impatiently.

"No—that's no good. I feel oppressed, nervy, somehow—perfectly idiotic, I know, but there it is. It's this—awful stillness, not even a fly in the room. Don't you feel it, too, Peter—or has this life got on my nerves till I'm imagining things?"

"Well—now you come to mention it, I've been feeling a little odd for some time. And now you point it out, it *is* curious, the absence of the—er—usual insect life around the lamp. It must be a storm brewing—or, as you say, we are both a little overdone."

The words were valiant, but there was trepidation in the little man's mild blue eyes—trepidation vague, formless but present. Mrs. Bond struck her hand on the wall in a spasm of irritation, born of the quick inrush of fear that had now seized her, like a stealthy enemy rendered suddenly bolder, at the discovery that the same creeping dread had been working its spell upon her husband's peace of mind as well.

"Peter!" She spoke firmly. "This is either sheer foolishness on our part, of which we ought to be thoroughly ashamed—or else someone is trying to play tricks upon us . . . for doing our duty as Christians to our flock, despite their ignorant prejudices."

It was odd how, instinctively, it seemed, her mind reverted to the matter of Takkari and Mefren—the former's menacing, sullen eyes.

The little clergyman looked frankly frightened.

"You mean you think Takkari! . . ." His sentence was unfinished.

"Oh, I don't mean anything *really*—what's-its-name—uncanny!" Mrs. Bond snapped. "I should hope I'm too good a Christian for that—but I wouldn't be surprised if Takkari and some of her precious friends tried to work some of their jugglers' tricks on us, to frighten us . . . pure nastiness, of course! Nothing else is possible. . . ."

Her tone was a shade too decided; against her will as she talked, partly at random, she could not but realise that the weight and monotony of the silence seemed rising like a sea about them—and . . . was it so, or was it a trick of her agitated imagination? The fresh lamp now seemed to cast a ring of smaller size, of decreased brilliance; shadows, surely, surely, loomed more deeply in the corners behind the bamboo chairs! There was a curious break in Peter Bond's voice as he answered—a little quake of fear.

"Are you sure, Matilda? I thought so . . . but tonight, I kept thinking of the witch who tempted Samuel—the Witch of Endor . . . of Our Lord's strange words of wickedness in high places. . . . And I wondered . . ."

With a decisive movement, Mrs. Bond strode over to the window and slammed it to, pulling the curtains together to shut out the night—and reeled away with a strangled shriek of terror! Rushing to her assistance, her frightened husband peered out into the darkness, but all was still, save the faint rustling among the tamarisks as the little wind crept through them.

There was no light in the distant hut that housed Takkari and her sullen anger. At the table Mrs. Bond shivered and gasped, gradually regaining her self-control.

"What, my dear . . . what happened?" The dead silence, the crowding shadows, seemed to listen for her reply. With a huge effort the woman sat up and gulped down her terrors, replying with a steadiness that spoke well for her pluck.

"Peter—something—something awful seized my wrist as I pulled those curtains! Now don't you tell me I'm mad—I was never saner! I grant I was feeling a little nervy—things seem odd to-night somehow—but just at that moment I was perfectly balanced. What—what you said about the . . . well, you know what you said—suddenly made me realise we were allowing ourselves to become—well, foolishly, unchristianly frightened at nothing at all—it *must* be nothing at all!—and I went to pull the curtains, to shut out the night and the wind and make ourselves cosy and sensible. I was going to suggest we played Patience . . . and all of a sudden a hand took me by the wrist, strongly, and tried to prevent the curtains being pulled! I told you Takkari was up to something . . . though how . . ."

Her eyes, frightened, angry, bewildered, met her husband's—and read there a greater terror than hers.

"Wait!" His voice was a mere whisper. "I can tell you now . . . but I did not dare to tell you, Matilda, lest it be a mere hallucination on my part. I know"—the humiliated tears were very near—"alas, I am a weak man, Matilda! . . . I thought perhaps the stillness of the night and—and my own foolish fears, for I must freely admit that I have been far from easy the whole of the evening—were working upon me till I saw, or thought I saw . . ."

"What?" Mrs. Bond's face was strained; beads of perspiration speckled the little chaplain's lean jaw as he answered, in a voice that shook uncontrollably in the now definitely gathering gloom.

"Something—something swathed and indefinite, but Something that wasn't a shadow—I swear—stand beside you and bend over to watch you write!"

Mrs. Bond shrank back with an involuntary cry of terror. The bald statement was horrible, and the woman shuddered as she listened.

The Rev. Peter's knees were shaking, his voice gathering speed, a hoarse whisper as he rushed on, his frightened eyes seeking from side to side . . . and still the lamp sank lower and the silence gathered, fold on fold, about the trembling pair.

"I stared and stared . . . and looked away and forced myself to write. I prayed and sweated and dared not look again, dared not speak for fear it was hallucination and you might think my brain going with the heat and work—till you spoke. Then I dared look—and it was gone! Thank God . . . I spoke, I believe, rationally enough . . . and then you rose to draw the curtain, and Matilda, as I am a priest of God and hope for salvation, suddenly It rose at your side again, and Its face pressed close to yours . . . and the horror of it was Its face was no human face at all, but a gilded mask!"

The hurrying voice rose high and culminated in a half shriek—for on the last word the lamp, now a dying flicker on the table, went out, and with one stride darkness entered the room.

Utterly unnerved, Peter Bond collapsed whimpering on the table, but although shaking in every limb, his wife rose dauntlessly, and biting her lips to still their quivering, faced the darkness that had entered into possession of the room. Silence, dead, heavy, menacing, ruled supreme, broken only by the sobs of the terrified chaplain, the heavy breathing of his wife. Like a cornered creature at bay, she backed sturdily against the table, panting hard, turning her head from side to side, her hands clammy with moisture, clenching and unclenching. There was, indeed, something pathetically valiant about this woman driven thus to fight so hopelessly one-sided a battle, for, in the dire, stealthy strength of the Force that she now dimly realised was arrayed against her, all her shivering, gallant bravery went for no more than a reed's feeble stand against the gale. Upright in the swirling shadows that clustered about her, she stood, clutching hard at her sanity, her self-control, while her little narrow soul shrank within her and grew shrivelled and puny with terror, like a last year's walnut in its shell. She knew now—she knew the Thing behind all this—in some way some streak of lightning clarity had told her—somewhere behind this awful manifestation moved Something that belonged to Egypt, that had demanded Its right of Its land, and had through her been denied it . . . yet, though sweating with terror, shaking in every limb, Mrs. Bond, true to her stern type, held grimly to her convictions, and her shaking lips muttered prayer on prayer, while her soul crawled in terror, but not regret. . . . But the end was at hand, and mercifully. With a final huge effort to throw off the spell, with some vague idea that even to try and light the lamp, anything humdrum, ordinary, might break the influence that held her so bound, Mrs. Bond stretched out a fumbling hand along the table for the matches . . . and touched another hand! Dry and cold and leathery, with sharply pointed nails, it lay alongside hers, and as she touched it, withdrew sharply, but it was too late. Even as Mrs. Bond, her last quivering defences down, opened her mouth to shriek. It grew beside her swiftly in the darkness, indefinite, macabre, and of a terror unspeakable; a Thing swathed and clumsy and vague, shapeless, yet dreadfully, appallingly powerful, a blind Horror seeking vengeance. . . .

In a frenzy of fear the woman flung herself backwards across the table where crouched poor little Peter Bond, gibbering, hysterical, in his panic . . . but the Shape rose above her against the moving dark, the crowding shadows, and she saw It clearly, bulbous eyes in a horrible still face of gleaming gold, sinister and pitiless as It bent over her and . . . as her senses mercifully left her, laid Its ghastly cheek to hers!

Frith knocked out his pipe. As the echoes of his voice died away into the tense silence a little ripple stirred the intent group of listeners, held in the grip of sheer horror. Dennison, the soldier, was the first to find his voice.

"Good Lord—what a beastly yarn! But go on, Frith—that can't be the end? You've got us all on tenterhooks!"

Frith smiled drily.

"That's just where the clever storyteller should leave his audience! I'd rather leave things where they are—on the pitch of the climax, but, of course, there is an aftermath. Fact is, I happened to be strolling near the chapel that night and heard Mrs. Bond scream—rushed in and found her lying in a faint, with poor little Bond perfectly hysterical at her side, burbling wildly, and quite unstrung—for the moment a complete lunatic. Oh, yes, the lamp flared up again just as I got inside the room—no, I saw nothing; but I tell you what I *did* notice—the awful smell in the room!"

"What sort of a smell?" asked Hellier sharply.

"Bitumen," said Frith simply. "Bitumen and natron and dried spices and the intolerably ancient smell of the grave—the smell of the burial rites of old Egypt—stern, undying. The place stank like a newly-opened tomb!"

"But what, actually, was it? The Thing with the gold face, I mean?" My curiosity was greater than my shyness as I put the question.

Frith raised his eyebrows as he poured himself out another liqueur brandy.

"Ah——well, that no one can say for certain. Egypt keeps her secrets now as well as ever she did, but I think I can give a good guess, at least. If I knew the history of Takkari, a strange old daughter of the Nile sands, with the blood, perhaps, of Pharaohs dead ten thousand years ago in her veins . . . you see, it's true that the system of embalmment died out long ago, yet, like other strange ceremonies, religions, beliefs, no one can swear, even now, that it is utterly dead and forgotten . . . and who knows what age-old memories, what instincts, what fears, may have haunted those two women from the mysterious Desert as they suffered and agonised over the Stillborn!"

We fell silent, spellbound, as he went on, his voice thrilling, his eyes distant on the blue-gold ancient country he so greatly loved. "You see—in the old days, unless the body of a stillborn child, immediately on its birth, was embalmed with the full ritual, the swathings, the amulets, the golden mask, all the strange symbolic trappings and ceremonies of a full grown being—the Ka, the soul that it had meant to incarnate, would rise in rage and anger at the neglect of the honours due to it, and turn against the house where it was born and all therein, become the evil demon, the Maleficence haunting the unfortunate being who had dared to do it this wrong. . . ."

"Then you think this was the direct result of Mrs. Bond's insisting on Christian burial—that Takkari and her daughter, urged by who knows what instinctive dread and knowledge, meant to secretly steal away with their dead to the Desert, to bury it there with spices and cerements and ceremony to propitiate the Ka thwarted by death of its incarnation?"

Hellier's eyes were alight with interest—Frith nodded.

"Yes. That's what I do think, frankly. In utter ignorance, blundering and narrow, Mrs. Bond forced her weak husband to pit his puny might against a great and ancient Force, and thwarted of its right, the outraged Ka rose against these presumptuous ones . . . and won . . . very dreadfully won. In the morning the grave was found empty; the women had dug up the body of their dead in the night and fled with it to the silence of the Desert, which opened and swallowed them. There, perhaps, they laid it to rest in their own way—in Egypt's way. At least the Horror, having worked its will upon those poor well-meaning fools, passed away. I spent many nights after that in the house, and it was perfectly normal. Poor Mrs. Bond—she has paid bitterly enough for her folly, poor soul. She has never been able to tell me what she felt at that supreme moment of horror, when the Thing rose over her and pressed its cheek to hers, except that it was utterly impalpable, no actual touch at all, but a ghastly coldness that scored and burnt like the searing finger of an icicle . . . then she lost consciousness, thank Heaven. But that terrible moment has left a mark on her that she will never lose. When I picked her up I saw her face was twisted, all wried sideways . . . where the Gilded Mask had touched."

ALAN W. LEAR
Dance! Dance! The Shaking of the Sheets

Alan W. Lear (b.1953) has had several of his unusual horror and ghost stories published in Ghosts & Scholars *and various other magazines and anthologies.*

It had no eyes, but it could see him in the dark; no nose, but if he tried to hide it would snuffle him out. There was no brain behind the green-white dome of its brow, but it knew his thoughts and it would find him wherever he ran.

The night was hot and silent. The air wasn't stirring at all in the narrow bedroom with its sloping roof and meagre pallet stuffed with straw. On the top of the bed, Wat crouched. His feet were bare, his patched nightshirt drenched in sweat that had already gone cold. His eyes were wide and staring—a rabbit's watching a stoat. Framed in the doorway, the grim white shape reached out its hand of bones, and beckoned.

Wat was twelve. His father was a Master of the Guild of Canterbury Drapers, an important man. Wat was his only child. Once there had been two little sisters—giggling white bundles for Wat to tickle or smack according to his mood—but the measles had carried them both off when he was nine. The year after, his big roguish brother Geoff had shouldered his bow and strode off to France with the Black Prince. The light in his eyes darkened at Crecy.

Wat's mother turned dreamy after that; at times she'd talk to the loaves while she baked them, and she was seldom aware that her husband and her last remaining child were in the house. Wat's father threw himself angrily into his business dealings. He talked a lot, when he talked at all, about his chances of being elected alderman. Wat himself was sent to school at Master Thomas's by the West Gate. He was much beaten and learned little.

355

And then this strange, hushed summer came upon Canterbury. Folk said it was the hottest ever. The sky stretched from horizon to horizon a hard, unreal blue, without a cloud or a breath of wind, and the birds lost the will to sing. Butter and cheese turned rancid and stank, even in the cool cellars under the flags. The River Stour declined to a thick, dun trickle, choked with pallid weeds and rank frogspawn.

The town began to sniff the air and look over its shoulder. Speaking softly got to be the fashion. The monks in the Cathedral took to praying all day long, but their chants hardly carried over the heavy, smothering air. Children stopped running and laughing in the streets and meadows.

One day a packman from Dover came over the hill and set about crying his wares in the Butter Market: lace for the ladies, bowstrings, little bottles of scent from France. The townsfolk clustered round him, glad of a diversion from their forebodings . . . in the middle of his huckstering, the packman staggered and passed a hand across his face. He begged a sip of water and sat down dazed upon the ground.

Two days later he was buried, and by then a dozen townsfolk lay sick as well.

The symptoms never varied: headaches, dizziness and exhaustion, then the discovery of a hard swelling in armpit or groin. The sufferer would cough and sweat profusely, and his breath and body exuded the stench of corruption. Soon black blotches broke out all over his skin, like blackberries, and after that Death held off three days at the most.

Panic clutched the city as simple folk and gentry and even the Church fell victim in their scores. Some locked themselves in their houses and barricaded the doors. Others crowded into the Cathedral and the chapels to wail up masses and pleas for Divine mercy; at the close of every service, a corpse or two would be lifted up from the consecrated floor.

Priests found excuses for not visiting the sick. The Archbishop let it be known that for the duration of the emergency, Final Confession might without sacrilege be heard by a layman. Doctors sitting at bedsides fell from their stools and died before their clients.

On Wednesday of the third week, Wat's mother went into the yard to draw water. Her husband was sitting over his account books, muttering the figures to himself as though saying a rosary. Wat crouched in a corner, hunting for a flea beneath his doublet. It was a long search, but he was a patient lad, and in the end he caught and killed it. Only then did he notice that his mother hadn't come back.

The sunlight was hard and white on the plaster of the yard walls, and there was a hum of flies. Wat's mother stood clinging to the handle of the well, peering into the distance with a puzzled expression. It seemed she was trying to make sense of some shape she thought she ought to recognise. She jumped when her husband touched her arm.

"It's only that I'm hard worked!" she snapped tightly. "That's all. Man, you know how much I've to do in the house, and never a hand raised to help me—why would I *not* be tired? By St James, a woman might well feel dizzy times in a summer like this one!"

The man laid an arm around her shoulder. "Come you into the house, Alice," he said wearily. "Wat'll fetch the water."

They wrapped her corpse two nights later, in fine linen as was proper for a Master Draper's wife, and laid it outside the door. They went to their beds, lying helplessly awake until curfew, and they listened as the big clumsy cart creaked to a halt, and the carters grunted with the weight of their burden.

That same night, Wat found a swelling under his left arm.

He spoke of it to no one, nor of the dizzy spells or the spear-thrusts of pain which began, ever more frequently as the day progressed, to take him unawares and leave him gasping. While his fears were mewed up in his head, unspoken, they might still just be a boy's imaginings; other fears had, when he was smaller. The day passed. He kept his silence.

But that night he woke to find his father's face looming over him, vague and pale like the moon. There was a hectic, determined glitter in the drawn man's eyes.

"I'm out the back door and over the wall tonight," he said briskly. "Heading north. Maybe Scotland. There must be *some* place in the world free from this pestilence yet."

He paused a moment, chewing his lip in something like exasperation. "Ach, Wat!" he complained. "Don't curse your father. I'd have taken you if the Lord had allowed. You're young to be joining the dance, pitiful young . . . your sisters were younger, God knows. What's to be said about it all? A man can't sit in corners and weep every tear he's cause to shed. I've wept myself dry; I must be doing.

"Listen now boy, don't tell me you've not been taught prayers enough in your time. Now's when you should be looking to that. There's a butt of water by the bed, and the last of the apples . . ." He coughed, dry and painfully.

"There's this: you're too young to have any but little sins on you. And your ma's gone on before to plead your cause. So God by you, son. Ach, you were a scamp times, but I ——"

The voice faltered; the looming pale shape flitted away into the darkness. Wat wanted to call out, but his mouth was dry as old straw.

The night passed, and the next day. Wat prayed, sipped the cool water, ate half an apple. It seemed to him that only the weight of the thin sheet stopped his body flying up to the ceiling like a bird set free.

Sometimes there were other folk in the room with him, jostling throngs like on market day, all talking and laughing at once. And now he was back in Master Thomas's schoolroom. It was wintertime, and he was shaking all over with cold, and Master Thomas was coming for him with the birch rod in his hand.

But later he was lying in the long grass at the side of the Stour, in gentle, caressing sunlight, and his fine big brother Geoff was asleep at his side, and the world was kind and warming and calm.

He was stark awake. Night had fallen—moonless, airless and owlless—and by the unsteady starlight he saw a figure standing in the bedroom doorway, gaunt and greenish-white. Wat could make out the shadows on the landing through the spars of its naked ribs. It was contemplating him out of sockets that had no eyes in them, and grinning with a toothy mouth that had no lips.

Wat struggled to his knees. The hairs on the back of his neck were lifting one by one in stiff spears. He needed no schoolmaster to instruct him: he knew well What had come.

The figure took a step forward.

A dry rattle of foot-bones pattering against the wooden floor.

It neared Wat's bed. Stretched out a long, ivory hand.

With a sudden wordless shriek Wat was out of bed. His legs were running before his footsoles hit the floor. His bladder emptied as his nightshirt was held, but then he was free and out of the bedroom and scampering along the landing to the stairs.

One thought in his mind—a mad thought, but all he had. Listen: this thing that had come, it didn't have all night, did it? There were thousands pricked down before dawn in the Weald of Kent alone. Kings and Cardinals lay waiting for the bony night-comer.

How long could Death afford to spend chasing an unimportant small boy?

At the head of the stairs Wat looked round. The figure was outside the bedroom door. It still had its hand stretched out, beckoning.

The rail of the landing balustrade was polished oak. It gleamed dully in the darkness, on a level with the skeleton's shoulder. Wat frowned. He'd seen his father and his father's friends often enough on that landing, and the balustrade reached no higher than their waists.

Death was a dwarf, then.

Or a child.

How old, would you reckon? Eleven? Maybe twelve, if he was on the stunted side?

Wat shot a glance at the coaxing right hand of the figure, then desperately down at this own. At his index finger, bent at a slight angle as a result of a fall on the ice when he was six.

He flung himself down the stairs, a moan like plainsong issuing unbidden from his slack mouth. He slammed headfirst into the street door and stunned himself, and then his fingers turned clumsy and rebellious and made all sorts of trouble with the heavy bar of the latch. He could hear the rattling behind him as he struggled: an unhurried, remorseless descent.

Then he was out of the house, and the street was full of music and dancers.

The still, stifling air was vibrant with crumhorns and shawms, harps and rebecks and pipes, all wailing together in a sorrowful, stately pavane.

They passed the draper's house two by two. Wat recognised Mistress Philippa from the bakery. She was a notorious shrew; twice she'd been ducked on the stool while the townsfolk looked on and laughed. She wasn't scolding now. Her face was grave and composed, her progress dignified, as she danced down the street hand in hand with her own naked bones.

Behind her came a fat priest, looking as big as a hill beside his partner. And next, Master Thomas the schoolmaster, with hardly an ounce more flesh on his niggardly body than on the gaunt thing at his side.

The stars looking down that airless night saw how all Europe thronged with dancers. In London and Paris, mocking the men of power. In Ghent and Hamburg, Avignon, even Rome: thousand upon thousand, moving stately to the rebecks of eternity.

A dry, sharp-edged hand slid into the hand of Wat the draper's son. The music filled his mind. He forgot everything. Everything but the dance.

There was a vacant space at Master Thomas's back. And it was Wat who occupied it: Wat, in perfect step with his own small, bespoken Death, part now forever of the grim processional that filled the streets of Canterbury.

J. SHERIDAN LE FANU
The Fortunes of Sir Robert Ardagh

Joseph Sheridan Le Fanu (1814–73), *great-nephew of the dramatist Richard Brinsley Sheridan, was unequalled in the Victorian era as a writer of mystery and supernatural tales. In the words of M.R.James, he 'stands absolutely in the first rank as a writer of ghost stories'. Among his many classics in the genre are "The Familiar", "Green Tea", and "A Strange Event in the Life of Schalken the Painter".*

"The Fortunes of Sir Robert Ardagh", from The Watcher and Other Weird Tales (1894), *originally appeared in* the Dublin University Magazine, *March 1838.*

> The earth hath bubbles as the water hath——
> And these are of them.

In the south of Ireland, and on the borders of the county of Limerick, there lies a district of two or three miles in length, which is rendered interesting by the fact that it is one of the very few spots throughout this country in which some vestiges of aboriginal forests still remain. It has little or none of the lordly character of the American forest, for the axe has felled its oldest and its grandest trees; but in the close wood which survives live all the wild and pleasing peculiarities of nature: its complete irregularity, its vistas, in whose perspective the quiet cattle are browsing; its refreshing glades, where the grey rocks arise from amid the nodding fern; the silvery shafts of the old birch-trees; the knotted trunks of the hoary oak, the grotesque but graceful branches which never shed their honours under the tyrant pruning-hook; the soft green sward; the chequered light and shade; the wild luxuriant weeds; the lichen and the moss—all are beautiful alike in the green freshness of spring or in the sadness and sere of autumn. Their beauty is of that kind which makes the heart full with joy—appealing to the affections with a power which belongs to nature only. This wood runs up, from below the base, to the ridge of a long line of irregular hills, having perhaps, in primitive times, formed but the skirting of some mighty forest which occupied the level below.

But now, alas! whither have we drifted? whither has the tide of civilization borne us? It has passed over a land unprepared for it—it has left nakedness behind it; we have lost our forests, but our marauders remain; we have destroyed all that is picturesque, while we have retained everything that is revolting in barbarism. Through the midst of this woodland there runs a deep gully or glen, where the stillness of the scene is broken in upon by the brawling of a mountain-stream, which, however, in the winter season, swells into a rapid and formidable torrent.

There is one point at which the glen becomes extremely deep and narrow; the sides descend to the depth of some hundred feet, and are so steep as to be nearly perpendicular. The wild trees which have taken root in the crannies and chasms of the rock are so intersected and entangled, that one can with difficulty catch a glimpse of the stream which wheels, flashes, and foams below, as if exulting in the surrounding silence and solitude.

This spot was not unwisely chosen, as a point of no ordinary strength, for the erection of a massive square tower or keep, one side of which rises as if in continuation of the precipitous cliff on which it is based. Originally, the only mode of ingress was by a narrow portal in the very wall which overtopped the precipice, opening upon a ledge of rock which afforded a precarious pathway, cautiously intersected, however, by a deep trench cut out with great labour in the living rock; so that, in its pristine state, and before the introduction of artillery into the art of war, this tower might have been pronounced, and that not presumptuously, impregnable.

The progress of improvement and the increasing security of the times had, however, tempted its successive proprietors, if not to adorn, at least to enlarge their premises, and about the middle of the last century, when the castle was last inhabited, the original square tower formed but a small part of the edifice.

The castle, and a wide tract of the surrounding country, had from time immemorial belonged to a family which, for distinctness, we shall call by the name of Ardagh; and owing to the associations which, in Ireland, almost always attach to scenes which have long witnessed alike the exercise of stern feudal authority, and of that savage hospitality which distinguished the good old times, this building has become the subject and the scene of many wild and extraordinary traditions. One of them I have been enabled, by a personal acquaintance with an eye-witness of the events, to trace to its origin; and yet it is hard to say whether the events which I am about to record appear more strange and improbable as seen through the distorting medium of tradition, or in the appalling dimness of uncertainty which surrounds the reality.

Tradition says that, sometime in the last century, Sir Robert Ardagh, a young man, and the last heir of that family, went abroad and served in foreign armies; and that, having acquired considerable honour and emolument, he settled at Castle Ardagh, the building we have just now attempted to describe. He was what the country people call a *dark* man; that is, he was considered morose, reserved, and ill-tempered; and, as it was supposed from the utter solitude of his life, was upon no terms of cordiality with the other members of his family.

The only occasion upon which he broke through the solitary monotony of his life was during the continuance of the racing season, and immediately subsequent to it; at which time he was to be seen among the busiest upon the course, betting deeply and unhesitatingly, and invariably with success. Sir Robert was, however, too well known as a man of honour, and of too high a family, to be suspected of any unfair dealing. He was, moreover, a soldier, and a man of intrepid as well as of a haughty character; and no one cared to hazard a surmise, the consequences of which would be felt most probably by its originator only.

Gossip, however, was not silent; it was remarked that Sir Robert never appeared at the race-ground, which was the only place of public resort which he frequented, except in company with a certain strange-looking person, who was never seen elsewhere, or under other circumstances. It was remarked, too, that this man, whose relation to Sir Robert was never distinctly ascertained, was the only person to whom he seemed to speak unnecessarily; it was observed that while with the country gentry he exchanged no further communication than what was unavoidable in arranging his sporting transactions, with this person he would converse earnestly and frequently. Tradition asserts that, to enhance the curiosity which this unaccountable and exclusive preference excited, the stranger possessed some striking and unpleasant peculiarities of person and of garb—though it is not stated, however, what these were—but they, in conjunction with Sir Robert's secluded habits and extraordinary run of luck—a success which was supposed to result from the suggestions and immediate advice of the unknown—were sufficient to warrant report in pronouncing that there was something *queer* in the wind, and in surmising that Sir Robert was playing a fearful and a hazardous game, and that, in short, his strange companion was little better than the Devil himself.

Years rolled quietly away, and nothing very novel occurred in the arrangements of Castle Ardagh, excepting that Sir Robert parted with his odd companion, but as nobody could tell whence he came, so nobody could say whither he had gone. Sir Robert's habits, however, underwent no consequent change; he continued regularly to frequent the race meetings, without mixing at all in the convivialities of the gentry, and immediately afterwards to relapse into the secluded monotony of his ordinary life.

It was said that he had accumulated vast sums of money—and, as his bets were always successful and always large, such must have been the case. He did not suffer the acquisition of wealth, however, to influence his hospitality or his house-keeping—he neither purchased land, nor extended his establishment; and his mode of enjoying his money must have been altogether that of the miser—consisting merely in the pleasure of touching and telling his gold, and in the consciousness of wealth.

Sir Robert's temper, so far from improving, became more than ever gloomy and morose. He sometimes carried the indulgence of his evil dispositions to such a height that it bordered upon insanity. During these paroxysms he would neither eat, drink, nor sleep. On such occasions he insisted on perfect privacy, even from the intrusion of his most trusted servants; his voice was frequently heard, sometimes in earnest supplication, sometimes raised, as if in loud and angry altercation with some unknown visitant. Sometimes he would for hours together walk to and fro throughout the long oak-wainscoted apartment which he generally occupied, with wild gesticulations and agitated pace, in the manner of one who has been roused to a state of unnatural excitement by some sudden and appalling intimation.

These paroxysms of apparent lunacy were so frightful, that during their continuance even his oldest and most faithful domestics dared not approach him; consequently his hours of agony were never intruded upon, and the mysterious causes of his sufferings appeared likely to remain hidden for ever.

On one occasion a fit of this kind continued for an unusual time; the ordinary term of their duration—about two days—had been long past, and the old servant who generally waited upon Sir Robert after these visitations, having in vain listened for the well-known tinkle of his master's hand-bell, began to feel extremely anxious; he feared that his master might have died from sheer exhaustion, or perhaps put an end to his own existence during his miserable depression. These fears at length became so strong, that having in vain urged some of his brother servants to accompany him, he determined to go up alone, and himself see whether any accident had befallen Sir Robert.

He traversed the several passages which conducted from the new to the more ancient parts of the mansion, and having arrived in the old hall of the castle, the utter silence of the hour—for it was very late in the night—the idea of the nature of the enterprise in which he was engaging himself, a sensation of remoteness from anything like human companionship, but, more than all, the vivid but undefined anticipation of something horrible, came upon him with such oppressive weight that he hesitated as to whether he should proceed. Real uneasiness, however, respecting the fate of his master, for whom he felt that kind of attachment which the force of habitual intercourse not unfrequently engenders respecting objects not in themselves amiable, and also a latent unwillingness to expose his weakness to the ridicule of his fellow-servants, combined to overcome his reluctance; and he had just placed his foot upon the first step of the staircase which conducted to his master's chamber, when his attention was arrested by a low but distinct knocking at the hall-door. Not, perhaps, very sorry at finding thus an excuse even for deferring his intended expedition, he placed the candle upon a stone block which lay in the hall and approached the door, uncertain whether his ears had not deceived him. This doubt was justified by the circumstance that the hall entrance had been for nearly fifty years disused as a mode of ingress to the castle. The situation of this gate also, which we have endeavoured to describe, opening upon a narrow ledge of rock which overhangs a perilous cliff, rendered it at all times, but particularly at night, a dangerous entrance. This shelving platform of rock, which formed the only avenue to the door, was divided, as I have already stated, by a broad chasm, the planks across which had long disappeared, by decay or otherwise; so that it seemed at least highly improbable that any man could have found his way across the passage in safety to the door, more particularly on a night like this, of singular darkness. The old man, therefore, listened attentively, to ascertain whether the first application should be followed by another. He had not long to wait. The same low but singularly distinct knocking was repeated; so low that it seemed as if the applicant had employed no harder or heavier instrument than his hand, and yet, despite the immense thickness of the door, with such strength that the sound was distinctly audible.

The knock was repeated a third time, without any increase of loudness; and the old man, obeying an impulse for which to his dying hour he could never account, proceeded to remove, one by one, the three great oaken bars which secured the door. Time and damp had effectually corroded the iron chambers of the lock, so that it afforded little resistance. With some effort, as he believed, assisted from without, the old servant succeeded in opening the door; and a low, square-built figure, apparently that of a man wrapped in a large black cloak, entered the hall. The servant could not see much of this visitor with any distinctness; his dress appeared foreign, the skirt of his ample cloak was thrown over one shoulder; he wore a large felt hat, with a very heavy leaf, from under which escaped what appeared to be a mass of long sooty-black hair; his feet were cased in heavy riding-boots. Such were the few particulars which the servant had time and light to observe. The stranger desired him to let his master know instantly that a friend had come, by appointment, to settle some business with him. The servant hesitated, but a slight motion on the part of his visitor, as if to possess himself of the candle, determined him; so, taking it in his hand, he ascended the castle stairs, leaving the guest in the hall.

On reaching the apartment which opened upon the oak-chamber he was surprised to observe the door of that room partly open, and the room itself lit up. He paused, but there was no sound; he looked in, and saw Sir Robert, his head and the upper part of his body reclining on a table, upon which two candles burned; his arms were stretched forward on either side, and perfectly motionless; it appeared that, having been sitting at the table, he had thus sunk forward, either dead or in a swoon. There was no sound of breathing; all was silent, except the sharp ticking of a watch, which lay beside the lamp. The servant coughed twice or thrice, but with no effect; his fears now almost amounted to certainty, and he was approaching the table on which his master partly lay, to satisfy himself of his death, when Sir Robert slowly raised his head, and, throwing himself back in his chair, fixed his eyes in a ghastly and uncertain gaze upon his attendant. At length he said, slowly and painfully, as if he dreaded the answer,——

"In God's name, what are you?"

"Sir," said the servant, "a strange gentleman wants to see you below."

At this intimation Sir Robert, starting to his feet and tossing his arms wildly upwards, uttered a shriek of such appalling and despairing terror that it was almost too fearful for human endurance; and long after the sound had ceased it seemed to the terrified imagination of the old servant to roll through the deserted passages in bursts of unnatural laughter. After a few moments Sir Robert said,——

"Can't you send him away? Why does he come so soon? O Merciful Powers! let him leave me for an hour; a little time. I can't see him now; try to get him away. You see I can't go down now; I have not strength. O God! O God! let him come back in an hour; it is not long to wait. He cannot lose anything by it; nothing, nothing, nothing. Tell him that! Say anything to him."

The servant went down. In his own words, he did not feel the stairs under him till he got to the hall. The figure stood exactly as he had left it. He delivered his master's message as coherently as he could. The stranger replied in a careless tone:

"If Sir Robert will not come down to me; I must go up to him."

The man returned, and to his surprise he found his master much more composed in manner. He listened to the message, and though the cold perspiration rose in drops upon his forehead faster than he could wipe it away, his manner had lost the dreadful agitation which had marked it before. He rose feebly, and casting a last look of agony behind him, passed from the room to the lobby, where he signed to his attendant not to follow him. The man moved as far as the head of the staircase, from whence he had a tolerably distinct view of the hall, which was imperfectly lighted by the candle he had left there.

He saw his master reel, rather than walk, down the stairs, clinging all the way to the banisters. He walked on, as if about to sink every moment from weakness. The figure advanced as if to meet him, and in passing struck down the light. The servant could see no more; but there was a sound of struggling, renewed at intervals with silent but fearful energy. It was evident, however, that the parties were approaching the door, for he heard the solid oak sound twice or thrice, as the feet of the combatants, in shuffling hither and thither over the floor, struck upon it. After a slight pause, he heard the door thrown open with such violence that the leaf seemed to strike the side-wall of the hall, for it was so dark without that this could only be surmised by the sound. The struggle was renewed with an agony and intenseness of energy that betrayed itself in deep-drawn gasps. One desperate effort, which terminated in the breaking of some part of the door, producing a sound as if the door-post was wrenched from its position, was followed by another wrestle, evidently upon the narrow ledge which ran outside the door, overtopping the precipice. This proved to be the final struggle; it was followed by a crashing sound as if some heavy body had fallen over, and was rushing down the precipice through the light boughs that crossed near the top. All then became still as the grave, except when the moan of the night-wind sighed up the wooded glen.

The old servant had not nerve to return through the hall, and to him the darkness seemed all but endless; but morning at length came, and with it the disclosure of the events of the night. Near the door, upon the ground, lay Sir Robert's sword-belt, which had given way in the scuffle. A huge splinter from the massive door-post had been wrenched off by an almost superhuman effort—one which nothing but the gripe of a despairing man could have severed—and on the rocks outside were left the marks of the slipping and sliding of feet.

At the foot of the precipice, not immediately under the castle, but dragged some way up the glen, were found the remains of Sir Robert, with hardly a vestige of a limb of feature left distinguishable. The right hand, however, was uninjured, and in its fingers were clutched, with the fixedness of death, a long lock of coarse sooty hair—the only direct circumstantial evidence of the presence of a second person.

L.A. LEWIS
Haunted Air

Squadron-Leader Leslie Allin Lewis (1899–1961)
was a veteran of both world wars, flying Sopwith
Camels over France in 1918 and Hurricanes over
England in 1940. He was also one of the very
best writers in the macabre and supernatural genre
between the wars. A collection of his unusual and
excellent stories was published in 1934 under the
title Tales of the Grotesque, *from which the*
following story is taken.

"**W**ell, Blake, we can't do your stuff yet. What about another 'tonic' while we wait?"

Pitchmann, air-record breaker and taxi-pilot of international repute, pushed his empty tankard over the counter and strolled to the window, where he stood looking glumly through rain-blurred glass across the sodden aerodrome.

Violent gusts howled in paroxysms about the angles of the Club House, and the wind-stocking above the hangars stood out horizontally threshing like a mad thing.

"Okay," said the press photographer laconically. "My squeak, I think. Two more cans, please, steward."

Pitchmann moved back to the bar.

"Bloody nuisance hanging about this god-forsaken dive for a shot of that blasted crash," he complained. "Why the hell didn't Carr pick some tin-pot shopkeeper for a passenger instead of an M.P.? Your rag would have given 'em a three-line par and let me out of this 'picnic'."

Blake shrugged and took a pull at his beer. He knew Pitchmann as well as anyone could claim to know him, having been his passenger on many rush jobs across Europe, and he knew when the big pilot expected an answer—which was not often.

Pitchmann half emptied his tankard at a gulp and swept the four other occupants of the room with a contemptuous glance, favouring the Club Instructor with a nod as nearly cordial as the latter might care to believe.

"Better join us, Jacobs," he remarked acidly, with an imperious gesture to the barman. "You seem to think it's too breezy for your nestful of stiffs to take the air—so why waste good beer-time?"

Jacobs hitched his chair forward and murmured, "Thanks. A pink gin," endeavouring to sound as casual as he could. He hated Pitchmann's intolerant grey eyes and air of conscious superiority, but knew that his directors expected tact from him—perhaps even more than flying ability. He was not obliged to agree with all Pitchmann's opinions, but it would not do to offend the fellow.

"Shot if I'm going up solo in this gale, anyway," said young Remington, who, as an owner-pilot with private means, held aces in no particular esteem.

Pitchmann pointedly ignored him, rousing the boy to quick anger.

"Call it what you like," he went on heatedly, "it was taking a chance yesterday in this sort of damned weather that killed Carr, threw his passenger clean out of the machine, and brought you vultures up here to get photos of his wreckage." His second remark drew the badger. Pitchmann accorded him a supercilious stare.

"That poor mutt!" he replied witheringly. "He was for the high jump all his flying career. Windy as hell. Fair weather pilot from A to Z. That's the only way he lasted so long. I've seen him turn down local joy-rides on account of a bit of ground mist when Imperials were getting through from Le Bourget in pea-soup stuff. You blokes who play at flying for a hobby can go up and sun yourselves on fine days like damned butterflies, but the professional has to fly in anything—*anything*," he repeated loudly, "otherwise aviation ceases to be a business." He turned his back on Remington and glanced at Jacobs for confirmation. The latter nodded judicially.

"That's true up to a point," he agreed, "but we all have our different jobs. Mine's training pupils at present, and I'm not expected to risk their necks and the machines in these conditions. He glanced out of the window and added, "Incidentally, the sun *is* breaking through a bit, though the wind's increasing!"

"Come on, Blake," said Pitchmann, slamming down his

tankard. "It's visibility we want. Damn the wind! Let's get your plates exposed, and we can be back in Town by evening!"

He stooped to pick up his gloves and turned impatiently to the press photographer, who was finishing his drink. "Get a jerk on, man. I want to be away."

The door slammed after them.

"He's rather wonderful, don't you think?" observed the only lady member present, looking up from the pages of *Air Events*, and emerging from daydreams of a celebrated woman pilot's latest exploit. "I mean," she continued diffidently as nobody vouchsafed a reply, "a man has to be big—really big in himself—to talk quite so—so ruthlessly, to—to lay down the law like Captain Pitchmann."

"Damn good pilot, anyway," said Jacobs, breaking an awkward silence. The barman was heard to grunt non-committally. Young Remington lit a cigarette and blew a smoke ring ceilingwards.

"You may think he's wonderful, Mrs. Conyer," he volunteered, "*I* think he's a disease. After all, '*De Mortuis nil nisi bonum.*' I didn't know Carr personally, but that was no way to talk of a bloke who's just passed out. . . ."

The roar of an engine drowned the rest of his sentence and Pitchmann's plane flashed past one of the windows, staggering drunkenly in the tremendous gusts that assailed it. As the noise dwindled the fourth occupant of the lounge broke in for the first time.

"Thanks, laddie. I *did* know Carr personally. We were, in fact, very old friends. But it's no good arguing with a man like Pitchmann. A good pilot, yes—very good—but absolutely without sentiment, so one can't expect any consideration from him." He paused and stared after the disappearing aircraft.

"Pitchmann," he resumed thoughtfully, "accused Carr of being 'windy', and implied that it was lack of *technique* in bad conditions that killed him. I *know* how he was killed, and, if you like, I will tell you at the risk of straining your credulity. . . . Do any of you believe in ghosts?" he wound up with apparent irrelevance.

"Suggesting a supernatural explanation of the crash?" Jacobs countered, "because, if so, Beckett, you're wrong. Carr was caught in a bad 'bump'—a 'sinker' and thrown out of control. I know the air pockets there, and they're fierce enough even in a normal breeze.

"Haven't you seen that Air Ministry notice advising pilots not to cross the Ridgeway in a high wind under two thousand feet? They have quite a few spots black-listed that way now—one near 'Gib', for instance—another up the Forth. Queer things bumps."

"First of all," said Beckett, settling back with the persistence of a born raconteur and totally disregarding Jacobs' remark, "I must say in fairness to Carr that he was not a fair-weather pilot. When I was his observer in France, in 1916, we were up more than a few times in this sort of thing"—he waved a hand towards the window—"and in a type of machine that would fall to bits on you for two pins. Carr never funked his job then, but as he explained to me when I met him years later in civil flying, he didn't see the force of taking unreasonable risks in peace time for the sake of publicity. He preferred knocking up a modest three or four hundred a year in his own way to undertaking spectacular flights for big money which he might not live to enjoy. Hence his reputation as quoted by Pitchmann and his failure to get work with the more progressive concerns. He and Pitchmann often used to meet at Croydon, and the great man never missed a chance of using Carr as a foil for his own prowess. He would watch Carr take a passenger to a thousand feet for a couple of loops, and then go up and cut the air all shapes, at a quarter the height. Carr could have done it as well, and *had* done later in the War, when he was on 'scouts', but people didn't know that, and his caution lost him a lot of trade, not that he seemed to care. I guess his wife knocked the personal ambition out of him—but that's by the way.

"Now, I'm going to tell you something about Carr that I'll bet he never admitted to a soul except myself; but first I must digress to explain what helped me to believe his story. You look interested, Mrs. Conyer, and if you two blokes don't want to listen, you can play darts. We shan't fly yet, anyway.

"Well, I had a brother who was a pilot in the East, after the War, operating from a hill station—frontier stuff you know—and he was killed in much the same way as poor old Carr. One night, after the rains, a pretty extensive landslide occurred in his district, a few thousand tons of soil falling on a native settlement, and my brother was sent up to survey the damage. When he failed to return after a due interval, two machines went to look for him. Of these, only one returned, the pilot reporting that his companion had first sighted my brother's plane, badly smashed up among some rocks, and had dived down ostensibly for a closer investigation. Seeing that there was no possible landing-place at hand, the reporting pilot had kept his altitude and circled round waiting for the other to climb up again when his survey had finished. To his astonishment the machine below suddenly began to perform the most crazy aerobatics, throwing several loops and rolls at a very low altitude and finally flying for some distance on its back, from which position it presently nose-dived with great violence into the rocks, and burst into flames. After debating for some time the advisability of investigating both crashes more closely, he concluded that they might have been caused by abnormal wind eddies, and that it would be wiser to send a land party. This the C.O. decided to go, and after considerable difficulty the crashes were brought in, and the usual court enquiry held. Both pilots had evidently been killed instantly, but from my brother's machine, which had not fired, it was deduced that there had been no structural failure, and the verdict was 'Crashed out of control, owing to exceptional atmospheric phenomena associated with the contours'. Within a few weeks three more pilots were killed at or near the same spot, after which it was mapped out as a prohibited area, and the matter officially closed. It was only when I met an officer from the same squadron on leave during the following year that I heard about the native version as related by a fanatical old tribesman, who had made a pilgrimage to the aerodrome especially to implore the C.O. to stop flying over the landslide, and had talked a lot of guff about *Things which are Enemies of Man and Beast Creation* and the earth having "*Given Outlet to That which the Prophet had Sealed Down*'. " 'Guff', we called it then," said Beckett quietly. "I'm not so sure now."

It was a tribute to the man's personality and to the conviction in his voice that no word of interruption was spoken as he slowly filled his pipe.

"As you, no doubt, are aware," he went on presently, "there was a landslide on this saddle called the Ridgeway some ten days ago, but what you may not know is that Carr was the first pilot to fly over it after the occurrence. He read the account of it in a newspaper, and, having his joy-ride plane parked in a field relatively near to the scene, he elected to go up and view the subsidence from the air. It is of interest that his machine was an Avro three-seater, convertible for dual control by removing the middle seat, flooring and all, so as to expose the second rudder-bar and joystick socket. Carr had been giving instruction to some local resident the previous evening, and he took the Avro over the Ridgeway, flying from the front seat, without bothering to remove the dual controls. Well, he found the place without difficulty—a big brown gash in the green hillside, as he described it, but nothing much as a spectacle. Beyond blocking a short length of road in the valley, the fallen earth seemed to have done little harm, and he was about to turn back to his field when he caught sight of something moving in the air, between his plane and the ground, which looked extremely odd, and, as he told me, gave him an unaccountable feeling of goose-flesh, even before he saw what sort of thing it was.

"Apart from its extraordinary shade of pulsating, unnatural green, the object was quite evidently not a bird, and he might momentarily have dubbed it a grotesque toy balloon, like the flying pigs they shoot down at the Hendon Pageant, but for the fact that it was so obviously—and somehow *horribly*—alive. Carr described it as resembling a monstrous monkey, clambering with incredible speed up an invisible rope. It appeared to be *wriggling* vertically upwards, and as he watched it in fascinated wonder his lower wing passed over and hid it from view. He banked steeply to the left, failed to see it, and as quickly whipped into a right-hand turn—but the green thing had vanished. He made a complete circle, still without success, and finally, the air being calm, took his hands from the controls and half raised himself in his seat, the better to see over the engine cowling. As he did so, the machine's nose rose abruptly, and he had to grab the joystick in a hurry to avoid a stall.

"Carr told me that he was too intent on watching for the reappearance of the weird object to realize at once how queerly the aeroplane had behaved. It was so rigged that, without ballast in the rear cockpit, the nose should have dropped. As soon as this dawned on him, he again released the stick, which, to his utter amazement, began to move rapidly from side to side, the Avro wallowing in unison with it, as the ailerons took effect. So pronounced and regular was the movement that it could only be caused by someone moving the dual stick in the other cockpit—but he had taken off *solo*!

"Carr said that several things happened to his brain during the next few seconds, but in what order he could not remember. Ill-defined fear numbed his faculties, so that he could do nothing but stare stupidly at the shifting controls, but at the same time a corner of his mind, working with crystal clarity, was aware that the green thing had somehow got into the machine with him, that it was definitely alive, though equally definitely not human, and, worst of all, that it was *intelligently* operating stick and rudder! He felt his hair crawling under his tightly strapped helmet, and dared not look behind him.

"Presently he heard the engine open out, and dully realized that the throttle lever was correspondingly moving forward while, at the same time, the joystick came back slowly towards him, and the Avro began to climb. He seems at this period to have fallen into a sort of coma, in which state his physical senses were blanked out, and only some deep recess of his brain continued to record intuitive impressions. He knew that, whatever creature was riding behind him, it was age-old, and somehow *belonged* to the air. He also knew that it had been long imprisoned, and was exultant at release, while he understood, too, that there was no novelty in this nightmare situation.

"Either it had happened before, or, his subconscious self had contained a fore-knowledge of it, hitherto mercifully concealed. . . . His next physical impression was seeing the needle of the altimeter standing at five thousand feet, and simultaneously feeling the plane nose down into a power dive, engine at full throttle, and stick pressing the dash-board. For a few seconds it held this course, then swept up and over in a perfect loop. As the stick came back into the pit of his stomach he clutched it feebly—childishly—and attempted to force it away, but it was locked as though in a vice. While the sunlit vista of Earth whirled over his head, the stick did go forward again, but Carr knew *he* had not moved it. An instant later, the Avro executed a flick roll, stalled, and fell into a spin.

"Carr said that as fast as the thought flashed into his brain, that this was the end, it was followed by a positive assurance that his strange captor would let him live—at least for a time. He felt, in some fashion, that this same horror had befallen other pilots whose deaths had never been satisfactorily accounted for, and that, becoming demented with fear, they had roused contemptuous anger in these green things, and so courted instant death. He, by showing no physical reaction, had whetted the appetite of this monstrosity for a cat-and-mouse game. He said he felt like a raw pupil receiving a lesson in aerobatics from a masterly instructor.

"Carr said the culmination of nausea was reached when the thing touched him for the first time (I gather it forced other assignations on him, though of these he did not speak). Powerless to make physical resistance, he felt a pad-like extremity brush his cheek clammily, and expected a stranglehold, but realized with extreme repugnance, that the touch was in the nature of a petting. The viscous paw passed smoothly over his face, covering his eyes, where it lingered caressingly, obscuring his vision. Then, to his profound disgust, he felt a gelatinous mouth pressed against his own! The shudder that passed through him at the contact somehow restored his muscular control, and, uttering a word of loathing, he again clutched the controls, dimly aware that the green thing was crawling sinuously over the side to the port lower plane, where it wreathed itself about the gap strut and stood regarding him. Carr described it as resembling a human or ape in build, having a flexible trunk, four limbs ending in flat, webbed pads, and a grotesquely tiny wet head, with round, mouse-like ears. Its mouth was a yellow slit, and its eyes lidless, and opaque. It was nude and hairless, but of indeterminate sex, as it possessed the faculty of altering its shape in any direction, like those glutinous, transparent things one finds in ponds. When he at last brought himself to look directly at it, the creature grinned at him, and hopped along the wing, where it gripped an aileron and shook it up and down, causing the machine to rock. Next, it stretched two of its rubber-like limbs the full length of the fuselage, to seize rudder and elevators, which it proceeded to operate by direct pressure against Carr's efforts with the controls. From this unique position it once more put the plane through all its imaginable paces. During the whole performance its face radiated a sort of perverse glee, reminding Carr, through the mist of horror that wrapped him, of a mischievous child playing with a toy. Finally it slithered back along the wing, and gazed intently and for a long time into Carr's face. Carr said that its telepathic influence was strongest at that time. He knew as well as if it had spoken aloud what it was thinking. There was a damnable, triumphant possessiveness in its eyes which told him that he now belonged to the green thing for all Eternity. It recalled, he said, the way some women look at a man when they have him in their power. I suppose he spoke from experience. Finally the creature released its hold, and drifted down into the abyss of air, still staring up at him with an expression of gloating ownership.

"Carr said he must have found his way back to his field, and landed there quite automatically. His next conscious recollection was of leaning against a tree sobbing like a baby, while an alarmed mechanic offered him a cup of water."

Beckett came to an abrupt halt, but, seeing that the others were waiting for him to continue, added briefly: "That was all Carr told me. I never saw him alive again."

"My God!" whispered Mrs. Conyer. "What a ghastly idea!" She stopped, looked helplessly at the others, and went on, "Forgive me, Mr. Beckett, but did—did your friend drink?"

Beckett shook his head.

"No more than I do—or any of us here. Personally, I believe Carr's account. You must please yourselves what construction you put on it."

He relapsed into thoughtful silence.

"Why in God's name did he go back to the Ridgeway yesterday?" asked young Remington, obviously deeply impressed. Beckett shrugged.

"Nobody could guess the active range of such a—manifestation," he replied. "Carr's flight started in the opposite direction, and maybe the green thing found him and took him there. The passenger fell out, you know, nearly two miles away, and *that* hasn't been explained. *I* think he *jumped*!

Jacobs had been staring moodily at the carpet during the whole of Beckett's recital. Now he straightened up, and gave him a very curious glance.

"Sorry," he began, "but this is right outside my experience or understanding. I see you're sincere, Beckett, and I won't be such a swine as to laugh, especially after Pitchmann's behaviour. But no! Sorry, I can't——!"

The harsh "burr" of the telephone interrupted him. The barman picked up the receiver, and they heard him answering the call.

"Yes. Speaking. What's that? Whereabouts? Good Lord! Both of them? What's that? A mile?"

He turned from the instrument to Jacobs. "Ridge Village Police, Sir," he announced, "Captain Pitchmann's crashed."

Mrs. Conyer and Remington sprang spontaneously to their feet.

"Where?" Jacobs demanded.

"On the Ridgeway, sir, close to Mr. Carr's Avro."

"Are they—all right?" Jacobs managed with an effort. The barman shook his head gravely. "No. Both killed. The Sergeant thinks the gale got them out of control. Mr. Blake was flung out a mile away."

Beckett crossed his legs, and knocked out his pipe on his boot-heel.

"As you remarked just now, Jacobs," he put in quietly. "Queer things—Bumps."

R.H. MALDEN
The Coxswain of the Lifeboat

Richard Henry Malden (1879–1951) *was Chaplain to King George V, Canon of Ripon Cathedral, and Dean of Wells. He wrote several theological books and a fine collection of supernatural tales,* Nine Ghosts (1943), *published as a tribute to M.R.James, his friend for over thirty years.*

There is upon the coast of Suffolk a church which is locally believed to be haunted. The rector is a friend of mine, and as I do not want to expose him to the attentions of the Phantasmagorical Association or any similar body, I will not describe the place particularly. I will only say that the church is a large building in the Perpendicular style of architecture constructed of grey flint. The neighbourhood is popular with artists. If these details are sufficient to enable anyone to identify it he is entitled to any reward for his ingenuity which he can secure.

The ghost has never, so far as I know, had a name put to him and nobody knows anything of his antecedents. He has never actually been seen. But he may be heard very often. He dances and chuckles, not upon the whole malevolently, but is always careful to keep a pillar or some equally solid object between himself and his audience. He is very agile and no one has ever succeeded in cornering him. It is on record that once when the sexton was locking up he chased the ghost (who was being noisier than usual) from pillar to pillar all down the nave. Then up the tower staircase as far as the belfry. Still there was nothing to be seen. By this time the sexton was hot and out of breath, so he said rather crossly—"Hey, what are you a sniggerin' at?" A clear voice from amongst the bells replied—"It's not funny enough for two." The rest, as Hamlet once remarked, is silence.

If the story of what befell me a good many years ago within sight of that church is not interesting enough for two, I must apologize. But I think it sufficiently out of the way to be worth putting on paper.

The church is not particularly rich in monuments. But near the font there is a mural tablet worth attention. It commemorates the crew of the lifeboat from 1850–69. During those years they underwent no change and rescued no less than four hundred and fifty-two shipwrecked mariners. That particular stretch of coast is still, I believe, regarded by seafarers as unusually dangerous. There is no anchorage within thirty miles and about four miles out there is a maze of sandbanks. A sailing ship which gets among them in bad weather is lost and even a steamship finds escape difficult. There has been talk of putting a light there more than once, but nothing has come of it. When there was more coastwise traffic (for the most part in small brigs) than there is now, the calls upon the lifeboat must have been incessant during the winter months.

After nineteen years of beneficent activity (I am quoting from the tablet) disaster came. On 31 October, 1869, the boat was lost with all hands. No bodies were recovered except that of Henry Rigg, the coxswain. I had often wondered what lay behind this. Had they gone on too long and allowed familiarity with danger to blind them to the fact that they had become too old for the work—as is said to be not unknown in the case of Swiss guides? Had the coxswain's nerve and judgment, upon which everything depended, failed at some critical moment? Although it was unlikely that anyone would ever be able to answer these queries, I put them to myself more than once. For some reason, which I could not explain, I felt sure that there was a story behind this catastrophe which removed it from the category of ordinary hazards of the sea, and I wished very much that I knew what it was. Irrational as I knew the desire to be, it refused to be dislodged. In fact it became stronger every time I saw the tablet.

One day when I was wandering, rather aimlessly I must admit, in the churchyard, I suddenly found myself opposite Henry Rigg's grave. I don't know why I had never thought of looking for it before. Perhaps I had assumed that in view of his station in life there would be no headstone, or at least a small and inconspicuous one which would be difficult to find. In fact, it was a large and massive slab of the pink granite which was popular for such purposes about the middle of the last century. Personally I have always thought it one of the ugliest monumental materials known to man, especially when it is polished so highly that it looks wet. There is a striking example in the memorial to the O.W.s who fell in the Crimean War outside Dean's Yard. In 1869 it must have been about the most expensive material which could be procured. The inscription was brief:

IN MEMORY OF
HENRY RIGG.

For nineteen years coxswain of the Life Boat
Who was drowned with all his crew off the
Anchor Shoal 31 October, 1869, aged 62 years.

When thou passest through the waters I will be with thee.

There was no suggestion that the stone had been erected by public subscription. Had it been, the names of the crew would have been recorded. I concluded that the Rigg family had paid for it, and wondered idly how they had managed to find the money. This led to some reflections on funeral expenditure in general. These might have been prolonged considerably and even have reached a pitch of moral elevation sufficient to justify their committal to paper, had I not had a sudden feeling that there was somebody close behind me. Of course that churchyard was a public place and anyone might have come up without my hearing his step upon the grass. It might be somebody who had some business with another grave; or an idler like myself who wondered what I was staring at so intently and had allowed his curiosity to get the better of his manners. Nothing could be more reasonable than either of these hypotheses. But all the same I was conscious of a feeling of discomfort; almost of alarm. I turned round quickly, but there was no one there. I think this disturbed me quite as much as any presence, however malevolent, could have done. I had felt so certain that there was someone. However, as there was nothing to be seen I walked away. When I had gone a little distance I glanced back. It was between three and four on a November afternoon, so the light was failing. But for a moment I could have sworn that there was an animal of some kind, either a black cat or a black dog, I couldn't see which, sitting on the grave. It was gone in a moment whatever it was. "Some trick of shadow," I said aloud, more to reassure myself than because I believed it, and walked on;

perhaps a little more briskly. I did not look behind me again and was glad when I was out on the high-road and only a few hundred yards from my inn, *The Flood Tide*.

I had stayed there often before and was on good terms with the landlord. If business was slack I would sometimes ask him into my sitting-room after supper. He knew a good deal about the neighbourhood, and was seldom reluctant to impart his knowledge. In perpetuity he might have been a bore. But as an occasional visitor I found him very good company.

I told him that I had come upon Henry Rigg's grave in the churchyard that afternoon.

"Ah," he said, "that's fine stone. Must have cost a deal of money to put that up."

"Yes, so I thought. Did his family pay for it, or was there a public subscription?"

"No, Sir. It were not his family, for he hadn't none. Never married and kep' himself very much to himself, if you take my meaning. When he die a lawyer chap come over from Saxmundham and say he were executioner for the Will. And he have the stone put and choose the text. No, there were no talk of any subscription, for he were not liked. No, he were not. They couldn't hardly get bearers for the coffin, I believe, and there was some as said he didn't ought to be buried in the churchyard at all. But rector he didn't pay no heed to they. All he say were—Well, he'll be safer there than anywhere else I du suppose. And so it were done. But no, he were not liked, not even by his own crew, though he were a good seaman—to give the devil his doo—as the sayin' goes" (the last four words seemed to be added hurriedly as an obvious afterthought).

At this point a servant knocked at the door and said that the landlord was wanted in the bar. I have not mentioned that his name was Rust. He went off, not altogether unwillingly I thought, and about half an hour afterwards I went to bed. Sea air always makes me sleepy.

The next two or three days were unusually fine for the time of year and I spent them bicycling about the country. I was taking a belated holiday, having been kept in London all through the summer months by a book which I was writing: an occupation which necessitated frequent and lengthy visits to the library of the British Museum. The manuscript was now in the hands of the printer and I felt that a change of air and scene would equip me to deal with the proof. I took care not to go near the part of the churchyard where Henry Rigg's body reposed. This seemed to me to be a wise precaution, though I must confess that I felt rather ashamed of myself for adopting it. All the same I thought I should like to elicit some more information about him. So one evening I invited Mr. Rust to join me again. After a little miscellaneous conversation I came to the point. I think he was expecting me to do so.

"Well, Sir," he said, "I don't know as I can tell you much more. I were only a lad at the time." (You could, but don't mean to, was my unspoken comment.) "But by what I've 'eard he was a close-fisted old chap. And then his language. The fishermen aren't so particular as what you or me have to be with a position to keep up. But they du say that the way he went on at his boat's crew was like, well, like nothing—if you take my meaning. They wouldn't ha' stood it, but that he were good seaman: and you don't find them under gooseberry bushes neither; no nor yet on apple-trees. And he live all alone, with one big black cat what were fierce enough to scrat your eyes out. And nobody knowed what he did to pass the time away, except that he were never seen in church. And then when he die and it come out that he had a mort o' money in the bank at Saxmundham—well, that made more talk. How'd he come by it and why didn't he spent it? That's what people wanted to know. But the lawyer wouldn't tell 'em and the bank wouldn't tell 'em, so they was a wise as they begun."

"What happened to the money?" I asked.

"Why, he left it all to an old lady somewhere Acle way. But she hadn't hardly got it when the house where she lived all alone got on fire and she were burned dead to a cinder. So she didn't get no good by it neither. And as she were interstit, what they term, and 'adn't no relations, Queen Victoria took it. There was some as thought she did ought to be warned. But I never'eard that it done 'er no 'arm. You'd ha' thought she had pretty nigh enough already, wouldn't you, Sir? But there, she had a long family to put out, and a widow-woman too.

"There were an auction of Rigg's bits of things. But nobody wouldn't bid for 'em, not a penny piece. So the lawyer chap he have them taken away in a cart. And the man what drove the cart slip somehow, and the wheel went over his leg, and broke that in two places. Went lame all his life, he did.

"Then nobody wouldn't take the house till the agent he got some strangers. And they didn't stop no more than a week. So then Lord S.—what own all this part —he say—Pull that down. And it were done. There's been nothing of it these many years 'cept a few mounds just outside the village. The old people say it's no place now; specially after dark. But that's as may be, for what I know."

"Well," I said, "he must have been an odd character. Is there anyone left who could tell me any more about him?"

Mr. Rust looked at me for a moment without speaking. Then—"Odd, well, yes he were. And if I was you, Sir, I'd leave it be so. But there's old Dan Rix what were in the coastguard when that happen. He come up here now and again and if you was to stand him a pot of beer and a screw of tobacco he mought get talkin'. And then again he moughtn't."

Luckily, Mr. Rix honoured *The Flood Tide* with a visit about noon on the following day. I was in as I had happened to have a number of letters to write. An introduction was effected without difficulty and I followed Mr. Rust's advice with good results. I will summarize the story I got in my own words.

Yes. He had known Henry Rigg for several years. Probably as well as anybody. Nobody knew him well. He did not like him. Nobody did. But as coxswain of the lifeboat there was no one to touch him. He (Rix) remembered the day of the disaster very well. He was wakened about dawn by the distress signals of a ship. One of the worst gales he ever remembered. Wind north-east by east; the most dangerous quarter. The lifeboat was launched as quickly as possible, Rigg swearing and cursing more than usual. By the time the boat was away it was quite light, so he watched through his telescope. The ship was a small brig. Foreign certainly: perhaps Russian. She was on the Anchor Shoal and didn't look as if she could last an hour. He could see the men clinging to the rigging. There was a very nasty sea, but Rigg's steering was wonderful. The devil himself couldn't have bettered it. One funny thing he noticed. More than once he could have sworn that there was someone sitting beside the coxswain. Must have been the way the old boat-cloak he always wore was blown by the wind. All went well until the lifeboat was nearly up to the distressed ship. Then all of a sudden the helm was put right over. The boat broached and was gone in a moment. This was before the days of the modern self-righting boats. (I have omitted some maritime technicalities with which the story as told to me was embellished. It will be enough to say that the act amounted to murder and suicide. A shore-going equivalent would be for the driver of a car to turn it off the road at fifty miles an hour.)

The ship went to pieces a few minutes afterwards. There were no survivors, and nothing by which she could be identified ever came ashore.

"Curious," I said, "that Rigg himself, who seems to have been entirely responsible for the disaster, was the only one who—well, I can't say 'escaped' exactly, but lived (if you can put it that way) to receive Christian burial." Mr. Rix took a long draught of beer, and put down his empty mug. "Ar: there's some as the sea can't drown, and others as it won't keep!" With which oracular utterance he stumped off.

After lunch the wind had risen considerably, so I thought that a walk would be pleasanter than a bicycle ride. I would go northwards along the top of the low sandy cliffs and return with the wind behind me along the beach. The tide would not, I knew, be high till six o'clock, so there would be a strip of firm sand available. I walked for a little over an hour, and it was past three o'clock when I turned down to the beach and set my face for home. There was every prospect of a stormy night, and the white water on the Anchor Shoal was very visible under a grey and lowering sky. Naturally my mind ran on the story I had heard. Local opinion evidently held that there was more in it than met the eye. But what more it seemed unlikely I should find out. It was solitary down there. On my right hand the cliffs were high enough to cut off any view inland. On my left lay the sea. Some three miles in front there was a small projection, you could hardly dignify it by calling it a headland, screening the village for which I was bound. Naturally I had the beach to myself. No one was likely to be about in the gathering dusk and rising storm. On the whole I was glad of that. The company, or even the sight, of another human being might be welcome. But on the other hand there might be people about whom I should not care to meet. Once I thought of turning up to the top of the cliffs again. But that would be rather silly, and the particular stretch which I was passing then did not look very accessible. I certainly wasn't going to turn back to where I had come down. So I held on.

Presently I saw a figure some little distance in front of me. He was standing at the very edge of the water. I was surprised that I hadn't noticed him before, and allowed myself to wonder for a moment whether he had just come up from the sea. But of course that was nonsense. He must have been sheltering, resting perhaps, on the lee side of one of the groynes which crossed the beach at intervals. I could not make out whether he was going in my direction or coming to meet me. After a time I saw that he was walking up and down; like a man keeping an appointment. An odd and uncomfortable rendezvous, I thought, and no one else in sight—I hope he isn't waiting for me.

I did not like his looks, so decided to strike up along the shingle until I had passed him, though it meant heavy going and climbing the groynes, instead of turning them at the seaward end.

When I got a little nearer I saw that he was dressed like a seaman of the last (by which I mean the eighteenth) century. In fact he reminded me of the illustrations in a copy of *Treasure Island* which I had had when I was a schoolboy. He wore a three-cornered hat, a boat-cloak wrapped round him and sea-boots. But for the fact that he had two legs he might have been Long John Silver himself. His hat was pulled down over his forehead and the collar of his cloak turned up: naturally enough as the wind had risen to nearly a gale and was very cold. I could see nothing of his face, for which I was thankful. There was something indescribably sinister, worse than sinister, downright evil about him. However, he took no notice of me. I looked back once or twice when I had passed him to make sure that he was not coming after me. The last I saw of him he was still pacing up and down.

When I got round the little headland there were, as usual, a number of fishing-boats drawn up near the bottom of the slipway which led from the beach to the village. As I made my way through them I received the impression that there was somebody dodging about among them. But as the light had now failed considerably I could not see him distinctly. In fact I could not be sure whether there was anyone there or not. But I thought so; though whenever I looked steadily at the point where I had seen him last there was nothing. Anyhow, whoever he was and whatever he was up to, it was no business of mine and I did not feel called to interfere. Pusillanimous perhaps. But if, as

I more than half suspected, he had an appointment to keep in the direction from which I had come, interference on any pretext would not be likely to be very fruitful. I won't pretend that I was not more than ordinarily glad to find myself safely back at *The Flood Tide*.

After tea I settled down to read that grim, if entertaining, work of Anatole Le Braz—*La légende de la Mort en Basse Bretagne*—which was one of the few books I had brought with me. The inn-library consisted principally of Sunday School prizes acquired from time to time by various members of the house of Rust. From one standpoint the collection was very gratifying, but except for *Little Henry and his Bearer* (which I was delighted to meet again) it was not in the first rank as literature. For the moment at any rate I preferred the sombre stories of Anatole Le Braz. Now, the reader who gets as far as this may assert, when he has heard the rest of what I have to say, that I fell asleep. I cannot prove that I did not. I can only say that I repudiate the suggestion entirely. I *know* that I did not. Even if I did, my "dreams" would not be easy to account for.

Quite suddenly I seemed to be looking through the pages of my book at a scene beyond. Every detail was very sharp, though the whole picture was on a small scale. It was exactly like what one used to see in the *camera obscura* when I was a child. Some ingenious arrangement of lenses, and mirrors too I suppose, threw a picture of what was passing outside on to a table in a darkened room. I suppose such a thing hardly exists now. It could not hope to compete with the films; though as a matter of fact I came upon one only about ten years ago in a queer old house in Edinburgh, not far from the Castle. The first thing I saw was a sandy beach. The light was beginning to fail and there were unmistakable signs of gathering storm. Plainly a reproduction of what I had looked upon not much more than an hour before. And here was the sinister-looking seaman whom I had passed. As before, I did not see him come. He was suddenly in the picture, walking up and down. I was intensely interested, as I felt sure that the other party to the appointment would make his appearance before long. I was right. After not more than a minute or two I saw someone coming from the direction of the village. He kept as close as possible to the bottom of the cliffs, which suggested that he was anxious to avoid being seen. That part of the beach consisted of loose shingle, and if there is worse going than loose shingle to be found anywhere in the world I should like to know where and what it is. (I will not dispute the abstract possibility: I merely repeat—I should like to know where and what it is.) He came on slowly, and presently the old seaman saw him and stood still near the seaward end of a groyne. When the newcomer reached the landward end he turned and ran down it with surprising speed, bending double. He would have been quite invisible from the far side, and not easy to pick out from the other, or from the top of the cliff. The general effect suggested an animal rather than a human being and was extraordinarily repulsive. He seemed to be dressed like a fisherman, but as he too had a boat-cloak wrapped about him I could make out no details. I could not see his face. He struck me as unusually short, almost a dwarf, and I thought he was slightly hump-backed. When the two men met they spoke a few words. (Which of course I could not hear.) Then something which looked like a small bag changed hands. The second man stowed it somewhere about his person and started to return as he had come. Then everything became dark and I could see no more.

I felt sure that there was more to come, so waited, looking down at the pages of my book. I did not have to wait long. The next picture was the living-room of a cottage; rather larger and better furnished than the average, but not particularly noteworthy in any way. In the middle of the room was a small round table above which hung an oil lamp. There was a good fire of wood and coal on the hearth and I noticed the little blue flames which old ship-timbers always give off. (Whether this is due to the salt which they have absorbed, or to the tar, or to both, or neither, I cannot say.) Between the table and the fire a man was sitting in an easy chair smoking a long clay pipe. Beside him on the table was a long tumbler nearly half empty from which an inviting steam went up. I had no doubt that this was the second man I had seen on the beach. Now that I could see him plainly I saw that I had been right in thinking that he was almost a dwarf and, if he were not actually hump-backed, very round-shouldered. He was swarthy, almost as if he had gipsy blood in him, and his face was not a pleasant one. It was mean and sly. At the same time, however, the jaw suggested courage and determination. I could not decide whether I should dislike him more as a friend or as an enemy.

His surroundings were comfortable enough, but it was soon obvious that he was ill at ease. From time to time he fidgeted in his chair and seemed to mutter something to himself. Once or twice he looked sharply over his shoulder. The only other occupant of the room was a large black cat which was pacing to and fro in regular quarter-deck fashion on the side of the room farthest from the fire. But for the light catching its eyes from time to time I should not have known that it was there. They glowed very green and very bright. It seemed fairly clear that the man was expecting a visitor—and not a welcome one either. This suspicion was confirmed when he got up, tried the fastenings of the shutters and satisfied himself that the door was locked and bolted. When he sat down he mixed himself another drink. Before he had finished it a very strange thing happened. I saw the key in the lock of the door turn and I saw the bolts slide back. I am as certain of that as I have ever been of anything. The door opened slowly and a man came in. Of course it was the first man I had seen on the beach—and I did not like him any the better at closer quarters. He did not take off his hat or turn down the collar of his boat-cloak. So I could make no more of his face than I had before. But I was quite sure that two more unpleasant characters can seldom have been found in the same room.

The little man was obviously horribly affected by the entrance of his visitor. But he stood up as if determined to put the best face upon it. (By this time I think he was at least half-drunk; or, as he might have put it himself, Three sheets in the wind.) The men did not shake hands and no word was spoken. The newcomer drew up a chair to the table and produced a pack of cards. The little man turned himself towards it and they began to play. The cat jumped up upon the table and sat watching with a baleful stare. I do not know what the game was and could not follow it very well. But it became clear that the ace of spades was the master-card, and the visitor held it every time. As hand succeeded hand the face of the little man became more and more ghastly until it was hardly human. If a cat can laugh I swear that that cat, which I was coming to dislike as much as either of the men, was laughing to itself. Suddenly the visitor stood up. He seemed to have grown larger and his head almost touched the ceiling. He was between me and the lamp, and his cloak seemed to fly out like the wings of a great bird, so that I could see nothing but blackness. I thought I understood what is meant by *darkness which may be felt* in the account of the ninth of the plagues of Egypt.

When the scene cleared there was a new picture. I was looking at a churchyard, which I had no difficulty in recognizing. There was an open grave and a man standing near it; presumably the sexton. One detail struck me as curious. There were several spades lying on the grass beside him as if a whole party of diggers had been at work. Then I saw the funeral procession, headed by the clergyman, approaching from the lych-gate. It came straight towards the grave. The corpse was not to be taken into the church. The coffin was carried by four bearers and there were no mourners following. As soon as the service was over each of the bearers took a spade and helped the sexton to fill the grave in. All five men worked with immense energy, as if there were not a moment to be lost. The clergyman (this also I thought unusual) stood by and watched them. As soon as the work was finished the party dispersed as rapidly as was consistent with decency. In fact they might almost be said to have run away. Once or twice while this was going on I thought I saw a figure of some kind just outside the lych-gate. But it was so indistinct, that I could make nothing of it. I could not even be sure whether there was anybody there at all.

When this picture disappeared I felt sure there was nothing more to come, and soon afterwards the maid came in to lay the table for supper. As this was my last evening I had Mr. Rust in later to help me pass it. We talked of general matters pleasantly enough and no mention of Henry Rigg was made. But I think we both felt the other was somehow *en garde*. Next morning I returned to London.

Well, there is my story. I could not make it more interesting except by some unwarrantable excursion into the realm of romance. I cannot pretend to say why my adventure (if you can call it that) befell me, nor to explain any of the details. But I think I can guess why Henry Rigg was not popular in his lifetime and why his memory was still odious in the pleasant little village of H—more than thirty years after his death. And I have sometimes wondered whether the text which the lawyer from Saxmundham had placed on his tombstone had any secret and sinister significance.

GUY de MAUPASSANT
On the River

*Guy de Maupassant (1850–93) was one of the
leading geniuses of French literature and a supreme
master of short story writing. Many of his tales,
like "Was He Mad?", "Who Knows?". "He?"
and "The Horla", reflect his phobias and fear
of incipient madness, an obsession that became
reality a few months before his premature end in
a mental hospital.*

I had rented, last summer, a little country house on the banks
of the Seine a few miles from Paris, and I used to go down
there every night to sleep. In a few days I made the acquaintance
of one of my neighbours, a man between thirty and forty, who
was certainly the most curious type that I had ever met. He was
an old rowing man, crazy about rowing, always near the water,
always on the water, always in the water. He must have been
born in a boat, and he would certainly die in one.

While we were walking together along the Seine, I asked him
to tell me some stories about his life upon the river; and at
that the good man suddenly became animated, transfigured,
eloquent, almost poetical! In his heart there was one great
passion, devouring and irresistible—the river.

"Ah!" said he to me, "how many memories I have of that
river which is flowing there beside us. You people who live in
streets, you don't know what the river is. But just listen to a
fisherman simply pronouncing the word. For him it is the thing
mysterious, the thing profound, unknown, the country of mirage
and of phantasmagoria, where one sees, at night, things which
do not exist, where one hears strange noises, where one trembles
causelessly, as though crossing a graveyard. And it is, indeed,
the most sinister of graveyards—a graveyard where there are no
tombstones.

"To the fisherman the land seems limited, but of dark nights,
when there is no moon, the river seems limitless. Sailors have

no such feeling for the sea. Hard she often is and wicked, the great Sea; but she cries, she shouts, she deals with you fairly, while the river is silent and treacherous. It never even mutters, it flows ever noiselessly, and this eternal flowing movement of water terrifies me far more than the high seas of ocean.

"Dreamers pretend that the Sea hides in her breast great blue regions where drowned men roll to and fro among the huge fish, in the midst of strange forests and in crystal grottoes. The river has only black depths, where one rots in the slime. For all that it is beautiful when it glitters in the rising sun or swashes softly along between its banks where the reeds murmur.

"The poet says of the ocean:

" 'O seas, you know sad stories! Deep seas, feared by kneeling mothers, you tell the stories to one another at flood tides! And that is why you have such despairing voices when at night you come towards us nearer and nearer.'

"Well, I think that the stories murmured by the slender reeds with their little soft voices must be yet more sinister than the gloomy dramas told by the howling of the high seas.

"But, since you ask for some of my recollections, I will tell you a curious adventure which I had here about ten years ago.

"I then lived, as I still do, in the house of the old lady Lafon, and one of my best chums, Louis Bernet, who has now given up for the Civil Service his oars, his low shoes, and his sleeveless jersey, lived in the village of C——, two leagues farther down. We dined together every day—sometimes at his place, sometimes at mine.

"One evening as I was returning home alone and rather tired, wearily pulling my heavy boat, a twelve-footer, which I always used at night, I stopped a few seconds to take breath near the point where so many reeds grow, down that way, about two hundred meters before you come to the railroad bridge. It was a beautiful night; the moon was resplendent, the river glittered, the air was calm and soft. The tranquillity of it all tempted me; I said to myself that to smoke a pipe just here would be extremely nice. Action followed upon the thought; I seized my anchor and threw it into the stream.

"The boat, which floated down again with the current, pulled the chain out to its full length, then stopped; and I seated myself in the stern on a sheepskin, as comfortable as possible. One heard no sound—no sound; only sometimes I thought I was aware of a low, almost insensible lapping of the water along the bank, and I made out some groups of reeds which, taller than their fellows, took on surprising shapes, and seemed from time to time to stir.

"The river was perfectly still, but I felt myself moved by the extraordinary silence which surrounded me. All the animals— the frogs and toads, those nocturnal singers of the marshes— were silent. Suddenly on my right, near me, a frog croaked; I started; it was silent; I heard nothing more, and I resolved to smoke a little by way of a distraction. But though I am, so to speak, a regular blackener of pipes, I could not smoke that night; after the second puff I sickened of it, and I stopped. I began to hum a tune; the sound of my voice was painful to me; so I stretched myself out in the bottom of the boat and contemplated the sky. For some time I remained quiet, but soon the slight movements of the boat began to make me uneasy. I thought that it was yawing tremendously, striking now this bank of the stream, and now that; then I thought that some Being or some invisible force was dragging it down gently to the bottom of the water, and then was lifting it up simply to let it fall again. I was tossed about as though in the midst of a storm; I heard noises all around me; with a sudden start I sat upright; the water sparkled, everything was calm.

"I saw that my nerves were unsettled, and I decided to go. I pulled in the chain; the boat moved; then I was conscious of resistance; I pulled harder; the anchor did not come up, it had caught on something at the bottom of the river and I could not lift it. I pulled again—in vain. With my oars I got the boat round upstream in order to change the position of the anchor. It was no use; the anchor still held. I grew angry, and in a rage I shook the chain. Nothing moved. There was no hope of breaking the chain, or of getting it loose from my craft, because it was very heavy, and riveted at the bow into a bar of wood thicker than my arm; but since the weather continued fine, I reflected that I should not have to wait long before meeting some fisherman, who would come to my rescue. My mishap had calmed me; I sat down, and I was now able to smoke my pipe. I had a flask of brandy with me; I drank two or three glasses, and my situation made me laugh. It was very hot, so that, if needs must, I could pass the night under the stars without inconvenience.

"Suddenly a little knock sounded against the side. I started, and a cold perspiration froze me from head to foot. The noise came, no doubt, from some bit of wood drawn along by the current, but it was enough, and I felt myself again overpowered by a strange nervous agitation. I seized the chain, and I stiffened myself in a desperate effort. The anchor held. I sat down exhausted.

"But, little by little, the river had covered itself with a very thick white mist, which crept low over the water, so that, standing up, I could no longer see either the stream or my feet or my boat, and saw only the tips of the reeds, and then, beyond them, the plain, all pale in the moonlight, and with great black stains which rose towards heaven, and which were made by clumps of Italian poplars. I was as though wrapped to the waist in a cotton sheet of a strange whiteness, and there began to come to me weird imaginations. I imagined that some one was trying to climb into my boat, since I could no longer see it, and that the river, hidden by this opaque mist, must be full of strange creatures swimming about me. I experienced a horrible uneasiness, I had a tightening at the temples, my heart beat to suffocation; and, losing my head, I thought of escaping by swimming; then in an instant the very idea made me shiver with fright. I saw myself lost, drifting hither and thither in this impenetrable mist, struggling among the long grass and the reeds which I should not be able to avoid, with a rattle in my throat from fear, not seeing the shore, not finding my boat. And it seemed to me as though I felt myself being drawn by the feet down to the bottom of this black water.

"In fact, since I should have had to swim up stream at least five hundred meters before finding a point clear of rushes and reeds, where I could get a footing, there were nine chances to one that, however good a swimmer I might be, I should lose my bearings in the fog and drown.

"I tried to reason with myself. I realized that my will was firmly enough resolved against fear; but there was something in me beside my will, and it was this which felt afraid. I asked myself what it could be that I dreaded; that part of me which was courageous railed at that part of me which was cowardly; and I never had comprehended so well before the opposition between those two beings which exist within us, the one willing, the other resisting, and each in turn getting the mastery.

"This stupid and inexplicable fear grew until it became terror. I remained motionless, my eyes wide open, with a strained and expectant ear. Expecting—what? I did not know save that it would be something terrible. I believe that if a fish, as often happens, had taken it into his head to jump out of the water, it would have needed only that to make me fall stark on my back into a faint.

"And yet, finally, by a violent effort, I very nearly recovered the reason which had been escaping me. I again took my brandy-flask, and out of it I drank great draughts. Then an idea struck me, and I began to shout with all my might, turning in succession towards all four quarters of the horizon. When my throat was completely paralyzed, I listened. A dog howled, a long way off.

"Again I drank; and I lay down on my back in the bottom of the boat. So I remained for one hour, perhaps for two, sleepless, my eyes wide open, with nightmares all about me. I did not dare to sit up, and yet I had a wild desire to do so; I kept putting it off from minute to minute. I would say to myself: 'Come! get up!' and I was afraid to make a movement. At last I raised myself with infinite precaution, as if life depended on my making not the slightest sound, and I peered over the edge of the boat.

"I was dazzled by the most marvellous, the most astonishing spectacle that it can be possible to see. It was one of those phantasmagoria from fairy-land; it was one of those visions described by travellers returned out of far countries, and which we hear without believing.

"The mist, which two hours before was floating over the water, had gradually withdrawn and piled itself upon the banks. Leaving the river absolutely clear, it had formed, along each shore, long low hills about six or seven meters high, which glittered under the moon with the brilliancy of snow, so that one saw nothing except this river of fire coming down these two white mountains; and there, high above my head, a great, luminous moon, full and large, displayed herself upon a blue and milky sky.

"All the denizens of the water had awaked; the bull-frogs croaked furiously, while, from instant to instant, now on my right, now on my left, I heard those short, mournful, monotonous notes which the brassy voices of the marsh-frogs give forth to the stars. Strangely enough, I was no longer afraid;

I was in the midst of such an extraordinary landscape that the most curious things could not have astonished me.

"How long the sight lasted I do not know, because at last I had grown drowsy. When I again opened my eyes the moon had set, the heaven was full of clouds. The water lashed mournfully, the wind whispered, it grew cold, the darkness was profound.

"I drank all the brandy I had left; then I listened shiveringly to the rustling of the reeds and to the sinister noise of the river. I tried to see, but I could not make out the boat nor even my own hands, though I raised them close to my eyes.

"However, little by little the density of the blackness diminished. Suddenly I thought I felt a shadow slipping along near by me; I uttered a cry; a voice replied—it was a fisherman. I hailed him; he approached, and I told him of my mishap. He pulled his boat alongside, and both together we heaved at the chain. The anchor did not budge. The day came on—somber, gray, rainy, cold—one of those days which bring always a sorrow and a misfortune. I made out another craft; we hailed it. The man aboard of it joined his efforts to ours, then, little by little, the anchor yielded. It came up, but slowly, slowly, and weighted down by something very heavy. At last we perceived a black mass, and we pulled it alongside.

"It was the corpse of an old woman with a great stone round her neck."

J.C.MOORE
Things

John Cecil Moore (1907–67) *is one of the
most popular "country writers" this country has
produced, a worthy successor to Richard Jefferies
and Edward Thomas. He achieved his greatest
fame with* Portrait of Elmbury (1945) *and* Bren-
sham Village (1946), *but his earlier work is lesser
known today. The* English Review *was the first
magazine to publish any of his stories, beginning
with three in 1928, including "Decay" (which has
often been anthologised) and the equally fine and
poetic "Things".*

My friend Sam, the poacher, can hardly be credited with
a very vivid imagination. Indeed, the exigencies of his
trade do not permit him to possess one; for the silence of the
woods at night is a queer silence, and small sounds are apt to
shatter it suddenly, sounds that would make some men jump.
And when one is trying to be particularly still and quiet, and
the light in the keeper's cottage gleams ominously through the
trees, it is just as well not to jump. In fact, a start might be fatal.
Jays are noisy birds. Perhaps it is that an imagination of this
sort—the kind that makes one jump when a fox rustles through
the bracken—is akin to, if not dependent upon, a conscience;
and by a divine ordinance Sam has not been given a conscience.
He simply cannot understand such a thing.

Now, if you or I, whose sins occupy perhaps half a page of
the Recording Angel's ledgers in comparison with Sam's twenty
volumes, were to walk at midnight through the Long Copse,
or across the moor, beside the river, or down by the Silent
Pool, it is quite possible that our nerves would become just a
little strained, just a little sharpened and on edge. We should
not be frightened of course, but—well, taut. Taut; waiting for
something to happen, and then starting when a jay squawked or
an owl screeched close at hand. We should hear Things rustling

in the grasses, Things splashing in the water, Things moaning softly in the bushes, Things sighing queerly in the trees. To us, they are just Things; rather terrifying because of our ignorance of them. But Sam catalogues them specifically and particularly. He knows the rustle of a sliding snake from that of a gliding weasel; knows the bat's squeak and the jay's call, the nightjar's and the owl's; the splash of wallowing bream and the sough of the early morning wind through the trees. What are Things to us are birds and beasts and insects to Sam. I suppose it is partly a matter of knowledge, partly of conscience. I remember most of my sins; Sam could not possibly remember one-half of his; so conveniently forgets them all.

However it may be, this rather lengthy prelude is designed to show that Sam is not in the habit of seeing and hearing and feeling Things; though his sharp eyes miss few rabbits, and his keen ears fail to warn him of few footsteps. And it is just this that makes his queer story all the queerer.

I must give it in my own words; not that they are better than Sam's rather colourful oratory—I do not think they are—but simply because Sam's special variety of prose is not for all occasions and all audiences. It is reserved for one or two favoured folk like myself, down in the "Green Dragon" bar, over a pint of the landlord's best, half an hour after closing time—but that is another matter entirely. The frequent personal allusions, the queer idiom, the allegory, the metaphor, the simile: all would be lost upon the average reader. And above all, the favourite expletive——

It was early in the autumn of last year that Sam decided to try for a snipe down by the Silent Pool. The excursion was in the nature of a holiday from the much more serious business of poaching my pheasants and the pheasants of all my neighbours; for the marshy swamps around the Silent Pool were neglected and unfrequented, and no one had ever bothered about the shooting rights within the memory of man. Not even the osiers were tended—the place was four miles from a main road, and at one and threepence a bundle (and a bundle must be forty-two inches round its waist) it simply did not pay.

The Silent Pool is the biggest of several ponds which lie close together in the middle of a large withy-bed. Popular superstition has it that it is bottomless; however that may be, it is a gloomy place enough, overgrown with sallows and hedged in with bulrushes, so that no wind ever reaches it to ruffle the oily calm of its dark waters. A solitary poplar, sentinel-like, stands up at its farthermost edge.

The pools are joined together by a network of dykes and runnels. The whole place is a marsh, and there are spots where one could sink up to one's neck in slimy, black mud in half a minute. One ill-defined path runs parallel with the biggest of the runnels, and circles the pool itself; the rest is an untrodden wilderness. One feature by its very incongruity increases the impression of gloom and solitude. A single telephone wire, run across country to the old Manor House at the bottom of the valley, traverses the top end of the swamp and violates the branches of the sentinel poplar.

It is, indeed, a spot

> as lonely and enchanted
> As e'er beneath a waning moon was haunted
> By woman wailing for her demon lover.

But there is no traditional ghost connected with the place. It could tell tales, perhaps, of suicide and murder, and the ends of babies whose birth has been an inconvenience; but for my part I think its story would be one of gloom and solitude, silence and darkness, and gloom and unending solitude again. It is as if the pond were dead, when not even a breeze can ruffle the dark mirror of its surface, which reflects nothing but the lonely poplar and the changeless, ever-changing, sky.

There were few spots within his district that were not subject to Sam's periodical scrutiny, and the Silent Pool was no exception. He had marked down a brace of snipe breeding in the osier-bed in the spring, and there were mallard come to the pool to roost. So one evening in mid-September he took his gun, called his dog, and tramped off across the meadows towards the pool, following the line of the hedges. He avoided footpaths and open country generally; and Sam on a main road always reminded me somehow of an owl caught blinking in a tree in the sunlight, terrified of the mob of tits and sparrows.

His bitch, Jane, followed so closely at his heels that one could see her pad-marks impressed regularly upon his footprints.

Their tracks, in this respect, were the only things that Sam and the keepers had in common.

This Jane was, indeed, a lady fallen from virtue. She had been born of parents of excellent pedigree, but the owner, during his absence on the Riviera, had entrusted the chauffeur to look after Jane's mother, and when he received a respectful letter to say that Brackenhurst Bountiful had a litter of four puppies he saw no reason to doubt the statement. Actually, she had had six; and the chauffeur thus ingeniously provided himself with, as he put it, two "buckshee" ones which he proceeded to dispose of to his friends.

Sam was the recipient of one; and the little ball of black fur renounced the honourable title of, say, Brackenhurst Ballet-dancer, and became plain Jane. As she grew up into a very handsome Cocker, she acquired all the furtive, slinking characteristics of the poacher's dog; became, in fact, as disreputable a person as Sam himself. She had an entirely illegitimate litter of puppies by a shepherd's collie, each member of which grew up as shameful and shameless as herself. The eldest amused itself by making violent love to all the keepers' bitches in the neighbourhood, whose consequent mongrel offspring surprised and disgusted the owners beyond words. But it was a risky sport, and one day a charge of No. 5 shot rolled him over like a rabbit.

But to get back to Jane and her disreputable owner.

Sam followed his devious course and entered the swamp at the leeward end, more out of habit than because of the wind; for the evening was almost calm, with that tense stillness which comes only in the autumn.

Mists rose up like sinuous wraiths marking the courses of the dykes, and hanging like blots and smudges over the pools. In the west the sun was sinking through the haze into a crimson lake.

Sam took the only clear path and fought his way through the branches of projecting sallows, which met like an archway of crossed swords above his head.

"Seek in—seek," he called softly, and Jane went crashing through the undergrowth down to the runnel; questing among the rushes, splashing in the water. And "Seek, seek," called Sam so softly, yet so shrilly.

A mallard rose with a whirr of wings, but the sallows hid it from view, and when at last it swept back overhead, it was high up out of range, and Sam knew better than to waste a shot on it.

He crept along the rough pathway until he reached the Silent Pool. Now and then the "plop" of a diving water-rat broke the silence, and Jane's inquisitive sniff as she tested each clump of reeds. For the rest, it was very still, and the sun had set. The first evening chills crept across the swamp, and the labyrinthine pattern of the mists over the runnels became less clearly defined, their edges melting everywhere into shadows. It seemed to Sam that the dusk came very suddenly.

Two moorhens swam about in the middle of the pool, but there was no other sign of life. It was duck-light now, and Sam called Jane to his heels and set himself to wait patiently for the mallard. He waited for a quarter of an hour; the twilight deepened. Once a moth fluttered against his face with a soft caress of downy wings, and Sam so far forgot himself as to strike at it irritably with his hand. The utter stillness seemed to him rather queer. He began to think that it would be very easy to trip over one of the stumps in the darkness on the way back; and that there was no saying that the hammer of his gun might not catch in his coat as he fell, from which it needed no great stretch of imagination to visualize the gun thrown up in such a position that it would blow his brains out. Such a death seemed to Sam peculiarly unpleasant. For one would lie there, lie there for days and weeks and months, and no one would be any the wiser. Sam was not the sort of person for whom they would send out search-parties; his absences, generally in gaol, were too frequent to excite comment.

Some such notion came into Sam's head, and the more he thought of it, the less he liked it. Slowly one would rot, half in the water and half in the mud, with Jane watching restlessly over one's body, sniffing, scratching, whimpering impatiently. One's skeleton would remain there for ever in that horrible stillness—

The idea did not appeal to Sam, who had, like many pagans, an earnest desire for a decent burial. He opened his gun and took out the cartridges; it was too late for a shot, even if the duck did come. The only sounds now were the occasional croak of a moorhen, the wallow of gigantic fish in the pool, and the gurgle and bubble of marsh-gas rising up through the mud. Sam noticed for the first time that some foul miasma seemed to hang about the place; there was an odour of death and corruption in the air, a stench of mud and rotting things. He made up his mind to go back while there was yet some glimmer of daylight; and then suddenly, Jane, who had been lying quietly at his feet, sprang up and froze. Involuntarily Sam froze, too.

It seemed at first as if a wind had got up and was sighing through the dry leaves of the poplar and rustling among the bulrushes. And then swish-swish—something passed over the pool with a sighing moan and the water was ruffled and churned into spray for a second. Jane growled softly, and Sam saw that she was shivering. A bitter cold seemed to envelop him. He felt another moth brush against his face, then another and another. But he could not see the blurred dusky forms, though it was still light, and when he struck at them, he felt nothing. His hands beat like flails, striking the emptiness of air.

All at once it struck Sam that they were not moths.

Again and again the Things touched him. He felt them all over his face and neck, felt them brushing against his legs through his trousers. There were Things abroad with a vengeance now, rustling in the dry reeds, sighing in the trees, swishing over the water. It was as if the atmosphere was charged with electricity gone mad. Jane kept up a low growling. A cold sweat broke out on Sam's forehead. Remember, he was not accustomed to Things. He told himself that the sound was the whistle of ducks' wings, and that the ducks were circling overhead before they alighted on the pond. But he knew too well that it was nothing of the sort. One needs an imagination to deceive oneself.

Sam turned hurriedly to go; as he did so, a strange climax, "twang!" went the telephone wire, and there was a sudden stillness. The rustlings, the sighings, the moanings died in mid career.

The ensuing horrible silence was too much for Sam. For the first and only time in his life he lost his head. He called to Jane in a shrill querulous tone, which he scarcely recognized as his own voice, and away he went down the dark pathway towards the open country. He ran blindly, heedless of the branches which sprang back catapult-like into his face, careless of the stumps that tripped him up and the muddy ditches into which he fell. Again and again he went headlong into the black mud or slipped sideways into a dyke. Again and again the stumps bruised his shins and the supple branches of the sallows lashed his face. His clothes were torn and muddy, soaking wet from repeated immersion in the dykes; his face was cut and bleeding, his legs and hands were scratched and bruised. Jane followed madly behind him, terrified of the thing that had frightened her master.

He got out safely at last, and once again in the open his courage returned. He stood at the edge of the swamp listening; but the silence within was unbroken—not even a moorhen's croak nor a bat's squeak nor the heavy splash and wallow of the big carp and bream in the pools.

And that was uncommon queer, says Sam.

At each stile on the way home Sam found a pair of lovers; and he says that he was never so glad to see anybody as that first couple huddled in each other's arms not two meadows away from the Silent Pool. It was like coming back to sanity after madness; returning from that weird and gloomy haunt of nameless things to the sane old earth, where flowers blossomed and corn was gathered in sheaves, and men and women loved as other men and women have done since the human race began. Sam says he could have put a fatherly arm round the two of them and hugged them yet closer together, if that were possible; equally he was prepared to cry; but as it was, he contented himself with a broad grin and a merry "Goodnight" just to hear his normal voice again. But they were too much engrossed in their business of loving even to notice him.

So with Jane once more returned to her senses and padding meticulously at his heels, over the Summer Leasow, across the Twenty Acres, down over Starveall, up over the Quitch Meadow, along Honeysuckle Lane—Sam went home.

Oddly enough, most urgent business took Sam back to the Silent Pool next morning, when the bright sun had dispelled the previous evening's fears; for hounds were cubbing in the osiers, and there's never such a good time to pick up a rabbit or a hare as when hounds are drawing, and game is disturbed, and everybody's attention is riveted upon foxes. Besides, should anyone, knowing your vocation, ask you what you're doing there, what easier than to reply: "Watching the hounds, sir; and surely you don't grudge a poor man his bit of honest sport?" and then if it's the Master, you tell him confidentially of that vixen you have spotted in the hazel brake, and so perhaps get half-a-crown in addition to your hare. . . .

Sam stayed outside the covert. Hounds did not find, and no wonder, says Sam, for they bunched together at the edge of the osiers and never tried the thick beds around the Silent Pool at all. But it was reassuring to hear the huntsman's clear voice waking the echoes in that desolate place.

Now, it may be that there is a natural, logical explanation of all that Sam felt and heard and saw down by the Silent Pool. It may be that for the first time in his life Sam's imagination ran riot and his senses played him false. But let me remind you once more that there are few natural phenomena that Sam does not know the meaning of (since the wind and the storm and the sun and the moon are his playmates); and, further, that he is not in the habit of seeing and hearing and feeling Things.

Sam is constitutionally averse to publicity. So he did not go home on that evening in mid-September and sit down to pen letters to the newspapers and the Society for Psychical Research. Instead, he reserves his story for those rare evenings down in the "Green Dragon" bar, in the company of one or two favoured folk like myself, over a pint of the landlord's best, half-an-hour after closing time—but that, as I said before, is another matter entirely.

EDITH NESBIT
The Ebony Frame

Edith Nesbit (1858–1924) is best remembered for her children's classics, notably The Story of the Treasure Seekers (1899), The Railway Children (1906), *and* Five Children and It (1902), *dramatised on BBC TV earlier this year. Early in her career she contributed some excellent ghost stories to* Argosy, Illustrated London News, *and other magazines, and the best of these were collected in* Grim Tales (1893), *including "Man-Size in Marble", "John Charrington's Wedding", and "The Ebony Frame".*

To be rich is a luxurious sensation, the more so when you have plumbed the depths of hard-up-ness as a Fleet Street hack, a picker-up of unconsidered pars, a reporter, an unappreciated journalist; all callings utterly inconsistent with one's family feeling and one's direct descent from the Dukes of Picardy.

When my Aunt Dorcas died and left me seven hundred a year and a furnished house in Chelsea, I felt that life had nothing left to offer except immediate possession of the legacy. Even Mildred Mayhew, whom I had hitherto regarded as my life's light, became less luminous. I was not engaged to Mildred, but I lodged with her mother, and I sang duets with Mildred and gave her gloves when it would run to it, which was seldom. She was a dear, good girl, and I meant to marry her some day. It is very nice to feel that a good little woman is thinking of you—it helps you in your work—and it is pleasant to know she will say "Yes," when you say, "Will you?"

But my legacy almost put Mildred out of my head, especially as she was staying with friends in the country.

Before the gloss was off my new mourning, I was seated in my aunt's armchair in front of the fire in the drawing-room of my own house. My own house! It was grand, but rather lonely.

I *did* think of Mildred just then.

The room was comfortably furnished with rosewood and damask. On the walls hung a few fairly good oil paintings, but the space above the mantelpiece was disfigured by an exceedingly bad print, "The Trial of Lord William Russell," framed in a dark frame. I got up to look at it. I had visited my aunt with dutiful regularity, but I never remembered seeing this frame before. It was not intended for a print, but for an oil-painting. It was of fine ebony, beautifully and curiously carved.

I looked at it with growing interest, and when my aunt's housemaid—I had retained her modest staff of servants—came in with the lamp, I asked her how long the print had been there.

"Mistress only bought it two days before she was took ill," she said; "but the frame—she didn't want to buy a new one—so she got this out of the attic. There's lots of curious old things there, sir."

"Had my aunt had this frame long?"

"Oh, yes, sir! It must have come long before I did, and I've been here seven years come Christmas. There was a picture in it. That's upstairs too—but it's that black and ugly it might as well be a chimney-back."

I felt a desire to see this picture. What if it were some priceless old master, in which my aunt's eyes had only seen rubbish?

Directly after breakfast next morning, I paid a visit to the attic.

It was crammed with old furniture enough to stock a curiosity shop. All the house was furnished solidly in the Mid-Victorian style, and in this room everything not in keeping with the drawing-room suite ideal was stowed away. Tables of papier-maché and mother-of-pearl, straight-backed chairs with twisted feet and faded needle-work cushions, fire-screens of gilded carving and beaded banners, oak bureaux with brass handles, a little work-table with its faded, moth-eaten, silk flutings hanging in disconsolate shreds; on these, and the dust that covered them, blazed the full daylight as I pulled up the blinds. I promised myself a good time in re-enshrining these household gods in my parlour, and promoting the Victorian suite to the attic. But at present my business was to find the picture as "black as the chimney back"; and presently, behind a heap of fenders and boxes, I found it.

Jane, the housemaid, identified it at once. I took it downstairs carefully, and examined it. Neither subject nor colour was distinguishable. There was a splodge of a darker tint in the middle, but whether it was figure, or tree, or house, no man could have told. It seemed to be painted on a very thick panel bound with leather. I decided to send it to one of those persons who pour on rotting family portraits the water of eternal youth; but even as I did so, I thought—why not try my own restorative hand at a corner of it.

My bath-sponge soap and nail-brush, vigorously applied for a few seconds, showed me that there was no picture to clean. Bare oak presented itself to my persevering brush. I tried the other side, Jane watching me with indulgent interest. The same result. Then the truth dawned on me. Why was the panel so thick? I tore off the leather binding, and the panel divided and fell to the ground in a cloud of dust. There were two pictures—they had been nailed face to face. I leaned them against the wall, and the next moment I was leaning against it myself.

For one of the pictures was myself—a perfect portrait—no shade of expression or turn of feature wanting. Myself—in the dress men wore when James the First was King. When had this been done? And how, without my knowledge? Was this some whim of my aunt's?

"Lor', sir!" the shrill surprise of Jane at my elbow; "what a lovely photo it is! Was it a fancy ball, sir?"

"Yes," I stammered. "I—I don't think I want anything more now. You can go."

She went; and I turned, still with my heart beating violently, to the other picture. This was a beautiful woman's picture—very beautiful she was. I noted all her beauties—straight nose, low brows, full lips, thin hands, large, deep, luminous eyes. She wore a black velvet gown. It was a three-quarter-length portrait. Her arms rested on a table beside her, and her head on her hands; but her face was turned full forward, and her eyes met those of the spectator bewilderingly. On the table by her were compasses and shining instruments whose uses I did not know, books, a goblet, and a heap of papers and pens. I saw all this afterwards. I believe it was a quarter of an hour before I could turn my eyes from hers. I have never see any other eyes like hers; they appealed, as a child's or a dog's do; they commanded, as might those of an empress.

"Shall I sweep up the dust sir?" Curiosity had brought Jane back. I acceded. I turned from her my portrait. I kept between her and the woman in the black velvet. When I was alone again I tore down "The Trial of Lord William Russell," and I put the picture of the woman in its strong ebony frame.

Then I wrote to a frame-maker for a frame for my portrait. It had so long lived face to face with this beautiful witch that I had not the heart to banish it from her presence; I suppose I *am* sentimental—if it be sentimental to think such things as that.

The new frame came home, and I hung it opposite the fireplace. An exhaustive search among my aunt's papers showed no explanation of the portrait of myself, no history of the portrait of the woman with the wonderful eyes. I only learned that all the old furniture together had come to my aunt at the death of my great-uncle, the head of the family; and I should have concluded that the resemblance was only a family one, if everyone who came in had not exclaimed at the "speaking likeness." I adopted Jane's "fancy ball" explanation.

And there, one might suppose, the matter of the portraits ended. One might suppose it, that is, if there were not evidently a good deal more written here about it. However, to me then the matter seemed ended.

I went to see Mildred; I invited her and her mother to come and stay with me. I rather avoided glancing at the picture in the ebony frame. I could not forget, nor remember without singular emotion, the look in the eyes of that woman when mine first met them. I shrank from meeting that look again.

I reorganised the house somewhat, preparing for Mildred's visit. I brought down much of the old-fashioned furniture, and after a long day of arranging and re-arranging, I sat down before the fire, and lying back in a pleasant languor, I idly raised my eyes to the picture of the woman. I met her dark, deep, hazel eyes, and once more my gaze was held fixed as by strong magic—the kind of fascination that keeps one sometimes staring for whole minutes into one's own eyes in the glass. I gazed into her eyes, and felt my own dilate, pricked with a smart like the smart of tears.

"I wish," I said, "oh, how I wish you were a woman and not a picture! Come down! Ah, come down!"

I laughed at myself as I spoke; but even as I laughed, I held out my arms.

409

I was not sleepy; I was not drunk. I was as wide awake and as sober as ever was a man in the world. And yet, as I held out my arms, I saw the eyes of the picture dilate, her lips tremble—if I were to be hanged for saying it, it is true.

Her hands moved slightly; and a sort of flicker of a smile passed over her face.

I sprang to my feet. "This won't do," I said aloud. "Firelight does play strange tricks. I'll have the lamp."

I made for the bell. My hand was on it, when I heard a sound behind me, and turned—the bell still unrung. The fire had burned low and the corners of the room were deeply shadowed; but surely, there—behind the tall worked chair—was something darker than a shadow.

"I must face this out," I said, "or I shall never be able to face myself again." I left the bell, I seized the poker, and battered the dull coals to a blaze. Then I stepped back resolutely, and looked at the picture. The ebony frame was empty! From the shadow of the worked chair came a soft rustle, and out of the shadow the woman of the picture was coming—coming towards me.

I hope I shall never again know a moment of terror as blank and absolute. I could not have moved or spoken to save my life. Either all the known laws of nature were nothing, or I was mad. I stood trembling, but, I am thankful to remember, I stood still, while the black velvet gown swept across the hearthrug towards me.

Next moment a hand touched me—a hand, soft, warm, and human—and a low voice said, "You called me. I am here."

At that touch and that voice, the world seemed to give a sort of bewildering half-turn. I hardly know how to express it, but at once it seemed not awful, not even unusual, for portraits to become flesh—only most natural, most right, most unspeakably fortunate.

I laid my hand on hers. I looked from her to my portrait. I could not see it in the firelight.

"We are not strangers," I said.

"Oh, no, not strangers." Those luminous eyes were looking up into mine, those red lips were near me. With a passionate cry, a sense of having recovered life's one great good, that had seemed wholly lost, I clasped her in my arms. She was no ghost, she was a woman, the only woman in the world.

"How long," I said, "how long is it since I lost you?"

She leaned back, hanging her full weight on the hands that were clasped behind my head.

"How can I tell how long? There is no time in hell," she answered.

It was not a dream. Ah! no—there are no such dreams. I wish to God there could be. When in dreams do I see her eyes, hear her voice, feel her lips against my cheek, hold her hands to my lips, as I did that night, the supreme night of my life! At first we hardly spoke. It seemed enough

> . . . after long grief and pain,
> To feel the arms of my true love,
> Round me once again.

It is very difficult to tell my story. There are no words to express the sense of glad reunion, the complete realisation of every hope and dream of a life, that came upon me as I sat with my hand in hers, and looked into her eyes.

How could it have been a dream, when I left her sitting in the straight-backed chair, and went down to the kitchen to tell the maids I should want nothing more—that I was busy, and did not wish to be disturbed; when I fetched wood for the fire with my own hands, and, bringing it in, found her still sitting there—saw the little brown head turn as I entered, saw the love in her dear eyes; when I threw myself at her feet and blessed the day I was born, since life had given me this.

Not a thought of Mildred; all other things in my life were a dream—this, its one splendid reality.

"I am wondering," she said, after a while, when we had made such cheer, each of the other, as true lovers may after long parting—"I am wondering how much you remember of our past?"

"I remember nothing but that I love you—that I have loved you all my life."

"You remember nothing—really nothing?"

"Only that I am truly yours; that we have both suffered; that—tell me, my mistress dear, all that you remember. Explain it all to me. Make me understand. And yet—No, I don't want to understand. It is enough that we are together."

If it was a dream, why have I never dreamed it again?

She leaned down towards me, her arm lay on my neck, and drew my head till it rested on her shoulder. "I am a ghost, I suppose," she said, laughing softly; and her laughter stirred memories which I just grasped at and just missed. "But you and I know better, don't we? I will tell you everything you have forgotten. We loved each other—ah! no, you have not forgotten that—and when you came back from the wars, we were to be married. Our pictures were painted before you went away. You know I was more learned than women of that day. Dear one, when you were gone, they said I was a witch. They tried me. They said I should be burned. Just because I had looked at the stars and gained more knowledge than other women, they must needs bind me to a stake and let me be eaten by the fire. And you far away!"

Her whole body trembled and shrank. Oh love, what dream would have told me that my kisses would soothe even that memory?

"The night before," she went on, "the devil did come to me. I was innocent before—you know it, don't you? And even then my sin was for you—for you—because of the exceeding love I bore you. The devil came, and I sold my soul to eternal flame. But I got a good price. I got the right to come back through my picture (if anyone, looking at it, wished for me), as long as my picture stayed in its ebony frame. That frame was not carved by man's hand. I got the right to come back to you, oh, my heart's heart. And another thing I won, which you shall hear anon. They burned me for a witch, they made me suffer hell on earth. Those faces, all crowding round, the crackling wood and the choking smell of the smoke—"

"Oh, love, no more, no more!"

"When my mother sat that night before my picture, she wept and cried, 'Come back, my poor, lost child!' And I went to her with glad leaps of heart. Dear, she shrank from me, she fled, she shrieked and moaned of ghosts. She had our pictures covered from sight, and put again in the ebony frame. She had promised me my picture should stay always there. Ah, through all these years your face was against mine."

She paused,

"But the man you loved?"

"You came home. My picture was gone. They lied to you, and you married another woman; but some day I knew you would walk the world again, and that I should find you."

"The other gain?" I asked.

"The other gain," she said slowly, "I gave my soul for. It is this. If you also will give up your hopes of heaven, I can remain a woman, I can remain in your world—I can be your wife. Oh my dear, after all these years, at last—at last!"

"If I sacrifice my soul," I said slowly, and the words did not seem an imbecility, "if I sacrifice my soul I win you? Why, love, it's a contradiction in terms. You *are* my soul."

Her eyes looked straight into mine. Whatever might happen, whatever did happen, whatever may happen, our two souls in that moment met and became one.

"Then you choose, you deliberately choose, to give up your hopes of heaven for me, as I gave up mine for you?"

"I will not," I said, "give up my hope of heaven on any terms. Tell me what I must do that you and I may make our heaven here, as now?"

"I will tell you to-morrow," she said. "Be alone here to-morrow night—twelve is ghost's time, isn't it?—and then I will come out of the picture, and never go back to it. I shall live with you, and die, and be buried, and there will be an end of me. But we shall live first, my heart's heart."

I laid my head on her knee. A strange drowsiness overcame me. Holding her hand against my cheek, I lost consciousness. When I awoke, the grey November dawn was glimmering, ghost-like, through the uncurtained window. My head was pillowed on my arm, and rested—I raised my head quickly—ah! not on my lady's knee, but on the needle-worked cushion of the straight-backed chair. I sprang to my feet. I was stiff with cold and dazed with dreams, but I turned my eyes on the picture. There she sat, my lady, my dear love. I held out my arms, but the passionate cry I would have uttered died on my lips. She had said twelve o'clock. Her lightest word was my law. So I only stood in front of the picture, and gazed into those grey-green eyes till tears of passionate happiness filled my own.

"Oh! my dear, my dear, how shall I pass the hours till I hold you again?"

No thought, then, of my whole life's completion and consummation being a dream.

I staggered up to my room, fell across my bed, and slept heavily and dreamlessly. When I awoke it was high noon. Mildred and her mother were coming to lunch.

I remembered, at one o'clock, Mildred coming and her existence.

Now, indeed the dream began.

With a penetrating sense of the futility of any action apart from *her*, I gave the necessary orders for the reception of my guests. When Mildred and her mother came I received them with cordiality; but my genial phrases all seemed to be someone else's. My voice sounded like an echo; my heart was not there.

Still, the situation was not intolerable, until the hour when afternoon tea was served in the drawing-room. Mildred and her mother kept the conversational pot boiling with a profusion of genteel commonplaces, and I bore it, as one in sight of heaven can bear mild purgatory. I looked up at my sweetheart in the ebony frame, and I felt that anything which might happen, any irresponsible imbecility, any bathos of boredom, was nothing, if, after all, *she* came to me again.

And yet, when Mildred, too, looked at the portrait and said: "Doesn't she think a lot of herself? Theatrical character, I suppose? One of your flames, Mr. Devigne?" I had a sickening sense of impotent irritation which became absolute torture when Mildred—how could I ever have admired that chocolate-box barmaid style of prettiness—threw herself into the high-backed chair, covering the needlework with ridiculous flounces, and added, "Silence gives consent! Who is it, Mr. Devigne? Tell us all about her: I am sure she has a story."

Poor little Mildred, sitting there smiling, serene in her confidence that her every word charmed me—sitting there with her rather pinched waist, her rather tight boots, her rather vulgar voice—sitting in the chair where my dear lady had sat when she told me her story! I could not bear it.

"Don't sit there," I said, "it's not comfortable!"

But the girl would not be warned. With a laugh that set every nerve in my body vibrating with annoyance, she said, "Oh, dear! mustn't I even sit in the same chair as your black-velvet woman?"

I looked at the chair in the picture. It *was* the same, and in her chair Mildred was sitting. Then a horrible sense of the reality of Mildred came upon me, Was all this a reality after all? But for fortunate chance, might Mildred have occupied, not only her chair, but her place in my life? I rose.

"I hope you won't think me very rude," I said, "but I am obliged to go out."

I forget what appointment I alleged. The lie came readily enough.

I faced Mildred's pouts with the hope that she and her mother would not wait dinner for me. I fled. In another minute I was safe, alone, under the chill, cloudy, autumn sky—free to think, think, think of my dear lady.

I walked for hours along streets and squares; I lived over and over again every look, word and hand-touch—every kiss; I was completely, unspeakably happy.

Mildred was utterly forgotten; my lady of the ebony frame filled my heart, and soul, and spirit.

As I heard eleven boom through the fog, I turned and went home.

When I got to my street, I found a crowd surging through it, a strong red, light filling the air.

A house was on fire. Mine!

I elbowed my way through the crowd.

The picture of my lady—that, at least, I could save.

As I sprang up the steps, I saw, as in a dream—yes, all this was *really* dream-like—I saw Mildred leaning out of the first-floor window, wringing her hands.

"Come back, sir," cried a fireman; "we'll get the young lady out right enough."

But *my* lady? The stairs were crackling, smoking, and as hot as hell. I went up to the room where her picture was. Strange to say, I only felt that the picture was a thing we should like to look on through the long, glad, wedded life that was to be ours. I never thought of it as being one with her.

As I reached the first floor I felt arms about my neck. The smoke was too thick for me to distinguish features.

"Save me," a voice whispered. I clasped a figure in my arms and bore it with a strange disease, down the shaking stairs and out into safety. It was Mildred. I knew *that* directly I clasped her.

"Stand back," cried the crowd.

"Everyone's safe," cried a fireman.

The flames leaped from every window. The sky grew redder and redder. I sprang from the hands that would have held me. I leaped up the steps. I crawled up the stairs. Suddenly the whole horror came to me. "*As long as my picture remains in the ebony frame.*" What if picture and frame perished together?

I fought with the fire and with my own choking inability to fight with it. I pushed on. I must save my picture. I reached the drawing-room.

As I sprang in, I saw my lady, I swear it, through the smoke and the flames, hold out her arms to me—to me—who came too late to save her, and to save my own life's joy. I never saw her again.

Before I could reach her, or cry out to her, I felt the floor yield beneath my feet, and I fell into the flames below.

How did they save me? What does that matter? They saved me somehow—curse them. Every stick of my aunt's furniture was destroyed. My friends pointed out that, as the furniture was heavily insured, the carelessness of a nightly-studious housemaid had done me no harm.

No harm!

That was how I won and lost my only love.

I deny, with all my soul in the denial, that it was a dream. There are no such dreams. Dreams of longing and pain there are in plenty; but dreams of complete, of unspeakable happiness— ah, no—it is the rest of life that is the dream.

But, if I think that, why have I married Mildred and grown stout, and dull, and prosperous?

I tell you, it is all *this* that is the dream; my dear lady only is the reality. And what does it matter what one does in a dream?'

AMYAS NORTHCOTE
The Downs

*Amyas Northcote (1864–1923) was the seventh
son of the First Earl of Iddesleigh (Disraeli's
Chancellor of the Exchequer), and was for several
years a Justice of the Peace in Buckinghamshire.
He wrote diverse articles with such titles as "Among
French Cathedrals" and "Utter Corruption in
American Politics" for magazines like* Blackwoods
and the Nineteenth Century. *Surprisingly, for a
man with such a variety of interests, he produced
only one book—a collection of supernatural stories*
In Ghostly Company, *published in 1922 shortly
before his death.*

I am venturing to set down the following personal experience,
inconclusive as it is, as I feel that it may interest those
who have the patience to study the phenomena of the unseen
world around us. It was my first experience of a psychical
happening and its events are accordingly indelibly imprinted
on my memory.

The date was, alas, a good many years ago, when I was still
a young man and at the time was engaged in reading hard for a
certain examination. My friend J. was in similar plight to myself
and together we decided to abjure home and London life and
seek a quiet country spot, where we might devote ourselves to
our work amidst pleasant and congenial surroundings.

J. knew of such a place: a farm belonging to a Mr. Harkness,
who was a distant connection of his own by marriage.
Mr. Harkness was a childless widower and lived much to himself
at Branksome Farm, attended to only by an elderly housekeeper
and one or two servants. Although he called himself a farmer and
did in fact farm fairly extensively, he was a man of cultivated and
even learned tastes, widely read and deeply versed in the history
and folklore of his neighbourhood. At the same time, although
good-natured, he was the most reserved and tactiturn man I ever

met, and appeared to have a positive horror of communicating his very considerable fund of local knowledge to outsiders like ourselves. However, he was glad to welcome us as paying guests for the sake of his relationship to J., and he and his housekeeper certainly took great care to make us comfortable and happy.

Branksome Farm is a large old-fashioned house, surrounded by the usual farm buildings and situated in a valley winding its way among the Downs. The situation is beautiful and remote, and it would astonish many of our City dwellers to know that within two or three hours' railway journey from London there still are vast stretches of open Downland on which one may walk for hours without sight of a human being, and traversed only by winding roads which run from one small town or hamlet to another, linking a few lonely cottages or farms to civilization on their route. Behind the house Branksome Down, the highest in the neighbourhood, rises steeply, and beyond it at a distance of about three miles is Willingbury, the nearest town, whence the railway runs to London.

It is necessary to describe the geography of the country between Willingbury and Branksome a little more closely. The two places lie, as is usually the case in the Down country, in valleys between the hills and by road are distant from each other about six to seven miles, being separated by the long ridge of Branksome Down. But actually the distance between them does not exceed three miles across the Down: the path from Branksome, a mere sheep-track, leading up to the top of Branksome Down whence the wanderer sees before him a wide shallow dip in the Down, nearly circular, about three-quarters of a mile across and at the other side sloping up to another gentle ridge. Arrived at the summit of this second elevation the traveller gazes down on the Willingbury-Overbury road and following another sheep-track down the hill-side he reaches the road about a mile outside Willingbury.

The whole Down is covered with sweet, short turf, unbroken by trees or shrubs and, at the time of my story, was unmarred by fencing of any form. Flocks of sheep tended by shepherds and their watchful dogs were almost its sole inhabitants, save for the shy, wild life that clings to all natural shelters. Of the beauty of this Down and, in fact, of the whole neighbourhood it is useless to speak. To anyone who has once felt the fascination of a walk in the fresh, pure air, over the springy and centuries-old turf, and who has allowed his eyes to wander over the miles and miles of open Down, studded here and there with rare belts of trees, and has watched the shifting lights play over the near and distant hills, it is needless to speak, and to anyone who has never yet been fortunate enough to find himself in Downland in fine weather one can hardly make its fascination clear in words, and one can only advise him to go and explore its beauties for himself.

Well, it was at Branksome Farm that J. and I took up our abode and commenced a course of steady reading, tempered and varied by long walks about the country. Our time passed pleasantly and profitably, and we discovered one day with regret that more than half of it had elapsed. Dismayed at this discovery we began to set our wits to work to find an excuse for prolonging our stay at Branksome, when suddenly an event happened which entirely altered our plans.

Returning one day from our accustomed walk, J. found a telegram waiting for him, which called him to London without delay and the contents of which appeared to indicate the probability of his being unable to return to Branksome. No time was to be lost in making a start if he was to catch the afternoon train at Willingbury and, as it was really quicker to walk across the Down than to drive round the roads behind Mr. Harkness' rather slow old mare, he threw a few clothes hastily into a bag and departed for the station. I accompanied him to see him off and we made the best possible speed to Willingbury. But we had miscalculated the time; the afternoon train had gone, and we found on inquiry that there would be no other until the night mail for London, which passed through Willingbury shortly before 11 p.m.

J. urged me not to wait for this but to leave him at the little inn and go back to Branksome before dark, but I was anxious to keep him company and cheer up his rather depressed spirits, so finally we agreed to dine together at the *Blue Lion* and spend the evening there until the train left. I was perfectly confident in my ability to find my way back over the Down to Branksome at night, as the path was very familiar to us, and I expected to be aided by the light of the moon which would rise about ten o'clock. In due course the train arrived, and having seen J. safely on his way to London I turned my steps towards the Willingbury-Overbury road and its junction with the Branksome sheeptrack.

It was a little after 11 p.m. when I left Willingbury on my homeward way, and I was disappointed to find that the moon had failed me, being completely hidden behind a thick canopy of cloud. The night was profoundly still as well as being very dark, but I was confident in my powers of finding my way and I strode contentedly along the road till I reached the point where it was necessary I should diverge on to the Down. I found the commencement of the sheep-track without difficulty, as my eyes were now accustomed to the surrounding obscurity, and set myself to climbing the Down as quickly as possible.

I must make it clear that up to the present time I had been in my usual state of health and spirits, although the latter were somewhat depressed at J.'s sudden departure and the break up of our pleasant association together. Up to this night, also, I had never in the least suspected that I was possessed of any special psychic intelligence. It is true that I had known that I was in the habit of occasionally dreaming very vividly and consecutively, but I had never given this faculty a serious thought, nor, like most young men in their twenties, had I ever given any consideration to psychic matters. It must be remembered also that I am writing of nearly forty years ago, when an intelligent interest in the potentialities of unseen beings and kindred topics was far less common than it is to-day.

Well, I commenced my ascent of the hill, and I had not gone very far when I became aware of a certain peculiar change taking place in myself. I fear I shall find it very difficult to describe my sensations in a fashion intelligible to those who have never experienced anything similar, whilst to those who have undergone psychic ordeals my description will probably appear bald and inadequate.

I seemed to be in some mysterious fashion divided into a dual personality. One, the familiar one, was myself, my body, which continued to walk up the sheep-track, keenly alive to the need to keep a sharp look out against losing my way or stumbling over some obstruction. This personality also felt loneliness and a certain degree of nervousness. The darkness, silence and immensity of the empty country round me were oppressive. I feared something, I was not quite sure what, and I anxiously wished I was at the end of my journey with the farm lights shining out to welcome me. My other personality was more vague and ill-defined; it seemed to be separated from my body and from my outer consciousness and to be floating in a region where there was neither space nor time. It seemed to be aware of another world, a world surrounding and intermingling with this one, in which all that is or was or will be was but one moment and in which all places near or far, the Down and the remotest of the invisible stars, were but one spot. All was instantaneous and all was eternal. I am not clear how long this mood lasted, but it was probably only a few minutes before my earthly self was brought or appeared to be brought into entire control of my personality by a sudden shock.

As I walked I became aware that I was not alone. There was a man moving parallel with me on my right at the distance of some four or five yards. So suddenly and so silently had he appeared that he seemed to have risen from the earth. He was walking quite quietly at my own pace abreast of me, but apparently taking no notice of me, and I observed that his footsteps made no sound on the soft turf. The dim light made it difficult to see him at all distinctly, but he was evidently a tall, powerfully built fellow, dressed in a long cloak, which, partly covering his face, fell nearly to his feet. On his head he wore a queer-shaped, three-cornered hat and in his hand he carried what appeared to be a short, heavy bludgeon.

I was greatly startled. I am a small and by no means robust man and the apparition of this odd-looking stranger on these lonely Downs was disquieting. What did he want? Had he followed me down the road from Willingbury, and, if so, for what purpose? However, I decided it was best not to appear alarmed and after taking another glance at the man, I wished him good evening.

He took not the faintest notice of my salutation, which he appeared not even to have heard, but continued to advance up the hill by my side in dead silence.

After a few moments I spoke again; and this time my voice sounded strange in my own ears, as if it did not come from my lips, but from somewhere far away.

"A dark night," I said.

And now he answered. In a slow, measured voice, but one in which there sounded a note of hopelessness and misery, he said:

"It is dark to you. It is darker for me."

I scarcely knew what to reply, but I felt that my courage was at an ebb and that I must maintain it by endeavouring to keep up a conversation, difficult though this might prove. Accordingly I went on:

"This is a strange place to walk in at night. Have you far to go?"

He did not turn his head or look at me.

"Your way is short and easy, but mine is long and hard. How long, O Lord, how long?" he cried. As he uttered the last words his voice rose to a cry and he tossed his arms above his head, letting them fall to his side with a gesture of despair.

We had now almost reached the top of the Down, and as we neared the summit I became aware that the wind was rising. At the moment we were sheltered from it by the brow of the hill, but I could hear its distant roaring, and as we reached the summit it broke upon us with a rush.

With it and mingled in its sounds came other sounds, the sounds of human voices, of many voices, in many keys. There were sounds of wailing, of shouting, of chanting, of sobbing, even at times of laughter. The great, shallow bowl of Branksome Down was alive with sounds. I could see nothing, save my strange companion, who continued to move steadily forward; and I, dreading his company and yet dreading even more to be left alone, accompanied him. The night was still profoundly dark and, though as I advanced the voices often sounded quite near, I saw nothing until after we had passed the centre of the depression and were mounting the opposite slope. At that moment the wind tore aside the clouds and the moon streamed down full upon the Downs. By her light I saw a marvellous and a terrifying sight. The whole of Branksome Down was alive with people hurrying hither and thither, some busy and absorbed in their occupations, whatever they might be, others roaming aimlessly and tossing their arms into the air with wild and tragic gesticulations. The crowd appeared to be of all sorts and conditions and to be dressed in the fashions of all the ages, though ancient costumes seemed to predominate. Here I saw a group of persons clothed apparently in the priestly robes of ancient Britain; there walked a soldier wearing the eagle-crested helmet of Rome. Other groups there were in dresses of later date, the steel-clad knight of the Middle Ages, the picturesque dress and flowing hair of a cavalier of the Seventeenth Century. But it was impossible to fix the shifting crowd. As I gazed, absorbed, at one figure, it melted and was gone and another took its place, to fade likewise as I watched.

My companion paid no heed to the throng. Steadily he passed on towards the crest of the hill, at intervals raising his arms and letting them fall with his old gesture of despair and uttering at the same time time his mournful cry of "How long, how long?"

We passed onward and upward and reached the top of the Down, my companion now a few yards in front of me. As he reached the crest of the hill, he stopped and, lifting his arms above his head, stood motionless. Suddenly he wavered, his figure expanded, its lines became vague and blurred against the background, it faded and was gone. As it vanished the wind dropped suddenly, the sound of human voices ceased and gazing round me I saw the plain bare and still in the moonlight.

I was now at the top of the hill, and looking downwards I saw a light burning in a window of Branksome Farm. I stumbled down the hill in haste, and as I approached the house saw Mr. Harkness standing at the open door. He looked at me strangely as I entered.

"Have you come across Branksome Down to-night," he exclaimed, "to-night of all the nights in the year?"

"Yes," I replied.

"I should have warned you," he said, "but I expected you back before dark. Branksome Down is an ill place to-night and men have vanished upon it before now and never been heard of again. No shepherd will set foot upon it to-night, for this is the night in the year when, folk say, all those that ever died violent deaths upon the Downs come back to seek their lost rest."

FITZ-JAMES O'BRIEN
The Pot of Tulips

Fitz-James O'Brien (1826?–62), *Irish-born son of a lawyer, emigrated in 1852 to the United States, where he soon became the leading American writer of horror stories in the period immediately following the death of Edgar Allan Poe. His most reprinted tales have been "The Diamond Lens", "The Wondersmith", and "What Was It?"; less familiar is his traditional ghost story, one of the best of the Victorian era, "The Pot of Tulips" (1855).*

Twenty-eight years ago I went to spend the summer at an old Dutch villa which then lifted its head from the wild country that, in present days, has been tamed down into a site for a Crystal Palace. Madison Square was then a wilderness of fields and scrub oak, here and there diversified with tall and stately elms. Worthy citizens who could afford two establishments rusticated in the groves that then flourished where ranks of brown-stone porticos now form the landscape; and the locality of Fortieth Street, where my summer palace stood, was justly looked upon as at an enterprising distance from the city.

I had an imperious desire to live in this house ever since I can remember. I had often seen it when a boy, and its cool verandas and quaint garden seemed, whenever I passed, to attract me irresistibly. In after years, when I grew up to man's estate, I was not sorry, therefore, when one summer, fatigued with the labours of my business, I beheld a notice in the papers intimating that it was to be let furnished. I hastened to my dear friend, Jaspar Joyce, painted the delights of this rural retreat in the most glowing colours, easily obtained his assent to share the enjoyments and the expense with me, and a month afterward we were taking our ease in this new paradise.

Independent of early associations, other interests attached me to this house. It was somewhat historical, and had given shelter to George Washington on the occasion of one of his visits to

424

the city. Furthermore, I knew the descendants of the family to whom it had originally belonged. Their history was strange and mournful, and it seemed to me as if their individuality was somehow shared by the edifice. It had been built by a Mr Van Koeren, a gentleman of Holland, the younger son of a rich mercantile firm at the Hague, who had emigrated to this country in order to establish a branch of his father's business in New York, which even then gave indications of the prosperity it has since reached with such marvellous rapidity. He had brought with him a fair young Belgian wife; a loving girl, if I may believe her portrait, with soft brown eyes, chestnut hair, and a deep, placid contentment spreading over her fresh and innocent features. Her son, Alain Van Koeren, had her picture—an old miniature in a red gold frame—as well as that of his father; and in truth, when looking on the two, one could not conceive a greater contrast than must have existed between husband and wife. Mr Van Koeren must have been a man of terrible will and gloomy temperament. His face—in the picture—is dark and austere, his eyes deep-sunken, and burning as if with a slow, inward fire. The lips are thin and compressed, with much determination of purpose; and his chin, boldly salient, is brimful of power and resolution. When first I saw those two pictures I sighed inwardly and thought, "Poor child! you must often have sighed for the sunny meadows of Brussels, in the long, gloomy nights spent in the company of that terrible man!"

I was not far wrong, as I afterward discovered. Mr and Mrs Van Koeren were very unhappy. Jealousy was his monomania, and he had scarcely been married before his girl-wife began to feel the oppression of a gloomy and ceaseless tyranny. Every man under fifty, whose hair was not white and whose form was erect, was an object of suspicion to this Dutch Bluebeard. Not that he was vulgarly jealous. He did not frown at his wife before strangers, or attack her with reproaches in the midst of her festivities. He was too well-bred a man to bare his private woes to the world. But at night, when the guests had departed and the dull light of the quaint old Flemish lamps but half illuminated the nuptial chamber, then it was that with monotonous invective Mr Van Koeren crushed his wife. And Marie, weeping and silent, would sit on the edge of the bed listening to the cold, trenchant irony of her husband, who, pacing up and down the room, would now and then stop in his walk to gaze with his burning eyes upon the pallid face of his victim. Even the evidences that Marie gave of becoming a mother did not check him. He saw in that coming event, which most husbands anticipate with mingled joy and fear, only an approaching incarnation of his dishonour. He watched with a horrible refinement of suspicion for the arrival of that being in whose features he madly believed he should but too surely trace the evidences of his wife's crime.

Whether it was that these ceaseless attacks wore out her strength, or that Providence wished to add another chastening misery to her burden of woe, I dare not speculate; but it is certain that one luckless night Mr Van Koeren learned with fury that he had become a father two months before the allotted time. During his first paroxysm of rage, on the receipt of intelligence which seemed to confirm all his previous suspicions, it was, I believe, with difficulty that he was prevented from slaying both the innocent causes of his resentment. The caution of his race and the presence of the physicians induced him, however, to put a curb upon his furious will until reflection suggested quite as criminal, if not as dangerous, a vengeance. As soon as his poor wife had recovered from her illness, unnaturally prolonged by the delicacy of constitution induced by previous mental suffering, she was astonished to find, instead of increasing his persecutions, that her husband had changed his tactics and treated her with studied neglect. He rarely spoke to her except on occasions when the decencies of society demanded that he should address her. He avoided her presence, and no longer inhabited the same apartments. He seemed, in short, to strive as much as possible to forget her existence. But if she did not suffer from personal ill-treatment it was because a punishment more acute was in store for her. If Mr Van Koeren had chosen to affect to consider her beneath his vengeance, it was because his hate had taken another direction, and seemed to have derived increased intensity from the alteration. It was upon the unhappy boy, the cause of all this misery, that the father lavished a terrible hatred. Mr Van Koeren seemed determined, that, if this child sprang from other loins than his, the mournful destiny which he forced upon him should amply avenge his own existence and the infidelity of his mother. While the child was an infant his plan seemed to have been formed. Ignorance and neglect were the two deadly influences with which he sought to assassinate the moral nature of this boy; and his terrible campaign against the virtue of his own son was, as he grew up, carried into execution with the most consummate generalship. He gave him money, but debarred him from education. He allowed him liberty of action, but withheld advice. It was in vain that his mother, who foresaw the frightful consequences of such a training, sought in secret by every means in her power to nullify her husband's attempts. She strove in vain to seduce her son into an ambition to be educated. She beheld with horror all her agonized efforts frustrated, and saw her son and only child becoming, even in his youth, a drunkard and a libertine. In the end it proved too much for her strength; she sickened, and went home to her sunny Belgian plains. There she lingered for a few months in a calm but rapid decay, whose calmness was broken but by the one grief; until one autumn day, when the leaves were falling from the limes, she made a little prayer for her son to the good God, and died. Vain orison! Spendthrift, gamester, libertine, and drunkard by turns, Alain Van Koeren's earthly destiny was unchangeable. The father, who should have been his guide, looked on each fresh depravity of his son's with a species of grin delight. Even the death of his wronged wife had no effect upon his fatal purpose. He still permitted the young man to run blindly to destruction by the course into which he himself had led him.

As years rolled by, and Mr Van Koeren himself approached to that time of life when he might soon expect to follow his persecuted wife, he relieved himself of the hateful presence of his son altogether. Even the link of a systematic vengeance, which had hitherto united them, was severed, and Alain was cast adrift without either money or principle. The occasion of this final separation between father and son was the marriage of the latter with a girl of humble, though honest extraction. This was a good excuse for the remorseless Van Koeren, so he availed himself of it by turning his son out of doors. From that time forth they never met. Alain lived a life of meagre dissipation, and soon died, leaving behind him one child, a daughter. By a coincidence natural enough, Mr Van Koeren's death followed his son's almost immediately. He died as he had lived, sternly. But those who were around his couch in his last moments mentioned some singular facts connected with the manner of his death. A few moments before he expired, he raised himself in the bed, and seemed as if conversing with some person invisible to the spectators. His lips moved as if in speech, and immediately afterward he sank back, bathed in a flood of tears. "Wrong! wrong!" he was heard to mutter, feebly; then he implored passionately the forgiveness of some one who, he said, was present. The death struggle ensued almost immediately, and in the midst of his agony he seemed wrestling for speech. All that could be heard, however, were a few broken words. "I was wrong. My—unfounded—For God's sake look in—You will find—" Having uttered these fragmentary sentences, he seemed to feel that the power of speech had passed away forever. He fixed his eyes piteously on those around him, and, with a great sigh of grief, expired. I gathered these facts from his granddaughter and Alain's daughter, Alice Van Koeren, who had been summoned by some friend to her grandfather's dying couch when it was too late. It was the first time she had seen him, and then she saw him die.

The results of Mr Van Koeren's death were a nine days' wonder to all the merchants in New York. Beyond a small sum in the bank, and the house in which he lived, which was mortgaged for its full value, Mr Van Koeren had died a pauper! To those who knew him and knew his affairs, this seemed inexplicable. Five or six years before his death he had retired from business with a fortune of several hundred thousand dollars. He had lived quietly since then,—was known not to have speculated, and could not have gambled. The question then was, where had his wealth vanished to. Search was made in every secretary, in every bureau, for some document which might throw a light on the mysterious disposition that he had made of his property. None was found. Neither will, nor certificates of stock, nor title deeds, nor bank accounts, were anywhere discernible. Inquiries were made at the offices of companies in which Mr Van Koeren was known to be largely interested; he had sold out his stock years ago. Real estate that had been believed to be his was found on investigation to have passed into other hands. There could be no doubt that for some years past Mr Van Koeren had been steadily converting all his property into money, and what he had done with that money no one knew. Alice Van Koeren and her mother, who at the old gentleman's death were at first looked on as millionaires, discovered, when all was over, that they were no better off than before. It was evident that the old man, determined that one whom, though bearing his name, he believed not to be of his blood, should never inherit his wealth or any share of it, had made away with his fortune before his death—a posthumous vengeance which was the only one by which the laws of the State of New York relative to inheritance could be successfully evaded.

I took a peculiar interest in the case, and even helped to make some researches for the lost property, not so much, I confess, from a spirit of general philanthropy, as from certain feelings which I experienced toward Alice Van Koeren, the heir to this invisible estate. I had long known both her and her mother, when they were living in honest poverty and earning a scanty subsistence by their own labor; Mrs Van Koeren working as an embroideress, and Alice turning to account, as a preparatory governess, the education which her good mother, spite of her limited means, had bestowed on her.

In a few words, then, I loved Alice Van Koeren, and was determined to make her my wife as soon as my means would allow me to support a fitting establishment. My passion had never been declared. I was content for the time with the secret consciousness of my own love, and the no less grateful certainty that Alice returned it, all unuttered as it was. I had, therefore, a double interest in passing the summer at the old Dutch villa, for I felt it to be connected somehow with Alice, and I could not forget the singular desire to inhabit it which I had so often experienced as a boy.

It was a lovely day in June when Jasper Joyce and myself took up our abode in our new residence; and as we smoked our cigars on the piazza in the evening we felt for the first time the unalloyed pleasure with which a townsman breathes the pure air of the country.

The house and grounds had a quaint sort of beauty that to me was eminently pleasing. Landscape gardening, in the modern acceptation of the term, was then almost unknown in this country, and the "laying out" of the garden that surrounded our new home would doubtless have shocked Mr Loudon, the late Mr Downing, or Sir Thomas Dick Lauder. It was formal and artificial to the last degree. The beds were cut into long parallelograms, rigid and severe of aspect, and edged with prim rows of stiff dwarf box. The walks, of course, crossed always at right angles, and the laurel and cypress trees that grew here and there were clipped into cones, and spheres, and rhomboids. It is true that, at the time my friend and I hired the house, years of neglect had restored to this formal garden somewhat of the raggedness of nature. The box edgings were rank and wild. The clipped trees, forgetful of geometric propriety, flourished into unauthorized boughs and rebel offshoots. The walks were green with moss, and the beds of Dutch tulips, which had been planted in the shape of certain gorgeous birds, whose colours were represented by masses of blossoms, each of a single hue, had transgressed their limits, and the purple of a parrot's wings might have been seen running recklessly into the crimson of his head; while, as bulbs, however well-bred, will create other bulbs, the flower-birds of this queer old Dutch garden became in time abominably distorted in shape;—flamingoes with humps, golden pheasants with legs preternaturally elongated, macaws afflicted with hydrocephalus—each species of deformity being proportioned to the rapidity with which the roots had spread in some particular direction. Still, this strange mixture of raggedness and formality, this conglomerate of nature and art, had its charms. It was pleasant to watch the struggle, as it were, between the opposing elements, and to see nature triumphing by degrees in every direction.

The house itself was pleasant and commodious. Rooms that, though not lofty, were spacious; wide windows, and cool piazzas extending over the four sides of the building; and a collection of antique carved furniture, some of which, from its elaborateness, might well have come from the chisel of Master Grinling Gibbons. There was a mantelpiece in the dining-room, with which I remember being very much struck when first I came to take possession. It was a singular and fantastical piece of carving. It was a perfect tropical garden, menagerie, and aviary, in one. Birds, beasts, and flowers were sculptured on the wood with exquisite correctness of detail, and painted with the hues of nature. The Dutch taste for colour was here fully gratified. Parrots, love-birds, scarlet lories, blue-faced baboons, crocodiles, passion-flowers, tigers, Egyptian lilies, and Brazilian butterflies, were all mixed in gorgeous confusion. The artist, whoever he was, must have been an admirable naturalist, for the ease and freedom of his carving were only equalled by the wonderful accuracy with which the different animals were represented. Altogether it was one of those oddities of Dutch conception, whose strangeness was in this instance redeemed by the excellence of the execution.

Such was the establishment that Jasper Joyce and myself were to inhabit for the summer months.

"What a strange thing it was," said Jasper, as we lounged on the piazza together the night of our arrival, "that old Van Koeren's property should never have turned up!"

"It is a question with some people whether he had any at his death," I answered.

"Pshaw! every one knows that he did not or could not have lost that with which he retired from business."

"It is strange," said I, thoughtfully; "yet possible search has been made for documents that might throw light on the mystery. I have myself sought in every quarter for traces of this lost wealth, but in vain."

"Perhaps he buried it," suggested Jasper, laughing; "if so, we may find it here in a hole one fine morning."

"I think it much more likely that he destroyed it," I replied. "You know he never could be got to believe that Alain Van Koeren was his son, and I believe him quite capable of having flung all his money into the sea in order to prevent those whom he considered not of his blood inheriting it, which they must have done under our laws."

"I am sorry that Alice did not become a heriess, both for your sake and hers. She is a charming girl."

Jasper, from whom I concealed nothing, knew of my love.

"As to that," I answered, "it is little matter. I shall in a year or two be independent enough to marry, and can afford to let Mr Van Koeren's cherished gold sleep wherever he has concealed it."

"Well, I'm off to bed," said Jasper, yawning. "This country air makes one sleepy early. Be on the lookout for trap-doors and all that sort of thing, old fellow. Who knows but the old chap's dollars will turn up. Good night!"

"Good night, Jasper!"

So we parted for the night. He to his room, which lay on the west side of the building; I to mine on the east, situated at the end of a long corridor and exactly opposite to Jasper's.

The night was very still and warm. The clearness with which I heard the song of the katydid and the croak of the bull-frog seemed to make the silence more distinct. The air was dense and breathless, and, although longing to throw wide my windows, I dared not; for, outside, the ominous trumpetings of an army of mosquitoes sounded threateningly.

I tossed on my bed oppressed with the heat; kicked the sheets into every spot where they ought not to be; turned my pillow every two minutes in the hope of finding a cool side;—in short did, everything that a man does when he lies awake on a very hot night and cannot open his window.

Suddenly, in the midst of my miseries, and when I had made up my mind to fling open the casement in spite of the legion of mosquitoes that I knew were hungrily waiting outside, I felt a continuous stream of cold air blowing upon my face. Luxurious as the sensation was, I could not help starting as I felt it. Where could this draught come from? The door was closed; so were the windows. It did not come from the direction of the fireplace, and, even if it did, the air without was too still to produce so strong a current. I rose in my bed and gazed round the room, the whole of which, though only lit by a dim twilight, was still sufficiently visible. I thought at first it was a trick of Jasper's, who might have provided himself with a bellows or a long tube; but a careful investigation of the apartment convinced me that no one was present. Besides, I had locked the door, and it was not likely that any one had been concealed in the room before I entered it. It was exceedingly strange; but still the draught of cool wind blew on my face and chest, every now and then changing its direction—sometimes on one side, sometimes on the other. I am not constitutionally nervous, and had been too long accustomed to reflect on philosophical subjects to become the prey of fear in the presence of mysterious phenomena. I had devoted much time to the investigation of what are popularly called supernatural matters, by those who have not reflected or examined sufficiently to discover that none of these apparent miracles are *super*-natural, but all, however singular, directly dependent on certain natural laws. I became speedily convinced, therefore, as I sat up in my bed peering into the dim recesses of my chamber, that this mysterious wind was the effect of forerunner of a supernatural visitation, and I mentally determined to investigate it, as it developed itself, with a philosophical calmness.

"Is any one in this room?" I asked, as distinctly as I could. No reply; while the cool wind still swept over my cheek. I knew, in the case of Elizabeth Eslinger, who was visited by an apparition while in the Weinsberg jail, and whose singular and apparently authentic experiences were made the subject of a book by Dr Kerner, that the manifestation of the spirit was invariably accompanied by such a breezy sensation as I now experienced. I therefore gathered my will, as it were, into a focus, and endeavored, as much as lay in my power, to put myself in accord with the disembodied spirit, if such there were, knowing that on such conditions alone would it be enabled to manifest itself to me.

Presently it seemed as if a luminous cloud was gathering in one corner of the room—a sort of dim phosphoric vapour, shadowy and ill-defined. It changed its position frequently, sometimes coming nearer and at others retreating to the furthest end of the room. As it grew intenser and more radiant, I observed a sickening and corpse-like odour diffuse itself through the chamber, and, despite my anxiety to witness this phenomenon undisturbed, I could with difficulty conquer a feeling of faintness which oppressed me.

The luminous cloud now began to grow brighter and brighter as I gazed. The horrible odour of which I have spoken did not cease to oppress me, and gradually I could discover certain lines making themselves visible in the midst of this lambent radiance. These lines took the form of a human figure—a tall man, clothed in a long dressing-robe, with a pale countenance, burning eyes, and a very bold and prominent chin. At a glance I recognized the original of the picture of old Van Koeren that I had seen with Alice. My interest was now aroused to the highest point; I felt that I stood face to face with a spirit, and doubted not that I should learn the fate of the old man's mysteriously concealed wealth.

The spirit presented a very strange appearance. He himself was not luminous, except some tongues of fire that seemed to proceed from the tips of his fingers, but was completely surrounded by a thin gauze of light, so to speak, through which his outlines were visible. His head was bare, and his white hair fell in huge masses around his stern, saturnine face. As he moved on the floor, I distinctly heard a strange crackling sound, such as one hears when a substance has been overcharged with electricity. But the circumstance that seemed to me most incomprehensible connected with the apparition was that Van

Koeren held in both hands a curiously painted flower-pot, out of which sprang a number of the most beautiful tulips in full blossom. He seemed very uneasy and agitated, and moved about the room as if in pain, frequently bending over the pot of tulips as if to inhale their odour, then holding it out to me, seemingly in the hope of attracting my attention to it. I was, I confess, very much puzzled. I knew that Mr Van Koeren had in his lifetime devoted much of his leisure to the cultivation of flowers, importing from Holland the most expensive and rarest bulbs; but how this innocent fancy could trouble him after death I could not imagine. I felt assured, however, that some important reason lay at the bottom of this spectral eccentricity, and determined to fathom it if I could.

"What brings you here?" I asked audibly; directing mentally, however, at the same time, the question to the spirit with all the power of my will. He did not seem to hear me, but still kept moving uneasily about, with the crackling noise I have mentioned, and holding the pot of tulips toward me.

"It is evident," I said to myself, "that I am not sufficiently in accord with this spirit for him to make himself understood by speech. He has, therefore, recourse to symbols. The pot of tulips is a symbol. But of what?"

Thus reflecting on these things I continued to gaze upon the spirit. While observing him attentively, he approached my bedside by a rapid movement, and laid one hand on my arm. The touch was icy cold, and pained me at the moment. Next morning my arm was swollen, and marked with a round blue spot. Then, passing to my bedroom-door, the spirit opened it and went out, shutting it behind him. Catching for a moment at the idea that I was the dupe of a trick, I jumped out of bed and ran to the door. It was locked with the key on the inside, and a brass safety-bolt, which lay above the lock, shot safely home. All was as I had left it on going to bed. Yet I declare most solemnly, that, as the ghost made his exit, I not only saw the door open, but *I saw the corridor outside, and distinctly observed a large picture of William of Orange that hung just opposite to my room*. This to me was the most curious portion of the phenomena I had witnessed. Either the door had been opened by the ghost, and the resistance of physical obstacles overcome in some amazing manner—because in this case the bolts must have been replaced when the ghost was *outside* the door—or he must have had a sufficient magnetic accord with my mind to impress upon it the belief that the door was opened, and also to conjure up in my brain the vision of the corridor and the picture, features that I should have seen if the door had been opened by any ordinary physical agency.

The next morning at breakfast I suppose my manner must have betrayed me, for Jasper said to me, after staring at me for some time, "Why, Harry Escott, what's the matter with you? You look as if you had seen a ghost!"

"So I have, Jasper."

Jasper, of course, burst into laughter, and said he'd shave my head and give me a shower-bath.

"Well, you may laugh," I answered; "but you shall see it to-night, Jasper."

He became serious in a moment—I suppose there was something earnest in my manner that convinced him that my words were not idle—and asked me to explain. I described my interview as accurately as I could.

"How did you know that it was old Van Koeren?" he asked.

"Because I have seen his picture a hundred times with Alice," I answered, "and this apparition was as like it as it was possible for a ghost to be like a miniature."

"You must not think I'm laughing at you, Harry," he continued, "but I wish you would answer this. We have all heard of ghosts—ghosts of men, women, children, dogs, horses, in fact every living animal; but hang me if ever I heard of the ghost of a flower-pot before."

"My dear Jasper, you would have heard of such things if you had studied such branches of learning. All the phenomena I witnessed last night are supportable by well-authenticated facts. The cool wind has attended the appearance of more than one ghost, and Baron Reichenbach asserts that his patients, who you know are for the most part sensitive to apparitions, invariably feel this wind when a magnet is brought close to their bodies. With regard to the flower-pot about which you make so merry, it is to me the least wonderful portion of the apparition. When a ghost is unable to find a person of sufficient receptivity, in order to communicate with him by speech it is obliged to have recourse to symbols to express its wishes. These it either creates by some mysterious power out of the surrounding atmosphere, or it impresses, by magnetic force on the mind of the person it visits, the form of the symbol it is anxious to have represented. There is an instance mentioned by Jung Stilling of a student at Brunswick, who appeared to a professor of his college, with a picture in his hands, which picture had a hole in it that the ghost thrust his head through. For a long time this symbol was a mystery; but the student was persevering, and appeared every night with his head through the picture, until at last it was discovered that, before he died, he had got some painted slides for a magic lantern from a shopkeeper in the town, which had not been paid for at his death; and when the debt had been discharged, he and his picture vanished forevermore. Now here was a symbol distinctly bearing on the question at issue. This poor student could find no better way of expressing his uneasiness at the debt for the painted slides than by thrusting his head through a picture. How he conjured up the picture I cannot pretend to explain, but that it was used as a symbol is evident."

"Then you think the flower-pot of old Van Koeren is a symbol?"

"Most assuredly, the pot of tulips he held was intended to express that which he could not speak. I think it must have had some reference to his missing property, and it is our business to discover in what manner."

"Let us go and dig up all the tulip beds," said Jasper, "who knows but he may have buried his money in one of them?"

I grieve to say that I assented to Jasper's proposition, and on that eventful day every tulip in that quaint old garden was ruthlessly uprooted. The gorgeous macaws, and ragged parrots, and long-legged pheasants, so cunningly formed by those brilliant flowers, were that day exterminated. Jasper and I had a regular *battue* amidst this floral preserve, and many a splendid bird fell before our unerring spades. We, however, dug in vain. No secret coffer turned up out of the deep mould of the flower-beds. We evidently were not on the right scent. Our researches for that day terminated, and Jasper and myself waited impatiently for the night.

It was arranged that Jasper should sleep in my room. I had a bed rigged up for him near my own, and I was to have the additional assistance of his senses in the investigation of the phenomena that we so confidently expected to appear.

The night came. We retired to our respective couches, after carefully bolting the doors, and subjecting the entire apartment to the strictest scrutiny, rendering it totally impossible that a secret entrance should exist unknown to us. We then put out the lights, and awaited the apparition.

We did not remain in suspense long. About twenty minutes after we retired to bed, Jasper called out, "Harry, I feel the cool wind!"

"So do I," I answered, for at that moment a light breeze seemed to play across my temples.

"Look, look, Harry!" continued Jasper in a tone of painful eagerness, "I see a light—there in the corner!"

It was the phantom. As before, the luminous cloud appeared to gather in the room, growing more and more intense each minute. Presently the dark lines mapped themselves out, as it were, in the midst of this pale, radiant vapour, and there stood Mr. Van Koeren, ghastly and mournful as ever, with the pot of tulips in his hands.

"Do you see it?" I asked Jasper.

"My God! yes," said Jasper, in a low voice. "How terrible he looks!"

"Can you speak to me, to-night?" I said, addressing the apparition, and again concentrating my will upon my question. "If so, unburden yourself. We will assist you, if we can."

There was no reply. The ghost preserved the same sad, impassive countenance; he had heard me not. He seemed in great distress on this occasion, moving up and down, and holding out the pot of tulips imploringly toward me, each motion of his being accompanied by the crackling noise and the corpse-like odour. I felt sorely troubled myself to see this poor spirit torn by an endless grief,—so anxious to communicate to me what lay on his soul, and yet debarred by some occult power from the privilege.

"Why, Harry," cried Jasper after a silence, during which we both watched the motions of the ghost intently, "why, Harry, my boy, there are *two* of them!"

Astonished by his words, I looked around, and became immediately aware of the presence of a second luminous cloud, in the midst of which I could distinctly trace the figure of a pale but lovely woman. I needed no second glance to assure me that it was the unfortunate wife of Van Koeren.

"It is his wife, Jasper," I replied; "I recognize her, as I have recognized her husband, by the portrait."

"How sad she looks!" exclaimed Jasper in a low voice.

She did indeed look sad. Her face, pale and mournful, did not, however, seem convulsed with sorrow, as was her husband's. She seemed to be oppressed with a calm grief, and gazed with a look of interest that was painful in its intensity, on Van Koeren. It struck me, from his air, that, though she saw him, he did not see her. His whole attention was concentrated on the pot of tulips, while Mrs. Van Koeren, who floated at an elevation of about three feet from the floor, and thus overtopped her husband, seemed equally absorbed in the contemplation of his slightest movement. Occasionally she would turn her eyes on me, as if to call my attention to her companion, and then, returning, gaze on him with a sad, womanly, half-eager smile, that to me was inexpressibly mournful.

There was something exceedingly touching in this strange sight;—these two spirits so near, yet so distant. The sinful husband torn with grief and weighed down with some terrible secret, and so blinded by the grossness of his being as to be unable to see the wife-angel who was watching over him; while she, forgetting all her wrongs, and attracted to earth by perhaps the same human sympathies, watched from a greater spiritual height, and with a tender interest, the struggles of her suffering spouse.

"By Jove!" exclaimed Jasper, jumping from his bed, "I know what it means now."

"What does it mean?" I asked, as eager to know as he was to communicate.

"Well, that flower-pot that the old chap is holding—" Jasper, I grieve to say, was rather profane.

"Well, what of that flower-pot?"

"Observe the pattern. It has two handles made of red snakes, whose tails twist round the top and form a rim. It contains tulips of three colours, yellow, red, and purple."

"I see all that as well as you do. Let us have the solution."

"Well, Harry, my boy! don't you remember that there is just such a flower-pot, tulips, snakes and all, carved on the queer old painted mantelpiece in the dining-room."

"So there is!" and a gleam of hope shot across my brain, and my heart beat quicker.

"Now as sure as you are alive, Harry, the old fellow has concealed something important behind that mantelpiece."

"Jasper, if ever I am Emperor of France, I will make you chief of police; your inductive reasoning is magnificent."

Actuated by the same impulse, and without another word, we both sprang out of bed and lit a candle. The apparitions, if they remained, were no longer visible in the light. Hastily throwing on some clothes, we rushed down stairs to the dining-room, determined to have the old mantelpiece down without loss of time. We had scarce entered the room when we felt the cool wind blowing on our faces.

"Jasper," said I, "they are here!"

"Well," answered Jasper, "that only confirms my suspicions that we are on the right track this time. Let us go to work. See! here's the pot of tulips."

This pot of tulips occupied the centre of the mantelpiece, and served as a nucleus round which all the fantastic animals sculptured elsewhere might be said to gather. It was carved on a species of raised shield, or boss, of wood, that projected some inches beyond the plane of the remainder of the mantel-piece. The pot itself was painted a brick colour. The snakes were of bronze colour, gilt, and the tulips—yellow, red, and purple—were painted after nature with the most exquisite accuracy.

For some time Jasper and myself tugged away at this projection without any avail. We were convinced that it was a movable panel of some kind, but yet were totally unable to move it. Suddenly it struck me that we had not yet twisted it. I immediately proceeded to apply all my strength, and after a few seconds of vigorous exertion I had the satisfaction of finding it move slowly round. After giving it half a dozen turns, to my astonishment the long upper panel of the mantelpiece fell out toward us, apparently on concealed hinges, after the manner of the portion of escritoires that is used as a writing-table. Within were several square cavities sunk in the wall, and lined with wood. In one of these was a bundle of papers.

We seized these papers with avidity, and hastily glanced over them. They proved to be documents vouching for property to the amount of several hundred thousand dollars, invested in the name of Mr. Van Koeren in a certain firm at Bremen, who, no doubt, thought by this time that the money would remain unclaimed forever. The desires of these poor troubled spirits were accomplished. Justice to the child had been given through the instrumentality of the erring father.

439

The formulas necessary to prove Alice and her mother sole heirs to Mr. Van Koeren's estate were briefly gone through, and the poor governess passed suddenly from the task of teaching stupid children to the envied position of a great heiress. I had ample reason afterward for thinking that her heart did not change with her fortunes.

That Mr. Van Koeren became aware of his wife's innocence, just before he died, I have no doubt. How this was manifested I cannot of course say, but I think it highly probable that his poor wife herself was enabled at the critical moment of dissolution, when the link that binds body and soul together is attenuated to the last thread, to put herself in accord with her unhappy husband. Hence his sudden starting up in his bed, his apparent conversation with some invisible being, and his fragmentary disclosures, too broken, however, to be comprehended.

The question of apparitions has been so often discussed that I feel no inclination to enter here upon the truth or fallacy of the ghostly theory. I myself believe in ghosts. Alice—my wife—believes in them firmly; and if it suited me to do so I could overwhelm you with a scientific theory of my own on the subject, reconciling ghosts and natural phenomena.

VINCENT O'SULLIVAN
The Burned House

Vincent O'Sullivan (1868–1940) *is remembered chiefly today as the writer of* Aspects of Wilde *(1936), an excellent study of the 1890s literary scene. He contributed a large number of poems, essays, and short stories to* fin-de-siècle *periodicals, and wrote many strange and macabre tales which can be found in such collections as* A Book of Bargains *(1896; a very rare book which contains a frontispiece by Aubrey Beardsley) and* A Dissertation Upon Second Fiddles *(1902). "The Burned House", one of several later ghost stories by O'Sullivan which were never collected in book form, is taken from the Christmas number of the* Premier *magazine published at the end of 1916.*

O ne night at the end of dinner, the last time I crossed the Atlantic, somebody in our group remarked that we were just passing over the spot where the *Lusitania* had gone down. Whether this were the case or not, the thought of it was enough to make us rather grave, and we dropped into some more or less serious discussion about the emotions of men and women who see all hope gone, and realise that they are going to sink with the vessel.

From that the talk wandered to the fate of the drowned. Was not theirs, after all, a fortunate end? Somebody related details from the narratives of those who had been all-but drowned in the accident of the war. A Scotch lady inquired fancifully if the ghosts of those who are lost at sea ever appear above the waters and come aboard ships. Would there be danger of seeing one when the light was turned out in her cabin? This put an end to all seriousness, and most of us laughed. But a little, tight-faced man, bleak and iron-grey, who had been listening attentively, did not laugh. The lady noticed his decorum, and appealed to him for support.

"You are like me—you believe in ghosts!" she asked lightly.
He hesitated, thinking it over.

"In ghosts?" he repeated slowly. "N-no, I don't know as I do.
I've never had any personal experience that way. I've never seen
the ghost of anyone I knew. Has anybody here?"

No one replied. Instead, most of us laughed again—a little
uneasily, perhaps.

"All the same, strange enough things happen in life," resumed
the man, "even if you leave out ghosts, that you can't clear up by
laughing. You laugh till you've had some experience big enough
to shock you, and then you don't laugh any more. It's like being
thrown out of a car—"

At this moment there was a blast on the whistle, and
everybody rushed up on deck. As it turned out, we had only
entered into a belt of fog. On the upper deck I fell in again with
the little man, smoking a cigar and walking up and down. We
took a few turns together, and he referred to the conversation
at dinner. Our laughter evidently rankled in his mind.

"So many strange things happen in life that you can't account
for," he protested. "You go on laughing at faith-healing, and at
dreams, and this and that, and then something comes along that
you just can't explain. You have got to throw up your hands
and allow that it doesn't answer to any tests our experience has
provided us with. Now, I'm as matter-of-fact a man as any of
those folks down there; but once I had an experience which I
had to conclude was out of the ordinary. Whether other people
believe it or not, or whether they think they can explain it, don't
matter. It happened to me, and I could no more doubt it than
I could doubt having had a tooth pulled after the dentist had
done it. If you will sit down here with me in this corner, out of
the wind, I'll tell you how it was.

"Some years ago I had to be for several months in the North
of England. I was before the courts; it does not signify now what
for, and it is all forgotten by this time. But it was a long and
worrying case, and it aged me by twenty years. Well, sir, all
through the trial, in that grimy Manchester court-room, I kept
thinking and thinking of a fresh little place I knew in the Lake
district, and I helped to get through the hours by thinking that
if things went well with me I'd go there at once. And so it was
that on the very next morning after I was acquitted I boarded
the north-bound train.

"It was the early autumn; the days were closing in, and it was night and cold when I arrived. The village was very dark and deserted; they don't go out much after dark in those parts, anyhow, and the keen mountain wind was enough to quell any lingering desire. The hotel was not one of those modern places which are equipped and upholstered like the great city hotels. It was one of the real old-fashioned taverns, about as uncomfortable places as there are on earth, where the idea is to show the traveller that travelling is a penitential state, and that, morally and physically, the best place for him is home. The landlord brought me a kind of supper, with his hat on and a pipe in his mouth. The room was chilly, but when I asked for a fire, he said he guessed he couldn't go out to the woodshed till morning. There was nothing else to do, when I had eaten my supper, but to go outside, both to get the smell of the lamp out of my nose and to warm myself by a short walk.

"As I did not know the country well, I did not mean to go far. But although it was an overcast night, with a high north-east wind and an occasional flurry of rain, the moon was up, and, even concealed by clouds as it was, it yet lit the night with a kind of twilight grey—not vivid, like the open moonlight, but good enough to see some distance. On account of this, I prolonged my stroll, and kept walking on and on till I was a considerable way from the village, and in a region as lonely as anywhere in the country. Great trees and shrubs bordered the road, and many feet below was a mountain stream. What with the passion of the wind pouring through the high trees and the shout of the water racing among the boulders, it seemed to me sometimes like the noise of a crowd of people. Sometimes the branches of the trees became so thick that I was walking as if in a black pit, unable to see my hand close to my face. Then, coming out from the tunnel of branches, I would step once more into a grey clearness which opened the road and surrounding country a good way on all sides.

"I suppose it might be some three-quarters of an hour I had been walking when I came to a fork of the road. One branch ran downward, getting almost on a level with the bed of the torrent; the other mounted in a steep hill, and this, after a little idle debating, I decided to follow. After I had climbed for more than half a mile, thinking that if I should happen to lose track of one of the landmarks I should be very badly lost, the path—for it was now no more than that—curved, and I came out on a broad plateau. There, to my astonishment, I saw a house. It was a good-sized house, three storeys high, with a verandah round two sides of it, and from the elevation on which it stood it commanded a far stretch of country.

"There were a few great trees at a little distance from the house, and behind it, a stone's-throw away, was a clump of bushes. Still, it looked lonely and stark, offering its four sides unprotected to the winds. For all that, I was very glad to see it. 'It does not matter now,' I thought, 'whether I have lost my way or not. The people in the house will set me right.'

"But when I came up to it I found that it was, to all appearance, uninhabited. The shutters were closed on all the windows; there was not a spark of light anywhere. There was something about it, something sinister and barren, that gave me the kind of shiver you have at the door of a room where you know that a dead man lies inside, or if you get thinking hard about dropping over the rail into that black waste of waters out there. This feeling, you know, isn't altogether unpleasant; you relish all the better your present security. It was the same with me standing before that house. I was not *really* frightened. I was alone up there, miles from any kind of help, at the mercy of whoever might be lurking behind the shutters of that sullen house; but I felt that by all the chances I was perfectly alone and safe. My sensation of the uncanny was due to the effect on the nerves produced by wild scenery and the unexpected sight of a house in such a very lonely situation. Thus I reasoned, and, instead of following the road farther, I walked over the grass till I came to a stone wall, perhaps two hundred and fifty yards in front of the house, and rested my arms on it, looking forth at the scene.

"On the crests of the hills far away a strange light lingered, like the first touch of dawn in the sky on a rainy morning or the last glimpse of twilight before night comes. Between me and the hills was a wide stretch of open country. On my right hand was an apple orchard, and I observed that a stile had been made in the wall of piled stones to enable the house people to go back and forth.

"Now, after I had been there leaning on the wall some considerable time, I saw a man coming towards me through the orchard. He was walking with a good, free stride, and as he drew nearer I could see that he was a tall, sinewy fellow between twenty-five and thirty, with a shaven face, wearing a slouch hat, a dark woollen shirt, and gaiters. When he reached the stile and began climbing over it I bade him goodnight in neighbourly fashion. He made no reply, but he looked me straight in the face, and the look gave me a qualm. Not that it was an evil face, mind you—it was a handsome, serious face—but it was ravaged by some terrible passion: stealth was on it, ruthlessness, and a deadly resolution, and at the same time such a look as a man driven by some uncontrollable power might throw on surrounding things, asking for comprehension and mercy. It was impossible for me to resent his churlishness, his thoughts were so certainly elsewhere. I doubt if he even saw me.

"He could not have gone by more than a quarter of a minute when I turned to look after him. He had disappeared. The plateau lay bare before me, and it seemed impossible that, even if he had sprinted like an athlete, he could have got inside the house in so little time. But I have always made it a rule to attribute what I cannot understand to natural causes that I have failed to observe. I said to myself that no doubt the man had gone back into the orchard by some other opening in the wall lower down, or there might be some flaw in my vision owing to the uncertain and distorting light.

"But even as I continued to look towards the house, leaning my back now against the wall, I noticed that there were lights springing up in the windows behind the shutters. They were flickering lights, now bright—now dim, and had a ruddy glow like firelight. Before I had looked long I became convinced that it was indeed firelight—the house was on fire. Black smoke began to pour from the roof; the red sparks flew in the wind. Then at a window above the roof of the verandah the shutters were thrown open, and I heard a woman shriek. I ran towards the house as hard as I could, and when I drew near I could see her plainly.

"She was a young woman; her hair fell in disorder over her white nightgown. She stretched out her bare arms, screaming. I saw a man come behind and seize her. But they were caught in a trap. The flames were licking round the windows, and the smoke was killing them. Even now the part of the house where they stood was caving in.

"Appalled by this horrible tragedy which had thus suddenly risen before me, I made my way still nearer the house, thinking that if the two could struggle to the side of the house not bounded by the verandah they might jump, and I might break the fall. I was shouting this at them; I was right up close to the fire; and then I was struck by—I noticed for the first time an astonishing thing—the flames had no heat in them!

"I was standing near enough to the fire to be singed by it, and yet I felt no heat. The sparks were flying about my head; some fell on my hands, and they did not burn. And now I perceived that, although the smoke was rolling in columns, I was not choked by the smoke, and that there had been no smell of smoke since the fire broke out. Neither was there any glare against the sky.

"As I stood there stupefied, wondering how these things could be, the whole house was swept by a very tornado of flame, and crashed down in a red ruin.

"Stricken to the heart by this abominable catastrophe, I made my way uncertainly down the hill, shouting for help. As I came to a little wooden bridge spanning the torrent, just beyond where the roads forked, I saw what appeared to be a rope in loose coils lying there. I saw that part of it was fastened to the railing of the bridge and hung outside, and I looked over. There was a man's body swinging by the neck between the road and the stream. I leaned over still farther, and then I recognised him as the man I had seen coming out of the orchard. His hat had fallen off, and the toes of his boots just touched the water.

"It seemed hardly possible, and yet it was certain. That was the man, and he was hanging there. I scrambled down at the side of the bridge, and put out my hand to seize the body, so that I might lift it up and relieve the weight on the rope. I succeeded in clutching hold of his loose shirt, and for a second I thought that it had come away in my hand. Then I found that my hand had closed on nothing, I had clutched nothing but air. And yet the figure swung by the neck before my eyes!

"I was suffocated with such horror that I feared for a moment I must lose consciousness. The next minute I was running and stumbling along that dark road in mortal anxiety, my one idea being to rouse the town, and bring men to the bridge. That, I say, was my intention; but the fact is that when I came at last in sight of the village I slowed down instinctively and began to reflect. After all, I was unknown there; I had just gone through a disagreeable trial in Manchester, and rural people were notoriously given to groundless suspicion. I had had enough of the law, and of arrests without sufficient evidence. The wisest thing would be to drop a hint or two before the landlord, and judge by his demeanour whether to proceed.

"I found him sitting where I had left him, smoking, in his shirt-sleeves, with his hat on.

" 'Well,' he said slowly, 'I didn't know where you had got to.'

"I told him I had been taking a walk. I went on to mention casually the fork in the road, the hill, and the plateau.

" 'And who lives in that house?' I asked with a good show of indifference, 'on top of the hill?'

"He stared.

" 'House? There ain't no house up there,' he said positively. 'Old Joe Snedeker, who owns the land, says he's going to build a house up there for his son to live in when he gets married; but he ain't begun yet, and some folks reckon he never will.'

" 'I feel sure I *saw* a house,' I protested feebly. But I was thinking—no heat in the fire, no substance in the body. I had not the courage to dispute.

"The landlord looked at me not unkindly. 'You seem sort of done up,' he remarked. 'What you want is to go to bed.' "

The man who was telling me the story paused, and for a moment we sat silent, listening to the pant of the machinery, the thrumming of the wind in the wire stays, and the lash of the sea. Some voices were singing on the deck below. I considered him with the shade of contemptuous superiority we feel, as a rule, towards those who tell us their dreams or what some fortune-teller has predicted.

"Hallucinations," I said at last, with reassuring indulgence. "Trick of the vision, toxic opthalmia. After the long strain of your trial your nerves were shattered."

"That's what I thought myself," he replied shortly, "especially after I had been out to the plateau the next morning, and saw no sign that a house had ever stood there."

"And no corpse at the bridge?" I said; and laughed.

"And no corpse at the bridge."

He tried to get a light for another cigar. This took him some little time, and when at last he managed it, he got out of his chair and stood looking down at me.

"Now listen. I told you that the thing happened several years ago. I'd got almost to forget it; if you can only persuade yourself

447

that a thing is a freak of imagination, it pretty soon gets dim inside your head. Delusions have no staying power once it is realised that they are delusions. Whenever it did come back to me, I used to think how near I had once been to going out of my mind. That was all.

"Well, last year, being up north, I went up to that village again. I went to the same hotel, and found the same landlord. He remembered me at once as 'the feller who stayed with him and thought he saw a house,' 'I believe you had the jim-jams,' he said.

"We laughed, and the landlord went on:

" 'There's been a house there since, though.'

" 'Has there?'

" 'Yes; an' it ha' been as well if there never had been. Old Snedeker built it for his son, a fine big house with a verandah on two sides. The son, young Joe, got courting Mabel Elting from Windermere. She'd gone down to work in a shop somewhere in Liverpool. Well, sir, she used to get carrying on with another young feller 'bout here, Jim Travers, and Jim was wild about her; used to save up his wages to go down to see her. But she chucked him in the end, and married Joe; I suppose because Joe had the house, and the old man's money to expect. Well, poor Jim must ha' gone quite mad. What do you think he did? The very first night the new-wed pair spent in that house he burned it down. Burned the two of them in their bed, and he was as nice and quiet a feller as you want to see. He may ha' been full of whisky at the time.'

" 'No, he wasn't,' I said.

" 'The landlord looked surprised.

" 'You've heard about it?'

" 'No; go on.'

" 'Yes, sir, he burned them in their bed. And then what do you think he did? He hung himself at the little bridge half a mile below. Do you remember where the road divides? Well, it was there. I saw his body hanging there myself the next morning. The toes of his boots were just touching the water.'"

C.D. PAMELY
The Unfinished Masterpiece

This charming story by Carl Douglas Pamely *is taken from his rare collection* Tales of Mystery and Terror (1926).

> *Chiaro mi fu allor com' ogni dove*
> *In cielo è paradiso.*
>
> Dante

He was an old man when he first took up his abode in a humble quarter of that old-world village of Provence. His face bore marked traces of many years' sorrow and suffering, but intermingled with this there was a wistful expression which attracted and yet puzzled beholders. He gave the name of Claude Roubouc when he rented his room, never entered into conversation with anybody about his own affairs, or enquired about those of other people, procured the materials for his frugal meals from the shops, and enjoyed them in the open air among the lovely surroundings of the village. He received no letters beyond an occasional government one marked "Banque de France," and was regarded as a man of mystery by the inhabitants. Yet there was a mingled air of superiority, refinement, and resignation about the stranger which effectually prevented people from importuning him with awkward questions.

From his affectionate treatment of certain portraits in his room, the proprietor of his apartment presumed that he had suffered the calamity of the loss of his wife and two children, but otherwise nothing was known about the mysterious newcomer.

Every morning at sunrise he went out of the village and proceeded along the road beneath the scanty shade of the scorched and dusty plane-trees, past the ancient church, until he turned aside and was lost to view amid a clump of chestnut trees. With him he bore his easel, palette, canvas, colours, and brushes, carefully wrapped up to protect them from the intense heat of the sun. He set up his easel at a remote spot beneath the shade of a tall fig-tree on the height, whence he had an uninterrupted view of the lovely panorama before him, the vineyards and the fields of olives gently sloping down to the hollow beneath, in the midst of which nestled the white houses and walls of the village, while in the distance the calm blue waters of the Mediterranean could be seen sparkling beneath the rays of the southern sun. He did not return to his apartment in the village until late in the afternoon, still carrying his paraphernalia with the same care as in the morning.

All through the spring and the long hot summer he went regularly at sunrise to his favourite spot beneath the giant fig-tree on the height, bearing with him his artist's equipment and the materials for his frugal meals. No one knew what was depicted on the canvas, for it was always encased in a frame and thickly wrapped in brown paper when seen in the hands of the artist, until one day a countryman, happening to traverse the grove on the height in proceeding from his vineyard to the dusty road, saw, in passing behind the fig-tree, the artist at work on his theme.

The peasant comprehended but vaguely the meaning of the objects depicted in such beautiful colouring on the canvas, but on his return to the village he spread the report that a celestial vision could be seen on the canvas of the unknown artist, more glorious than anything portrayed on the painted glass of the church windows. Soon (all unknown to the painter, who was absorbed in his work) people crept stealthily through the thicket to the spot behind the fig-tree and gazed from various points of vantage at the uncompleted handiwork of Claude Roubouc.

On the canvas was depicted a fair paradise, bright with green meadows, and resplendent with the gorgeous colours of various trees and flowers. Laughing blossoms and golden fruits flourished in the halcyon spring-time, while multi-coloured birds with magnificent plumage flitted among the branches of the trees. The picture contained obvious reminiscences of classical scenery and associations, but the rich colours spread on the canvas with such careful judgment and sound artistic sense were all the painter's own. The paradise was thronged with joyous crowds of people basking in the sunshine of the meadows or reclining beneath the trees of the groves. Underneath a clump of myrtle trees in the centre of the canvas was depicted the form of a beautiful woman in the prime of life, holding two comely children, a boy and a girl, by the hand. They were disporting themselves on a bed of amaranths and roses and lilies, and their mid-nineteenth century costumes formed a striking contrast to the mythological associations of their surroundings. The paradise was surrounded by a wall of glittering gold, and all was happiness within, from the radiant countenances of the mother and the two children to the sunshine of the meadows and the gorgeous colours of the fruits and flowers.

The painting was obviously a masterpiece, and the beholders were transported with admiration at the sight of the rich, variegated tints of green, red, brown, gold, and purple employed in the representation of this Elysium, and the expressions of divine happiness depicted on the faces of the mother and children, mingled withal with a perplexing suggestion of wistfulness as they gazed on their lovely surroundings. The inhabitants of the village marvelled at the way in which the mysterious artist had kept the secret of his genius. It might, indeed, have remained for ever unknown but for the chance discovery of the peasant behind the fig-tree. The features of the artist were quietly and unobtrusively scanned with eager curiosity every morning and afternoon as he went to and fro, and many were the people who secretly watched him with increased interest and wonder at work on his picture.

Yet the painting remained unfinished. Fully a third of the canvas on the right-hand side had been left uncovered by the artist. The spectators watched intently while he touched up the colouring on the paradisal scene here and there, and speculation grew rife as to what objects would be represented by the painter to fill in the blank.

Meanwhile the long hot summer advanced and waned, and the leaves of the trees became scorched and brown. The artist had become more and more oblivious to and negligent of his own comfort. His visits to the village shops for provisions became less frequent and more spasmodic; he would often entirely forget to carry any food with him in the morning when he left his apartment, and had no sustenance during the day except the wild fruits which were found in profusion on the trees in that favoured region. His sojourns beneath the fig-tree on the hillside became more lengthy, and he did not return until the roseate and gorgeous colours of the sunset gave warning that darkness was impending.

He languished visibly, yet he grew wild in the ardour of his task. A strange light flashed in his eyes, and he would stand for hours beneath the fig-tree mixing the colours on the palette and transferring them to the canvas, without pausing for rest or refreshment, utterly oblivious to everything around him, obsessed with a burning desire to finish the magnificent creation of his imagination before it was too late. Rarely did he turn his eyes from the canvas, his whole being seemed absorbed in the completion of his life's work. One or two of the bolder spirits in the village ventured to remonstrate with him, and urged him to be more careful about his health, but he shook his head as if he did not understand, and remained absorbed in reflection as before.

And now he began to fill up the blank space on the canvas, and the watchers saw the crystal waters of a stream, whose bed was gleaming with jewels, flow around the walls of the golden paradise. When the limpid current had been portrayed on the right hand side of the picture, it was noticed that the mother and the two beautiful children were gazing in that direction with the same suggestively wistful expression of countenance which had previously puzzled beholders. The painter began to outline the further margin of the stream, and speculation again grew rife as to what he would portray on the other side.

In his zeal for his art he had for some time neglected the simplest precautions for the care of his health, and became oblivious to everything except the spreading of the tints on the canvas before him. His form was haggard and wasted, but his eyes shone with a bright radiance not of this earth, and he seemed like a man whose decrepit frame could no longer keep back the soaring spirit within. He seemed to realise that he was engaged in a pitiless race with time, and he strove with his whole remaining strength to complete his masterpiece in the brief time which he knew was decreed to him . . .

But death overtook him. One morning they found him lying dead beneath the fig-tree, with a serene expression on his worn and pinched features, still clutching his brushes and palette overspread with bright pigments, his mighty task uncompleted. The easel had fallen over, and the canvas lay face upwards on the ground. He had just begun the outline of a figure, apparently

that of a man with hands raised in supplication, on the further
margin of the stream. They reverently lifted his corpse from the
ground, and bore it to the village for burial, then they returned
to gather up the unfinished masterpiece on the canvas, and the
painter's equipment.

But a strange thing had happened in their absence. The
burning rays of the southern sun, shining down through the
interstices in the foliage of the fig-tree, had scorched the canvas
in places, and when they picked up the unfinished *chef d'oeuvre*,
the faint outline of the man's figure on the brink had become
obliterated in the scorched brown of the canvas, while the solar
rays had faintly traced the figure of a man just emerging from
the crystal river before the gate of gold which gave admittance
to the fair paradise within.

To all appearance it was the shadowy form of the painter
himself! And when they examined the foot of the canvas,
they found these words traced in faint and uncertain letters
of gold—obviously the last effort of the artist when he felt the
sands of life running out: *J'ai achevé ma journée*.

JAMES PLATT
The Witches' Sabbath

*James Platt (1861–1910) was, like his con-
temporary M.R. James, renowned as one of the
greatest scholars of his generation. Fluent in every
European language by the age of 25, he went
on to study most of the little known languages
of Africa and North America, and contributed
many invaluable etymological insights to the new
edition of the* Oxford English Dictionary. *Platt's
six extraordinary* Tales of the Supernatural *(1894)
could only have been written by a scholar steeped
in Mediaevalism and the wild traditions of folklore
and demonology. "If Stevenson and Poe had
worked together", wrote his biographer, "backed
by a profound knowledge of their subject, these are
the kind of stories they would have produced".*

O ur scene is one of those terrific peaks set apart by tradition
as the trysting place of wizards and witches, and of every
kind of folk that prefers dark to day.

It might have been Mount Elias, or the Brocken, associated
with Doctor Faustus. It might have been the Horsel or Venus-
berg of Tannhaeuser, or the Black Forest. Enough that it was
one of these.

Not a star wrinkled the brow of night. Only in the distance
the twinkling lights of some town could be seen. Low down in
the skirts of the mountain rode a knight, followed closely by
his page. We say a knight, because he had once owned that
distinction. But a wild and bloody youth had tarnished his
ancient shield, the while it kept bright and busy his ancestral
sword. Behold him now, little better than a highwayman.
Latterly he had wandered from border to border, without
finding where to rest his faithful steed. All authority was
in arms against him; Hageck, the wild knight, was posted
throughout Germany. More money was set upon his head than

454

had ever been put into his pocket. Pikemen and pistoliers had dispersed his following. None remained to him whom he could call his own, save this stripling who still rode sturdily at the tail of his horse. Him also, the outlaw had besought, even with tears, to abandon one so ostensibly cursed by stars and men. But in vain. The boy protested that he would have no home, save in his master's shadow.

They were an ill-assorted pair. The leader was all war-worn and weather-worn. Sin had marked him for its own and for the wages of sin. The page was young and slight, and marble pale. He would have looked more at home at the silken train of some great lady, than following at these heels from which the gilded spurs had long been hacked. Nevertheless, the music of the spheres themselves sings not more sweetly in accord than did these two hearts.

The wild knight, Hageck, had ascended the mountain as far as was possible to four-legged roadsters. Therefore he reined in his horse and dismounted, and addressed his companion. His voice was now quite gentle, which on occasion could quench mutiny, and in due season dry up the taste of blood in the mouths of desperate men.

"Time is that we must part, Enno."

"Master, you told me we need never part."

"Let be, child, do you not understand me? I hope with your own heart's hope that we shall meet again to-morrow in this same tarrying place. But I have not brought you to so cursed a place without some object. When I say that we must part, I mean that you must take charge of our horses while I go further up the mountain upon business, which for your own sake you must never share."

"And is this your reading of the oath of our brotherhood which we swore together?"

"The oath of our brotherhood, I fear, was writ in water. You are, in fact, the only one of all my company that has kept faith with me. For that very reason I would not spare your neck from the halter, nor your limbs from the wheel. But also for that very reason I will not set your immortal soul in jeopardy."

"My immortal soul! Is this business then unhallowed that you go upon? Now I remember me that this mountain at certain seasons is said to be haunted by evil spirits. Master, you also are bound by our oath to tell me all."

455

"You shall know all, Enno, were oaths even cheaper than they are. You have deserved by your devotion to be the confessor of your friend."

"Friend is no name for companionship such as ours. I am sure you would die for me. I believe I could die for you, Hageck."

"Enough, you have been more than brother to me. I had a brother once, after the fashion of this world, and it is his envious hand which has placed me where I stand. That was before I knew you, Enno, and it is some sweets in my cup at any rate, that had he not betrayed me I should never have known you. Nevertheless, you will admit that since he robbed me of the girl I loved, even your loyal heart is a poor set off for what fate and fraternity took from me. In fine, we both loved the same girl, but she loved me, and would have none of my brother. She was beautiful, Enno—how beautiful you can never guess that have not yet loved."

"I have never conceived any other love than that I bear you."

"Tush, boy, you know not what you say. But to return to my story. One day that I was walking with her my brother would have stabbed me. She threw herself between and was killed upon my breast."

He tore open his clothes at the throat and showed a great faded stain upon his skin.

"The hangman's brand shall fade," he cried, "ere that wash out. Accursed be the mother that bore me seeing that she also first bore him! The devil squat down with him in his resting, lie with him in his sleeping, as the devil has sat and slept with me every noon and night since that deed was done. Never give way to love of woman, Enno, lest you lose the one you love, and with her lose the balance of your life."

"Alas! Hageck, I fear I never shall."

"Since that miscalled day, blacker than any night, you know as well as any one the sort of death in life I led. I had the good or evil luck to fall in with some broken men like myself, fortune's foes and foes of all whom fortune cherishes, you among them. Red blood, red gold for a while ran through our fingers. Then a turn of the wheel, and, presto, my men are squandered to every wind that blows—I am a fugitive with a price upon my head!"

"And with one comrade whom, believe me, wealth is too poor to buy."

"A heart above rubies. Even so. To such alone would I confide my present purpose. You must know that my brother was a student of magic of no mean repute, and before we quarrelled had given me some insight into its mysteries. Now that I near the end of my tether I have summed up all the little I knew, and am resolved to make a desperate cast in this mountain of despair. In a word, I intend to hold converse with my dead sweetheart before I die. The devil shall help me to it for the love he bears me."

"You would invoke the enemy of all mankind?"

"Him and none other. Aye, shudder not, nor seek to turn me from it. I have gone over it again and again. The gates of Hell are set no firmer than this resolve."

"God keep Hell far from you when you call it!"

"I had feared my science was of too elementary an order to conduct an exorcism under any but the most favourable circumstances. Hence our journey hither. This place is one of those where parliaments of evil are held, where dead and living meet on equal ground. To-night is the appointed night of one of these great Sabbaths. I propose to leave you here with the horses. I shall climb to the topmost peak, draw a circle that I may stand in for my defence, and with all the vehemence of love deferred, pray for my desire."

"May all good angels speed you!"

"Nay, I have broken with such. Your good wish, Enno, is enough."

"But did we not hear talk in the town about a hermit that spent his life upon the mountain top, atoning for some sin in day-long prayer and mortification? Can this evil fellowship of which you speak still hold its meetings upon a spot which has been attached in the name of Heaven by one good man?"

"Of this hermit I knew nothing until we reached the town. It was then too late to seek another workshop. Should what you say be correct, and this holy man have purged this plague spot, I can do no worse than pass the night with him, and return to you. But should the practices of witch and wizard continue as of yore, then the powers of evil shall draw my love to me, be she where she may. Aye, be it in that most secret nook of heaven where God retires when He would weep, and where even archangels are never suffered to tread."

"O all good go with you!"

"Farewell, Enno, and if I never return count my soul not so lost but what you may say a prayer for it now and again, when you have leisure."

"I will not outlive you!"

The passionate words were lost on Hageck, who had already climbed so far as to be out of hearing. He only knew vaguely that something was shouted to him, and waved his hand above his head for a reply. On and on he climbed. Time passed. The way grew harder. At last exhausted, but fed with inward exaltation, he reached the summit. It was of considerable extent and extremely uneven. The first thing our hero noticed was the cave of the hermit. It could be nothing else, although it was closed with an iron door. A new departure, thought Hageck to himself, as he hammered upon it with the pommel of his sword, for a hermit's cell to be locked in like a fortress.

"Open, friend," he cried, "in heaven's name, or in that of the other place if you like it better."

The noise came from within of a bar being removed. The door opened. It revealed a mere hole in the rock, though large enough, it is true, to hold a considerable number of persons. Furniture was conspicuous by its absence. There was no sign even of a bed, unless a coffin that grinned in one corner served the occupant's needs. A skull, a scourge, a crucifix, a knife for his food, what more does such a hermit want? His feet were bare, his head was tonsured, but his eyebrows were long and matted, and fell like a screen over burning maniacal eyes. A fanatic, every inch of him. He scrutinised the invader from top to toe. Apparently the result was unsatisfactory. He frowned.

"A traveller," said he, "and at this unholy hour. Back, back, do you not know the sinister reputation of this time and place?"

"I know your reputation to be of the highest, reverend father; I could not credit what rumour circulates about this mountain top when I understood that one of such sanctity had taken up a perpetual abode here."

"My abode is fixed here for the very reason that it is a realm of untold horror. My task is to win back, if I can, to the dominion of the church this corner, which has been so long unloved that it cries aloud to God and man. This position of my own choice is no sinecure. Hither at stated times the full brunt of the Sabbath sweeps to its rendezvous. Here I defy the Sabbath. You see that mighty door?"

"I had wondered, but feared to ask, what purpose such a barrier could serve in such a miserable place."

"You may be glad to crouch behind it if you stay here much longer. At midnight, Legion, with all the swirl of all the hells at his back, will sweep this summit like a tornado. Were you of the stuff that never trembles, yet you shall hear such sounds as shall melt your backbone. Avoid hence while there is yet time."

"But you, if you remain here, why not I?"

"I remain here as a penance for a crime I did, a crime which almost takes prisoner my reason, so different was it from the crime I set out to do, so deadly death to all my hopes. I am on my knees throughout the whole duration of this pandemonium that I tell you of, and count thick and fast my beads during the whole time. Did I cease for one second to pray, that second would be my last. The roof of my cavern would descend and efface body and soul. But you, what would you do here?"

"I seek my own ends, for which I am fully prepared. To confer with a shade from the other world I place my own soul in jeopardy. For the short time that must elapse, before the hour arrives when I can work, I ask but a trifle of your light and fire."

"The will-o'-the-wisp be your light, Saint Anthony's your fire! Do you not recognise me?"

The wild knight bent forward and gazed into the hermit's inmost eye, then started back, and would have fallen had his head not struck the iron door. This recalled him to his senses, and after a moment he stood firm again, and murmured between his teeth, "My brother!"

"Your brother," repeated the holy man, "your brother, whose sweetheart you stole and drove me to madness and crime."

"I drove you to no madness, I drove you to no crime. The madness, the crime you expiate here, were all of your own making. She loved me, and me alone—you shed her blood, by accident I confess, yet you shed it, and not all the prayers of your lifetime can gather up one drop of it. What soaked into my own brain remains there for ever, though I have sought to wash it out with an ocean of other men's blood."

"And I," replied the hermit, and he tore his coarse frock off his shoulders, "I have sought to drown it with an ocean of my own."

He spoke truth. Blood still oozed from his naked flesh, ploughed into furrows by the scourge.

"You, that have committed so many murders," he continued, "and who have reproached me so bitterly for one, all the curses of your dying victims, all the curses I showered upon you before I became reformed have not availed to send you yet to the gibbet or to the wheel. You are one that, like the basil plant, grows ever the rifer for cursing. I remember I tried to lame you, after you left home, by driving a rusty nail into one of your footsteps, but the charm refused to work. You were never the worse for it that I could hear. They say the devil's children have the devil's luck. Yet some day shall death trip up your heels."

"Peace, peace," cried the wild horseman, "let ill-will be dead between us, and the bitterness of death be passed, as befits your sacred calling. Even if I see her for one moment to-night, by the aid of the science you once taught me, will you not see her for eternity in heaven some near day?"

"In heaven," cried the hermit, "do I want to see her in heaven? On earth would I gladly see her again and account that moment cheap if weighted against my newly discovered soul! But that can never be. Not the art you speak of, not all the dark powers which move men to sin, can restore her to either of us as she was that day. And she loved you. She died to save you. You have nothing to complain of. But to me she was like some chaste impossible star."

"I loved her most," muttered the outlaw.

"You loved her most," screamed the hermit. "Hell sit upon your eyes! Put it to the test. Look around. Do you see anything of her here?"

The other Hageck gazed eagerly round the cave, but without fixing upon anything.

"I see nothing," he was forced to confess.

The hermit seized the skull and held it in front of his eyes.

"This is her dear head," he cried, "fairer far than living red and white to me!"

The wild knight recoiled with a gasp of horror, snatched the ghastly relic from the hand of his brother, and hurled it over the precipice. He put his fingers over his eyes and fell to shaking like an aspen. For a moment the hermit scarcely seemed to grasp his loss. Then with a howl of rage he seized his brother by the throat.

"You have murdered her," he shrieked in tones scarcely recognisable, "she will be dashed to a hundred pieces by such a fall!"

He threw the outlaw to the ground and, retreating to his cave, slammed the door behind him, but his heart-broken sobs could still be heard distinctly. It was very evident that he was no longer in his right mind. The wild knight rose somewhat painfully and limped to a little distance where he perceived a favourable spot for erecting his circle. The sobbing of the crazed hermit presently ceased. He was aware that his rival had entered upon his operations. The hermit re-opened his door that he might more clearly catch the sound of what his foe was engaged upon. Every step was of an absorbing interest to the solitary as to the man who made it. Anon the hermit started to his feet. He fancied he heard another voice replying to his brother. Yes, it was a voice he seemed to know. He rushed out of the cave. A girlish figure clad in a stained dress was clasped in his brother's arms. Kiss after kiss the wild knight was showering upon brow, and eye, and cheek, and lip. The girl responded as the hermit had surely seen her do once before. He flew to his cave. He grasped the knife he used for his food. He darted like an arrow upon the startled pair. The woman tried to throw herself in front of her lover, but the hermit with a coarse laugh, "Not twice the dagger seeks the same breast," plunged it into the heart of her companion. The wild knight threw up his arms and without a cry fell to the ground. The girl uttered a shriek that seemed to rive the skies and flung herself across her dead. The hermit gazed at it stupidly and rubbed his eyes. He seemed like one dazed, but slowly recovering his senses. Suddenly he started, came as it were to himself, and pulled the girl by the shoulder.

"We have not a minute to lose," he cried, "the great Sabbath is all but due. If his body remains out here one second after the stroke of twelve, his soul will be lost to all eternity. It will be snatched by the fiends who even now are bound to it. Do you not see yon shadowy hosts—but I forget, you are not a witch."

"I see nothing," she replied, sullenly, rising up and peering round. The night was clear, but starless.

"I have been a wizard," he answered, "and once a wizard always a wizard, though I now fight upon the other side. Take my hand and you will see."

She took his hand, and screamed as she did so. For at the instant there became visible to her these clouds of loathsome beings that were speeding thither from every point of the compass. Warlock, and witch, and wizard rode past on every conceivable graceless mount. Their motion was like the lightning of heaven, and their varied cries—owlet hoot, caterwaul, dragon shout—the horn of the Wild Hunter, and the hurly of risen dead—vied with the bay of Cerberus to the seldseen moon: A forest of whips was flourished aloft. The whirr of wings raised dozing echoes. The accustomed mountain shook and shivered like a jelly, with the fear of their onset.

The girl dropped his hand and immediately lost the power of seeing them. She had learned at any rate that what he said was true.

"Help me to carry the body to the cave," cried he, and in a moment it was done. The corpse was placed in the coffin of his murderer. Then the hermit crashed his door to its place. Up went bolts and bars. Some loose rocks that were probably the hermit's chairs and tables were rolled up to afford additional security.

"And now," demanded the man, "now that we have a moment of breathing space, tell me what woman-kind are you whom I find here with my brother? That you are not her I know (woe is me that I have good reason to know) yet you are as like her as any flower that blows. I loved her, and I murdered her, and I have the right to ask, who and what are you that come to disturb my peace?"

"I am her sister."

"Her sister! Yes, I remember you. You were a child in those days. Neither I nor my brother (God rest his soul!), neither of us noticed you."

"No, he never took much notice of me. Yet I loved him as well as she did."

"You, too, loved him," whispered the hermit, as if to himself; "what did he do to be loved by two such women?"

"Yes, I loved him, though he never knew it, but I may confess it now, for you are a priest of a sort, are you not, you that shrive with steel?"

"You are bitter, like your sister. She was always so with me."

"I owe you my story," she replied more gently; "when she died and he fell into evil courses and went adrift with bad companions, I found I could not live without him, nor with anyone else, and I determined to become one of them. I dressed in boy's clothes and sought enlistment into his company of free lances. He would have driven me from him, saying it was no work for such as I, yet at last I wheedled it from him. I think there was something in my face (all undeveloped as it was and stained with walnut juice) that reminded him of her he had lost. I followed him faithfully through good and evil, cringing for a look or word from him. We were at last broken up (as you know) and I alone of all his sworn riders remained to staunch his wounds. He brought me hither that he might wager all the soul that was left to him on the chance of evoking her spirit. I had with me the dress my sister died in, that I had cherished through all my wanderings, as my sole reminder of her life and death. I put it on after he had left me, and followed him as fast as my strength would allow me. My object was to beguile him with what sorry pleasure I could, while at the same time saving him from committing the sin of disturbing the dead. God forgive me if there was mixed with it the wholly selfish yearning to be kissed by him once, only once, in my true character as loving woman, rid of my hated disguise! I have had my desire, and it has turned to apples of Sodom on my lips. You are right. All we can do now is to preserve his soul alive."

She fell on her knees beside the coffin. The hermit pressed his crucifix into her hands.

"Pray!" he cried, and at the same moment the distant clock struck twelve. There came a rush of feet, a thunder at the iron door, the cave rocked like a ship's cabin abruptly launched into the trough of a storm. An infernal whooping and hallooing filled the air outside, mixed with it imprecations that made the strong man blanch. The banner of Destruction was unfurled. All the horned heads were upon them. Thrones and Dominions, Virtues, Princes, Powers. All hell was loose that night, and the outskirts of Hell.

The siege had begun. The hermit told his beads with feverish rapidity. One Latin prayer after another rolled off his tongue in drops of sweat. The girl, to whom these were unintelligible, tried in vain to think of prayers. All she could say, as she pressed the Christ to her lips, was "Lord of my life! My Love." She scarcely heard the hurly-burly that raged outside. Crash after crash resounded against the door, but good steel tempered with holy water is bad to beat. Showers of small pieces of rock fell from the ceiling and the cave was soon filled with dust. Peals of hellish cachinnation resounded after each unsuccessful attempt to break down that defence. Living battering rams pressed it hard, dragon's spur, serpent's coil, cloven hoof, foot of clay. Tall Iniquities set their backs to it, names of terror, girt with earthquake. All the swart crew dashed their huge bulk against it, rakchelly riders, humans and superhumans, sin and its paymasters. The winds well nigh split their sides with hounding of them on. Evil stars in their courses fought against it. The seas threw up their dead. Haunted houses were no more haunted that night. Graveyards steamed. Gibbets were empty. The ghoul left his half-gnawn corpse, the vampire his victim's throat. Buried treasures rose to earth's surface that their ghostly guardians might swell the fray. Yet the hermit prayed on, and the woman wept, and the door kept its face to the foe. Will the hour of release never strike? Crested Satans now lead the van. Even steel cannot hold out for ever against those in whose veins instead of blood, runs fire. At last it bends ever so little, and the devilish hubbub is increased tenfold.

"Should they break open the door—" yelled the hermit, making a trumpet of his hands, yet she could not hear what he shouted above the abominable din, nor had he time to complete his instructions. For the door did give, and that suddenly, with a clang that was heard from far off in the town, and made many a burgher think the last trump had come. The rocks that had been rolled against the door flew off in every direction, and a surging host—and the horror of it was that they were invisible to the girl—swept in.

The hermit tore his rosary asunder, and scattered the loose beads in the faces of the fiends.

"Hold fast the corpse!" he yelled, as he was trampled under foot, and this time he made himself heard. The girl seized the long hair of her lover pressed it convulsively, and swooned.

Years afterwards (as it seemed to her) she awakened and found the chamber still as death, and—yes—this was the hair of death which she still clutched in her dead hand. She kissed it a hundred times before it brought back to her where she was and what had passed. She looked round then for the hermit. He, poor man, was lying as if also dead. But when she could bring herself to release her hoarded treasure, she speedily brought him to some sort of consciousness. He sat up, not without difficulty, and looked around. But his mind, already half way to madness, had been totally overturned by what had occurred that woeful night.

"We have saved his soul between us," she cried. "What do I not owe you for standing by me in that fell hour?"

He regarded her in evident perplexity. "I cannot think how you come to be wearing that blood-stained dress of hers," was all he replied.

"I have told you," she said, gently, "but you have forgotten that I cherished it through all my wanderings as my sole memento of her glorious death. She laid down the last drop of her blood for him. She chose the better part. But I! my God! what in the world is to become of me?"

"I had a memento of her once," he muttered. "I had her beautiful head, but I have lost it."

"That settles it," she said, "you shall cut off mine."

EDGAR ALLAN POE
Metzengerstein

Edgar Allan Poe (1809–49), America's out-standing writer of horror literature, inspired and influenced countless later writers with his pathological and macabre stories and poems. "Metzengerstein" (1832), Poe's first published tale, is his most Gothic story, featuring a dissolute Hungarian baron and a ghostly demonic horse.

Pestis eram vivus—moriens tua mors ero.
Martin Luther

Horror and fatality have been stalking abroad in all ages. Why then give a date to the story I have to tell? Let it suffice to say, that at the period of which I speak, there existed, in the interior of Hungary, a settled although hidden belief in the doctrines of the Metempsychosis. Of the doctrines themselves—that is, of their falsity, or of their probability—I say nothing. I assert, however, that much of our incredulity (as La Bruyère says of all our unhappiness) *"vient de ne pouvoir être seuls."*[1]

But there were some points in the Hungarian superstition which were fast verging to absurdity. They—the Hungarians—differed very essentially from their Eastern authorities. For example. *"The soul,"* said the former—I give the words of an acute and intelligent Parisian—*"ne demeure qu'une seule fois dans un corps sensible: au reste—un cheval, un chien, un homme même, n'est que la ressemblance peu tangible de ces animaux."*

The families at Berlifitzing and Metzengerstein had been at variance for centuries. Never before were two houses, so

---

[1] Mercier, in *L'An deux mille quatre cent quarante,* seriously maintains the doctrines of the Metempsychosis, and J. D'Israeli says that "no system is so simple and so little repugnant to the understanding." Colonel Ethan Allen, the "Green Mountain Boy," is also said to have been a serious metempsychosist.

illustrious, mutually embittered by hostility so deadly. The origin of this enmity seems to be found in the words of an ancient prophecy—"A lofty name shall have a fearful fall when, as the rider over his horse, the mortality of Metzengerstein shall triumph over the immortality of Berlifitzing."

To be sure, the words themselves had little or no meaning. But more trivial causes have given rise—and that no long while ago—to consequences equally eventful. Besides, the estates, which were contiguous, had long exercised a rival influence in the affairs of a busy government. Moreover, near neighbours are seldom friends; and the inhabitants of the Castle Berlifitzing might look from their lofty buttresses into the very windows of the Palace Metzengerstein. Least of all had the more than feudal magnificence, thus discovered, a tendency to allay the irritable feelings of the less ancient and less wealthy Berlifitzings. What wonder, then, that the words, however silly, of that prediction, should have succeeded in setting and keeping at variance two families already predisposed to quarrel by every instigation of hereditary jealousy? The prophecy seemed to imply—if it implied anything—a final triumph on the part of the already more powerful house; and was of course remembered with the more bitter animosity by the weaker and less influential.

Wilhelm, Count Berlifitzing, although loftily descended, was, at the epoch of this narrative, an infirm and doting old man, remarkable for nothing but an inordinate and inveterate personal antipathy to the family of his rival, and so passionate a love of horses, and of hunting, that neither bodily infirmity, great age, nor mental incapacity, prevented his daily participation in the dangers of the chase.

Frederick, Baron Metzengerstein, was, on the other hand, not yet of age. His father, the Minister G—, died young. His mother, the Lady Mary, followed him quickly. Frederick was, at that time, in his eighteenth year. In a city, eighteen years are no long period; but in a wilderness—in so magnificent a wilderness as that old principality, the pendulum vibrates with a deeper meaning.

From some peculiar circumstances attending the administration of his father, the young Baron, at the decease of the former, entered immediately upon his vast possessions. Such estates were seldom held before by a nobleman of Hungary. His castles were without number. The chief in point of splendour and extent was the "Palace Metzengerstein." The boundary line of his dominions was never clearly defined; but his principal park embraced a circuit of fifty miles.

Upon the succession of a proprietor so young, with a character so well known, to a fortune so unparalleled, little speculation was afloat in regard to his probable course of conduct. And, indeed, for the space of three days the behaviour of the heir out-Heroded Herod, and fairly surpassed the expectations of his most enthusiastic admirers. Shameful debaucheries—flagrant treacheries—unheard-of atrocities—gave his trembling vassals quickly to understand that no servile submission on their part—no punctilios of conscience on his own—were thenceforward to prove any security against the remorseless fangs of a petty Caligula. On the night of the fourth day, the stables of the Castle Berlifitzing were discovered to be on fire; and the unanimous opinion of the neighbourhood added the crime of the incendiary to the already hideous list of the Baron's misdemeanours and enormities.

But during the tumult occasioned by this occurrence, the young nobleman himself sat apparently buried in meditation, in a vast and desolate upper apartment of the family palace of Metzengerstein. The rich although faded tapestry hangings which swung gloomily upon the walls represented the shadowy and majestic forms of a thousand illustrious ancestors. *Here*, rich-ermined priests and pontifical dignitaries, familiarly seated with the autocrat and the sovereign, put a veto on the wishes of a temporal king, or restrained with the fiat of papal supremacy the rebellious sceptre of the Arch-enemy. *There*, the dark, tall statures of the Princes Metzengerstein—their muscular war-coursers plunging over the carcasses of fallen foes—startled the steadiest nerves with their vigorous expression; and *here*, again, the voluptuous and swan-like figures of the dames of days gone by floated away in the mazes of an unreal dance to the strains of imaginary melody.

But as the Baron listened, or affected to listen, to the gradually increasing uproar in the stables of Berlifitzing—or perhaps pondered upon some more novel, some more decided act of audacity—his eyes were turned unwittingly to the figure of an enormous, and unnaturally coloured horse, represented in the tapestry as belonging to a Saracen ancestor of the family of his rival. The horse itself, in the foreground of the design, stood motionless and statue-like—while, farther back, its discomfited rider perished by the dagger of a Metzengerstein.

On Frederick's lip arose a fiendish expression, as he became aware of the direction which his glance had, without his consciousness, assumed. Yet he did not remove it. On the contrary, he could by no means account for the overwhelming anxiety which appeared falling like a pall upon his senses. It was with difficulty that he reconciled his dreamy and incoherent feelings with the certainty of being awake. The longer he gazed the more absorbing became the spell—the more impossible did it appear that he could ever withdraw his glance from the fascination of that tapestry. But the tumult without becoming suddenly more violent, with a compulsory exertion he diverted his attention to the glare of ruddy light thrown full by the flaming stables upon the windows of the apartment.

The action, however, was but momentary; his gaze returned mechanically to the wall. To his extreme horror and astonishment, the head of the gigantic steed had, in the meantime, altered its position. The neck of the animal, before arched, as if in compassion, over the prostrate body of its lord, was now extended at full length, in the direction of the Baron. The eyes, before invisible, now wore an energetic and human expression, while they gleamed with a fiery and unusual red; and the distended lips of the apparently enraged horse left in full view his sepulchral and disgusting teeth.

Stupefied with terror, the young nobleman tottered to the door. As he threw it open, a flash of red light, streaming far into the chamber, flung his shadow with a clear outline against the quivering tapestry; and he shuddered to perceive that shadow—as he staggered awhile upon the threshold—assuming the exact position, and precisely filling up the contour, of the relentless and triumphant murderer of the Saracen Berlifitzing.

To lighten the depression of his spirits, the Baron hurried into the open air. At the principal gate of the palace he encountered three equerries. With much difficulty, and at the imminent peril of their lives, they were restraining the convulsive plunges of a gigantic and fiery-coloured horse.

"Whose horse? Where did you get him?" demanded the youth, in a querulous and husky tone, as he became instantly aware that the mysterious steed in the tapestried chamber was the very counterpart of the furious animal before his eyes.

"He is your own property, sire," replied one of the equerries, "at least he is claimed by no other owner. We caught him flying, all smoking and foaming with rage, from the burning stables of the Castle Berlifitzing. Supposing him to have belonged to the old Count's stud of foreign horses, we led him back as an estray. But the grooms there disclaim any title to the creature; which is strange, since he bears evident marks of having made a narrow escape from the flames."

"The letters W. V. B. are also branded very distinctly on his forehead," interrupted a second equerry; "I suppose them, of course, to be the initials of William Von Berlifitzing—but all at the castle are positive in denying any knowledge of the horse."

"Extremely singular!" said the young Baron, with a musing air, and apparently unconscious of the meaning of his words. "He is, as you say, a remarkable horse—a prodigious horse! although, as you very justly observe, of a suspicious and untractable character; let him be mine, however," he added, after a pause, "perhaps a rider like Frederick of Metzengerstein may tame even the devil from the stables of Berlifitzing."

"You are mistaken, my lord; the horse, as I think we mentioned, is *not* from the stables of the Count. If such had been the case, we know our duty better than to bring him into the presence of a noble of your family."

"True!" observed the Baron, dryly; and at that instant a page of the bedchamber came from the palace with a heightened colour, and a precipitate step. He whispered into his master's ear an account of the sudden disappearance of a small portion of the tapestry, in an apartment which he designated; entering, at the same time, into particulars of a minute and circumstantial character; but from the low tone of voice in which these latter were communicated, nothing escaped to gratify the excited curiosity of the equerries.

The young Frederick, during the conference, seemed agitated by a variety of emotions. He soon, however, recovered his composure, and an expression of determined malignancy settled upon his countenance, as he gave peremptory orders that the apartment in question should be immediately locked up, and the key placed in his own possession.

"Have you heard of the unhappy death of the old hunter, Berlifitzing?" said one of his vassals to the Baron, as, after the departure of the page, the huge steed which that nobleman had adopted as his own, plunged and curveted, with redoubled fury, down the long avenue which extended from the palace to the stables of Metzengerstein.

"No!" said the Baron, turning abruptly toward the speaker, "dead! say you?"

"It is indeed true, my lord; and, to the noble of your name, will be, I imagine, no unwelcome intelligence."

A rapid smile shot over the countenance of the listener. "How died he?"

"In his rash exertions to rescue a favourite portion of the hunting stud, he has himself perished miserably in the flames."

"I-n-d-e-e-d-!" ejaculated the Baron, as if slowly and deliberately impressed with the truth of some exciting idea.

"Indeed," repeated the vassal.

"Shocking!" said the youth, calmly, and turned quietly into the palace.

From this date a marked alteration took place in the outward demeanour of the dissolute young Baron Frederick Von Metzengerstein. Indeed, his behaviour disappointed every expectation, and proved little in accordance with the views of many a manœuvring mamma; while his habits and manner, still less than formerly, offered anything congenial with those of the neighbouring aristocracy. He was never to be seen beyond the limits of his own domain, and, in this wide and social world, was utterly companionless—unless, indeed, that unnatural, impetuous, and fiery-coloured horse, which he henceforward continually bestrode, had any mysterious right to the title of his friend.

Numerous invitations on the part of the neighbourhood for a long time, however, periodically came in. "Will the Baron honour our festivals with his presence?" "Will the Baron join us in a hunting of the boar?"—"Metzengerstein does not hunt;" "Metzengerstein will not attend," were the haughty and laconic answers.

These repeated insults were not to be endured by an imperious nobility. Such invitations became less cordial—less frequent—in time they ceased altogether. The widow of the unfortunate Count Berlifitzing was even heard to express a hope "that the Baron might be at home when he did not wish to be at home, since he disdained the company of his equals; and ride when he did not wish to ride, since he preferred the society of a horse." This, to be sure, was a very silly explosion of hereditary pique;

and merely proved how singularly unmeaning our sayings are apt to become, when we desire to be unusually energetic.

The charitable, nevertheless, attributed the alteration in the conduct of the young nobleman to the natural sorrow of a son for the untimely loss of his parents;—forgetting, however, his atrocious and reckless behaviour during the short period immediately succeeding that bereavement. Some there were, indeed, who suggested a too haughty idea of self-consequence and dignity. Others again (among whom may be mentioned the family physician) did not hesitate in speaking of morbid melancholy, and hereditary ill-health; while dark hints, of a more equivocal nature, were current among the multitude.

Indeed, the Baron's perverse attachment to his lately acquired charger—an attachment which seemed to attain new strength from every fresh example of the animal's ferocious and demon-like propensities—at length became, in the eyes of all reasonable men, a hideous and unnatural fervour. In the glare of noon—at the dead hour of night—in sickness or in health—in calm or in tempest—the young Metzengerstein seemed riveted to the saddle of that colossal horse, whose intractable audacities so well accorded with his own spirit.

There were circumstances, moreover, which, coupled with late events, gave an unearthly and portentous character to the mania of the rider, and to the capabilities of the steed. The space passed over in a single leap had been accurately measured, and was found to exceed, by an astounding difference, the wildest expectations of the most imaginative. The Baron, besides, had no particular *name* for the animal, although all the rest in his collection were distinguished by characteristic appellations. His stable, too, was appointed at a distance from the rest; and, with regard to grooming and other necessary offices, none but the owner in person had ventured to officiate, or even to enter the enclosure of that horse's particular stall. It was also to be observed, that although the three grooms, who had caught the steed as he fled from the conflagration at Berlifitzing, had succeeded in arresting his course by means of a chain-bridle and noose—yet not one of the three could with any certainty affirm that he had, during that dangerous struggle, or at any period thereafter, actually placed his hand upon the body of the beast. Instances of peculiar intelligence in the demeanour of a noble and high-spirited horse are not to be supposed capable of exciting unreasonable attention, but there were certain circumstances which intruded themselves perforce upon the most sceptical and phlegmatic; and it is said there were times when the animal caused the gaping crowd who stood around to recoil in horror from the deep and impressive meaning of his terrible stamp—times when the young Metzengerstein turned pale and shrunk away from the rapid and searching expression of his human-looking eye.

Among all the retinue of the Baron, however, none were found to doubt the ardour of that extraordinary affection which existed on the part of the young nobleman for the fiery qualities of his horse; at least, none but an insignificant and misshapen little page, whose deformities were in everybody's way, and whose opinions were of the least possible importance. He (if his ideas are worth mentioning at all) had the effrontery to assert that his master never vaulted into the saddle without an unaccountable and almost imperceptible shudder; and that, upon his return from every long-continued and habitual ride, an expression of triumphant malignity distorted every muscle in his countenance.

One tempestuous night, Metzengerstein, awaking from a heavy slumber, descended like a maniac from his chamber, and, mounting in hot haste, bounded away into the mazes of the forest. An occurrence so common attracted no particular attention, but his return was looked for with intense anxiety on the part of his domestics, when, after some hours' absence, the stupendous and magnificent battlements of the Palace Metzengerstein were discovered crackling and rocking to their very foundation, under the influence of a dense and livid mass of ungovernable fire.

As the flames, when first seen, had already made so terrible a progress that all efforts to save any portion of the building were evidently futile, the astonished neighbourhood stood idly around in silent if not apathetic wonder. But a new and fearful object soon riveted the attention of the multitude, and proved how much more intense is the excitement wrought in the feelings of a crowd by the contemplation of human agony, than that brought about by the most appalling spectacles of inanimate matter.

Up the long avenue of aged oaks which led from the forest to the main entrance of the Palace Metzengerstein, a steed, bearing an unbonneted and disordered rider, was seen leaping with an impetuosity which outstripped the very Demon of the Tempest.

The career of the horseman was indisputably, on his own part, uncontrollable. The agony of his countenance, the convulsive struggle of his frame, gave evidence of superhuman exertion; but no sound, save a solitary shriek, escaped from his lacerated lips, which were bitten through and through in the intensity of terror. One instant, and the clattering of hoofs resounded sharply and shrilly above the roaring of the flames and the shrieking of the winds—another, and, clearing at a single plunge the gateway and the moat, the steed bounded far up the tottering staircases of the palace, and, with its rider, disappeared amid the whirlwind of chaotic fire.

The fury of the tempest immediately died away, and a dead calm sullenly succeeded. A white flame still enveloped the building like a shroud, and, streaming far away into the quiet atmosphere, shot forth a glare of preternatural light; while a cloud of smoke settled heavily over the battlements in the distinct colossal figure of—*a horse*.

K. and H. PRICHARD
The Story of Saddler's Croft

Kate and Hesketh Prichard were a very successful mother-son writing team, publishing many adventure and mystery stories under both their real names and also the pseudonym "E. and H. Heron". Hesketh was also a noted explorer, big-game hunter, and county cricketer. In the wake of the success of Sherlock Holmes, he devised the genre's first regular psychic investigator (or "ghost buster"), Flaxman Low, to solve all the inexplicable and supernatural cases outside the range of the Great Detective! Among the many psychic sleuths destined to follow Flaxman Low's example were Algernon Blackwood's John Silence, William Hope Hodgson's Carnacki, and Margery Lawrence's Miles Pennoyer. "The Story of Saddler's Croft" first appeared in Pearson's Magazine, *February 1899.*

Although Flaxman Low has devoted his life to the study of psychical phenomena, he has always been most earnest in warning persons who feel inclined to dabble in spiritualism, without any serious motive for doing so, of the mischief and danger accruing to the rash experimenter. Extremely few persons are sufficiently masters of themselves to permit of their calling in the vast unknown forces outside ordinary human knowledge for mere purposes of amusement.

In support of this warning the following extraordinary story is laid before our readers.

Deep in the forest land of Sussex, close by an unfrequented road, stands a low half-timbered house, that is only separated from the roadway by a rough stone wall and a few flower borders. The front is covered with ivy, and looks out between two conical trees upon the passers-by. The windows are many of them diamond-paned, and an unpretentious white gate leads up to the front door. It is a quaint, quiet spot, with an old-world suggestion about it which appealed strongly to pretty Sadie Corcoran as she drove with her husband along the lane. The Corcorans were Americans, and had to the full the American liking for things ancient. Saddler's Croft struck them both as ideal, and when they found out that it was much more roomy and comfortable than it looked from the road, and also that it had large lawns and grounds attached to it, they decided at once on taking it for a year or two.

When they mentioned the project to Phil Strewd, their host, and an old friend of Corcoran, he did not favour it. Much as he should have liked to have them for neighbours, he thought that Saddler's Croft had too many unpleasant traditions connected with it. Besides, it had lain empty for three years, as the last occupants were spiritualists of some sort, and the place was said to be haunted. But Mrs. Corcoran was not to be put off, and declared that a flavour of ghostliness was all that Saddler's Croft required to make it absolutely the most attractive residence in Europe.

The Corcorans moved in about October, but it was not till the following July that Flaxman Low met Mr. Strewd on the Victoria platform.

"I'm glad you're coming down to Andy Corcoran's," Strewd began. "You must remember him? I introduced you to him at the club a couple of years ago. He's an awfully decent fellow, and an old friend of mine. He once went with an Arctic expedition, and has crossed Greenland or San Josef's Land on snowshoes or something. I've got the book about it at home. So you can size him up for yourself. He's now married to a very pretty woman, and they have taken a house in my part of the world.

"I didn't want them to rent Saddler's Croft, for it had a bad name some years ago. Some of your psychical folk used to live there. They made a sort of Greek temple at the back, where they used to have queer goings on, so I'm told. A Greek was living with them called Agapoulos, who was the arch-priest of their sect, or whatever it was. Ultimately Agapoulos died on a moonlight night in the temple, in the middle of their rites. After that his friends left, but, of course, people said he haunted the place. I never saw anything myself, but a young sailor, home on leave about that time, swore he'd catch the ghost, and he was found next morning on the temple steps. He was past telling us what had happened, or what he had seen, for he was dead. I'll never forget his face. It was horrible!"

"And since then?"

"After that the place would not let, although the talk of the ghost being seen died away until quite lately. I suppose the old caretaker went to bed early, and avoided trouble that way. But during the last few months Corcoran has seen it repeatedly himself, and—in fact, things seem to be going on very strangely. What with Mrs. Corcoran wild on studying psychology, as she calls it——"

"So Mrs. Corcoran has a turn that way?"

"Yes, since young Sinclair came home from Ceylon about five months ago. I must tell you he was very thick with Agapoulos in former times, and people said he used to join in all the ruffianism at Saddler's Croft. You'll see the rest for yourself. You are asked down ostensibly to please Mrs. Corcoran, but Andy hopes you may help him to clear up the mystery."

Flaxman Low found Corcoran a tall, thin, nervy American of the best type; while his wife was as pretty and as charming as we have grown accustomed to expect an American girl to be.

"I suppose," Corcoran began, "that Phil has been giving you all the gossip about this house? I was entirely sceptical once; but now—do you believe in midsummer madness?"

"I believe there often is a deep truth hidden in common beliefs and superstitions. But let me hear more."

"I'll tell you what happened not twenty-four hours ago. Everything has been working up to it for the last three months, but it came to a head last night, and I immediately wired for you. I had been sitting in my smoking-room rather late reading. I put out the lamp and was just about to go to bed when the brilliance of the moonlight struck me, and I put my head through the window to look over the lawn. Directly I heard chanting of a most unusual character from the direction of the temple, which lies at the back of that plantation. Then one voice, a beautiful tenor, detached itself from the rest, and seemed to approach the house. As it came nearer I saw my wife cross the grass to the plantation with a wavering, uncertain gait. I ran after her, for I believed she was walking in her sleep; but before I could reach her a man came out of the grass alley at the other side of the lawn.

"I saw them go away together down the alley towards the temple, but I could not stir, the moonbeams seemed to be penetrating my brain, my feet were chained, the wildest and most hideous thoughts seemed rocking—I can use no other term—in my head. I made an effort, and ran round by another way, and met them on the temple steps. I had strength left to grasp at the man—remember I saw him plainly, with his dark, Greek face—but he turned aside and leapt into the underwood, leaving in my hand only the button from the back of his coat.

"Now comes the incomprehensible part. Sadie, without seeing me, or so it appeared, glided away again towards the house; but I was determined to find the man who had eluded me. The moonlight poured upon my head; I felt it like an absolute touch. The chanting grew louder, and drowned every other recollection. I forgot Sadie, I forgot all but the delicious sounds, and I—I, a nineteenth-century, hard-headed Yankee—hammered at those accursed doors to be allowed to enter. Then, like a dream, the singing was behind me and around me—some one came, or so I thought, and pushed me gently in. The moon was pouring through the end window; there were many people. In the morning I found myself lying on the floor of the temple, and all about me the dust was undisturbed but for the mark of my own single footstep and the spot where I had fallen. You may say it was all a dream, Low, but I tell you some infernal power hangs about that building."

"From what you tell me," said Flaxman Low, "I can almost undertake to say that Mrs. Corcoran is at present nearly, if not quite, ignorant of the horrible experience you remember. In her case the emotions of wonder and curiosity have probably alone been worked upon as in a dream."

"I believe in her absolutely," exclaimed Corcoran, "but this power swamps all resistance. I have another strange circumstance to add. On coming to myself I found the button still in my hand. I have since had the opportunity of fitting it to its right position in the coat of a man who is a pretty constant visitor here," the American's lips tightened, "a young Sinclair, who does tea-planting in Ceylon when he has the health for it, but is just now at home to recruit. He is the son of a neighbouring squire, and in every particular of face and figure unlike the handsome Greek I saw that night."

"Have you spoken to him on the subject?"

"Yes; I showed him the button, and told him I had found it near the temple. He took the news very curiously. He did not look confused or guilty, but simply scared out of his senses. He offered no explanation, but made a hasty excuse, and left us. My wife looked on with the most perfect indifference, and offered no remark."

"Has Mrs. Corcoran appeared to be very languid of late?" asked Low.

"Yes, I have noticed that."

"Judging from the effect produced by the chanting upon you, I should say that you were something of a musician?" said Low irrelevantly.

"Yes," replied the other, astonished.

"Then, this evening, when I am talking with Mrs. Corcoran, will you reproduce the melody you heard on that night?"

Corcoran agreed, and the conversation ended with a request on the part of Mr. Low to be permitted to make the acquaintance of Mrs. Corcoran, and further, to be given the opportunity of talking to her alone.

Sadie Corcoran received him with effusion.

"O Mr. Low, I'm just perfectly delighted to see you! I'm looking forward to the most lovely spiritual talks. It's such fun! You know I was in quite a psychical set before I married, but afterwards I dropped it, because Andy has some effete old prejudices."

Flaxman Low inquired how it happened that her interest had revived.

"It is the air of this dear old place," she replied, with a more serious expression. "I always found the subject very attractive, and lately we have made the acquaintance of a Mr. Sinclair, who is a—" she checked herself with an odd look, "who knows all about it."

"How does he advise you to experiment?" asked Mr. Low. "Have you ever tried sleeping with the moonlight on your face?"

She flushed, and looked startled.

"Yes, Mr. Sinclair told me that the spiritualists who formerly lived in this house believed that by doing so you could put

479

yourself into communication with—other intelligences. It makes one dream," she added, "such strange dreams."

"Are they pleasant dreams?" asked Flaxman Low gravely.

"Not now, but by and by he assures me that they will be."

"But you must think of your dreams all day long, or the moonlight will not affect you so readily on the next occasion, and you are obliged to repeat a certain formula? Is it not so?"

She admitted it was, and added: "But Mr. Sinclair says that if I persevere I shall soon pass through the zone of the bad spirits and enter the circle of the good. So I choose to go on. It is all so wonderful and exciting. Oh, here is Mr. Sinclair! I'm sure you will find many interesting things to talk over."

The drawing-room lay at the back of the house, and overlooked a strip of lawn shut in on the further side by a thick plantation of larches. Directly opposite to the French window, where they were seated, a grass alley which had been cut through the plantation gave a glimpse of turf and forest land beyond. From this alley now emerged a young man in riding-breeches, who walked moodily across the lawn with his eyes on the ground. In a few minutes Flaxman Low understood that young Sinclair had a pronounced admiration for his hostess, the reckless, headstrong admiration with which a weak-willed man of strong emotions often deceives himself and the woman he loves. He was manifestly in wretched health and equally wretched spirits, a combination that greatly impaired the very ordinary type of English good-looks which he represented.

While the three had tea together Mrs. Corcoran made some attempt to lead up to the subject of spiritualism, but Sinclair avoided it, and soon Mrs. Corcoran lost her vivacity, which gave place to a well-marked languor, a condition that Low shortly grew to connect with Sinclair's presence. Presently she left them, and the two men went outside and walked up and down smoking for a while till Flaxman Low turned down the path between the larches. Sinclair hung back.

"You'll find it stuffy down there," he said, with curved nostrils.

"I rather wanted to see what building that roof over the trees belongs to," replied Low.

With manifest reluctance Sinclair went on beside him. Another turn at right angles brought them into the path leading up to the little temple, which Low found was solidly built of stone. In shape it was oblong, with a pillared Ionic façade. The trees stood closely round it, and it contained only one window, now void of glass, set high in the further end of the building. Low asked a question.

"It was a summer-house made by the people who lived here formerly," replied Sinclair, with brusqueness. "Let's get away. It's beastly damp."

"It is an odd kind of summer-house. It looks more like—" Low checked himself. "Can we go inside?" He went up the low steps and tried the door, which yielded readily, and he entered to look round.

The walls had once been ornamented with designs in black and some glittering pigment, while at the upper end a daïs nearly four feet high stood under the arched window, the whole giving the vague impression of a church. One or two peculiarities of structure and decoration struck Low. He turned sharply on Sinclair.

"What was this place used for?"

But Sinclair was staring round with a white, working face; his glance seemed to trace out the half-obliterated devices upon the walls, and then rested on the daïs. A sort of convulsion passed over his features, as his head was jerked forward, rather as if pushed by some unseen force than by his own will, while, at the same time, he brought his hand to his mouth, and kissed it. Then with a strange, prolonged cry he rushed headlong out of the temple, and appeared no more at Saddler's Croft that day.

The afternoon was still and warm with brooding thunderstorm, but at night the sky cleared. Now it happened that Andy Corcoran was, amongst many other good things, an accomplished musician, and, while Flaxman Low and Mrs. Corcoran talked at intervals by the open French window, he sat down at the piano and played a weird melody. Mrs. Corcoran broke off in the middle of a sentence, and soon she began swaying gently to the rhythm of the music, and presently she was singing. Suddenly, Corcoran dropped his hand on the notes with a crash. His wife sprang from her chair.

"Andy! Where are you? Where are you?" And in a moment she had thrown herself, sobbing hysterically, into his arms, while he begged her to tell him what troubled her.

"It was that music. Oh, don't play it any more! I liked it at first, and then all at once it seemed to terrify me!" He led her back towards the light.

"Where did you learn that song, Sadie? Tell me."

She lifted her clear eyes to his.

"I don't know! I can't remember, but it is like a dreadful memory! Never play it again! Promise me!"

"Of course not, darling."

By midnight the moon sailed broad and bright above the house. Flaxman Low and the American were together in the smoking-room. The room was in darkness. Low sat in the shadow of the open window, while Corcoran waited behind him in the gloom. The shade of the larches lay in a black line along the grass, the air was still and heavy, not a leaf moved. From his position, Low could see the dark masses of the forest stretching away into the dimness over the undulating country. The scene was very lovely, very lonely, and very sad.

A little trill of bells within the room rang the half-hour after midnight, and scarcely had the sound ceased when from outside came another—a long cadenced wailing chant of voices in unison that rose and fell faint and far off but with one distinct note, the same that Low had heard in Sinclair's beast-like cry earlier in the day.

After the chanting died away, there followed a long sullen interval, broken at last by a sound of singing, but so vague and dim that it might have been some elusive air throbbing within the brain. Slowly it grew louder and nearer. It was the melody Sadie had begged never to hear again, and it was sung by a tenor voice, vibrating and beautiful.

Low felt Corcoran's hand grip his shoulder, when out upon the grass Sadie, a slim figure in trailing white, appeared advancing with uncertain steps towards the alley of the larches. The next moment the singer came forward from the shadows to meet her. It was not Sinclair, but a much more remarkable-looking personage. He stopped and raised his face to the moon, a face of an extraordinary perfection of beauty such as Flaxman Low had never seen before. But the great dark eyes, the full powerfully moulded features, had one attribute in common with Sinclair's face, they wore the same look of a profound and infinite unhappiness.

482

"Come." Corcoran gripped Flaxman Low's shoulder. "She is sleep-walking. We will see who it is this time."

When they reached the lawn the couple had disappeared. Corcoran leading, the two men ran along under the shadow of the house, and so by another path to the back of the temple.

The empty window glowed in the light of the moon, and the hum of a subdued chanting floated out amongst the silent trees. The sound seized upon the brain like a whiff of opium, and a thousand unbidden thoughts ran through Flaxman Low's mind. But his mental condition was as much under his control as his bodily movements. Pulling himself together he ran on. Sadie Corcoran and her companion were mounting the steps under the pillars. The girl held back, as if drawn forward against her will; her eyes were blank and open, and she moved slowly.

Then Corcoran dashed out of the shadow.

What occurred next Mr. Low does not know, for he hurried Mrs. Corcoran away towards the house, holding her arm gently. She yielded to his touch, and went silently beside him to the drawing-room, where he guided her to a couch. She lay down upon it like a tired child, and closed her eyes without a word.

After a while Flaxman Low went out again to look for Corcoran. The temple was dark and silent, and there was no one to be seen. He groped his way through the long grass towards the back of the building. He had not gone far when he stumbled over something soft that moved and groaned. Low lit a match, for it was impossible to see anything in the gloom under the trees. To his horror he found the American at his feet, beaten and battered almost beyond recognition.

The first thing next morning Mr. Strewd received a note from Flaxman Low asking him to come over at once. He arrived in the course of the forenoon, and listened to an account of Corcoran's adventures during the night, with an air of dismay.

"So it's come at last!" he remarked, "I'd no idea Sinclair was such a bruiser."

"Sinclair? What do you suppose Sinclair had to do with it?"

"Oh, come now, Low, what's the good of that? Why, my man told me this morning when I was shaving that Sinclair went home some time last night all covered in blood. I'd half a guess at what had happened then."

"But I tell you I saw the man with whom Corcoran fought. He was an extraordinarily handsome man with a Greek face."

Strewd whistled.

"By George, Low, you let your imagination run away with you," he said, shaking his head. "That's all nonsense, you know."

"We must try to find out if it is," said Low.

"Will you come over to-night and stay with me? There will be a full moon."

"Yes, and it has affected all your brains! Here's Mrs. Corcoran full of surprise over her husband's condition! You don't suppose that's genuine?"

"I know it is genuine," replied Low quietly. "Bring your Kodak with you when you come, will you?"

The day was long, languorous, and heavy; the thunderstorm had not yet broken, but once again the night rose cloudless. Flaxman Low decided to watch alone near the temple while Strewd remained on the alert in the house, ready to give his help if it should be needed.

The hush of the night, the smell of the dewy larches, the silvery light with its bewildering beauty creeping from point to point as the moon rose, all the pure influences of nature, seemed to Low more powerful, more effective, than he had ever before felt them to be. Forcing his mind to dwell on ordinary subjects, he waited. Midnight passed, and then began indistinct sounds, shuffling footsteps, murmurings, and laughter, but all faint and evasive. Gradually the tumultuous thoughts he had experienced on the previous evening began to run riot in his brain.

When the singing began he does not know. It was only by an immense effort of will that he was able to throw off the trance that was stealing over him, holding him prisoner—how nearly a willing prisoner he shudders to remember. But habits of self-control have been Low's only shield in many a dangerous hour. They came to his aid now. He moved out in front of the temple just in time to see Sadie pass within the temple door. Waiting only a moment to make quite sure of his senses, and concentrating his will on the single desire of saving her, he followed. He says he was conscious of a crowd of persons at either side; he knew without looking that the pictures on the wall glowed and lived again.

Through the high window opposite him a broad white shaft of light fell, and immediately under it, on the daïs, stood the man whom Mr. Low in his heart now called Agapoulos. Supreme in its beauty and its sadness that beautiful face looked across the bowed heads of those present into the eyes of Mr. Flaxman Low. Slowly, very slowly, as a narrow lane opened up before him amongst the figures of the crowd, Low advanced towards the daïs. The man's smile seemed to draw him on; he stretched out his hand as Flaxman Low approached. And Low was conscious of a longing to clasp it even though that might mean perdition.

At the last moment, when it seemed to him he could resist no longer, he became aware of the white-clad figure of Sadie beside him. She also was looking up at the beautiful face with a wild gaze. Low hesitated no longer. He was now within two feet of the daïs. He swung back his left hand and dealt a smashing half-arm blow at the figure. The man staggered with a very human groan, and then fell face forward on the daïs. A whirlwind of dust seemed to rise and obscure the moonlight; there was a wild sense of motion and flight, a subdued sibilant murmur like the noise of a swarm of bats in commotion, and then Flaxman Low heard Phil Strewd's loud voice at the door, and he shouted to him to come.

"What has happened?" said Strewd, as he helped to raise the fallen man. "Why, whom have we got here? Good heavens, Low, it is Agapoulos! I remember him well!"

"Leave him there in the moonlight. Take Mrs. Corcoran away and hurry back with the Kodak. There is no time to lose before the moon leaves this window."

The moonlight was full and strong, the exposure prolonged and steady, so that when afterwards Flaxman Low came to develop the film—but we are anticipating, for the night and its revelations were not over yet. The two men waited through the dark hour that precedes the dawn, intending when daylight came to remove their prisoner elsewhere. They sat on the edge of the daïs side by side, Strewd at Low's request holding the hand of the unconscious man, and talked till the light came.

"I think it's about time to move him now," suggested Strewd, looking round at the wounded man behind him. As he did so, he sprang to his feet with a shout.

"What's this, Low? I've gone mad, I think! Look here!"

Flaxman Low bent over the pale, unconscious face. It bore no longer the impress of that exquisite Greek beauty they had seen an hour earlier; it only showed to their astonished gaze the haggard outlines of young Sinclair.

Some days later Strewd rubbed the back of his head energetically with a broad hand, and surmised aloud.

"This is a strange world, my masters," and he looked across the cool shady bedroom at Andy Corcoran's bandaged head.

"And the other world's stranger, I guess," put in the American drily, "if we may judge by the sample of the supernatural we have lately had.

"You know I hold that there is no such thing as the supernatural; all is natural," said Flaxman Low. "We need more light, more knowledge. As there is a well-defined break in the notes of the human voice, so there is a break between what we call natural and supernatural. But the notes of the upper register correspond with those in the lower scale; in like manner, by drawing upon our experience of things we know and see, we should be able to form accurate hypotheses with regard to things which, while clearly pertaining to us, have so far been regarded as mysteries."

"I doubt if any theory will touch this mystery," Strewd objected. "I have questioned Sinclair, and noted down his answers as you asked me, Low. Here they are."

"No, thank you. Will you compare my theory with what he has told you? In the first place, Agapoulos was, I fancy, one of a clique calling themselves Dianists, who desired to revive the ancient worship of the moon. That I easily gathered from the symbol of the moon in front of the temple and from the half-defaced devices on the walls inside. Then I perceived that Sinclair, when we were standing before the daïs, almost unconsciously used the gesture of the moon worshippers. The chant we heard was the lament for Adonis. I could multiply evidences, but there is no need to do so. The fact also tells that the place is haunted on moonlight nights only."

"Sinclair's confession corroborates all this," said Strewd at this point.

Corcoran turned irritably on his couch.

"Moon-worship was not exactly the nicest form of idolatry," he said in a weary tone; "but I can't see how that accounts for the awkward fact that a man who not only looks like Agapoulos, but was caught, and even photographed as Agapoulos, turns out at the end of an hour or so, during which there was no chance of substituting one for the other, to be another person of an entirely different appearance. Add to this that Agapoulos is dead and Sinclair is living, and we have an array of facts that drive one to suspect that common-sense and reason are delusions. Go on, Low."

"The substitution, as you call it, of Agapoulos for Sinclair is one of the most marked and best attested cases of obsession with which I have personally come into contact," answered Flaxman Low. "You will notice that during Sinclair's absence in Ceylon nothing was seen of the ghost—on his return it again appeared."

"What is obsession? I know what it is supposed to be, but—" Corcoran stopped.

"I should call it in this case as nearly as possible an instance of spiritual hypnotism. We know there is such a thing as human hypnotism; why should not a disembodied spirit have similar powers? Sinclair has been obsessed by the spirit of Agapoulos; he not only yielded to his influence in the man's lifetime, but sought it again after his death. I don't profess to claim any great knowledge of the subject, but I do know that terrible results have come about from similar practices. Sinclair, for his own reasons, invited the control of a spirit, and, having no inherent powers of resistance, he became its slave. Agapoulos must have possessed extraordinary will-force; his soul actually dominated Sinclair's. Thus not only the mental attributes of Sinclair but even his bodily appearance became modified to the likeness of the Greek. Sinclair himself probably looked upon his experiences as a series of vivid dreams induced by dwelling on certain thoughts and using certain formulae, until this morning when his condition proved to him that they were real enough."

"That is perhaps all very well so far as it goes," put in Strewd, "but I fail to understand how a seedy, weakly chap like Sinclair could punish my friend Andy here, as we must suppose he has done, if we accept your ideas, Low."

"You are aware that under abnormal conditions, such as may be observed in the insane, a quite extraordinary reserve of latent strength is frequently called out from apparently weak persons. So Sinclair's usual powers were largely reinforced by abnormal influences."

"I have another question to ask, Low," said Corcoran. "Can you explain the strange attraction and influence the temple possessed over all of us, and especially over my wife?"

"I think so. Mrs. Corcoran, through a desire for amusement and excitement, placed herself in a degree of communication with the spiritual world during sleep. Remember, the Greek lived here, and the thoughts and emotions of individuals remain in the *aura* of places closely associated with them. Personally, I do not doubt that Agapoulos is a strong and living intelligence, and those persons who frequent the vicinity of the temple are readily placed in rapport with his wandering spirit by means of this *aura*. To use common words, evil influences haunt the temple."

"But this is intolerable. What can we do?"

"Leave Saddler's Croft, and persuade Mrs. Corcoran to have no more to do with spiritism. As for Sinclair, I will see him. He has opened what may be called the doors of life. It will be a hard task to close them again, and to become his own master. But it may be done."

LENNOX ROBINSON
The Face

Lennox Robinson (1886–1958) was one of Ireland's leading playwrights, long associated with the Abbey Theatre (Dublin), and best known for his outstanding plays The Lost Leader (1918) *and* The Whiteheaded Boy (1920). *He also wrote biographies, novels, dramatic criticism, and several tales of the supernatural.* "The Face" (1913) *is taken from his collection* Eight Short Stories (1919).

Never in the daytime or in bright sunlight could you see it, but sometimes just before sunset when some sinking ray of the sun was reflected from the rock to the lake's dark surface, and always in moonlight and on clear starry nights then, lying flat on the top of the cliff and peering over you could see the face quite clearly.

It lay in the deep pool at the foot of the cliff, a few yards from the shore and apparently a foot or two deep in the water. First it appeared as a piece of white rock with a film of lakeweed floating across it, then gradually your vision cleared and you saw the pale features distinctly, the closed eyes and the long dark lashes, the curved eyebrows, the gentle mouth and the fair hair which half hid the white neck and which sometimes drifted like a veil across the face; below the neck the pool lay in deeper shadow, and no one had ever been able to tell the shape of the beautiful creature that lay there.

It was a precipitous climb down the face of the cliff and no one but Jerry Sullivan had ventured it, but as he touched with his fingers the water of the pool the face shivered away, and stretching his arm deep into the water it met nothing except a tendril of lake-weed. Only once had he climbed down because he was afraid that if he probed too deeply the face would disappear for ever—for it was days after he touched the water before he saw it again; for the future he was content to gaze at it from above.

He had known it all his life. He could not have been more than six years old when his father had led him to the cliff's edge and shown him the sleeping face in the water. He had never been afraid of it as were some of the other boys, on the contrary when he was sent to drive the sheep from one hill to another he would contrive to pass the lake either coming or going, he would loiter there until the sun sank and risk a scolding when he got home; but hardly a week passed without his seeing the face.

Up among those lonely mountains he saw few women. There was only his mother, old now and grey, and a mile or two to the west the MacCarthy's cottage with the two girls Peg and Ellen, coarsely featured both with thick black hair, and the few other women he saw from time to time were either coarsely dark or foxy red. Was it any wonder that he turned from them to the fair face floating in the water? any wonder that as he grew older he judged every woman's face by that hard standard and found them all wanting.

His father died when he was eighteen years old and Jerry lived on with his mother, tilling the little bit of land, cutting turf on the side of the mountain, driving the sheep. It was a lonely, silent life—for he was an only child—and his mother often urged him to take a wife, but he made the excuse that while she was there he wanted no other woman in the house, and though she remonstrated with him she was well content to remain sole mistress of the cottage to the day of her death. He never told her of those hours he spent by the lake; hidden in a fold of the hills no one saw him go there, the neighbours shunned the place as haunted, and as the years crept by the face grew to be more and more particularly his own.

Fifteen years after his father's death his mother died, and when the funeral was over he climbed the mountain and stared for a long time into the water. It was a stormy winter evening and as the sun went down a pale young moon appeared. Never had the face been so clear, never had it looked more lovely. He had felt very lonely when the earth was thrown on his mother's coffin, now he felt quietly content. He had nothing left in the world to love except this face. It had no rival now, he could pour out all the love of his heart in adoration of it.

And so for three years it went on like this: more and more he shunned the neighbours, more and more time he spent by the lake. He began to neglect the farm, for what pleasure was

490

there in working only for himself? and to the overtures of the match-makers he was either morosely silent or roughly violent. He spent now whole nights on the cliff; sometimes he thought he saw a stirring of the eyelids and the fancy grew in him that after sufficient concentration of devotion on his part the eyes would open; already the cheeks seemed less pale, the mouth had parted slightly, he thought he saw a gleam of white teeth.

He grew worn with watching. The woman in the water seemed to draw her vitality from him, and as her cheeks grew fuller his own grew thin, and as her face flushed his paled until one evening gazing down at those closed eyes he saw the lids stir and stir again and at last very slowly they opened. The eyes behind them were dazzlingly blue and they met his grey ones with a long comprehending look. Everything he had ever hoped to see in a woman's eyes was there, and half in terror, half in joy, he gave a cry and drew back from the cliff; when he looked again a second later the face had vanished.

He thought he would see it the next night, but he looked in vain. He was frantic. There had been weeks before when on account of the weather or some trick of light he had been unable to see the face, but always through those dark days he had been conscious that it was waiting for him in the water, ready to re-appear at any moment; now he was only conscious of a great blank, an emptiness, a desolation. He ran round the lake like a distracted man, he looked into other pools—in vain. With the opening of her eyes she had fled and the little lake was as deserted as a last year's nest.

It was three days later at the fair of Coolmore that he found her. She was standing with her back to the wall outside the post-office, and a little curious crowd was round her questioning her and touching her clothes. There was a strangeness, a foreignness about her, and when the village policeman came and began to question her the crowd gathered closer, but her replies were incoherent; she did not know her name or where she had come from or where she was going; she stood there lonely and aloof and her blue eyes kept searching every face piteously, like a blind man feeling with his stick for the pavement's edge. Then she lifted her eyes and beyond the fringe of the crowd they met Jerry's eyes. He again saw that look, he strode to her pushing the crowd away roughly to right and left, he put his arm into hers and led her to his house.

The priest married them and they lived in perfect contentment and happiness. She had been pale and fragile when he brought her home, but she grew every day stronger and more beautiful. She knew nothing of housework or farmwork and learned but little, preferring to sit in the shadow of a rock in the field while Jerry worked and in the winter to crouch in the corner near the fire or sit in the window in the moonlight. He was quite content to have her so and gladly did the work of two; he liked the mystery of her, he liked to feel her different from the neighbours. She never could tell him where she came from and he soon ceased to question her; he told her of the face in the water, but it seemed to awaken no memory in her mind, and yet sometimes, looking at her—especially when she sat in the moonlight—the texture of her body would seem to become fluidic, her face would appear as if floating, and behind it he would seem to see that other face with its closed eyes. That face had disappeared from the lake and he never went to the cliff now.

In the second November after their marriage when the moon was full a child was born to them, a child as fragile as a moon-ray, that lay in the cradle hardly stirring, never crying.

The fair of Coolmore was held ten days later and Jerry had to bring some cattle to it to sell. Coolmore lay fifteen miles away across the mountain, and he got up very early in the morning, lit the fire, left food and drink for his wife, and started. Peg MacCarthy had promised to look in at her once or twice during the day and he knew she would want for nothing.

He sold his cattle, but there was a delay about payment and it was after four o'clock when he left Coolmore village. He walked quickly, the money was heavy in his pocket, his mind was strangely anxious about his wife and he made the best pace he could. The evening grew colder and colder, yellowish-grey clouds came up from the north-east, the rushes in the lonely bogs bent to the wind, and as he reached the top of the pass it began to snow. It was early in the year for snow, but this was a heavy shower and the big flakes half blinded him as he pushed doggedly on. But his boots grew clogged, he had to walk more and more slowly, and when he was three miles from home he determined to take a short cut across the hills which would shorten his road by half a mile. It was wild walking but he knew every foot of the path, it led him along the top of the cliff above the lake, and he stopped for a minute there to get his breath. The snow had ceased to fall, the sky was clearing, a few stars shone out and the lake lay black at his feet. Something—old habit perhaps—made him fall on his knees and peer over, and there in the pool below he saw the face. It was there just as it had always been with closed eyes and floating hair. He rose to his feet vaguely troubled. He had never seen it since his marriage.

Half a mile from his house he met Peg MacCarthy walking quickly towards him. "Thank God it's yourself, Jerry" she said. "The wife, God help me, is gone. I saw her just before milking time and she was sitting by the fire; I said you'd have a bad walk home and she said she wished she could go and meet you; then afterwards, and I sitting at my tea, a step passed on the road and now when I went to your house she's gone."

Hardly stopping to answer her he ran home. It was true, she was not there. The child lay quietly sleeping in its cradle. Then he thought of the face in the lake and he ran up the road and along the path and over the breast of the hill to the cliff's edge. The face was there still, and again as he had done years before he climbed down to the rock. He still saw the face, he touched the water, the face did not vanish, he plunged in his arms and drew his wife's body to the shore.

In the water the face had appeared living, out of it with the wet hair clinging about it it was cold and dead. Had she come to meet him and fallen in? He could see no hurt on her. Or had she fled from him back to the element to which she belonged? The wet form in his arms seemed less his than the woman in the water. Every impulse of his nature urged him to lay her back. He did so and she sank in the deep pool till only her face was seen.

He climbed the cliff and walked home. He felt strangely bewildered. He hardly grieved. Had he lost her or had he ever had her? Was this only the evening of his mother's funeral and had he, kneeling on that cliff, fallen into a dream and dreamed of the face's awakening, of the marriage, of the child? No, this last was real at any rate, and he took it from the cradle and held it in his arms and stood by the window looking out at the dying moon. And yet—was it only fancy—or, as the sickly moon sank did the child really grow lighter and lighter in his arms, and would he find when morning broke that he was only clasping a tangle of wet lake-weed wrapped in an old quilt?

DAVID G.ROWLANDS
A Fisher of Men

David G.Rowlands (b.1941) has contributed many fine ghost stories to anthologies and magazines over the past twenty years, and has been a regular contributor to Ghosts and Scholars *and the* Holly Bough *annual Christmas numbers of the* Cork Examiner. *Several of these tales are related by the Catholic priest Father O'Connor. "A Fisher of Men" (which first appeared in the* Holly Bough, *Christmas 1984) is an intriguing extension to the legend of the 6th-century Irish saint and hero who voyaged across the Atlantic to the "Promised Land of the Saints", subsequently named "St.Brendan's Island".*

The ten o'clock news was full of the rescue bid to aid a yachtsman whose attempt to sail single-handed across the Atlantic had come to grief.

"Hmm", I grunted to my old friend Fr. O'Connor, "another fool risking other lives as well as his own. If I were in the rescue services I'd get pretty fed-up with having to stand by every time some lunatic decided to cross the Atlantic on a biscuit tin, or some other silly stunt".

The old priest was more tolerant than I. "Well, now, it would be a pity to see the spirit of adventure stifled. There will always be those carried along by a zest for risks". He chuckled. "Without such foolhardiness by Irish monks like St. Columba, most of Europe might have remained pagan for centuries—it always was very backward! Columba's voyages were epics, you know . . . Then look again at the miraculous voyages of St. Brendan in the sixth century, when he and his chosen companions went boldly off in search of the Promised Land way up through the Hebrides, Shetlands, and Faroes; maybe as far as Iceland, or even come to that, America".

"Come now, Father", I scoffed, "surely those are no more than old Celtic legends?".

"Well you must remember", said he gently, "that if it had not been for Severin's epic voyage (which you would call foolhardy) from Brandon Creek to Newfoundland in 1976, the scoffers could still say the legend of Brendan discovering America was impossible. We now know that it is possible".

"But I thought Brendan was just a Kerry monk, who journeyed to Iona and then became the Abbot of Llancarvon, only returning to Kerry to die?"

"Ah, but you see even three centuries after Brendan's death, Viking raiders found Irish monks in Iceland and their loot included Irish bells and, allegedly, Brendan's miraculous Crozier". He smiled, rising to leave. "At any rate I have a story about St. Brendan for you, so remind me on your next visit".

The next time I visited the old priest, I reminded him of the promised story. He rose and crossed to a wall cupboard from which he withdrew a small carving. "What do you make of this?" he asked, handing it to me.

I examined it carefully—a salt-water-hardened, yellowish lump of wood that a skilled hand had carved in to a small rounded boat. There was a deck at one end, with a mast, and six figures filling the bows, one of whom towered over the others, holding the tiller and pointing forward. "Fine work", I said, handing it back. "St. Brendan and his crew, I take it"?

The old priest nodded. "Well, yes and no. It was given to me by an old monk at Melrose". He smiled in amused recollection. "Brother Sebastian was a real character and had seen a lot of the world before taking up monastic life. He had been profiteer, mercenary, adventurer, soldier (or I should say sailor) of fortune, for 'old salt' described him to a 't'. Dear me, I can see the old fellow with his ruddy, wind-beaten face now! He was a carpenter at Melrose and said this wood came from the beach of Brendan's Isle—Oilean Bhran—and that he carved it in memory of an adventure there."

"Brendan's Isle", said I musingly, "I didn't know there was one".

Fr. O'Connor laughed. "Nor did I, but it seems there are several in fact. Medieval maps show one situated to the far

West. This one of Bro. Sebastian's seems to have been beyond Sula Sgeir, toward Iceland. At any rate he was adamant about its exsistence and it certainly reformed his life.

"I have hinted" (continued Fr O'Connor) "that Sebastian was originally a bit of a rough character. It seems that at a tavern in Mallaig, he and his fishermen crew fell in with another of their kind who was unable to keep to himself a yarn about some outer island where there was a vast treasure for anyone to bespoil. They would have scoffed—and did for a while—until the old seaman produced (with much stealth and sideways glances) a handful of old coins and rings and jewellery settings. Tarnished and stained it's true, but genuine enough to convince Sebastian of the truth of at least a part of the old chap's ramblings. According to the legend of the place, Abbot Brendan had miraculously directed that the sea should yield its tithe of flotsam and jetsam from the occasional wrecked shipping on to the island rocks, down through the centuries. The sea's bounty should include not only food (and fish thrown up on the shore) but also treasures and valuables, driftwood in abundance to keep fires alight (for there were no trees to the island) and for building huts and altars and that humans who survived the perils of drowning and being dashed on the awful rocks that girt the island should join the community established there by Brendan himself, and contribute to its devotions and welfare.

Sebastian and his cronies plied the old seadog with drink until he drew for them—in liquor spilled on the table—the location of this magic island, up through the North Minch and toward Sula Sgeir. They didn't reckon much to the miracles, but there was no denying the treasures it seemed, and a visit to this 'treasure island' would certainly be worthwhile. They had that fatality of view that marks the seasoned fishermen and those who 'occupy their business in deep waters'. Their new friend by now seemed incapable of moving himself, so they dragged him along, after naturally relieving him of his valuables! Had they been more sober themselves, perhaps they would not have begun the voyage . . . who knows? But dirty weather is so much part-and-parcel of fishing around the Minches that they take it for granted.

At any rate, set sail they did . . . and somewhere up beyond Lewis they ran into what was bad weather even by their standards! The fact that they were in a Force 6 south westerly gale, and thrown about mercilessly by big white-capped waves effectively sobered them. They were convinced that they would be smashed on the huge rocks which stuck up from the boiling sea like giant teeth, or worse, ground upon those that were revealed only as the seas receded momentarily before the next crushing swell broke over them.

They had forgotten their involuntary passenger, but in the fury of the storm he was suddenly standing among them, in full sobriety and mastery of the situation! He took the helm, staring fixedly ahead although the visibility in flying spray and spindrift was virtually nil and steered the little boat which was tossed about like a cork over the foaming wave crests. Was it, only minutes, or was it hours later that they sighted dimly, lying low in the water, an island surrounded by a turmoil of water where the ebb tide and wind were in direct conflict? Toward this the boat headed, flung forward by wind and rollers, and rebuffed by the ebb. It was over in an instant, but Sebastian swears that their navigator guided them to a spot between two headlands where the sea lay uncannily black and still, yet turned the boat about, so that a great comber smashed them on to the guardian rocks, ripping the bottom out of their craft . . . and they were flung forward into the strangely still 'harbour', from where it was easy to swim ashore, clamber over mossy rocks and to sprawl, exhausted, on to the shore.

After a few minutes, Sebastian and the others were helped to their feet by their erstwhile captive. He smiled benignly upon them . . .

'I am Brother Brendan. Welcome to my Island.'

In the grey light of day and squalling wind it was an unprepossessing place—no trees or vegetation other than mosses and some scrubby grass—bleak and barren. 'Here you will find treasures indeed—the joys of serving God and of forgetting yourselves. Your minds will grow pure and unsullied by lucre and you will come to rejoice in praying for others. Once this was a community of blessed souls . . . but if the seas do not bring me alumni, then I must needs go out and about to find them. You see I am truly a fisher of men . . . you swallowed my bait and I have landed you safe here for God'.

'But you were drunk', protested Sebastian reaching for his knife to deal with this lunatic. 'And see here mister . . . what about the treasure?'

Brother Brendan smiled sweetly. 'Spiritous liqueurs do not affect me, my son . . . but I think I may claim a little talent for acting. As for the treasures, they are here. Come, I will show you the island, then you shall eat'.

There was not much to show! The island was but a couple of miles in area, rocky and with central high ground. There, in a sheltered cleft, was a cluster of primitive stone dwellings, badly in need of repair, and a spring of running water. One of the huts was a store of provisions brought by the tide. 'The sea provides us from her bounty', said Brendan. There were indeed treasures too, at which the comrades gaped—washed ashore from wrecked ships of all ages, and piled round an altar at which Brendan knelt briefly. He set them to building a fire of driftwood to dry themselves . . . 'When you have eaten, I will begin your lessons', he smiled 'there is plenty of time. Your daily Offices performed will ensure a supply of necessities from the sea, but (here he frowned) be warned . . . any lapse from grace and humility in your prayers for others and the sea will cease to provide'.

So, incredibly, it seemed to work out. The cut-throats had no option but to stay and form the community that Brother Brendan desired, for the island was well away from regular fishing routes and there was no chance of repairing their boat—the smashed ribs of which they could see at certain times of day beyond the coastal lagoon. Indeed, all dried out wreckage and driftwood had to be salvaged and husbanded carefully for the communal fire.

There was a magnetism about Brother Brendan and his teachings and they sat at his feet and listened to his exhortations and homilies, between their sessions of prayer for the welfare of seafarers, and the necessary domestic work.

It was equally miraculous that whenever they sought to rebel—as occasionally happened of course—(particularly after breaching the rum casks washed ashore in some previous age), the fish forsook the shores, and the waves brought no jetsam. This punishment they could have sustained for some time on their existing provisions, but the wind and rain squalled, and the fire went out, and Brother Brendan appeared to reprimand them. It was simpler in every way to comply . . . and Brother Brendan took to visiting them less and less. They never saw him approach. They would turn from a task, and there he was. He said he had other communities to visit, but how he came and went was a mystery. Sebastian did not know then how long they were on the island. It might have been four months or forty years; but in fact it was about three years. The chance of rescue came with the arrival of a Geological Survey party (this was pre WW1 interposed Fr. O'Connor). But Sebastian's comrades had found contentment in their isolated life and decided to hide. He himself had been conscious of a growing conviction that he must follow where Brendan led and win other seafarers for the Lord, so he returned with the Survey team to Western Scotland. He served some years with the Missions to Seamen at parish work before finishing his days at Melrose, where I met him. He died in the full conviction that he would join the Blessed Brendan's 'Press-gang'.

And that was when he gave me this carving as a memento of his story".

"Oh, come now, Father", I protested, coming back to reality as the old man finished speaking. "You aren't expecting me to believe that story, surely? And that it was Saint Brendan himself in 1910 or 1911 who took his new recruits to that island? Why, it's as nonsensical as the 'whale island' in The Voyages of Brendan the Abbot' ".

"Well now", said the priest; smiling at my vehemence, "Brother Sebastian had no doubts. I keep an open mind." He picked up the carved wooden boat and looked at it. "You know David, our Blessed Brendan is the patron of mariners, and somehow I like the notion that he haunts the seafarers' taverns and ports whenever he needs to replenish his communities. He follows in the footsteps of Christ—not only as a navigator—and remember the storm on Galilee!—but as a fisher of men . . . and the most down-to-earth and forthright of men; men in need of salvation, in fact".

He sighed. "If only one knew when he needed men, it would be worth trying to meet him . . ."

MARK RUTHERFORD
A Mysterious Portrait

Mark Rutherford (*pseudonym of William Hale White, 1831–1913*) *acquired a very large and enthusiastic public for a sequence of autobiographical fictions written in middle age, notably* The Autobiography of Mark Rutherford (1881) *and* Mark Rutherford's Deliverance (1885). *His last important novel*, Clara Hopgood (1896), *was accused of immorality, and also enjoyed great success.*

I remember some years ago that I went to spend a Christmas with an old friend who was a bachelor. He might, perhaps, have been verging on sixty at the time of my visit. On his study wall hung the portrait—merely the face—of a singularly lovely woman. I did not like to ask any questions about it. There was no family likeness to him, and we always thought that early in life he had been disappointed. But one day, seeing that I could hardly keep my eyes off it, he said to me, "I have had that picture for many years, although you have never seen it before. If you like, I will tell you its history." He then told me the following story.

"In the year 1817, I was beginning life, and struggling to get a living. I had just started in business. I was alone, without much capital, and my whole energies were utterly absorbed in my adventure. In those days the master, instead of employing a commercial traveller, often used to travel himself, and one evening I had to start for the North to see some customers. I chose to go by night in order to save time, and as it was bitterly cold and I was weak in the chest, I determined to take a place inside the coach. We left St. Martin's-le-Grand at about half-past eight, and I was the sole passenger. I could not sleep, but fell into a kind of doze, which was not sufficiently deep to prevent my rousing myself at every inn where we changed horses. Nobody intruded upon me, and I continued in the same drowsy, half-waking, half-slumbering condition till we came to the last stage before reaching Eaton Socon. I was then thoroughly awake, and continued awake until after the coach started. But presently I fell sound asleep for, perhaps, half-an-hour, and woke suddenly. To my great surprise I found a lady with me. How she came there I could not conjecture. I was positive that she did not get in when the coach last stopped. She sat at the opposite corner, so that I could see her well, and a more exquisite face I thought I had never beheld. It was not quite English—rather pale, earnest and abstracted, and with a certain intentness about the eyes which denoted a mind accustomed to dwell upon ideal objects. I was not particularly shy with women, and perhaps if she had been any ordinary, pretty girl I might have struck up a conversation with her. But I was dumb, for I hardly dared to intrude. It would have been necessary to begin by some commonplaces, and somehow my lips refused the utterance of commonplaces. Nor was this strange. If I had happened to find myself opposite the great Lord Byron in a coach I certainly should not have thrust myself upon him, and how should I dare to thrust myself upon a person who seemed as great and grand as she, although I did not know her name? So I remained perfectly still, only venturing by the light of the moon to watch her through my half-shut eyes. Just before we got to Eaton, although I was never more thoroughly or even excitedly awake in my life, I must have lost consciousness for a minute. I came to myself when the coach was pulling up at an inn. I looked round instantly, and my companion was gone. I jumped out on pretence of getting something to eat and drink, and hastily asked the guard where the lady who had just got out was put into the coach. He said they had never stopped since they had last changed horses, and that I must have been dreaming. He knew nothing about the lady, and he looked at me suspiciously, as if he thought I was drunk. I for my part was perfectly confident that I had not been deluded by an apparition of my own brain. I had never suffered from ghost-like visitations of any kind, and my thoughts, owing to my preoccupation with business, had not run upon women in any way whatever. More convincing still, I had noticed that the lady wore a light blue neckerchief; and when I went back into the coach I found that she had left it behind her. I took it up, and I have it to this day. You may imagine how my mind dwelt upon that night.

I got to Newcastle, did what I had to do, came back again, and made a point this time of sleeping at Eaton Socon in order to make inquiries. Everybody recollected the arrival of the down coach by which I travelled, and everybody was perfectly sure that no lady was in it. I produced the scarf, and asked whether anybody who lived near had been observed to wear it. Eaton is a little village, and all the people in it were as well known as if they belonged to one family, but nobody recognised it. It was certainly not English. I thought about the affair for months, partly because I was smitten with my visitor, and partly because I was half afraid my brain had been a little upset by worry. However, in time, the impression faded.

Meanwhile I began to get on in the world, and after some three or four years my intense application was rewarded by riches. In seven or eight years I had become wealthy, and I began to think about settling myself in life. I had made the acquaintance of influential people in London, and more particularly of a certain baronet whom I had met in France while taking a holiday. Although I was in business I came of good family, and our acquaintance grew into something more. He had two or three daughters, to each of whom he was able to give a good marriage portion, and I became engaged to one of them. I don't know that there was much enthusiasm about our courtship. She was a very pleasant, good-looking girl, and although I can acquit myself of all mercenary motives in proposing to her, I cannot say that the highest motives were operative. I was as thousands of others are. I had got weary of loneliness; I wanted a home. I cast about me to see who amongst all the women I knew would best make me a wife. I selected this one, and perhaps the thought of her money may have been a trifle determinatory. I was not overmastered by a passion which I could not resist, nor was I coldly indifferent. If I had married her we should probably have lived a life of customary married comfort, and even of happiness; the same level, and perhaps slightly grey life which is lived by the ordinary English husband and wife. Things had gone so far that it was settled we were to be married in the spring of 1826, and I had begun to look out for a house, and make purchases in anticipation of house-keeping.

In 1825 I had to go to Bristol. I shall never forget to the day of my death one morning in that city. I had had my breakfast, and was going out to see the head of one of the largest firms in the city, with whom I had an appointment. I met him in the street, and I noted before he spoke that there was something the matter. I soon found out what it was. The panic of 1825 had begun; three great houses in London had failed, and brought him down. He was a ruined man, and so was I. I managed to stagger back to the hotel, and found letters there confirming all he had said. For some two or three days I was utterly prostrate, and could not summon sufficient strength to leave Bristol. One of the first things I did when I came to myself was to write to the baronet, telling him what had happened, that I was altogether penniless, and that in honour I felt bound to release his daughter from her engagement. I had a sympathising letter from him in return, saying that he was greatly afflicted at my misfortune, that his daughter was nearly broken-hearted, but that she had come to the conclusion that perhaps it would be best to accept my very kind offer. Much as she loved me, she felt that her health was far from strong, and although he had always meant to endow her generously on her marriage, her fortune alone would not enable her to procure those luxuries which, for her delicate constitution, alas! were necessaries. But the main reason with her was that she was sure that, with my independence, I should be unhappy if I felt that my wife's property was my support. His letter was long, but although much wrapped up, this was the gist of it. I went back to London, sold every stick I had, and tried to get a situation as clerk in some house, doing the business in which I had been engaged. I failed, for the distress was great, and I was reduced nearly to my last sovereign when I determined to go down to Newcastle, and try the friend there whom I had not seen since 1817.

It was once more winter, and, although I was so poor, I was obliged to ride inside the coach again, for I was much troubled with my ancient enemy—the weakness in the chest. The incidents of my former visit I had nearly forgotten till we came near to Eaton Socon, and then they returned to me. But now it was a dull January day, with a bitter thaw, and my fellow passengers were a Lincolnshire squire, with his red-faced wife, who never spoke a syllable to me, and by reason of their isolation seemed to make the thaw all the more bitter, the fen levels all the more dismally flat, and the sky all the more leaden. At last we came to Newcastle. During the latter part of the journey I was alone, my Lincolnshire squire and his lady having left me on the road. It was about seven o'clock in the evening when we arrived; a miserable night, with the snow just melting under foot, and the town was wrapped in smoke and fog.

I was so depressed that I hardly cared what became of me, and when I stepped out of the coach wished that I had been content to lie down and die in London. I could not put up at the coaching hotel, as it was too expensive, but walked on to one which was cheaper. I almost lost my way, and had wandered down a narrow street, which at every step became more and more squalid, and at last ended opposite a factory gate. Hard by was a wretched marine store shop, in the window of which were old iron, old teapots, a few old Bibles, and other miscellaneous effects. I stepped in to ask for directions to the Cross Key. Coming out, whom should I see crossing the road, as if to meet me, but the very lady who rode with me in the coach to Eaton some nine years ago. There was no mistaking her. She seemed scarcely a day older. The face was as lovely and as inspired as ever. I was almost beside myself. I leaned against the railing of the shop, and the light from the window shone full on her. She came straight towards me on to the pavement; looked at me, and turned up the street. I followed her till we got to the end, determined not to lose sight of her; and we reached an open, broad thoroughfare. She stopped at a bookseller's, and went in. I was not more than two minutes after her; but when I entered she was not there. A shopman was at the counter, and I asked him whether a lady, my sister, had not just left the shop. No lady, he said, had been there for half-an-hour. I went back to the marine store shop. The footsteps were still there which I saw her make as she crossed. I knelt down, tracing them with my fingers to make sure I was not deceived by my eyes, and was more than ever confounded. At last I got to my inn, and went to bed a prey to the strangest thoughts.

In the morning I was a little better. The stagnant blood had been stirred by the encounter of the night before, and though I was much agitated, and uncertain whether my brain was actually sound or not, I was sufficiently self-possessed and sensible to call upon my friend and explain my errand. He did what he could to help me, and I became his clerk in Newcastle. For a time I was completely broken, but gradually I began to recover my health and spirits a little. I had little or no responsibility, and nothing to absorb me after office hours. As a relief and an occupation, I tried to take up with a science, and chose geology. On Sundays I used to make long rambling excursions, and for a while I was pleased with my new toy. But by degrees it became less and less interesting. I suppose I had no real love for it. Furthermore, I had no opportunities for expression. My sorrow had secluded me. I demanded more from those around me than I had any right to expect. As a rule, we all of us demand from the world more than we are justified in demanding, especially if we suffer; and because the world is not so constituted that it can respond to us as eagerly and as sympathetically as we respond to ourselves, we become morose. So it was with me. People were sorry for me; but I knew that my trouble did not disturb them deeply, that when they left me, their faces, which were forcibly contracted while in my presence, instantly expanded into their ordinary self-satisfaction, and that if I were to die I should be forgotten a week after the funeral. I therefore recoiled from men, and frequently, with criminal carelessness and prodigality, rejected many an offer of kindness, not because I did not need it, but because I wanted too much of it.

My science, as I have said, was a failure. I cannot tell how it may be with some exceptionally heroic natures, but with me expression in some form or other, if the thing which should be expressed is to live, is an absolute necessity. I cannot read unless I have somebody to whom I can speak about my reading, and I lose almost all power of thinking if thought after thought remains with me. Expression is as indispensable to me as expiration of breath. Inspiration of the air is a necessity, but continued inspiration of air without expiration of the same is an impossibility. The geology was neglected, and at first I thought it was because it was geology, and I tried something else. For some months I fancied I had found a solace in chemistry. With my savings I purchased some apparatus, and began to be proficient. But the charm faded from this also; the apparatus was put aside, and the sight of it lying disused only made my dissatisfaction and melancholy the more profound. Amidst all my loneliness, I had never felt the least inclination to any baser pleasures, nor had I ever seen a woman for whom I felt even the most transient passion. My spectral friend—if spectre she was—dominated my existence, and seemed to prevent not only all licentiousness, but all pleasure, except of the most superficial kind, in other types of beauty. This need be no surprise to anybody. I have known cases in which the face of a singularly lovely woman, seen only for a few moments in the street, has haunted a man all through his life, and deeply affected it. In time I was advanced in my position as clerk, and would have married, but I had not the least inclination thereto. I did not believe in the actual reality of my vision, and had no hope of ever meeting in the flesh the apparition of the coach and the dingy street; I felt sure that there was some mistake, something wrong with me—the probabilities were all in favour of my being deceived; but still the dream possessed me, and every woman who for a moment appealed to me was tried by that standard and found wanting.

After some years had passed, during which I had scarcely been out of Newcastle, I took a holiday, and went up to London. It was about July. I was now a man on the wrong side of fifty, shy, reserved, with a reputation for constitutional melancholy, a shadowy creature, of whom nobody took much notice and who was noticed by nobody. While in London I went to see the pictures at the Academy. The place was thronged, and I was tired; I just looked about me, and was on the point of coming out wearied, when in a side room where there were crayon drawings, I caught sight of one of a face. I was amazed beyond measure. It was the face which had been my companion for so many years. There could be no mistake about it; even the neckerchief was tied as I remembered it so well, the very counterpart of the treasure I still preserved so sacredly at home. I was almost overcome with a faintness, with a creeping sensation all over the head, as if something were giving way, and with a shock of giddiness. I went and got a catalogue, found out the name of the artist, and saw that the picture had merely the name of "Stella" affixed to it. It might be a portrait, or it might not. After gazing myself almost blind at it, I went instantly to the artist's house. He was at home. He seemed a poor man, and was evidently surprised at any inquiry after his picture so late in the season. I asked him who sat for it. "Nobody," he said; "it was a mere fancy sketch. There might be a reminiscence in it of a girl I knew in France years ago; but she is long since dead, and I don't think that anybody who knew her would recognise a likeness in it. In fact, I am sure they would not." The price of the drawing was not much, although it was a good deal for me. I said instantly I would have it, and managed to get the money together by scraping up all my savings out of the savings bank.

That is the very picture which you now see before you. I do not pretend to explain everything which I have told you. I have long since given up the attempt, and I suppose it must be said that I have suffered from some passing disorder of the brain, although that theory is not sound at all points, and there are circumstances inconsistent with it."

The next morning my friend went to his office, after an early breakfast. His hours were long, and I was obliged to leave Newcastle before his return. So I bade him good-bye before he left home. I never saw him again. Two years afterwards I was shocked to see an announcement in the *Times* of his death. Knowing his lonely way of life, I went down to Newcastle to gather what I could about his illness and last moments. He had caught cold, and died of congestion of the lungs. His landlady said that he had made a will, and that what little property had remained after paying his funeral expenses had been made over to a hospital. I was anxious to know where the picture was. She could not tell me. It had disappeared just before his death, and nobody knew what had become of it.

PAMELA SEWELL
Ward 8

Pamela Sewell is among the best of the new ghost story writers, and has contributed several to magazines and anthologies.

J anice glanced at her watch. It was going to be a long night. Half the staff had gone down with the 'flu. Including Muriel: so she would be on her own tonight.

She shivered as she walked down the ward. Doctor Rivers had told her that the ward was haunted. Nothing too much to worry about, he said, but she should take care. Though having heard what had happened the other night, she was disinclined to believe him.

Peggy and Irene, the two other student nurses in the wing, had been on duty last night: they had still been shaking when they came in for breakfast. They, too, had heard that the ward was haunted; Irene had just been walking to the little room on the end, to see if the patients needed anything, when she saw something white fluttering against the window. She had quickly gone to fetch Peggy: together, they had stood at the window, watching, almost too scared to go in. Then they had heard something scratching behind them. . . .

They had been too scared to scream: and had been furious when they had seen one of the junior doctors behind them, laughing. He had walked into the little room, and switched on the light: there were no patients. The sole occupant was the lecture skeleton, wearing a white coat . . . Apparently, it was a long-running joke—first of all, to tell new students about the ghost, and then then to set up the lecture skeleton as "the ghost". Still, at least she had had the warning: they wouldn't frighten her now. Besides, there was a patient in the little room, tonight. No chance for any jokes.

Even so, she would have been glad of Muriel's company. The night stretched out endlessly, when you were on duty alone; although she could cope with six or seven patients on her own, it was always easier with two.

She sighed, swinging her legs under the heavy oak desk. She had done the last drugs round half an hour ago, marking their notes and the ward book; her report was up to date. Nothing else to do, there. And it had been over an hour since the doctor's final round. They had had just enough time for a quick chat—warning her to mind the white coats in the end room!—and had left; the ward was full of sleeping patients. The silence was eerie, punctuated with a few snores and soft murmurs.

The minutes ticked on. Janice wished that she had brought her knitting. It would have helped to pass the time. Though Matron had told off Peggy, the other night, for bringing in her sewing. Unhygienic. And a book was a bad idea. It was too easy to become engrossed, forgetting where you were, or to relax and become drowsy. Another reason why it was better to have two on duty: you had each other to talk to, keep awake. Test each other on anatomy, even, for the exams.

Time to check the beds again. She stood up, and walked slowly down the centre of the ward, her flat shoes making no noise: the patients all seemed comfortable enough. Mr. Mason—poor old thing—was coughing slightly in his sleep: bronchitis. And Mr. Ellis: hernia. She moved slowly down the beds, remembering the names, the ailments. All varying in ages, from old Mr. Williams with his prostate trouble, to their new patient, Ricky Moore, the road accident victim. Bruised ribs, leg fractured in two places. And then there was Mr. Stevens; he had kidney trouble. In a lot of pain, too: Matron had advised her to give him a little morphine when he woke. Helped to take away the pain, let him sleep.

That was the one thing about being in the general ward: the variety, Janice mused. She had learned more there in the past three weeks than she had in the previous six months. And Matron Allen wasn't a bad sort: some of them were real dragons, but she gave you a bit more confidence, saying that you were quite capable of doing the job. Even Irene—always a bit nervous—had seemed to blossom on Matron Allen's ward.

A cold shiver ran up Janice's back as she approached the little room: they had put Mr. Stevens there, so that he wouldn't be disturbed by any noise from the ward. The junior doctors had admitted that their story about the end room was just a joke. Even so. . . .

She chided herself mentally: of course the ward wasn't haunted. The noise she could hear was probably Mr. Stevens trying to settle; her face softened with pity. Matron had said that he found it hard to sleep, and that morphine helped the pain; it was just as well she had brought the morphine with her.

The youngish man in the bed smiled a little sheepishly at her as she walked in.

"How are you feeling?"

He half closed his eyes. "Not too bad."

And not too good, either, Janice thought: though he was trying bravely not to show it. "Can't sleep?"

He shook his head. "I try, but every time I try to get comfortable. . . ."

"It hurts," Janice finished. "Well, that's what I'm here for: to make you more comfortable." So saying, she poured out a small measure from the bottle. "This should help."

She marked the dosage on the board at the end of his bed, and smiled at him. "Would you like anything else?"

"Some more water would be nice," he admitted, glancing at the empty jug on his bedside table. "If it's not too much trouble, that is."

Janice smiled back at him. He had already become a favourite on the ward: he was one of the least demanding patients, with a ready appreciation of any kindness, however small. "Of course not. I'll be back in a tick."

She walked quickly up the ward, meaning to be only a moment; a sudden spasm of coughing from the direction of Mr. Mason's bed stopped her in her tracks. She hurried over to him, and helped him sit up; the old man closed his eyes in pain as another fit of coughing seized him. She held his hand, comforting him, until his breathing became calm again, and passed him a drink of water, sitting with him until he had finished.

He smiled gratefully at her, and settled down again; a muffled moan from the next bed made her turn. Little Ricky Moore: Irene had said something about nightmares. Sympathy rose in Janice. He wasn't much older than her baby brother. The accident had been fairly nasty. No wonder he was crying in his sleep.

She walked over towards him, and sat on the edge of his bed. They weren't supposed to do that: the sister in charge had told Muriel about that, the other week. Still, there was no-one to chide her. And if it would help her patient, then that was what mattered most.

Gently, she stroked the hair from his eyes: he was shivering and sweating. Probably reliving the crash. "It's all right, it's all over now," she soothed, patting his hand. "Come on, it's all right."

The young boy shuddered, and began to relax, though still clutching Janice's hand; she stayed with him for a while, until his breathing was calm and he seemed to be sleeping deeply. Gently, she disengaged her hand, and stood up again. She glanced at her watch, wondering how late it was, and started as she realised the time. Poor Mr. Stevens—she had promised him a drink, over half an hour ago! She quickly went into the kitchen, filled a jug with water, and walked back down to the little room.

"I'm so sorry," she apologised. "A couple of the others were taken badly."

Mr. Stevens smiled back at her, half drowsy. "It's all right. The other nurse got it for me: look." He gestured to the full water jug beside him.

Janice nodded. "That's all right, then. Is there anything else I can get you?"

He shook his head. "Nothing, thanks."

She left him to sleep, and walked back towards the old oak desk, suddenly relieved. So Muriel had made it in, after all. At least she wouldn't have to spend the whole night on her own. Though it was surprising that she hadn't seen her friend come in. She could have been busy at the time, of course, helping Mr. Mason—but Muriel was more likely to have come and given her a hand, not just gone to see Mr. Stevens. . . .

Her puzzled frown deepened as she reached the desk: where was Muriel? There was no sign of her. Only one cloak hung on the coat-hooks, and that was Janice's own. She shivered. So who had Mr. Stevens seen? Maybe Doctor Rivers hadn't been joking, after all. . . Janice shook herself. Ridiculous: of course he hadn't been serious. He had, after all, been responsible for Irene and Peggy's fright, the night before. She had given Mr. Stevens morphine: it had probably made him relax, lose track of time, think that she had already given him the water.

Even so, on her next walk round the ward, a chill gripped her. All the patients were sleeping: as before, she could only hear the odd snore, and deep nasal breathing. Almost nervously, she opened the door to the little room, as quietly as she could; as she put her head around the door, she realised that Mr. Stevens was awake.

"Not asleep, yet?" She tutted at him. "What am I going to do with you, eh?" She smiled in response to his sheepish grin. "If you need anything, you know you can always press the bell by your bed. That's what I'm here for."

He shook his head. "It's all right, Nurse, really; the other lady's been looking after me."

Janice felt her blood run cold. The mysterious nurse, again. She swallowed, and summoned a smile. "Which one was that, Mr. Stevens? My friend Muriel was supposed to be on duty with me, tonight, but she's in bed with the 'flu. I'm afraid I haven't had a chance to see the nurse who's doing her shift, yet. We've been that busy tonight!"

He frowned. "I'm not really sure; I don't think I've seen her, before. She had a kind face, though. And dark hair. Her uniform was a bit like yours, but grey, if that's any help?"

"Oh, yes—I know." Janice nodded reassuringly. "Everything's fine. Are you sure that I can't get you anything?" Mr. Stevens nodded.

"Sleep well, then." She walked out of the little room again, goose bumps rising on her skin. No Muriel. And a grey lady? It was probably the morphine making him see things, that was all. Though she could have sworn that the water jug was empty when she left him, the first time. . . . Then again, she could have filled it herself, before Mr. Mason had started coughing. You sometimes forget things like that, when there's a rush.

All the same, when the next shift came on at seven o'clock, they noticed the pallor on her face. "Not going down with the 'flu, Janice?" one of them asked, concerned.

"Oh, no." Janice frowned. "I'm worried about the patient in the end room, though. He's wandering a bit."

"Oh?"

"Mm. He's convinced that a lady in grey's been looking after him, all night—and my uniform's blue!"

The staff nurse suddenly paled; Janice looked at her. "What's wrong?"

"Well—you know young Rivers told you that the ward was haunted?" Janice nodded, listening intently. "Actually, he wasn't joking. You see, many years ago, a patient on this ward—in the end room—was given laudanum, to ease his pain. The nurse gave him an overdose, by mistake; he died. She was disciplined: but she couldn't take the shame. They found her, the next day, in the little room. She had hanged herself."

She paused for a moment; seeing the look on the student nurse's face, she continued. "Whenever a patient is given morphine or laudanum, she comes back to look after him, to make sure it never happens again."

Janice looked at her, frowning. "They used to have grey uniforms, didn't they?" At the other nurse's nod, she bit her lip. "Mr. Stevens is in the end room: and I gave him morphine, last night. . . ."

A.E.D. SMITH
The Coat

A.E.D. Smith, *a Civil Servant by profession, served in the Dardanelles, Egypt, and the Balkans, during the First World War. He later contributed a number of short stories to magazines and literary periodicals. "The Coat", which was based on a vivid dream, first appeared in the anthology* Powers of Darkness (1934), *and remains one of the most memorable ghost stories of its time.*

I am quite aware that the other fellows in the office regard me as something of an oddity—as being rather a "queer bird," in fact. Well, of course, a man who happens to be of a studious disposition, who dislikes noise and prefers his own company to that of empty-headed companions, and who, moreover, is compelled by defective vision to wear thick glasses, is always liable to be thus misjudged by inferior minds; and ordinarily, I treat the opinion of my colleagues with the contempt it deserves. But at this particular moment I was beginning to think that perhaps, after all, there might be something to be said for their view. For, though I might still repudiate the "queer bird" part of the business, undoubtedly I was an ass—a first-class chump; otherwise I should have been spending my holidays in a nice comfortable way with the rest of the normal world, listening to the Pierrots or winking at the girls on the promenade of some seaside resort at home, instead of having elected to set out alone on this idiotic push-bike tour of a little-known part of France. Drenched, hungry and lost; a stranger in a strange land; dispiritedly pushing before me a heavily-laden bicycle with a gashed tyre—such was the present result of my asinine choice.

The storm had overtaken me miles from anywhere, on a wild road over a spur of the Vosges, and for nearly two hours I had trudged through the pelting rain without encountering a living soul or the least sign of human habitation.

And then, at long last, rounding a bend, I glimpsed just ahead of me the chimney-pots and gables of a fair-sized house. It was a lonely, desolate-looking place standing amid a clump of trees a little way back from the road, and somehow, even at a distance, did not convey a very inviting impression. Nevertheless, in that wilderness, it was a welcome enough sight, and in the hope of finding temporary shelter and possibly a little badly-needed refreshment, I quickened my pace towards it. Two hundred yards brought me to the entrance gates, and here I suffered a grievous disappointment; for the roofless porter's lodge, the dilapidated old gates hanging askew on their hinges, and the over-grown drive beyond, plainly indicated that the place was no longer inhabited.

I speedily comforted myself, however, with the reflection that in the circumstances even a deserted house was not to be despised as a refuge. Once under cover of some kind, I might make shift to wring out my drenched clothing and repair my damaged mount; and without further ado I pushed my bicycle up the long-neglected drive and reached the terrace in front of the house itself. It proved to be an old château, half smothered in creepers and vines that had long gone wild, and, judging by the carved stone coat-of-arms over the main entrance, had once been occupied by a person of some quality. Mounted on a pedestal on either side of the iron-studded front door stood a rusty carronade—trophies, probably, of some long-forgotten war in which the former occupier had played a part. Most of the windows had been boarded up, and it was evident that the place had stood empty for many years.

I tried the front door. To my surprise it was unfastened, and a thrust of my shoulder sent it creaking grudgingly back on its hinges. My nostrils, as I stepped into the dim, wide hall, were at once assailed by the stale, disagreeable odour of rotting woodwork and mouldy hangings and carpets. For a moment or two I stood peering uncertainly about me, with the slight feeling of eeriness that one usually experiences when entering an old, empty house. Facing me was a broad staircase, with a long, stained-glass window, almost opaque with dirt and cobwebs, at its head. I mounted the stairs, and throwing open the first door at hand, found myself looking into a spacious, handsomely furnished room that had evidently once been the chief apartment of the house, though long neglect and disuse had now reduced it to a sorry state. The ornate cornice hung here and there in strips, and in one corner the plaster of the ceiling had come down altogether. Green mould covered the eighteenth-century furniture; curtains and draperies hung in tatters; and one-half of the beautiful old Persian carpet, from a point near the door right across to the fireplace, was overspread by an evil-smelling, bright orange fungus.

The fireplace gave me an idea. Could I but find fuel I might light a fire, make myself a hot drink, and get my clothes properly dried.

A little searching in the outbuildings discovered a sufficient quantity of old sticks to serve my purpose, and with a bundle of them under my coat I re-entered the house and briskly made my way upstairs again. But on the threshold of the big room, without quite knowing why, I suddenly checked. It was as though my legs, of their own volition, had all at once become reluctant to carry me further into the apartment—as if something quite outside of me were urging me to turn about and retreat. I laid the sticks down at my feet, and for a moment or two stood there uncertainly in the doorway. I was beginning to sense some subtle suggestion of danger in the atmosphere of the place. Everything was apparently just as I had left it; yet I had an uneasy sort of feeling that during my brief absence something evil had entered that room and left it again.

I am neither a nervous nor a superstitious person; yet I found myself, a moment later, rather shamefacedly picking up my sticks and moving back towards the head of the stairs. Actually, it was not so much fear as a vague, precautionary sense of uneasiness that prompted me. It had occurred to me that perhaps I might feel more comfortable if I remained nearer to the front door, and made my fire in one of the rooms on the ground floor. If—it was an idiotic fancy, I know—but . . . well, if anything—er—queer DID happen, and I had to make a sudden bolt for it, I could get out quicker that way.

It was on this second descent of the stairs, as I faced the light from the open front door, that I suddenly noticed something that pulled me up with a decided start. Running up the centre of the staircase, and quite fresh in the thick dust, was a broad, broken sort of track, exactly as though someone had recently trailed up an empty sack or something of that nature.

From the foot of the staircase I traced this track across the hall to a spot immediately below an old, moth-eaten coat that hung from one of a row of coat-pegs on the opposite wall. And then I saw that similar tracks traversed the hall in various directions, some terminating before the doors on either side, others leading past the foot of the stairs to the rear regions of the house, but all seeming to radiate from the same point below the coat-pegs. And the queerest thing about it all was that of footprints, other than my own, there was not a sign.

Uneasiness once more assailed me. The house appeared to be uninhabited, and yet, plainly some one, or something, had recently been in the place. Who, or what, was the restless, questing creature that had made those strange tracks to and from the old coat? Was it some half-witted vagrant—a woman possibly—whose trailing draperies obliterated her own footprints?

I had a closer look at the old garment. It was a military greatcoat of ancient pattern, with one or two tarnished silver buttons still attached to it, and had evidently seen much service. Turning it round on its peg with a gingerly finger and thumb, I discovered that just below the left shoulder there was a round hole as big as a penny, surrounded by an area of scorched and stained cloth, as though a heavy pistol had been fired into it at point-blank range. If a pistol bullet had indeed made that hole, then obviously, the old coat at one period of its existence had clothed a dead man.

A sudden repugnance for the thing overcame me, and with a slight shudder I let go of it. It may have been fancy or not, but all at once it seemed to me that there was more than an odour of mould and rotting cloth emanating from the thing—that there was a taint of putrefying flesh and bone. . . .

A taint of animal corruption—faint but unmistakable—I could sniff it in the air; and with it, something less definable but no less real—a sort of sixth-sense feeling that the whole atmosphere of the place was slowly becoming charged with evil emanations from a black and shameful past.

With an effort I pulled myself together. After all, what was there to be scared about? I had no need to fear human marauders, for in my hip pocket I carried a small but serviceable automatic; and as for ghosts, well, if such existed, they didn't usually "walk" in the daytime. The place certainly felt creepy, and I shouldn't have cared to spend the night there; but it would be ridiculous to allow mere idle fancies to drive me out again into that beastly rain before I'd made myself that badly needed hot drink and mended my bicycle.

I therefore opened the door nearest to me, and entered a smallish room that apparently had once been used as a study. The fireplace was on the side opposite to the door, and the wide, ancient grate was still choked with the ashes of the last log consumed there. I picked up the poker—a cumbersome old thing with a knob as big as an orange—raked out the ashes, and laid my sticks in approved Boy Scout fashion. But the wood was damp, and after I had used up half my matches, refused to do more than smoulder, whilst a back-draught from the chimney filled the room with smoke. In desperation I went down on my hands and knees and tried to rouse the embers into flame by blowing on them. And in the middle of this irksome operation I was startled by a sound of movement in the hall—a single soft "flop," as though some one had flung down a garment.

I was on my feet in a flash, listening with every nerve a-taut. No further sound came, and, automatic in hand, I tiptoed to the door. There was nothing in the hall; nothing to be heard at all save the steady swish of the rain outside. But from a spot on the floor directly below the old coat the dust was rising in a little eddying cloud, as though it had just been disturbed.

"Pah! A rat," I told myself, and went back to my task.

More vigorous blowing on the embers, more raking and poking, more striking of matches—and, in the midst of it, again came that curious noise—not very loud, but plain and unmistakable.

Once more I went into the hall, and once more, except for another little cloud of dust rising from precisely the same spot as before, there was nothing to be seen. But that sixth-sense warning of imminent danger was becoming more insistent. I had the feeling now that I was no longer alone in the old, empty hall—that some unclean, invisible presence was lurking there, tainting the very air with its foulness.

"It's no use," I said to myself. "I may be a nervous fool, but I can't stand any more of this. I'll collect my traps and clear out whilst the going's good."

With this, I went back into the room, and keeping a nervous eye cocked on the door, began with rather panicky haste to re-pack my haversack. And just as I was in the act of tightening the last strap there came from the hall a low, evil chuckle, followed

518

by the sound of stealthy movement. I whipped out my weapon and stood where I was in the middle of the floor, facing the door, with my blood turning to ice. Through the chink between the door hinges I saw a shadow pass; then the door creaked a little, slowly began to open, and round it there came—the COAT.

It stood there upright in the doorway, as God is above me—swaying a little as though uncertain of its balance—collar and shoulders extended as though by an invisible wearer—the old, musty coat I had seen hanging in the hall.

For a space that seemed an eternity I stood like a man of stone, facing the Thing as it seemed to pause on the threshold. A dreadful sort of hypnotism held me rooted to the spot on which I stood—a hypnotism that completely paralysed my body, and caused the pistol to slip from my nerveless fingers, and yet left my brain clear. Mingled with my frozen terror was a feeling of deadly nausea. I knew that I was in the presence of ultimate Evil—that the very aura of the Hell-engendered Thing reared there in the doorway was contamination—that its actual touch would mean not only the instant destruction of my body, but the everlasting damnation of my soul.

And now It was coming into the room—with an indescribable bobbing sort of motion, the empty sleeves jerking grotesquely at its sides, the skirts flopping and trailing in the dust, was slowly coming towards me; and step by step, with my bulging eyes riveted in awful fascination on the Thing, I was recoiling before it. Step by step, with the rigid, unconscious movement of an automaton, I drew back until I was brought up with my back pressed into the fireplace and could retreat no further. And still, with deadly malevolent purpose, the Thing crept towards me. The empty sleeves were rising and shakily reaching out towards my throat. In another moment they would touch me, and then I knew with the most dreadful certainty that my reason would snap. A coherent thought somehow came into my burning brain—something that I had read or heard of long ago . . . the power . . . of the . . . holy sign . . . against . . . the forces of evil. With a last desperate effort of will I stretched out a palsied finger and made the sign of the Cross. . . . And in that instant, my other hand, scrabbling frenziedly at the wall behind me, came into contact with something cold and hard and round. It was the knob of the old, heavy poker.

The touch of the cold iron seemed to give me instant

519

repossession of my faculties. With lightning swiftness I swung up the heavy poker and struck with all my force at the nightmare Horror before me. And lo! on the instant, the Thing collapsed, and became an old coat—nothing more—lying there in a heap at my feet. Yet, on my oath, as I cleared the hellish thing in a flying leap, and fled from the room, I saw it, out of the tail of my eye, gathering itself together and making shape, as it were to scramble after me.

Once outside that accursed house I ran as never man ran before, and I remember nothing more until I found myself, half fainting, before the door of a little inn.

"Bring wine, in the name of God!" I cried, staggering inside.

Wine was brought, and a little wondering group stood round me while I drank.

I tried to explain to them in my bad French. They continued to regard me with puzzled looks. At length a look of understanding came into the landlord's face.

"Mon Dieu!" he gasped. "Is it possible that monsieur has been in *that place*! Quick, Juliette! Monsieur will need another bottle of wine."

Later, I got something of the story from the landlord, though he was by no means eager to tell it. The deserted house had once been occupied by a retired officer of the first Napoleon's army. Judging from the landlord's story, he must have been one of the worst men that God ever allowed to walk the earth. "Most certainly, monsieur, he was a bad man—that one," concluded my host. "He killed his wife and tortured every living thing he could lay hands on—even, it is said, his own daughters. In the end, one of them shot him in the back. The old château has an evil name. If you offered a million francs, you would not get one of our country-folks to go near the place."

As I said at the beginning, I know that the other fellows in the office are inclined, as it is, to regard me as being a bit queer; so I haven't told any of them this story. Nevertheless, it's perfectly true.

My brand-new bicycle and touring traps are probably still lying where I left them in the hall of that devil-ridden château. Anybody who cares to collect them may keep them.

LEWIS SPENCE
A Voice in Feathers

Lewis Spence (1874–1955), *renowned poet and folklorist, wrote several books on Atlantis, a monumental* Encyclopaedia of Occultism (1920), *and a series of attractively bound volumes on the mythologies of the North American Indians, Mexico, Peru, Ancient Egypt, Babylonia and Assyria, and other countries. He also contributed many occult and supernatural tales to the* Grand, Cornhill *and other magazines of the 1920s. "A Voice in Feathers" originally appeared in* Hutchinson's Mystery-Story Magazine, *August 1923.*

K nud Arensen's black house looked down upon the wind-swept wharf of Westervick, where the trawlers lay huddled in the ice-blue water. As he climbed the hill for his midday meal he glanced back darkly at the harbour and then upwards and even more grimly at the tarred cottage of timber with the white window-sashes.

Only one of the boats below was now his, and within the hour he had assured himself that it was a lame duck. He had once owned three trawlers, but hereditary meanness had made him procrastinate in the matter of repairs and a harsh and battering winter had completed what his miserliness had begun—the ruin of his little flotilla.

It was a hard thought for a selfish man. He knew that his aged father who lay in the great bed in the kitchen had a tidy hoard somewhere. Indeed he would not have harboured him had he not thought that by doing so he would ultimately reap a rich return for the few basins of broth which kept the old man in life.

Of late, however, he had buoyed himself up with the hope that he might be able by judicious pressure to acquire at least a portion of the money while yet his father was alive. But hard as Knud was, his sire was even more flinty of heart, and the endeavours the younger man had made to coax him out of a part of his store had, so far, met with failure almost ludicrous.

Nor could he discover where the money had been bestowed. By careful inquiry he had ascertained that it was not in the keeping of the local bankers, and by a process of elimination he had come to the conclusion that Magnus Arensen, in true peasant fashion, had concealed the savings of years in or around the black house on the hill which, for nearly fifty years, had been the patrimonial dwelling.

The trampling of Knud's great sea-boots on the plank flooring aroused not the slightest interest in the three persons who had awaited his coming—his father, who lay in the great bed, his mass of white hair and beard giving him a strikingly patriarchal aspect; his wife, a wooden-faced, heavy house-woman; and his son Ragnor, a lad of fifteen, in whom the dull grasping mentality of the family had degenerated into a witlessness allied to lunacy.

Knud threw himself upon the settle by the stove and looked hard at the old man in the bed, gazing from beneath his thick brows at the wizened, shrewd face with its great, beak-like nose and mocking eyes that leered fixedly into vacancy. Turning sharply to his wife, he demanded food, and fell hungrily on the plate of herrings which she set before him.

"You can go to the village," he said gruffly, "and take the lad with you. I wish to speak with my father."

"As you please," she replied evenly. "I will require money for coffee and flour."

"I have none to give you," he snapped. "Money, always money. I tell you that the *Ran's* engines have broken down again. I used to be a rich man, and now——"

"Very well," she sighed, and went to dress herself.

When at last they had gone a queer silence fell between father and son. The clock ticked away nearly twenty minutes before Knud spoke. During this time the old man recognised his presence not at all, but continued to gaze at the wall opposite.

Knud rose and tramped the room, the noise of his clumsy going growing louder and louder as he gradually worked himself into the passion without which he never dared to face the calm, mocking face on the pillows.

"Father," he broke out at last, "I must have money. The *Ran* is a wreck inside, and unless the engines are repaired she must rot in the harbour and we must starve."

"As it is I starve," growled the old man. "I have always starved. You eat too much, you younger people. Sell the *Ran* for what she will fetch and ship with someone else."

"That is the advice you gave when the other boats went to the broker," Knud said thickly. "If the engines were repaired I could soon retrieve my old position. But if I sell the boat I shall be a poor man for the rest of my days, always working for someone else."

The thought seemed to madden him. He stared wildly at the old man. That this useless creature who had lived his life should have the wherewithal to help him, to rescue him from the years of comparative slavery which he saw stretching before him, and yet would not, drove him frantic.

"Curse you!" he spat out suddenly, "you have the money and yet you won't lend me an ore. You want to sell me into slavery, me and the boy."

He stood menacingly over the figure on the bed.

"Tell me where you have put your money!" he almost whispered, so tense was the quality of his passion. "Tell me, or—"

"You will not frighten me," cackled the old man in senile malice. "You will not get an ore out of me, Knud Arensen, alive or dead."

His old eyes sparkled with wicked glee, his frail body shook with triumphant laughter. It was more than such flesh and blood as Knud's could bear. He seized the scraggy, bearded throat and shook it in a frenzy of homicidal passion. There was just a little movement beneath his sinewy hands—and then there was none.

"Curse him," gasped Knud as he threw the body back on the bed, "what has he made me? It was his own fault, the old miser. I will not be blamed for it—I need not be blamed for it. There isn't a single sign. He might have died any day."

Dazed, trembling, but terribly practical, he composed the body. The bearded throat concealed the accusing finger-marks. The struggle had been so slight as to leave none of the horrid insignia of murder behind it. Knud took a spade and went to dig in the garden. He seemed to go on digging for hours. His wife and son, returning from the village, passed him, but he gave no sign of their presence. A cry from the house aroused him at last.

"Knud, Knud, come at once. Your father—"

He slouched into the house.

"Well, what is it?" he asked coolly, advancing to the bed.

"He is not breathing," said his wife fearfully.

"Dead people don't breathe," said Knud.

"Is he dead?" asked the boy.

"Quite," answered Knud. "He must have died while I was digging in the garden. I, for one, expected him to die any day."

The woman crossed the dead hands over the breast and covered the face, which, even in the repose of death seemed instinct with malicious glee.

"What must we do now?" she asked of her husband.

"We must carry him to the spare bedroom," said Knud. "Tomorrow I will go to the pastor—and the carpenter."

"And his money?" whispered the woman.

"Ah, we must search for that, I suppose?"

"Were you talking about money when I was out?" she inquired, in a frightened tone, looking at him askance.

"No," he answered carelessly, "we were speaking about the *Ran* and how best to dispose of her. We do not need to trouble about that now—if we can find the money. We *must* find it," he added so fiercely that she shrank from him.

Next morning Knud Arensen went into the village, and after he had seen the pastor he walked into the workshop of Atterbom, the carpenter. Atterbom had heard of the death and greeted him solemnly.

But it was difficult to keep solemn in that place, as Atterbom was a bird-fancier, and the air was rent with the screaming of parrots and cockatoos and the whistling, shrilling and piping of other feathered things, ranged round the wall in cages of every size. For Atterbom's sympathy Knud affected a manly unconcern, and began to scrutinise the occupants of the cages.

"You always promised me a bird, Sigmund," he complained during a momentary lull, "but I've never seen it yet. I must believe that you don't intend to keep your promise. Come, I'll buy one from you. Something that will speak and sing and brighten up our dull house. I'll have money now, you know. If I can find it."

Atterbom looked at him strangely.

"You're growing generous, Knud Arensen," he said with an uneasy laugh. "Well, look here. Your father's burying—poor man—will cost you more than a trifle, and the money will drop into my pocket, so I will be generous likewise. You see this pair of white cockatoos? Well, they hatched out a young one this morning. I don't believe that such a thing has happened in Norway before. At least it hasn't happened to me. Look."

He touched the tail of the sitting hen so that she made to rise, and Knud, staring with all his eyes, saw a little bundle of fluff and flesh, a scraggy neck, and a beak out of all proportion to the body. He laughed.

"What use is that to anyone?" he asked. "You don't expect me to rear that, do you?"

"Not in that cold house of yours," admitted Atterbom. "But listen. They are all imported from abroad and consequently they all speak Spanish or Portuguese. Now I'll rear this one for you and, if it lives, it will be the first cockatoo trained to speak in Norwegian."

"They don't speak half so well as parrots, I'm told," said Knud in some disappointment.

"Nonsense," laughed the bird-fancier, "many of them speak far better—and swear far better too. Is it a bargain?"

"Oh, I suppose so," said Knud carelessly, turning away from the cage. "About the other business. You'll come up this afternoon?"

"Count on me," replied Atterbom, "though it's hardly necessary, as I've had a mental note of his measure for a long time."

Magnus Arensen was duly laid to rest with his fathers. About eight months afterwards Atterbom called one day at the black house on the hill, carrying something shrouded in a baize covering. This he drew off, and discovered a large metal cage in which perched a snow-white cockatoo.

When Ragnor saw it he danced round the cage in glee. Knud, who had half forgotten his arrangement with Atterbom, looked on sourly, in the belief that he was trying to sell him the bird. He had been searching for his father's hidden money all those months, but had not yet found the smallest trace of it, and the scanty store he had got from the sale of the *Ran* was speedily running out.

More and more gloomy he had grown, and when he heard the bird cackle a joke in hoarse Norwegian, it was with difficulty that he raised the ghost of a smile. But Ragnor and his mother were delighted. They thanked Atterbom profusely and hung the cage up in a prominent place in the kitchen—in the very place where Magnus Arensen's bed had once stood.

The bird soon became a favourite with the little household, at least with the woman and the boy, for Knud would scarcely look at it. He was unable to give any reason for the strange antipathy he had felt for the creature from the very first, but his wife told him that he disliked it because of the few pence worth of seed it consumed.

"We are all a burden to you," she said bitterly. "You grudge us the scraps we live on, even the Troll."

Ragnor had named the bird the Troll, the Norse name for an evil spirit, because, as he explained, of its ghostly appearance.

The months went by and still Knud searched for his father's money. He had dug up the entire garden and hunted every nook and cranny in the house, but so far without success. As the days wore on without result he grew more and more taciturn, more and more hopeless. At last he almost convinced himself that his father had amassed no treasure at all, and had been playing upon his cupidity.

One day he entered the kitchen and threw himself down heavily on the settle.

"It is all over with us," he said to his wife. "The money is not to be found. We must sell the house and go to America. There is nothing for us here."

She did not reply, for she had heard him in this strain often before. But Ragnor looked up.

"The Troll speaks about money," he giggled, "about hidden money."

Knud looked at him darkly.

"He grows dafter, that one," he said. "He was always light-headed, but he grows worse."

"But I tell you it is true, father," insisted the lad.

Knud looked at the cockatoo's cage which had been covered up for the night, and laughed.

"Very likely," he grunted. "He has heard us speaking about money and has picked up the words. After all he knows as much about it as we do—and that is nothing."

Knud slouched by day round the harbour, borrowing tobacco from those of his old acquaintances who were sufficiently good-natured to tolerate him. One evening as he climbed the hill to the black house and opened the door suddenly he saw Ragnor standing in the little inner porch in an attitude of rapt attention. The boy held up a warning finger.

"What is it?" growled Knud.

"Hush," said Ragnor, "it is the Troll speaking—about money. Listen."

Knud, despite himself, strained his hearing faculties and remained as quiet and attentive as his son.

Silent moments passed. Then the bird spoke.

"The money," it cackled, "the money—is near—near at hand."

Knud craned his neck round the door and glanced into the kitchen. In the evening dusk the white bird seemed like a spirit.

He shivered. The voice he had heard was not the voice of the bird.

"The money is near—near at hand," it repeated.

Whose voice was that—in God's name, whose voice?

"You shall never find it, Knud Arensen. Never, never."

Knud fell rather than walked out of the house. He dared not re-enter. Down the path to the village he staggered, his brain in a whirl. As he ran a wild peal of laughter floated from the kitchen window. He recognised the laughter. He felt that madness was near him.

That night he came home late. He was not sober. The house was in complete darkness. He crawled into bed and lay awake all night, a prey to fears of the most terrible kind. With the first streak of dawn he rose, dressed himself and lurched into the kitchen.

He tore the cover off the cockatoo's cage and glared at it in the half-light. It was wide awake and returned his stare with its small, malicious eyes. Then it burst into a hoarse shriek of mocking laughter.

"You devil," he cried, "you thought to cheat me, but I'll have the secret out of you yet. Tell me where you have hidden the money, or I'll twist your neck as I did before."

For answer the bird laughed again. Knud inserted a murderous hand into the cage. The bird screamed louder and avoided his grasp. It pecked savagely at his fingers and as he withdrew his hand, fluttered out of the cage, and, flying through the window, perched on a birch tree at the edge of the garden, where it continued its cachinnations.

Knud ran out of doors, shaking his fist at it and swearing loudly. The hubbub awoke Ragnor, who came running into the garden.

"The old miser," yelled Knud, "he has come back to mock me. Boy, fetch my gun from above the stove. Quick."

Ragnor hurried inside and in a moment reappeared with the weapon. But as Knud sought to take it from him, the lad slipped. There was a loud explosion, and Knud Arensen fell writhing to the ground. The last sound he heard was the mocking laughter of the cockatoo.

That night the woman and the boy found enough money to buy a whole fleet of trawlers in an old pair of sea-boots which had belonged to Magnus Arensen.

DEREK STANFORD
A Dream of Porcelain

Derek Stanford (b.1918) is a distinguished critic, editor and poet, and author of studies on Muriel Spark, Dylan Thomas, Christopher Fry and John Betjeman. He has also published several anthologies and articles on the 1890s. Among his other writings are Movements in English Poetry 1900–1958 (1959) and Inside the Forties: Literary Memoirs, 1937–1957 (1977). Stanford has contributed many original stories dealing with the ghostly and paranormal to various anthologies.

Above all, for those readers to whom the house in the story will appear as a dear familiar domain.

How much love of one particular woman does a man in his early fifties need, when what he primarily seeks—in his encounter with her—is that which stimulates his creativity as a writer?

Roger had been living with Clarissa for ten years, and thought he knew the answer to this question. Which was why he had fled to Peacock Place—an artists' rest-home on the North Downs in Surrey — in order, as Clarissa ironically put it, to work out his crisis situation. That, she said, was what Roger seemed to think he was suffering from. Others might have termed it the male menopause. Well, a cow-pat by any other name would smell as sweet.

He saw his flight somewhat differently; he was all but certain that his stay in this place of sanctuary would verify the verdict he'd already arrived at.

Roger had made a somewhat late arrival at Peacock Place, phoning the comely housekeeper Margaret (whom he always spoke of as "the chatelaine") to leave him a plate of sandwiches, a thermos of coffee and a little rum, since he'd had a tiresome journey and thought an early night the best thing.

This supper snack had been placed in his room. Margaret had brought an hot-water bottle and Eric, her amiable consort whose kingdom was the garden, had carried his luggage upstairs for him.

Roger looked round the comfortable bedroom, with its good writing table, easy chairs, ample wardrobe and invaluable bedside-stand (for pills, glass of water, night-cap novel, spectacles, and other knick-knacks to have near one) . . . . yes, all was in apple-pie order for composition, meditation, recreation— or whatever he chose.

Two once-expensive suitcases lay on the bed unopened: he did not feel like extensive unpacking just now. His good friends, Margaret and Eric, had bidden him good-night and left him to get ready for bed. He fished for his pyjama top in one case, preferring V-front pants to pyjama trousers; and, pulling out his faded short gold-striped dressing-gown, dropped both cases by the side of the bed. No one, save himself, would occupy it. No Clarissa beside him or any other figure sharing its warmth or accommodating herself to the contours of his side. Well, he had wanted to be on his own. Had wooed this solitude like a lover with his imagination. And here it was: a vacancy awaiting him.

It was only about half-past ten when he padded in his slippers down to the bookshelves in the library and coffee-room. He'd bought a paper-back with him, Hardy's *The Woodlanders*, for bedside reading—a second time round with the author since his teens. Tonight, however, that old rustic pessimist's opinion of the cosmos appeared to stick out like a sore thumb from the text. The opening of Chapter Four had proved too much for him on this unexhilarating evening:

> "There was now a distant manifestation of morning in the air, and presently the bleared white visage of a sunless winter day emerged like a dead-born child."

After this, Roger felt the animating good cheer of Victorian melodrama might be more rewardingly sought in Conan Doyle. In the hall, before opening the library door, Roger's eye rested for a moment on the portrait of William Francis Rickett—the manufacturer of Rickett's Blue Washing Cubes, whose fortunes had led to the founding of this house as a rest-home for artists of all callings. The portrait in question had been painted by Orpen who—to the benign black-suited benefactor with his pipe and tooth-brush moustache—had mischievously added a background of that identical blue which his sitter's father had so profitably patented. Roger normally enjoyed the painting; was amused by it, and felt welcomed by the kindly look in the eye of the dead man (himself a good amateur painter.) Tonight, however, something seemed wrong. The friendly half-query on the founder's face seemed to be trembling on the verge of a frown or of some puzzled non-recognition. The rose in his buttonhole, which Roger recalled as red appeared to have lost its full blush and become a strangely pallid pink, And—something Roger had never noticed before—there was smoke coiling upwards from the pipe held in one hand—a blue ectoplasmic serpent of smoke.

All these were momentary impressions—produced perhaps by the low-lighting in the passage with only one lamp left on all night. As soon as he had chosen a book from the shelves—it happened to be a World Classics edition of *Sherlock Holmes: Selected Stories*—Roger, returning upstairs, could not help somewhat anxiously checking for these changes in the portrait on the wall.

The features remained the same as he had first known them. Roger must have been deceived by the half-light. But if your eyes can play you false, what about your other senses? How much trust can we place in our perceptions: one's prided intuitions?

Peacock Place had many engaging memories. He had met colleagues and made friends there; and from the library shelves he would take down, here and there, a volume presented by some author, acquainted with him, recording the productive association of the book with the house which had known its genesis or gestation. William Cooper had presented a copy of his *Scenes of Metropolitan Life* in "great appreciation"; Bryan Magee spoke of part of his magisterial study *The Philosophy of Schopenhauer* being written in this well-chosen spot and Denis Bardens' occult compendium *Mysterious Worlds: A Personal Investigation of the Weird, the Uncanny and the Unexplained* contained an expression of thanks for the researcher's "happy and grateful stay".

This night, however, he was the only guest; and though one of his most cherished visits to Peacock Place had been when the house was empty, save for the staff, and the February rains had filled all the dykes for days on end, tonight the pervasive thought of old companions—of long-familiar books and pictures intimately remembered—failed to cheer him as formerly. The homeliness, which he felt breathing out of the walls whenever he'd thought about the spot, no longer operated its domestic magic. Had these *lares et penates*, seeing that it was the third week in October—engaged in a short hibernatory nap?

Back in his room, he sat up to drain the last drops of rum and coffee. Much to his dismay, he found his thoughts deserting Dr. Watson (so much more clubbable than Holmes) in order to go over his "thing" with Clarissa. Quite unexpectedly and quite unforseeably, it appeared it was going to be one of those nights.

The elusive essence of inspiration . . . that was what Roger was always seeking. That was what hitherto he had found in Clarissa. For him, she had proved to be an ample amphora, containing and conveying those invisible fluids upon which his whole being was nurtured. With her palpably rounded figure, she conjured up, in his inner eye, the image of a kind of two-handed Roman wine-jar; an amphora in bed and about the house. Figuratively, he thought of this jar as containing wine, water, olive oil—three basic liquids, three sustainers and comforters—and all of them he received from her, liberally, when called for. No, he had not gone short. She had fed the inner man, as well as he who shared her bed and board. She nurtured him and the works he produced. He claimed these productions were their children; and she sensed in him the artist's almost inevitable selfishness. But his self-indulgence *was* creative; and she felt she was the mother to these offspring which were not of the flesh—though without the flesh and spirit of them both, they would not exist in their present form, if in any satisfactory fashion at all. This had been Clarissa's viewing of things—or, at least, how he had imagined it to be.

Such, then, had been the pattern of their communion throughout those years together. She had made herself an hospitable habit: something taken, appreciatively, and yet for granted; and all the more missed when it began to function uncertainly. Previous bestowals had been so sure.

But what was it, he asked himself, which was now in jeopardy? He could not fault the initial acts of transgression between them. It was just that what was transmitted did not proceed, as in the past, to become engaged in a transmuting process. Her giving—their interchange—ceased to colour and stir his thought. The chemistry of their closeness and coming together did not appear to be different: it was only that the former alchemy was absent.

He had first become aware of this when the springs of his own work began to behave intermittently. Promising starts petered out. Paragraphs, commencing lively enough, grew stodgy, turgid or faltered out completely. Ideas were there—a shower of likely notions. What was wanting was momentum; the mind's illusion of perpetual motion. This newly increased paucity occasioned a play-back in Roger's life with Clarrie. A lack of being able to draw on a former amplitude of responses now commenced to characterize their existence. Old magnanimities were no longer to be relied upon. A disturbing emotional stinginess made itself felt. Neither their hearts nor their senses indulged each other with the same kind of generosity they had exerted so naturally and for so long. The currency of Roger's thought and emotions, concerning her, grew devalued.

When he was writing well, or had been doing so, he felt grateful, tranquilized; and Clarrie became the prime centre of this emanation of approval. Contrary-wise, when he was writing, or believed himself to have written, inadequately, he felt dissatisfied, tense or barren; and it was Clarrie who received these negatory vibrations.

Then Roger took to getting up in the night. He would steal into the next room, brew himself a lemon herb tea; and, sometimes lose himself in the topiary of a few choice paragraphs. Contented, he would drain the honey-infused liquid at the bottom of the cup; and quietly tip-toe back to Clarrie. At others, heavy-headed or unsteady on his pins, he would sit regarding the pedestrian sentences he had composed with a desperate attempt to evade triteness or mediocrity by means of all-too recherché metaphor. Too often, he failed to claim the feeblest miniscule of elegance to set against the wasted hours of night, fit for sleep or tender closeness. When his prose had displayed one or two pretty paces, he returned to bed, inwardly purring at the feel of Clarrie's buttocks or thighs against him; and blessing her as his sweet companion or helpmate. When his words had refused to cartwheel, however, he lay miserably awake, his mind ticking away until Clarrie turned in her sleep and cuddled him in her lap. Drowsily he would murmur some endearment, but was awake again at dawn to renew the search for response from his uncertain daemon.

Latterly, the tempo of their love-making changed. At night, Roger was usually too dissatisfied with his unproductive day to find relief in Clarrie's ample body. He hoped only for a better day tomorrow, and for as quick an exit out of the present as possible. In the morning, he was amorous, often first thing on waking, if the night had provided him with a bonanza; Clarrie, though, while hugging him was still enmeshed in sleep. If the night had granted him no windfall, he wanted only to be up and doing, hoping to commit something to paper before his energies ran out. Age may be measured by the degree in which we become aware of the need for conserving our energies. Roger, now, was very conscious of that need; and, sometimes, it seemed that he and Clarrie were hardly granted time for love-making.

It ended up with him electing to stay two or three nights a week in the little guest-bedroom. Sometimes the experiment sparked something off, but just as often he spent a wordless loveless night. It was then that Clarrie came up with the suggestion that they should both go off for a holiday—apart. They would not communicate with each other for a full three weeks, even though each should possess the relevant address and telephone number.

"It should tell us something, either way," she insisted. "What I really mean it should tell *you* what you're wanting."

"And you, Clarrie?" he had asked her.

"Oh, me, well, perhaps what I wish for most of all is just to learn what you're really after."

The mind at midnight makes its précis, not always a very coherent one.

Roger's memory had just unwound the spool of the past and then rewound it again.

If sleep was to be bad, a Delmane was called for. Washing down the little grey-and-amber capsule, Roger invoked Morpheus; and, then, seeing it was a late October night, with mist between the trees and over the Downs, and a country cold making itself felt in the bedroom—(since he had been too lazy to take the little electric fire out of the cupboard) he decided, untowardly, he wanted to pee.

From previous stays at Peacock Place, Roger had found in the double-doored capacious wardrobe—a massive Victorian what-not which so many rooms possessed—a chamber-pot often dusty from disuse. From the little bedside lockers, these utensils of an earlier era had vanished entirely. The bathroom nearest to him was along a corridor in which the lights had been extinguished; and Roger was imagining how chill it would feel outside his room, as well as being aware of his reluctance to unlock his door and go pattering past all those deserted bedrooms.

With the pressure on his sphincter-muscle increasing, he switched on the bedside light and rummaged at the back of the big wardrobe. No, it looked as if those unhygienic conveniences of a former era had been discarded. Expecting to find the locker of his bedside table likewise empty, he opened the door and there—Eureka!—a fine Edwardian chamber-pot dawned upon his sight. It was of shining porcelain-smooth china, resplendent with garlands of roses and cupids around the rim; with Venus and Mars, in traditional nudity, emblazoned on the sides, and a large pink rose, nenuphar-like, glowing up at him from the vessel's bottom.

Roger was so amazed that, for a moment, he suspended his necessary performance. Roses around these comforting containers were known to him from days of childhood; but he failed to remember one such in which *putti* frolicked amid the flowers. This particular porcelain-like exhibit was more than an object of solace. It was, in terms of the potter's craft, very much a thing of beauty and, design-wise, unusually rare. It was also a two-handed vessel to make the disposal of contents easier, safer and more practical. Its maker had obviously believed that this object of easement should not become a burden.

In the sacramental materialism of everyday living, what domestic utensil symbolises the propinquity of two partners more than a shared *pot-de-chambre*? Roger's reflection, on this point before sleep, might have more fittingly applied to earlier epochs than the 'Nineteen-Nineties. But, there, he was not a man of his time but something of an old-fashioned social thinker!

He woke, in the morning to a greyish light emanating from sunshine strained through clouds and percolating between the not-quite-closed curtains. He thought to empty the jereboam in the bedside-locker before house-keeper Margaret or Mavis, her lieutenant, brought the tea. But when he opened the cupboard door, there was no night utensil there.

535

Had he, as the sleeping-pill submerged his perception, smuggled it, by any chance, back into the wardrobe? No; that, too, was empty. Had he dreamt up the whole affair? Just then, a tap came at the bedroom door and demure Mavis brought in his morning tray.

There was a dewy-dimness on the grass of the lawns this morning, and the paving-surrounded pool in the garden—where one might see the occasional fish-marauding heron—breathed off a brumy breath of autumn.

By ten, however, the sky had cleared so that its ethereal blue reminded Roger of the French poet Mallarmé: "Skies pale and pure which sad October knew." Was that it, or had he got it wrong? No matter! It was a long time since he had read that English translation from the Eighteen-Nineties.

The gardens of Peacock Place were extensive; and Roger was hoping that he might find a good place in which to write. He remembered a little locked summer-house or gazebo, which an English Buddhist monk, staying at the house, had once fitted up with rough wooden shelves on which he kept meditational manuals. These had long since vanished, when the *ersatz* guru had decamped rather suddenly in circumstances not clearly understood. The old chair and little table he had used now alone kept their place.

Roger went for the key; returned with it, and ensconced himself at the uneven table, with the door propped wide open to make the most of the Indian summer sun.

He had a story to tell which had been occupying him for some time. It was to be called *The True Life of Burlington Bertie*, and was planned as if Roger was recounting a piece of researched biography. The mask of apparent fact to conceal a fiction was something that appealed to his fancy. His notes were at hand, the place was auspicious, he felt unexpectedly rested and well (the sleeping-pills had seen him off nicely), and was accordingly looking forward to a serene progression of prose across the pages of his manuscript book.

Mavis tripped in with coffee at eleven; and still he had not set down a single word. Half an hour before the gong would sound for lunch, he decided to take a turn between the trees. Odd phrases seemed to be buzzing in his brain; and he hoped that by walking he could coax them down to his finger-tips. But when he returned with what he thought might prove a preliminary capful of them, he found the door of the summer-house locked. He could have sworn he had put the key on the top of a bookshelf after opening up. It was, in fact, still there, as he could see through the glass of the door; but, none the less, it would not open.

After lunch, he told Margaret of his predicament. She said the lock of the door must have jammed. Had he slammed it, perhaps? Or the wood had warped. She couldn't remember when it had last been in use. When Mr. Hall was staying here, he seemed to have locked himself in by mistake. They'd had to find a second key to get in, since he'd lost the first one given him.

After coffee in the lounge, she'd brought him a fresh shiny key unlike the old rusty one lying on the shelf inside. And there, through the afternoon, he'd waited for the words to arrive.

For their visitation he waited in vain. His lunch had been a light collation of avocado, cold chicken and celery-nut-and-sultana salad. He'd skipped dessert, and taken his coffee black as an added protection against post-prandial drowsiness. His head and bodily perceptions were clear, but his mind seemed to fasten on to every distraction available. He found himself fascinated by the slow gentle drone of an old two-seater bi-plane (obviously some amateur's joy) which was bumbling like a somnolent autumn-heavy bee. He noted, too, the lazy movements of a she-cat, once a wild stray, who lived in an out-house attached to the kitchen, and was too sluttish even to venture far for its scratch in the soft earth of the border unless carried there by Eric. Her functions disdainfully performed, she was now, with some show of reluctance, making her way back to the outhouse in the wake of Eric's retreating form. Other small details waylaid his attention: a green woodpecker on the trunk of an elm, and a late dragonfly which had so far unheeded the season's knell—though when he looked for it again it was gone. No question of his mind's non-attentiveness. It was just that all his consciousness lay on the surface, there being, so to speak, no lift working between ground-floor awareness and imagination's basement.

He looked at his watch; only three hours since lunch, and already the tea-trolley would have been put out in the library, so that one could brew oneself Darjeeling, Assam, Earl

Grey—take your pick!—and fill up with Elaine's fairy cakes or cream sponge.

Here he was, come to Peacock Place, to verify his belief that writing, and writing alone, would provide him with a sufficiency of companionship and emotional excitement, the solace and comfort which most men obtain from a variety of sources—few of them of a purely mental order. A flight from matrimonial trivias; and, so far, all he'd done was to put down two square meals, arise to meet an intermediary snack, and prepare for the thought of a third. This too, too solid flesh! Nor could he claim that the succulence of dessert had produced a pudding heaviness of mind.

Then, just as he was picking up the key to lock the door—one couldn't be too careful in this deserted garden!—he noticed a fawn which had emerged from the high hedge separating Peacock Place from Dovecotes, the Voysey-built house next door, and yet seemingly almost light years away, so silent were the neighbours beyond that green divide. The fawn—half-frightened, half-fastidious—lapped at the waters of the pool and questioningly nibbled a water-lily leaf.

Since he had arrived last night, Roger's thoughts had seemed to glance and glide solely on the top of things. One after another, minutiae had come into his ken without touching off any mood or meaning for him. The day had proved itself singularly non-creative. He was not aware of a single interesting thought which had visited him this morning. Not a single phrase had his pen hatched out. Only perceptions had occupied his mind. Yet with all this conscious passivity, he had a feeling that, before dark, something eventful might take place; but that, if it did, it would not be himself which set things in actions. Events would happen not through him, but to him. He sensed himself to be a target.

As he made his way from the little copse of trees in which the summer-house stood, past the lily-pond (the lapping fawn having quietly removed itself), across the grass and under the veranda into the capacious lounge with its cream-coloured flowerlet-worked armchairs and sofas, he became aware of something else that characterized this desultory afternoon and the odd inner vacancy of his own mind. It was the feeling, the realization that all these small intrusions into the garden stillness . . . the old-fashioned bi-plane bumbling into the blue, the sleazy cat, the investigatory fawn, the whirring of the power-mower cutting the thick grass between the fruit trees . . . all of these impressions had registered themselves in a way he had not experienced before. At the time, he had been lost in each simple individual perception; but now, sitting by the tea-trolley in the library, an emotion of acute unease crept up on him.

He felt that, in receiving each detail of the day, he had sacrificed something of himself. No, sacrificed was not the word, since that might suggest a willing offering; and this was something imposed from without. Something of himself had been transferred then; his possession, his ownership of himself withdrawn. In the hazy sunshine of the library, he shivered.

A cup of tea—the pragmatist's prescription, if not panacea, for all things. He brewed himself Earl Grey, and waited for its warmth to revive his feelings. Meanwhile, he cut himself a wadge of cream sponge. I eat and drink, therefore I am. Well, it was reassuring to be able to do something more than think. Of that capacity there seemed to be no absence. Could he rephrase his condition for himself?

It seemed to him—or so he conjectured—that he had lost that priority of status which humans command in the world of the non-human. As if he had become just one further phenomenon among these phenomena. Say, rather, taken in by these, and merged in the context of garden sights and sounds. To a point where his identity had been subtracted. He could even imagine himself become a part of the furniture or fitments of the house; and, yes, in his mind's eye, he saw himself depicted in a painting hanging on the wall of the passage outside the door of the billiard-room. There he was, in the picture, presented like some piece of still-life in the bell-jar of the garden gazebo. He saw it quite clearly though it didn't exist.

Pouring himself a second cup of Earl Grey, Roger wondered if this was fantasy running riot. Could it be his blocked creativity as a writer was enacting its fantasies in his own person? To ask this question was perhaps to provide himself with the hope of an escape—an escape from feeling himself lost in nature; lost in the multiplicity of things: a single tile or tessara in a mosaic extending beyond his mental vision. The best thing to do would be to ignore it; to feed the inner man with a second slice of Elaine's cream-sponge—and then to return to work, or try to.

It had been an early tea; and there was still a little while before the garden grew fumey and dense with dusk. Perhaps a surprise sentence might give him the note for tomorrow morning's writing. (He hated to compose creatively by lamplight; and kept artificial illumination for letters—above all, correspondence with accountants, bank managers and the Inland Revenue.)

But when he fitted the key into the lock of the summer-house and turned it, the handle of the door failed to open it. And, what was more, confronting him on the top-most shelf of the bookcase within, there stood a remarkable ceramic object which had certainly not been present when he left the shelter some thirty minutes earlier. Its rich dark bulk and incised decoration immediately made it a focal centre; and the abstract, semi-organic shapes depicted on its upper half filled the gazebo with powerful vibrations.

Roger stood looking at its shape, some two feet high and capaciously broad. It had a handle which joined the top of the jar to the short neck and mouth of the vessel, and seemed to recall objects of a like nature to Roger from their place in museum or art-galleries. He took it to be a cider-jar, probably of French or English manufacture, and deriving its line and design from African pottery.

The decoration was carried on circular bands incised upon the side of the jar. The first appeared just below its neck; and to Roger it seemed to resemble a male member between two spherical shapes which suggested testicles. Below this, and occupying more of the surface of the jar was a second motif, again repeating spherical and cylindrical forms; but this time, the shapes were larger and the cylindrical form more elongated, prompting the image of a phallus imprisoned between two female breasts. There was nothing in the way of anatomical exactness about these shapes—nothing, in the least clinical or, for that matter, pornographic. At the same time, the surprise which the jar's appearance created was undeniably erotic. It was primitive, potent and inexplicable.

Amazed, and not a little confounded, Roger tried the key a second time. Yes, it clicked as if he'd engaged the lock and opened it; but still, when he tried the door-handle, he found it impossible to obtain entry.

Keeping his eye on the jar for as long as the summer-house was in sight, he went back to the house to report these fresh proceedings. Something made him say nothing to Margaret about the jar—something that was not quite concerned with what he took its design to be. Possibly, someone else would not see these Freudian patternings.

Margaret returned with him to the hut, took the key and inserted it in the look. It turned, and she immediately flung open the door.

"Phew! What a smell of cider in here. Been having an afternoon swiggy, Mr. Daimler?"

But what appalled Roger, even more than the scent of cider still heavy on the red sundowning air, was the fact that the jar had absolutely vanished. It was bad enough, attempting to explain his second lock-out from the summer-house, without bringing the absconding jar into the picture. As it was, Margaret obviously thought that his difficulty with the key had been the result of his drinking. She was, though, given to open friendly humour, too discreet in her position as "lady of the manor" to ask him where he'd secreted the bottle.

Roger, left wondering in the gazebo, never managed that redeeming single sentence. He felt the impact of what a gifted writer[1] called "the malice of inanimate objects", and this fresh evidence of it deeply unnerved him. And, yet, what was essentially malicious about that oddly-patterned jar? It was only its sudden unaccountable appearance and equally inexplicable disappearance which made it a matter of puzzled foreboding. Things were asserting their secret primacy; and he wondered what manifestation might be making ready in the wings.

As it was, the night proved singularly restful. No rose-painted jereboams materialised for the specific solace of some belated time-traveller. An Irish coffee at eight and two Delmane sleeping-pills at eleven had proved a prophylactic against such encountering. Reading in his Conan Doyle of Sherlock Holmes injecting himself with "a seven-per-cent solution of cocaine", Roger fell asleep feeling almost normal.

By ten in the morning, he had digested his muesli, coffee, toast and smoked haddock; taken his short constitutional through the terraced garden, down to a lane at the bottom, chequered already with scanty fallen leaves, then back by road to the house from the front.

[1] M.R. James

541

This time he made up his mind to give that summer-house the go-by. Margaret said she'd had the lock oiled; but the prelude of a smile on her face suggested that she thought it was Roger who had been well-oiled the previous afternoon.

Instead, he decided to take a canvas chair, and place it against the espaliered wall in a warm corner nook where his thoughts could ripen. This was towards the bottom of the garden, in a little orchard close, midway on one of the descending terraces, between the lawn and the vegetable patch with its compost heap, tangle of blackberry bushes and a thick hedge which enfenced it from the lane.

There he planned to start his story, the whole scenario of which he had worked out in his mind, wanting only those compulsive words to give his naked thoughts their dress. But, once again, they proved not at beck and call; and the externalities of the scene—a profuse bush of Golden Rod and a mass of Michaelmas Daisies planted by chance among the fruit trees, occupied all his attention. Both were flowers he had loved from childhood; and the former, with its glowing crowd of flower-heads made him think of that cloud of airy sovereigns about to find access in Danae's open lap. Yes, that was how Correggio had painted Jove's descent!

The Michaelmas Daisies, with their melancholy mauves, seemed to symbolize the opposite of this: not impregnation, but a retirement into the underworld, the blossoms appearing like day-time torches of some commencing hibernation.

Just as Roger's observations began to take a downward turn, a wide-winged Red Admiral butterfly, perched on a branch of buddleia, took off; and, in slow majestic flight—drawn perhaps by the odour of rotting pears and apples on the compost-heap—flew over the orchard's red-brick south-wall into a waste-ground and vegetable patch consisting of the garden's lowest terrace.

Roger felt a fancy to follow the lovely creature, and see if he could detect its next perch. After all, there would not be so many more Red Admirals on the wing this year, this one being clearly of the rear-guard few.

He descended three steps into the garden's waste-plot, where all sorts of aromatic decompositions were in progress. He could not spot the kingly flier. The blackberries were long over; what had once been fruit now misted with mould. When was it the

Devil was said to blight them with his breath, after which they were not for eating? Was it Hallowe'en or St. Martin's Day? Well, this year he had visited well in advance.

Perhaps it was the damp of this little secluded region which led Roger to unbutton himself and urinate on a brown fungus-sprouting stump of a tree. Almost, like an echo, as he adjusted his dress, there came a trickling sound. Was it the fountain that functioned years back from a pool now dry and packed tight with bullrushes? Even if water still remained there, the jet, he was sure, had long ceased to operate. Then, he recalled how Clarrie—when using a public loo—would speak of having "a penny tinkle." That was what it sounded like.

The next moment and he had spotted the Red Admiral settled on something the colour of a flower-pot, behind a row of flowering onions. It was a larger-than-life-size figure of a naked woman, cast in unglazed ceramic, part organic and part abstract in form and composition. The Red Admiral had perched itself on the nipple of the left breast—with its wings opening and closing—as if its proboscis was extracting from that dry nodule as rich an ambrosia as any lepidoptera could expect from buddleia, tobacco-plant or night-scented stock.

When Roger's glance first fell on the sculpted figure, the eyes were two oval-shaped hollows in the ceramic face; but as the butterfly's tittilation of the breast continued, he noticed that eyelids of stoneware were closing over them as if in the ecstasy of lactation or love, and that the bent ceramic knees were easing themselves apart.

Roger could endure no more. He picked up his folding canvas chair, his notebook and his cardigan; and left the butterly in possession of that inanimate and yet responsive figure. He admitted to being very frightened at what he had seen and could make no sense of. A second part of the garden was become *verboten* to him.

"Very frightened" was an understatement. Within the house, without the house, he did not know what would happen next. He had come to this place of retreat only to find the sanctuary haunted. But was the haunting inherent in the place, or had he somehow brought it with him? And if it emanated from the place, why had it not been manifest before? How could he possibly remain?

That afternoon, he took a bus up to Box Hill. The woods were in their prime; and after tea—Darjeeling with toasted teacake and an unusual Danish pastry flavoured with ginger—he made his way down, from the chalet-restaurant, through the trees and winding track, to the main road. There, just outside the town of Dorking, Henry Hope—friend and patron of Disraeli—had built his fine mansion; and it was from Deepdene (as his host's splendid residence was called) that Dizzy had dated *Coningsby*. Roger—a sceptical anti-Thatcherite Tory—forgot about his hauntings in these fond associations. It was less than ten minutes back in the little diesel train to Reigate. He arrived at Peacock Place in time to take a bath before dinner.

That had been a stiffish trot-down from Box Hill for so sedentary a type as Roger. None the less, he was glad to have made it; happily congratulating himself that the happenings in the house had not extended their range of operation. Had they ceased their hanky-panky here also?

He had just undressed to step into the hot water, and had unclasped the lattice-window to let out the steam, when a large bluebottle, disturbed by the light and the movement of the curtains, alighted on his chest, just above the right nipple. There was something so peculiarly bloated and repellant about this seeming half-comatose insect that Roger felt a shiver of disgust—but more than plain disgust—pass over him. It was as if some putrefying touch, some death-in-life infection had contaminated him.

He brushed it off swiftly and roughly with a towel, and the thing fell to the floor as in a stupor. He tried to spot its whereabouts, ready with his slipper to swat it, but couldn't see it anywhere.

With the sensation of pollution still tingling in him, he clambered quickly into the bath and vigorously soaped his chest and nipple. The pleasure of relaxing his exercised muscles was spoiled for him by the recollection of that overblown fly. Even in the water, his flesh recalled its contact.

All that evening he was restless, pacing between the library and the lounge, and ferreting about among old periodicals kept in an ancient battered bookcase with brass handles and glass-panelled doors. The lock fastening one of these had ceased to work; and, to prevent it from swinging open, a little rubber wedge had been inserted at the bottom. The other door seemed permanently stuck, so that one had to grope with one's hand behind the glass in order to extricate the volume wanted. While trying to withdraw, from a line of Oxford histories on that subject, Margaret Whinney and Oliver Millard's book *On English Art 1625–1714*, he knocked down an odd number from a pile of old *Apollo's* which fell on the floor, its leaves open. What he saw filled him with amazement. He could not believe it—but there it was indubitably: a full-page coloured reproduction, in two separate illustrations, of that chamber-pot found so mysteriously in his bedside-cupboard, the first night of his stay. There were the same plump Cupids playing among the flowers, Mars and Venus naked as if for love; and, in a second depiction of the vessel, the inside of the pot with its curious rose, like some outspread water-lily, splendidly resplendent at the bottom. It had been photographed some twenty-five years back, on the occasion of some grand auction; and now, in all probability, adorned some American tycoon's dinner-table where it served as a glorified flower-bowl. As to its date, Roger had got it wrong. It was not Edwardian as he imagined, but Regency; and the designer and manufacturer were French.

These were all points of artistic interest; but, outweighing them all, was the incredible coincidence that the magazine should fall from the cupboard and open itself at the very page where the identical vesselfirst appearing then disappearing— was depicted. To have come across it was extraordinary enough; stranger still was its having absconded by morning; and now, by an utter act of chance, to encounter its total likeness: the three- reduced to the two-dimensional.

Roger went to bed that night feeling an anxiety close to utter panic. Was he on the brink of madness? It would be a couple of Delmanes, tonight, with a third if the initial charge didn't take.

He folded back the blanket and eiderdown to find the hot-water-bottle round which Mavis had put his pyjama-jacket to warm. There they were, all cozy to the touch; but something else was there also—the large repellant blowfly he had seen in the bathroom and which, he thought, had dropped to the floor there. Yet here it was, clearly dead, with its bloated body already shrinking and drying, right in the centre of the sheet above his night-clothes. He swept it off the bed with the cuff of his dressing-gown, and spent the next few minutes fighting down nausea.

The following morning, after a laggard breakfast— having tasted his Alpen, nibbled a corner of toast, swallowed less than half a cup of coffee, and leaving the kedgeree quite unexplored—Roger dragged himself into the library and sank wearily into an armchair.

Besides the fear of what was happening to him, he felt an acute dispiritedness at the thought of being driven out of Peacock Place—for he did not see how he could stay there longer.

These horrifically unexplainable happenings were infrequent and intermittant; and, in between their manifestation, the house and gardens lived on with a quietly well-ordered serene life of their own. It was he, his own inward agitation, his constantly suppressed state of expectedness, which prevented the healing spirit of the place from getting through and reassuring him.

He was, in addition, deeply mortified at being driven out of his celibate Eden, the problem he had brought with him (against all anticipation) unsolved. He had come up with a conjectured answer to his literary-domestic problem, and had looked to his stay at Peacock Place to provide ample verification. The proof of the rightness of his decision had singularly failed to reveal itself. He had been expecting that, on his own, he would write with ease and abundance; that those fountains, whose waters had flowed so unsteadily, would jet, for long periods, with effortless *élan*. Instead, the condition confronting him was that, here, with every convenience and inducement to hand, he had not succeeded in writing one word.

Seeking to exculpate himself, he wondered if the company of colleagues—one or two interesting and genial spirits—would have released that switched-off creativity. He had been here before—for two or three days, and, on one occasion, two weeks—with the house to himself and experienced neither loneliness nor writer's block.

Even so, he thought of the mental vivacity, the disburdening of one's thoughts in badinage, table talk, or soberer discussion. He called up the images of good companions known here: Brian Magee, his large impressive frame, with voice and thoughts as clear as a bell; Andrew Mackenzie, that engaging combination of the sceptical Scot with a touch of the Highlander's second sight; Charles Getty and Paul Chand, with their jokes and anecdotes of opera and stage; Clive Murphy who lived over an East End Pakistani restaurant and had written the life of an actress-loo-attendant; and rueful serious Fred Grubb with whom he had once broken a lance on the vexed issue of Marxism. To the image of these companions and colleagues, his memory turned on the spirit of communion. Perhaps the thought of them might lend him strength . . .

His eye alighted alphabetically on the B's in the bookcases: Sebastian Barker, Paul Binding, John Bowen, John Braine—the latter already with the shades. No; these good men, alive or dead, had no power to stem the rising panic in him. He rose, heavily, from the armchair, half feeling a kinship with those in the shadows.

And now, he supposed, there was nothing to do but go upstairs to his room and pack. Margaret and Eric had expected his stay would be longer; and he would have to invent some polite taradiddle to account for his early departure.

While he was rummaging at the back of his wardrobe for various oddments shoved into the recesses, his hand made contact with a book he did not remember being there before. He pulled it out and read the title: *A History of World Pottery* by Emmanuel Cooper, inscribed by the author in italic script. Seated only in a pair of shorts—his sun-loving back and torso basking—Emmanuel's image returned to Roger. He recalled him writing an article on the little-known nineteenth-century painter Tuke, as he sat at a small garden table between a box-hedge and a fig-tree, beside the verandah which led to the lounge.

The book was one of those coffee-table summaries for intelligent readers, plentifully illustrated; and he remembered taking it from the library when he had first met Emmanuel, some few years back. Someone must evidently have been looking at it, and forgot to replace it when he left.

Opening the volume, Roger flicked through the pages. At page 179, he suddenly stopped. *Earthenware cider jar with incised decoration, made at Winchcombe Pottery by Michael Cardene, 1936.* Roger's indifferent attention received a jab like that delivered by a dental syringe. Here, in photographic print was that identical jar, with strange half-abstract erotic markings, which he had seen through the panes of the summer-house and which had disappeared without a trace by the time he had fetched Margaret to fiddle with the key. On page 181 a greater shock awaited him. *"Woman" by Mary Frank. Unglazed ceramic. A strong and powerful sculptural piece Length 89 inches 1973.* This was the figure he had come upon in the garden, easing open its knees in response to the Red Admiral butterfly. The figure in this garden manifestation had also grown in magnitude, just as the measurements of the photographic figure were smaller than those of the ceramic original.

How, in heaven's name (or should it be hell's?) had these two-dimensional likenesses got from the page of Cooper's book to assume three-dimensional nature outside its pages? How, having assumed this extra dimension, had they got back into the book, vanishing without a trace after their brief appearance in the world of objects?

Roger knew there could be no answer; knew, too, that no one would believe these events, if he narrated them as they had happened. If these occasions possessed a logic, it would be one which was valid for him only. These happenings were like random-seeming phrases which only the grammar of personal emotion could place in meaningful sentence-order. That sentence Roger now thought he could construe.

The gist of it was amazingly simple. He, in his disturbed state of mind (with doubts and feelings he did not own to) acted as a kind of catalyst for objects which could conduct a psychic charge. It was this magnetic power in his sub-conscious which was responsible for their bi-location giving to the two-dimensional a momentary three-dimensional nature. Illustrations from a book and a magazine became the things they were likenesses of; then, having served their purpose, reverted to photographic state.

The Regency chamber-pot, from the pages of *Apollo*, had appeared in his bedside cupboard, drawn by suppressed feelings of the intimate life he had known with Clarissa—a life he was consciously bent on deserting. Likewise, the earthenware cider-jar, with its erogenous cryptograms, displaying itself in the summer-house, was a reminder of sex without love—an abstract paraphrase of erotic mechanics. Even more so, was the unglazed ceramic figure of a woman—wooed by the Red Admiral butterfly and flexing her knees in response to his courtship—suggestive of that propinquity which he was fore-going. Art offered the terracotta woman as an imaginary succubus of the imagination.

Roger recognised that he had sought to separate erotic and artistic experience; when, for his deepest nature, the one depended on the other. Moreover, to deny one—as Freud might have put it—was to deny life itself and to invoke death. Hence the blowfly whose dead body was found when he drew back the bedclothes. Sooner or later, Thanatos occupies every vacancy, every living cell which we fail to exercise.

What remained of the morning Roger devoted to writing: he felt it imperative to be in touch with Clarrie.

Should they ignore their contract and meet before the date they'd agreed on? There was so much he wanted to tell her: above all, the fact that he loved and needed her terribly.

At the end of his letter, he added a postscript very much in his orthodox-unorthodox style:

> *Have been reading Isaiah (Chap. 54)*
> "Sing, O barren, that didst not bear, break forth into singing and cry aloud, thou that didst not travail with child: for more are the children of the desolate than the children of married wife, saith the Lord."
>
> *I seem to have found a message here; though I'm not sure it's quite what the prophet intended. I went away to write but remained wordless. My barrenness has taught me to sing; It has shown me how desolate I was without you.*
>
> *Another verse, also, held out reprieve and promise:*
> "For a small moment have I forgotten thee; but with great mercies will I gather thee."
>
> *To me, I think, this was Providence speaking. I say something like this to you, too, dearest, hoping you'll forgive and take me back.*

Where Coppice Lane joined Manor Road stood a lonely pillar-box, as if on guard. Normally, it was emptied three times a day; but, in reality, Collection No. 2 often changed to No. 3 without the box being opened. This time, Roger was lucky. The postman was just collecting the midday mail, and duly popped the letter to Clarrie into his sack.

Tired, after his bad night, but infinitely easier in mind, Roger decided on a nap after lunch. Feeling himself no longer hunted by some monster within himself, he took *The Hound of the Baskervilles* to bed with him, believing he could digest its horrors with impunity. This belief proved correct; since, after five minutes' engagement with the terrifying canine, the book dropped from his hand, falling, unretrived, upon the floor.

Almost immediately, Roger found himself at the bottom of the garden, in that little wasteland of briars and compost. Beside the dried-up fountain overgrown with bull-rushes, he saw again that unglazed figure of a woman. There, too, as before, was a Red Admiral butterfly, its antennae engaging the left nipple of her breast.

Oh, God; was he back to Square One?

Yet, even as he started to shudder, he discovered that he had taken the butterfly's place, and was employing his tongue to titillate the ceramic nipple between his lips. No sooner was he kissing the earthenware breast, than he felt the unglazed anatomy beneath him becoming smoother; like flesh but firmer.

He had closed his eyes since the touch of the nipple between his lips incited his senses, though the sight of the ceramic breast was not appealing. Now, with the form beneath him changing in texture and density, he opened them to find himself half-mounted on a porcelain woman, the ivory glow of its flesh warmed with a half-blush of rose.

Between his lips the porcelain tips became an erected bud of flesh. Beneath him, the body was undergoing a miraculous transformation. The sun-kissed porcelain turned to sun-kissed flesh, undulating and moving responsively.

He recognised the pulsating form as warm, since—with a dream's transition—he knew himself also naked. Then, very lightly, he felt his right thigh pinched and pressed by this strange *al fresco* partner. But with that touch, all strangeness disappeared: it was one of Clarrie's fondling gestures which he had known her to employ at this particular point of amatory manoeuvres. It was answered by him, instinctively, with another procedural signal. Her nipple still between his lips, he removed the hand that was holding her breast like a drinking-cup, and squeezed her crotch. Then he was inside her, waking without full redress to find his seed pulsing from him.

Tantalizing though this moment was, he knew himself to be

a happy man. The dream and its speeded-up conclusion was a libation to his rediscovered love, a deep sub-conscious homage to Clarrie and his inescapable need of her.

His bags already packed the next morning, he came down to find a letter waiting for him on the table outside the breakfast room. With its characteristic loops, which reminded him of Clarrie's generous breasts, Roger knew it was from her.

He carried it to his place at the table, poured himself a cup of coffee, then slit the envelope open. By the time he gave his attention to breakfast, the coffee had appreciably cooled, so astounding were the contents of Clarrie's letter:

> Dearest,
>
> I am breaking our pact of not writing because of a dream I had last night. Nothing I've ever dreamt before was like it.
>
> It has, I'm sure, a meaning for me; and, perhaps, for you also. At any rate, I think I should tell you about it.
>
> I seemed to be in an ancient orchard. The trees were old, and had mostly lost their leaves, yet, at the same time, some of them were still bearing fruit—apples and pears, some ripe, some rotten.
>
> All together, things seemed topsy-turvy. There was a blue sky, and the sun was shining on the grass and tree-tops; yet, the air felt cold: it was like winter and summer rolled into one.
>
> I was on a lie-low in what should have been a warm protected corner of a south-facing wall. There was a blanket over my knees, and I pulled it up over my lap. Then I felt a nip—it was almost a love-bite—just below my right nipple. I pulled up my jersey to see what it was, and discovered I was wearing no bra and that a Red Admiral butterfly had settled on my bust and was examining my nipple with its antennae.
>
> It was, somehow, something alarming and exciting. Then I found I had no clothes on; and the beautiful and resplendent creature, with its black satin red-bordered wings, was fluttering down my body till it reached my parts. I was in a state of terror and ecstasy; and then I heard you speak to me. "Clarrie, my love," I heard you

cry. I felt something stir inside me, and woke up to the orgasm which had started in my dream. I knew you were my Red Admiral butterfly and that I loved you, Roger, sweet-heart.

If this dream makes the same sort of sense to you as it did to me, I think we should meet as soon as possible. Ring me if you agree. (I'll be in till 12 and again from 2 to 6).

Your love,
Clarissa.

Marvellous, marvellous; an absolute miracle! All right: their letters had crossed; but what about the amazing way their dreams had paralleled each other, with such perfect matching of detail. Telepathy and coincidence? And what was telepathy—a sympathetic pairing of mental currents? Whatever way one looked at it, it seemed a bloody miracle!

By ten o'clock he had phoned Clarrie, and planned to return in the afternoon. Eric had told him to leave his cases in the room, and Roger had arranged for a taxi to collect him at Eleven.

His thoughts and feelings were so tumultous that he went out for a short walk to calm the racing pulse in his head. He made his way down the lawn, past what he called the haunted gazebo, through the little orchard and the wild patch at the bottom of the garden, where he had seen the ceramic woman flexing her earthenware knees in amorous excitement. All now was natural; calm, uninterfered with. He unlatched the garden-gate into the lane at the back, and completed his short walk, approaching the house from the front. By the time he had returned, Roger's joy had reached an even higher pitch; but, as it ascended, his recent abnormal experience yielded to a more rational state of mind. The utter weirdness of all that had happened was in process of being rationalized away. His mind was so taken over by joy that it had no room for horror and terror.

Inside the hall, he found Eric waiting for him. "I moved your stuff down from your room, Mr. Daimler; but I couldn't find you anywhere about. Mavis brought a coffee to speed you on your way, but she couldn't find you either. Then I remembered I hadn't checked to see if you'd left anything in the wardrobe. For some reason or other, I couldn't open the door. Next, a really crazy idea came to me. I was sure someone was inside, trying desperately to get out. I imagined you'd locked yourself in. I tried the handle again, but it wouldn't turn. Then I heard someone coming in, downstairs; and was I relieved to see you!"

Roger thanked Eric for his solicitude, and ran upstairs to his room. The handle of the wardrobe opened without difficulty. There was nothing inside, save a musty smell of stored fruit and drying roses which he had not noticed before.

He returned to the hall, shook hands with Eric, and told him the wardrobe lock must have jammed. It seemed to be working now all right.

At that moment, the taxi hooted outside in the drive; and Roger, with Eric's help, had bundled his baggage into the boot. Wise a good while after the events, and with Clarissa's fabulous letter in mind, he was inclined to put things down to coincidence and telepathy. That, plus the jittery state he was in—along with his inner conflict—might, conceivably, explain away the whole matter.

Might have done, were it not for the fact that, as the taxi turned out of the drive, he heard the harsh strident screech of a peacock. There were no peacocks at Peacock Place.

That is, if one discounted the peacock shaped by Eric with his shears out of a yew-bush by the front door.

HERBERT STEPHEN
No.11 Welham Square

Sir Herbert Stephen (1857–1932) *was a barrister, Clerk of Assize, and occasional writer of short stories in the tradition of Dickens, Collins, and Sheridan Le Fanu. This ghost story originally appeared anonymously (under the fictional guise of "Edward Masey") in the* Cornhill Magazine, *May 1885, with illustrations by George du Maurier.*

We were sitting in the drawing-room of our house at Bayswater one evening after dinner, in high good-humour. I had that day been appointed to a certain post at the British Museum which would afford me ample opportunity for the studies in which I was most interested, and put me in possession of what I expected to find an ample competence. We had been talking over my prospects, and the only cloud I could discern upon the horizon was that I should have to be at my post at an earlier hour in the morning than was comfortably compatible with the three-mile walk from our house to the Museum.

"What a pity," said my youngest sister Patricia, "that we don't still live in the dear old house in Welham Square! You could have got to the Museum from there in five minutes."

I was born after we left Welham Square, but Patricia was six years my senior, and could remember her nursery days there.

"Not at all," said my father, very abruptly; "the walk will do you all the good in the world."

As the old gentleman had been, to all appearance, fast asleep for at least ten minutes, I was rather surprised at the energy with which he spoke. Looking up, I saw my mother making anxious signals to Patricia, which she followed up by instantly changing the subject.

A few days afterwards, as I descended reluctantly into the bowels of the earth at the Edgware Road Metropolitan Station, on the way to my new work for the first time, this episode recurred to my mind, and I began to speculate upon what might be the reasons that made the mention of Welham Square distasteful to my parents. I determined to consult my eldest sister Ellen on the subject, and from her, and some other sources, I gradually accumulated the facts which I will present here in the form of a continuous narrative.

No. 11 Welham Square has always been the freehold property of my family. It was built, together with several adjoining houses, about the beginning of the eighteenth century by the owner of a plot of land in which the houses stand, a retired attorney, who had two nephews. These were Andrew Masey, my great-great-great-grandfather, and his cousin, Ronald Masey. Ronald, who was generally thought to be his uncle's favourite, and probable heir, was an exceedingly tall and powerful young man, with a forbidding and melancholy expression of countenance. As a boy he was singularly backward, and his incapacity for mental exertion seemed to develop, as he grew up, into something not far removed from downright idiocy. His weakness of mind caused him to be remarkably subject to the influence of those with whom he lived, and in particular his cousin Andrew, my ancestor, was supposed to exercise over him an influence almost amounting to fascination, and to be able to mould him to all the purposes of an exceptionally vigorous will. Shortly after the building of the houses in what is now Welham Square, the uncle of these young men died, and Andrew took possession of all his property under the provisions, as he asserted, of a will, the existence of which no one except Ronald had any interest in disputing, and which no one except Andrew, the sole executor and devisee, ever saw. Shortly before his uncle's death, Ronald had become engaged to a young lady named Lettice White, to whom he was passionately attached, and it was generally supposed among the neighbours that upon his accession to the avuncular wealth the marriage would take place. But when a barely decent interval had occurred since the old gentleman's obsequies, the fair Lettice was led to the altar, not by the impecunious Ronald, but by his more fortunate cousin Andrew. The newly married pair took up their residence in No. 11, and Ronald came to live with them.

When it was represented to Andrew by some of his few intimate acquaintances that this arrangement was so singular as almost to be thought improper, he curtly gave them to understand that Ronald's mental condition was not such as to permit of his only living relation allowing him to live alone, and that he was compelled by the merest considerations of family affection to take the unfortunate young man into his own household. So the three lived on in the stately and somewhat gaunt mansion, Andrew collecting his rents with methodical regularity, and otherwise giving his neighbours but little concern. As for Ronald, there soon came to be little doubt in anyone's mind of his confirmed imbecility. He appeared seldom, and when he did, was for the most part silent, regarding his cousin and former betrothed with an expression of the profoundest submission, which at times merged into a look of wild and hardly human apprehension, "like a terrified brute-beast," as it was put by an old lady who was one of the few friends occasionally privileged to partake of the gloomy hospitality of this uncomfortable establishment. Nothing more was ever known of the condition in which my ancestor, his wife, and his cousin lived, and no one was specially interested when, about six years after the marriage, Ronald, who had not been seen for many months, died, and was buried in a frugal manner.

Before he had been dead a year, Andrew and Lettice suddenly left their house and took up their abode elsewhere, and after a while a tenant was found for No. 11 Thirty years later, the lease of the house having expired, Andrew's son, who had succeeded to his father's property, came to reside there, but not for long. He left the house suddenly after a few years, and a rumour went abroad that it was haunted, probably by the ghost of the unfortunate Ronald. From this time No. 11 descended from father to son, the adjoining property being sold piecemeal as the family necessities dictated. Occasionally the successive freeholders made attempts to live there, but they never stayed more than a few months, and on each occasion of their removal the rumours of ghostly possession were renewed. These, however, would die away, and tenants would after a time be found, who never suffered from any inconvenience. The last occupation by the owner was that of my father, who moved into the house when my sister Patricia was a little girl. After living there a year he left precipitately, but Ellen could give me no particulars of his reasons for doing so, and knew only that he disliked any reference to the house, and never mentioned it himself. The house was now let to a stockbroker with a family.

2

Five years had elapsed since the conversation I related at the beginning of the previous chapter. My parents had both died, and Patricia was married and living with her husband in a provincial town. My career at the Museum had been a prosperous one, and I was now entrusted with a more responsible and better paid office. The tenant of No. 11 Welham Square had just given me notice of his intention to depart from it, and it occurred to me that it would be interesting to follow what seemed to be the family destiny, and try living in the house myself, to say nothing of the fact that it was admirably suited to my requirements. I felt fully capable of confronting any number of ghosts, and my wife was neither timid nor superstitious. Accordingly at the beginning of the new year we established ourselves, with our two babies, and my sister Ellen, who lived with us, in Welham Square, greatly delighted with the proximity of my work, with the solid masonry, spacious apartments, and roomy passages of our new abode, and with the remnant of eighteenth-century fashion and grandeur which seemed to pervade the neighbourhood. And in Welham Square we lived prosperously, without any kind of disturbance, for upwards of six months.

In the course of July my wife and the children left home to spend a couple of months at the seaside. I intended to join them when the time came to take my holiday, and in the meantime I stayed in London, going daily to my work. Ellen stayed on with me to keep house in the absence of her sister-in-law.

One evening, four or five days after my wife's departure, I was sitting in my study, a large room with a door leading into the drawing-room, and a heavy curtain hung over my side of the door. It was past eleven; my sister had retired half an hour before, and the two maids who were left in the house were presumably in bed and asleep. I was therefore surprised to hear heavy and somewhat slow footsteps, apparently those of a large man, ascending the stairs from the ground-floor. The front door I knew was locked and chained, nor had I heard anyone ring. The steps paused for a moment on the landing outside my door, and then I heard the intruder proceed to go up the next flight of stairs leading to the bedrooms on the second floor. I sprang up, seized a candle, and opened the door. As I stood on the threshold of my room I seemed to hear footsteps, as of a man heavily mounting the stairs at the top of the flight leading up from my door. But, though I held the light above my head, I could see no one. Everything wore its usual aspect. I walked quickly up the stairs, but nobody was visible. I searched all the empty rooms, but with no result. I called up Ellen and the maids, but none of them had seen or heard anything. I am ashamed to say that I made a specially rigorous investigation of a large room at the back of the house, which we used for a night nursery, and which tradition declared to have been the abode of my ill-fated kinsman Ronald Masey. I then went downstairs and completed my search of the entire premises. Everything was in order, and at the end of an hour I went back to my study and my book, rather annoyed with myself for having spent so much time in so fruitless an exploration, and determined to think nothing more about the matter.

It was the next night after this that I suddenly started up very wide awake with a conviction that somebody was in my bedroom. I seemed to hear still ringing in my ears the sound of a long-drawn human sigh. I sat up, trembling with excitement, and looked about in the dim twilight of dawn in late July. I could see no one, but I did not feel alone. The feeling of suspense became unbearable. I jumped out of bed, and walked with nervous determination to the window, where I turned round and faced the room, such light as there was being behind me. I saw no one. Again I walked across the room, and as I did so I felt unmistakably that wave of air that meets one walking in the streets when someone on foot passes close to him in the opposite direction. I seemed to feel the light graze of a passing substance against my nightgown. I was dimly conscious of a faint, indescribable odour, calling up recollections of a time of life long but indefinitely past. And while I stood fixed to the spot with surprise and horror, my heart beating violently, I heard distinctly four long heavy steps passing from me towards the window. The floor creaked under their weight. The next instant I felt that I was alone. But it was not until long after the morning was as light as noon that I fell asleep again.

I awoke much troubled in mind, and doubting whether I should not, like my fathers, be compelled to leave this uncanny dwelling; but when in some measure restored by breakfast, I determined to say nothing to my sister at present, but to wait and see whether the situation would in any way develop itself. My resolution was fated to be put to the test sooner than I expected.

I did not get home that evening till close upon dinner-time. When I entered the drawing-room Ellen greeted me with, "Oh, Edward! What do you think has happened? Sikes is dead!"

Now Sikes was a grey parrot belonging to my wife. He was so called because when he first came to us it was affirmed of him, perhaps rather libellously, that, like the hero of Mr. Calverley's poem, he "habitually swore." He certainly did from time to time blaspheme somewhat unreservedly.

I was secretly not altogether sorry to hear of his demise. So I answered with much composure, "Did the cat eat him?"

"No," said Ellen, "he died in the most horrible convulsions."

I went up to get ready for dinner, thinking more of how to prevent my wife from replacing Sikes by another clamorous bird than of the manner of the lost one's death, but in the course of our meal it occurred to me that his fate was an odd one.

"How did Sikes come to have convulsions?" I asked.

"Why, it was most curious," answered Ellen. "I was going to tell you about it. I was in the drawing-room writing letters, and suddenly I heard a tremendous screaming and flapping, and I looked up, and there was Sikes turning over and over in the air, and pecking, and clawing, and flapping his wings, and screaming, and before I could get to him he suddenly twisted his head right round two or three times, and tumbled down dead on the floor."

"But do you mean," I said, "that he was carrying on these gymnastics up in the air?"

"Yes; when I saw him he was quite up above his cage, which was on the little table, and in his struggles he must have wrung his own neck."

"That seems rather remarkable."

"Yes; and another remarkable thing was that he must have opened the door of his cage and got out all by himself, which I never heard of his doing before, because I had been feeding him with cake after lunch, and I know the door was fastened then. I found it open when he was dead."

"Had he been out long?"

"No. He must have been seized almost directly he got out, because it so happened that about five minutes before he began to scream, I fancied I heard the door open, and looked up to see if anyone was coming in, and no one was there, but I happened to see the parrot, and he was in his cage just as usual."

"Well," I said, "I suppose he's dead, and there's an end of it; but it is a very singular catastrophe. I hope Marion won't be inconsolable."

During the rest of dinner I was conscious of being rather poor company. Following close upon the mysterious occurrences I have described, Sikes's unhappy fate troubled me. My suspicions were, however, so undefined, and seemed even to me, when I tried to contemplate them from an impartial point of view, so ridiculous, that I could not bring myself to communicate them to Ellen, and incur the contempt which would be the deserved portion of a grown-up man who confessed to being seriously disturbed by an odd sound in an empty house, and by a commonplace nightmare. I have no hesitation in revealing these sentiments now that subsequent events have justified them. But that evening I again determined to wait. I did not have to wait long.

It was a cold evening, and, after bidding good-night to my sister, I lighted a fire in my study and sat down to enjoy a new novel I had long been wishing to read. I was about halfway through my volume when I suddenly felt a sensation of cold. I looked up. The fire was burning brightly, but I did not feel its warmth. It was as though some opaque body, or a large glass screen, had been interposed between me and it. A moment afterwards I felt the heat fall on my face again. Had I heard the muffled sound of a footstep on the hearth-rug close to me? I put out my hand and felt nothing but the warmth of the fire. As I gazed about the room in surprise my eye fell on an armchair standing on the other side of the fire. It was a nearly new chair, which I had bought shortly after coming to Welham Square. It had a leather seat, smooth and unworn, with particularly good and yielding springs. Hung upon its back was an antimacassar, worked aesthetically in crewels. As I looked at this chair it struck me that the seat was considerably depressed, as though some one had recently sat down upon it, and the seat had failed to resume its ordinary level. This surprised me, for I had sat in the chair that morning and felt sure the springs had then been in good order. I looked at the antimacassar. Towards the top it was pushed up in wrinkles. As I looked, it occurred to me that it was impossible for it to hang in such a manner by itself. It looked for all the world as if an invisible but substantial human frame was then actually sitting in the chair. When this notion occurred to me, I sat dazed with an indescribable horror, staring stupidly at the chair, which did not move. In an access of frenzied terror, I hurled the book I was reading at the chair. Did it strike the seat, or did it glance away a few inches from the edge and fall on the hearth-rug? The next instant the seat of the chair rose up audibly to its normal level, and the antimacassar fell out into its usual folds, still preserving, however, the traces of its previous wrinkles. I started up, and rushing to the chair, began to prod it. I could discover nothing unusual in its condition. As I was doing so I felt a hand, beyond all doubt, laid steadily on my shoulder. I faced round and saw nothing. "Who are you?" I shouted. "What do you want?" But no answer came. I was alone.

I sat cogitating till one o'clock, and then I went to bed. Just as I was getting into bed it occurred to me that perhaps I might be annoyed in the dark, and though I had not yet seen anything, the prospect seemed rather awful, and with a slightly trembling hand I lighted a night-light. When I had done so, and got into bed, I was rather disposed to be ashamed of myself, and thought I would put it out, but, partly no doubt from a disinclination to get out of bed, I determined that in any case it would do no harm, and that I would leave it as it was. It occurred to me what an odd thing it is that one feels safer in bed than anywhere else, whereas in fact one is never in a more defenceless situation. Then I went to sleep.

I do not know what time I woke. It seemed to me that the air was blowing in upon my chest where the bedclothes should have covered me up. And—yes, certainly there was an odd depression in my pillow, close in front of my face, as if some heavy weight were pressing it down. I put up my hand to investigate. I touched something on the pillow. I caught hold of it, and turned cold with terror. For I held tightly in my hand, another hand, neither cold nor warm, but large and solid. My light was still burning, and there was no one to be seen. The hand was suddenly jerked away from me. I sprang out of bed, and rushed to the fireplace with a despairing feeling that someone followed close behind me. I seized the poker, turned round, and struck wildly at the air. Whether I hit anything or not I do not know. I remember only that as I was recovering myself from a frantic lunge at nothing, I received a sharp and stunning blow on the back of my head. When I came to myself it was six in the morning, and I was lying on the floor where I had fallen. The night-light was out, and the morning sunlight was streaming in at my window. There was a very large and painful bruise where I had been struck.

3

I felt that this was getting beyond a joke. It was all very well to frighten me, but when my ghostly enemy took to knocking me down like a ninepin, I was not going to keep it to myself any longer. I had no intention of surrendering, for the blood of the Maseys was up, and the fact that each of my ancestors since the house was built had sooner or later evacuated the premises made me all the more determined not to be driven away without making some further resistance. So I revealed to my sister Ellen the whole of my experience in the matter. She was decidedly sceptical about the ghost, if ghost it could be called, and suggested that I was not well. I vowed that I was as well as any man with a great hole in the back of his head could be, and she consented to the arrangement that I proposed—that she should sit up for a night or two in the drawing-room, while I was in my study, with the door open between us, and that if any remarkable incident occurred, I should call her in. In order not to be wholly without male assistance in case I should be attacked, I invited a college friend of mine named Prescott, a strong, sensible, and energetic young doctor who lived near us, to keep my sister company in the drawing-room. He, when he heard my story, was, as befitted a scientific young professional man, exceedingly facetious at my expense, but he willingly consented to share our watch, and to sleep in the house. That evening I sat up as usual in my study, while Prescott and Ellen beguiled the hours in the drawing-room with light literature, until about half-past two, when, nothing having occurred, we settled to go to bed, and separated; Prescott divided between high spirits at the temporary triumph of incredulity, and a tinge of disappointment at the non-occurrence of anything in the shape of a row, and Ellen rather indignant with me for having kept her up so long to no purpose. After the stormy experiences of the two preceding nights I thoroughly enjoyed an unbroken sleep.

I prevailed upon my sister and my friend to give the ghost one more chance, and the next evening saw us again comfortably established in the two rooms, separated only by the curtain which hung over the door of communication.

It may have been eleven o'clock when I heard a board creak just behind my chair. Uttering a shout, I sprang up, and dashed at the spot from which the noise had come. I came into heavy contact with what felt like a gigantic human figure. Prescott and Ellen hurried into the room and beheld me wildly grappling, apparently with nothing at all. "By Jove!" said Prescott, "he has got them." "Them" I believe meant some kind of hallucinations upon which Prescott professed to be an authority, but I was struggling furiously with my unseen antagonist, and had no breath for explanations.

"Seize him! seize him!" I cried.

At that moment my prey burst from me, hurling me with prodigious violence across the room.

Prescott rushed forward, and as he did so was tripped up by what he afterwards described as a heavy kick from an unseen foot, and sent sprawling on the floor. Fortunately I was prostrate at the other end of the room, and could not be suspected of having had a hand, or a foot, in this outrage.

As we struggled to our feet, while Ellen stared wildly about, we all heard two or three hurried steps, as of a man running; there was a tremendous crash, and all was still. But the curtains had swung violently back into the window, and the window itself, plate-glass, frame, and all, was burst clean away outwards.

Prescott was as white as a sheet, and the sensible and strong-minded Ellen was actually crying, which impressed me more than anything else in the scene.

"Let us leave this horrible house," she said; "something worse will happen if we stay."

But I was filled with an unreasonable kind of courage at having, as it seemed, put our inexplicable visitor to flight; and I was besides conscious of a certain degree of pride in the assurance that Prescott had been converted, and would hardly talk again about my having "got them."

"We can't go tonight," I said, "and as our gentleman seems to have taken himself off for the present, we had better consider what's to be done next. I am sure Prescott wants to stay and investigate the phenomenon."

We shut the shutters over the wreck of the window, and sat talking over the event until late at night. By degrees I contrived to infuse into my companions some of my courage, and at last, no further disturbance having taken place, we all went to bed in pretty good spirits. I placed a loaded double-barrelled pistol on the table by my bedside, thinking that if a ghost could be struggled with, he ought to be able to be shot, and Prescott placed within reach a large bowie-knife, which he had brought back from America, and had long been wishing for an opportunity to make use of.

When I woke I thought my last hour had come. My throat was tightly grasped by two extremely strong hands. A crushing weight was on my chest. I tried to shout, but could not. I was rapidly being strangled. And as I lay writhing, my eyes, forced half out of their sockets, glared through the light of the night-light at the opposite wall, which looked precisely as usual, except that, as the squeezing of my throat grew more and more intolerable, my view of the room slowly darkened. But of the horrible and only too palpable from that was killing me I could see no trace. In unavailing despair I clutched at the iron wrists that held me down. In another moment I believe I should have become unconscious. Then, a last gleam of hope, the thought of my pistol, flashed through my mind. I stretched out my hand, and as I lay I could just reach the end of the barrel. I drew it towards me, and with an expiring effort pushed the muzzle of it close against what I took to be the invisible body of my tormentor, and fired. We never found the bullet, or any trace of it afterwards. Instantly the hands relaxed their grip on my throat a little, and with a violent effort I wrenched my neck away; then a heavy body fell sideways from my bed to the ground, and I fell too, grappling with it. At that moment Ellen and Prescott, who had been aroused by the sound of the shot, burst into the room. There they saw me struggling, partly on the floor, and partly kneeling apparently on space. They rushed to my assistance. Both of them felt the thing, both of them grappled with it. The struggles of our enemy became fainter. Managing to get one hand free I repossessed myself of the pistol, which had fallen on the floor, and emptied the second barrel into what I judged to be the breast of the spectre. I fired straight downwards, apparently at the floor, but of that bullet we saw no more than of the other. Meanwhile Prescott stabbed furiously with the bowie-knife, and each time he dashed the blade down its progress was arrested before it reached the carpet. Then the struggles ceased, and nothing was heard except our rapid panting. We were all kneeling on and holding down what looked like space, and felt like the form of a tall and athletic man.

"We've done for it, whatever it is," said I hoarsely.

Prescott burst into a foolish giggle. "By Jove!" he said, "we'll make a cast of it and see what it's like."

As he spoke the form of our victim was agitated by a desperate convulsion, which shook us all off. Before we could seize it again a deep groan burst from the place where we had held it, and the word "Lettice!" rang through the room in a tone of sepulchral melancholy. Then there was silence.

I threw myself on the floor—not, as I had intended, on the prostrate figure. We searched the room, and then the house, but we could find absolutely nothing. Nor from that day to this has anyone, to the best of my knowledge, seen, heard, or felt anything whatever of this ghastly being.

After much consideration we determined to keep the adventure to ourselves, for a time at any rate. Indeed, it was only last summer, when we had lived in the house for a good number of years without any kind of ghostly interruption, that I described the circumstances herein narrated to my wife. She doesn't believe them, and I am sorry I told her.

Was it the ghost of Ronald Masey? Did it voluntarily depart and leave us alone because it considered that the annoyances it had inflicted upon my ancestors and me were sufficient, and that the tale of its vengeance upon our house, for the wrongs, whatever they were, inflicted upon Ronald in his lifetime by Andrew and Lettice, was complete? Or did we actually kill it? Perhaps we did. He was a poor weak creature when he was alive.

FRANK R. STOCKTON
The Bishop's Ghost and the Printer's Baby

Frank Richard Stockton (1834–1902) *was a leading American novelist who established his reputation with the humorous novel* Rudder Grange *in 1879. His best-known short story was "The Lady or the Tiger?" (1884), and his many other highly imaginative tales are still read and enjoyed today for their lively style. His collections include* The Bee-man of Orn (1887), The Chosen Few (1895), A Story-teller's Pack (1897), John Gayther's Garden (1902) *and* The Magic Egg (1907). *The following story appeared in* Chapman's Magazine of Fiction, *June 1895*.

Around the walls of a certain old church there stood many tombs, and these had been there so long that the plaster with which their lids were fastened down had dried and crumbled, so that in most of them there were long cracks under their lids, and out of these the ghosts of the people who had been buried in the tombs were in the habit of escaping at night.

This had been going on for a long time, and, at the period of our story, the tombs were in such bad repair that every night the body of the church was so filled with ghosts that before daylight one of the sacristans was obliged to come into the church and sprinkle holy water everywhere. This was done to clear the church of ghosts before the first service began, and who does not know that if a ghost is sprinkled with holy water it shrivels up? This first service was attended almost exclusively by printers on their way home from their nightly labours on the journals of the town.

The tomb which had the largest crack under its lid belonged to a bishop who had died more than a hundred years before, and who had a great reputation for sanctity; so much so, indeed, that people had been in the habit of picking little pieces of plaster from under the lid of his tomb and carrying them away as holy relics to prevent diseases and accidents.

This tomb was more imposing than the others, and stood upon a pedestal, so that the crack beneath its lid was quite plain to view, and remarks had been made about having it repaired.

Very early one morning, before it was time for the first service, there came into the church a poor mason. His wife had recently recovered from a severe sickness, and he was desirous of making an offering to the church. But having no money to spare, he had determined that he would repair the bishop's tomb, and he consequently came to do this before his regular hours of work began.

All the ghosts were out of their tombs at the time, but they were gathered together in the other end of the church, and the mason did not see them, nor did they notice him; and he immediately went to work. He had brought some plaster and a trowel, and it was not long before the crack under the lid of the tomb was entirely filled up, and the plaster made as smooth and neat as when the tomb was new.

When his work was finished, the mason left the church by the little side door which had given him entrance.

Not ten minutes afterwards the sacristan came in to sprinkle the church with holy water. Instantly the ghosts began to scatter right and left, and to slip into their tombs as quickly as possible, but when the ghost of the good bishop reached his tomb, he found it impossible to get in. He went around and around it, but nowhere could he find the least little chink by which he could enter. The sacristan was walking along the other side of the church scattering holy water, and in great trepidation the bishop's ghost hastened from tomb to tomb, hoping to find one which was unoccupied into which he could slip before the sprinkling began on that side of the church. He soon came to one which he thought might be empty, but he discovered to his consternation that it was occupied by the ghost of a young girl who had died of love.

"Alas! alas!" exclaimed the bishop's ghost. "How unlucky! who would have supposed this to be your tomb?"

"It is not really my tomb," said the ghost of the young girl. "It is the tomb of Sir Geoffrey of the Marle, who was killed in battle nigh two centuries ago. I am told that it has been empty for a long time, for his ghost has gone to Castle Marle. Not long ago I came into the church, and, finding this tomb unoccupied, I settled here."

"Ah, me!" said the bishop's ghost, "the sacristan will soon be round here with holy water. Could not you get out and go to your own tomb; where is that?"

"Alas, good father," said the ghost of the young girl, "I have no tomb; I was buried plainly in the ground, and I do not know that I could find the place again. But I have no right to keep you out of this tomb, good father; it is as much yours as it is mine, so I will come out and let you enter: truly you are in great danger. As for me it does not matter very much whether I am sprinkled or not."

So the ghost of the young girl slipped out of Sir Geoffrey's tomb, and the bishop's ghost slipped in, but not a minute before the sacristan had reached the place. The ghost of the young girl flittered from one pillar to another until it came near to the door, and there it paused, thinking what it should do next. Even if it could find the grave from which it had come, it did not want to go back to such a place; it liked churches better.

Soon the printers began to come in to the early morning service. One of them was very sad, and there were tears in his eyes. He was a young man, not long married, and his child, a baby girl, was so sick that he scarcely expected to find it alive when he should reach home that morning.

The ghost of the young girl was attracted by the sorrowful printer, and when the service was over and he had left the church it followed him, keeping itself unseen. The printer found his wife in tears; the poor little baby was very low. It lay upon the bed, its eyes shut, its face pale and pinched, gasping for breath.

The mother was obliged to leave the room for a few moments to attend to some household affair, and her husband followed to comfort her, and when they were gone, the ghost of the young girl approached the bed and looked down on the little baby. It was nearer death than its parents supposed, and scarcely had they gone before it drew its last breath.

The ghost of the young girl bowed its head; it was filled with pity and sympathy for the printer and his wife; in an-instant, however, it was seized with an idea, and in the next instant it had acted upon it. Scarcely had the spirit of the little baby left its body, than the spirit of the young girl entered it.

Now a gentle warmth suffused the form of the little child, a natural colour came into its cheeks, it breathed quietly and regularly, and when the printer and his wife came back, they found their baby in a healthful sleep. As they stood amazed at the change in the countenance of the child, it opened its eyes and smiled upon them.

"The crisis is past!" cried the mother. "She is saved; and it is all because you stopped at the church instead of hurrying home, as you wished to do." The ghost of the young girl knew that this was true, and the baby smiled again.

It was eighteen years later and the printer's baby had grown into a beautiful young woman. From her early childhood she had been fond of visiting the church, and would spend hours among the tombs reading the inscriptions, and sometimes sitting by them, especially by the tomb of Sir Geoffrey of the Marle. There, when there was nobody by, she used to talk with the bishop's ghost.

Late one afternoon she came to the tomb with a happy smile on her face. "Holy father," she said, speaking softly through the crack, "are you not tired of staying so long in this tomb which is not your own?"

"Truly I am, daughter," said the bishop's ghost, "but I have no right to complain: I never come back here in the early morning without a feeling of the warmest gratitude to you for having given me a place of refuge. My greatest trouble is caused by the fear that the ghost of Sir Geoffrey of the Marle may some time choose to return. In that case I must give up to him his tomb. And then, where, oh where shall I go?"

"Holy father," whispered the girl, "do not trouble yourself; you shall have your own tomb again and need fear no one."

"How is that?" exclaimed the bishop's ghost. "Tell me quickly, daughter."

"This is the way of it," replied the young girl. "When the mason plastered up the crack under the lid of your tomb he seems to have been very careful about the front part of it, but he didn't take much pains with the back where his work wasn't likely to be seen, so that there the plaster has crumbled and loosened very much, and with a long pin from my hair I have picked out ever so much of it, and now there is a great crack at the back of the tomb where you can go in and come out, just as easily as you ever did. As soon as night shall fall you can leave this tomb and go into your own."

The bishop's ghost could scarcely speak for thankful emotions, and the happy young girl went home to the house of her father, a prosperous man, now the head-printer of the town.

The next evening the young girl went to the church and hurried to the bishop's tomb. Therein she found the bishop's ghost, happy and contented.

Sitting on a stone projection at the back of the tomb, she had a long conversation with the bishop's ghost, which, in gratitude for what she had done, gave her all manner of good advice and counsel. "Above all things, my dear daughter," said the bishop's ghost, "do not repeat your first great mistake; promise me that never will you die of love."

The young girl smiled. "Fear not, good father," she replied. "When I died of love, I was, in body and soul, but eighteen years old, and knew no better; now, although my body is but eighteen, my soul is thirty-six. Fear not, never again shall I die of love."

BRAM STOKER
The Secret of the Growing Gold

Bram Stoker (1847–1912), author of Dracula—*the greatest and most influential horror novel of the past hundred years—also wrote some of the best weird and supernatural short stories of the 1890s, notably "The Judge's House", "The Squaw", "The Burial of the Rats", and "The Secret of the Growing Gold" which originally appeared in the* Black and White *magazine, 23 January 1892, with graphic illustrations by Paul Hardy.*

When Margaret Delandre went to live at Brent's Rock the whole neighbourhood awoke to the pleasure of an entirely new scandal. Scandals in connection with either the Delandre family or the Brents of Brent's Rock, were not few; and if the secret history of the county had been written in full both names would have been found well represented. It is true that the status of each was so different that they might have belonged to different continents—or to different worlds for the matter of that—for hitherto their orbits had never crossed. The Brents were accorded by the whole section of the country an unique social dominance, and had ever held themselves as high above the yeoman class to which Margaret Delandre belonged, as a blue-blooded Spanish hidalgo out-tops his peasant tenantry.

The Delandres had an ancient record and were proud of it in their way as the Brents were of theirs. But the family had never risen above yeomanry; and although they had been once well-to-do in the good old times of foreign wars and protection, their fortunes had withered under the scorching of the free trade sun and the "piping times of peace." They had, as the elder members used to assert, "stuck to the land," with the result that they had taken root in it, body and soul. In fact, they, having chosen the life of vegetables, had flourished as vegetation does—blossomed and thrived in the good season and suffered in the bad. Their holding, Dander's Croft, seemed to have been worked out, and to be typical of the family which had inhabited it. The latter had declined generation after generation, sending out now and again some abortive shoot of unsatisfied energy in the shape of a soldier or sailor, who had worked his way to the minor grades of the services and had there stopped, cut short either from unheeding gallantry in action or from that destroying cause to men without breeding or youthful care—the recognition of a position above them which they feel unfitted to fill. So, little by little, the family dropped lower and lower, the men brooding and dissatisfied, and drinking themselves into the grave, the women drudging at home, or marrying beneath them—or worse. In process of time all disappeared, leaving only two in the Croft, Wykham Delandre and his sister Margaret. The man and woman seemed to have inherited in masculine and feminine form respectively the evil tendency of their race, sharing in common the principles, though manifesting them in different ways, of sullen passion, voluptuousness and recklessness.

The history of the Brents had been something similar, but showing the causes of decadence in their artistocratic and not their plebeian forms. They, too, had sent their shoots to the wars; but their positions had been different, and they had often attained honour—for without flaw they were gallant, and brave deeds were done by them before the selfish dissipation which marked them had sapped their vigour.

The present head of the family—if family it could now be called when one remained of the direct line—was Geoffrey Brent. He was almost a type of a worn-out race, manifesting in some ways its most brilliant qualities, and in others its utter degradation. He might be fairly compared with some of those antique Italian nobles whom the painters have preserved to us with their courage, their unscrupulousness, their refinement of lust and cruelty—the voluptuary actual with the fiend potential. He was certainly handsome, with that dark, aquiline, commanding beauty which women so generally recognise as dominant. With men he was distant and cold; but such a bearing never deters womankind. The inscrutable laws of sex have so arranged that even a timid woman is not afraid of a fierce and haughty man. And so it was that there was hardly a woman of any kind or degree, who lived within view of Brent's Rock, who did not cherish some form of secret admiration for the handsome wastrel. The category was a wide one, for Brent's Rock rose up steeply from the midst of a level region and for a circuit of a hundred miles it lay on the horizon, with its high old towers and steep roofs cutting the level edge of wood and hamlet, and far-scattered mansions.

So long as Geoffrey Brent confined his dissipations to London and Paris and Vienna—anywhere out of sight and sound of his home—opinion was silent. It is easy to listen to far off echoes unmoved, and we can treat them with disbelief, or scorn, or disdain, or whatever attitude of coldness may suit our purpose. But when the scandal came close home it was another matter; and the feelings of independence and integrity which is in people of every community which is not utterly spoiled, asserted itself and demanded that condemnation should be expressed. Still there was a certain reticence in all, and no more notice was taken of the existing facts than was absolutely necessary. Margaret Delandre bore herself so fearlessly and so openly—she accepted her position as the justified companion of Geoffrey Brent so naturally that people came to believe that she was secretly married to him, and therefore thought it wiser to hold their tongues lest time should justify her and also make her an active enemy.

The one person who, by his interference, could have settled all doubts was debarred by circumstances from interfering in the matter. Wykham Delandre had quarrelled with his sister—or perhaps it was that she had quarrelled with him—and they were on terms not merely of armed neutrality but of bitter hatred. The quarrel had been antecedent to Margaret going to Brent's Rock. She and Wykham had almost come to blows. There had certainly been threats on one side and on the other; and in the end Wykham overcome with passion, had ordered his sister to leave his house. She had risen straightway, and, without waiting to pack up even her own personal belongings, had walked out of the house. On the threshold she had paused for a moment to hurl a bitter threat at Wykham that he would rue in shame and despair to the last hour of his life his act of that day. Some weeks had since passed; and it was understood in the neighbourhood that Margaret had gone to London, when she suddenly appeared driving out with Geoffrey Brent, and the entire neighbourhood knew before nightfall that she had taken up her abode at the Rock. It was no subject of surprise that Brent had come back unexpectedly, for such was his usual custom. Even his own servants never knew when to expect him, for there was a private door, of which he alone had the key, by which he sometimes entered without anyone in the house being aware of his coming. This was his usual method of appearing after a long absence.

Wykham Delandre was furious at the news. He vowed vengeance—and to keep his mind level with his passion drank deeper than ever. He tried several times to see his sister, but she contemptuously refused to meet him. He tried to have an interview with Brent and was refused by him also. Then he tried to stop him in the road, but without avail, for Geoffrey was not a man to be stopped against his will. Several actual encounters took place between the two men, and many more were threatened and avoided. At last Wykham Delandre settled down to a morose, vengeful acceptance of the situation.

Neither Margaret nor Geoffrey was of a pacific temperament, and it was not long before there began to be quarrels between them. One thing would lead to another, and wine flowed freely at Brent's Rock. Now and again the quarrels would assume a bitter aspect, and threats would be exchanged in uncompromising language that fairly awed the listening servants. But such quarrels generally ended where domestic altercations do, in reconciliation, and in a mutual respect for the fighting qualities proportionate to their manifestation. Fighting for its own sake is found by a certain class of persons, all the world over, to be a matter of absorbing interest, and there is no reason to believe that domestic conditions minimise its potency. Geoffrey and Margaret made occasional absences from Brent's Rock, and on each of these occasions Wykham Delandre also absented himself; but as he generally heard of the absence too late to be of any service, he returned home each time in a more bitter and discontented frame of mind than before.

At last there came a time when the absence from Brent's Rock became longer than before. Only a few days earlier there had been a quarrel, exceeding in bitterness anything which had gone before; but this, too, had been made up, and a trip on the Continent had been mentioned before the servants. After a few days Wykham Delandre also went away, and it was some weeks before he returned. It was noticed that he was full of some new importance—satisfaction, exaltation—they hardly knew how to call it. He went straightway to Brent's Rock, and demanded to see Geoffrey Brent, and on being told that he had not yet returned, said, with a grim decision which the servants noted:

"I shall come again. My news is solid—it can wait!" and turned away. Week after week went by, and month after month; and then there came a rumour, certified later on, that an accident had occurred in the Zermatt valley. Whilst crossing a dangerous pass the carriage containing an English lady and the driver had fallen over a precipice, the gentleman of the party, Mr. Geoffrey Brent, having been fortunately saved as he had been walking up the hill to ease the horses. He gave information, and search was made. The broken rail, the excoriated roadway, the marks where the horses had struggled on the decline before finally pitching over into the torrent—all told the sad tale. It was a wet season, and there had been much snow in the winter, so that the river was swollen beyond its usual volume, and the eddies of the stream were packed with ice. All search was made, and finally the wreck of the carriage and the body of one horse were found in an eddy of the river. Later on the body of the driver was found on the sandy, torrent-swept waste near Täsch; but the body of the lady, like that of the other horse, had quite disappeared, and was—what was left of it by that time—whirling amongst the eddies of the Rhone on its way down to the Lake of Geneva.

Wykham Delandre made all the enquiries possible, but could not find any trace of the missing woman. He found, however, in the books of the various hotels the name of "Mr. and Mrs. Geoffrey Brent." And he had a stone erected at Zermatt to his sister's memory, under her married name, and a tablet put up in the church at Bretten, the parish in which both Brent's Rock and Dander's Croft were situated.

There was a lapse of nearly a year, after the excitement of the matter had worn away, and the whole neighbourhood had gone on its accustomed way. Brent was still absent, and Delandre more drunken, more morose, and more revengeful than before.

Then there was a new excitement. Brent's Rock was being made ready for a new mistress. It was officially announced by Geoffrey himself in a letter to the Vicar, that he had been married some months before to an Italian lady, and that they were then on their way home. Then a small army of workmen invaded the house; and hammer and plane sounded, and a general air of size and paint pervaded the atmosphere. One wing of the old house, the south, was entirely re-done; and then the great body of the workmen departed, leaving only materials for the doing of the old hall when Geoffrey Brent should have returned, for he had directed that the decoration was only to be done under his own eyes. He had brought with him accurate drawings of a hall in the house of his bride's father, for he wished to reproduce for her the place to which she had been accustomed. As the moulding had all to be re-done, some scaffolding poles and boards were brought in and laid on one side of the great hall, and also a great wooden tank or box for mixing the lime, which was laid in bags beside it.

When the new mistress of Brent's Rock arrived the bells of the church rang out, and there was a general jubilation. She was a beautiful creature, full of the poetry and fire and passion of the South; and the few English words which she had learned were spoken in such a sweet and pretty broken way that she won the hearts of the people almost as much by the music of her voice as by the melting beauty of her dark eyes.

Geoffrey Brent seemed more happy than he had ever before appeared; but there was a dark, anxious look on his face that was new to those who knew him of old, and he started at times as though at some noise that was unheard by others.

And so months passed and the whisper grew that at last Brent's Rock was to have an heir. Geoffrey was very tender to his wife, and the new bond between them seemed to soften him. He took more interest in his tenants and their needs than he had ever done; and works of charity on his part as well as on his sweet young wife's were not lacking. He seemed to have set all his hopes on the child that was coming, and as he looked deeper into the future the dark shadow that had come over his face seemed to die gradually away.

All the time Wykham Delandre nursed his revenge. Deep in his heart had grown up a purpose of vengeance which only waited an opportunity to crystallise and take a definite shape. His vague idea was somehow centred in the wife of Brent, for he knew that he could strike him best through those he loved, and the coming time seemed to hold in its womb the opportunity for which he longed. One night he sat alone in the living-room of his house. It had once been a handsome room in its way, but time and neglect had done their work and it was now little better than a ruin, without dignity or picturesqueness of any kind. He had been drinking heavily for some time and was more than half stupefied. He thought he heard a noise as of someone at the door and looked up. Then he called half savagely to come in; but there was no response. With a muttered blasphemy he renewed his potations. Presently he forgot all around him, sank into a daze, but suddenly awoke to see standing before him some one or something like a battered, ghostly edition of his sister. For a few moments there came upon him a sort of fear. The woman before him, with distorted features and burning eyes seemed hardly human, and the only thing that seemed a reality of his sister, as she had been, was her wealth of golden hair, and this was now streaked with grey. She eyed her brother with a long, cold stare; and he, too, as he looked and began to realise the actuality of her presence, found the hatred of her which he had had, once again surging up in his heart. All the brooding passion of the past year seemed to find a voice at once as he asked her:—

"Why are you here? You're dead and buried."

"I am here, Wykham Delandre, for no love of you, but because I hate another even more than I do you!" A great passion blazed in her eyes.

"Him?" he asked, in so fierce a whisper that even the woman was for an instant startled till she regained her calm.

"Yes, him!" she answered. "But make no mistake, my revenge is my own; and I merely use you to help me to it." Wykham asked suddenly:

"Did he marry you?"

The woman's distorted face broadened out in a ghastly attempt at a smile. It was a hideous mockery, for the broken features and seamed scars took strange shapes and strange colours, and queer lines of white showed out as the straining muscles pressed on the old cicatrices.

"So you would like to know! It would please your pride to feel that your sister was truly married! Well, you shall not know. That was my revenge on you, and I do not mean to change it by a hair's breadth. I have come here to-night simply to let you know that I am alive, so that if any violence be done me where I am going there may be a witness."

"Where are you going?" demanded her brother.

"That is my affair! and I have not the least intention of letting you know!" Wykham stood up, but the drink was on him and he reeled and fell. As he lay on the floor he announced his intention of following his sister; and with an outburst of splenetic humour told her that he would follow her through the darkness by the light of her hair, and of her beauty. At this she turned on him, and said that there were others beside him that would rue her hair and her beauty too. "As he will," she hissed; "for the hair remains though the beauty be gone. When he withdrew the lynch-pin and sent us over the precipice into the torrent, he had little thought of my beauty. Perhaps his beauty would be scarred like mine were he whirled, as I was, among the rocks of the Visp, and frozen on the ice pack in the drift of the river. But let him beware! His time is coming!" and with a fierce gesture she flung open the door and passed out into the night.

Later on that night, Mrs. Brent, who was but half-asleep, became suddenly awake and spoke to her husband:

"Geoffrey, was not that the click of a lock somewhere below our window?"

But Geoffrey—though she thought that he, too, had started at the noise—seemed sound asleep, and breathed heavily. Again Mrs. Brent dozed; but this time awoke to the fact that her husband had arisen and was partially dressed. He was deadly pale, and when the light of the lamp which he had in his hand fell on his face, she was frightened at the look in his eyes.

"What is it, Geoffrey? What dost thou?" she asked.

"Hush! little one," he answered, in a strange, hoarse voice. "Go to sleep. I am restless, and wish to finish some work I left undone."

"Bring it here, my husband," she said; "I am lonely and I fear when thou art away."

For reply he merely kissed her and went out, closing the door behind him. She lay awake for awhile, and then nature asserted itself, and she slept.

Suddenly she started broad awake with the memory in her ears of a smothered cry from somewhere not far off. She jumped up and ran to the door and listened, but there was no sound. She grew alarmed for her husband, and called out: "Geoffrey! Geoffrey!"

After a few moments the door of the great hall opened, and Geoffrey appeared at it, but without his lamp.

"Hush!" he said, in a sort of whisper, and his voice was harsh and stern. "Hush! Get to bed! I am working, and must not be disturbed. Go to sleep, and do not wake the house!"

With a chill in her heart—for the harshness of her husband's voice was new to her—she crept back to bed and lay there trembling, too frightened to cry, and listened to every sound. There was a long pause of silence, and then the sound of some iron implement striking muffled blows! Then there came a clang of a heavy stone falling, followed by a muffled curse. Then a dragging sound, and then more noise of stone on stone. She lay all the while in an agony of fear, and her heart beat dreadfully. She heard a curious sort of scraping sound; and then there was silence. Presently the door opened gently, and Geoffrey appeared. His wife pretended to be asleep; but through her eyelashes she saw him wash from his hands something white that looked like lime.

In the morning he made no allusion to the previous night, and she was afraid to ask any question.

From that day there seemed some shadow over Geoffrey Brent. He neither ate nor slept as he had been accustomed, and his former habit of turning suddenly as though someone were speaking from behind him revived. The old hall seemed to have some kind of fascination for him. He used to go there many times in the day, but *grew* impatient if anyone, even his wife, entered it. When the builder's foreman came to inquire about continuing his work Geoffrey was out driving; the man went into the hall, and when Geoffrey returned the servant told him of his arrival and where he was. With a frightful oath he pushed the servant aside and hurried up to the old hall. The workman met him almost at the door; and as Geoffrey burst into the room he ran against him. The man apologised:

"Beg pardon, sir, but I was just going out to make some enquiries. I directed twelve sacks of lime to be sent here, but I see there are only ten."

"Damn the ten sacks and the twelve too!" was the ungracious and incomprehensible rejoinder.

The workman looked surprised, and tried to turn the conversation.

"I see, sir, there is a little matter which our people must have done; but the governor will of course see it set right at his own cost."

"What do you mean?"

"That 'ere 'arth-stone, sir: Some idiot must have put a scaffold pole on it and cracked it right down the middle, and it's thick enough you'd think to stand hanythink." Geoffrey was silent for quite a minute, and then said in a constrained voice and with much gentler manner:

"Tell your people that I am not going on with the work in the hall at present. I want to leave it as it is for a while longer."

"All right sir. I'll send up a few of our chaps to take away these poles and lime bags and tidy the place up a bit."

"No! No!" said Geoffrey, "leave them where they are. I shall send and tell you when you are to get on with the work." So the foreman went away, and his comment to his master was:

"I'd sent in the bill, sir, for the work already done. 'Pears to me that money's a little shaky in that quarter."

Once or twice Delandre tried to stop Brent on the road, and, at last, finding that he could not attain his object rode after the carriage, calling out:

"What has become of my sister, your wife." Geoffrey lashed his horses into a gallop, and the other, seeing from his white face and from his wife's collapse almost into a faint that his object was attained, rode away with a scowl and a laugh.

That night when Geoffrey went into the hall he passed over to the great fireplace, and all at once started back with a smothered cry. Then with an effort he pulled himself together and went away, returning with a light. He bent down over the broken hearth-stone to see if the moonlight falling through the storied window had in any way deceived him. Then with a groan of anguish he sank to his knees.

There, sure enough, through the crack in the broken stone were protruding a multitude of threads of golden hair just tinged with grey!

He was disturbed by a noise at the door, and looking round, saw his wife standing in the doorway. In the desperation of the moment he took action to prevent discovery, and lighting a match at the lamp, stooped down and burned away the hair that rose through the broken stone. Then rising nonchalantly as he could, he pretended surprise at seeing his wife beside him.

For the next week he lived in an agony; for, whether by accident or design, he could not find himself alone in the hall for any length of time. At each visit the hair had grown afresh through the crack, and he had to watch it carefully lest his terrible secret should be discovered. He tried to find a receptacle for the body of the murdered woman outside the house, but someone always interrupted him; and once, when he was coming out of the private doorway, he was met by his wife, who began to question him about it, and manifested surprise that she should not have before noticed the key which he now reluctantly showed her. Geoffrey dearly and passionately loved his wife, so that any possibility of her discovering his dread secrets, or even of doubting him, filled him with anguish; and after a couple of days had passed, he could not help coming to the conclusion that, at least, she suspected something.

That very evening she came into the hall after her drive and found him there sitting moodily by the deserted fireplace. She spoke to him directly.

"Geoffrey, I have been spoken to by that fellow Delandre, and he says horrible things. He tells to me that a week ago his sister returned to his house, the wreck and ruin of her former self, with only her golden hair as of old, and announced some fell intention. He asked me where she is—and oh, Geoffrey, she is dead, she is dead! So how can she have returned? Oh! I am in dread, and I know not where to turn!"

For answer, Geoffrey burst into a torrent of blasphemy which made her shudder. He cursed Delandre and his sister and all their kind, and in especial he hurled curse after curse on her golden hair.

"Oh, hush! hush!" she said, and was then silent, for she feared her husband when she saw the evil effect of his humour. Geoffrey in the torrent of his anger stood up and moved away from the hearth; but suddenly stopped as he saw a new look of terror in his wife's eyes. He followed their glance, and then he, too, shuddered—for there on the broken hearth-stone lay a golden streak as the points of the hair rose through the crack.

"Look, look!" she shrieked. "Is it some ghost of the dead! Come away—come away!" and seizing her husband by the wrist with the frenzy of madness, she pulled him from the room.

That night she was in a raging fever. The doctor of the district attended her at once, and special aid was telegraphed for to London. Geoffrey was in despair, and in his anguish at the danger of his young wife almost forgot his own crime and its consequences. In the evening the doctor had to leave to attend to others; but he left Geoffrey in charge of his wife. His last words were:

"Remember, you must humour her till I come in the morning, or till some other doctor has her case in hand. What you have to dread is another attack of emotion. See that she is kept warm. Nothing more can be done."

Late in the evening, when the rest of the household had retired, Geoffrey's wife got up from her bed and called to her husband.

"Come!" she said. "Come to the old hall! I know where the gold comes from! I want to see it grow!"

Geoffrey would fain have stopped her, but he feared for her life or reason on the one hand, and lest in a paroxysm she should shriek out her terrible suspicion, and seeing that it was useless to try to prevent her, wrapped a warm rug around her and went with her to the old hall. When they entered, she turned and shut the door and locked it.

"We want no strangers amongst us three to-night!" she whispered with a wan smile.

"We three! nay we are but two," said Geoffrey with a shudder; he feared to say more.

"Sit here," said his wife as she put out the light. "Sit here by the hearth and watch the gold growing. The silver moonlight is jealous! See it steals along the floor towards the gold—our gold!" Geoffrey looked with growing horror, and saw that during the hours that had passed the golden hair had protruded further through the broken hearth-stone. He tried to hide it by placing his feet over the broken place; and his wife, drawing her chair beside him, leant over and laid her head on his shoulder.

"Now do not stir, dear," she said; "let us sit still and watch. We shall find the secret of the growing gold!" He passed his arm round her and sat silent; and as the moonlight stole along the floor she sank to sleep.

He feared to wake her; and so sat silent and miserable as the hours stole away.

Before his horror-struck eyes the golden-hair from the broken stone grew and grew; and as it increased, so his heart got colder and colder, till at last he had not power to stir, and sat with eyes full of terror watching his doom.

In the morning when the London doctor came, neither Geoffrey nor his wife could be found. Search was made in all the rooms, but without avail. As a last resource the great door of the old hall was broken open, and those who entered saw a grim and sorry sight.

There by the deserted hearth Geoffrey Brent and his young wife sat cold and white and dead. Her face was peaceful, and her eyes were closed in sleep; but his face was a sight that made all who saw it shudder, for there was on it a look of unutterable horror. The eyes were open and stared glassily at his feet, which were twined with tresses of golden hair, streaked with grey, which came through the broken hearth-stone.

MARK VALENTINE
The Ash Track

*Mark Valentine (b.1959), one of Britain's modern
exponents of the ghost story tradition, has written
several supernatural tales featuring Ralph Tyler,
psychic investigator and a most worthy successor
to Prichard's Flaxman Low, Blackwood's John
Silence and Lawrence's Miles Pennoyer. Some of
the Tyler stories were collected in* 14 Bellchamber
Tower *(1987); and the following new tale is a
notable addition to the canon.*

The Ash Track is a curious remnant of a once long and
well-used green lane, which ran from the neighbouring
county of Bedfordshire deep into our own area, passing through
and connecting a number of straggling settlements. Much of
this ancient route has now disappeared. Some of it has been
superceded by a major road which, however, eschews the almost
aimless curvings and contortions of the older way, and imposes
instead a more rational line across the countryside, as straight
as was negotiable. Thus, fragments of the green lane are left
forlorn and stranded in the middle of fields, moorland or woods.

The Ash Track is one such; there is access to it by a public
footpath from the main road, it ambles along for a little over a
mile, and then comes to an abrupt halt in the middle of private
pastures. There is no alternative, without trespass, to turning
and retracing your steps. It is an oddity, a leftover, but one
carefully preserved by the local hikers' group, who jealously
guard the popular privilege in this matter, and ensure the path
is walked at regular intervals.

The landowner whose field sees the sudden end of the path is
tolerant but firm. He makes no attempt, as did his predecessor,
to prove by archival research and legal representation that the
right-of-way is a chimera; he has reconciled himself to the
intrusion upon his domain. But, nonetheless, he declines to
allow the footpath's extension across his lands by about a quarter

of a mile, which would take it to a gate onto a by-road not far from the village of Fernho.

The usual theory concerning the Ash Track is that it did indeed extend further once; but successive ages witnessed the requisitioning of great stretches of it by unopposed landowners, until the definitive survey earlier this century could only accept the present anomalous conditions.

Even local opinion differs regarding the Ash Track's name; some attribute it to the trees of that type which grow at intervals along it, whilst others note the dark, dusty topsoil of the lane, and say that this so resembles cinders, as to be responsible for the title.

An acquaintance of mine is a leading light in the walking club I have already mentioned, and as I have a passing interest in the hobby too, we occasionally exchange talk about our latest rambles, forthcoming events, natural history notes and so on. I knew that Stephen Hope was rather inclined to enjoy the seemingly pointless stroll along the Ash Track, and it was usually he that watched for any depredation upon the public rights there. Indeed, he was in a real sense the sole warden of this historic vestige, for few other people had cause or desire to tread upon it. My attention was stirred beyond the usual, therefore, when he remarked, during a lull in conversation when I was paying him a call:

"There's something rather worrying about that dead end lane up by Fernho."

"How do you mean?" I responded.

"Well, whenever I'm down there lately, there seems to be a sort of whirring in the air. At first I thought my hearing was getting defective, but I never have any problems anywhere else. Then, I wondered if it might be the wind in the trees, but it just isn't like that. It seems to rise to a certain pitch, then falter and break apart. I can't fathom it."

"Farm machinery?" I suggested.

"I've never noticed any. Anyway, it doesn't strike you as mechanical."

I shrugged. "What else?"

"Oh, nothing much, probably. It's just that . . . have you ever noticed wheel ruts about halfway along, very deeply sunk into the ground? They've been there for ages. But it only really occurred to me the other day that no vehicle uses the track, it would be a futile and rather tricky exercise anyway, its so narrow and overgrown and stony."

"Not a tractor?"

"No, the grooves are far thinner than that would make."

"Motor-bike? A bit of amateur scrambling perhaps?"

"No, the tracks are a set of two wheels. And no treadmarks that I could tell."

I gave up accounting for the incidental curiosities associated with the Ash Track, and the talk turned to other matters; however, I asked Stephen Hope to let me know if much else turned up to foster his suspicions. I had in mind that it was from such inconsequential beginnings that stranger matters might emerge, and so told my friend Ralph Tyler of what I had heard.

It was evident to me that the polite attention he gave my account of Hope's comments masked a more eager interest. Some weeks had elapsed since our last involvement in any "case" and the fond recollection of success in past incidents was beginning to strike pale. Ralph was never more absorbed than when some disturbing occurrence demanded his energies and intuition, even more so when the matter lay close to home, in the region which was our own.

It was therefore not so great a jolt for either of us when Hope fairly burst into number 14, Bellchamber Tower at the late hour of 11.30 p.m. one night, a few days later. We had been mulling over an intriguing geometric board game which Ralph had been recommended by a correspondent of his, one of those with whom he frequently exchanged notes about their mutual pastime of games of skill. The flow of play kept us deeply immersed and insensible to the passing of the hours, and we were both snatched abruptly out of our pensive attention to the board when a rapid, loud noise at the door announced Hope's arrival. He rather breathlessly spluttered out terse explanations—

"Glad you're still here, went round to your place but they said you were still at Ralph's, look, eh, sorry to barge in right at this time of night only it's quite important, you see, well, you remember what I said about the Ash Track . . ."

Ralph took advantage of this brief pause to motion Hope into a seat, and himself assume his favourite, slumped attitude in the grey-flecked, disreputable armchair that had seen better days.

"There were wheel marks and an odd undertone of humming the last I heard" Ralph confirmed, and I nodded.

Our visitor's nervous agitation seemed to have subsided a little now, and he said quite calmly—

"I have seen something down there. I don't know if its a delusion, a hallucination or what. Well, it was so blurred, I am hardly sure now."

"*When* did you see—it?" demanded Ralph, eager to ascertain the full facts.

"Tonight. I'll start from the beginning. I'm sorry, I haven't really taken it all in yet."

We waited as Stephen Hope appeared to collect his thoughts.

"I was in Fernho with some mates. We went for a drink at the New Inn. I stayed for about an hour-and-a-half I suppose, left a little after ten. I only had two pints and as you know that's nowhere near enough to get to me. Well, I thought as I was out that way I might as well take a turn down the Ash Track, the cool night air would be very refreshing and its quite an enjoyable sensation, being utterly alone under the stars just walking along . . ." here our visitor grinned ruefully as if in embarassment.

"I hadn't gone so far along when I was struck by the solemn silence I was in. That's not unnatural of course, given my situation, gone ten at night in remote countryside, but I feel it was more than that. Anyway, I was lingering in the experience of it when there came over me the impression that the lane ahead was growing blacker, more opaque. I remember stopping, unsure if I should go on any further. Although the way is so familiar to me, I suddenly felt as if it were a yawning abyss in front, daring me to take another step. Nervousness swept over me.

"As I peered, hesitating, I caught sight of a flicker of flesh in the dim distance as if a face had appeared briefly, then been hidden again. I took a few more faltering steps. And then the same image, only greatly multiplied, splashes of face as it were, emerging, hovering, disappearing all along the lane ahead, like masks hung on the bushes. Well, then I must have been rooted to the spot in morbid fascination. Telling it to you now, I can see normally I'd have run like hell. Something held me there, I suppose it was sheer fright.

"As I watched, I began to make out that these faces, sort of shivering, sort of blurred, belonged to bodies, but *they* were all dressed so darkly it was hard to tell where their forms ended, they seemed to fade into the atmosphere. The more I looked, the more I seemed to see.

"It was like two long rows of people, on both sides of the way, dotted at intervals, receding into the dim horizon as though like a tunnel. And they were all just standing there, still. I don't really know how it came to an end, the scene just sort of swayed inward and went away, without a sound. Then I bolted, got in the car, drove away pretty recklessly, pulled in to a lay-by a few miles on, tried to make sense of what happened, got very unhappy and frustrated, and so I've come straight here. I hope you don't mind . . ."

Stephen Hope looked at us eagerly, as if fully realising for the first time the strangeness of his situation, and half-wondering how we would respond.

Ralph murmured, hardly looking up from his sprawling repose: "If you were able to see actual people in your . . . vision . . . what did they look like? Ordinary, everyday?"

"Its so hard to tell. The clothing was dark, I remember that. Mmmm, it didn't seem to be a proper modern way of dressing. Maybe I just imagined that though. I don't know. Everything was so . . . sort-of smudged."

"The faces then. Could you see individual characteristics? Expressions?"

"Ye—es. Yes. I could see they were all different. Men and women, a few children. And it was all so heavily serious, that was very distinct, a great impression of solemnity."

"Stern? Or sad?"

"Well both. But now you mention it, there was a feeling of sorrow in there. Despair almost, just underneath, like an unspoken hidden emotion." Ralph considered this for a while. Then:

"You know the track better than most. What could be responsible for this incident?" But Stephen Hope shook his head.

"I've been trying to puzzle that out. There's nothing. But I mean there can't have been a *real* crowd of people like that in the old lane for over a century. Longer than that."

"Hmmm," Ralph mused, "Then is that how it seemed to you? A scene from long ago?"

Our visitor hesitated. "I suppose so."

"But nothing happened to you? You didn't feel in any way

threatened? This mass apparition, it didn't seem to be for your benefit? It just happened; and you were there?"

"All that is absolutely true. Of course I was scared at the unfamiliarity of it all. So I ran. But I never seemed to be in any danger. I wasn't harmed."

Ralph got up. "Thank you for coming so soon after your experience. Those first impressions are invaluable. I ask you to give me a few days. I will be in touch with you both . . ." he nodded to me as a sign for my departure too, "as soon as I have anything to report."

"In the meantime, should I go near the Ash Track?" enquired Hope anxiously.

"Entirely up to you," was my friend's reply.

It was, unusually, several days before I heard from Ralph Tyler again, concerning this matter. From past cases, I had grown accustomed to Ralph's habit of examining a scene of an apparent incident at the earliest opportunity. I assumed, therefore, that he would be in touch with me very quickly after our meeting with Stephen Hope. But it was not until four days had passed that a message was left for me to pay him a visit at his flat in Bellchamber Tower. On arrival in the early evening, after work, I found that Stephen Hope was there before me. We exchanged greetings, and desultory comments, before Ralph, pacing within the limited floor space of his confined accommodation, summarised the purpose of our gathering:-

"I have already explained to Stephen that I feel we will be enlightened if we visit the Ash Track tonight, abiding as closely as possible to the conditions of his previous experience, with the sole exception . . ." here Ralph grinned wryly, "that we cannot take in two pints of intoxicating refreshment beforehand. I am perfectly assured that what Stephen drank in the New Inn was of no account, so far as the later occurrence is concerned, but we must be *certain* of our faculties this time.

"We have already discussed the probability that the vision, or apparition, which he encountered is of no harm. It is my expectation that our only role tonight should be that of watching—there may even be disappointment, although I don't think so. I'm sorry that I don't feel it would be fair to give you anything of my theory, yet. Later perhaps,"

Frankly, I did not necessarily share my friend's implication that the absence of any manifestation would be a source of disappointment. The description that had been evoked by Stephen Hope, so freshly after the event, was a little unnerving at best. Flickering faces in dark, sombre rows waiting ahead so far as the eye could see, in a narrow green hollow of a lane, for no known reason? But as usual the prospect of once more becoming involved in a deeply intriguing matter overcame my instinctive caution, and I trusted to Ralph Tyler's singular intuition and methodical approach.

Heavy clouds were in the process of suppressing the feeble yellow glimmerings of a close-to-full moon as we left Stephen Hope's car in a gateway and tramped up the short access path to the Ash Track. It was not long after ten, fierce gusts of wind blew about us, stirring the leaves and twigs of the trees and the hedgerow, setting up swathes of whispering and moaning that hardly assisted to soothe our trepidation. It was not an exceptionally cold night, but the very remoteness of our situation seemed to bring on a sense of vulnerability and I shivered quite distinctly.

We had not progressed far onto the Ash Track itself before I knew once again pangs of deep unease. My strained vision, almost clamouring to see something, kept picking up slight movements caused by the strong breeze, and reinterpreting them as sinister or unnatural. In this state of edgy anticipation my responses could scarcely be deemed reliable.

But the vision, when finally it began to emerge, happened so calmly and quietly that it seemed perfectly proper and acceptable. Stephen Hope had just murmured that it could not have been much further along that he had begun to see the apparition before, when Ralph, after a few strides more, halted, held up a hand, then pointed ahead. I gazed intently at the dim green alley in front, my heart jumped awkwardly as a blurred splash of hovering flesh formed itself unmistakeably out of the atmosphere, and was followed, as if like an echo, by many others, in pale shimmering rows. Hope's expression mingled stubborn determination with deep unease; I must have looked pretty sickly; Ralph Tyler was glancing gravely around, seeking a cause, a hint, a clue; but none of us seemed able to venture any further forward, into the field of the vision, nor yet to tear ourselves away.

And there swelled from the air that thronging drone which Stephen Hope had previously identified, a bewildering cluster of dull tones quite unlike any sound I could clearly place. Staring hard at the lane ahead, I knew that some stronger, more tangible change had taken place, for the insubstantial masks of faces were now supported by stolid bodies, stock still, like dark columns. And the faces themselves seemed to gather expressions and character, seemed to become individual; and every one was grim and heavy.

As the squall of groans, deep, despairing and sonorous, struck through the silence with painful weight and force, I saw from out of my own trancelike condition, Ralph Tyler moving rapidly aside, mouthing words I could not hear. The next thing I knew was a dizzying fall into the thick undergrowth of the ditch, and both he and Stephen Hope followed suit, sprawling awkwardly in the damp wilderness of weeds and brambles. Before I could remonstrate rather forcibly at this abrupt treatment, jolted out of my morbid fascination by the sudden physical sensation, my angry oaths faltered away at the sudden switch of pitch in the sound, which began soaring to a high whine, then seemed to disintegrate and could only be heard in irregular spasms.

Just above us, on the old lane, passed a cart pulled by a donkey, whose head was held by an old man; and by his side stumbled a woman of similar age, her grey hair fluttering in wisps from out of a coarse brown shawl. On the grimy boards of the cart was a bundle of rags. This humble procession seemed to take an age to pass, the reluctant beast paced at one with the tortuously slow shuffling of the couple, their heads bowed. What I can still recall is the bleak clarity of this scene; every tint of colour, every creak of sound, the almost tangible sense of presence, the vivid decrepitude and desolation of the elderly man and woman, the rattling, bumping cart and its huddled pile; yet this too was a vision, an ethereal work, for it plodded beyond us and into the swarm of waiting figures, seeming to become absorbed within them all as those dark forms which had been still as statues swayed inwards, taking the cart and the donkey and the broken, aged beings into an abyss of utter silence. One last glimpse was afforded to each of us as we scrambled from our hiding place, the cart succumbing to the depths of the vision; it was of the load it carried, crumpled on its crude planks; not a jumble of rags, but the twisted, torn body of a boy, hideously contorted and barely concealed by a hasty, makeshift winding sheet.

"The obvious place to start," commented Ralph, when we had returned to number 14, Bellchamber Tower, partaken of some fortification and emerged some hours later from a cramped, bleary sleep in his armchairs, to demand some kind of explanation, "was the nearby village of Fernho. If the vision Stephen had seen did recall some past event, as he seemed to sense, then all of the people must have come from there. I tried the church guidebook for hints of any religious ceremonies or folk customs that might have been held, which would warrant such a gathering in the lane. Nothing. There's a brief history of the area in the library, from 1877, but it spends most of its time discussing the local squire and his lineage, doubtless because he substantially funded the treatise; and this was of little help. But it gave me the idea that maybe there was once a turnout of the village to honour some eminent visitor; so I followed that up, but without success. Then I had the bright idea of sketching on the map the rough route the old Green Lane used to take up to so far as Fernho. It joins the "A" road for a good while then winds away again, becomes bridleways, narrow strips of field and so on, crosses the county border and disappears into the outskirts of Bedford. I let my gaze idle along the pencil line I'd drawn when one name pulled me up sharply—Furze Farm. Look, its here . . ."

Ralph pointed to a place on the map which he had spread out on the table.

"As you see, about five miles from Bedford. Now that meant something to me. I rummaged through my files . . ."

"Your what?" I enquired.

"Well, alright, that box of paper cuttings and jottings," my friend conceded, "It may not be very orderly, but it's fairly exhaustive . . . anyway, I turned up this." He wafted a faded, rather tatty press extract in the air, ". . . A minor matter, two paragraphs in a giveaway paper, never taken up elsewhere or followed through. The owner of Furze Farm, out in the fields, mid-afternoon, hears 'someone in great distress' not far off. Looks about, can't see anybody. Never does find out who it was. A curiosity item, six years ago. But interestingly it would be within a few days of the same time of year as our own little matter. A coincidence? Same lane, same time, same . . ."

"Channel?" I suggested, facetiously, recalling the old television slogan.

"Yes," said Ralph, not at all abashed, "Yes, same wavelength in a certain sense."

"So now I turned my attention beyond just the Ash Track, and Fernho, and looked at the Green Lane as a whole. There are intriguing episodes here and there. It took me hours to unearth it all from the library archives. One in particular is evoked tantalisingly in a record of an enquiry in 1851. The villagers of Turnmead were fighting a losing struggle to prevent their part of the Lane, a short cut, from being absorbed within a gentleman's sprawling parkland. The reporter, who fancies himself an antiquary, has a high time belittling the complaints of the local folk, in particular the assertion of an aged inhabitant that quite apart from the fact that the path had been used from time immemorial, *a corpse had passed along it*, too, which proved a right-of-way.

Upon it being enquired when this had transpired, the witness muttered; "Ned Rook", at which the Commissioner interposed and said he hardly felt the passage of the remains of an executed felon constituted legal precedent. Our wit-ridden chronicler adds his own retort, that since Ned Rook must certainly, by dint of his criminal past, have laid down a trail to Hell, was it in the minds of the assiduous villagers to follow him along *that* route too? But the old man's claim faithfully represents a not uncommon belief in rural parts, that a *corpse-way*, the route followed by the bearers of a coffin or a funeral cortege, to a burial place, was henceforth free of access to all. Scenes are even recorded of landowners resolutely refusing to allow hearses or processions across their land for fear of falling foul of this custom. But that was not what especially stirred me here. I had found the missing link in the chain I was sure. Distress at one end of the lane, a dark, solemn gathering at the other, mention of a corpse way inbetween. It seemed inconceivable, but I was faced with a funeral procession which apparently traversed all of the Lane till Furtho.

Now, then, the story of Ned Rook. There's several of those bloodthirsty gloating broadsheets which tell all, in the library. And an "edifying" account in the news chronicle of the time.

Edward Rook was born in the village of Fernho, and his parents are described as "of honest, hard-working stock". At the age of 15 he went out to find work as a farm labourer, and was taken on at a hiring fair by an employer whose holdings were over the border in Bedfordshire. So there he went to work, paying what snatched visits he might to his home some 18 miles away. Well, it seems that all the hands under this particular landowner's sway were maltreated—poorly and grudgingly paid, badly fed and hovelled, subject to arbitrary harshness. Natural resentment simmered a good long time before some of the labourers took matters into their own hands and staged a minor revolt, more or less physically forcing their employer to make concessions. Whether Ned Rook was a ringleader or not we are not told, but as he is later described as a "bright and lively youth", it may be presumed so. At any event, within a few weeks of the confrontation, a haystack, or barn (accounts differ) quite close to the private residence was found ablaze; arson was suspected; Rook was accused, evidence of some sort contrived; he was convicted and, as was the penalty in those Christian times, sentenced to death. He was 17. The execution was carried out before a large crowd in Bedford, but by a "merciful dispensation", the body was cut down almost directly after and delivered to the grieving parents.

They then began the long journey back to their village, the remains of their child carried in an old cart pulled by a donkey. This pitiful procession creaked with painful slowness all along the Green Lane, sometimes flocked by sightseers, other times by sympathetic mourners, for there was no lack of bitterness at the hideous sentence and the detested landowner. They at length, very late that night, trundled into sight of Fernho, and to their astonishment, no doubt, despite the hour, virtually the entire village had gathered sombrely to share their distress and give them what comfort they could. The child was given an unmarked burial."

Ralph paused and lit a cigarette, drawing upon it reflectively.

"Their anguish has lingered in the Green Lane, and takes tangible form at intervals. Who knows what other incidents happen at other points along the route? Unrecorded, unnoticed. What is called 'the supernatural' cannot be just what we see, it must go on all the time whether we happen to be present or not. There are hints of this grim tragedy elsewhere along the Lane, but even where anyone has been around to notice, much might be dismissed as harmless or inexplicable, but hardly disturbing. It is only the concentration of the images near the end, Fernho, the final resting place, the journey's goal, together with the presence of someone to notice, that has at last brought everything to the surface. For all we know, and I believe it may be so, the vision Stephen and then ourselves saw is repeated every year. It begins not long before the anniversary of the original event, gains in strength, and eventually becomes a spectral reconstruction.

"The noise, of course, is the distorted representation of the villagers' grief; there is no other explanation for its deeply tragic quality. The wheel ruts which have no material origin must be a tangible, scarred preservation of the passing of the cart."

"And what are we to do?" I wondered.

"Nothing."

I was taken by surprise. "Why?"

"So far as I am concerned, this apparition is a record of a village and a family's pure, honest grief at a brutal act. Who am I to even attempt to deny it or destroy it? If it harmed anyone today, I might—I say again, might—, go about to intervene. But even then—we sometimes need to be reminded of what our ancestors have done, and what lurks in us still—in any event I shall let the vision continue unhindered by my meddling."

"But, if it becomes known, won't it end up as a ritual for thrill-seekers?" I suggested.

"Perhaps. If the story spreads. But that is not necessarily wrong. Thrill-seekers, as you call them, are actually quite often searching for something rather more, and even if they are not, they might find it anyway. This haunting in a complete sense immortalises a victim who is not some perfect pious saint but a confused, courageous child. Let it stay."

E.H. VISIAK
In a Nursing Home
(A Euthanasian Subject)

E.H. Visiak (1878–1972) was considered the world's greatest authority on Milton, and yet at the same time he was a very underrated and neglected writer. His peak came in 1929 with the publication of his novel Medusa. *In the 1930s his only champion was John Gawsworth, the young poet who arranged for several of Visiak's stories to appear in anthologies of the period.*

Visiak, who numbered the writers Arthur Machen and David Lindsay and explorer Ernest Shackleton among his friends, spent his last years in a rest home in Hove, writing to the end.

"In a Nursing Home" was probably the last story Visiak wrote, and it was read to an assembly of relatives and friends on his 94th birthday party, a month before he died. It has never appeared in print and this marks its first publication. I am very grateful to Mrs. Helen Beere, a close friend of Visiak in his last years, for making this short story available for publication. Mrs. Beere explains the background to the story as follows: "The nurse and barrister are in love, but for no obvious reason unable to marry. The mystery lies in the fact that the nurse belongs to a select band recruited by an eminent physician, secretly (it is against the law, hence the reference to a Mansion House enquiry) to practice euthanasia, also secretly on terminal patients, especially of cancer, to save them suffering, the nurses being bribed with presents of priceless jewellery, and large cheques. This particular nurse is afraid that if she gives way to her passion and marries, she may betray them

*all." Visiak had a dread of cancer, though not a
sufferer, and appeared to come down on the side of
euthanasia, referring to the "humanitarian" doctor
as a "great good man".*

T he room in the Nursing Home, before the young man
casually came into it, was comparable in solitary boredom
to Colin Wilson's appalling "Black Room". The coming and
going with professional celerity—and professional kindness—of
the female nurses, was farcical; for, as I remarked on one
occasion, "You call me 'dear' or 'darling'; but if I fell down
dead at your feet at this moment, you wouldn't give a damn!"

There was one nurse, however, who seemed different and
genuinely humane, with exquisitely dark features, and coppery
shining hair, and it soon became evident that she and the new
young man allotted to the room were deeply in love; in the
looks—love objects—that passed between them, this became
obvious; nor did either of them essay to conceal the matter from
me, an aged and not unsympathetic observer. It came indeed,
between all these factors, at length, to be an "open secret".

The young man was a barrister, one possessed of ample
finances; the young woman was no less wealthy as if in token
of which she wore upon her finger a great uncut emerald that
must have been worth ten thousand pounds.

It was clear that the obstacle to their union was not financial.
There were times when under the stress of the great mystery
the young barrister became forensic, and addressed me as if
cross-questioning me in a court of law. But what in the strange
obscurity of the case could I do, or say?

An old patient dropped in, as she herself expressed it, at
an apposite moment; herself voluble, if attenuated, nor am
I writing with levity, nor sarcastically, when I assert that her
observations—which were mainly balderdash—put me to sleep.
And, in that sleep I suffered from nightmare.

It seemed actually, horrifically, that I was undergoing a
forensic inquisition: "Do you assert that you actually saw this
apparition?" I was asked. "You have asserted, asseverated, that
his black beard fell upon his waistcoat, was filmy, like a picture
on TV; that he had an enormous uncut ruby on his finger; that
there was a sailor's knotted black bow on his stiffly starched,
snowy white shirt front; that he drew a lethal pill from his

lefthand pocket of that waistcoat, and a cheque for a million pounds from his notebook, and that he presented pill and cheque to—WHOM? The emphasis on the word 'whom' was as terrific as it was unexpected and startling. The reverberation was strong in my ears as I awoke—I tried to murmur at the same moment "to a young woman", my lips working.

"What are you trying to say?" came the voice of the young barrister.

The man in my nightmare, the ghost having the great black beard, with his waistcoat pockets stuffed with treasure, represented (as it turned out) a real human being, a humanitarian, a "good great man", and this in such sort, as in riches—his "El Dorado" represented London or New York. That his waistcoat pockets were also stuffed with lethal pills had great bearing upon the matter. The man, who had a secret agency of hospital and nursing-home nurses, influenced their many lives.

This came out at the Mansion House enquiry in relation to the great mortality in bone cancer. However the case remained unproven.

It is no wonder, in the circumstance, that the women, who were as intelligent as they were beautiful and attractive, were strictly on guard.

EDGAR WALLACE
The Stranger of the Night

Edgar Wallace (1875–1932) *was the most prolific writer of popular fiction of his day, with countless mystery novels, short stories, plays, and non-fiction articles to his name. "The Stranger of the Night" (later reprinted as "The Man of the Night") originally appeared in the* Weekly Tale Teller, *15 October 1910.*

The little instrument on the table by the inspector's desk went "tick-tock." Then it stopped, as though considering how it should word the message it had to give.

It was very still in the charge-room, so still that the big clock above the fireplace was audible. That, and the squeaky scratching of the inspector's quill pen as it moved slowly over the yellow paper on the desk before him, were the only sounds in the room.

Outside it was raining softly, the streets were deserted, and the lines of lamps stretching east and west emphasized the loneliness.

"Tick-tock," said the instrument on the table excitedly, "tick-tock, tick-tock!"

The inspector's high stool creaked as he sat up, listening.

There was a constable at the door, and he, too, heard the frantic call.

"What's that, Gill?" demanded the inspector testily.

The constable came into the charge-room with heavy footsteps.

"Ticketty-ticketty-tick-tock," babbled the instrument, and the constable wrote the message.

'All stations arrest and detain George Thomas, on ticket-of-leave, aged 35, height 5 ft. 8 in., complexion and hair dark, eyes brown, of gentlemanly appearance. Suspected of being concerned in warehouse robbery. Walthamstow and Canning Town especially note this and acknowledge. S.Y.'

"In the middle of the night!" exclaimed the inspector despairingly. "They call me up to tell me what I've told them hours and hours ago! What a system!"

He nodded his head hopelessly.

Outside, in the thin rain a man was coming along the street, his hands deep in his pockets, his coat collar turned up, his head on his breast. He shuffled along, his boots squelching in the rain, and slackened his pace as he came up to the station. The policeman he expected to find at the door was absent.

The man stood uneasily at the foot of the steps, set his teeth, and mounted slowly.

He halted again in the passage out of which the charge-room opened. . . .

"It's a rum thing about Thomas," said the inspector's voice. "I thought he was trying to go straight."

"It's his wife, sir," said the constable, and there was a long silence, broken by the loud ticking of the clock.

"Then why did his wife give him away?" asked the inspector.

"Did she, sir?"

There was surprise in the constable's voice, but the man in the passage did not hear that. He was leaning against the painted wall, his hand at his throat, his thin, unshaven face a dirty white, his lips trembling.

"She gave him away," said the inspector. He spoke with the deliberation of a man enjoying the sensation of dispensing exclusive news. "Know her?"

"Slightly, sir," said the policeman's voice.

"Handsome woman—she might have done better than Thomas."

"I think she has," said the constable dryly, and they both laughed.

"That's the reason, is it? Wants to put him under screw—well, I've heard of such cases. . . ."

The man in the passage crept quietly out. He was shaking in every limb; he almost fell at the last step, and clutched the railings that bordered the station house to keep himself erect.

The rain was pouring down but he did not notice it; he was hocked, paralysed by his knowledge. He had broken into a warehouse because she had laughed to scorn his attempt at reformation. He had tried to go straight and she had made him go crooked . . . and then, when the job was done, with all the old cleverness so that he left no trace of his identity, she had gone straight away to the police and put him away. But that was nothing. Women had done such things before; out of jealousy, in a fit of insane anger at some slight, real or fancied, but she had done it deliberately, wickedly, because she loved some man better than she loved him.

He was cool now, seeing things very clearly, and quickened his walk until he was stepping out briskly and lightly, holding his head erect as he had in the days when he was a junior in a broker's office, and she had been a novel-reading miss of Balham.

The rain streamed down his face, the cuffs of his thin jacket clung to his wrists, his trousers were soaked from thigh to ankle. He knew a little shop off the Commercial Road where they sold cheese and butter and wood. He had purchased for a penny a morsel of bread and cheese; he remembered that the woman behind the counter had cut the cheese with a heavy knife, newly whetted and pointed . . . he thought the matter out as he turned in the direction of the shop. Such knives are usually kept in a drawer, next to the till, with the bacon saw and the milk tester, and the little rubber stamp which is used for branding margarine in accordance with the law.

He knew the shop would be shuttered, the door locked, and he had no instrument to force an entrance. The "kit" was in the hands of the police—he had wondered how the splits[1] had found them—now he knew.

He gulped down a sob.

Still, there must be a way. The knife was necessary. He was still weak from his last term of penal servitude; he could not kill her with his hands, she was so strong and beautiful—oh, so beautiful!

Thinking disconnectedly, he came to the shop.

It stood in a little side street. There was one street lamp giving light to the thoroughfare. There was no sound but the dismal drip of rain, nobody in sight. . . . There was a skylight above the shuttered door, it was the only way, he saw that at

[1] Detectives.

once. Sometimes these are left unfastened. He stood on tiptoe and felt gingerly along the lower part of the sash. His fingers encountered something that lay on the ledge, and his heart leapt. It was a key. . . . He had guessed this to be a "lock-up" shop; he knew enough of the casual character of these little shopkeepers not to be surprised at the ease with which an entry might be effected. He slipped the key into the lock, turned it, and stepped in, closing the door behind him softly.

The air of the shop was hot and stuffy, full of the pungent scent of food-stuffs . . . cheese and ham, and the resinous odour of firewood. He had matches in his pocket, but they were sodden and would not strike. He fumbled round the shelves and came upon a packet. He struck a light, guarding the flame with his hand. The shop had been swept and made tidy for the night. The weights were neatly arranged on either side of the scales, there was a piece of muslin laid over the butter on the slat slab. On the counter, conspicuously displayed, was a note. It contained instructions, written in pencil in a large, uneducated hand, to "Fred." He was to light the fire, put the kettle on, take in the milk, and serve "Mrs. Smith."

Fred was the boy, the early comer in the morning, for whom the key had been placed. It was remarkable that he settled all these particulars to his own satisfaction, as, lighting match after match, he sought the heavy knife with the sharp point and the newly whetted edge. He even felt a certain exultation in the ease with which he had gained admission to the shop, and had an insane desire to whistle and talk.

He found the knife. It was under the counter, with a greatly scarred cutting-board and a steel. He wrapped it up carefully in a sheet of newspaper, then remembered he was hungry. He broke off a wedge of cheese. There was no bread, but an open tin of children's biscuits was handy.

With the food in his hand, with the knife in his pocket, he continued his exploration. Behind the shop was a little parlour. The door was unlocked, and he entered.

He struck match after match, hesitated a moment, then lit the gas. It was a tiny room, cheaply but neatly furnished. There were china ornaments on the mantel-shelf, a few cheap lithographs on the wall, and a loudly ticking clock. There was a clock at the police-station . . . he made a grimace as though he were in pain, felt with his hand for the knife and smiled.

He sat at a little table in the middle of the room and ate the food mechanically, staring hard at the wall ahead of him.

He had done everything for her; his first crime . . . the few sovereigns extracted from the cash-box. . . . She had inspired that. Her little follies, her little extravagances, her vanities, these had been at the bottom of every step he had taken . . . staring blankly at the wall with wide-opened eyes, he traced his descent.

There was a text on the wall; he had been staring at it all this time, an ill-printed text, black-and-gold, green and vivid crimson, sadly out of register, and bearing in the bottom left-hand corner the conspicuous confession that it was "Printed in Saxony."

His thoughts were elaborate thoughts, but inclined to dive sideways into inconsequent bypaths; insensibly he had fixed his eyes on the text, in a subconscious attempt to concentrate his thoughts. One half of his brain pursued the deadly course of retrospection, the other half grappled half-heartedly with the words on the wall. He read only those that were in capital letters.

> Behold . . . Lamb . . . God . . . taketh Away . . . Sins . . . World.

Three years' penal servitude for burglary, two terms of six months for breaking and entering. . . . She had been at his elbow . . . years ago he was a member of a church, sang in the choir, and religious matters had some significance to him. It is strange how such things drop away from a grown man, how the sweet bloom of faith is rubbed off. . . . He married her at a registry office in Marylebone, and they went to Brighton for their honeymoon. She knew well enough that he could not afford to live as they were living; he had never dreamt that she guessed that he was robbing his employer; and when coolly, and with some amusement, she revealed her knowledge, he was shocked, stunned.

"Behold . . . Lamb . . ."

Might religion have helped him had he kept closer to its teachings? He wondered, slowly munching his biscuit and cheese, with his eyes on the garish text.

He found some milk and drank it, then he rose. Where he had sat were two little pools of water, one on the floor, the other on the table where his arm had rested. He turned out the light, walked softly through the shop, listened, and opened the door gently. There was nobody in sight, and he stepped out, closing and locking the door behind him. He put the key on the ledge where he had found it, and went quickly to the main road, the heavy knife, newly whetted and with a sharp point, bumping against his thigh with every step he took.

He had an uneasy feeling, and strove to analyse it down to a first cause. He decided it was the text, and smiled; then of a sudden the smile froze on his lips. He was not alone.

A man had come from the night, swiftly, silently, and walked with him, step for step.

He stopped dead, his hand wandered down to the pocket where the knife lay.

"What do you want?" he asked harshly.

The other made no reply; his face was in the shadow. What clothes he wore, what manner of man he was, Thomas could not say, only that, standing there, he was tall, gracefully proportioned, easy of movement.

There was a silence, then:

"Come," said the man from the night, and the burglar accompanied him without question.

They walked in silence, and Thomas observed that the stranger moved in the direction he himself would have taken.

"I shall give myself up—afterwards," he said, speaking feverishly fast. "I will end all this—end it—end it!"

It did not strike him as curious that he should plunge into most secret depths, revealing the innermost thoughts of his heart; he accepted without wonder the conviction that the stranger knew all.

"She led me down from step to step, down, down!" sobbed Thomas, as they walked side by side through the narrow streets that led to the river. "It used to worry me at first, but she strangled my conscience—she laughed at my fears. She is a devil, I tell you."

"Other men have said, 'The woman tempted me,'" said the stranger gently. "Yet a man has thought and will of his own."

Thomas shook his head doggedly.

"I had no will where she was," he said. "When I have killed her, I shall be a man again." He tapped his pocket, the knife was still there. "If we had children it might have made a difference, but she hated children."

"If you were free of her, you might be a man," said the stranger. His voice was sweet and deep and sad.

"Yes, yes!" The other turned on him eagerly. "That is what I mean; she is in my way. If I kill her, I can start all over again, can't I? I could go back and face the world and say, 'I've killed the bad part of me, give me another chance'—look!" He fumbled in his pocket and brought forth the knife. The rain came pitter-patter on the paper wrapping, and his hand trembled in his excited eagerness to display the strong blade, with the silvery edge and the needle-like point.

"I could not kill her with my hands," he said, breathing quickly, "so I got this knife. I feel I've got to do it, though I hate killing things. I once killed a rabbit when I was a kiddie, and it haunted me for days."

"If you were free of her, you might be a man," said the stranger again.

"Yes, yes," the thief nodded, "that is what I say—I could go back—back to the old people," his voice broke. "They don't know how far I've gone under."

They turned corner after corner, crossing main thoroughfares, diving through alleys where costers' barrows were stacked, chained wheel to wheel, into mean streets, and across patches of waste ground.

Once, through a little passage they came in sight of the river, saw three barges moored side by side, rising and falling slowly with the tide. Out in mid-river a steamer lay, three lights glimmering feebly.

"I shall go into the house from the back," Thomas said. "There's nobody else in the house but an old woman—or there oughtn't to be. My wife sleeps in the front room."

"If you were free of her, you might be a man," said the stranger.

"Yes, yes, yes!" The convict was impatient. "I know that—when I am free . . ." He laughed happily.

"She dragged you down to the deeps," said the man of the night softly. "Every step you took for good, she clogged and hindered—"

"That's right—that is the truth," said the other.

"Yet you could never escape her; you were loyal and faithful and kind."

"God knows that is true," said the man, and wept.

"For better or worse, for richer or poorer," he said, and it seemed to him that the stranger was saying these words at the same time.

At last they reached a street that was more dark, more wretched than any of its neighbours.

The man stopped at a narrow passage which led to the back of the houses.

"I am going in now," he said simply. "You wait for me here, and when I come back we will start our new life all over again. I shall kill her quickly."

The man of the night made no reply, and Thomas went through the passage, turned at right angles along a narrower strip of path between wooden fences, and so came to a rickety back gate.

He opened it and went in. He was in a dirty little yard, littered with the jettison of a poor household. There was a tumbledown fowl run, and as he walked stealthily to the house, a cock crew loudly.

The back room was empty, as he knew. He pushed up the window. It squeaked a little. He waited for the cock to crow again and mask the sound. Then he swung himself up to the window-sill and entered the room.

The point of the knife cut through the thin clothing he wore and he felt a sharp pain in his leg.

He took the knife from his pocket and felt the edge—then he became conscious of the fact that there was somebody in the room.

He gripped the knife tightly and peered through the darkness.

"Who's there?" he whispered.

"It is I," said a voice he knew, the voice of the man of the night.

"How—how did you get in?"

He was amazed and bewildered.

"I came with you," said the voice. "Let us free ourselves of this woman—she dragged you down, she is the weed that chokes your soul."

"Yes—yes," Thomas whispered, and reaching out, found the stranger's hand.

Hand in hand they came to the woman's room.

A cheap night-light was burning on the mantel-shelf. She lay with one bare arm thrown out of bed, her breast rose and fell regularly. (He had seen something else that had risen and fallen monotonously; what was it? Yes, barges on the river.)

She was handsome in a coarse way, and as she slept she smiled. Some movement of the man disturbed her, for she stirred and murmured a name—it was not the name of him who stood above her, a knife in his shaking hand.

"Do you love her?"

The stranger's voice was very soft.

The husband shook his head.

"Once—I thought so—now . . ." He shook his head again.

"Do you hate her?"

The thief was looking at the sleeping woman earnestly.

"I do not hate her," he said simply. "I served her because it was my duty. . . ."

"Come," said the stranger, and they left the room together.

Thomas unfastened the street door and they passed again into the dreary night.

"I do not love her: I do not hate her," he said again, half to himself. "I went to her because it was my duty—I worked and stole, and she betrayed me—so I thought I would kill her."

The knife was still in his hand.

In silence they traversed the way they came, until they reached a little passage that led to the river.

They turned into this.

At the end of the passage was a flight of stone steps, and they heard the "clug-clug" of water as it washed them.

Thomas raised his hand and sent the knife spinning into the river, and a voice hailed him from the foot of the steps.

"That you, Cole?"

His heart almost stopped beating. The voice was hard and metallic. He blinked as though awakened from a sleep.

"Is that you, Cole—who is it?"

Thomas saw a boat at the bottom of the steps. There were four men in it, and one was holding fast with a boat-hook to an iron ring let into the stone.

"Me," said the thief.

"It ain't Cole," said another voice disgustedly. "Cole won't turn up—he's drunk."

There was a whispering in the boat, then an authoritative voice demanded:

"Want a job, my lad?"

Thomas went down two steps and bent forward.

"Yes—I want a job," he said.

A querulous voice said something about missing the tide.

"Can you cook?"

"Yes—I can cook."

He had been employed in this capacity in prison.

"Jump in—sign you on to-morrow—we are going to Valparaiso—steam—how does that suit you?"

Thomas was silent.

"I don't want to come back—here," he said.

"We'll get a better man for the return voyage—jump in."

He got into the boat awkwardly, and the officer at the stern gave an order.

The boat pushed off and then the thief remembered the man of the night.

He could see him plainer than ever he had seen him before. He was a radiant figure standing on the dark edge of the water, his hands outstretched in farewell.

Thomas saw the face, beautiful and benevolent: he saw the faint light that seemed to surround him.

"Behold . . ." muttered the man in the boat. "It's strange how that text . . . Good-bye, good-bye sir. . . ."

"Who are you talking to, mate?" asked the sailor who was rowing.

"The—the man who was with me," said Thomas.

"There was no man with you," said the sailor scornfully. "You were by yourself."

EDITH WHARTON
The Triumph of Night

Edith Wharton (1862–1937), the distinguished American novelist and short-story writer, was much influenced by the work of her friend Henry James. Her novels include The House of Mirth, The Fruit of the Tree, The Age of Innocence, *and* The Children, *which has been turned into a major film (starring Ben Kingsley, Kim Novak and Geraldine Chaplin). Her ghost stories, including "The Triumph of Night" (1914), are among the . best to be found in American literature.*

It was clear that the sleigh from Weymore had not come; and the shivering young traveller from Boston, who had counted on jumping into it when he left the rain at Northridge Junction, found himself standing alone on the open platform, exposed to the full assault of night-fall and winter.

The blast that swept him came off New Hampshire snow-fields and ice-hung forests. It seemed to have traversed interminable leagues of frozen silence, filling them with the same cold roar and sharpening its edge against the same bitter black-and-white landscape. Dark, searching and sword-like, it alternately muffled and harried its victim, like a bull-fighter now whirling his cloak and now planting his darts. This analogy brought home to the young man the fact that he himself had no cloak, and that the overcoat in which he had faced the relatively temperate air of Boston seemed no thicker than a sheet of paper on the bleak heights of Northridge. George Faxon said to himself that the place was uncommonly well-named. It clung to an exposed ledge over the valley from which the train had lifted him, and the wind combed it with teeth of steel that he seemed actually to hear scraping against the wooden sides of the station. Other building there was none: the village lay far down the road, and thither—since the Weymore sleigh had not come—Faxon saw himself under the necessity of plodding through several feet of snow.

He understood well enough what had happened: his hostess had forgotten that he was coming. Young as Faxon was, this sad lucidity of soul had been acquired as the result of long experience, and he knew that the visitors who can least afford to hire a carriage are almost always those whom their hosts forget to send for. Yet to say that Mrs. Culme had forgotten him was too crude a way of putting it. Similar incidents led him to think that she had probably told her maid to tell the butler to telephone the coachman to tell one of the grooms (if no one else needed him) to drive over to Northridge to fetch the new secretary; but on a night like this, what groom who respected his rights would fail to forget the order?

Faxon's obvious course was to struggle through the drifts to the village, and there rout out a sleigh to convey him to Weymore; but what if, on his arrival at Mrs. Culme's, no one remembered to ask him what this devotion to duty had cost? That, again, was one of the contingencies he had expensively learned to look out for, and the perspicacity so acquired told him it would be cheaper to spend the night at the Northridge inn, and advise Mrs. Culme of his presence there by telephone. He had reached this decision, and was about to entrust his luggage to a vague man with a lantern, when his hopes were raised by the sound of bells.

Two sleighs were just dashing up to the station, and from the foremost there sprang a young man muffled in furs.

"Weymore?—No, these are not the Weymore sleighs."

The voice was that of the youth who had jumped to the platform—a voice so agreeable that, in spite of the words, it fell consolingly on Faxon's ears. At the same moment the wandering station-lantern, casting a transient light on the speaker, showed his features to be in the pleasantest harmony with his voice. He was very fair and very young—hardly in the twenties, Faxon thought—but his face, though full of a morning freshness, was a trifle too thin and fine-drawn, as though a vivid spirit contended in him with a strain of physical weakness. Faxon was perhaps the quicker to notice such delicacies of balance because his own temperament hung on lightly quivering nerves, which yet, as he believed, would never quite swing him beyond a normal sensibility.

"You expected a sleigh from Weymore?" the newcomer continued, standing beside Faxon like a slender column of fur.

Mrs. Culme's secretary explained his difficulty, and the other brushed it aside with a contemptuous "Oh, *Mrs. Culme!*" that carried both speakers a long way toward reciprocal understanding.

"But then you must be—" The youth broke off with a smile of interrogation.

"The new secretary? Yes. But apparently there are no notes to be answered this evening." Faxon's laugh deepened the sense of solidarity which had so promptly established itself between the two.

His friend laughed also. "Mrs. Culme," he explained, "was lunching at my uncle's today, and she said you were due this evening. But seven hours is a long time for Mrs. Culme to remember anything."

"Well," said Faxon philosophically, "I suppose that's one of the reasons why she needs a secretary. And I've always the inn at Northridge," he concluded.

"Oh, but you haven't, though! It burned down last week."

"The deuce it did!" said Faxon; but the humour of the situation struck him before its inconvenience. His life, for years past, had been mainly a succession of resigned adaptations, and he had learned, before dealing practically with his embarrassments, to extract from most of them a small tribute of amusement.

"Oh, well, there's sure to be somebody in the place who can put me up."

"No one *you* could put up with. Besides, Northridge is three miles off, and our place—in the opposite direction—is a little nearer." Through the darkness, Faxon saw his friend sketch a gesture of self-introduction. "My name's Frank Rainer, and I'm staying with my uncle at Overdale. I've driven over to meet two friends of his, who are due in a few minutes from New York. If you don't mind waiting till they arrive I'm sure Overdale can do you better than Northridge. We're only down from town for a few days, but the house is always ready for a lot of people."

"But your uncle—?" Faxon could only object, with the odd sense, through his embarrassment, that it would be magically dispelled by his invisible friend's next words.

"Oh, my uncle—you'll see! I answer for *him!* I daresay you've heard of him—John Lavington?"

John Lavington! There was a certain irony in asking if one had heard of John Lavington! Even from a post of observation as obscure as that of Mrs. Culme's secretary the rumour of John Lavington's money, of his pictures, his politics, his charities and his hospitality, was as difficult to escape as the roar of a cataract in a mountain solitude. It might almost have been said that the one place in which one would not have expected to come upon him was in just such a solitude as now surrounded the speakers—at least in this deepest hour of its desertedness. But it was just like Lavington's brilliant ubiquity to put one in the wrong even there.

"Oh, yes, I've heard of your uncle."

"Then you *will* come, won't you? We've only five minutes to wait," young Rainer urged, in the tone that dispels scruples by ignoring them; and Faxon found himself accepting the invitation as simply as it was offered.

A delay in the arrival of the New York train lengthened their five minutes to fifteen; and as they paced the icy platform Faxon began to see why it had seemed the most natural thing in the world to accede to his new acquaintance's suggestion. It was because Frank Rainer was one of the privileged beings who simplify human intercourse by the atmosphere of confidence and good humour they diffuse. He produced this effect, Faxon noted, by the exercise of no gift but his youth, and of no art but his sincerity; and these qualities were revealed in a smile of such sweetness that Faxon felt, as never before, what Nature can achieve when she deigns to match the face with the mind.

He learned that the young man was the ward, and the only nephew, of John Lavington, with whom he had made his home since the death of his mother, the great man's sister. Mr. Lavington, Rainer said, had been "a regular brick" to him—"But then he is to every one, you know"—and the young fellow's situation seemed in fact to be perfectly in keeping with his person. Apparently the only shade that had ever rested on him was cast by the physical weakness which Faxon had already detected. Young Rainer had been threatened with tuberculosis, and the disease was so far advanced that, according to the highest authorities, banishment to Arizona or New Mexico was inevitable. "But luckily my uncle didn't pack me off, as most people would have done, without getting another opinion. Whose? Oh, an awfully clever chap, a young doctor with a lot of

612

new ideas, who simply laughed at my being sent away, and said I'd do perfectly well in New York if I didn't dine out too much, and if I dashed off occasionally to Northridge for a little fresh air. So it's really my uncle's doing that I'm not in exile—and I feel no end better since the new chap told me I needn't bother." Young Rainer went on to confess that he was extremely fond of dining out, dancing and similar distractions; and Faxon, listening to him, was inclined to think that the physician who had refused to cut him off altogether from these pleasures was probably a better psychologist than his seniors.

"All the same you ought to be careful, you know." The sense of elder-brotherly concern that forced the words from Faxon made him, as he spoke, slip his arm through Frank Rainer's.

The latter met the movement with a responsive pressure. "Oh, I *am:* awfully, awfully. And then my uncle has such an eye on me!"

"But if your uncle has such an eye on you, what does he say to your swallowing knives out here in this Siberian wild?"

Rainer raised his fur collar with a careless gesture. "It's not that that does it—the cold's good for me."

"And it's not the dinners and dances? What is it, then?" Faxon good-humouredly insisted; to which his companion answered with a laugh: "Well, my uncle says it's being bored; and I rather think he's right!"

His laugh ended in a spasm of coughing and a struggle for breath that made Faxon, still holding his arm, guide him hastily into the shelter of the fireless waiting-room.

Young Rainer had dropped down on the bench against the wall and pulled off one of his fur gloves to grope for a handkerchief. He tossed aside his cap and drew the handkerchief across his forehead, which was intensely white, and beaded with moisture, though his face retained a healthy glow. But Faxon's gaze remained fastened to the hand he had uncovered: it was so long, so colourless, so wasted, so much older than the brow he passed it over.

"It's queer—a healthy face but dying hands," the secretary mused: he somehow wished young Rainer had kept on his glove.

The whistle of the express drew the young men to their feet, and the next moment two heavily-furred gentlemen had descended to the platform and were breasting the rigour of the night. Frank Rainer introduced them as Mr. Grisben and

Mr. Balch, and Faxon, while their luggage was being lifted into the second sleigh, discerned them, by the roving lantern-gleam, to be an elderly gray-headed pair, of the average prosperous business cut.

They saluted their host's nephew with friendly familiarity, and Mr. Grisben, who seemed the spokesman of the two, ended his greeting with a genial—"and many many more of them, dear boy!" which suggested to Faxon that their arrival coincided with an anniversary. But he could not press the enquiry, for the seat allotted him was at the coachman's side, while Frank Rainer joined his uncle's guests inside the sleigh.

A swift flight (behind such horses as one could be sure of John Lavington's having) brought them to tall gateposts, an illuminated lodge, and an avenue on which the snow had been levelled to the smoothness of marble. At the end of the avenue the long house loomed up, its principal bulk dark, but one wing sending out a ray of welcome; and the next moment Faxon was receiving a violent impression of warmth and light, of hot-house plants, hurrying servants, a vast spectacular oak hall like a stage-setting, and, in its unreal middle distance, a small figure, correctly dressed, conventionally featured, and utterly unlike his rather florid conception of the great John Lavington.

The surprise of the contrast remained with him through his hurried dressing in the large luxurious bedroom to which he had been shown. "I don't see where he comes in," was the only way he could put it, so difficult was it to fit the exuberance of Lavington's public personality into his host's contracted frame and manner. Mr. Lavington, to whom Faxon's case had been rapidly explained by young Rainer, had welcomed him with a sort of dry and stilted cordiality that exactly matched his narrow face, his stiff hand, and the whiff of scent on his evening handkerchief. "Make yourself at home—at home!" he had repeated, in a tone that suggested, on his own part, a complete inability to perform the feat he urged on his visitor. "Any friend of Frank's . . . delighted . . . make yourself thoroughly at home!"

2

In spite of the balmy temperature and complicated conveniences of Faxon's bedroom, the injunction was not easy to obey. It was wonderful luck to have found a night's shelter under the opulent roof of Overdale, and he tasted the physical satisfaction to the full. But the place, for all its ingenuities of comfort, was oddly cold and unwelcoming. He couldn't have said why, and could only suppose that Mr. Lavington's intense personality—intensely negative, but intense all the same—must, in some occult way, have penetrated every corner of his dwelling. Perhaps, though, it was merely that Faxon himself was tired and hungry, more deeply chilled than he had known till he came in from the cold, and unutterably sick of all strange houses, and of the prospect of perpetually treading other people's stairs.

"I hope you're not famished?" Rainer's slim figure was in the doorway. "My uncle has a little business to attend to with Mr. Grisben, and we don't dine for half an hour. Shall I fetch you, or can you find your way down? Come straight to the dining-room—the second door on the left of the long gallery."

He disappeared, leaving a ray of warmth behind him, and Faxon, relieved, lit a cigarette and sat down by the fire.

Looking about with less haste, he was struck by a detail that had escaped him. The room was full of flowers—a mere "bachelor's room", in the wing of a house opened only for a few days, in the dead middle of a New Hampshire winter! Flowers were everywhere, not in senseless profusion, but placed with the same conscious art that he had remarked in the grouping of the blossoming shrubs in the hall. A vase of arums stood on the writing-table, a cluster of strange-hued carnations on the stand at his elbow, and from bowls of glass and porcelain clumps of freesia-bulbs diffused their melting fragrance. The fact implied acres of glass—but that was the least interesting part of it. The flowers themselves, their quality, selection and arrangement, attested on some one's part—and on whose but John Lavington's?—a solicitous and sensitive passion for that particular form of beauty. Well, it simply made the man, as he had appeared to Faxon, all the harder to understand!

The half-hour elapsed, and Faxon, rejoicing at the prospect of food, set out to make his way to the dining-room. He had not noticed the direction he had followed in going to his room, and was puzzled, when he left it, to find that two staircases, of apparently equal importance, invited him. He chose the one to his right, and reached, at its foot, a long gallery such as Rainer had described. The gallery was empty, the doors down its length were closed; but Rainer had said: "The second to the left", and Faxon, after pausing for some chance enlightenment which did not come, laid his hand on the second knob to the left.

The room he entered was square, with dusky picture-hung walls. In its centre, about a table lit by veiled lamps, he fancied Mr. Lavington and his guests to be already seated at dinner; then he perceived that the table was covered not with viands but with papers, and that he had blundered into what seemed to be his host's study. As he paused Frank Rainer looked up.

"Oh, here's Mr. Faxon. Why not ask him—?"

Mr. Lavington, from the end of the table, reflected his nephew's smile in a glance of impartial benevolence.

"Certainly. Come in, Mr. Faxon. If you won't think it a liberty—"

Mr. Grisben, who sat opposite his host, turned his head toward the door. "Of course Mr. Faxon's an American citizen?"

Frank Rainer laughed. "That's all right! . . . Oh, no, not one of your pin-pointed pens, Uncle Jack! Haven't you got a quill somewhere?"

Mr. Balch, who spoke slowly and as if reluctantly, in a muffled voice of which there seemed to be very little left, raised his hand to say: "One moment: you acknowledge this to be—?"

"My last will and testament?" Rainer's laugh redoubled. "Well, I won't answer for the 'last'. It's the first, anyway."

"It's a mere formula," Mr. Balch explained.

"Well, here goes." Rainer dipped his quill in the inkstand his uncle had pushed in his direction, and dashed a gallant signature across the document.

Faxon, understanding what was expected of him, and conjecturing that the young man was signing his will on the attainment of his majority, had placed himself behind Mr. Grisben, and stood awaiting his turn to affix his name to the instrument. Rainer, having signed, was about to push the paper across the table to Mr. Balch; but the latter, again raising his hand, said in his sad imprisoned voice: "The seal—?"

"Oh, does there have to be a seal?"

Faxon, looking over Mr. Grisben at John Lavington, saw a faint frown between his impassive eyes. "Really, Frank!" He seemed, Faxon thought, slightly irritated by his nephew's frivolity.

"Who's got a seal?" Frank Rainer continued, glancing about the table. "There doesn't seem to be one here."

Mr. Grisben interposed. "A wafer will do. Lavington, you have a wafer?"

Mr. Lavington had recovered his serenity. "There must be some in one of the drawers. But I'm ashamed to say I don't know where my secretary keeps these things. He ought to have seen to it that a wafer was sent with the document."

"Oh, hang it—" Frank Rainer pushed the paper aside: "It's the hand of God—and I'm as hungry as a wolf. Let's dine first, Uncle Jack."

"I think I've a seal upstairs," said Faxon.

Mr. Lavington sent him a barely perceptible smile. "So sorry to give you the trouble—"

"Oh, I say, don't send him after it now. Let's wait till after dinner!"

Mr. Lavington continued to smile on his guest, and the latter, as if under the faint coercion of the smile, turned from the room and ran upstairs. Having taken the seal from his writing-case he came down again, and once more opened the door of the study. No one was speaking when he entered—they were evidently awaiting his return with the mute impatience of hunger, and he put the seal in Rainer's reach, and stood watching while Mr. Grisben struck a match and held it to one of the candles flanking the inkstand. As the wax descended on the paper Faxon remarked again the strange emaciation, the premature physical weariness, of the hand that held it: he wondered if Mr. Lavington had ever noticed his nephew's hand, and if it were not poignantly visible to him now.

With this thought in his mind, Faxon raised his eyes to look at Mr. Lavington. The great man's gaze rested on Frank Rainer with an expression of untroubled benevolence; and at the same instant Faxon's attention was attracted by the presence in the room of another person, who must have joined the group while he was upstairs searching for the seal. The newcomer was a man of about Mr. Lavington's age and figure, who stood just behind his chair, and who, at the moment when Faxon first saw him, was gazing at young Rainer with an equal intensity of attention. The likeness between the two men—perhaps increased by the fact that the hooded lamps on the table left the figure behind the chair in shadow—struck Faxon the more because of the contrast in their expression. John Lavington, during his nephew's clumsy attempt to drop the wax and apply the seal, continued to fasten on him a look of half-amused affection; while the man behind the chair, so oddly reduplicating the lines of his features and figure, turned on the boy a face of pale hostility.

The impression was so startling that Faxon forgot what was going on about him. He was just dimly aware of young Rainer's exclaiming: "Your turn, Mr. Grisben!" of Mr. Grisben's protesting: "No—no; Mr. Faxon first", and of the pen's being thereupon transferred to his own hand. He received it with a deadly sense of being unable to move, or even to understand what was expected of him, till he became conscious of Mr. Grisben's paternally pointing out the precise spot on which he was to leave his autograph. The effort to fix his attention and steady his hand prolonged the process of signing, and when he stood up—a strange weight of fatigue on all his limbs—the figure behind Mr. Lavington's chair was gone.

Faxon felt an immediate sense of relief. It was puzzling that the man's exit should have been so rapid and noiseless, but the door behind Mr. Lavington was screened by a tapestry hanging, and Faxon concluded that the unknown looker-on had merely had to raise it to pass out. At any rate he was gone, and with his withdrawal the strange weight was lifted. Young Rainer was lighting a cigarette, Mr. Balch inscribing his name at the foot of the document, Mr. Lavington—his eyes no longer on his nephew—examining a strange white-winged orchid in the vase at his elbow. Everything suddenly seemed to have grown natural and simple again, and Faxon found himself responding with a smile to the affable gesture with which his host declared: "And now, Mr. Faxon, we'll dine."

3

"I wonder how I blundered into the wrong room just now; I thought you told me to take the second door to the left," Faxon said to Frank Rainer as they followed the older men down the gallery.

"So I did; but I probably forgot to tell you which staircase to take. Coming from your bedroom, I ought to have said the fourth door to the right. It's a puzzling house, because my uncle keeps adding to it from year to year. He built this room last summer for his modern pictures."

Young Rainer, pausing to open another door, touched an electric button which sent a circle of light about the walls of a long room hung with canvases of the French impressionist school.

Faxon advanced, attracted by a shimmering Monet, but Rainer laid a hand on his arm.

"He bought that last week. But come along—I'll show you all this after dinner. Or *he* will, rather—he loves it."

"Does he really love things?"

Rainer stared, clearly perplexed at the question. "Rather! Flowers and pictures especially! Haven't you noticed the flowers? I suppose you think his manner's cold; it seems so at first; but he's really awfully keen about things."

Faxon looked quickly at the speaker. "Has your uncle a brother?"

"Brother? No—never had. He and my mother were the only ones."

"Or any relation who—who looks like him? Who might be mistaken for him?"

"Not that I ever heard of. Does he remind you of someone?"

"Yes."

"That's queer. We'll ask him if he's got a double. Come on!"

But another picture had arrested Faxon, and some minutes elapsed before he and his young host reached the dining-room. It was a large room, with the same conventionally handsome furniture and delicately grouped flowers; and Faxon's first glance showed him that only three men were seated about the dining-table. The man who had stood behind Mr. Lavington's chair was not present, and no seat awaited him.

When the young men entered, Mr. Grisben was speaking, and his host, who faced the door, sat looking down at his untouched soup-plate and turning the spoon about in his small dry hand.

"It's pretty late to call them rumours—they were devilish close to facts when we left town this morning," Mr. Grisben was saying, with an unexpected incisiveness of tone.

Mr. Lavington laid down his spoon and smiled interrogatively. "Oh, facts—what *are* facts? Just the way a thing happens to look at a given minute . . ."

"You haven't heard anything from town?" Mr. Grisben persisted.

"Not a syllable. So you see . . . Balch, a little more of that *petite marmite*. Mr. Faxon . . . between Frank and Mr. Grisben, please."

The dinner progressed through a series of complicated courses, ceremoniously dispensed by a prelatical butler attended by three tall footmen, and it was evident that Mr. Lavington took a certain satisfaction in the pageant. That, Faxon reflected, was probably the joint in his armour—that and the flowers. He had changed the subject—not abruptly but firmly—when the young men entered, but Faxon perceived that it still possessed the thoughts of the two elderly visitors, and Mr. Balch presently observed, in a voice that seemed to come from the last survivor down a mine-shaft: "If it *does* come, it will be the biggest crash since '93."

Mr. Lavington looked bored but polite. "Wall Street can stand crashes better than it could then. It's got a robuster constitution."

"Yes; but—"

"Speaking of constitutions," Mr. Grisben intervened: "Frank, are you taking care of yourself?"

A flush rose to young Rainer's cheeks.

"Why, of course! Isn't that what I'm here for?"

"You're here about three days in a month, aren't you? And the rest of the time it's crowded restaurants and hot ballrooms in town. I thought you were to be shipped off to New Mexico?"

"Oh, I've got a new man who says that's rot."

"Well, you don't look as if your new man were right," said Mr. Grisben bluntly.

Faxon saw the lad's colour fade, and the rings of shadow deepen under his gay eyes. At the same moment his uncle turned to him with a renewed intensity of attention. There was such solicitude in Mr. Lavington's gaze that it seemed almost to fling a shield between his nephew and Mr. Grisben's tactless scrutiny.

"We think Frank's a good deal better," he began; "this new doctor—"

The butler, coming up, bent to whisper a word in his ear, and the communication caused a sudden change in Mr. Lavington's expression. His face was naturally so colourless that it seemed not so much to pale as to fade, to dwindle and recede into something blurred and blotted-out. He half rose, sat down again and sent a rigid smile about the table.

"Will you excuse me? The telephone. Peters, go on with the dinner." With small precise steps he walked out of the door which one of the footmen had thrown open.

A momentary silence fell on the group; then Mr. Grisben once more addressed himself to Rainer. "You ought to have gone, my boy; you ought to have gone."

The anxious look returned to the youth's eyes. "My uncle doesn't think so, really."

"You're not a baby, to be always governed by your uncle's opinion. You came of age today, didn't you? Your uncle spoils you . . . that's what's the matter . . ."

The thrust evidently went home, for Rainer laughed and looked down with a slight accession of colour.

"But the doctor—"

"Use your common sense, Frank! You had to try twenty doctors to find one to tell you what you wanted to be told."

A look of apprehension overshadowed Rainer's gaiety. "Oh, come—I say! . . . What would *you* do?" he stammered.

"Pack up and jump on the first train." Mr. Grisben leaned forward and laid his hand kindly on the young man's arm. "Look here: my nephew Jim Grisben is out there ranching on a big scale. He'll take you in and be glad to have you. You say your new doctor thinks it won't do you any good; but he doesn't pretend to say it will do you harm, does he? Well, then—give it a trial. It'll take you out of hot theatres and night restaurants, anyhow . . . And all the rest of it . . . Eh, Balch?"

"Go!" said Mr. Balch hollowly. "Go *at once*," he added, as if a closer look at the youth's face had impressed on him the need of backing up his friend.

Young Rainer had turned ashy-pale. He tried to stiffen his mouth into a smile. "Do I look as bad as all that?"

Mr. Grisben was helping himself to terrapin. "You look like the day after an earthquake," he said.

The terrapin had encircled the table, and been deliberately enjoyed by Mr. Lavington's three visitors (Rainer, Faxon noticed, left his plate untouched) before the door was thrown open to re-admit their host.

Mr. Lavington advanced with an air of recovered composure. He seated himself, picked up his napkin and consulted the gold-monogrammed menu. "No, don't bring back the filet . . . Some terrapin; yes . . ." He looked affably about the table. "Sorry to

621

have deserted you, but the storm has played the deuce with the wires, and I had to wait a long time before I could get a good connection. It must be blowing up for a blizzard."

"Uncle Jack," young Rainer broke out, "Mr. Grisben's been lecturing me."

Mr. Lavington was helping himself to terrapin. "Ah—what about?"

"He thinks I ought to have given New Mexico a show."

"I want him to go straight out to my nephew at Santa Paz and stay there till his next birthday." Mr. Lavington signed to the butler to hand the terrapin to Mr. Grisben, who, as he took a second helping, addressed himself again to Rainer. "Jim's in New York now, and going back the day after tomorrow in Olyphant's private car. I'll ask Olyphant to squeeze you in if you'll go. And when you've been out there a week or two, in the saddle all day and sleeping nine hours a night, I suspect you won't think much of the doctor who prescribed New York."

Faxon spoke up, he knew not why. "I was out there once: it's a splendid life. I saw a fellow—oh, a really *bad* case—who'd been simply made over by it."

"It *does* sound jolly," Rainer laughed, a sudden eagerness in his tone.

His uncle looked at him gently. "Perhaps Grisben's right. It's an opportunity—"

Faxon glanced up with a start: the figure dimly perceived in the study was now more visibly and tangibly planted behind Mr. Lavington's chair.

"That's right, Frank: you see your uncle approves. And the trip out there with Olyphant isn't a thing to be missed. So drop a few dozen dinners and be at the Grand Central the day after tomorrow at five."

Mr. Grisben's pleasant gray eye sought corroboration of his host, and Faxon, in a cold anguish of suspense, continued to watch him as he turned his glance on Mr. Lavington. One could not look at Lavington without seeing the presence at his back, and it was clear that, the next minute, some change in Mr. Grisben's expression must give his watcher a clue.

But Mr. Grisben's expression did not change: the gaze he fixed on his host remained unperturbed, and the clue he gave was the startling one of not seeming to see the other figure.

Faxon's first impulse was to look away, to look anywhere else, to resort again to the champagne glass the watchful butler had already brimmed; but some fatal attraction, at war in him with an overwhelming physical resistance, held his eyes upon the spot they feared.

The figure was still standing, more distinctly, and therefore more resemblingly, at Mr. Lavington's back; and while the latter continued to gaze affectionately at his nephew, his counterpart, as before, fixed young Rainer with eyes of deadly menace.

Faxon, with what felt like an actual wrench of the muscles, dragged his own eyes from the sight to scan the other countenances about the table; but not one revealed the least consciousness of what he saw, and a sense of mortal isolation sank upon him.

"It's worth considering, certainly—" he heard Mr. Lavington continue; and as Rainer's face lit up, the face behind his uncle's chair seemed to gather into its look all the fierce weariness of old unsatisfied hates. That was the thing that, as the minutes laboured by, Faxon was becoming most conscious of. The watcher behind the chair was no longer merely malevolent: he had grown suddenly, unutterably tired. His hatred seemed to well up out of the very depths of balked effort and thwarted hopes, and the fact made him more pitiable, and yet more dire.

Faxon's look reverted to Mr. Lavington, as if to surprise in him a corresponding change. At first none was visible: his pinched smile was screwed to his blank face like a gas-light to a whitewashed wall. Then the fixity of the smile became ominous: Faxon saw that its wearer was afraid to let it go. It was evident that Mr. Lavington was unutterably tired too, and the discovery sent a colder current through Faxon's veins. Looking down at his untouched plate, he caught the soliciting twinkle of the champagne glass; but the sight of the wine turned him sick.

"Well, we'll go into the details presently," he heard Mr. Lavington say, still on the question of his nephew's future. "Let's have a cigar first. No—not here, Peters." He turned his smile on Faxon. "When we've had coffee I want to show you my pictures."

"Oh, by the way, Uncle Jack—Mr. Faxon wants to know if you've got a double?"

"A double?" Mr. Lavington, still smiling, continued to address himself to his guest. "Not that I know of. Have you seen one, Mr. Faxon?"

Faxon thought: "My God, if I look up now they'll *both* be looking at me!" To avoid raising his eyes he made as though to lift the glass to his lips; but his hand sank inert, and he looked up. Mr. Lavington's glance was politely bent on him, but with a loosening of the strain about his heart he saw that the figure behind the chair still kept its gaze on Rainer.

"Do you think you've seen my double, Mr. Faxon?"

Would the other face turn if he said yes? Faxon felt a dryness in his throat. "No," he answered.

"Ah? It's possible I've a dozen. I believe I'm extremely usual-looking," Mr. Lavington went on conversationally; and still the other face watched Rainer.

"It was . . . a mistake . . . a confusion of memory . . ." Faxon heard himself stammer. Mr. Lavington pushed back his chair, and as he did so Mr. Grisben suddenly leaned forward.

"Lavington! What have we been thinking of? We haven't drunk Frank's health!"

Mr. Lavington reseated himself. "My dear boy! . . . Peters, another bottle . . ." He turned to his nephew. "After such a sin of omission I don't presume to propose the toast myself . . . but Frank knows . . . Go ahead, Grisben!"

The boy shone on his uncle. "No, no, Uncle Jack! Mr. Grisben won't mind. Nobody but *you*—today!"

The butler was replenishing the glasses. He filled Mr. Lavington's last, and Mr. Lavington put out his small hand to raise it . . . As he did so, Faxon looked away.

"Well, then—All the good I've wished you in all the past years . . . I put it into the prayer that the coming ones may be healthy and happy and many . . . and *many*, dear boy!"

Faxon saw the hands about him reach out for their glasses. Automatically, he reached for his. His eyes were still on the table, and he repeated to himself with a trembling vehemence: "I won't look up! I won't . . . I won't . . ."

His fingers clasped the glass and raised it to the level of his lips. He saw the other hands making the same motion. He heard Mr. Grisben's genial "Hear! Hear!" and Mr. Balch's hollow echo. He said to himself, as the rim of the glass touched his lips: "I won't look up! I swear I won't!—" and he looked.

The glass was so full that it required an extraordinary effort to hold it there, brimming and suspended, during the awful interval before he could trust his hand to lower it again, untouched, to the table. It was this merciful preoccupation which saved him, kept him from crying out, from losing his hold, from slipping down into the bottomless blackness that gaped for him. As long as the problem of the glass engaged him he felt able to keep his seat, manage his muscles, fit unnoticeably into the group; but as the glass touched the table his last link with safety snapped. He stood up and dashed out of the room.

4

In the gallery, the instinct of self-preservation helped him to turn back and sign to young Rainer not to follow. He stammered out something about a touch of dizziness, and joining them presently; and the boy nodded sympathetically and drew back.

At the foot of the stairs Faxon ran against a servant. "I should like to telephone to Weymore," he said with dry lips.

"Sorry, sir; wires all down. We've been trying the last hour to get New York again for Mr. Lavington."

Faxon shot on to his room, burst into it, and bolted the door. The lamplight lay on furniture, flowers, books; in the ashes a log still glimmered. He dropped down on the sofa and hid his face. The room was profoundly silent, the whole house was still: nothing about him gave a hint of what was going on, darkly and dumbly, in the room he had flown from, and with the covering of his eyes oblivion and reassurance seemed to fall on him. But they fell for a moment only; then his lids opened again to the monstrous vision. There it was, stamped on his pupils, a part of him forever, an indelible horror burnt into his body and brain. But why into his—just his? Why had he alone been chosen to see what he had seen? What business was it of *his*, in God's name? Any one of the others, thus enlightened, might have exposed the horror and defeated it; but *he*, the one weaponless and defenceless spectator, the one whom none of the others would believe or understand if he attempted to reveal what he knew—*he* alone had been singled out as the victim of this dreadful initiation!

Suddenly he sat up, listening: he had heard a step on the stairs. Someone, no doubt, was coming to see how he was—to urge him, if he felt better, to go down and join the smokers. Cautiously he opened his door; yes, it was young Rainer's step. Faxon looked down the passage, remembered the other stairway and darted to it. All he wanted was to get out of the house. Not another instant would he breathe its abominable air! What business was it of *his*, in God's name?

He reached the opposite end of the lower gallery, and beyond it saw the hall by which he had entered. It was empty, and on a long table he recognized his coat and cap. He got into his coat, unbolted the door, and plunged into the purifying night.

The darkness was deep, and the cold so intense that for an instant it stopped his breathing. Then he perceived that only a thin snow was falling, and resolutely he set his face for flight. The trees along the avenue marked his way as he hastened with long strides over the beaten snow. Gradually, while he walked, the tumult in his brain subsided. The impulse to fly still drove him forward, but he began to feel that he was flying from a terror of his own creating, and that the most urgent reason for escape was the need of hiding his state, of shunning other eyes till he should regain his balance.

He had spent the long hours in the train in fruitless broodings on a discouraging situation, and he remembered how his bitterness had turned to exasperation when he found that the Weymore sleigh was not awaiting him. It was absurd, of course; but, though he had joked with Rainer over Mrs. Culme's forgetfulness, to confess it had cost a pang. That was what his rootless life had brought him to: for lack of a personal stake in things his sensibility was at the mercy of such trifles . . . Yes; that, and the cold and fatigue, the absence of hope and the haunting sense of starved aptitudes, all these had brought him to the perilous verge over which, once or twice before, his terrified brain had hung.

Why else, in the name of any imaginable logic, human or devilish, should he, a stranger, be singled out for this experience? What could it mean to him, how was he related to it, what bearing had it on his case? . . . Unless, indeed, it was just because he was a stranger—a stranger everywhere—because he had no personal life, no warm screen of private egotisms to shield him from exposure, that he had developed this abnormal sensitiveness to the vicissitudes of others. The thought pulled

him up with a shudder. No! Such a fate was too abominable; all
that was strong and sound in him rejected it. A thousand times
better to regard himself as ill, disorganized, deluded, than as the
predestined victim of such warnings!

He reached the gates and paused before the darkened lodge.
The wind had risen and was sweeping the snow into his face. The
cold had him in its grasp again, and he stood uncertain. Should
he put his sanity to the test and go back? He turned and looked
down the dark drive to the house. A single ray shone through
the trees, evoking a picture of the lights, the flowers, the faces
grouped about that fatal room. He turned and plunged out into
the road . . .

He remembered that, about a mile from Overdale, the
coachman had pointed out the road to Northridge; and he
began to walk in that direction. Once in the road he had
the gale in his face, and the wet snow on his moustache and
eyelashes instantly hardened to ice. The same ice seemed to be
driving a million blades into his throat and lungs, but he pushed
on, the vision of the warm room pursuing him.

The snow in the road was deep and uneven. He stumbled
across ruts and sank into drifts, and the wind drove against him
like a granite cliff. Now and then he stopped, gasping, as if an
invisible hand had tightened an iron band about his body; then he
started again, stiffening himself against the stealthy penetration
of the cold. The snow continued to descend out of a pall of
inscrutable darkness, and once or twice he paused, fearing he
had missed the road to Northridge; but, seeing no sign of a turn,
he ploughed on.

At last, feeling sure that he had walked for more than a mile,
he halted and looked back. The act of turning brought immediate
relief, first because it put his back to the wind, and then because,
far down the road, it showed him the gleam of a lantern. A sleigh
was coming—a sleigh that might perhaps give him a lift to the
village! Fortified by the hope, he began to walk back toward the
light. It came forward very slowly, with unaccountable zigzags
and waverings; and even when he was within a few yards of it he
could catch no sound of sleigh-bells. Then it paused and became
stationary by the roadside, as though carried by a pedestrian who
had stopped, exhausted by the cold. The thought made Faxon
hasten on, and a moment later he was stooping over a motionless
figure huddled against the snow-bank. The lantern had dropped

from its bearer's hand, and Faxon, fearfully raising it, threw its light into the face of Frank Rainer.

"Rainer! What on earth are you doing here?"

The boy smiled back through his pallor. "What are *you*, I'd like to know?" he retorted; and, scrambling to his feet with a clutch on Faxon's arm, he added gaily: "Well, I've run you down!"

Faxon stood confounded, his heart sinking. The lad's face was gray.

"What madness—" he began.

"Yes, it *is*. What on earth did you do it for?"

"I? Do what? . . . Why I . . . I was just taking a walk . . . I often walk at night . . ."

Frank Rainer burst into a laugh. "On such nights? Then you hadn't bolted?"

"Bolted?"

"Because I'd done something to offend you? My uncle thought you had."

Faxon grasped his arm. "Did your uncle send you after me?"

"Well, he gave me an awful rowing for not going up to your room with you when you said you were ill. And when we found you'd gone we were frightened—and he was awfully upset—so I said I'd catch you . . . You're *not* ill, are you?"

"Ill? No. Never better." Faxon picked up the lantern. "Come; let's go back. It was awfully hot in that dining-room."

"Yes; I hoped it was only that."

They trudged on in silence for a few minutes; then Faxon questioned: "You're not too done up?"

"Oh, no. It's a lot easier with the wind behind us."

"All right. Don't talk any more."

They pushed ahead, walking, in spite of the light that guided them, more slowly than Faxon had walked alone into the gale. The fact of his companion's stumbling against a drift gave Faxon a pretext for saying: "Take hold of my arm," and Rainer obeying, gasped out: "I'm blown!"

"So am I. Who wouldn't be?"

"What a dance you led me! If it hadn't been for one of the servants happening to see you—"

"Yes; all right. And now, won't you kindly shut up?"

Rainer laughed and hung on him. "Oh, the cold doesn't hurt me . . ."

For the first few minutes after Rainer had overtaken him, anxiety for the lad had been Faxon's only thought. But as each labouring step carried them nearer to the spot he had been fleeing, the reasons for his flight grew more ominous and more insistent. No, he was not ill, he was not distraught and deluded—he was the instrument singled out to warn and save; and here he was, irresistibly driven, dragging the victim back to his doom!

The intensity of the conviction had almost checked his steps. But what could he do or say? At all costs he must get Rainer out of the cold, into the house and into his bed. After that he would act.

The snow-fall was thickening, and as they reached a stretch of the road between open fields the wind took them at an angle, lashing their faces with barbed thongs. Rainer stopped to take breath, and Faxon felt the heavier pressure of his arm.

"When we get to the lodge, can't we telephone to the stable for a sleigh?"

"If they're not all asleep at the lodge."

"Oh, I'll manage. Don't talk!" Faxon ordered; and they plodded on . . .

At length the lantern ray showed ruts that curved away from the road under tree-darkness.

Faxon's spirits rose. "There's the gate! We'll be there in five minutes."

As he spoke he caught, above the boundary hedge, the gleam of a light at the farther end of the dark avenue. It was the same light that had shone on the scene of which every detail was burnt into his brain; and he felt again its overpowering reality. No—he couldn't let the boy go back!

They were at the lodge at last, and Faxon was hammering on the door. He said to himself: "I'll get him inside first, and make them give him a hot drink. Then I'll see—I'll find an argument . . ."

There was no answer to his knocking, and after an interval Rainer said: "Look here—we'd better go on."

"No!"

"I can, perfectly—"

"You shan't go to the house, I say!" Faxon redoubled his blows, and at length steps sounded on the stairs. Rainer was leaning against the lintel, and as the door opened the light from the hall flashed on his pale face and fixed eyes. Faxon caught him by the arm and drew him in.

"It *was* cold out there," he sighed; and then, abruptly, as if invisible shears at a single stroke had cut every muscle in his body, he swerved, drooped on Faxon's arm, and seemed to sink into nothing at his feet.

The lodge-keeper and Faxon bent over him, and somehow, between them, lifted him into the kitchen and laid him on a sofa by the stove.

The lodge-keeper, stammering: "I'll ring up the house," dashed out of the room. But Faxon heard the words without heeding them: omens mattered nothing now, beside this woe fulfilled. He knelt down to undo the fur collar about Rainer's throat, and as he did so he felt a warm moisture on his hands. He held them up, and they were red . . .

5

The palms threaded their endless line along the yellow river. The little steamer lay at the wharf, and George Faxon, sitting in the verandah of the wooden hotel, idly watched the coolies carrying the freight across the gang-plank.

He had been looking at such scenes for two months. Nearly five had elapsed since he had descended from the train at Northridge and strained his eyes for the sleigh that was to take him to Weymore: Weymore, which he was never to behold! . . . Part of the interval—the first part—was still a great gray blur. Even now he could not be quite sure how he had got back to Boston, reached the house of a cousin, and been thence transferred to a quiet room looking out on snow under bare trees. He looked out a long time at the same scene, and finally one day a man he had known at Harvard came to see him and invited him to go out on a business trip to the Malay Peninsula.

"You've had a bad shake-up, and it'll do you no end of good to get away from things."

When the doctor came the next day it turned out that he knew of the plan and approved it. "You ought to be quiet for a year. Just loaf and look at the landscape," he advised.

Faxon felt the first faint stirrings of curiosity.

"What's been the matter with me, anyway?"

"Well, over-work, I suppose. You must have been bottling up for a bad breakdown before you started for New Hampshire last December. And the shock of that poor boy's death did the rest." Ah, yes—Rainer had died. He remembered . . .

He started for the East, and gradually, by imperceptible degrees, life crept back into his weary bones and leaden brain. His friend was patient and considerate, and they travelled slowly and talked little. At first Faxon had felt a great shrinking from whatever touched on familiar things. He seldom looked at a newspaper and he never opened a letter without a contraction of the heart. It was not that he had any special cause for apprehension, but merely that a great trail of darkness lay on everything. He had looked too deep down into the abyss . . . But little by little health and energy returned to him, and with them the common promptings of curiosity. He was beginning to wonder how the world was going, and when, presently, the hotel-keeper told him there were no letters for him in the steamer's mail-bag, he felt a distinct sense of disappointment. His friend had gone into the jungle on a long excursion, and he was lonely, unoccupied and wholesomely bored. He got up and strolled into the stuffy reading-room.

There he found a game of dominoes, a mutilated picture-puzzle, some copies of *Zion's Herald* and a pile of New York and London newspapers.

He began to glance through the papers, and was disappointed to find that they were less recent than he had hoped. Evidently the last numbers had been carried off by luckier travellers. He continued to turn them over, picking out the American ones first. These, as it happened, were the oldest: they dated back to December and January. To Faxon, however, they had all the flavour of novelty, since they covered the precise period during which he had virtually ceased to exist. It had never before occurred to him to wonder what had happened in the world during that interval of obliteration; but now he felt a sudden desire to know.

To prolong the pleasure, he began by sorting the papers chronologically, and as he found and spread out the earliest number, the date at the top of the page entered into his consciousness like a key slipping into a lock. It was the 17th of December: the date of the day after his arrival at Northridge. He glanced at the first page and read in blazing characters:

"Reported Failure of Opal Cement Company. Lavington's Name Involved. Gigantic Exposure of Corruption Shakes Wall Street to Its Foundations."

He read on, and when he had finished the first paper he turned to the next. There was a gap of three days, but the Opal Cement "Investigation" still held the centre of the stage. From its complex revelations of greed and ruin his eye wandered to the death notices, and he read: "Rainer. Suddenly, at Northridge, New Hampshire, Francis John, only son of the late . . ."

His eyes clouded, and he dropped the newspaper and sat for a long time with his face in his hands. When he looked up again he noticed that his gesture had pushed the other papers from the table and scattered them at his feet. The uppermost lay spread out before him, and heavily his eyes began their search again. "John Lavington comes forward with plan for reconstructing Company. Offers to put in ten millions of his own—The proposal under consideration by the District Attorney."

Ten millions . . . ten millions of his own. But if John Lavington was ruined? . . . Faxon stood up with a cry. That was it, then—that was what the warning meant! And if he had not fled from it, dashed wildly away from it into the night, he might have broken the spell of iniquity, the powers of darkness might not have prevailed! He caught up the pile of newspapers and began to glance through each in turn for the head-line: "Wills Admitted to Probate." In the last of all he found the paragraph he sought, and it stared up at him as if with Rainer's dying eyes.

That—*that* was what he had done! The powers of pity had singled him out to warn and save, and he had closed his ears to their call, and washed his hands of it, and fled. Washed his hands of it! That was the word. It caught him back to the dreadful moment in the lodge when, raising himself up from Rainer's side, he had looked at his hands and seen that they were red . . .

MARY E. WILKINS
The Hall Bedroom

Mary Eleanor Wilkins (1852–1930) was a highly acclaimed American author who wrote about New England village life with sympathy and realism. Apart from many novels, she wrote more than two hundred short stories including several classics of the supernatural, some of which appeared in The Wind in the Rose-Bush (1903). *Her later works appeared under her married name Mary E. Wilkes Freeman. The American Academy of Arts and Letters awarded her the Howells medal for fiction in 1926. The following story is taken from* American Short Story Classics (1905).

My name is Mrs. Elizabeth Jennings. I am a highly respectable woman. I may style myself a gentlewoman, for in my youth I enjoyed advantages. I was well brought up, and I graduated at a young ladies' seminary. I also married well. My husband was that most genteel of all merchants, an apothecary. His shop was on the corner of the main street in Rockton, the town where I was born, and where I lived until the death of my husband. My parents had died when I had been married a short time, so I was left quite alone in the world. I was not competent to carry on the apothecary business by myself, for I had no knowledge of drugs, and had a mortal terror of giving poisons instead of medicines. Therefore I was obliged to sell at a considerable sacrifice, and the proceeds, some five thousand dollars, were all I had in the world. The income was not enough to support me in any kind of comfort, and I saw that I must in some way earn money. I thought at first of teaching, but I was no longer young, and methods had changed since my school days. What I was able to teach, nobody wished to know. I could think of only one thing to do: take boarders. But the same objection to that business as to teaching held good in Rockton. Nobody wished to board. My husband had rented a house with a number of bedrooms, and I advertised, but nobody applied. Finally my cash was running very low, and I became desperate. I packed my furniture, rented a large house in this town, and moved there. It was a venture attended with many risks. In the first place the rent was exorbitant; in the next I was entirely unknown. However, I am a person of considerable ingenuity, and have inventive power, and much enterprise when the occasion presses. I advertised in a very original manner, although that actually took my last penny, that is, the last penny of my ready money, and I was forced to draw on my principal to purchase my first supplies, a thing which I had resolved never on any account to do. But the great risk met with a reward, for I had several applicants within two days after my advertisement appeared in the paper. Within two weeks my boarding-house was well established, I became very successful, and my success would have been uninterrupted had it not been for the mysterious and bewildering occurrences which I am about to relate. I am now forced to leave the house and rent another. Some of my old boarders accompany me, some, with the most unreasonable nervousness, refuse to be longer associated in any way, however indirectly, with the terrible and uncanny happenings which I have to relate. It remains to be seen whether my ill luck in this house will follow me into another, and whether my whole prosperity in life will be forever shadowed by the Mystery of the Hall Bedroom. Instead of telling the strange story myself in my own words, I shall present the Journal of Mr. George H. Wheatcroft. I shall show you the portions beginning on January 18 of the present year, the date when he took up his residence with me. Here it is:

"*January 18, 1883*. Here I am established in my new boarding-house. I have, as befits my humble means, the hall bedroom, even the hall bedroom on the third floor. I have heard all my life of hall bedrooms, I have seen hall bedrooms, I have been in them, but never until now, when I am actually established in one, did I comprehend what, at once, an ignominious and sternly uncompromising thing a hall bedroom is. It proves the ignominy of the dweller therein. No man at thirty-six (my age) would be domiciled in a hall bedroom unless he were himself ignominious, at least comparatively speaking. I am proved by this means incontrovertibly to have been left far behind in the race. I see no reason why I should not live in this hall bedroom for the rest of my life, that is, if I have money enough to pay the landlady, and that seems probable, since my small funds are invested as safely as if I were an orphan-ward in charge of a pillar of a sanctuary. After the valuables have been stolen, I have most carefully locked the stable door. I have experienced the revulsion which comes sooner or later to the adventurous soul who experiences nothing but defeat and so-called ill luck. I have swung to the opposite extreme. I have lost in everything—I have lost in love, I have lost in money, I have lost in the struggle for preferment, I have lost in health and strength. I am now settled down in a hall bedroom to live upon my small income, and regain my health by mild potations of the mineral waters here, if possible; if not, to live here without my health—for mine is not a necessarily fatal malady—until Providence shall take me out of my hall bedroom. There is no one place more than another where I care to live. There is not sufficient motive to take me away, even if the mineral waters do not benefit me. So I am here and to stay in the hall bedroom. The landlady is civil, and even kind, as kind as a woman who has to keep her poor womanly eye upon the main chance can be. The struggle for money always injures the fine grain of a woman; she is too fine a thing to do it; she does not by nature belong with the gold grubbers, and it therefore lowers her; she steps from heights to claw and scrape and dig. But she cannot help it oftentimes, poor thing, and her deterioration thereby is to be condoned. The landlady is all she can be, taking her strain of adverse circumstances into consideration, and the table is good, even conscientiously so. It looks to me as if she were foolish enough to strive to give the boarders their money's worth, with the due regard for the main chance which is inevitable. However, that is of minor importance to me, since my diet is restricted.

"It is curious what an annoyance a restriction in diet can be even to a man who has considered himself somewhat indifferent to gastronomic delights. There was to-day a pudding for dinner, which I could not taste without penalty, but which I longed for. It was only because it looked unlike any other pudding that I had ever seen, and assumed a mental and spiritual significance. It seemed to me, whimsically no doubt, as if tasting it might give me a new sensation, and consequently a new outlook. Trivial things may lead to large results: why should I not get a new outlook by means of a pudding? Life here stretches

before me most monotonously, and I feel like clutching at
alleviations, though paradoxically, since I have settled down
with the utmost acquiescence. Still, one cannot immediately
overcome and change radically all one's nature. Now I look at
myself critically and search for the keynote to my whole self, and
my actions, I have always been conscious of a reaching out, an
overweening desire for the new, the untried, for the broadness
of further horizons, the seas beyond seas, the thought beyond
thought. This characteristic has been the primary cause of all
my misfortunes. I have the soul of an explorer, and in nine
out of ten cases this leads to destruction. If I had possessed
capital and sufficient push, I should have been one of the
searchers after the North Pole. I have been an eager student
of astronomy. I have studied botany with avidity, and have
dreamed of new flora in unexplored parts of the world, and
the same with animal life and geology. I longed for riches in
order to discover the power and sense of possession of the rich.
I longed for love in order to discover the possibilities of the
emotions. I longed for all that the mind of man could conceive
as desirable for man, not so much for purely selfish ends, as from
an insatiable thirst for knowledge of a universal trend. But I have
limitations, I do not quite understand of what nature—for what
mortal ever did quite understand his own limitations, since a
knowledge of them would preclude their existence?—but they
have prevented my progress to any extent. Therefore behold
me in my hall bedroom, settled at last into a groove of fate
so deep that I have lost the sight of even my horizons. Just
at present, as I write here, my horizon on the left, that is my
physical horizon, is a wall covered with cheap paper. The paper
is an indeterminate pattern in white and gilt. There are a few
photographs of my own hung about, and on the large wall space
beside the bed there is a large oil painting which belongs to my
landlady. It has a massive tarnished gold frame, and, curiously
enough, the painting itself is rather good. I have no idea who the
artist could have been. It is of the conventional landscape type
in vogue some fifty years since, the type so fondly reproduced
in chromos—the winding river with the little boat occupied by
a pair of lovers, the cottage nestled among trees on the right
shore, the gentle slope of the hills and the church spire in the
background—but still it is well done. It gives me the impression
of an artist without the slightest originality of design, but much

of technique. But for some inexplicable reason the picture frets me. I find myself gazing at it when I do not wish to do so. It seems to compel my attention like some intent face in the room. I shall ask Mrs. Jennings to have it removed. I will hang in its place some photographs which I have in a trunk.

"*January 26.* I do not write regularly in my journal. I never did. I see no reason why I should. I see no reason why anyone should have the slightest sense of duty in such a matter. Some days I have nothing which interests me sufficiently to write out, some days I feel either too ill or too indolent. For four days I have not written, from a mixture of all three reasons. Now, to-day I both feel like it and I have something to write. Also I am distinctly better than I have been. Perhaps the waters are benefiting me, or the change of air. Or possibly it is something else more subtle. Possibly my mind has seized upon something new, a discovery which causes it to react upon my failing body and serves as a stimulant. All I know is, I feel distinctly better, and am conscious of an acute interest in doing so, which is of late strange to me. I have been rather indifferent, and sometimes have wondered if that were not the cause rather than the result of my state of health. I have been so continually balked that I have settled into a state of inertia. I lean rather comfortably against my obstacles. After all, the worst of the pain always lies in the struggle. Give up and it is rather pleasant than otherwise. If one did not kick, the pricks would not in the least matter. However, for some reason, for the last few days, I seem to have awakened from my state of quiescence. It means future trouble for me, no doubt, but in the meantime I am not sorry. It began with the picture—the large oil painting. I went to Mrs. Jennings about it yesterday, and she, to my surprise—for I thought it a matter that could be easily arranged—objected to having it removed. Her reasons were two; both simple, both sufficient, especially since I, after all, had no very strong desire either way. It seems that the picture does not belong to her. It hung here when she rented the house. She says, if it is removed, a very large and unsightly discoloration of the wall paper will be exposed, and she does not like to ask for new paper. The owner, an old man, is travelling abroad, the agent is curt, and she has only been in the house a very short time. Then it would mean a sad upheaval of my room, which would disturb me. She also says that there is no place in the house where she can store the picture, and there is not a vacant space in another room for one so large. So I let the picture remain. It really, when I came to think of it, was very immaterial after all. But I got my photographs out of my trunk, and I hung them around the large picture. The wall is almost completely covered. I hung them yesterday afternoon, and last night I repeated a strange experience which I have had in some degree every night since I have been here, but was not sure whether it deserved the name of experience, but was not rather one of those dreams in which one dreams one is awake. But last night it came again, and now I know. There is something very singular about this room. I am very much interested. I will write down for future reference the events of last night. Concerning those of the preceding nights since I have slept in this room, I will simply say that they have been of a similar nature, but, as it were, only the preliminary stages, the prologue to what happened last night.

"I am not depending upon the mineral waters here as the one remedy for my malady, which is sometimes of an acute nature, and indeed constantly threatens me with considerable suffering unless by medicine I can keep it in check. I will say that the medicine which I employ is not of the class commonly known as drugs. It is impossible that it can be held responsible for what I am about to transcribe. My mind last night and every night since I have slept in this room was in an absolutely normal state. I take this medicine, prescribed by the specialist in whose charge I was before coming here, regularly every four hours while awake. As I am never a good sleeper, it follows that I am enabled with no inconvenience to take any medicine during the night with the same regularity as during the day. It is my habit, therefore, to place my bottle and spoon where I can put my hand upon them easily without lighting the gas. Since I have been in this room, I have placed the bottle of medicine upon my dresser at the side of the room opposite the bed. I have done this rather than place it nearer, as once I jostled the bottle and spilled most of the contents, and it is not easy for me to replace it, as it is expensive. Therefore I placed it in security on the dresser, and, indeed, that is but three or four steps from my bed, the room being so small. Last night I wakened as usual, and I knew, since I had fallen asleep about eleven, that it must be in the neighbourhood of three. I wake with almost clock-like regularity, and it is never necessary for me to consult my watch.

"I had slept unusually well and without dreams, and I awoke fully at once, with a feeling of refreshment to which I am not accustomed. I immediately got out of bed and began stepping across the room in the direction of my dresser, on which I had set my medicine bottle and spoon.

"To my utter amazement, the steps which had hitherto sufficed to take me across my room did not suffice to do so. I advanced several paces, and my outstretched hands touched nothing. I stopped and went on again. I was sure that I was moving in a straight direction, and even if I had not been I knew it was impossible to advance in any direction in my tiny apartment without coming into collision either with a wall or a piece of furniture. I continued to walk falteringly, as I have seen people on the stage: a step, then a long falter, then a sliding step. I kept my hands extended; they touched nothing. I stopped again. I had not the least sentiment of fear or consternation. It was rather the very stupefaction of surprise. 'How is this?' seemed thundering in my ears. 'What is this?'

"The room was perfectly dark. There was nowhere any glimmer, as is usually the case, even in a so-called dark room, from the walls, picture-frames, looking-glass or white objects. It was absolute gloom. The house stood in a quiet part of the town. There were many trees about; the electric street lights were extinguished at midnight; there was no moon and the sky was cloudy. I could not distinguish my one window, which I thought strange, even on such a dark night. Finally I changed my plan of motion and turned, as nearly as I could estimate, at right angles. Now, I thought, I must reach soon, if I kept on, my writing-table underneath the window; or, if I am going in the opposite direction, the hall door. I reached neither. I am telling the unvarnished truth when I say that I began to count my steps and carefully measure my paces after that, and I traversed a space clear of furniture at least twenty feet by thirty—a very large apartment. And as I walked I was conscious that my naked feet were pressing something which gave rise to sensations the like of which I had never experienced before. As nearly as I can express it, it was as if my feet pressed something as elastic as air or water, which was in this case unyielding to my weight. It gave me a curious sensation of buoyancy and stimulation. At the same time this surface, if surface be the right name, which I trod, felt cool to my feet with the coolness of vapour or fluidity, seeming to overlap the soles. Finally I stood still; my surprise was at last merging into a measure of consternation. 'Where am I?' I thought. 'What am I going to do?' Stories that I had heard of travellers being taken from their beds and conveyed into strange and dangerous places, Middle Age stories of the Inquisition flashed through my brain. I knew all the time that for a man who had gone to bed in a commonplace hall bedroom in a very commonplace little town such surmises were highly ridiculous, but it is hard for the human mind to grasp anything but a human explanation of phenomena. Almost anything seemed then, and seems now, more rational than an explanation bordering upon the supernatural, as we understand the supernatural. At last I called, though rather softly, 'What does this mean?' I said quite aloud, 'Where am I? Who is here? Who is doing this? I tell you I will have no such nonsense. Speak, if there is anybody here.' But all was dead silence. Then suddenly a light flashed through the open transom of my door. Somebody had heard me—a man who rooms next door, a decent kind of man, also here for his health. He turned on the gas in the hall and called to me. 'What's the matter?' he asked, in an agitated, trembling voice. He is a nervous fellow.

"Directly, when the light flashed through my transom, I saw that I was in my familiar hall bedroom. I could see everything quite distinctly—my tumbled bed, my writing-table, my dresser, my chair, my little washstand, my clothes hanging on a row of pegs, the old picture on the wall. The picture gleamed out with singular distinctness in the light from the transom. The river seemed actually to run and ripple, and the boat to be gliding with the current. I gazed fascinated at it, as I replied to the anxious voice:

" 'Nothing is the matter with me,' said I. 'Why?'

" 'I thought I heard you speak,' said the man outside. 'I thought maybe you were sick.'

" 'No,' I called back. "I am all right. I am trying to find my medicine in the dark, that's all. I can see now you have lighted the gas."

" 'Nothing is the matter?'

" 'No; sorry I disturbed you. Good-night.'

" 'Good-night.' Then I heard the man's door shut after a minute's pause. He was evidently not quite satisfied. I took a pull at my medicine bottle, and got into bed. He had left the hall gas burning. I did not go to sleep again for some time. Just before I did so, someone, probably Mrs. Jennings, came out in the hall and extinguished the gas. This morning when I awoke everything was as usual in my room. I wonder if I shall have any such experience to-night.

"*January 27.* I shall write in my journal every day until this draws to some definite issue. Last night my strange experience deepened, as something tells me it will continue to do. I retired quite early, at half-past ten. I took the precaution, on retiring, to place beside my bed, on a chair, a box of safety matches, that I might not be in the dilemma of the night before. I took my medicine on retiring; that made me due to wake at half-past two. I had not fallen asleep directly, but had had certainly three hours of sound, dreamless slumber when I awoke. I lay a few minutes hesitating whether or not to strike a safety match and light my way to the dresser, whereon stood my medicine bottle. I hesitated, not because I had the least sensation of fear, but because of the same shrinking from a nerve shock that leads one at times to dread the plunge into an icy bath. It seemed much easier to me to strike that match and cross my hall bedroom to my dresser, take my dose, then return quietly to my bed, than to risk the chance of floundering about in some unknown limbo either of fancy or reality.

"At last, however, the spirit of adventure, which has always been such a ruling one for me, conquered. I rose. I took the box of safety matches in my hand, and started on, as I conceived, the straight course for my dresser, about five feet across from my bed. As before, I travelled and travelled and did not reach it. I advanced with groping hands extended, setting one foot cautiously before the other, but I touched nothing except the indefinite, unnameable surface which my feet pressed. All of a sudden, though, I became aware of something. One of my senses was saluted, nay, more than that, hailed, with imperiousness, and that was, strangely enough, my sense of smell, but in a hitherto unknown fashion. It seemed as if the odour reached my mentality first. I reversed the usual process, which is, as I understand it, like this: the odour when encountered strikes first the olfactory nerve, which transmits the intelligence to the brain. It is as if, to put it rudely, my nose met a rose, and then the nerve belonging to the sense said to my brain, 'Here is a rose.' This time my brain said, 'Here is a rose,' and my sense then recognized it. I say rose, but it was not a rose, that is, not the fragrance of any rose which I had ever known. It was undoubtedly a flower odour, and rose came perhaps the nearest to it. My mind realized it first with what seemed a leap of rapture. 'What is this delight?' I asked myself. And then the ravishing fragrance smote my sense. I breathed it in and it seemed to feed my thoughts, satisfying some hitherto unknown hunger. Then I took a step further and another fragrance appeared, which I liken to lilies for lack of something better, and then came violets, then mignonette. I cannot describe the experience, but it was a sheer delight, a rapture of sublimated sense. I groped further and further, and always into new waves of fragrance. I seemed to be wading breast-high through flower beds of Paradise, but all the time I touched nothing with my groping hands. At last a sudden giddiness as of surfeit overcame me. I realized that I might be in some unknown peril. I was distinctly afraid. I struck one of my safety matches, and I was in my hall bedroom, midway between my bed and my dresser. I took my dose of medicine and went to bed, and after a while fell asleep and did not wake till morning.

"*January 28.* Last night I did not take my usual dose of medicine. In these days of new remedies and mysterious results upon certain organizations, it occurred to me to wonder if possibly the drug might have, after all, something to do with my strange experience.

"I did not take my medicine. I put the bottle as usual on my dresser, since I feared if I interrupted further the customary sequence of affairs I might fail to wake. I placed my box of matches on the chair beside the bed. I fell asleep about quarter past eleven o'clock, and I waked when the clock was striking two—a little earlier than my wont. I did not hesitate this time. I rose at once, took my box of matches and proceeded as formerly. I walked what seemed a great space without coming into collision with anything. I kept sniffing for the wonderful fragrances of the night before, but they did not recur. Instead, I was suddenly aware that I was tasting something, some morsel of sweetness hitherto unknown, and, as in the case of the odour, the usual order seemed reversed, and it was as if I tasted it first in my mental consciousness. Then the sweetness rolled under my tongue. I thought involuntarily of 'Sweeter than honey or the honeycomb' of the Scripture. I thought of the Old Testament manna. An ineffable content as of satisfied hunger seized me. I stepped further, and a new savour was upon my palate. And so on. It was never cloying, though of such sharp sweetness that it fairly stung. It was the merging of a material sense into a spiritual one. I said to myself, 'I have lived my life and always have I gone hungry until now.' I could feel my brain act swiftly under the influence of this heavenly food as under a stimulant. Then suddenly I repeated the experience of the night before. I grew dizzy, and an indefinite fear and shrinking were upon me. I struck my safety match and was back in my hall bedroom. I returned to bed, and soon fell asleep. I did not take my medicine. I am resolved not to do so longer. I am feeling much better.

"*January 29*. Last night to bed as usual, matches in place; fell asleep about eleven and waked at half-past one. I heard the half-hour strike; I am waking earlier and earlier every night. I had not taken my medicine, though it was on the dresser as usual. I again took my match-box in hand and started to cross the room, and, as always, traversed strange spaces, but this night, as seems fated to be the case every night, my experience was different. Last night I neither smelled nor tasted, but I heard—my Lord, I heard! The first sound of which I was conscious was one like the constantly gathering and receding murmur of a river, and it seemed to come from the wall behind my bed where the old picture hangs. Nothing in nature except a river gives that impression of at once advance and retreat. I could not mistake it. On, ever on, came the swelling murmur of the waves; past and ever past they died in the distance. Then I heard above the murmur of the river a song in an unknown tongue which I recognized as being unknown, yet which I understood; but the understanding was in my brain, with no words of interpretation. The song had to do with me, but with me in unknown futures for which I had no images of comparison in the past; yet a sort of ecstasy as of a prophecy of bliss filled my whole consciousness. The song never ceased, but as I moved on I came into new sound-waves. There was the pealing of bells which might have been made of crystal, and might have summoned to the gates of heaven. There was music of strange instruments, great harmonies pierced now and then by small whispers as of love, and it all filled me with a certainty of a future of bliss.

"At last I seemed the centre of a mighty orchestra which

constantly deepened and increased until I seemed to feel myself being lifted gently but mightily upon the waves of sound as upon the waves of a sea. Then again the terror and the impulse to flee to my own familiar scenes were upon me. I struck my match and was back in my hall bedroom. I do not see how I sleep at all after such wonders, but sleep I do. I slept dreamlessly until daylight this morning.

"*January 30*. I heard yesterday something with regard to my hall bedroom which affected me strangely. I cannot for the life of me say whether it intimidated me, filled me with the horror of the abnormal, or rather roused to a greater degree my spirit of adventure and discovery. I was down at the Cure, and was sitting on the veranda sipping idly my mineral water, when somebody spoke my name. 'Mr. Wheatcroft?' said the voice politely, interrogatively, somewhat apologetically, as if to provide for a possible mistake in my identity. I turned and saw a gentleman whom I recognized at once. I seldom forget names or faces. He was a Mr. Addison whom I had seen considerable of three years ago at a little summer hotel in the mountains. It was one of those passing acquaintances which signify little one way or the other. If never renewed, you have no regret; if renewed, you accept the renewal with no hesitation. It is in every way negative. But just now, in my feeble, friendless state, the sight of a face which beams with pleased remembrance is rather gratifying. I felt distinctly glad to see the man. He sat down beside me. He also had a glass of the water. His health, while not as bad as mine, leaves much to be desired.

"Addison had often been in this town before. He had in fact lived here at one time. He had remained at the Cure three years, taking the waters daily. He therefore knows about all there is to be known about the town, which is not very large. He asked me where I was staying, and when I told him the street, rather excitedly inquired the number. When I told him the number, which is 240, he gave a manifest start, and after one sharp glance at me sipped his water in silence for a moment. He had so evidently betrayed some ulterior knowledge with regard to my residence that I questioned him.

" 'What do you know about 240 Pleasant Street?' said I.

" 'Oh, nothing,' he replied, evasively, sipping his water.

"After a little while, however, he inquired, in what he evidently tried to render a casual tone, what room I occupied.

'I once lived a few weeks at 240 Pleasant Street myself,' he said. 'That house always was a boarding-house, I guess.'

"'It had stood vacant for a term of years before the present occupant rented it, I believe,' I remarked. Then I answered his question. 'I have the hall bedroom on the third floor,' said I. 'The quarters are pretty straitened, but comfortable enough as hall bedrooms go.'

"But Mr. Addison had showed such unmistakable consternation at my reply that then I persisted in my questioning as to the cause, and at last he yielded and told me what he knew. He had hesitated both because he shrank from displaying what I might consider an unmanly superstition, and because he did not wish to influence me beyond what the facts of the case warranted. 'Well, I will tell you, Wheatcroft,' he said. 'Briefly all I know is this: When last I heard of 240 Pleasant Street it was not rented because of foul play which was supposed to have taken place there, though nothing was ever proved. There were two disappearances, and—in each case—of an occupant of the hall bedroom which you now have. The first disappearance was of a very beautiful girl who had come here for her health and was said to be the victim of a profound melancholy, induced by a love disappointment. She obtained board at 240 and occupied the hall bedroom about two weeks; then one morning she was gone, having seemingly vanished into thin air. Her relatives were communicated with; she had not many, nor friends either, poor girl, and a thorough search was made, but the last I knew she had never come to light. There were two or three arrests, but nothing ever came of them. Well, that was before my day here, but the second disappearance took place when I was in the house—a fine young fellow who had overworked in college. He had to pay his own way. He had taken cold, had the grip, and that and the overwork about finished him, and he came on here for a month's rest and recuperation. He had been in that room about two weeks, a little less, when one morning he wasn't there. Then there was a great hullabaloo. It seems that he had let fall some hints to the effect that there was something queer about the room, but, of course, the police did not think much of that. They made arrests right and left, but they never found him, and the arrested were discharged, though some of them are probably under a cloud of suspicion to this day. Then the boarding-house was shut up. Six years ago nobody would have boarded there, much less occupied that hall bedroom, but now I suppose new people have come in, and the story has died out. I dare say your landlady will not thank me for reviving it.'

"I assured him that it would make no possible difference to me. He looked at me sharply, and asked bluntly if I had seen anything wrong or unusual about the room. I replied, guarding myself from falsehood with a quibble, that I had seen nothing in the least unusual about the room, as indeed I had not, and have not now, but that may come. I feel that that will come in due time. Last night I neither saw, nor heard, nor smelled, nor tasted, but I—felt. Last night, having started again on my exploration of, God knows what, I had not advanced a step before I touched something. My first sensation was one of disappointment. 'It is the dresser, and I am at the end of it now,' I thought. But I soon discovered that it was not the old painted dresser which I touched, but something carved, as nearly as I could discover with my unskilled finger-tips, with winged things. There were certainly long keen curves of wings which seemed to overlay an arabesque of fine leaf and flower work. I do not know what the object was that I touched. It may have been a chest. I may seem to be exaggerating when I say that it somehow failed or exceeded in some mysterious respect of being the shape of anything I had ever touched. I do not know what the material was. It was as smooth as ivory, but it did not feel like ivory; there was a singular warmth about it, as if it had stood long in hot sunlight. I continued, and I encountered other objects I am inclined to think were pieces of furniture of fashions and possibly of uses unknown to me, and about them all was the strange mystery as to shape. At last I came to what was evidently an open window of large area. I distinctly felt a soft, warm wind, yet with a crystal freshness, blow on my face. It was not the window of my hall bedroom, that I know. Looking out, I could see nothing. I only felt the wind blowing on my face.

"Then suddenly, without any warning, my groping hands to the right and left touched living beings, beings in the likeness of men and women, palpable creatures in palpable attire. I could feel the soft silken texture of their garments which swept around me, seeming to half enfold me in clinging meshes like cobwebs. I was in a crowd of these people, whatever they were, and whoever they were, but, curiously enough, without seeing one of them I had a strong sense of recognition as I passed among them. Now and then a hand that I knew closed softly over mine; once an arm passed around me. Then I began to feel myself gently swept on and impelled by this softly moving throng; their floating garments seemed to fairly wind me about, and again a swift terror overcame me. I struck my match, and was back in my hall bedroom. I wonder if I had not better keep my gas burning to-night? I wonder if it be possible that this is going too far? I wonder what became of those other people, the man and the woman who occupied this room? I wonder if I had better not stop where I am?

"*January 31*. Last night I saw—I saw more than I can describe, more than is lawful to describe. Something which nature has rightly hidden has been revealed to me, but it is not for me to disclose too much of her secret. This much I will say, that doors and windows open into an out-of-doors to which the outdoors which we know is but a vestibule. And there is a river; there is something strange with respect to that picture. There is a river upon which one could sail away. It was flowing silently, for to-night I could only see. I saw that I was right in thinking I recognized some of the people whom I encountered the night before, though some were strange to me. It is true that the girl who disappeared from the hall bedroom was very beautiful. Everything which I saw last night was very beautiful to my one sense that could grasp it. I wonder what it would all be if all my senses together were to grasp it? I wonder if I had better not keep my gas burning to-night? I wonder—"

This finishes the journal which Mr. Wheatcroft left in his hall bedroom. The morning after the last entry he was gone. His friend, Mr. Addison, came here, and a search was made. They even tore down the wall behind the picture, and they did find something rather queer for a house that had been used for boarders, where you would think no room would have been let run to waste. They found another room, a long narrow one, the length of the hall bedroom, but narrower, hardly more than a closet. There was no window, nor door, and all there was in it was a sheet of paper covered with figures, as if somebody had been doing sums. They made a lot of talk about those figures, and they tried to make out that the fifth dimension, whatever that is, was proved, but they said afterward they didn't prove anything. They tried to make out then that somebody had murdered poor Mr. Wheatcroft and hid the body, and they arrested poor Mr. Addison, but they couldn't make out anything against him. They proved he was in the Cure all that night and couldn't have done it. They don't know what became of Mr. Wheatcroft, and now they say two more disappeared from that same room before I rented the house.

The agent came and promised to put the new room they discovered into the hall bedroom and have everything new—papered and painted. He took away the picture; folks hinted there was something queer about that, I don't know what. It looked innocent enough, and I guess he burned it up. He said if I would stay he would arrange it with the owner, who everybody says is a very queer man, so I should not have to pay much if any rent. But I told him I couldn't stay if he was to give me the rent. That I wasn't afraid of anything myself, though I must say I wouldn't want to put anybody in that hall bedroom without telling him all about it; but my boarders would leave, and I knew I couldn't get any more. I told him I would rather have had a regular ghost than what seemed to be a way of going out of the house to nowhere and never coming back again. I moved, and, as I said before, it remains to be seen whether my ill luck follows me to this house or not. Anyway, it has no hall bedroom.

WILLIAM J. WINTLE
The Ghost at the "Blue Dragon"

William James Wintle (1861–1934) was a prolific journalist, whose many books include Nights with an Old Lag, Continental Dishes, *and* Armenia and its Sorrows. *While resident at the Priory on Caldy Island, he told ghost stories to the young novitiates on Sunday nights over a wood fire. These stories "were so fortunate as to meet with approval from their rather critical audience. Truth to tell, the gruesome ones met with the best reception." Wintle's supernatural stories were published together in* Ghost Gleams *(1921).*

The "Blue Dragon" was one of the oldest and best hotels in Saltminster; and that was saying a good deal. Long before Saltminster became popular as a seaside resort; long before people got into the habit of going to the seaside for holidays or for health; the old market town had been a busy place, and its inns were both numerous and good. New ones had sprung up of recent years to meet the needs of the visitors; and as these styled themselves hotels, the older ones had to fall into line and adopt the more ambitious name as well.

But although the "Blue Dragon" now called itself an hotel, and found itself doing more and better business than ever, it had changed very little in the course of the years. It was still a delightfully old-fashioned place; the quaint old rooms remained unaltered; the old English cookery was still the same; and you would look in vain for anything foreign or new-fangled. The French cook and the German waiter had never found entrance; and that was one of the reasons why the place was in such repute. You needed to book your room well in advance if you wished to stay at the "Blue Dragon."

Now Professor Latham wanted to stay at the "Blue Dragon"; for he knew a good thing when he found it. At Cambridge, where he occupied the chair of Assyrian History, he was better

649

known for his ability as a judge of port than as a lecturer; and, when he recommended an hotel, you might be quite sure that both table and cellar would prove to be above reproach. So he booked his room well in advance, and made his way to Saltminster in the middle of July to spend a quiet six weeks and incidentally to revise the manuscript of his forthcoming book.

At the "Blue Dragon" he found that he had been allotted a room which met with his full approval. It was in the quietest and most retired part of the house, at the end of a long corridor, and looked out upon the salt marshes that ran down to the sea. It was well away from the busier parts of the house, and was on the side remote from the road. And it was furnished in the style of our grandparents—exactly the style that Professor Latham admired and loved.

But it had one drawback, which gave the newcomer a distinct shock when he saw it. There were two beds in the room! Having only one body, he had no use for two beds. Nor had he the least intention of sharing his room with anyone else. But mine host quickly reassured him. The room was occasionally let to people who required an extra bed, and thus had been provided with one; but of course it would not be in use while the Professor occupied the room. Mine host trusted the bed would not be in the Professor's way: it was only kept furnished with the usual bedding because a dismantled bed looked so uncomfortable. The Professor assured him that he did not mind in the least if the bed was not used: it would do to put things on.

So he proceeded to unpack his bag and to throw the contents about the room in the careless style that was the despair of his housekeeper at Cambridge. The spare bed was soon pretty well concealed beneath scattered articles of clothing, books, bundles of manuscript and other things.

Then he went for a walk, located the principal streets and buildings with the aid of the local map which was always his first purchase on arriving at any strange place, noted sundry second-hand book shops and curio shops for further investigation at leisure, and finally made his way down to the shore, gazed with disapproval at the mixed bathing, and then absorbed himself in the alleged history of the town as set forth in a local guide-book.

Now Professor Latham was an authority on history, and had a keen scent for fiction masquerading as fact. So he duly appreciated a detailed account of the visit of Queen Elizabeth to the town, and her stay at the "Blue Dragon," at a date when she was unquestionably lying ill at the Old Palace at Richmond, which she was never to leave alive. But he cared less for various ghost stories, all of which seemed to be connected in one way or another with the "Blue Dragon." If they were all to be believed, that famous hostelry must have been a somewhat exciting place to stay at in the olden days.

The Professor did not believe in ghosts. He dealt in facts and had no use for fancies. He had never yet met with a ghost story that would stand looking into, or even telling a second time. Tales of that sort always crumbled to bits when you began to ask questions. Nobody whom he had met had ever seen a ghost, though plenty of them knew other people who had seen one: and he knew the worthlessness of second-hand evidence. Still, it was a little amusing to find that the "Blue Dragon" had been the scene of so many legends of this kind. It was just as well that he knew better than to trouble about such absurdities; or he might not have slept well. He would be able to tell his friends that he had stayed in a very nest of ghosts, and had proved by experience that there was nothing at all in it.

He returned to the hotel in time to dress for dinner, and at once noticed that the things he had left on the spare bed had been removed and placed carefully on the table. Evidently the chambermaid had been at work in his absence; but he rather wished she would leave things alone. He put them back on the bed and hoped she would take the hint. Then he dressed and went down to dinner.

The dinner met with his entire approval. The turbot was perfection, and the saddle of mutton was exactly as it should be. He sampled the famous fifty-eight port, of which he had heard good accounts; and he fully endorsed the accounts. He also finished the bottle. Professor Latham knew a good thing when he met it, and he never let it go to waste. Then he smoked a leisurely cigar, drank his coffee to the accompaniment of some particularly fine old brandy, and went up to bed on excellent terms with himself and with all the world beside.

When he reached his room, he paused and reflected. Surely he put those things back on the bed before he went down to dinner. And now they were on the table again! Confound that chambermaid! But was he quite sure that he put them back? He thought so—but really that port was uncommonly fine . . .

and the brandy was the genuine article . . . but did he put those things back, or did he only intend to do so? Really it was too absurd that he could not remember a simple little thing like that . . . let's see, what was the date? Fifty-eight, of course: but why should the waiter meddle with his arrangements of the bedroom? No, not the waiter: it must have been the chambermaid. Or were the things on the table after all? Why couldn't he remember a simple little thing like that? It must be the sea air. Better go to bed and not bother any more about it.

So Professor Latham threw the things back on the bed, except those that fell on the floor, and turned into the other bed. He murmured "Fifty-eight" twice, and then slept the sleep of the man who has dined. Not for worlds would we suggest that Professor Latham was either merry, elevated, well oiled, three sheets in the wind, or anything other than as sober as a judge after an assize dinner.

Thus it can only be regarded as remarkable that his sleep should have been disturbed by persistent dreams. And it was still more remarkable that all his dreams had to do with that other bed. He dreamed that it was occupied. He dreamed that he was aroused by the sound of—well, heavy breathing; and the sound came from the other bed. He struck a match and lit the candle that stood by his bedside. When it had left off spluttering he saw that the things he had laid on the other bed were no longer there. But a mountain seemed to have arisen in the midst of the bed. It was occupied! Now, who could have had the confounded impertinence . . . he would have a few plain words with the landlord in the morning about this.

Then he thought that he got carefully out of bed, said things to himself as his bare foot trod on a collar stud that some fool must have thrown on the floor, and made his way to the other bed to see who the intruder was. He had already noted that the man was an ugly looking fellow, red-headed and provided with a nose whose colour suggested that water disagreed with him. Probably some drunken roisterer who had come home late and had mistaken the room. He would enlighten him on the subject.

He took the candle to the bedside of the intruder, turned back the sheet to reveal the face more completely, and saw—himself! Then he seized himself by the shoulder and shook himself, with the result that himself woke up and hit him in the eye. A tremendous tussle followed. Himself jumped out of bed and knocked him down, but he got up again and tripped himself up and got the head of himself into chancery. When himself got free, it was clear that both of him were in a distinctly nasty temper. A stand-up fight followed, resulting in considerable damage to both himself and him; but finally he knocked himself down with a crash that shook the universe—and woke up Professor Latham.

The Professor was quite annoyed. He usually slept well and was rarely troubled by dreams. He struck a light to see the time; and then noticed that all the things he had thrown on the other bed were now lying in a heap on the floor. Now this was beyond a joke. It could not be the chambermaid this time. Was it possible that when he threw the things on the bed over night his aim was not quite straight? The thought was not an agreeable one to a man like himself of strictly sober habits.

Anyway, the things could not lie on the floor: so he got out and once more put them on the other bed. Then he turned in and dozed and dreamed until the morning. And his dreams were still occupied with that second bed, which seemed fated to destroy his rest.

When he rose next morning, the first thing that met his eye was that troublesome bed: and what he saw made him rub his eyes and wonder if he were awake or asleep. The things he had put on it during the night were now once more scattered about the floor. But this was not all. The bed had apparently been slept in! The bed clothes were thrown back, as if someone had just risen; and there was a depression in the middle of the bed and on the pillow which could only be accounted for by someone having slept there.

But the thing was simply impossible. Professor Latham went straight to the door, and found that it was locked as he had left it over night. No one could have come in. Who then slept in that other bed? It was an uncomfortable kind of question.

There seemed to be only three possible explanations of the affair. He might have risen in his sleep and changed into the other bed. But if so, he must have changed back again, for he was in the right bed when he woke up. He was not addicted to walking in his sleep; and the thing seemed very improbable. Or the bed might have been disturbed without anyone sleeping in it. But, if so, who disturbed it? No one could have done it but himself: so this did not help matters much. The third possible explanation was that someone other than himself had really been lying in that bed at some time during the night, but had gone before he woke up. But, if so, it must have been someone who could enter a locked room and leave it again without making any sign. This was an unpleasant kind of suggestion; and he did not dwell on it. As we have said, he did not believe in ghosts: and besides, who ever heard of a ghost sleeping in a bed—or anywhere else for the matter of that?

He thought and thought; and the more he thought, the less he liked it. Mysteries were not in his line, and he did not want to be mixed up in any. So he dismissed the matter from his mind, with a private resolve to avoid the fifty-eight port at dinner, and went downstairs to breakfast. On his way he met the chambermaid and learnt from her that she had not moved any things off the bed in his room.

After breakfast, he went up to his room in search of a book that he intended to take with him and read out of doors, and was just going to enter when he heard someone talking in the room. He paused and listened. Yes, there was certainly someone there, and he seemed out of temper. What he was saying Professor Latham could not hear; but the tone of the voice was distinctly unamiable. And the oddest thing about it was that it sounded just like his own voice as he had once heard it in a gramophone!

But, whoever the intruder might be, he had no right in that room; and the Professor entered with the full intention of telling him so in unmistakable terms. He went in with a frown on his brow; but this changed at once to a stare of astonishment. The room was empty. But apparently somebody had recently been there, for the very book he had come for had been thrown into the fireplace! And his pet cigar case was lying beside it!

Yet the door of the room had been locked till he opened it. No one could have entered the room, except the chambermaid who was provided with a master key; but inquiry proved that she had been in another part of the house since Professor Latham went down to breakfast. It was of course possible that some thief might have provided himself with a skeleton key; but there was nothing to suggest any attempt at robbery. Nothing had been interfered with, except the articles that were thrown into the fireplace. Besides, the Professor had heard the voice of the intruder immediately before entering the room.

The landlord was called, and he listened to the story with a patient smile. His explanation was a very simple one; but it did not convey much consolation to his guest.

"My dear Sir," he said, "in an old house like this, full of long passages and odd corners communicating with one another, all kinds of small sounds get carried along and mixed up; so that the echo of a voice or sound in one part of the house seems to come from another. If we were to take any notice of all the slight sounds that one hears when all is quiet at night, we should begin to think that every room in the place was haunted. All those silly tales about this house in the local guide-book have no doubt been started in this way. We simply take no notice of them."

But this did not explain the removal of the things from the bed, nor the disturbance of the bed clothes, nor the throwing of the book and cigar case into the fireplace; and it did not impress Professor Latham much. So he shrugged his shoulders, took up his book, and started for his walk. And then another queer thing happened.

Passing a photographer's shop, he was startled to see in the window an excellent portrait of himself! As he had never been to the place before, and had never in his life been photographed with his hat on his head—as this portrait represented him—he was considerably astonished. He went into the shop, and remarked:

"I see you have in your window a photograph of Professor Latham of Cambridge. May I ask when it was taken?"

"I fear you are mistaken, Sir," said the photographer. "We do not know the name and have certainly not taken any gentleman giving that name. Would you mind pointing out the portrait?"

The bewildered professor indicated the photograph, and received the explanation that it was that of a gentleman who had stayed at the "Blue Dragon" two years before, and who declined to give any name.

"But it is really a very good portrait of yourself," said the photographer. "Possibly it is yours, and you have forgotten the occurrence?"

Professor Latham could only assure him that he had never been in Saltminster before, and had certainly not sat for that portrait. It could only be regarded as a very curious and extraordinary coincidence. He wondered if he possessed a double.

Then another odd thing happened. In the course of his walk he met a man who raised his hat and said, "Let me take the opportunity of apologising for my clumsiness in colliding with you in the hotel last night. It was caused by catching my foot in the edge of the carpet."

The Professor assured him that he was mistaken. No one had collided with him: it must have been someone else. But the man persisted that it was he whom he had knocked against just outside the door of room No. 39, which was that which Professor Latham was occupying. These mistakes were very strange.

But a still more curious mistake awaited him on his return to the hotel. On entering his room, he found the chambermaid putting an extra blanket on the spare bed. He asked what this meant, as the bed was not to be used, and was told that he himself had asked her to do it as he felt cold in the night. The Professor denied this, and pointed out that he slept in the other bed. The maid said that both of the beds had been slept in, which she did not understand, and that she was quite sure she had seen him about half an hour previously, coming out of the room, and that he had been very particular to explain which bed was to have the extra blanket!

The bewildered Professor could not make it out at all. Had all the world gone mad in Saltminster? Or was he in the throes of a nightmare and would presently wake up and find it all a dream? And then came another shock. He presently went to the mirror to brush his hair; and over his shoulder he distinctly saw the exact double of himself going out through the door of the room. He turned quickly and was just in time to see the door close. He ran across the room and flung the door open; but no one was visible in the corridor. Yet he had been so quick, and the corridor was so long, that no one could have got away in the time.

A few minutes later he went down to lunch. As he entered the dining-room, he noticed that the waiter looked at him with some surprise. Then the man asked if he had changed his mind about lunching. The Professor asked what he meant, and was informed that as he went out of the house a few minutes before he had said in answer to the waiter's inquiry that he would not be in to lunch. Things were getting complicated. Evidently someone was being mistaken for him. This might be accounted for by personal resemblance; but what about the incidents in the bedroom? And these things were not happening after dinner; so that the blame could not be laid at the door of the fifty-eight port.

The rest of the day was uneventful. Professor Latham dined with as much satisfaction as on the day before, but he drank a lighter wine than port; he had a game at billiards after dinner; he avoided the old brandy; and he retired to rest in good time.

The sea air had made him sleepy, and he hoped to make amends for the restlessness of the previous night. On the whole he slept soundly, but twice in the night he was disturbed by dreams that he heard someone breathing heavily in the room. On thinking the matter over afterwards he was not quite sure whether he dreamed this or actually heard it when half awake. He was inclined to think that the latter was the case; for in the morning he found to his disgust that the spare bed had evidently been slept in again.

And there was a fresh development. On a chair beside the spare bed lay a piece of paper, torn out of the Professor's pocket book as it proved; and on this had been scribbled some verses of a music-hall song of a particularly ribald and vulgar character. And the handwriting was that of Professor Latham! He could not deny it. Though the song was quite unknown to him and was of a kind that he would never think of either writing or repeating, he could not get away from the fact that the handwriting was his own. He began to feel thankful that he had not left his cheque-book about.

But during the day things took a still more unpleasant turn. The landlord sought an interview with him; and after some hesitation told him that he must ask him to find other accommodation. He indignantly inquired the reason, and was told that a gentleman who attempted to kiss the chambermaid on the stairs was not the kind of patron that was desired at the "Blue Dragon"! Imagine the feelings of Professor Latham, who was the last man in the world to do such a thing! But the chambermaid persisted in her story, in spite of his denials and assurances that it must have been someone else; and the unfortunate man had to agree to leave the next day. By this time he had had more than enough of Saltminster, and decided to return to Cambridge rather than seek other accommodation in the place. But the delay till the next day was to prove very nearly fatal to him.

That same evening, as he went up to bed, he distinctly heard muttered laughter in his room just before he opened the door to go in; and he found that the clothes of the spare bed had been turned back as if someone was about to get into it. He also noticed that one of his razors had been taken out of its case and was lying open on the dressing-table. He put it back—and it was as well for him that he did so.

He undressed and was about to get into bed when he turned to the window to see what kind of weather it was. The moon was shining brightly, and he stood there for a minute of two with the window open. Then he suddenly found himself caught in the grip of someone behind him; and at the same moment an accidental glance at the mirror showed him the face of his antagonist over his shoulder. It was his own face!

He saw at once that it was to be a struggle for life. The horror that had him in its grip was evidently trying to throw him out through the window. For some minutes the issue was uncertain. Twice he was pressed against the window-sill and was almost over; but each time by a supreme effort he managed to get back into the room. Dressing-table and chairs were overturned in the struggle, and no doubt a great noise was thus made; but he was unconscious of everything but the struggle for life.

But the noise was the saving of Professor Latham. It attracted the notice of other guests, who came out of their rooms to see what it was. Then followed a loud knocking at his door; and at the same moment he found himself alone!

He left Saltminster the next morning; and he has expressed no opinion on ghost stories since. Nor has he ever been known to recommend the "Blue Dragon" as a nice quiet place for a holiday.